ITAL

'I expect my nurses to be women of intelligence, not blonde ragamuffins,' Dr Rodrigo Vitale tells Staff Nurse Sharon Craig on her arrival at his hospital above the Bay of Naples. After such an unfortunate introduction how can she hope to convince him that she's a competent nurse and not a dizzy blonde?

ITALIAN NURSE

BY

LYDIA BALMAIN

MILLS & BOON LIMITED
London · Sydney · Toronto

First published in Great Britain 1984
by Mills & Boon Limited, 15–16 Brook's Mews,
London W1A 1DR

© Lydia Balmain 1984

Australian copyright 1984
Philippine copyright 1984

ISBN 0 263 74758 1

Set in 10 on 10½ pt Linotron Times
03–0784–57,000

Photoset by Rowland Phototypesetting Ltd
Bury St Edmunds, Suffolk
Made and printed in Great Britain by
Richard Clay (The Chaucer Press) Ltd
Bungay, Suffolk

For Bryn Harrison
and the gallant team
of surgeons who
removed Jasper's spleen.

CHAPTER ONE

'HERE we are, Signorina, this is the *ospedale*.'

The ancient taxi screeched to a halt before the big building and Staff Nurse Sharon Craig drew in an incredulous breath.

'It's beautiful! It doesn't look much like a hospital, though.'

The Villa L'Arancia was built of warm, apricot-coloured stone. It had cupolas, ornate balustrades and round towers on its four corners. The front of the building was shaded by a canopy of bougainvillaea, its scarlet leaves forming a vivid contrast to the darker foliage. From where she stood on the freshly raked gravel of the entrance sweep, Sharon could see, behind it, the dark blue of the Bay of Naples whilst above the turrets the sky was brassy with the full heat of noon. Palm trees edged a half glimpsed terrace which, she guessed, must be built directly over the 600 foot high cliffs and when she glanced to her right she could see a terraced garden with ancient olive trees, figs and almonds, their shade cool and inviting.

The wizened little Italian driver who had brought her from the station to the small town of Sant' Agnello smiled at the blue-eyed blonde with approval as he began to heave her suitcases out of the car, talking in broken but perfectly understandable English as he did so.

'Ah, but this is the *English* 'ospital, Signorina, not a big place for all, like the *ospedale* in our city. My sister Barbèrina work as *l'infermiera* at the big 'spedale, and there it is jus' like the 'ospitals I see in London when I visit your country five year ago. This place, this Villa L'Arancia, was a nobleman's *casa* which was made into 'ospital. *Capisce*?'

'Yes, I understand. It does happen sometimes in England, I think.' Sharon picked up her overnight bag and made for the revolving doors at the entrance. 'Can you manage both those cases?'

'*Si*, Signorina, they are as feathers.' He stumped into the hallway behind her, carrying the cases with surprising ease and crashed them down on the black and white tiles. '*Attenzione*, Signorina Russano!'

The striking blonde behind the big reception desk pursed her lips and put down her magazine. She raised her brows, staring coldly at them.

'*Si? Cosa desidera?*'

'I'm sorry, I don't . . .' Sharon was beginning, when the driver broke in.

'This is Mees Craig, English Nurse,' he said briskly. 'This is English *'spedale*, Signorina Russano; let us remember this.'

At the implied reproof the blonde's cheeks flushed faintly, but she continued to stare coldly at Sharon.

'Why did you bring your cases here, Signorina? Do you expect to live in the hospital? Surely you were told that your living quarters would be in the nurses' flats?'

'Yes, but I wasn't told where the nurses' flats were,' Sharon said. She tried a friendly smile. It was not echoed in the cold, lovely countenance opposite. 'If you will direct me, Signorina, I'll go there at once. But I *was* told to report to the hospital as soon as I arrived!'

There was no reply from the blonde, who turned to the driver and addressed him sharply in a flood of Italian. He, with a sigh, heaved both suitcases up once more and jerked his head at Sharon.

'Come with me, Signorina. When you have found your flat and left your cases you can return.'

Outside, the driver slung the cases back in the car and then turned, to give Sharon an apologetic glance.

'I'm sorry, Signorina, that you should find Signorina Rossano so . . .' his English deserted him momentarily. 'So *antipatico*. She is very reech lady with very reech

padre—father, who work here only sometime. She
should have gone with you to the flats, but . . .' an
expressive shrug spoke volumes. 'Never min', Signorina, you are better with Guiseppe, no?'

'I'm sure I am.' The two of them climbed back into the
car and Guiseppe drove back down the drive and about
twenty feet further along the pavement before swinging
into another short drive.

'See, it is not far. Your flats, Signorina.'

This time, it was a modern block with a few trees
growing around it. Uniformly green balconies and shutters broke the white stucco of the frontage, and the
whole place looked deserted. Sharon and the driver
climbed out and went into the small entrance hall,
Guiseppe once more carrying the suitcases.

'What number, Signorina?'

'Oh dear, she didn't say!'

'*Cosa dice mai!* Well, this will, perhaps, take a few
moments, but we will try every door, and . . .'

He was interrupted. Someone came clattering down
the stairs and stopped a few steps from the bottom. It
was a girl in the uniform of a staff nurse and she smiled at
them, her grey eyes twinkling. She had a pleasant face
and the uniform with its blue and white dress and navy
belt revealed a neat figure.

'Hello, Guiseppe, is this our new staff nurse?' She did
not wait for a reply but swooped down on Sharon and
grabbed the heavy overnight bag. 'You'll be Sharon
Craig; I'm Julie Drummond, your flat-mate, we're on
the first floor, number 3. The dreaded Fortuna rang over
and told me to expect you. Bring the cases up, *amico*,
and I'll offer you a real cup of tea!'

'*Si*, Signorina,' Guiseppe said happily, hurrying up
the stairs in their wake. 'Aha, Mees Craig, this one is
quite different from that other, eh?'

'I gather from that remark that Fortuna was her usual
self.' Julie threw open the door of a pleasant living room.
'Come in, rest your toes, and I'll put the kettle on.'

But Guiseppe, it appeared, had another client waiting so Sharon pressed some crumpled lire notes into his hand and thanked him and the two girls waved him away. Only then did Sharon ask the question uppermost in her mind.

'Guiseppe said Signorina Russano only worked here sometimes. Who is she, and why only sometimes?'

'She's one of the surgeon's fancy bits, if you ask me,' Julie said. The kitchen and living room had a dividing door and she went through into the kitchen, raising her voice so that they could continue the conversation. 'Rodrigo Vitale runs the hospital, it was his idea, and when a part-time receptionist was needed he pushed Fortuna forward.'

'I see. This Vitale, what did you mean, the hospital was his idea?'

'Well, it was. Mind you, I don't know whether he actually thought of it or whether it was someone in the insurance business, but he took up the suggestion, offered the Villa L'Arancia, which was one of the family homes, for conversion, and although he still operates up at the big *ospedale*, he spends most of his time here.'

'I see. The taxi driver said the Russanos were rich.'

'Mm hm, so they are. Rumour has it that what the Russanos don't own, the Vitales do. And our chap's got a lot going for him, he's outstandingly handsome, marvellous physique, all that sort of thing, plus the family wealth. Add that he's one of the best surgeons in the province, and you can see why he's so demanding and arrogant with his staff.'

'Oh, like that, is he? What do the patients think of him?'

'Adore him. The nurses worship from afar, too, except when he's on the warpath about something, and then even his dishiness avails him nothing and everyone keeps out of his way. Except for Fortuna, who whisks off in his Lamborghini from time to time, looking insufferably pleased with herself.'

'I'd look pleased with myself if someone whisked me off in a car like that,' Sharon admitted. 'Will I see much of Vitale?'

'You will indeed, Wisteria is his main ward.' Julie re-entered the room, a cup of tea slopping over a little in either hand. 'Quick, grab this before I tip it all over my feet!'

Presently, the tea drunk, Julie took Sharon on a tour of inspection.

'The flats are tiny but nice,' she informed her new friend. 'Two cupboards with beds in are euphemistically called our bedrooms, another cupboard with a shower and a loo in it is the bathroom. But, as you can see, the kitchen's as big as the living room and beautifully airy, and the balconies still thrill me to bits, though I've been over here eighteen months now.'

'Yes, a balcony does seem a luxury,' Sharon admitted as they made their way back towards the hospital. 'I'm going to love it here, particularly the weather. What's the ward like, though, and Sister? I start work first thing tomorrow morning, I believe.'

'Sister's a darling—Sister Young, that is, the day-sister. You were warned that we have to do the odd bit of shift work, I hope? There are two night sisters, and both of them are all right, but Sister Crown is a bit of a tartar. Still, you won't come up against her much.'

'Well, nights are a bore, but I daresay I'll survive,' Sharon said comfortably as they entered the foyer of the hospital. 'What's the ratio of staff to patients like?'

'Very good, the wards are small, you see—Wisteria only has fourteen beds, split into three four-bedded wards and two single ones. But Vitale insists that one nurse whose first language is English shall be available on every ward for twenty-four hours a day. And that does sometimes lead to difficulties.'

'I wonder why?' Sharon glanced at Fortuna, who was painting her scarlet nails, not deigning to glance up as they clicked across the marble tiles. 'Don't the local girls make good nurses?'

'None better, but Vitale maintains that in an emergency one would revert to one's mother tongue, and almost ninety percent of our patients are British. Even the best of the Italian nurses can be puzzled by some of the more idiosyncratic English expressions, you know, and children sometimes use funny words to mean quite basic things.'

They had climbed the stairs and were on the first floor, facing a wing of the great house which must, Sharon guessed, overlook the terrace. Julie tapped on the nearest door.

'Here we are, this is Wisteria Ward and this is Sister's office.' She did not wait for an invitation to enter but opened the door and gestured Sharon in. 'Sister, I've brought your new nurse,' she said brightly.

Sister Young was sitting behind the desk, tapping away at a brand new electronic typewriter, her brow furrowed with concentration, but as soon as she saw Sharon she smiled and stood up, holding out her hand. She was middle-aged, with greying hair and a plump little figure, but her eyes were shrewd and her smile kindly. Sharon liked her on sight.

'Good afternoon, Nurse, did you have a pleasant journey? Now you'll want to know all about the ward.'

Her briefing was efficient and businesslike, but as soon as she was sure that Sharon was fully informed as to her methods and the general running of the ward, she turned to Julie.

'Sister Brett's given you an hour off, she told me, so could you hold the fort here whilst I introduce Nurse Craig to the patients and the rest of the staff? It won't take more than ten minutes, we're not full.'

Upon Julie agreeing the two of them set off, Sister bustling ahead.

'This is room No 1, for female patients in for short stays,' she explained. 'Both patients are breast biopsies and will be out in forty-eight hours, and both, as it happens, are Italians who prefer the quiet of our smaller hospital. Room 2 is for longer stay female patients, you'll meet the ladies tomorrow, and Room 3 is male surgical. The only patient there liable to cause you much trouble is Mr Reynolds. Cheeky young man here on holiday from Birmingham. Thinks the world revolves for him!' But there was that in her tone which made Sharon suspect that Sister Young had a soft spot for the redoubtable Mr Reynolds.

The two of them glanced into the four-bed wards, all of which were pleasant and airy rooms, cool despite the full heat of the noonday sun. Sharon remarked on this. Sister Young smiled.

'We're air-conditioned, of course, but you'll find that though the Italian patients will keep the windows tightly shut and the shutters across for most of the day, the English patients will throw open the windows and push back the shutters the moment the sun moves round. And now for my single rooms.'

They walked the length of the corridor to where two doors faced them. They would lead, Sharon guessed, to the turret rooms she had glimpsed upon her arrival. But instead of entering, Sister Young stopped outside, lowering her voice to a rather more confidential note than the carrying tones she had used until now.

'I'd just like a word with you, Nurse, before we go in here. These rooms are usually reserved for the very rich, or the very sick, or the reclusive, but the patient here at the moment is none of these things. She's a nine-year-old child.'

'And she's all alone? Why on earth . . . ?'

'She's Susan Ridgeway, daughter of the film star, Morena Morasco, and the director, Ian Ridgeway. They divorced when Susan was only a few months old. As luck would have it, they were coming to the Sorrentine peninsula to make a film this summer, and it seemed an ideal opportunity for Susan to see them both, so she was sent for. Unfortunately, she was involved in a car accident within forty-eight hours of arriving in Italy, so now she's here, with a stitched-up cheek and a fractured femur. She's on Hamilton Russell traction.'

'Poor scrap! A broken shaft will mean she'll be immobilised for twelve weeks or so, of course. And all alone, too!'

'Precisely. And her mother hasn't visited her once since she's been put on traction. I just wish we could put her in a real children's ward, or in with other patients at least, but the mother won't hear of it.'

'Why not? It seems very cruel!'

'Because the regular children's ward is in the big *spedale* in the city and Morena Morasco won't have her child mixing with all the brats of the Sorrentine peninsula—her very words. So, at the moment, our hands are tied, though I'm hoping that when the father turns up things may change.'

'Oh?' Sharon looked her query. 'I thought you said he was in Italy too?'

'So he is, but in Rome at a conference at the moment. We'd better go in now, and you know what to expect—she's sharp as a needle, our Susan.'

Sister tapped briskly on the door and opened it and the two of them entered the room. It was the tower room, with windows on three sides, all overlooking the bay. At the foot of the bed a television set flickered soundlessly and on the bedside locker a small portable radio chattered out an Italian pop-song. Susan herself, propped up with pillows, her leg hoisted high, turned and grinned lopsidedly at them.

'Hello, Sister! Hello, Nurse! Are you the new Staff they've been talking about?'

She was not a pretty child, this offspring of one of the loveliest women in the world. She was small for her age and sallow skinned, with limp brown hair and brown eyes, and her cheek and forehead marred, at the moment, by a 'C' shaped line of stitches. But when she smiled at them, charm and character made you forget her plainness.

'That's right, Susan, this is Nurse Craig. You'll be seeing quite a bit of her, I daresay, so I hope you'll be friends.'

'Hello, Susan,' Sharon said. She took the small hand held out to her, then kissed the child's uninjured cheek. 'We're both new here, I understand, so you can tell me all about everyone and show me the ropes. I bet you know everything, tied up as you are!'

'I do, because people pop in—other patients, I mean,' Susan said. She patted the bed. 'Can you stay for a bit? Do, do, Sister says it does me good to see a fresh face!'

'Very well, you stay here with Susan, Nurse, and I'll send Nurse Drummond along to you presently,' Sister said. She opened the door, then paused in the doorway. 'Nurse has come all the way from England today, dear, so don't overtire her.'

'I won't, Sister, I'll do all the talking.' They heard Sister chuckle as the door closed, then Susan turned eagerly to Sharon. 'Can you imagine, I'm here for twelve whole weeks! I can tell you, it's hell to be lying here all useless when you thought you'd be up to your neck in water and having fun all summer. I *adore* swimming and I'm good at it, and then Daddy's here and he indulges me, Mummy says, so I thought I'd probably get some horseriding, and I told the other girls I was going to get Daddy to buy a boat and teach me how to waterski, and now it's all come to this. What's more,' she went on, before Sharon could reply, 'Mummy's lead is Pete Powers, he's my favourite film star. I'm going to marry him one day and he's got the best seat on a horse you ever did see, and he promised *faithfully* that he'd show me how to ride like cowboys do, you know, with long stirrups and no rising in the saddle, and . . . Oh, Craigie, twelve *weeks*!'

Sharon, taking 'Craigie' on the chin without a blink, nodded sympathetically.

'It is hard luck, I quite agree, but we'll do our best for you. There's a nice young man in Ward 3, I believe, he might come down and talk to you. He's in his twenties and . . .'

'Geoff Reynolds, do you mean? The one who had this frightful pain in his thingy, and he thought it was appendicitis, and then . . .'

'Yes, Geoff Reynolds, that's the one,' Sharon said hurriedly. 'So he's managed to stagger down here, has he?'

'Yes, he came down the very day after his hernia operation,' Susan said triumphantly. 'He's lovely, Geoff is. I wish I was in *his* ward, but he'll go much sooner than I will, of course. You should have been here when he first started to walk—he was all doubled over and he used to swear like anything. He's cross over his holiday, of course, but he won't go home until he's had his fortnight, he says he has to get some sun and drink some vino and find himself a willing chick.' She paused, to eye Sharon curiously. 'Chicks are girls—did you know that? And isn't his voice funny? When I first heard him talking I hardly bothered to listen because I thought it was Italian or German or something.'

'I believe he's from Birmingham,' Sharon said. 'Yes, it can be a difficult accent to understand until you get used to it.'

'Yes, Brummy, that's what he said. It's a *lovely* accent, isn't it? Get him to say "Where's me shirt?" for you, that's really *great*!' Julie's head, peering round the door, caused Susan to give an anxious squeak and seize Sharon's hand. 'Oh, *don't* go! I get so lonely you wouldn't believe, and Geoff won't come until after five o'clock because he's snoozing on the balcony. Or at least that's what he tells Sister, but really he's got his binoculars, and he's watching the chicks on the beach. He says there's one he fancies, and he's waiting for her to do him a favour and go topless, isn't he, Julie?'

'I suppose you can't help listening, but you really

shouldn't repeat all Geoff's remarks,' Julie said. 'I've got to take Nurse Craig away now, Susan, honestly I have, or Sister will get cross with us all, to say nothing of Dottore Vitale. Be good, and I'll come back for a natter this evening, when I'm officially off duty.'

Sharon stood up and Susan sighed, but attempted no further delaying tactics.

'Oh, all right. It was nice of you to stay with me at all, Craigie, and nice of old Drumsticks there to leave you here. Could you just pop in to Room No. 3 and give Geoff my dear love and remind him he's got a date with me at five o'clock?'

'We'll do that,' Julie promised, shepherding Sharon out of the room. 'And don't think you'll be left in peace for long because Ivonne's coming round with cool drinks and sugar biscuits, and probably she'll stop for a bit. Dottore Vitale's done his round today, hasn't he?'

'He has. Oh frabjous day,' Susan carolled, picking up a notebook. 'I'll write my diary until she arrives.'

'She's awfully precocious for nine, but such a charmer that it doesn't matter a bit,' Julie said as they closed the door behind them and walked back along the cool corridor, with only their footsteps and the air conditioner's hum to disturb the noon silence. 'Vitale disapproves of her being on the ward, he wants to force the issue and take her in to the city hospital, but, quite honestly, I don't think it would work. She scarcely speaks two words of Italian, and though her mother insists on her staying here for all the wrong reasons, that doesn't mean it would be right to move her. You'll have to watch your step, though.'

'Me? Why?'

'Because Vitale insists that the Wisteria staff must not give her more than her fair share of their time. That's why I spend such a lot of my off-duty here. If he catches you playing with her, there'll be ructions, and it isn't worth the unpleasantness.'

Sharon raised her brows.

'What makes you think I shall play with her?'

'What a question! She knows a soft touch when she sees one—young Susan will have you eating out of her hand in no time at all.'

'Hm, you could be right. If only another child could be transferred from the *ospedale*—but that wouldn't work, either. She needs someone—or something.'

'Got younger sisters?' Julie enquired, leading Sharon out into the sunshine at the hospital entrance. 'It sounds as if you know a thing or two about little 'uns.'

'Yes. Two. Even a budgerigar, she could teach it to talk, would be company for her.' She stopped short. 'Where are we going? I thought you were taking me back to the flat!'

'No, we're going to the terrace. Sister said you were to rest out here for about an hour and she's told a maid to bring out a tray of tea. And then she's going to treat us both to dinner at the Moonlight Trattoria. She's a good sort, and she knows I'm on duty until five although normally I would have been off. We're a bit shorthanded on Virginia at present.'

'That's awfully kind of her.' They reached the terrace and Sharon sank onto a generously upholstered swing seat and glanced approvingly round her at the wrought-iron tables and the comfortable, sagging wicker chairs with their cushioned seats and well-worn arm rests. 'Isn't this bliss? I feel like a film star myself sitting out here!'

'Well, make the most of it, because by the time Dr Vitale has bawled you out you'll feel like a student again,' Julie advised cheerfully. 'He believes in nursing by the book, but life just isn't like that and from time to time there's an explosion of wrath over something. At the moment your junior, Ivonne Lenghi, cringes at the sound of his footstep. She was giggling with one of the male patients, probably Geoff Reynolds from what Susan was saying, and Dr Vitale came in and spoke to her. She jumped, stepped backwards, and cannoned into the trolley which was fully laden with all the impedimenta of a dressing change. There was hell to pay.'

'I shan't do that, I'm far too old a bird,' Sharon protested, moving the swing seat gently backwards and forwards with one sandalled foot. 'I gave up being terrified of surgeons when I started my SRN training. Incidentally, we aren't going straight out to dinner are we? I don't fancy spending the evening in this.' She indicated her brief orange sundress and the flimsy sandals that went with it.

'Of course not, I'm not walking through the town in uniform and nor would Sister. Aha, here comes your tea, I'd better make myself scarce!' She raised her voice to the girl who stood, blinking, on the edge of the terrace. 'Over here, Maria! Now I'll love you and leave you.'

'Here ees your tea, Nurse Craig.'

Maria was a pretty, sturdy woman with a broad smile and black hair coiled on top of her head in a bun. She smiled at Sharon and put the tray down on the table in front of her.

'*Grazie*, Maria. It all looks delicious.'

'*Prego.*' Maria beamed. 'It weel not be long, Signorina, before you spik very good Italian.'

'I hope you're right. I'll bring the tray back when I've finished.'

Sharon settled down to enjoy her tea and presently she carried the tray back to the kitchen through the doorway from which Maria had emerged. She went confidently along the corridor, guided by the sounds of washing up, and left the tray with the kitchen staff after an exchange of fulsome compliments – at least, they had been compliments on her part, she could only hope that the girls in the kitchen had been as friendly as they seemed!

Returning to the terrace, she took stock of her surroundings. The Villa L'Arancia slept in the sun, most of the windows either shuttered or at least with the shutters

pulled half across. Looking up at her own ward, she saw
that air-conditioning had not prevailed upon the men, at
least, to close their windows or draw their shutters, and
she smiled to herself, imagining Geoff Reynolds up
there, his binoculars trained on the beach. Though the
beach, in mid-afternoon, could surely contain little of
interest to such an ardent womaniser?

The views from the terrace were unrivalled. On her
left there was a mind-bending drop down to a tiny beach
hundreds of feet below, whilst if one looked out to sea
the cliffs went straight down into the depths of the blue
water. To the right, the terraced garden went in giant-
steps almost down to sea level, with every step cultivated
with vegetables, fruit, or orchard trees.

Sharon went and leaned on the left-hand balcony. The
tiny beach looked miles below her, a bite of golden sand
out of the azure sea. It was private, so private that she
supposed no one ever frequented it, since it could only
be reached by boat or by swimming round from the
public beach which was further back still. This was
deserted at this time of the day, save for a brave holidaymaker or two who lolled in the water, scarcely daring
to climb out onto the baking hot sand. There were
probably people in the shade of the bright blue umbrellas which dotted the beach at regular intervals, but
they were invisible from here.

As she leaned over, speculating idly, she heard a cry.
Tiny, faint, but quite definitely a cry. Sharon glanced
round her. Seagulls? Of course, it must be—but where
were they? She could not see so much as a sparrow, let
alone a gull! She leaned further over the balustrade.
Perhaps the gulls came here to nest, and perhaps they
had young—that would account for the thinness and
frailty of the cry, the hint of desperation which she
imagined it had contained. Young gulls were always
hungry.

Then she saw the steps, and for a moment her mind
was diverted. So one *could* get down to the tiny bay,

someone had carved a flight of steep steps into the rock-face. She leaned out further, and was able to see that they did not begin at terrace-level, but from somewhere further down. She frowned. Odd! And then, when she had stopped even thinking about the cry, she saw the kitten.

Pure white and the size of a clenched fist, it crouched on a tiny ledge, at least six feet down the cliff. Sharon felt the hair rise on the nape of her neck. Poor little thing! She could not imagine how it had ever got there, but one thing was certain, it would never get back unaided. It had gone as far as it could along the incredibly narrow ledge and now, despite its best efforts, it could not turn back. Ahead lay a sheer drop down into the sea, dwarfed by distance into silky calm. In reality, the kitten would never survive the force with which it would hit the water, even if it could have withstood the waves. There was no way down to it, or no way that a sensible person would take. She looked wildly round her. No one. The house drowsed in the sunlight and the kitten was staring down over the edge of its precarious perch as if hypnotised by the gently moving waves so far below.

As she looked, as if attracted by her gaze, the kitten glanced up. It caught her eye, and she saw its own eyes widen hopefully. Sharon sighed, then wriggled on top of the balustrade. She could not just watch it die, she would have to do her best to rescue it!

CHAPTER TWO

ON THE far side of the balustrade, the distance between herself and the kitten seemed less, but far more dangerous. She knelt down, clutching the balustrade with one hand, and stretched out the other towards the kitten. It was as she realised the futility of this that she saw the tree. It grew up on the terrace, of course, but its roots, long and gnarled and reliable, reached quite halfway to the kitten. If she could swing across and get a good grip of the root with one hand, it would be possible, if not simple, to lean down towards the little creature.

The kitten stopped looking up and took a step nearer eternity. Sharon closed her eyes and leaned over, opening them in time to grab at the root and swing her body across, her feet finding a niche without too many false steps. Below her, the kitten looked up again, then fixed its gaze on the waves, miniaturised by distance into tiny, smooth movements. Did it realise that the waves were not within paw-patting distance? A cold sweat broke out and Sharon's hands slid a little on the root. Gulping, she called down to the kitten in her most authoritative voice.

'Puss! Pussy! Come here, there's a good little puss!'

The kitten looked up. It had eyes as blue as the sea below and the expression on its small white face was at once both innocent and intensely curious. Very slowly, Sharon began to stretch out her hand towards it. Her fingers were still several inches above the kitten's ledge. But its curiosity might save the little thing, if only she could arouse it sufficiently. She curled her fingers, as if there was something interesting hidden in the palm of her hand.

'Here, puss, see what Sharon's got for you!'

And against all the odds, the kitten stood up on its

hind legs and extended its small pink nose to sniff at its rescuer's hand.

Sharon grabbed. Her fingers closed round the kitten's thin neck and ignoring its sudden squawk she picked it up and pulled herself back into a vertical position once more, her heart thundering. Her comfort was not increased by the fact that the kitten had claws like tiny pins and seemed intent on getting as good a hold on Sharon as she had on it. With a squeak of her own, Sharon shifted her grip from its neck to its scrawny middle. Having got so far, she had no desire to let her wriggling captive plunge them both down to test the sea temperature together!

It had been a mixture of courage, impulse and ignorance which had sent her down to rescue the kitten but now, standing on the tiny ledge and clinging grimly to the tree root, Sharon realised that getting back was not going to be easy. There was a slight bulge in the cliff above her which she had not even noticed from the terrace and burdened as she was with the kitten in one hand, it was going to prove quite a climb.

She had two tries, then acknowledged that she could not do it, not with the kitten hampering her right hand. She gave a small whimper of exasperation, then straightened her back resolutely. What on earth was the matter with her, all she needed to do was to use a little imagination! She was wearing a sundress with a tie belt—she would tie one end of the belt round her wrist and the other round the kitten, and then she would have both hands free to climb with.

But it did not work. When she tried to tie the kitten in the belt she had to leave go of the tree root, and the kitten became mad with fear when she began to manoeuvre it. Sharon sighed, frowned, and looked all round her. There *must* be a way! She did not intend to abandon the kitten now that it was so nearly safe—

'Put the kitten inside the upper part of your dress, Signorina.'

The deep, calm voice nearly frightened Sharon out of her wits; for a moment she truly thought that Heavenly intervention was at hand and much though she wanted to be rescued, the thought of an angel with a flaming sword was not precisely soothing! But after her first start, she looked up at the terrace she had so recently vacated. Leaning over the balustrade was a man. Dark hair fell across his forehead, and his eyes were fixed on hers. She could see nothing more, but there was something in his voice, in the way he was watching, that gave her confidence. She felt safe, as though it would only be a matter of time, now, before she was back on the terrace once more.

'Oh, you startled me! What am I to do, Signor? I cannot pull myself back with only one hand, and the kitten won't let me tie it up in my belt!'

'Put the kitten into the bosom of your dress, Signorina. Then tie the belt and hold up both your hands to me.'

'Down the bosom . . . oh!' Sharon looked down at her sundress. 'There isn't much room in there, Signor. I don't want to squash the kitten.'

'I can see you're right, Signorina.' There was a tremor of laughter in the man's voice and for the first time Sharon realised what her remark had implied, and blushed. 'But the kitten is small and if you pull some material through the belt to form a small bag, I think it will travel up the cliff-face comparatively painlessly. Hurry, your arms must be very tired.'

'I will.' Sharon pushed the kitten, spitting and swearing, down the front of her dress, where it formed a protuberant third. Then she took a step up onto the next tiny ledge she had earmarked for her ascent, and grabbed a bit higher with her left hand. Her right hand, waving above her head, was seized in an iron grip.

'I've got you, Signorina. Move the left hand further up, and now you must trust me to bear your weight while I give you a strong, even pull so that you come a little higher still. Don't wriggle, don't panic, just stay quite still.'

She moved her left hand up the root and felt her wrist
caught and held. Then—and it was as difficult as anything she had done that day—she forced herself to
simply hang limply in the man's hold as he drew her up
over the cliff bulge and to a place where, once more, she
could use her feet, jamming them into tiny crevices,
letting him guide her fingers onto the top of the balustrade. From there, with her scrambling and clutching
and her rescuer employing his considerable strength, she
was pulled to safety. The man stood back, his chest
heaving, his head lowered and Sharon, quite without
meaning to, swayed and then collapsed onto the cream-
coloured paving whilst the kitten dug its little claws into
her breasts unregarded.

Hands on her shoulders brought her to her senses.
Hard hands, that shook her and then took her beneath
her armpits, dragging her to her feet.

'I could say no word of reproach when a false move
might have plunged you to your death, but do you know
what a dam' fool thing you've just done?' The man's face
was very close to hers, his mouth grim, his eyes narrowed. 'You could have killed yourself over a scrap of a
cat—there are a million such.' As if unable to contain
himself, he seized her shoulders and shook her until her
hair fell over her eyes and the kitten uttered a wail of
alarm. 'You stupid little bitch, you could have been
killed—I could have been killed too trying to get you!'
He then added a couple of sentences in Italian whose
meaning escaped her, though the sentiments did not.
'Well? What have you got to say for yourself?'

'I'm sorry, I simply acted on impulse, it never occurred to me that I'd have difficulty in getting back. And
the kitten—I couldn't just leave it there to die!'

She looked earnestly into his face, and noticed, for the
first time, that he was the best looking man she had ever
seen. Dark hair sprung, thick and curly, from a broad,
tanned brow, his eyes were dark, fringed with thick,
black lashes, his mouth was firm, perhaps might be

sensuous when he was not blazingly angry.

'Well? Can you say nothing but that you acted on impulse? What the hell are you doing here, for a start? You aren't a patient, no patient could have gone over that balustrade, so I suppose you're a visitor, another love-starved holidaymaker chasing after one of the patients, and you've no right whatsoever . . .'

'I'm a nurse.' Sharon felt a cold and terrible knowledge strike her. Without having to ask, she knew who this must be. It would be just her luck to get on the wrong side of Dottore Vitale, a man she had been warned did not suffer fools gladly!

'A nurse! I expect my nurses to be people of good sense! Not little blonde ragamuffins who climb down cliff faces to rescue unwanted kittens! I want women of intelligence and understanding, not untried girls; how *dare* you . . .'

'I *am* intelligent!' Sharon's blue eyes began to sparkle with annoyance. How dared he link her blondeness with brainlessness! Nothing annoyed her more than the old cliché, a dumb blonde, particularly when it was thrown at her by a man who knew nothing whatsoever about her! 'You shouldn't judge people by their appearance, Dottore Vitale! I'm a fully trained State Registered Nurse, I'm twenty-one years old, and I'm fully responsible for my actions! You say the kitten was unwanted; well, you're wrong, that kitten isn't only wanted, it's needed! I happen to be an animal lover, and . . .'

She stopped short. Something warm and wet was trickling down . . .

'Oh, my God!' She stepped back from the man, one hand going to the front of her dress. 'Now look what you've done, why don't you just go away and leave me to get the kitten out of my dress? Oh, oh!'

'I saved your life, you ungrateful, scatty . . .' he grabbed her arm and swung her round to face him, for she had been about to fly from the scene to somewhere where she might remove the soggy kitten from her now soggy person. For a second he stared at her, then his eyes dropped, and he saw the spreading patch of wet at her waist. She felt his fingers tighten, then saw that he was actually laughing! 'Good Lord, it's wetted you—perhaps you were well-served for your recklessness, after all.' He began to stride towards the villa, pulling her after him. 'Come on, you've had a bad time, now let's get you cleaned up!'

'I can manage! I don't need any h-help to clean up!' Sharon's voice was wavering and she knew that if she did not escape quickly she would start to cry and make a complete fool of herself, convince the surgeon that she was in truth a dumb blonde. She tried to wrench herself out of his grasp but his fingers continued to bite into the soft flesh of her upper arm. He hurried her along the passage but they went straight past the kitchens she had visited earlier and into a room she had not seen before, a room a little like a study and a little like a surgery. His consulting room. He sat her down on a chair, then held out a commanding hand.

'Give me the kitten.'

'How can I?'

Sharon stared defiantly up at him. It had been quite easy to pop the kitten down the front of her dress, but to get it out, against its wishes, might prove extremely embarrassing! However, it seemed he could be understanding enough when he wished, for he nodded his head slowly, though she could see his lips twitching.

'I see. If I were you, I'd undo the belt and let the kitten drop downwards. I'll just go through to the dispensary and get something to calm you down, and fetch some tea. I shan't be long.'

As soon as he had disappeared Sharon fished the kitten, wild-eyed and rumpled, out of her clothing. It was a resourceful little creature, though. After all its adventures it merely shook itself, licked its shoulder and began to purr, and when she sank back onto the chair again it jumped on her lap and settled itself comfortably, as though it had known her all its short life.

'Better?' The voice behind her made her jump, but she nodded casually as he came round to stand before her.

'Definitely. Better out than in, as you doubtless tell your patients. You *are* Dottore Vitale?'

He nodded, then handed her the cup which he was carrying. It contained hot and steamingly fragrant tea.

'I'm Vitale. And you're Nurse Craig, of course. Drink the tea, which really *is* good for shock, and take these two tablets. They'll help you to relax. Later, I'll give you some sleeping pills.'

'Thanks for the tea, but I won't bother with the tablets, if you don't mind, I'm not the nervy sort.' She smiled demurely, sipping her tea. 'If I had been, I'd scarcely have gone over that cliff!'

He raised a brow, his expression sardonic.

'Independant! But you look better, apart from being filthy and damp, of course.'

'Oh, I know, but . . .' Sharon drank the tea quickly, burning her tongue. 'Thank you, Signor, for your help, and . . . well, for saving the kitten's life, because if you hadn't helped me I might have been forced to abandon it, and . . .'

'You won't admit that I saved your life?' For the first time, he smiled at her and a shock, almost of recognition, coursed through her veins. No wonder he gave the impression of being arrogant, he must be well used to women swooning at his feet when he looked at them like that! However, she was made of sterner stuff!

'Well, I suppose . . .'

'Very well, I don't want to humiliate you any further, just let's say I'm an animal-lover too, particularly human animals.'

'I'm sorry.' Sharon stood up, cradling the kitten in her arms. 'I was churlish; thank you for saving my life and the kitten's. And now, if you'll excuse me . . .'

He stood up too, towering over her. He put his hand beneath her elbow. 'I'm taking you back to your flat,

young woman, so don't try to be *too* independant,
please. You're having a bath and then you're going to
bed with a mild sleeping pill, otherwise you'll dream
about that cliff and what might have happened all night
and come to work tomorrow in no fit state to nurse my
patients.'

'It's very kind of you, but I'm being taken out to
dinner tonight, and I don't see . . .'

'Really?' The sarcastic inflection was back at full
power. 'You *are* a fast worker, Nurse Craig! Who's the
fortunate man?'

Sharon smiled demurely. Sarcasm deserved a set-
down and she would make sure he got one!

'Sister Young of Wisteria Ward, Signor. She asked
Nurse Drummond and I out for a meal so that we
wouldn't have to cook on my first night.'

If he considered this to be a set-down, he gave no sign
of it. Instead, he gave an approving nod.

'Excellent, I'll give Sister a ring and explain and she'll
send a nurse down to see that you obey my orders.'

Sharon said nothing. She had no intention of going to
bed, she was hungry, and though the moment on the cliff
had been frightening and her muscles ached dreadfully,
she would be quite all right to walk slowly and sedately
to the Trattoria and have a quiet dinner. Indeed, her
stomach rumbled protestingly already at the thought of
being sent to bed hungry, like a naughty child—she was
longing for a plate piled high with lasagne, or canelloni,
or spaghetti Bolognese!

He picked up the phone and dialled. 'Sister? Vitale
here.' He outlined the story briefly, listened for a moment, they nodded, said goodbye, and replaced the
receiver. He turned to Sharon.

'She's just come off duty so she'll come here and take
you back with her.' He smiled grimly. 'You won't twist
Sister round your little finger, Nurse, so don't you
imagine that you'll be dining by candlelight tonight!
Now what do you intend to do with that cat?'

'Keep it, if it hasn't got an owner,' Sharon said. 'Do you think it belongs to someone in the hospital? Or someone in one of the surrounding villas, perhaps?'

'It'll be the last of the litter Rafaello found in the wine cellars; this one must have escaped, somehow. No one's going to claim it.'

'Right, then I have a use for it.'

He shrugged, but looked indifferent.

'I can't imagine what use anyone could have for such a small kitten, but . . . Ah, Sister!'

Sister Young entered the room. She was still in uniform but had shed her cap and carried a shopping basket over one arm.

'You are in a state, Nurse Craig.' Her eyes lit on the kitten. 'Don't tell me, you were rescuing that animal from the results of its own stupidity.'

'That's right. And Dr Vitale rescued me. But I'm all right, really I am.'

'Take her away, Sister, and make sure she takes these once she's tucked up in bed.' Vitale handed Sister Young the tablets. 'And be firm over that kitten – if you think she'll neglect her work for the creature just you take it away and let it run wild. After all, nine out of ten of the cats in Sant' Agnello manage to scrape a living without anyone bothering overmuch about them.'

'I do *not* approve of the way the local people treat cats,' Sister Young said firmly. 'And very well you know it, Signor! As for my nurse, she'll do exactly as I say, of course. And the kitten's a pretty little thing, we'll contrive something suitable.' She took Sharon's arm. 'Come along, my dear, back to the flat!'

Sharon found herself quite glad, in the end, to submit to the wills of all the dictatorial people by whom she was surrounded and go meekly to bed. Not supperless, however, despite her fears, for Sister Young made an omelette, fluffy without and creamy within, and generously garnished with mushrooms and ham, and Julie ran down the road to the little local shop and came back with a large helping of walnut icecream, smothered in dark chocolate sauce. After eating her share of this feast, Sharon privately thought that she did not need the sleeping tablet which Dr Vitale had insisted that she take, but at any rate she slumbered the night away dreamlessly, waking next morning to bright sunlight and Julie, standing at the head of her bed with a tray in her hands.

'Come along, Craigie, you're due on the ward in less than an hour! I've brought you breakfast in bed as a special treat—weak lemon tea and a slightly stale scone—so do sit up.'

'Great!' Sharon sat up, rubbed her eyes, stretched and yawned. 'Does bacon and eggs follow?'

'No it doesn't, you greedy cat! And talking of cats, your kitten performed in that tray of earth you put down for it as if it had been using trays of earth all its life. When it noticed I was watching, though, it gave me the coldest look and turned its back, for all the world as though I were some sort of *voyeur*! I can't wait to see Susan's face when you give it to her.'

'Nor me. It's the ideal pet for her now, though, whilst she's so inactive. It's terribly small and skinny and it'll do it a lot of good to be stuffed with nice food and smothered with affection. Did Sister tell you that it had probably broken its back leg at some time or other?'

'Yes, she did. She said that the less exercise it got the better, until the break has healed completely—not that it will stay quiet for long, knowing kittens. And children with kittens, of course.'

'Oh, well, we'll see.' Sharon drank her tea, and bit into the scone, then gave an exclamation and jumped out of bed.

'My scones aren't *that* bad—what's up?'

'I am—and about time too—I've just remembered, I want to have the kitten settled in with Susan before I start work, so I'll have to get a move on. Thanks a million for the tea, Julie, though why lemon?'

'No milk,' Julie said briefly. 'We do tend to run out of things and locally more goat's milk is drunk than cow's, and I hate goat's milk in tea, though it isn't too bad in coffee. Look, if you're going to have a shower and dress now, I'll leave you in peace and go and put my makeup on. Then we'll walk over to L'Arancia together.'

'Right. I shan't be long.'

Presently, neatly uniformed, the two girls set off across the road for the hospital, Sharon with the kitten in a cardboard box tucked beneath one arm. Its muffled protests were loud and pathetic by the time they reached the foyer, but no one was around yet to hear, so Sharon bade Julie goodbye and set off for Susan's room.

Susan, washed and breakfasted, was sitting up in bed, lethargically knitting. Her work was an indeterminate size, shape and colour, and it did not need much imagination to prove that she was not a keen knitter. But her face lit up when she saw Sharon.

'Craigie, guess who's coming to see me tomorrow? Daddy! Yes, he rang last night and said his work in Rome is finished. He's travelling back up here or should it be down? We're nearer the toe here, aren't we—the toe of Italy, I mean, so perhaps it should be down. Well, anyway, he's coming back today, and he'll be in to see me first thing tomorrow.' She cast her knitting down. 'What a long day this will be! I say, Craigie, what's in that box?'

The kitten, either lulled or knocked unconscious by its journey, was quiet. Sharon put the box down on the bed and drew back the lid.

'He's yours, if you'd like him. Whilst you're stuck here, anyway. When you leave, perhaps he'd better live with me.'

'A kitten!' Susan had the kitten out of the box in a trice and cradled in her arms. 'For me? My very own? Oh Craigie, I've wanted a kitten all my life!'

'Well, you've got one for as long as you're here. Afterwards, you'll have to see what your parents think.

There's quarantine, though, if you wanted to take it back to England—perhaps the best thing would be to let me keep him, and then whenever you're in Italy you can claim him again.'

Susan's mouth tightened. 'He's mine, and I shall keep him. I don't understand too much about quarantine, but I'm sure there's a way round it. Thank you, Craigie, thank you!'

'Yes, well . . .' Sharon felt that this was neither the time nor the place for a lecture on the dangers of rabies. 'What are you going to call him?'

'Snowflake,' Susan said promptly. 'I've always known if I was lucky enough to get a white kitten, I'd call it Snowflake, a black one would have been Carbonel, after a cat in a book, a ginger one would have been Rufus . . .'

'You really do like cats, don't you?' Sharon said, watching as the cat, with extended neck and eyes black with curiosity, began to explore the mysteries of traction. 'This kitten had a ghastly ordeal yesterday, but it's rather a long story and I can't tell it now, so take care of him, don't let him fall off the bed and injure himself—his back leg's been broken, Sister Young thinks—and I'll come back again in my lunch-hour.'

'Or earlier, if you have to do some nursing for me?' Susan said eagerly, as Sharon stood up. '*Someone* has to rub cream into my elbows and things, and it might as well be you—then you could tell me Snowflake's story.'

'Well, perhaps,' Sharon was beginning, when the door opened and Dr Vitale strode into the room. His expression, as it fell on Susan, was pleasant and friendly enough, but it froze when he took in Sharon's presence and that of the kitten. His eyes raked her from the tip of her cap to her sensible shoes, and somehow managed to convey icy disapproval.

'Good morning, Susan! What are you doing here, Nurse? With that . . . that animal?'

'Oh, I'm just . . . well, I *am* on duty actually and

Susan is one of my patients.' Sharon tried to sound
nonchalant but merely succeeding in sounding defensive. 'As for the kitten . . .'

'It's mine,' Susan cut in eagerly, 'and he's my dearest
friend and my very own pet.' Her lower lip trembled and
she cast the surgeon an appealing look. 'You *said* it
would do me good to have someone to play with, you
said it wasn't right to keep a child cooped up in a room by
itself all day, you *said* . . .'

'Did I say you should have an animal in here? Did I?'
He turned to Sharon. 'More interference of your making, Nurse, I can see that! And what will Sister say when
she finds herself unwillingly hosting a small, scruffy cat?'

'Sister knows, and she doesn't . . .' Sharon began,
then stopped. Susan, without fuss or noise, was crying.
Huge tears ran down the thin brown cheeks and dripped
off her pointed chin. Her lips were turned down and her
frail shoulders were shaking. Sharon reached the bed in
one quick movement. 'Susan? It's all right, pet, Dr
Vitale didn't mean . . .'

But quick though she was, she was no quicker than the
surgeon. His arm was around the child and he was
bending over her, picking the kitten up in one hand,
examining the little scrap with well-simulated interest.

'Sister doesn't mind? Then why should I complain?
And you couldn't have chosen a better kitten if you'd
had your pick of a hundred! Look at those blue eyes, and
the fur's as white as snow! What are you going to call it?'

'S-Snowflake,' Susan said, rubbing her face dry with
the backs of her hands. 'Do you have a kitten at home,
Signor?'

'Not at present. You must watch that I don't kidnap
this fine little creature, mustn't you?'

'Well, if you like my kitten, why were you shouting at
Craigie?' Susan asked, her voice still a trifle querulous. 'I
th-thought you were going to be like my mother, and say
I c-couldn't keep this darling, *clean* little cat!'

'Nothing was further from my mind,' asserted Vitale,

appearing not to notice Sharon's eyes widening at this blatant lie. 'I didn't want to annoy Sister, you see, and hadn't realised that she approved. Now, Nurse, I'm sure you have work to do.'

'Of course.' Sharon headed for the door. 'I'll see you later, Susan.'

But she had gone no more than six feet from the door when it opened and an imperious voice addressed her.

'Nurse!'

'Yes, Signor?' She turned back reluctantly, to find Vitale softly closing Susan's door behind him.

'Ah, Nurse, I could scarcely speak to you further on the subject when the patient was becoming so distressed, but I want you to know that I shall hold you entirely responsible for that kitten—entirely! If it becomes a nuisance, it must go, and you must see that it does. And you'll have to take care of it at night—I refuse to allow the animal to career around my hosital at night.'

'Very well. Although, Signor, since you are so passionately fond of cats, with a particular fondness for white ones, I'll *quite* understand if you feel you'd like to have him for the odd weekend, when I'm off!'

A dark eyebrow shot up. Sharon felt she had scored, but was speedily proved wrong.

'Him? What makes you assume it's a male?'

'Oh!' Sharon remembered the brevity of the surgeon's glance at the kitten and took courage. She smiled mockingly. 'And what makes you so sure it isn't?'

'Biology, Nurse, or don't they teach you the difference between the male and female of the species when you're doing your training?'

'Well, not of cats,' Sharon admitted. 'Do you mean it really is a female?'

'It really is.' The dark eyes raked her again, but this time the glance was mocking, intimate. 'I am very aware of the difference, Nurse, whether it is amongst cats or people—*vive la difference*, as the French say.'

'Oh, well, whether it's male or female, it'll have to be

neutered,' Sharon said, preparing to leave him, though with heightened colour. 'I'll pay for the operation when the time comes, don't worry.'

The dark brows rose once more, but this time the eyes fixed on hers were dancing with amusement. He had noticed her blush, she could see that!

'Operation? Aha, you mean the operation performed by so many veterinary surgeons in your country upon defenceless cats and dogs. You will find, Nurse, that in Italy no vet would dream of ruining the natural function of an animal.'

'Natural function! There's nothing natural about cats producing litters of kittens every six months and dying before they're more than a few years old. And the kittens being drowned, or allowed to roam wild, or . . .'

'More crusading, Nurse? I wonder when you'll have time for your work at the hospital? Because putting Italy to rights, neutering all our cats and dogs, could easily become a full-time job. Especially as you'll have to perform all the operations yourself!'

'Don't be ridiculous,' Sharon snapped, turning away. 'All I'm concerned about is one small kitten and one small patient.' She turned back, her chin raised. 'And you, Signor, though you may try very hard to pretend otherwise, are every bit as concerned over that child as I am!'

'More, Nurse, very much more.' His expression had lost its mockery, his dark eyes were stern. 'I can understand far more easily than you how lonely and misunderstood that child is.'

Before she could so much as answer him, he had turned on his heel and walked back into Susan's room, closing the door firmly behind him.

'Well, Nurse, you settling in nicely?' Geoff Reynolds' cheerful tones greeted Sharon as she entered Room 3. Signor Vitale was operating today, and had intimated that he would do a ward round before he started his list, and ever since their encounter over the kitten, Sharon had been on her metal, eager to prove to him that she was neither dumb nor dizzy, but a competent nurse. This, however, had been her first opportunity, since in the five days she had worked at the L'Arancia, she had managed to miss his ward round by some fluke.

'I'm fine, Mr Reynolds. I've just come from Susan's room—she wants to know if you'll take your coffee down to her room when elevenses come round.'

She popped the thermometer into his mouth, effectively silencing him.

Geoff Reynolds was in his mid-twenties, a sturdy, athletic man with toffee-coloured hair and a ready smile. He must have found the restrictions placed on him by his recent operation very irksome, but being blessed with a sunny and uncritical disposition, he simply made the best of it. He was disappointed over the start to what should have been the holiday of a lifetime, but since he had every intention of remaining in Italy once he was fit, this period in hospital was merely a delaying of the fun. He was keenly interested in women, made no secret of his affection for the opposite sex, and had both the young Italian nurses blushing and giggling every time he glanced in their direction. In fact, the girls vied for his attention and both had offered him hospitality the moment he left the Villa L'Arancia.

'You tell young Susan I'll 'ave me coffee with her if you'll be there too, Nurse Craig,' he said as soon as the thermometer was out of his mouth. 'Nicest little chick I've seen since me accident!'

'Indeed? What about Ivonne and Carmella? To say nothing of Maria and Giuseppina, and . . .'

'Aw, they all adore me, that's the trouble,' Geoff said. He was sitting on his bed in his pyjama trousers, the jacket being discarded the second Sister left Room 3. He stuck out his chest now and flexed one brawny arm in a Mr Universe pose. 'Look at that, Craigie! Gals go down like ninepins after one glimpse of me biceps.'

'Really, Mr Reynolds?' Sharon, slipping the thermometer in the next patient's mouth, winked at him. Little Mr Mapp, down for theatre later, smiled and winked back. 'I'm afraid I'm made of sterner stuff, I don't go down at the sight of a few muscles.' She wheeled the blood pressure apparatus over to his bed and wound the band of the sphyg around his upper arm. 'As soon as I've taken your b.p., however, you can strut around the hospital and watch all the other nurses swoon.'

'Aren't you hard, Craigie?' Geoff did his best to look soulful. 'Cold, too. Blondes are all alike.' He burst into song. 'Lovely to look at, delightful to hold, but ever so cold!' He watched her as, undeterred by his foolery, she filled in his chart and moved back to Mr Mapp's bedside. 'Aw, come on, Craigie, admit I'm gorgeous and I knock you out!'

'Not today, I'm too busy. When do you go home, Mr Reynolds? You look pretty fit to me!'

'Home? I'm going to have me holiday first, don't you forget that! Vitale says he'll give me a medical certificate to send back to the factory so that they know it's all genuine, and Carmella's mum says I can stay at their flat, and I've all me insurance money to come, besides the bread I'd got for holiday spends. So I'll be around for a bit yet!'

'Ah well, nothing in life is perfect, they say.' Sharon took the thermometer from Mr Mapp's mouth, read it, and returned it to its slot above his bed. Then she wheeled the b.p. trolley over. 'How do you feel, Mr Mapp? Has the anaesthetist been in to see you?'

'Yes, he's been. I feel fitter now than I shall in an hour or so, I daresay,' Mr Mapp said. 'Mind, I believe Vitale's a first-rate surgeon, but even so . . . I'll be glad when it's over.'

'Yes, you're down for theatre before noon. A nasty case of sepsis, Sister said. You'll be glad to get rid of it, I daresay.'

'Aye. Ingrown toenail gone rotten, that's what it is. More or less. And you're right, I'll be glad to get rid of it and be able to walk in comfort.'

'That's the spirit.' Sharon filled in his chart and moved on to the third bed. Mr Weston was due to leave in a few days, his cholecystectomy having been performed satisfactorily some ten days earlier. Proof positive, if such were needed, reposed on his bedside locker in the form of a small bottle containing the offending gall-stones. 'And how's Mr Weston this fine morning?'

'All the better for seeing you, Nurse Craig,' Mr Weston said gallantly. He held out a plump arm for the sphyg. 'Start my holiday all over again, Dr Vitale says—the best treatment, he reckons.' He sighed happily. 'Plenty of sun, good food in moderation, and I'll be fit as a fiddle in no time.'

'Wouldn't we all?' Sharon approached her last patient in Room No. 3. 'You're for theatre too, Mr Hobbs, so if you two gentlemen would like to stay here, we'll pack the other two off and have the room to ourselves.'

'Why, Nurse? What are you going to do to them?' Geoff Reynolds leered at her. 'If it's anything intimate, we'd just as soon stay!'

'Certainly you can stay, but you'll have to be prepped too,' Sharon said, entering into the spirit of his badinage. 'Come along, then, hop back into bed—and put that pyjama jacket on at once, before Dr Vitale catches you improperly dressed in a nurse's presence!'

'I'll go, I'll go,' Geoff said hastily. He left the room and Sharon went down to the sluice and called Ivonne to bring the trolley.

Sister Young and Sharon were in the laundry room. Because there was less back-up from home here, with the majority of the patients holidaymakers who could not easily lay their hands on the required number of towels, nightgowns and bedjackets, the linen room was larger and better stocked than in most hospitals. Sharon had already taken a pair of clean sheets, a draw-sheet, two regulation pillowslips and two towels, but now she turned doubtfully to Sister.

'How well equipped will Mrs Humphries be? She's coming from the big *spedale*, isn't she?'

'She's a resident, so she'll bring everything she should, including towels.' Sister took the towels off Sharon's pile and put them back on the shelf. 'Take the bedding straight to Carmella and she and Ivonne can do the bed, then later I'll go over the patient's notes with you and you can prepare a trolley. Dr Vitale wants to see her as soon as she's settled.'

'Very well. In the meantime, I'll take my coffee up to Susan's room and have a chat whilst I drink it.'

It was a moment's work to hand over the bedding to Carmella and to hurry along the corridor to the kitchen, where she picked up a tray with two coffees on it, a milky one for Susan and one for herself. She was balancing the tray on her hip preparatory to opening Susan's door when it shot open and there was Geoff, obviously waiting for her. He winked.

'Hi, beautiful! Told you she couldn't resist me, young Susan,' he added over his shoulder. 'Brought us a cup of coffee, too!'

Sharon swept regally into the room, smiled at Susan, and put the tray down on the bedside locker. She turned to Geoff, who had come in behind her and shut the door.

'This is *my* coffee, Mr Reynolds, if you want a cup there's plenty in the dayroom, Susan and I won't keep you.' Her voice dropped to a softer note. 'Hello, Snowflake? How's my favourite kitten, then?'

'Scrawny little brute, isn't it?' Geoff said, sitting on the end of the bed and taking the kitten from Susan. 'All bones and eyes!'

The two girls cried out at this and Sharon tried to take the kitten from him but Geoff was in a teasing mood and promptly got to his feet and held the kitten out of her reach.

'Give us a kiss and you can have the animal. Come on, prove I'm your favourite feller!'

'You aren't.' Sharon put her cup down and Geoff

promptly handed her the kitten and removed her cup. 'Oh, come on, Mr Reynolds, I'm terribly thirsty and I don't have all morning to drink mine, like you can. Hand it over!'

Geoff shook his head, his face alight with amusement.

'Not on your life! A kiss is me price! Deliver the goods or your coffee will go all cold and nasty!'

Sharon grabbed, caught his arm, and watched the coffee slop dangerously against the sides of the cup as her fingers closed round it. She smiled up at Geoff, looking enchantingly pretty with the sunshine gleaming on her pale gold hair and her eyes sparkling with fun.

'Come on, admit you're beaten, I've got the cup and . . .'

Geoff swung her into his arms, ignoring her squeak of horror as the coffee leapt onto the tiled floor. His mouth, half-teasing still, came down over hers.

'Just what are you doing, Nurse Craig?'

She would have known that icy voice anywhere. Sharon wrenched herself free, her cheeks burning. Trust Vitale to catch her in that most compromising of positions, actually in a patient's arms! No amount of explanation would mitigate her sin, fooling around with the male patients was a crime which no surgeon, however understanding, would tolerate.

'I'm sorry, Signor, I came down here with my coffee, and . . .'

She noticed, with a calm part of her mind, that though he had come straight from theatre he was as cool and unruffled as though he had just risen from a quiet half-hour of television viewing. His greens had been left downstairs presumably, but he had donned a crisp white coat and his stethoscope hung round his neck. Help! She had forgotten the ward round—he had been forced to cancel the early round he had planned because an emergency had come in. Her confusion was complete.

But help was at hand. Geoff Reynolds stepped forward.

'Don't blame Nurse Craig, Signor. I kidnapped her coffee and I was kidding her she'd have to kiss me to get it back. I didn't mean to do it, either, I don't know what came over me, honest.'

Dr Vitale stared at him for a moment, then the slow smile dawned. He sighed.

'I daresay her confusion was irresistible. Nevertheless, my nurses ought to be able to keep patients under control without resorting to . . . to horseplay. Don't let it happen again.'

'I won't, Signor.'

'Good.' The surgeon beckoned to Sharon. 'Come with me, Nurse.'

He led her briskly down the corridor and into Sister's room, which was empty. They faced one another. He had smiled at Geoff, but now his eyes, beneath heavy lids, were travelling over her in a speculative manner, as though he was wondering just what made her tick. It put her on the defensive and made her sound truculent when she spoke.

'Well, Signor? Do you want to remind me that nurses are responsible people who never drop their guard before the patients?'

He raised a brow and the speculative look increased.

'It seems, Nurse, that mere words make very little impression upon your volatile personality! We'll say no more about it, however. I've brought you here to tell you a little about the transfer abdominal surgery in No. 2.'

'Mrs Humphries, you mean,' Sharon said stiffly. She disapproved of patients being known by their ailments or operations. 'Sister was going to speak to me about her.'

'Well, I'm doing it instead. Have you any objection?'

'No, of course n-not . . .' Sharon stammered, knowing she was blushing. She seemed to say the wrong thing by instinct when she was talking to Vitale! She took a deep breath and began again. 'I'm sorry if I sounded rude, I didn't mean to be. I did wonder why Mrs Humphries was coming here since she's had the operation, though.'

'Yes. Sit down, will you, this may take a little while.' Sharon sat on the edge of the visitor's chair and Vitale leaned across the desk and addressed her earnestly.

'Mrs Humphries is in her sixties and a widow, and before she knew she had to have surgery she was planning another marriage. She's broken off her engagement to the elderly man who wanted to marry her and she won't see him or talk about the affair. She's old-fashioned, narrow-minded, rather silly I suppose, but she's full of courage and humour. I believe that with understanding and sympathy, we may yet persuade her to go through with her arrangements and marry Signor Pappalardo.'

'I see. But that doesn't altogether explain why she's coming to the Villa L'Arancia.'

'Mrs Humphries has lived here for twenty years or more but still speaks almost no Italian, so she desperately needs care from someone who speaks her language. A conviction that she would die under the anaesthetic and would be no use, post-operatively, to Signor Pappalardo, was what made her break off her engagement. But now . . . well, she's rapidly improving and is going to be as fit as she ever was, so it's mainly obstinacy. Despite your faults, Nurse, I've been impressed by your dedication towards your work and by your undoubted efficiency with the sick. I believe you could prove to be Mrs Humphries salvation.'

Making her way down to Room No. 2, Sharon's heart felt light and her step came perilously close to a skip. He had accepted Geoff's story, he did not think her an irresponsible flirt, and he had actually admitted that she was dedicated and efficient. She would do her very best with Mrs Humphries, she would jolly her out of all her fears and foolishness and try to get the engagement mended, and Dr Vitale would be pleased with her.

It had become important to win his approval, though she could not have said why.

CHAPTER THREE

DUE TO a hold up in the system for passing a patient from the big hospital to the smaller one, Mrs Humphries did not arrive in Wisteria Ward for two days, but Sharon was well prepared when she went down to greet her in the foyer.

The stretcher was brought in from the ambulance by two Italian porters and for the first time Sharon appreciated the difficulties which patients must suffer when they do not speak the same language as medical staff. The porters adjured Mrs Humphries to lie still, to keep her hands inside the stretcher in the lift, and told her they would only be a moment—all in rapid and incomprehensible Italian. Sharon, hastily translating, only guessed what they were saying because it was what all stretcher bearers say when their patients are so obviously ill-at-ease.

Once Mrs Humphries was comfortably installed in bed Sharon went to Sister's office and rang down for Dr Vitale as she had been instructed. Fortuna said she would pass the message on, and then Sharon returned to her new patient.

'Dr Vitale will be up in a moment, to make sure the journey hasn't upset you in any way,' she said soothingly, smiling down at Mrs Humphries. 'As soon as he's finished with you I'll get you a nice cup of tea, I daresay you could do with one.'

'That'd be lovely, Nurse. Oh, the pleasure of hearing English spoken, and so nicely, too,' Mrs Humpries said. She, was a pretty, plump little woman with big brown eyes, a rosebud mouth and an abundance of feathery grey curls. It was no wonder that the Italian had fallen for her, Sharon thought.

'You'll hear plenty of English now,' Sharon said, lingering by the bedside. 'But your surgeon's an Italian, though he does speak very good English.'

'Ah, Vitale's only half Eyetalian. His mother was as English as you or I, that's why he spent such a lot of his childhood in England. He was at school there, you know, and when his mother died and his father married again he stayed on there for a bit, living with his grand-parents. A difficult business, I daresay, finding yourself with a stepmother, I believe he had quite a chip on his shoulder for a bit.' She gave Sharon a conspiratorial look. 'He's ever so lovely, isn't he? All that Latin charm and machis . . . what's the word?'

'Machismo, I expect you mean,' Sharon said, looking as amused as she felt. 'He's certainly very handsome, but I'm not so sure about the machismo; he's very arrogant with us nurses, you know!'

'That's surgeons for you,' Mrs Humphries said comfortably. 'They're important people, my dear, with the power of life and death in their hands. They don't suffer fools gladly.'

Sharon, aware that she had just been called a fool in the nicest possible way, decided to change the subject.

'That's true.' She glanced around the almost empty room. 'I'm sorry none of your room-mates are here at the moment, except for Mrs Snelling and, as you can see, she's very soundly asleep indeed, but I'll introduce you to the others when they come in. Or perhaps you'd like to go along to the day-room, when you've seen Dr Vitale.'

'We'll see, Nurse.' Mrs Humphries could almost be seen to cling to her sheets. 'It doesn't do to hurry things.'

Sharon, agreeing, glanced at her wristwatch. Ten minutes had passed since she had phoned down and there was still no sign of the surgeon. Was it possible that Fortuna had not passed on the message? But just as she was contemplating telephoning down again, the door opened.

'Ah, Nurse, a message for you. Signor Vitale's been called away to see a patient on another ward. He'll be with you in thirty minutes.'

'I see. Thank you, Sister.' Sharon walked over to the door, smiling at Sister Young. 'I'd better get on with the rest of my work, then, and come back later.'

There was a wail of protest from Mrs Humphries and Sister winked.

'All right, Nurse, stay here and do the obs, and I'll send the girl through with some tea for your patient. You can get a trolley ready, too, for when the consultant arrives.'

Sharon, busily taking Mrs Humphries' blood pressure, temperature and pulse and then setting up the trolley, thought that the wink bestowed on her by Sister had a very definite meaning. *Get to know the woman*, that wink implied. *She may be silly, but get to know her*. She would do just that.

'You've lived in Italy a long time, Mrs Humphries. Do you like it here? I've barely been in Sant' Agnello a week, but I love it already.'

'You don't know it as I do, my dear. Oh, I won't deny the weather is very nice and the people friendly as can be, but there's times I'd give a good deal to see Manchester on a rainy Monday morning, or hear the coster-folk and the old rag and bone men or the flower sellers shouting their wares in good old Lancashire accents, with a joke now and then. Just so long as it was English they were talking.'

'That's homesickness, I suppose,' Sharon said wisely. 'But you don't feel like that often, do you?'

'Not often; not at all, perhaps, until this operation happened. But from the moment I knew I'd got to be cut open I wanted to go back. Not that I'd find much that I left, I daresay, for I've got a beautiful house and a garden the Queen would envy me, could she but see it.'

'And you must have friends, too,' Sharon suggested.

'You can't have lived here so long without making friends.'

'Yes, I've good friends here, though scarce a word of the language do I speak,' Mrs Humphries said with a measure of pride. 'When I'm sensible, I know I'd be an ill old woman at home, probably crippled with arthritis, so I've much to be thankful for.'

'What made you come?' Sharon asked curiously. 'What made you choose Italy?'

'It's a long story . . .' Mrs Humphries said, with the air of one who firmly intends to relate every last word of it.

The late Mr Humphries, it transpired, was a good deal older than his wife and had fought in Italy in the Second World War. He had been befriended by an Italian family during his time in the country, and the farmer's eldest son had saved his life and very nearly lost his own in so doing. He had always meant to go back and thank them, and on his deathbed, he had asked his wife to return to Italy and convey his thanks to the family.

'Give 'em some money, Florrie,' he had said. 'They could do with a bit and we've no children, we won't miss some of the cash we've put by.'

Mrs Humphries and her husband had been only children, so there were no near relatives. She had sold up her little house in Manchester and within three months, shares which her husband had bought and never even thought about, had soared in value. She found herself a rich woman, with the world at her feet and very little to do except to see that her husband's dying wish was granted. She came to Italy, fell in love with the country and the whole boisterous, affectionate peasant family, and decided to stay. She soon realised that it would not be tactful to simply hand money to the Marcheses, however. Instead, she bought a share in the farm, paying, she told Sharon cheerfully, an exorbitant price for it by local standards at that time, and insisting that they let her help by advising on the investment of the money she had paid, as well as buying a good deal of modern farm machinery.

'It snowballed, after that,' she confided. 'I bought land and built my present home and ten years ago the old people retired and moved in near me, leaving the farming to the younger ones. I've been very fortunate.'

'And very brave, very kind, very generous,' Sharon said gently. 'It would have been easy to give the family money and run off home, wouldn't it? But you cared too much for their dignity to do that, so you stayed. And you've been rewarded, haven't you? Because they've given you two things that money can't buy—love and trust. I daresay they treat you just like a member of the family, too.'

Mrs Humphries smiled and dabbed at her eyes with a small lace hanky.

'Yes, they do, you're quite right. Visiting times, the ward will hum with my family—and they all speak English, Nurse. Even the youngest grandchild who's only five, though he's a bit shaky.'

'That's wonderful. Then when you've recuperated and are well enough to leave here you'll have a ready-made family to take care of you.'

'Except that now I live in the city it isn't so easy—they're a good twenty miles away. Apart from the old 'uns of course, and it takes them all their time to take care of themselves.' She glanced slyly at Sharon beneath her lashes. 'I thought I wasn't going to be around for long after the operation, so I didn't bother to make arrangements. Or rather, I made arrangements which I might have regretted.'

Sharon smiled encouragingly at her patient.

'Now what sort of arrangements . . .'

The opening of the door stopped her in mid-sentence. Vitale entered, giving his patient an approving smile.

'Settling in, Mrs Humphries? Good, good, you'll find Nurse Craig will soon have you on your feet again! Just let me take a look at my handiwork and then you can go along to the day-room and meet your fellow patients.'

'I don't know whether I want to go mixing with . . .' Mrs Humphries began, but was cut short by Sharon whisking the curtains round her bed and siting the trolley conveniently close. The surgeon waited whilst she pulled back the covers and exposed the wound, peeling back the dressing, and then he bent over his patient.

'Excellent, this is healing just as it ought. I want to keep you here for a few weeks since we don't have any convalescent homes where English is spoken locally, and then you can go back and take up your life just where you left off.' He beckoned to Sharon. 'A new dressing please, Nurse, and then Mrs Humphries will go along to the day-room.'

'Very good, Signor,' Sharon murmured, as he disappeared through the curtains. She saw that Mrs Humphries was not looking too pleased, but removed the dressing and picked up her kidney basin and swabs. 'Just let me tidy you up, Mrs Humphries, and then I'll walk with you to the day-room and introduce you to the other patients.'

The job was soon done and Mrs Humphries helped into a very pretty negligee in soft blue with an Elizabethan ruffle round the neck. Despite her reluctance, Sharon found it easy enough to jolly her patient along to the point where the two of them were making their way down the corridor to meet the other patients. To do Mrs Humphries credit, when she found that it was a mixed ward, with men as well as ladies in the day-room, she seemed to perk up a bit.

'A mixed ward, Nurse? Well I never! But I daresay it will do me good to meet some gentlemen, keep me on my metal. I do have a . . . a gentleman friend in Italy, though I daresay we shan't see him here, since we had words.' She patted Sharon's hand and shuffled into the day-room. 'Introduce me, there's a dear good girl!'

In the office, Vitale was waiting. He raised a brow as she entered, then gestured her to a chair.

–'Well?'

'She's in the day-room. She's very sweet, and almost pathetically grateful for anyone who speaks English— the language barrier's very real when you're ill, isn't it? And people do get odd ideas over major surgery,' Sharon added diffidently. 'She didn't mention Signor Pappalardo by name, but she did hint that she and her "gentleman friend" had fallen out.'

'Give her time. You'll get the whole story in due course.' He had been sitting behind the desk in Sister's chair but now he stood up. 'A job well done, Nurse.' He walked over to the door, opened it, and held it for her As she passed him he put a hand on her arm. 'I've been meaning to ask you, Nurse, if . . .'

'Signor, the man with the nosebleed, what are we to do with him? The theatre's engaged, Dr Malpense's operating and the foyer is no place for such a man.'

Signorina Russano stood at the head of the stairs, her aristocratic features set in distaste. She shot a malevolent glance at Sharon, making that young person suddenly aware that the surgeon's hand was still resting on her arm. She moved and Vitale's grip tightened, then he let her go.

'Nurse Craig and I are about to go to Room 3 Signorina, where there is now a spare bed. Kindly have the man brought to us there, I'll deal with him on the ward since the small theatre is in use and I don't want to occupy the large one for an epistaxis.'

The receptionist hesitated. She really *is* possessive, Sharon thought with amusement, reading in Fortuna's glance the other girl's reluctance to go downstairs and leave her alone with Vitale. But the surgeon's hard stare caused the receptionist to look uneasily away.

'But Rod . . . oh, very well.' She turned and descended the stairs whilst Vitale continued to lead Sharon down the corridor, saying as he did so: 'I was about to tell you, Nurse, that the young fellow suffering from epistaxis needs plugging. He's had it before and this attack was probably brought on by the flight, but when they couldn't stop the bleeding at the hotel they brought him straight here—very sensible. So if you'll lay up a trolley for me with Lignocaine, Simpson noseplugs and nasal-angled forceps, I'll do the work on the ward. Tell Sister we'll keep the chap in overnight just to be on the safe side.'

'Yes, Signor,' Sharon said. She watched him turn into Room 3, then went towards Sister's office once more. What had he been going to ask her, before Fortuna had appeared at the head of the stairs? She shrugged, then re-entered the office and picked up the internal telephone. Sister was down on Virginia Ward, having a cup of tea with Sister Fox; she had better get in touch with her first and inform her of the surgeon's calm take-over of one of her beds, and then lay up that trolley.

For some days after Mrs Humphries' arrival Sharon continued to bask in Dr Vitale's approval and her relationship with the patient continued excellent, though Mrs Humphries still had not confided exactly what had gone wrong between her fiancé and herself. Sharon thought Mrs Humphries would make someone a lovely wife and would, furthermore, be much fitter and happier with a man to fuss over, but she could not do anything to further the romance until Mrs Humphries admitted to the relationship.

She also met and liked Ian Ridgeway, Susan's father. Tall, thin and bespectacled with light brown hair and a vague manner, he had all Susan's charm and a good deal of sex appeal into the bargain. Sharon thought he must have been badly hurt by Morena, otherwise such an attractive man would have remarried, long since.

Morena Morasco, on the other hand, though she was every bit as lovely off-screen as on, was heartily disliked by the nursing staff. She visited her daughter only occasionally, with a retinue of young men or a sour-faced secretary, but when she came it was usually not long before she had upset her daughter. Either she objected to the kitten, or she derided Susan's drawings or writing, or she managed to knock over a laboriously completed jigsaw.

'Anyone would think she hated the kid,' Julie Drummond complained one day, as she and Sharon sat in their kitchen eating a delicious pizza supplied by the Caffé Rosso. 'She goes out of her way to be difficult—I can't understand a judge giving her custody.'

'When children are tiny, fathers probably don't even consider trying to cope with them,' Sharon pointed out through a mouthful of ham and mushroom. 'Now that she's older though, it could be different. Why did you mention it?'

'Ian was talking about buying a farm in Surrey—I don't know whether it's just a dream or whether he's really considering it—and he said how nice it would be if he and Susan could live there, only of course, Morena has custody. It made me wonder, because he's so much more suitable to have charge of a child than that Morena.'

'What's this, Ian? I always call him Mr Ridgeway!'

Sharon was only half teasing, for much though she liked Ian Ridgeway, and fond though she was of Julie, it seemed to her that it might well be disastrous for Julie to fall in love with the older man. Julie was a darling and very popular, but she was plain and shy and Ian had once been married to a very beautiful woman and was still surrounded by film stars, extras and aspiring actresses. It was rather unlikely that he would look to Julie for anything but friendship.

'He asked me to call him Ian,' Julie said now. 'Remember, Craig, I visit Susan in my spare time and as a friend, but when you visit her it's bottoms up and let's check your traction.'

'Yes, I forgot that,' Sharon admitted, but she still felt unhappy with the situation. Julie might say what she liked, but her grey eyes behind her big spectacles sparkled at the sound of Ian's name. 'Mr Ridgeway's awfully nice, but he must be very settled in his ways. How old is he? Forty?'

'Thirty-eight. And if you mean he's got a girlfriend when you say he's settled in his ways, he hasn't, I'm sure.' Julie tossed her head. 'Anyway, I don't like him in *that* way, I enjoy his company.'

'Well, so long as that's all!' Sharon finished off her pizza and leaned back in her chair with a satisfied sigh. 'That was grand, Julie, no one warms up a pizza quite as well as you do.'

'Thank you, dear. Don't forget that tomorrow night you're going to venture into the city in search of food for me to cook, then I can display my real talent! And don't get carried away and spend the housekeeping on the beautiful marquetry you'll see in the shops, or on the marvellous clothes, just keep your mind on pasta, fruit and veg!'

'I will, even though it'll be my first trip to the city, though I do wish you could have come too. Wretched shift changes!'

'I know, it's the sheer uncertainty that makes nursing so exciting,' Julie said, grinning. 'Why we do it, I'll never know. Why did you came to Italy, anway? I've been meaning to ask for ages.'

'How can you ask? A glamorous job in a glamorous country with a good salary and a two-year contract renewable after twenty-two months. Anway, there's a recession which makes one's first job as a staff nurse not so easy to find as you'd think. I didn't have a boyfriend to miss or anything, either. How about you?'

Julie got up from her chair and walked over to the cooker, where she proceeded to pour the coffee from the gently bubbling pot.

'My best friend married the boy who'd been courting me for eight months,' she said bluntly. 'So you see, I'm not likely to make a fool of myself over Ian or anyone else. That's the snag with nursing, you make dates and then have to break them, you're working when everyone else is off and off when everyone else is working . . . But there, I came here and I've got no regrets. I want to stay here for years and years!'

'I'd like to see more of the country thàn I have so far, though,' Sharon said rather wistfully, taking the cup that Julie was proffering. 'Is it always as busy as this, or do we sometimes get the off-duty that's due to us?'

'Poor Sharon—of course we get time off! We usually work shifts of four days on and three off and we get very generous holidays so that we can get home once or twice a year. The trouble is this is right in the middle of the summer holidays and we're fearfully shorthanded. Well for instance, you've been on nights four times, haven't you?'

'Five, actually. Not that I mind, because it isn't as if I know anyone or want to go anywhere desperately, it's just that I'm genuinely feeling pretty tired.' She sipped her coffee and grinned over the top of the cup at her friend. 'Anyway, I'm not grumbling—I've got eight whole days off, after tomorrow!'

CHAPTER FOUR

'Is THERE anything you want in town, poppet?'

Sharon's head, appearing unexpectedly round the door, caused Susan to jump and emit a squeak. She was painting, and now the sun had got a long, crimson tail where her brush had trailed across the paper.

'O-oh, Craigie!'

Sharon continued to peer round the door.

'I'm sorry, did I startle you? I just wondered whether . . .'

'Yes, you jolly well did, and you've turned my sun into a comet.' Susan rested her brush carefully on the edge of her tray and flourished her drawing at Sharon, turning round to wag a reproving finger as she did so. 'People oughtn't to come half into rooms where patients are tied by the leg, it isn't fair.' She put on a coaxing expression. 'Come right in, Craigie, just for a moment, and we can have a little talk.'

'I really shouldn't, I'm . . .' Sharon glanced at her watch, then came fully into the room and moved over to the bed. 'Well, I was going to catch the early bus into Sorrento, but I suppose the next one will do. Or I could walk, it isn't far.' She picked up Susan's painting and scrutinised it. 'What's it supposed to be, anyway?'

'Sunrise. This morning's. There's the tree outside this window. Good, isn't it?'

'We-ell, it's cheerful,' Sharon conceded. 'What were you doing watching the sun rise, anyway? Good little patients should still be fast asleep.'

'I wake as soon as it's light,' Susan said, beginning to tint the sky a deeper blue. 'I like it then, the air's all fresh and quiet and everything's new. Why are you going into the city this evening, though, Craigie? I thought this was the first of your days leave, and you said you'd go up after lunch.'

'So it should have been, but I spent the morning helping in theatre. They were a nurse short and Dr Vitale was operating, and since I was on the premises, bringing Snowflake back to you after his night on the tiles, Sister asked if I could help out. Then this afternoon I put on my scruffiest clothes and cleaned the flat, which was how I'd meant to spend the morning, and then I went into Sant' Agnello and bought a tray of plants and some terracotta pots and turned our living room balcony into a thing of beauty.'

'What does that mean?'

'I put the plants into the pots and the pots onto the balcony. They may not look much now—well, they don't look much now—but in a few weeks that balcony will be a riot of colour. When's Daddy coming to see you?'

'Quite soon, I think. He came this afternoon and he and Drumsticks taught me to play whist. I won. I say, Craigie, what's it like working in the theatre? Did you watch Vitale sink his stethoscope into living flesh? I suppose you didn't faint? I bet I would, I bet I'd fall right across the patient with a crash at the first sign of blood!'

'Doctors don't operate with their stethoscopes, you duffer,' Sharon said, rumpling Susan's hair. 'They use knives and things. I know what you mean about feeling sick because when I first started I did used to get a bit queasy, but I'm used to it now and I don't actually watch more than I have to. I just move quickly and quietly and keep my wits about me, and the time flies. Dr Vitale's a very good surgeon, too, as quick and accurate as anyone I've worked with and a good deal more decisive than most.'

'When I'm a nurse, I shan't watch operations,' Susan said dreamily. 'Unless I'm an actress, of course. I wouldn't mind being an actress if Peter Powers was my leading man even though he is a bit old. Did you get an eyeful when he came down the wards yesterday morning? Isn't he dishy?'

'He's not bad.' Sharon privately thought that Peter Powers had far too high an opinion of his flashy looks, but he was good with Susan, never grudging her his time and presenting her with some really imaginative presents. 'Look, if there's nothing you want I'd better go. I might even catch that bus if I run.'

'That's right, go, leave me here by myself,' Susan said dolefully. 'Suppose Daddy can't get away? There you'll be, gadding around Sorrento, and I'll . . .'

The door opened and Ian Ridgeway entered the room, a book in one hand. Susan's tray shot across the bed and her painting fell, unregarded, to the floor.

'Daddy! Oh, I'm so glad you've come! You know Craigie, don't you?'

Ian Ridgeway was tall and thin, with large dark-rimmed spectacles. At first glance, one might wonder why Morena Morasco had married him, but at second glance his shy and charming smile, his dreamy brown eyes, and his charm made itself felt. He was, in fact, very like his daughter. Now he sat down on the bed and smiled up at Sharon.

'Do I know Nurse Craig, the prettiest nurse in the Villa L'Arancia? Yes, of course I do.'

'I thought you thought Drumsticks was the prettiest,' his daughter said accusingly. 'You were being very friendly to her yesterday. I thought you liked her best!'

'Ah, well, I know Drumsticks a good deal better than I know Craigie,' Ian Ridgeway replied, not in the least put out by his child's frankness. 'To tell the truth, Sue, I find most nurses irresistible. Now stop criticising me and see what I've brought you.'

Bidding the two goodbye, therefore, Sharon made her way out of the hospital. As she reached the main road the bus arrived at the stop and the only person waiting climbed aboard. The driver revved his engine and Sharon broke into a run.

But the bus was well away from the kerb and making for Sorrento like a bat out of hell before she had run more than a dozen yards. Sharon slowed, feeling the sweat beginning to trickle down her back. Damn and damn again she said crossly to herself. Now she would have to walk. Later, perhaps, the heat would lift, but right now it was still oppressively hot.

She was still standing at the kerb looking after the fast disappearing bus, when the car drew up beside her. She turned her head. A man with thick, wavy hair and pale skin was leaning across the car, his hand on the passenger door-handle.

'Signorina, is it that you've missed the autobus? Will you allow me to offer you a ride into Sorrento? I am going that way myself and it is a wretchedly hot evening for walking or for waiting thirty minutes. The breeze in an open car is very pleasant in weather such as this.'

Sharon looked hard at the man. He looked respectable enough, and he did have a pleasant, open smile.

'Well, if you really wouldn't mind,' she was beginning, when he swung out of his seat and came round to open the door for her.

'Not at all. You are a nurse from the *'spedale*?'

As he got behind the wheel again, Sharon turned to stare at him. She did hope that her profession had not begun to show on her face or person. Bedpan hands, she thought dismally. But the look which he was giving her did not speak of bedpans, it was a very Latin sort of look!

'Yes, I'm a nurse at the Villa L'Arancia, the English hospital,' she admitted. 'How did you know?'

'That's easy. You're English, but obviously not a holidaymaker or you would probably use the hotel bus and not local transport. You came up the Via Cappuccini, which is the way the nurses always come into town. And . . .' here the eyes turned on her own positively swam with emotion, '. . . and you remind me, a little bit, of Angela.'

'And Angela is . . . ?' Sharon prompted, since her

escort seemed about to go off into some private dream as he steered the car slickly round a bend.

'Ah, I'm sorry. Angela was a wonderful girl, I had the privilege to be her lover whilst she was in Sant' Agnello. I miss her very much now that she has gone back to England.'

'Oh, I see.' Sharon turned and looked at him again. Lover? Surely he must mean something different, less . . . less *Latin*?

'Yes, I miss her. We were very good friends, though I knew, of course, that she would go back to England quite soon.'

Sharon heaved a sigh of relief and settled more comfortably into the seat. Good friends, that was better!

'It's nice to have friends when you're in a foreign land,' she said. 'Everyone at the hospital is friendly, of course, but we don't mix a lot with the local people, except when they're ill, and that isn't quite the same.'

'You'll soon get to know plenty of Italians,' her new friend stated positively. 'Forgive me, but you are a very pretty, blonde girl, and Italian men like blonde ladies.' He sighed reminiscently. 'Angela was blonde.'

'Yes, so I understand. I expect most of the nurses up at the hospital know you, then?'

'Yes, they . . .' he clapped a hand to his brow and turned to Sharon, seeming oblivious of the fact that with his action the car had swerved right across the road. 'I have not introduced myself! I am Paolo Trapani at your service, Miss . . .'

'Craig, Sharon Craig,' Sharon said quickly. 'How do you do, Mr Trapani?'

'Paolo, please. And I may call you Sharon? It is a pretty name.'

'Yes, of course,' Sharon said nervously. She just wished that he would keep his eyes on the road and both hands on the wheel! 'Whereabouts will you put me down in Sorrento, Signor?'

'Right in the centre. In fact, I was about to suggest that

you might meet me later so that we can drive home together. Or do you have plans, a meeting, perhaps?'

'Oh, no, I'm only doing some household shopping. But you must have plans of your own, Signor, I couldn't possibly . . .'

'You are not meeting someone? A beautiful girl . . . but this must be remedied!' He put a hand on her knee. 'Signorina Craig, will you dine with me tonight? First I will take you shopping, see that you are not cheated, and then we will dine somewhere really good. What do you say?'

'Well, Signor . . .' Sharon hesitated. This was a pick-up, there could be no doubt about that, and a slick one, too, but he seemed a respectable young man. He spoke excellent English and wore his clothes with casual elegance, and anyway, from what she had seen so far, if she wanted to meet Italian men other than those who worked in the hospital she would have to get used to being picked up!

'Yes, Sharon? You will say yes, you will be my guest?'

'I'd love to, Paolo. But surely you had plans for this evening?'

'None. Or none of moment. I would have driven into the city, gone to a *caffé* where I am well known, drunk a little wine, talked . . . I daresay you know how a bachelor behaves when he has no woman with him to civilise him! But an evening with a person as charming as yourself would be memorable indeed!'

'There's no answer to that,' Sharon said lightly, and was rewarded to see him look startled.

'*Che cosa dice?* I don't quite . . .'

'It's only slang, I didn't mean anything, really. Why are we going in here?'

The car had turned into a dark and tree-lined drive to the right of the square.

'This is one of the finest hotels in Sorrento. My father used to supply all their wine, and now I do. That is one of the good things about a family business. They always keep a parking space for me, when I come into the city.'

'That must be convenient.'

'It is. It's one of the advantages of having lived all one's life in a place, though I've travelled more than most.' He drew to a halt and turned to her in the shade beneath the trees. 'When I was in London it was very different, I had to park a good deal less centrally and often I was persecuted by traffic wardens.'

'I expect you mean prosecuted . . . or perhaps not,' Sharon said as he came round and opened her door. 'Well, Signor, where do we go from here?'

'You shall choose. We can go into the bar here and have a drink first, or we can do your shopping.'

'Shopping first, please,' Sharon said. She had no desire to be taken into the enormous hotel where he doubtless knew everyone and would insist on introducing her. He seemed very nice, but she had the feeling that he was looking on her, at the moment, as an achievement rather than a person. A pretty blonde girl he had succeeded in grabbing as she passed by.

'Very well, we will shop and I will show you the sights.'

Signor Trapani was indefatigable in his efforts to show off his city. He led her across the main square, fringed with orange trees in full fruit, and into the Corso Italia.

'Here are some of our best and most expensive shops where you can buy marvellous clothes and rich and beautiful jewellery,' he said impressively. 'Also shoes —Italian shoes are famous. See, in that window there is coral, cut and shaped into pears, roses, all sorts of different things. Also very fine silver and gold, and see there, the earrings which look like jet? They are made from the rocks of Vesuvio when it last overwhelmed the land.'

'Vesuvius? The volcano?' Sharon stared at the glittering ornaments. 'I'll get some of them before I go home.'

'You like them? But they are nothing—the coral,

now, that is good, set in gold it is very good. See that necklace—I will buy it for you.'

'Oh no, thank you, I really couldn't . . .'

'Nonsense, of course I will buy it for you—it will be a little present to remind you of our first meeting. No, no, don't shake your head, it is not expensive, nothing that it would not be right to buy on first acquaintance. There could be nothing . . . I forget the word, but you would be unkind to refuse me the pleasure of buying you a gift.'

But over this at least, Sharon was firm. She explained that her mother would think it very odd for her to accept a gift from a man she had met barely an hour before, and this explanation seemed to satisfy him. Italians, she thought thankfully as they moved away from the shop, seemed to set more store by the wishes of absent mothers than an Englishman would!

'Now, Sharon, what did you want to buy? For meat, fish, fruit, I know all the best places.'

'Well, I want vegetables for soup, a piece of fish big enough for two, and some nice fruit.'

'Aha! What sort of fish did you want, Sharon?'

'I don't know the names, I'd just planned to point and say "Quanto?"' Sharon admitted. 'Julie knows the names and things, but she's on duty today. She's my flat-mate.'

'Well, today you will have the best,' Paolo said firmly. He took her arm. 'You know the Via S. Cesareo?'

'No. I don't know anywhere, except for the big square where we crossed over, and this road—the Via Italio, isn't it?'

'The Piazzo Tasso is the main square,' her escort told her instructively. 'I will take you now to the Via S. Cesareo, where you will see the best fish and vegetables.'

Sharon had thought Sorrento delightful as they drove into it, but now, in the dusk, with the street lamps casting a golden glow on the faces of the people in the streets, it was even lovelier and the Via S. Cesareo, a narrow alley crowded with both shops and people, seemed livelier and even more Italian than the rest of the city.

They found a shop selling fruit and vegetables and Sharon got better quality and paid less for it than she had expected. She glanced narrowly at Paolo, but he had certainly not handed the shopkeeper any money—perhaps it was just influence. Further up the alley a fishmonger was shouting his wares and weighing them out onto an old brass balance-scale whilst his customers, keen-eyed Italian housewives, looked on.

'Now, Sharon, what sort of fish would you like?' Paolo put an authoritative hand into a white enamelled dish and drew out a nightmare. Long, greyish tentacles, bulging, death-glazed eyes, a mottled, tubular body. 'How about some squid? Cooked properly, it's very good.'

'No thanks,' Sharon said hurriedly, averting her eyes from the squid's reproachful gaze. 'Something more ordinary, I think. Oh, what's that?'

'Umm, what is the English for . . . I know, it is a sword-fish. It's a very big one, you would need perhaps a kilo of the flesh. It's sweet and nutty in flavour. Shall I ask the price?'

But the sword-fish, on closer acquaintance, had a sad and noble air, and Sharon decided it would be almost as bad to eat such a creature as the squid, which would have come with eyes attached. She shook her head.

'No, I don't think . . . how about that?'

'Ah, now that's a good choice. That is the spignola. Do you know how to cook him?'

'Oh, is that a spignola? I've eaten him—it—baked, down at the Moonlight Trattoria, with mushrooms and tomatoes and those big purple things. I suppose you just put it under the grill?'

'First you clean him, then you butter him, and spread over his back onions, very finely shredded . . .' Paolo was practically smacking his lips. 'But would it not be

best, Sharon, if I came back to your flat and cooked him
for you? I'm an excellent cook, I assure you.'

Sharon showed the whites of her eyes. A pick-up was
one thing, allowing a strange young man to come into
her flat and cook for her another. Firmly, she shook her
head.

'It's awfully kind of you, Paolo, but Julie's a very good
cook, she'll know just how to . . . to treat a spignola.
How many do I need for the two of us, or do I buy it by
the kilo?'

'No, no, no, you must buy him whole.' He turned to
the fishmonger and addressed a flood of Italian at him,
then smiled down at Sharon. 'There, he will find you a
fish which is right for two persons.'

The fishmonger seized a fish, slung it on the scale, set
the appropriate weight in the opposite pan and then
reeled off the incredibly huge sum in lire which such a
fish cost. Sharon took a ten thousand lire note out of her
purse and proffered it, sincerely hoping that it would
cover the cost. The fishmonger raised his eyes to heaven
and said something in Italian—she did not need to speak
the language to know he was asking if she had anything
smaller, just as an English fishmonger would do if
offered a fiver for a twenty pence purchase.

She rooted in her purse, found a five thousand lire
note, and held it out. He accepted it and gave her a great
deal of change, and then she took the well-wrapped
parcel and the two of them set off down the narrow alley
once more, walking with care, for all the shops spilled
out onto the pavement and around the shop frontages
people surged and gossiped good-humouredly without a
thought for those trying to walk past.

'Now, shall we go first to the Marina Grande or the
Marina Piccola?' Paolo mused, as they emerged onto the
square once more. 'We could go down to sea-level in a
horse and cart, if that would please you?'

The horses wore straw hats or plumes and sad expressions, and the small, highly polished carriages that they

pulled were much-decorated and filled with brightly striped cushions. They stopped beside a dapple-grey pony pulling a carriage with a bright pink awning over the passenger seats and bright pink cushions. Sharon hung back.

'It's awfully tripperish, isn't it, to ride in one of those?'

'Nonsense, *mia bella*! Come along, up with you!'

Laughing, she allowed herself to be helped into the carriage whilst Paolo gave the driver instructions, and then they were off, swaying over the strip of cobbles and then making their way across the Piazzo Tasso to dive down a small, steep street which evidently led down to the harbour.

Halfway down, feeling as if she were going to be tipped straight into the sea, Sharon allowed Paolo to put an arm round her shoulders, though she was rather glad when they reached the quay and he let her go again.

'There! Did you enjoy your ride?' Sharon thanked Paolo, then went round and thanked their driver and caressed the pony's smooth, velvet nose. It snuffled hopefully at her hand and she remembered the fruit and asked Paolo if she might give the horse an apple.

Paolo asked the driver, who was agreeable, and Sharon fed the horse two ripe apples before watching the gay little equippage make its way up the steep little road again and back to the main square.

'I've told him to come back in an hour or so, and if we've finished our meal we'll ride up the hill again,' Paolo said, taking her arm. His fingers were firm on the soft flesh, and she did not dislike his touch. 'See the restaurant on that . . . I cannot think of the name, the one over the water? That's where we're going.'

'The one built on the pier? Oh, lovely, we'll have the sea on all sides of us as we eat!'

They went into the restaurant and the head waiter showed them to a table where they were only about a foot from the gently sighing sea, though a narrow balustrade separated them from it. It was very romantic,

Sharon thought, sitting here in the dark, with only the pale gold light of hanging lanterns and the moonlight to illumine the scene, whilst an excellent meal was set before them. As they ate, she glanced again and again at the lights which blinked and winked out to sea, and at the big, brilliant stars and at the silver disc of the moon. She had to keep reminding herself that it was she, Sharon Craig, sitting in this doubtless expensive and exclusive restaurant, with an Italian moon shining in the sky and the warm air caressing her bare shoulders. And with a very personable young Italian male eyeing her with increasing warmth!

'What are you thinking of, you pretty thing?'

Paolo's words jerked her back to reality, but she had a perfectly truthful answer ready.

'That island, Paolo, out in the bay—what's it called?'

He did not follow her pointing finger but stared at her incredulously, a slow smile dawning.

'Sharon, how long have you been in Sant' Agnello? You cannot tell me that no one has mentioned the name of that island?'

'Well, no, I'm sure no one's mentioned it,' Sharon assured him. 'Remember, Paolo, I'm a hard-working nurse, not a tourist. There's no mention of moons and heavenly food and warm seas, it's all paperwork and charts and medical practice. Conversation between us, in fact, consists mainly of the Twelve Best Ways to Remove a Kidney, or How to take out an Appendix Without Really Trying.'

Paolo's English was excellent, but humour was obviously beyond him. He looked impressed.

'Really? And you take part in such conversations?'

'But you've still not told me what the island's called,' Sharon reminded him.

'It is Capri. Some day I would be honoured if you would let me take you there to show you around. There is so much to see, the Blue Grotto, the home of your film star, Gracie Fields, the . . .'

'Your wine, Signor,' the waiter said in faultless English, and conversation was at an end for a time as Sharon and Paolo did justice both to the wine and to one of the best steaks Sharon had ever tasted.

'That was absolutely delicious,' Sharon sighed, as, an hour later, they left the restaurant together. 'The strawberries and cream just rounded the meal off nicely. Thank you very much, I'm sure I'll sleep like a log when I get home.'

And indeed, by the time the horse and carriage arrived back at the car, Sharon could scarcely keep her eyes open. She climbed in and sank onto her seat, hoping that she would manage to remain wakeful until they arrived home.

It was a pleasant drive back to Sant' Agnello. The night air was cool and pleasant, scented with pine and with the salty whiff of the sea, and Paolo, though he spoke little, hummed a tune as he drove. When he drew up beside the flats and leaned towards Sharon, she smiled up at him with genuine affection. How kind he had been and what a marvellous evening she had had—a goodnight kiss was most definitely in order. So when he leaned closer yet and took her in his arms she yielded her mouth, wanting to show him, in the time-honoured fashion, that she liked him and had enjoyed his company.

The trouble, it soon transpired, was that Paolo had no intention of stopping at a kiss or two. He seemed to be all over her, pressing her uncomfortably against the back of the seat, his mouth hot and demanding, his hands everywhere, now clutching her breast with such fervour that she gasped a protest, now sliding across her thighs, now seizing her chin and forcing it up so that her mouth was more accessible. Sharon, who had been worried in case she hurt his feelings at first, now found herself eager to hurt far more than that! Such an attack was unforgivable, she had done nothing to arouse such lust, nor had she given him any indication that she intended to assuage it. She got a hand free, scratched his neck, punched him on the side of the jaw and managed to detach her mouth from his suddenly limpet-like lips.

'Get off! Stop it! Let me go at . . .'

Undeterred by this lively defence, he returned to the attack once more and for a moment, Sharon was really frightened. What on earth did he intend to do—rape her within six feet of the nurses' flats? But then, suddenly, he was drawing back, smoothing down her skirt, pulling it into respectability once more though seconds earlier he had seemed intent on getting it round her neck. She was scrabbling to find the door handle and free herself when the door opened, it seemed, of its own accord and strong hands caught her beneath the arms and lifted her out of the car.

'Good evening, Nurse Craig, good evening, Signor Trapani! Forgive the intrusion, but I want a word with you, Nurse.'

It was Vitale, imperturbable as ever, though he was looking very grand now in a black dinner jacket and crisp white shirt. Sharon, turning in his arms, gave him a look blazing with gratitude.

'Oh, thank you, Signor—you weren t in-intruding, this g-gentleman is about to leave.'

She turned to the car and snatched her handbag and shopping basket off the back seat, to see that whatever madness had infected Paolo had vanished as suddenly as it had arrived. He shrugged, smiled, and then leaned forward to turn the key in the ignition.

'Very well, Sharon, thank you for your delightful company. I will telephone you, if I may, tomorrow or the day after.'

'You may not!' Sharon had to raise her voice above the roar of the engine, but she was sure he heard, though he only waved as the car shot off into the darkness.

Still trembling and in considerable disarray, Sharon turned to Vitale.

'Thank you very much, Signor, for your timely intervention I don't know what made him behave like that, but . . .'

'I imagine he was given cause to think his advances were not unwelcome, Signorina. Italian men only treat women as they wish to be treated.'

Vitale's voice was cold, impersonal. Sharon stared incredulously up into his dark, unsmiling face.

'*Wish* to be . . . Signor, if you think I encouraged him to . . . to . . .'

'Perhaps not intentionally, but Paolo is a man of good family, he would not have treated you like an easy conquest if you hadn't behaved like one.'

'I did nothing of the sort!' Sharon's voice cracked with indignation. 'I did nothing, said nothing, that he could have interpreted as encouragement. You are abominable, Signor!'

'Am I?' He took her arm. 'Let me take you back to your flat, Signorina.' He glanced down at her as they entered the lighted foyer and his lips quirked. 'You look . . . a little worse for wear. Is Nurse Drummond at home?'

'No, she isn't, but I'm quite capable of looking after myself, thank you.' She made her voice as frosty and furious as she could. 'Please don't bother to come up.'

'It is no bother.' He was leading her up the stairs now, stopping outside the door of the flat. 'Where's your key?'

'In my handbag, by my . . . oh!'

'What's the matter?'

'Nothing,' Sharon said, taking her key out of the bag. Her voice wavered. 'Nothing at all. Oh, do go away!'

He ignored this, taking the key from her shaking fingers, unlocking the door and pushing her inside.

'Go and clean up,' he ordered. 'I'll put the kettle on. A strong cup of coffee would probably keep you awake all night, and I can't keep prescribing sleeping tablets for you, so I'll make you hot chocolate. I don't approve of all the tea-drinking you English do.'

'All right. B-but . . .'

Suddenly he smiled and his face looked lighter, younger and very much nicer.

'Come on, what's the matter? Cat got your tongue?'

'It isn't important really, it's just that my purse must have fallen out of my handbag whilst Paolo and I were fighting in the car.'

His mouth twitched at her choice of words, but he patted her shoulder quite kindly.

'I shouldn't worry, Paolo's a Trapani and they're a very rich family, I don't think he'll be tempted to purloin your purse.'

'I know.' Sharon bit her lip and stared at her own feet. 'But I'll have to get in touch with him, arrange to meet him to get it back.'

'Well?' He walked over to her and tilted her chin with a finger so that she was forced to meet his eyes. 'What's wrong? He won't eat you, you silly child!'

'I don't ever want to see him again,' Sharon said vehemently. 'He scared me, really he did. No one's ever behaved like that to me before, whatever you may think.'

'They haven't?' He was standing very close, looking down into her face, his lids heavy over his eyes. 'Don't worry, I'll speak to him for you, I'll . . .'

He took her in his arms and slowly pulled her close. Sharon's mouth opened to protest, and his mouth came down over hers. There was no clutching or grabbing, no loose, wet lips. His mouth moved gently, his arms were firm, his hands caressed her back mesmerically. He made a little noise in the back of his throat, like the purr of a tiger, and pulses she had not known existed beat double time all over Sharon's body. As his mouth demanded, hers softened, as his body pushed forward she moulded herself against him, her heart thundering, lost to everything but the magic of the moment, the physical attraction between them which made his caresses not only delightful, but urgently wanted.

When he drew back she blinked up at him, completely disarmed, only to see him smiling scornfully down at her.

'Well? Why didn't you slap my face if no one's ever kissed you before?'

It was like a douche of cold water, the insinuation that she had welcomed his caresses, even if it was true. She felt the hot blood burn to her face, tide over her neck, felt tears of indignation brighten her eyes.

'Paolo wasn't just kissing me, Signor, and I think you know that very well! What he was trying to do was unforgivable, and you—you should not have behaved like that either! You took advantage of the fact that I was unhappy and afraid, otherwise I should have slapped your face quite as hard as you might wish!' She turned away from him and opened the bathroom door, then turned for one last remark. 'You might also remember that it's difficult for me to slap my boss!'

He caught her shoulder, ignoring her when she tried to tug free.

'You're right, and I apologise, I yielded to an uncontrollable impulse and then felt guilty over my behaviour so tried to blame you. Go and shower; I'll make that drink.'

She spent a long time in the shower, half dreading, half longing to see him again and hear what he had to say. He would be a marvellous lover, she thought dreamily as she washed, if that kiss was anything to go by. He had been rude, cruel, unfair—but his touch did things to her which she enjoyed, despite herself.

After twenty minutes she put on the towelling robe which hung behind the bathroom door and returned to the kitchen, wondering, and denying to herself that she wondered, whether he would kiss her again—in a quiet and friendly way, of course, not with the wild, demanding kiss which had crushed her lips and set her heart hammering. But she was doomed to disappointment, for it was Julie who sat at the table with a jug of hot chocolate and two cups before her. She looked up as the door opened and smiled at Sharon, then began to pour the hot drink.

'You poor sweet, Dr Vitale phoned the ward and told Night Sister that he wanted me for half an hour. He said you'd been the victim of the abominable Paolo Trapani, and needed tea and sympathy, so here I am. Well, it's hot chocolate, but the sympathy's there all right. Sit down, love, and tell Aunt Julie everything!'

But Sharon, sitting down, sipping chocolate and giving Julie a blow-by-blow account of her evening, could scarcely bring Paolo's iniquitous behaviour to mind without thinking of that other, much more welcome, embrace. And when at last she sank into bed, she knew that, however reprehensible Vitale's behaviour had been, she had still enjoyed it!

CHAPTER FIVE

THE day after her encounter with Paolo and the surgeon, Sharon spent quietly, sleeping late, having a leisurely breakfast, and then pottering round doing some half-hearted flat-cleaning. It was not until she was sitting at the kitchen table eating her solitary lunch, that she allowed herself to think about the previous evening. It was no use ignoring facts, Paolo had her purse and she would have to get it back or spend the remaining three days of her leave as quietly as she had spent this one. She could borrow some money from Julie, no doubt, but her purse was a capacious one with a pocket where she kept her cheque book and banker's card and it was always possible that Paolo might not have seen the purse, might have knocked it out of the car and driven away, and then where would she be?

Should she telephone the police and explain her loss? But the thought of being addressed in Italian by a police officer was not tempting. She was still standing, staring at the telephone as if it might bite her, when the doorbell rang.

Immediately, her heart lifted. It would be Paolo, coming to return her property! She ran across the living room and out in the hall and flung open the door, no longer caring that it would mean facing Paolo after their last embarrassing meeting.

But it was not Paolo standing in the corridor, it was Dr Vitale. In one hand he held her purse and in the other a large bouquet of flowers.

'It is I, Nurse Craig.' He gave her a charming smile. 'I was rude last night and thoughtless, and you were tired and perhaps rather quick to take offence. I went and fetched your purse and Paolo insisted that I brought along some flowers he had purchased for you. It seems he intended to bring them up to the hospital, with your purse, and leave them in reception, but he was happy to allow me to be his messenger. There's a note.'

'Thank you very much.' Sharon held out her hand and he put the purse into it but continued to hold the flowers.

'Think nothing of it. Are you going to forgive me? And Paolo, I suppose, though he must sue for his own terms.'

'Yes, of course.' The surgeon's demeanour, which was that of a man waiting and expecting to be invited inside, was too obvious to ignore any longer. 'Won't you come in? I'll put the kettle on.'

He passed her and went in to the kitchen, lying the flowers carefully on the draining board before detaching a small envelope from the stems and handing it to her.

'I gather the note explains Paolo's behaviour. You're very fortunate, he insisted on explaining it to me in person, which took quite a while. It appears his previous girlfriend was a nurse here, and her attitude to love-making has coloured—had coloured, I should say—his attitude towards English girls in general.'

'It's always a mistake to judge a nation by one member of it,' Sharon said rather coolly, remembering Dr Vitale's own attitude towards blondes. She opened the envelope and scanned the short note. 'Yes, that's more or less what he says. He's going to ring me up, so I'll be able to tell him he's forgiven and thank him for the flowers.' She tossed the note onto the table and turned to the sink. 'I'll just put them in water and then I'll make you some coffee, if you'd like some?'

'I don't think I'd better, I'm due to do a ward round in about fifteen minutes, and I've promised Fortuna that I'll run her back home before then.' But he sat down on the edge of the table, nevertheless. 'Or could you make it a very quick one?'

'I think so, I'd boiled the kettle just before you arrived,' Sharon said. 'I've got a coffee percolator but it'll have to be instant now, if you're in a hurry.'

'Instant will be fine. I spent a good part of my life in the Land of Instant, remember? What did you think of Sorrento last night?'

'America's the Land of Instant, not England,' Sharon said reproachfully. 'Sorrento? It's lovely, isn't it? I'd like to see more of the surrounding countryside, though. The trouble is when I'm off Julie isn't, and that means I have to look round alone, which isn't such fun.'

'That's true. Have you seen Herculaneum yet? I'm off tomorrow, and if you'd like to see the city I'd gladly take you—perhaps you might find the experience less ephemeral than flowers, which are the other way of saying one is sorry for bad behaviour.'

Sharon felt her cheeks warm. Did he think she had been hinting that she wanted company? But she was longing to see the Roman city and had wondered how she could manage it without transport of her own. She looked doubtfully across at him as she made two cups of coffee.

'I'd love to . . . but please don't think you owe me anything just because you sprang to a wrong conclusion! I mean . . . not flowers, or a ride to Herculaneum.'

A dark brow shot up. He looked satanic when he did that, she reflected uneasily. But she had not been rude, she was giving him a chance to retract.

'I owed you an apology, which I've duly delivered. Now I'm asking for the pleasure of your company. I would suggest Pompeii which is so much better known, but the recent earthquakes have left it in a very poor state, a good number of the roads and houses are closed and visitors miss a lot.'

He smiled at her, but she could see a trace of impatience in his face and reflected that it must be a novel experience for him to ask a woman out and not get an immediate and delighted response. Well, it would do him good, but she would have to accept! She had wanted to see the ancient cities all her life and to see

Herculaneum in Vitale's company would really be a thrill. Not, she reminded herself hastily, just because he was handsome and sexy, but because he was an educated and intelligent man. *And* handsome and sexy!

'Then I'll be happy to accept. To tell the truth, I belong to the vast majority—that is, I've heard lots about Pompeii but very little about Herculaneum, though someone on the aeroplane coming over told me that the latter is in a much better state of preservation. Does it have chariot wheel-tracks, though?'

'Aha, you've heard of the tracks, I see. Well, wait and see. I'll pick you up here at ten tomorrow morning, before the heat of the day is too oppressive.'

Shortly after that he left and Sharon tidied away the coffee cups and changed into a swimsuit so that she could sunbathe on the balcony. She fell asleep out there, which was as well, as it turned out, for the ringing of the telephone woke her and when she answered it, it was an apologetic Sister Young.

'I know you're officially on leave, Nurse, but could you possibly do the night-shift for me tonight? This place needs a larger staff than we've got at present, and a better administrator, those giggling society creatures who take it in turns to work in reception are useless!'

'Yes, of course I'll come in,' Sharon said at once. 'I've no plans for tonight. I'll have to see Julie about taking care of Snowflake, but other than that it will be fine.'

'I did have a word with Nurse Drummond,' Sister said rather apologetically. 'I wanted to see if we could arrange it so that the day off in lieu which you'll have for working the extra night could coincide with her time off, and we've managed that for you. She said she'd see to Snowflake.'

'Good. Then I'll catch up on some sleep now, and see you later.'

She managed to snatch a few words with Julie about Snowflake, and also told her about her outing with Signor Vitale the following day.

'That'll put Fortuna's nose out of joint,' Julie rather disappointingly observed. 'She thinks she owns Vitale, now she'll see she doesn't.'

'Is that all you can say? I was just thinking how clever I'd been to find a handsome Italian to give me the low-down on Herculaneum.'

'Vitale isn't just a handsome Italian, he's our boss,' Julie observed practically. 'It is quite odd, though, when I think about it. I've been here two years and I've never known him to take a member of the nursing staff out before, not even a sister. But you're very pretty, of course, and Italian men do like blondes.'

'That particular Italian man hasn't shown many signs of it,' Sharon said crossly. 'You haven't half made me feel small! Either he's taking me out because I'm yellow-headed, or to show Fortuna that she doesn't own him, which is it to be?'

'I didn't mean it like that! He must fancy you, though . . . only it seems an odd sort of place to take you for a romantic interlude! Unless you're a culture-vulture?'

'Who knows what else he's got in mind? A ramble through the ruins, a quiet meal in a secluded restaurant, and then a stroll along the moonlit beach, wine and kisses in his Lamborghini . . . I can't wait!'

'I thought you were off parked cars for ever,' Julie said, grinning affectionately at her friend. 'I thought Paolo had taught you a lesson you were never going to forget!'

'So he did, I forgot! Anyway, you're probably right and it'll be a quick canter round the ruins with one eye on Fortuna to make sure she's noticed, and then home. Ah well, I can dream, can't I?'

'Not about Vitale, it's too dangerous,' Julie said firmly. 'Men like that don't come our way, love!'

'No, and nor do film producers,' Sharon said quickly, seeing a way to warn Julie without being hurtful. 'They're a feather in our caps, but we mustn't set too much store by them.'

'Yes, you're right, we've probably both hooked sharks we're too young and inexperienced to land,' Julie said, giggling. 'But at least we can enjoy the sensation as they nibble at the bait!'

'That has to be the most provocative remark of the century,' Sharon said. 'No one's nibbling at *my* bait, or not without being bitten back, if you see what I mean! Look, are you on your way up to see Susan, because if so, you might as well take Snowflake now and save yourself a trip over later.'

'Yes, I'll do that.' The two girls had been standing in the corridor just outside Sister's office, now they set off up towards the turret rooms. 'Do you want to come, or are you just being polite? Or can it be that you're chaperoning me?'

'Chaper . . . oh, is Mr Ridgeway visiting?'

'He is.'

The two girls entered the room, to find Ian Ridgeway and his daughter puzzling over a large jigsaw spread out on Susan's tray. He looked up and smiled at them as they entered, but Sharon saw how warmly his eyes rested on Julie, and was worried for her friend.

'Hello, girls, come to help us with this confounded jigsaw?'

'Not really,' Julie said regretfully. 'Sharon's on nights and I'm going to take Snowflake home with me for a change.' She turned to Susan. 'Craigie's going to Herculaneum tomorrow—guess who with?'

'Geoff? If it's Geoff, Craigie, do tell him . . .'

'It isn't, Sue, it's Signor Vitale.'

'Well! Get a load of you!' Susan made a vulgar noise and then giggled at her father's expression. 'He's a big cheese, isn't he, Craigie?'

'He is, and I object to the inference that I'm a small mouse, which your friend Drumsticks has already made very plain,' Sharon said. 'I'll tell you all about it when I get back, though.'

'I've not seen Herculaneum yet,' Mr Ridgeway remarked. He glanced at Julie. 'Would you like to take me round, Nurse D? I'd treat you well and buy you a sandwich and a beer—I've got a hired car, too.'

'Yes, that would be lovely,' Julie said, only betraying by the slightest heightening of her colour how delighted she was. Sharon, seeing her out of the door, hissed 'culture-vulture', and then turned back to her patient.

'Well, now we're all going to see Herculaneum, except our poor little Susan,' she said briskly. 'Never mind, you'll go there when you're on your feet again, I'm sure. And now, Mr Ridgeway, I want to put some cream on Susan's pressure points, so if you'll hold the jigsaw for a moment . . .'

By half-past ten the next morning, Sharon was standing on the downward sloping path which led from the car-park into the city of Herculaneum itself, looking at the scene before her. It was so *modern*, she thought wonderingly, the small houses golden in the sun, the big pantiles on the roofs a deeper gold. The streets were dusty with a good deal of paving. Groves of palm trees, cypresses and flowering shrubs all added to the illusion that this was no centuries-old city buried long ago in the course of a volcano's eruption, but a living, thriving place. At any moment, she felt, a woman might pop out of one of the terracotta doorways, bang a mat against the stone balustrade which edged the upper road, and disappear once more into her neat Roman villa.

'Seen enough? Want to get closer?'

Vitale's voice in her ear made Sharon jump, so enthralled had she been by the scene before her. But she turned obediently as he took her arm and began the descent, looking all the time towards the city through the trees which edged the path. She did not know what these trees were, with their narrow, shiny dark leaves and their brilliant pink blossom, but they flourished all over the Peninsula, so Julie had told her.

'Well? What do you think now you can see the detail better?'

They had emerged from the trees and were actually standing in one of the streets. Sharon swallowed, then turned to look up into the dark face above her own.

'I'm sorry, Signor, I suppose I've been rude, but it . . . it takes my breath away! It's totally unexpected, so . . . well, so *real*!'

'I understand you. Wait till you see . . .' his fingers tightened round her arm, then his hand slid down to take her fingers. 'You're very fortunate.'

'Fortunate? Yes, but why do you say so now?'

'Because you are going to have the experience of seeing Herculaneum now, as an interested and intelligent adult. When I was first brought here I was eight, and I thought it dull, boring. The aunt who brought me lectured me about the past glories of Italy until I stopped listening. By the time I came to appreciate it, it had become part of my life and the sensations of reverence and astonishment which you feel, I could not. I appreciate it, but I shall never feel that first delighted shock which I saw in your face just now.'

'I know what you mean. It's the way I feel about Bath Abbey, I suppose. I was born in Bath and there is a stone sculpture on the front of the abbey showing angels, climbing a long ladder up into heaven—and falling, and slipping. When visitors want to stand and gape and talk about it, I *know* it's lovely and interesting, yet I feel no particular respect for it.'

'That's probably what I mean.' He led her down the street, past the homely, familiar front doors. They were almost the only people in the city this early and as she glanced at the dwellings, each one seemingly perfect, and at the shrubs and fountains, she knew again the lovely, exciting feeling that at any moment a door might open and a man in a toga or a woman in the flowing robes of a Roman matron might stroll into the street.

'This is the main street, the Decumanus Maximus,'

Vitale said. 'It was pedestrianised—the Romans knew all about traffic problems!'

'Pedestrianised? You're joking—how could you possibly know?'

'See those little things like milestones at either end of the street? You couldn't drive a chariot past them in a hurry! And see the horse trough, and the rails where you could tie up your horse and water it whilst you waited for your wife to finish her visit—or perhaps it was a slave who drove the lady of the house; he would sit on the edge of the trough and pick his teeth and hum a tune the soldiers sang and wish he was free.'

He spoke so convincingly that Sharon could almost see the slave, black-skinned, with a leather collar round his neck, dangling his feet over the cobbles as he waited for his mistress.

'Yes, I see how it could have been.' She turned to him impulsively. 'You must love this place!'

'I do. The eyes of love can shrink the years that have passed since this was a living city down to minutes, can't they?' He took her hand, as naturally as though they were old friends or lovers. 'Would you like to go shopping like a Roman matron did?'

'Oh, yes!'

'No doubts or questions this time, I see; that's good.' He led her along the street and then into a doorway. Inside, it was gloomy but not dark, for light flooded in through the doorway and through a square window. Vitale gestured, and she saw that the room was divided by a counter, marble topped, with three deep, bowl-like depressions in it. They looked very similar to modern ice-cream dispensers. Behind the counter the walls were shelved and pots, jars and jugs made of unglazed clay met her gaze.

'Well? What's this?'

'It's a shop, of course. Now I wonder what they sold?' Sharon pointed to the shelves. 'Wine? But if it's a Roman pub, why the holes in the counter? Unless they went in for salted peanuts and crisps in a big way, of course.'

He laughed, shaking her hand admonishingly in his.

'No, the thermopolia and taberna both sold wine, probably by the cup or glass as well as in the amorphas which you see on the shelves. This, then, would have been a thermopolia, with wine, oil and vinegar for sale on the shelves and probably the counter-bowls would have contained cereals—rice, lentils, that sort of thing. I'll show you a hot-food shop presently, which is more like our idea of a caffé or trattoria. You could buy food and hot drinks and sit on benches to eat it on the premises.'

'Come on, then. I wonder what sort of food they sold? Not Cornish pasties or hot-dogs, that's for sure!'

He laughed with her, and led her out into the sunshine again. Her hand lay in his still, and she would not for the world have removed it—it gave her such a feeling of security, of . . . well, of friendship, she told herself defiantly.

'One day, I'll take you into Naples proper, to the big museums,' he said as they strolled along the street. 'The city was full of treasures once, more so than Pompeii because Herculaneum was the place where the rich people lived even if they owned property or factories or some such thing in Pompeii. The trouble was, they were too easy to steal, and once things began to go, they were moved into Naples, to museums. It's a shame, but human nature, I suppose. You'd like to see them, wouldn't you? The carbonised remains of the people who lived here when the eruption occurred, their dogs their statues and artefacts?'

'I don't know,' Sharon said cautiously. 'Not if they look agonised I wouldn't.'

'They don't. Most of them look as though death caught them sleeping, but that may be because most of them lay down, covering themselves with cloaks or anything else that came to hand, thinking that the suffocating fumes would be held off by such means.'

'Poor souls. Let's not think of the eruption, though, let's think about it the way you did, earlier. The slave sitting on the horse trough, swinging his legs and whistling a tune he'd heard the legionnaires singing as they marched through the city. It's those things that make it come alive for me, not carbonised remains.'

He smiled.

'Right, I'll remember that.' He was wearing a short-sleeved white shirt, and he glanced at the watch round his wrist. 'Heavens, time does fly, look, we've just got time to see one or two more houses and then I'm whisking you off for lunch. I've booked a table, so we'll have to leave here promptly.'

'Oh, all right. And afterwards?'

'We'll come back, if you're agreeable.'

By the time they reached the huge city restaurant where Vitale had booked a table, Sharon was beginning to feel the effects of her sleepless night, but she said nothing and tucked into an excellent meal with a good appetite. They drank a white wine which tasted of the sun and the sea air, enjoyed a starter, the main course and a huge plate of vari-coloured icecream and finished off their meal with cappuchini and flat, pale green mints.

'That was delicious,' Sharon sighed, as they made their way back to the car. 'The trouble was, I ate too much and I feel sated and lazy and more like a siesta than anything else. Is this actually Naples, Signor?'

'It's Ramoros, on the outskirts of Naples. Not beautiful, but a centre of industry.' He held open the car door for her, inserting her into the seat with as much care as though she had been, in some way, precious to him. It gave her a good feeling. 'Well? Are you up to continuing our tour of Herculaneum?'

'Yes, I'm dying to see the rest.'

But despite her brave words, she fell asleep between Ramoros and the car park outside the ancient city and was only awoken by Vitale shaking her shoulder and calling her name.

'Sharon? Sharon! Come along, little one, culture calls!'

Sharon moaned and tried to settle herself deeper into what she fondly imagined was her bed, but the hot leather beneath her cheek brought her, blinking and stupefied by tiredness, back to reality. The car, the car park, and Vitale bending over her.

'How you sleep! Would you like to stay here for a little while, and rest? Or I could take you back to your flat and we could see the rest of the city another day.'

Sharon, now thoroughly wide awake, blushed, but spoke the truth.

'I'm sorry, Signor, I did night-duty last night since Sister Young was a nurse short, and then there was the wine . . . I'm afraid I'm behaving very badly, I shouldn't have drunk anything knowing I wasn't used to it. But I'm all right now.' She climbed, swaying, out of the car. 'See? I'm raring to go, honestly.'

He joined her, his expression remorseful.

'You should have told me you'd worked a night shift, I could have let you lie in this morning and then brought you here after lunch! But since we're here, we might as well finish the job. We'll see the baths, they shouldn't be missed, and the House of the Wooden Partition, and one or two other things.'

And Sharon, with his arm round her shoulders, found that she felt wonderfully refreshed after all and quite capable of continuing their tour! She admired the House of the Wooden Partition, and marvelled over its excellent state of preservation, the wooden stairs which led to the upper storey being complete and perfectly safe and the upper storey itself still containing a bed and a couch from those long-ago times.

In order to reach the Baths of the Forum they had to bend double and make their way in almost total darkness through a long tunnel. Sharon went ahead and was glad when they emerged once more into light. She had a vivid imagination and could not help a horrid feeling that, should Vitale suddenly turn into a werewolf, she was in the worst possible position to defend herself. The thought made her giggle, for werewolves, she believed, were more prone to attack the throat than the posterior, and when they stood upright once more she still had what was doubtless a very silly smirk on her face.

'What's the joke?' Vitale loomed over her, his expression quizzical. 'I'm not a bottom-pincher, like some of my compatriots, if that's why you kept suddenly shooting forward in the dark.'

'No, it wasn't . . .' Sharon choked and quickly turned to view the room in which they stood. 'Isn't this lovely?'

It was. There were marble benches round the walls with hooks above them for hanging clothing and the floor was decorated in mosaics to form a beautiful picture of a Triton and four dolphins, as well as an octopus and a squid engaged in a battle to the death.

'Yes. It's the Apodyterium or dressing room. Through that little doorway there you get into the tepidarium which was just what it sounds, warm but comfortable, and further through yet, into the calidarium, where you stewed in a really hot bath—all of you together.'

'How cosy,' Sharon said appreciatively. 'Can we go through?'

'Of course. Bend your head, these doorways weren't made for dwarves, as you might conclude, but for keeping the temperature in, so to speak.'

In the last room, the calidarium, he took her over to the marble bath and suggested that she should try it out.

'There's no water in there, of course, but just climb in and sit down and see what it felt like to bathe in a Roman turkish bath.'

Sharon climbed gingerly into the veined and mottled marble. 'I meant to ask you, why aren't there more people about? We've scarcely seen a soul here at all,' she said as he joined her in the bath.

'It's not one of the days for conducted tours,' he said briefly. 'Well, what do you think of it?'

'Weird.' Sharon looked up at the vaulted ceiling and pulled a face. 'I don't much like the corrugated-iron effect, either.'

'No, it isn't pretty, but it helped to build up the heat.' He climbed out of the bath and then leaned in and, before she could object, plucked her up and out and then stood with her in his arms, smiling down at her. 'My goodness, you weigh more than you appear to!'

'Then put me down,' Sharon said unsteadily. The feel of his arms about her and the thunder of his heart so close to hers were doing very unusual things to her metabolism, to say nothing of her heartbeat! He stood her down, but did not release her. Instead, smiling down into her eyes, he said softly: 'Shall I? Or will you scream the place down? Not that anyone would hear you, of course.'

'Wouldn't they?'

'No, because . . .'

But the reason was never revealed, because at that moment his lips claimed hers and once more she was floating, gliding, sinking, whilst her heart hammered double time and her whole body tingled at his touch.

When he released her she did not attempt to move away but stood still, leaning against him for a moment, before stepping back and smiling up at him.

'I'll never forget today,' she said quietly. 'Thank you for bringing me here, and for making it all come alive for me.'

He pushed her towards the dark little tunnel that would lead her back into the sunshine and then stepped before her.

'I'll go first, and then perhaps you won't be giggling when we reach the outside world.'

It was a kind thought, but Sharon's imagination was still working overtime and no sooner did she realise that there was no one behind her than she peopled the darkness at her rear with furious Roman ghosts, some of them armed with those pronged tridents that remind one of toasting forks. Her proximity to Vitale's doubled up figure was such, indeed, that on the two occasions that he stopped to call back to her, she actually bumped into him, giving a muffled shriek on each occasion and also pushing him rather more forcefully onward than was, perhaps, polite.

'What was the matter *that* time?' Vitale said as they emerged into the sunshine once more. His voice was testy but his face was not. Amusement tilted his mouth. Sharon blushed.

'Ghosts,' she said tersely.

'Ah, I *see*! In togas and laurel wreaths?'

'I don't know. But they had tridents.'

'That explains it. And you, of course, were in the rear.' He took her hand and began to lead her back along the Lower Decumanus Road. 'My poor child, spitted on a ghostly trident—no wonder you pushed me.'

He began to laugh softly, shaking with mirth, and Sharon, after a vain attempt to remain grave, joined in.

They were still laughing, off and on, when they climbed back into the car.

Sharon fell asleep again on the journey back to Sant' Agnello, but Vitale was soothing, pointing out that it was no fault of hers and cast no doubts on his ability to interest her.

'It is the fault of the staffing system in the Villa L'Arancia at the moment,' he told her. 'Things are always difficult in the summer, but we'll sort ourselves out soon, I'm sure.' He got out of the car and saw her into the foyer of the flats, but did not attempt to mount the stairs with her. 'Thank you for coming with me, I've enjoyed myself and I feel we know one another very much better, too. I hope you'll come out with me again.'

'I'd love to,' Sharon said sincerely. 'I can't tell you

how wonderful it s been! Are you sure you wouldn't like
to come up for a cup of coffee or a drink?'

'Not tonight. I've got to get over to the Villa; I
promised Fortuna that I'd give her a lift home, she
doesn't drive, you know, and it isn't always convenient
for the car to call for her. But I'll see you on the wards in
a couple of days.'

He raised a hand and was gone. Sharon began to
mount the stairs, a good deal of her golden happiness
fled. So he was going back to give Fortuna a lift home,
was he? Why could she not make her own arrangements,
as other people did, instead of butting in on a lovely day
out?

Unlocking her front door, it also occurred to her that
there had been no real need for Vitale to tell her why he
had to get back to the hospital. Had he regretted his
impulse to make love to her in the Baths? Was he telling
her, as kindly and tactfully as he could, that he had
enjoyed a pleasant and flirtatious interlude with her, but
that was all it was, just an interlude?

She was crossing the kitchen to put the kettle on when
the telephone rang. She ran across the living room and
lifted the receiver, praying that it would not be Sister,
asking her to do another night. If so, she really thought,
in fairness to her patients, that she would have to say no.
She was exhausted, all she wanted to do was to drop into
bed and fall miserably asleep.

'Hello? Sharon Craig speaking,' she said crossly into
the receiver.

'Hello, little one. I forgot to tell you to go straight to
bed, and to have sweet dreams.' There could be no
mistaking that deep, slightly accented voice. 'And no
tridents.'

'Oh, Signor, I will, and n-no tridents,' Sharon said,
her voice lifting with pleasure that he had thought of her.

'Goodnight, then.'

'Goodnight, Signor.'

She heard him chuckle softly, then he put the receiver

down and, after a moment of hugging her own receiver, she followed suit and returned to the kitchen. A quick cup of tea and then she really would take his advice and go to bed—but how happily, now!

She was almost asleep when another thought occurred to her. Suppose he had deliberately rung her from the hospital so that Fortuna would be in no doubt that he had taken another woman out? Just to teach her not to be so possessive?

But it was no use wondering, no use conjecturing, not when she was so tired. And whatever the reason, nothing could spoil that wonderful day!

CHAPTER SIX

As IT happened, Sharon and Dr Vitale did not meet for nearly two weeks after their day out in Herculaneum. Sister Young, conscience-stricken over the way her newest staff nurse had been working, gave her a double leave period and then, when she did come back, it seemed that Dr Vitale was on a course of some description in Rome.

'It was arranged months ago,' Sister Young explained comfortably, totally unaware of why Nurse Craig should be interested in the whereabouts of a surgeon who was not exactly every staff nurses' favourite. 'Dr Malpense is very efficient, though, you'll find. And Vitale would come back if there was an emergency.'

But what really put the cat amongst the pigeons was a further titbit of information which Sharon garnered from one of the constantly changing bevy of part-time receptionists. She was a curvy, lush beauty called Maddalena, and she told Sharon rather irritably that she was doing far more than her fair share of work on reception because Signorina Russano had seen fit to take a week off without warning anyone.

'Oh? I wonder why?' Sharon said idly, and without any real expectation of getting an answer.

'Why? Can you not guess, Sharon? She's gone to Rome with Vitale, of course! He is not a monk, you know.'

'Oh! But I thought Italian girls were far less liable to sleep around than the English are supposed to be.' Sharon said. 'Are you *sure*, Maddy?'

'Sure I'm sure, honey,' Maddalena said. She had learned her English from an American. 'Besides, Fortuna's not an innocent little thing, she's twenty-eight and

90

she's got around a bit. And anyway, Italian girls . . .'

'All right, I get the general idea,' Sharon said heavily. 'I'm on the ward in ten minutes, I'd better get moving. 'Bye, Maddy.'

That had been several days ago, and they had been miserable days for Sharon. It was obvious that she had been building castles in the air, he was no more interested in her than he was in Julie, he had just been showing her he was sorry for his strictures on her behaviour with Paolo.

On the day of his return, however, Sharon had determined to be fair. She would treat him with friendly caution, and if it seemed that he was inclined to treat her more warmly—well, she would have to ask him outright about Fortuna. She confided all this to Julie, who was sympathetic but sceptical.

'I don't believe he's having an affair with Fortuna, I bet she's taken the time off so that folk will think she's in Rome with him,' Julie said stoutly. 'Mind you, I wouldn't build too much on that day out in Herculaneum, love. He's thirty-eight, you know, he's had all the time in the world to learn how to lure a girl into his clutches and then to escape without pain. It's women who get hurt when they tangle with men like Vitale.'

So when she heard his voice outside in the corridor, Sharon, who was fetching clean sheets, repressed the urge to rush out and greet him and remained behind a rack of blankets in the linen cupboard. She told herself that presently she would go into the corridor and confront him normally, but by the time she had collected the necessary bedding and staggered beneath its weight out of the cupboard, Vitale was nowhere to be seen.

Carmella, hurrying past, hailed her instead.

'Is that the bedlinen for Rooms 2 and 3, Sharon? A man will be here in an hour and a Signora Porzio is in the waiting room now.'

'Yes, it is. The man's an appendectomy, isn't he?

Look, can you make up both beds whilst I do the admission on Signora Porzio? That way, we'll be all ready when the patient comes up from theatre.' She handed her burden over to Carmella, adding casually as she did so, 'Have you seen Dr Vitale yet? Does he look better for his holiday?'

'Better? He look jus' the same. And it wasn't a 'oliday, was it?'

'No, it was a course, Sister said.' Sharon smiled and turned towards Sister's office. 'Never mind, he'll do a ward round after theatre and I'll see him then.'

She went into the office where Sister was typing up reports and the staccato tap of the keys stopped at her entry.

'I've come for the file on Signora Porzio, Sister. She's a biopsy, I think. And I'll have the appendectomy too, if you've got the details from reception yet.'

'Porzio's file is here,' Sister said, handing over a buff folder, 'But Fortuna's back on reception after her week's holiday, so there will be a delay before Mr Wisden's notes come up. You'll do the admission?'

'Yes, and by the time the Signora's done, Mr Wisden's details should be up. He was an emergency, wasn't he? A holidaymaker?'

'That's right. Sudden pains which weren't that sudden; you'd be surprised at the number of people who come away on holiday feeling far from well and end up in a hospital bed! Nothing dire, usually, but it can be annoying when you're busy. Oh, by the way, can you pop in on Mrs Humphries and remind her to get some day-clothes from her people when they come tonight?'

Sharon agreed to pop in on Mrs Humphries since she knew that before he left for his trip to Rome, Vitale had suggested that the patient should get used to ordinary clothing once again, and it would give Carmella time to get Signora Porzio's bed made up. Mrs Humphries greeted the idea of having day-clothes with enthusiasm and assured Sharon that she quite understood the reasoning behind it.

'If all goes well and I go home in two or three weeks, it'll be a help if I'm used to tight belts and corsets and so on,' she said. 'I'll get several outfits and we'll see which is most comfortable.'

'Good idea, we'll have a mannequin parade. You're good at dressmaking aren't you, I remember you said so once. There may be some alterations to be made since a big operation almost invariably leads to some changes in the cut of one's clothing. It'll save time if you can get them done whilst you're still with us.'

'Yes, though . . .' Mrs Humphries gave Sharon a quick, shy glance. 'Once I'm dressed and feeling more . . . more myself, I wonder if the surgeon would agree . . . if he'd say it wouldn't hurt . . .'

'Carry on,' Sharon said encouragingly. How nice it would be if Mrs Humphries asked Signor Pappalardo to come visiting! Despite tactful encouragement and her own tendency to talk almost non-stop, Mrs Humphries had contrived never to mention her admirer's name to anyone.

'No, it was just a thought, I'll wait and see if I can still get into my blush-pink,' Mrs Humphries said disappointingly.

Going through the door once more, for the conversation had taken place in the day-room, Sharon came face to face with a slender, dark-haired girl who had just emerged from the waiting room. The girl smiled hesitantly and Sharon held out her hand.

'Signora Porzio? Do come with me, I'm sure your bed will have been made up by now, and we can admit you, which means that we'll fill in some forms together.'

She led her new patient along to Room 3 to find Carmella had indeed made the bed and hung a clean chart at the bottom of it, so she fished out her pen and checked the name at the top. Maria Porzio.

'Are you Nurse Craig? My brozzer knows you.'

Sharon stopped in the act of pulling the curtains around the bed.

'Really? Does he work at the hospital?'

'No, but he knows you. His name is . . .'

'Paolo Trapani, at your service, Sharon.'

Sharon spun round to find Paolo, looking like a naughty puppy, smiling at her from the doorway. After a pause, she smiled back. He was not a lot older than she herself, and he had apologised charmingly!

'Good morning, Paolo, I didn't know you had a married sister. I did ring you up to thank you for the beautiful flowers, but the lady who answered the phone . . .'

'That was *mia madre*—my mother,' Paolo exclaimed. 'I, too, rang you, Signorina, but only to your friend did I manage to speak—the charming Miss Drummond. She said to ring back later but later, alas, I was away, rushing off to Rome to buy wine.'

'Well, never mind, we're both here now,' Sharon said. 'And now I'm afraid I'll have to ask you to leave, Paolo, since I'm going to be busy with your sister for a little while.' He looked so crestfallen, however, that she relented. 'Look, if you want a quick word, wait in the waiting room and when I've finished with Signora Porzio, I'll come along and see you. Is that all right?'

When he had gone Sharon filled in the admission form with Signora Porzio's help, assisted her out of her clothing and into a filmy and glamorous nightie, and then went and fetched the trolley with all the paraphernalia for taking blood samples on it. Once more in the curtained cubicle, she saw that the girl was looking very apprehensive and smiled reassuringly at her.

'I'm going to take a little blood sample since you're having surgery, but you're not worried, are you? It says on your notes that you have a tiny cyst behind your ear which the surgeon wants to make sure is only what it seems.'

'Oh, no—it is the blood-taking which I do not like.'

'Well, I'm a dab hand with a 20 ml syringe.' Sharon wound the tourniquet round the girl's arm and deftly inserted the needle. 'There, the needle slips into the brachial artery, I fill the syringe, and it's all over.' She removed the full syringe and proceeded to squirt the blood first into the blood-count bottle and then into the ESR container. 'That's all I want for now, I'll send your brother through if you like and you can talk to him for a while.'

'My brozzer cannot wait,' the girl said. 'May I go and find the ozzer patients, Mees Craig?'

'Yes, of course, and do call me Sharon, your brother does,' Sharon said. 'I'll show you were the dayroom is on my way to tell your brother that he can take your case now.' She picked up the case, now full of the clothing Signora Porzio had brought in with her, and made her way down the corridor, despatching the girl into the dayroom as she passed it. She went in shyly, but she would soon settle in and she was so young and pretty that the men, at any rate, would speedily be vying for her attention.

Paolo rose to his feet as she entered the waiting room, his face a little anxious.

'Is she all right, Maria, I mean? She's such a shy little thing, I cannot help worrying about her. Though in Signor Vitale's hands she is sure of the best treatment.'

'Yes, and she's so sweet that we'll all make a fuss of her,' Sharon said warmly, touched by his obvious concern for his sister. 'She's only a babe, though—how long has she been married?'

'It must be nearly four months. She's past seventeen.'

'Gracious!' Sharon felt very old and worldly in comparison, yet the other girl was a married woman. 'Is her husband very young as well?'

'No. But he is very eligible, very rich,' Paolo said with obvious satisfaction. 'The family were pleased with the match. Tullo is in his mid-fifties—just the right husband for a pretty child like our Maria.'

'The right . . . honestly, Paolo, words fail me! There can be nothing right about an age gap of nearly forty years!'

Paolo looked surprised and a little hurt.

'Why ever not? Maria is Tullo's second wife, you understand, so he has learned just how to please a woman. He is handsome, sophisticated, and of course he worships her. He would give her the moon if she wanted it.'

'I see. What about you, then? Would you like a bride in her fifties?'

Paolo looked revolted.

'Of course not, the cases are very different. But if I was fifty, I've no doubt I'd enjoy a fresh young thing like Maria in my bed!' He caught Sharon's wrist, drawing her close to him. 'Don't be cross with me, my dearest, Maria was not cross at all! And anyway, it wasn't my sister I wanted to talk to you about, it was us! Will you come out with me again? I swear on my honour as a gentleman that I'll treat you with all the care and respect I would lavish on the daughter of family friends. There!'

He was so obviously pleased with this offer that Sharon melted towards him and, laughing, was about to say that she would be pleased to go out with him one evening provided that they went merely as friends, when the door opened. With her hands tightly held in Paolo's and her back towards the intruder, she still knew a frisson of feeling which told her who had entered.

'Nurse!'

Wrenching her hands free from Paolo's grasp and drawing away from him, she turned round. Vitale's face was like a thundercloud.

'Y-yes, Signor?'

'You *are* on duty? I suppose it means nothing to you that there's a very sick man lying in Room 3 whilst Carmella struggles to put up the drip and do the admission in a language not her own? Who is the Staff Nurse on duty this morning?'

'Well, me, but . . .'

'Nurse Craig was telling me about my sister, she's . . .' Paolo began loyally, but his explanation was brushed aside.

'It's time you left, Signor Trapani. Nurse, come with me.'

Sharon cast an apologetic glance at Paolo and then followed the surgeon. Why oh why did it have to be he who searched for her? Why couldn't he have seen to the drip himself and sent Carmella to hunt her out?

Once in Room 3 he dismissed Carmella with a curtness which sent that young person scurrying out of the room and then turned on Sharon with all the ferocity of a hungry tiger.

'So! This is how you behave the moment my back is turned!'

Sharon gritted her teeth and kept a hold on her already flaring temper.

'Please don't speak to me like that, Signor; it is perfectly true that Paolo's sister has just been admitted and that I was discussing her case with him. You have no right . . .'

'Holding hands? Gazing into each other's eyes? It is obvious to me, Nurse, that you're just like that little tart Angela—you're anyone's if they take you out and give you a good time.'

The patient, lying supine on the bed with the drip attached, might not have been there for all the notice the couple took of him. Sharon drew herself up to her full height.

'Anyone's? Well, you didn't have much luck, did you? And you'll never have the chance to see if you can score again, Signor!' She was trembling with fury, wanting to tell him how much she detested him, when the patient stirred. Mr Wisden's face was grey and drained from his recent ordeal, it would do him no good to find himself being fought over! She turned away from the bed, ignoring the surgeon's sharp repetition of her name. She would not remain to be slandered!

She made straight for the empty turret room next to Susan's, closed the door softly, and then went over to the window and gazed out at the blue beyond. She was still trembling with rage, but a small, still voice inside her was beginning to make itself heard. *Any senior member of staff would have been annoyed with you for shutting yourself into the waiting room with a young and attractive man*, the little voice said. *And you had been warned that Vitale was doing an emergency operation and that the patient would be on your ward shortly. If you had to go off for a few minutes to talk to a patient's anxious relative, you should have made sure that the rest of the staff knew where you were.*

On the other hand, to be called a tart, by a man who had just come back from an illicit week in Rome with a snooty, sharp-tongued cat like Fortuna was unforgivable. She knew it, and so would he, when he calmed down a bit. In fact, it could easily have been interpreted as jealousy, and the worst sort of jealousy too, the dog-in-the-manger sort. He might not want a permanent relationship with her, but he didn't want anyone else to have one either!

It was at this point in her reflections that the door opened. She stiffened, but did not turn away from her contemplation of the view.

'Nurse Craig?' She did not move until a hand touched her shoulder, and then she moved away, to stand facing the other window.

'Sharon, I shouldn't have called you . . . what I did. I know it isn't true, I'm sorry. But I can't have such unprofessional behaviour on my ward, you know.'

She turned at that. It was a handsome apology for a surgeon to make to a nurse and she knew he was right. It *was* unprofessional to behave as she had done. She would have smiled at him, except that his eyes were still as cold and angry as they had been when she looked into them across Mr Wisden's recumbent form. So the apology was a formal one only, then, to make it possible for them to work together! Well, probably it was as well. She had been in danger of losing her heart and her good sense over Vitale, now she would be her own woman again.

'It's all right, Signor. I'm very sorry too, I know it was silly to talk to Paolo as I did, though at the time I saw no harm in it.'

'No. Well then, we will shake hands and forget it.'

His handshake was firm and impersonal and he turned and left the room after it without a word or a smile. Sharon, following him slowly out, felt uncharacteristically miserable. They could never be anything but working colleagues now and she would miss his friendship.

For a week, Nurse Craig and Dr Vitale remained carefully polite to one another and took pains that their paths should cross as little as possible. Indeed, Vitale seemed more and more to plan his ward rounds so that they only took place when Sharon was busy elsewhere and though she told herself that this was sensible, her heart was sore because of it. Just to see him, vile though she told herself he was, gave her pleasure in an odd, heart-wrenching sort of way. I am *not* in love with him, she told herself half-a-dozen times a day, and knew she lied. Unfortunately, *he is not in love with me* completely convinced her, and sank her into the deepest depths of depression so that everyone noticed her new quietness.

And then Snowflake went missing. The kitten's leg was completely mended now and her curiosity as rampant as it had ever been. Someone must have left the door open a crack, though no one would admit to it, and Snowflake had sneaked out.

A great fuss was made by everyone, including the surgeon.

'He pretends he's worrying in case the cat sneaks into the theatre and ruins something, or trips a patient, or annoys the cook, but he's really worried because he's fond of Susan,' Sister Young said crossly to Sharon as the two of them laid up a trolley. 'I can't think what's the matter with the man lately, he's as cross as two sticks, never has a good word to say for anyone, and finds fault so constantly that even the theatre staff are noticing.'

'I expect he blames me, I brought the cat in in the first place,' Sharon said gloomily. 'To tell the truth, I blame myself every time I see Susan's tearful little face. How long's Snowflake been gone now?'

'Only twenty-four hours. It seems like weeks, though. You're doing a split shift today, aren't you? Well, if you'd like to oblige me, dear, could you pick me up some insoles in the chemist, if that's where they sell them. The soft ones that stop your feet from aching. I'll give you the money before you leave.'

'Yes, of course. To tell you the truth, I thought I'd have a look round Sant' Agnello and see if I can spot the kitten; she may have followed another cat and be living somewhere down by the beach, especially if the fishermen leave fish scraps lying about. And I could have a swim at the same time, I've only swum a couple of times since I got here.'

'That's an excellent idea.' Sister looked remorsefully up at Sharon. 'I do feel you've had a hard time of it, with Julie hardly ever being able to get her time off to coincide with yours. But it'll be better once the home leave's finished for the season.'

'So I understand. How's Mr Wisden this morning?'

The talk became technical and presently Sister and Staff Nurse hurried off to do their rounds of the ward.

But later, after a very busy morning, Sharon found herself free at last and hurrying back to the flat for a quick sandwich before going into Sant' Agnello to look around. She had accepted an invitation from Paolo to have dinner with him and then go dancing at the biggest hotel in Sorrento and another from Geoff Reynolds, still in Sant' Agnello, since he had found himself what he described as 'a cosy billet', acting as barman in a nightspot. Life was beginning to pick up, and what was even nicer, she had made another girl-friend. Julie was a dear, but so rarely available, and when Signora Porzio had suggested shyly that Sharon might like to go and see her lovely new house when she had some time off, Sharon was happy to accept. The two of them got on very well, and since the cyst on Maria's neck had proved to be non-malignant she had gone home after only three days on the ward and had either popped in to visit her new friend or had telephoned her, every day since.

So Sharon, strolling round the village, was in a sunny mood and ready to be pleased with everything. She was looking forward to her date with Paolo tomorrow evening, and to her date with Geoff the next. Although Susan had looked a little worried when she had told her about the date with Geoff.

'You won't *marry* him, Craigie, will you?' she had asked anxiously. 'I think he's nicer even than Peter Powers. I'd rather hoped to marry him myself.'

'Never fear, I'm beginning to think I'm not the marrying kind,' Sharon assured her. 'I'll give him your love, though.'

So now, peering into the shops half with a view to seeing what was on offer and half with the hope that she might see a white kitten lurking, Sharon ambled contentedly up and down the village street. She was quite surprised, nevertheless, to find herself hailed in English.

'Hi, Sharon!'

It was Geoff, darkly tanned now and with a huge yellow melon under one arm.

'Oh, hi, Geoff. Shopping? I didn't know you were self-catering!'

'I'm shopping for my landlady, honey! What are you doing this fine afternoon? Why don't we mosey off down to my pad and have a little lovin'?'

'What, in this heat? Don't even suggest it!'

'Cold as charity,' Geoff said, shaking his head mournfully. 'You'd be better than air-conditioning in my room!

Well, if you don't feel like a bit of slap and tickle, how about a swim?'

'No, sorry. You won't have heard the news, but Susan's kitten has gone missing. We've turned the hospital inside out, but no luck. So I'm going to spend the afternoon beachcombing to see if I can come up with anything.'

'So long as it isn't a body,' Geoff said grimly. 'That poor kid! How about if I find a substitute? A white kitten's a white kitten, after all.'

Sharon shook her head.

'We thought of it, but it wouldn't work. Snowflake's quite a character, Susan's taught her to do all sorts of things, she'd know a double at once. But thanks for the thought.'

'Tell you what, I'll nip in and spend an hour or two with the kid,' Geoff suggested. 'That might cheer her up.'

'It would. I suppose you've no idea where Snowflake could have gone?'

'Over the edge,' Geoff said grimly. 'That's where you found her, wasn't it? I'd take a bet on it, poor little blighter.'

'I hope you're wrong. Now I'd better buy Sister her insoles before I forget.'

It was not until she had returned to the flat for her bathing costume and towel that a thought struck Sharon. Geoff had said the kitten might well have gone over the balustrade, but was it not far likelier that Snowflake had found her way back to the old wine cellars, where her mother had given birth to her? She had found her way out of those wine cellars and onto the cliff, no one had been able to explain how. Suppose she had done it again, and was stuck out there, on a ledge which could not be seen from the terrace this time?

Sharon ran quickly down the stairs, out of the flats and across the road. She was going to the hospital, after all, there could be no harm in looking!

Sister thanked her for the insoles, slipped them inside her neat white shoes on the spot, and gave a sigh of relief.

'That's so much better! I'll see you again at about eight, shall I?'

'That's right. 'Bye, Sister!'

It did not occur to her until later that she had said nothing to Sister or anyone else about searching the villa's old wine cellars, nor that her swimming costume and towel, hidden in her straw basket, were unlikely to have been noticed by anyone. Thinking only of Snowflake, and of Susan's distress over the loss of her pet, she went straight down into the storerooms in the basement and began to search for the cellar door.

She found it soon enough and for a moment stared at it, dismayed. It was an immense thing, capable of withstanding a siege by the look of it and firmly locked, the great key still in the lock. How could a tiny kitten have got through that?

But she remembered that not only a tiny kitten but a full-sized cat expecting a litter had done it, so presumably there were times when the door was left open. She turned the key in the lock, and since it turned easily, with well-oiled smoothness, she realised that she must be right; the wine cellars were still used for something.

Through the doorway, she realised something else. The 'rooms' beyond were, in fact, caves, though whether they were natural or man-made she could not tell since they were very dark, only lit by the sunshine which poured through a smallish aperture at the very end of the furthest cave.

She had a small torch in her bag, however, and shone it around. The mystery of what was kept in the wine cellars was soon solved—it was wine, racks and racks of it, far more than the patients or staff could ever have hoped to drink—officially, at least. Probably it was Vitale wine, laid down years ago when the villa had been a private house, and probably the surgeon came down here from time to time and departed with a case or two. Other than that, it seemed that no one came here, at least from the thickness of the dust on the bottles and shelves.

'Snowflake? Snowy, love, are you here?' Sharon's little torch beam probed the shadows and once, something scuttled. She shone the beam in the direction of the noise and saw a grey shape gliding for cover. Rats! Oh Lord, and rats could eat a kitten, couldn't they? She found herself saying a fervent prayer that she would not presently come across a tiny, gnawed pile of bones.

But she did not, though neither did she find the kitten. Instead, she crossed the cellar and peered out of the aperture, then hastily drew back, her head spinning.

The drop beneath was apparently sheer down to the tiny beach below, and Sharon was on the verge of giving up and returning to the hospital itself when she remembered that it could *not* be sheer. Snowflake had got out there once, she could do so again.

This time, she did not just look out of the window, she looked all round it, and discovered that it was not really a window at all but an entrance of some sort. At any rate, there were steps leading up to it. Shuddering slightly, she climbed the steps, clinging tightly to the rocky ledge. and peered out. And there *were* steps out there as well, narrow to be sure, and steep, but steps nevertheless, which led, she would swear, right down to the beach below.

It took courage to step out of the aperture and onto those steps, but Sharon told herself firmly that she was not doing it for herself but for a sick child, and stepped. And once out there, it wasn't too bad. There was a hand-guide, for a start, an ancient rail fixed quite securely into the cliff-face, and the steps themselves, though steep and not very wide, were deep and dry and perfectly climbable.

It was, nevertheless, a relief to find dry sand beneath her feet and to know that she was indeed at the bottom of the cliff. Sharon stood still for a moment, looking back up at the steps which she had just descended. Ugh! But going back might not be too bad, at least she knew it was not only possible, but fairly painless. She turned away from the cliff face then, and surveyed her surroundings.

It was quite lovely, the sand was clean and uncluttered by people or sea-wrack, it lay there with the sea creaming against it in gentle waves, totally inviting. On the far side of the beach there were some crab or lobster pots, so presumably a fisherman used the place as a deposit for his gear from time to time, but otherwise it was as deserted as one could wish.

Sharon glanced around again. Marvellous, it was even out of sight of the Sant' Agnello beach, hidden by the jut of the cliff, and out to sea there was no one, of course. A daring idea formed in her brain, to be abruptly dismissed as she glanced upwards. No, nude bathing was out of the question when you remembered the terrace up there, and the possibility that anyone might stroll out and look over the edge! However, having climbed all the way down here, she might as well enjoy herself and have a swim and some sunbathing. She could not have found a more perfect spot for it.

She moved back against the cliff to change, mindful of possible eyeballing from on high, and then moved down to the water's edge. She was wearing a white bikini which enhanced her slight tan, but how much better it would look if she could just cook down here for a little while, and attain a really good, deep colour! Accordingly, she spread her pale yellow towel out on the sand so that presently she could go and lie on it, and ran into the sea.

She was a good swimmer, but even so, the unexpectedness of the shelf surprised her. One moment she was knee-deep in water, the next the bottom had simply disappeared and she was swimming. The sea, mild beneath the hot sun, was delightful, however, and she continued to swim out until she could see the crowded beach umbrellas on the public sands. Then, feeling that she had been in the water long enough, she returned to her own private bay, climbed out onto the shore, and flopped onto her towel.

She may have dozed a little, with the sun burning down on her; certainly, she could not think why she was suddenly alert. It had been a sound, like a seagull's cry, floating on the breeze which, slight though it was, goose-fleshed her skin. Or was it the breeze? Was it not that the cry reminded her of another time when she had thought she heard a gull, only it had really been the kitten?

She moved her head, and felt something against her nose. Another nose. Small and pink and damply quivering, it bumped her whilst a purr began to reverberate through a small, skinny body.

Sharon gave a squeak, sat upright, and hugged Snowflake to her now dry bikini. The little devil! She must have been on the beach all the time, probably hidden by the lobster pots or whatever they were, and when she saw Sharon come out of the water and lie down on her towel, she had decided to investigate. Oh, the little *devil*!

Snowflake, not at all put out by the hugs, put up her small head and licked Sharon's chin delicately, then, purring like distant thunder, she jumped down and headed determinedly for the cliff. It was immediately clear what had happened. Getting down the cliff path must have been half climb half slip, slide and scramble, but getting up again was different. Because not with the best will in the world could Snowflake reach the first, and steepest, step. In fact, there was an overhang at about eighteen inches from the sand which must have effectively prevented her from even realising where the steps were. Poor little creature, had it not been for Geoff's remark she might have starved down here!

Jubilantly, Sharon picked up her bag, stuffed the towel and her dress and sandals into it, and followed the kitten. Then she picked her up as well and began to climb.

Snowflake was very good during the climb, even though Sharon clutched her rather tightly. Perhaps she remembered that other journey, which had ended so happily for her. At any rate, she sat comfortably in Sharon's arms, occasionally craning her neck to peer down to the beach but making no attempt to get free. That was, until they reached the cellar. Then, one look at the darkness and Snowflake's blue-grey eyes dilated until they were all black, and she began to struggle.

'Don't be a silly little thing,' Sharon said severely, trying to keep a hold on the wriggling little body whilst stepping over the sill and retaining her grasp on her shopping basket. 'It's quite all right, you're nearly home.'

But Snowflake refused to be convinced. Just as Sharon slid into the cellar the kitten gave one last wriggle and dropped onto the floor with a small thud, to flash across the room like lightning and disappear behind the wine-racks.

'You little idiot!' Sharon's irritable voice did not tempt the kitten to reappear. 'What do you think you're doing? Come here at once!'

There was a flicker of movement behind the racks, but the kitten remained prudently hidden. Sharon tried flattery.

'Who's a lovely, brave little girl, then? Who's going to come with Sharon and get the biggest dinner she's seen for hours and hours? Who's . . . Oh, confound it, I'll open the door and you'll be able to smell cooking for yourself.'

It surprised her at first when the door didn't budge, and then, with cold conviction, she knew what had happened. Someone had come down into the storeroom, tried the door for some unguessable reason, and realised that it was unlocked when it should be locked. They had simply turned the key in the lock and gone off again, back about their rightful business. Leaving her and Snowflake firmly locked out!

She turned back to the cave once more, giving a small, involuntary shudder. It was cold in here, or cold after the heat outside, at any rate. It was annoying to be locked out, of course, but not fatal by a long chalk. There was little point in banging on the door or calling, she realised that, but on the other hand she was a strong swimmer and though it was annoying and would take time, she only had to climb down the cliff again, swim round to the public beach, and return to the hospital via the cliff-lift. Then she could go back to the store rooms, unlock the cellar door, and bring Snowflake through without any trouble at all.

Resolutely, she walked through to the cave with the window in it, calling Snowflake in her most blandishing tones as she did so, though it didn't matter really, since she had not the faintest intention of allowing the kitten to follow her down onto the beach again. She would block the window with her towel or something so that Snowflake wouldn't be tempted to try the descent.

And then, behind her, she heard the little scrabble of claws on rock and a tiny squeak. She whirled, and then broze into total stillness. Snowflake had emerged from the wine racks and was standing looking at her, ears pricked, eyes wide, tail erect. And behind her, scarcely a foot away, was the biggest rat Sharon had ever imagined. Its eyes glowed red in the reflected light from the window, and it was staring, with beady intensity, at Snowflake!

Sharon knew she must have cried a warning to the kitten, but her hand moved instinctively to grasp a weapon—and came up with a bottle of wine. She hurled, and it smashed on the wall just above the rat, which promptly scuttled towards Snowflake. Sharon uttered another banshee yell and another bottle whizzed through the air, this time causing the kitten to yell too, on a different note, as it was suddenly deluged with wine.

Another bottle crashed, then another. The rat was beginning to look more hunted than hunter, Sharon saw with satisfaction. In fact, when her sixth bottle sent a whole rack toppling, the rat proved her point. Totally unnerved—it must have led quite a sheltered life down in the cellars—it turned and scuttled as fast as it could for a tiny hole near the door, disappearing with such alacrity that it was probably not even splashed by the last, triumphant, wine bottle.

But someone else was. The door shot open and Vitale stood blinking down at her, screwing up his eyes to see further into the sudden darkness. Then, without more ado, he was beside her, grabbing her, shaking her!

'You're alive! Dear God, when they told me . . . I remembered the kitten, I knew what you'd done . . . gone scrambling to fetch it back, slipped, fallen . . .' He was hugging her tightly, his arms hard, but she could feel him shaking. 'You damned, bloody little fool!'

She could not say a word. Happiness was welling up almost painfully, bubbling like golden wine in her heart. He might be calling her names, but he was welcome to call her anything he liked if he did it with his arms round her and that wonderful warmth in his tone!

'No, I c-came down here, w-went down the steps. And I f-f-found her, too!'

Her voice was shaking so much that she was stuttering and she realised, at the same moment, that her knees were about to give. She had always loathed and feared rats, but it was only now that she realised how much. She bit back tears, but was unable to stop a small sob from escaping.

'You found her?'

From behind a wine rack, Snowflake came creeping. She gave a tiny, doubtful *miaow* and Sharon realised that the kitten probably had no idea at whom the wine bottles had been hurled; it might just as well have been at her! She heard Vitale gasp, then he hugged her again before putting her gently from him.

'Poor little creature, I'll put it out of its misery.' He went towards Snowflake and Sharon, suddenly realising what he must think, gave another shriek. The kitten was soaked in wine, of course—red wine!

'Don't! She's all right! It isn't blood!'

'So I see.' For the first time, the surgeon looked round the cellar. Sharon, following his gaze, saw it, for a moment, through his eyes. There was glass everywhere, and wine puddled the floor. One whole rack had been knocked over and the bottles had not yet stopped rolling gently about. Add one wine-soaked kitten, and it looked like some mad sort of orgy.

Vitale glanced back at her. One eyebrow rose almost into his hair.

'This was necessary, I suppose? Don't tell me, you hurled wine bottles at the kitten to prevent its escape? Or were you teaching it not to frighten us so badly again?'

'Of course not! There was a huge rat, immense, as big as . . . as anything. It was going to kill Snowflake, so I threw a bottle of wine at it.' His expression remained irate, so Sharon tried a more placatory tone. 'Two or three bottles, actually. Or four.'

'And the rat? Where is its body?'

'Oh, I didn't *hit* it,' Sharon said, relieved to be able to explain that she was not out to kill. 'I wouldn't want to hurt it—well, I wouldn't have minded stunning it but I didn't want it to *die*, poor thing. No, I just wanted it to go away.'

He was quiet for a moment, looking at the now empty wine rack. When he spoke, it was in even, almost thoughtful, tones.

'You just wanted it to go away! Did you try asking it? Before you proceeded to wreck my wine cellar, I mean?'

'If asking would have worked, it would have gone at the first wine bottle,' Sharon pointed out reasonably.

'I'm sorry if I've made a mess, but the truth is, I'm terrified of rats, and . . .'

'Well, well, the damage is done, I suppose I must just be grateful that it wasn't a Roman soldier. With a trident. You might have been forced to wreck the entire cellar to get rid of one of those!'

There was a pause whilst Sharon assimilated this, and when she spoke again, it was defensively.

'Signor, I did *not* imagine that rat, it was here, honestly—it went out through that hole near the door. And I've s-said I'm s-s-sorry for . . .'

He was beside her, grinning down at her, taking her arm.

'All right, all right, no need to get dignified! You've spared my Napoleon brandy, at least I've something to be grateful for, and the wine, though old and rare, is not irreplaceable. Come along, let's get you and that confounded kitten cleaned up. And I'd better tell Sister that the panic's over.'

'What panic?' Sharon said dreamily as he walked beside her through the store rooms. 'Gracious, Signor, let me hold Snowflake, she's getting wine all over your shirt.'

'It doesn't matter, the scent comforts me for my loss of the substance. What panic? My dear child, when a maid runs shrieking through a hospital announcing that there's a dead woman on the beach, and when a surgeon drops everything and simply disappears into the cellars . . . Well, that's my idea of a panic. I don't know that there's anyone else in the hospital who knows of the existence of those steps down onto the beach, you see, though nearly all the medical staff know about the cellars.'

'Perhaps they've concluded you felt you needed a stiff drink before investigating the dead woman,' Sharon said cheerfully. 'I do hope they aren't lowering a medical team over the balcony at this very moment!'

'No, they won't do that, they'll conclude, very sensibly, that a holidaymaker must have swum round to the private beach and fallen asleep on the sand, and then woken and swum away again.' He looked thoughtfully down at Sharon. 'Shall we let them think it, my child? I really don't want to find any more nurses risking their lives on that cliff face.'

'That suits me fine,' Sharon said. 'We can just say, truthfully, that you and I found Snowflake in the cellars.'

'Hmm. I think we'll leave it that you found her. And I went down to the cellars to fetch up some wine and we walked back together.'

'Right. What about the wine, though? The poor little thing's going to smell like a bottle of Chianti for days!'

'Chianti?' He winced slightly, then continued, 'We'll say she knocked a bottle over during her incarceration and it got broken. Any more objections?'

They had reached the foyer. Sharon smiled at him and resisted a strong urge to snuggle up. Fortuna was staring at them, the colour heightened in her cheeks.

'No, nothing more, Signor. I'll take the kitten straight up to Susan.'

She walked up the stairs, and it was not until she reached the upper landing that she realised why Fortuna had stared so. She was still clad in nothing but a very tiny white bikini!

CHAPTER SEVEN

'So ALL's well that ends well,' Sharon concluded at the end of her story of the kitten's rescue. 'But not a word beyond these four walls, or Dr Vitale will personally kill me first and Snowflake next. He doesn't want anyone to know about those steps.'

She was sitting on Susan's bed, with Julie perched on the windowsill and Ian Ridgeway in the visitor's chair, but in fact at this moment they were all three visiting, since Julie and Sharon both had the day off.

'I'm not surprised,' Julie said weakly, wiping her streaming eyes. Both she and the film producer had laughed until they cried, though Susan had thought it a very affecting story and not very funny at all. Rats were something that Susan did not much care for either.

'You're a crazy girl, Sharon, but a rather nice one,' Ian announced. He got to his feet. 'Julie and I are off into Sorrento—do you want a lift, or some shopping?'

'No, thanks. After the trauma of yesterday I'm going to have a nice, quiet day mooning around the flat and cooking a meal, before having a few hours' rest, of course. I'm on nights for a day or so, and sleeping in the day doesn't agree with me, but if I'm fairly inactive it usually means that I can keep awake all right.'

'All right, then. Take care of yourself, Susan, we'll pop in for half an hour after lunch.' Ridgeway and Julie went out, and Susan leaned back against her pillows and prepared her paper for her next drawing. Drawing was her present passion and she used masses of paper in her efforts to attain, if not perfection, at least a reasonable likeness.

'Well, Craigie, I've got a bit of gossip for you! Fortuna's feeling poorly, and the maids think it's very suspicious!'

'Suspicious? Why on earth should it be suspicious?'

'Well, apparently she's been feeling sick and odd, and complaining of aches and pains, and Stacy told Lucia that she'd been away with a man for a whole week, and what did she expect?'

Sharon experienced a cold, sinking feeling. Surely the maids did not think that Fortuna was pregnant? Worse, did Fortuna think she was pregnant? And if so, did she think that Vitale was the father? It must be a mistake, he could not be so light-minded as to get one girl into trouble whilst carrying on a flirtation with another. No, not a flirtation, she told herself severely, a *relationship*. He could not do such a thing. Could he?

The answer, of course, was that he could. Men had been tricked into marriage before by this sort of ploy. Fortuna could have followed him to Rome, thrown herself at his head, and now she could be about to blackmail him into marriage.

'What's the matter, Craigie? You've been staring at my drawing for five minutes, and it isn't that bad!'

'Oh! Sorry, I'm afraid my mind was wandering.' She stood up, unable to stay there any longer whilst doubts and fears chased through her head. Sister might know something . . . any one! 'I'll come back later, pet, I just want a word with someone.'

Her careful enquiries, however, led to no firm conclusion. Maddy was on the reception desk and though a forthcoming girl as a rule, she could not say more than that Fortuna did not seem well.

'But she's got an appointment to see Dr Vitale this afternoon,' she added. 'If she's putting it on to get time off, I can't see her asking for the appointment, and if she's really ill, Vitale will spot it. Unless . . .'

'Unless what?' Sharon said sharply, but Maddalena only shrugged and looked embarrassed.

'Unless nothing. It's just the way my mind works, sometimes. Forget it.'

Her mind isn't the only mind, Sharon thought distractedly. Oh, oh, I wish this afternoon was over!

In the end, hanging around the hospital had simply proved too nerveracking for Sharon, particularly once she had realised that Vitale did not intend to visit the ward that day. Instead, she went back to the flat, had a very early lunch, and took a sleeping tablet provided by Sister so that she could get some sleep. She woke at seven, when Julie came home, banging about the flat in a very cheerful manner, and talking hopefully of how Ian was planning to do this and that once Susan was out of hospital.

'Well, don't make too much of it,' Sharon said, disagreeable after her enforced sleep. 'Men are just about as dependable and trustworthy as cobras, if you ask me.'

Julie's eyebrows shot up.

'That sounded bitter! Poor Sharon, what's he done now?'

'He? I don't know who you mean.'

'Oh, what a liar you are! If you think it isn't obvious to all and sundry that you're head over heels in love with Vitale, you must be blind and mad.'

Sharon stared, her face slowly reddening.

'*Me?* In love with that . . . that sharp-tongued, irascible . . .'

'Yes, you.' Julie came across the kitchen where the two girls had been preparing their evening meal and put an arm round Sharon's shoulders. 'My poor old love, it stands out a mile!'

The kindness was more than Sharon could cope with. She sniffed, gulped, and burst into tears.

'Now what's the matter? There's nothing wrong with you being in love, you can't help it, it's like catching measles! Do stop howling, Sharon, and tell me what he's done!'

'N-nothing, not to m-me! But Fortuna . . . the maids think she's pregnant, and if so . . . they say she spent a week with Vitale in Rome, and . . . oh, Julie, if every-one knows how I feel about him, and he knows, then I'll die of shame if he has to marry that spiteful little bitch!'

'Vitale's no fool, I don't think for one moment that he's sleeping with Fortuna, but if he was, he'd make very sure there wasn't any likelihood of a baby! The man's a top surgeon, with a reputation to think about, apart from the fact that no man wants to feel trapped into marriage. Now stop being daft, do, and put this omelette into the pan.'

'All right. And at least I'll know what happened at the clinic this afternoon; Sandra was on duty and so by now it'll be all round the hospital.'

But when she got back to the Villa L'Arancia, Sharon had to go no further than Susan's room to find out most of what she wanted to know. Susan was sitting up in bed waiting for her, a look of pleased importance on her face.

'Guess what? Fortuna's been admitted, she's in the second turret room! Sister and Dr Vitale were talking about her in there earlier with the window open, and I stretched my ears like anything and heard every word! Vitale thinks she's panicking over one of those tummy bugs that have been going around but it seems her parents are away and she's alone in the house so he's said she's to stay in overnight for observation. What do you think of that? Everyone hates Fortuna, you know, so she won't get many staff visitors!'

'Oh, Lor, and I'm on nights,' groaned Sharon. 'I just hope she doesn't spend the entire twelve hours beefing to me about her aches and pains. I'd better pop in, though, and see how she seems.'

'They're going down like flies with that bug,' Susan said cheerfully. 'Sister Crown's down—that was poetry, Craigie!—and Sandra went home two hours early, and poor Dr Malpense was carried off in agony, and so was one of the receptionists. Just you wait, before the night's out you'll be rolling around on the floor begging me to get you help.'

'I shan't, you little horror,' Sharon said, belatedly remembering she was in here to rub cream into Susan's pressure points.

Presently, she tapped on the door of the second turret room and slipped in. Fortuna certainly did look pale, she had to give her that, and though she turned a glance of dislike on Sharon, it lacked the usual amount of icy disapproval.

'Oh, it's you,' she said ungraciously. 'The pain's awful now, it's really digging at me.'

'I'm sorry. Have you eaten or drunk anything since you came in? Are you thirsty now?'

'No I'm not,' Fortuna snapped. 'I had some beef tea earlier and then I was sick, I'm not going to touch anything else.' She groaned and held onto her side dramatically, but Sharon's sharp eyes took in the sweat that broke out on her brow; she really was in pain, though it was impossible to say how much. 'Turn my television on.'

'Right,' Sharon said peaceably, though she wished that Fortuna had said 'please'. 'Anything else?'

'No. Just leave me in peace.'

'Right.' Sharon bit back the words 'It'll be a pleasure', and left the room without another word.

The evening wore on, and was one of the busiest Sharon had ever experienced. At nine-thirty, Sister Harris, in charge of the downstairs ward, rang through to tell Sharon, in a voice charged with pain, that she was off home.

'It's the bug, all right,' she said weakly. 'I feel as if I'm being filleted, I'm no use to anyone like this, but it means leaving Nurse Pirra in charge. She's Italian, of course, and her English isn't too marvellous, but beggars can't be choosers. Keep an eye on my ward, there's a good

girl. I suppose you've not got anyone on who could stand
in for me?'

'No, I'm in the same boat myself,' Sharon admitted.
'I've got a nice kid with me, but she's young and new and
only speaks a few words of English.'

This was true, though Nurse Savelli would not have
agreed. The fact was that her English was so fractured
that Sharon herself had great difficulty in understanding
her, and the patients scarcely made the attempt. It
would be impossible to allow the girl to take charge of a
ward.

An hour later, the night resolved itself into nightmare.
Everything that could go wrong, did. Mr Wisden, who
was to leave the following day, turned a cup of hot
chocolate all over himself and his bed. No sooner had
Sharon cleaned him up and remade his bed with fresh
linen than Mr Crisp, who was only in for a couple of
nights whilst his broken leg was checked out after an
infection, fell over and cracked his plaster. As if to prove
that men did not hold the record for clumsiness Miss
Ethel Broadhead, a spare and vinegary spinster, managed to disconnect herself from her drip, and whilst
Sharon and Nurse Savelli were replacing the needle, the
telephone rang again, to report that Theatre Sister had
been sent home.

'Well, let's hope there are no emergencies,' Sharon
said gloomily, then put the phone down and headed for
Fortuna's room. She had better keep a close eye on the
woman, she did not want an adverse report being put in
to Vitale in the morning.

Fortuna was lying back with her eyes closed. She
looked almost peaceful until you noticed the sweat on
her brow and the fact that her teeth were clenched in
pain. Sharon felt her forehead. It was hot, but not, she
fancied, excessively so. Nevertheless, she would check
everything now she was here.

Fortuna's pulse, temperature and b.p. were a little up,
and whilst Sharon was still filling in her chart she sud-

denly vomited, but after that, she said she felt a little better.

'I suppose it must be this bug that Vitale spoke of,' she said crossly, settling down again. 'I shall see if I can sleep, now.'

Sharon left the room and rushed in to Susan. Just inside the door Snowflake was prowling, with typical feline awkwardness she had decided to wake up for the night and was looking black-eyed and alert. Sharon sighed, scooped up the kitten, and plonked her on Susan's bed.

'Susan love, I'm rushed off my feet, do keep Snowflake with you, it would be the end if she got out tonight! And I'm going to settle you down now and put your light off, because if I don't, heaven knows when I'll get round to it. I know it's boring for you, love, because you don't get tired with spending so much time lying still, but do try to sleep!'

'Don't blame me if I wake at two and want tea, then,' Susan said, reluctantly putting down her book. 'Do you mind if Nurse Savelli pops in later? She's teaching me to speak Italian and she usually gives me a lesson when things quieten down.'

'No, I don't mind, but I doubt if things are going to quieten down. There's no Sister or Staff on the other ward, and Theatre Sister's just gone off sick. However, I promise that if things do settle, one of us will come and see if you're still awake. How's that?'

'Thanks, Craigie.' Susan put her thumb in her mouth and spoke through it in a muffled whisper. 'G'night, then.'

'Goodnight, love.'

A quick tour of Rooms 1, 2 and 3, and then Sharon popped back to see Fortuna. She was lying quiet now, and actually smiled as Sharon's face appeared in the doorway.

'I'm feeling so much better,' she said weakly. 'All the pain's gone. It must have been the bug Vitale mentioned. I think I'll sleep all right now.'

'Good. I'll pop in from time to time.'

Sharon was letting herself out quietly when a thought that had been in the back of her mind came to the fore. *In a suspected appendicitis case, should the pain suddenly disappear, panic!* She could even visualise the face of Sister Tutor at St Paul's as she recited the words of wisdom to the young nurses in her class. Sharon hesitated, her hand still on the door knob. Was it possible that Fortuna's appendix had ruptured? She went cold at the thought—Theatre Sister was off, there was no Sister on the other ward, and Dr Abele, who was on duty tonight, was already in the small theatre, operating on someone who had just come in.

She could ring down and get a message through to Dr Abele, and he would come up when he'd finished operating and give her his opinion. But if the appendix had ruptured it might be too late!

Making up her mind, Sharon returned to the room and laid her hand gently on Fortuna's abdomen. It was hard as a board, and the flush on her face indicated that her temperature was still up, might even have risen.

A minute later she was in full flight down the corridor, hospital rules about running forgotten. One glance at the thermometer when she withdrew it was enough to make up her mind for her. Fortuna might have the bug, she might be about to start a false alarm, but she could not risk the girl's life by not alerting everyone.

She reached Sister's office, grabbed the telephone book, and found Vitale's number. She dialled it, and the phone was answered almost immediately. A deep, sleepy voice that she could never mistake for any other, even though it was speaking in Italian.

'Oh, Dr Vitale, it's Nurse Craig, Wisteria Ward. I think Fortuna's appendix has ruptured.'

There was perhaps half a second of stupefied silence before Vitale's voice barked in her ear: 'Abele?'

'In theatre. Signor . . .'

'I'll be with you in ten or fifteen minutes. Sharon, are you sure enough of your diagnosis to get the theatre set up for an emergency operation?'

'Well, I . . .' but her intuition was strong. 'Yes, I'm sure, Signor. Only there's hardly any qualified staff in the building, they've been going down like flies with the gastro-enteritis bug. Dr Abele will have taken the staff who were on call, too, for his emergency.'

'Right. Ring Sister Young in the nurses' flats and tell her to get anyone who isn't actually sick or away to come over. And then get yourself down to that theatre and start to set up.'

'Right away, Signor.'

She put the receiver down, then dialled Sister Young's number. Surprisingly quickly, it was answered.

'Sister Young here.'

Sharon outlined what had happened and what Signor Vitale had said, heard Sister Young promise to take care of the staffing end of things, then replaced her receiver once again and flew down the corridor.

'Savelli!'

The little, dark girl came out of the male ward, mouth opening in surprise at the abrupt call and the rapid patter of the staff nurse's feet.

'Yes, Staff?'

'I've got to get theatre prepared for Dr Vitale to do an emergency op. It's Fortuna, the girl in the second turret room. I think her appendix has ruptured. Can you prep her for theatre?'

'Of course. Has she eaten? And what about injections? I cannot give . . .'

'Sorry, sorry, I was forgetting. Look, just get her into a theatre gown, shave her and ring down to the porter to stand by. Sister Young's coming with anyone she can find to help. She'll see to injections and so on. The stomach'll be empty since everything she ate she brought up. Can you manage?'

Nurse Savelli nodded and smiled, so Sharon felt she

was justified in pattering rapidly back along the corridor towards the stairs. But her troubles were not yet over. Mrs Taylor, fat, fifty, fair, came out of Ward 1, her little face one big question mark.

'Nurse, all this noise! I wonder if you'd mind . . .'

'Not now, Mrs Taylor.' Sharon resisted an urge to scream a rude word and push Mrs Taylor down the stairs. Instead, she took the patient by the shoulders and moved her bodily out of her way. 'Sorry, but we've an emergency on here, you'll have to manage for a while.'

'An emergency?' Mrs Taylor's eyes gleamed. 'Not that dear little girl in the turret room, I hope? I've often said she's given too much freedom, mind, with that cat running in and out all day and . . .'

'No, it's the new patient, I don't think you've met her.' Sharon was halfway down the stairs by the time Mrs Taylor had thought of another question, and entering the operating theatre before the woman could have started to speak. Fortunately, Dr Abele had chosen to use the smaller of the two theatres, so Dr Vitale would be able to spread himself a bit more. She crossed the room, having switched on the huge overhead lights, and went into the ante-room where the staff changed into operating gowns. She turned on the lights in there too, checked that the sterilizer was burbling away quietly to itself, and then walked over to the basins, intending to scrub up.

'Ah, you're here! Amaryllis is up on Wisteria, supervising the patient, and Sister Brett's on her way to assist here. Now, let's get organised.'

'Oh, Sister, I could weep with relief,' Sharon said frankly, turning back from the basin. 'It's been the devil of a night so far, and when I saw Fortuna and guessed that she'd ruptured I really felt like running away.'

'But you didn't.' Sister had changed and was moving round laying up a trolley with speed and efficiency. 'Hope Brett gets a move on, I've not helped out in theatre on a big op for a while.'

'You don't seem to have forgotten much,' Sharon said, tying her belt firmly round her small waist. 'And how did you get into working gear so quickly?'

'Practice. I was a theatre sister for years, until I began to feel that I didn't have enough to do with the patients. Only saw them when they were out cold. Ah, I hear an arrival.'

Vitale came in, pulling his shirt over his head as he did so. Sister jerked her head, and Sharon went over to him obediently. He scrubbed up, then turned to her.

'Gown, Nurse!'

She helped him into the green gown, trying not to notice how his broad, muscular chest gleamed beneath the brilliant theatre lights.

'Gloves!'

She had a bit of a struggle with the gloves, because she had glanced up at him and seen his dark eyes gleaming down at her over his mask. He looked as though he might be smiling at her, and that was confusing, particularly when she was so nervous.

'Is the patient ready? I called in at the big *spedale* and brought their anaesthetist with me, he's gone up to see the patient and he'll be here any moment. Then he'll put her under and we can start. I hope your diagnosis was correct, Staff.'

For a moment Sharon's blood ran cold. Suppose she had made a mistake, suppose Fortuna had simply got gastro-enteritis as most of the nurses had? It was she, Sharon, who had put the whole hospital on general alert, she who had caused people to be dragged out of bed, she who had got the theatre set up, would presently have Fortuna anaesthetised. Suppose she had done it just for a tummy bug?

But he had turned away and was talking to a figure, gowned and masked, which Sharon thought must be Sister Brett, the day shift theatre sister. She was a small, fierce little creature with no patience, so the other nurses said, and a reputation for scathing speech. Sharon quailed at the thought of what Sister Brett might say—or do—if she found she had been brought out on a fool's errand by a mere staff nurse!

'I'll do a laparotomy, of course,' Vitale was saying to the sister. He spoke quite naturally, and not as though he had the slightest doubt that an operation was necessary. 'You can't be too careful with a woman, though it bears all the classic signs of a rupture . . .'

Relief flooded through Sharon and beneath her mask an enormous smile spread across her face. He *had* checked! She must have been mad to think that he would go ahead on her say-so—a girl in her early twenties who had only been at this hospital a few weeks. When the theatre doors parted and the comatose figure of Fortuna was wheeled in, Sharon went across to help to transfer her onto the operating table with a positive spring in her step. It was just possible that she had done the right thing at last!

'Well, Staff?'

Worn out almost as much with vicarious excitement as with her own endeavours, Sharon had difficulty in bringing herself out of the world of the brightly lit theatre and into the reality of the changing room. It was full of people getting back into their ordinary things and now Vitale was facing her, in dark trousers once more and ordinary shoes, having just pulled his shirt down over his head, careless of the strain this must put on his buttons. She wondered whether to admonish him, and knew that she really was worn out. What a thing to think!

'Sorry, Signor, I'm still wondering what hit me. It *was* a ruptured appendix, wasn't it? And she's going to be all right?'

'That's what it was, and we caught it in time, thanks to you.' He flung back his head, gave a huge yawn, and then took her arm and led her out into the quiet, moonlit foyer, calling back goodnights to the staff who were still changing. 'You're a good girl. Now, when did you last eat?'

'I don't know, I had a sandwich at about seven, I think. Why? What's the time now?'

'Two o'clock, and you've missed that ghastly meal, the night-shift lunch. Look, run up to the ward and get your coat and I'll take you back to your flat and cook you an omelette. It's the least I can do.'

Sharon was about to answer him when she remembered that Nurse Savelli had been alone on Wisteria Ward for over two hours. She tried to pull away from his hand on her arm.

'Oh, I can't, Signor, I have to go back, it's me that's supposed to be getting the patient back to bed, fixing the drip, seeing that the obs are done when they should be!'

He retained his hold on her without any apparent effort. He also shook her a little.

'Sharon, no one's indispensible, and Sister Young found a replacement for you, she told me who, only I've forgotten. Just calm down and come and check that they can manage without you for the rest of the night.'

'Well, if you think it's fair to land someone else with my night duty, I suppose I could ask.'

He accompanied her up the stairs and into Sister's office where Amaryllis sat behind the desk, reading a paperback. She slapped it down quickly as they entered and stood up.

'All's quiet, Signor. Savelli's sitting with the patient, though she came round some while ago and has gone back to a natural sleep now. Do you want to take a look at her?'

'Yes, I'd better just stroll down there. But my main reason for coming back to the ward was to find out if you can manage without Nurse Craig. She hasn't eaten and the canteen's closed again.'

'Yes, easily. In fact, Sister Young told me to work through until eight and then to take the morning off.' She smiled at Sharon. 'If I'm not down with the bug by then, of course. Goodnight to you both—you don't need me to come down to the turret room, do you?'

'No, I think we can manage,' Vitale said gravely. 'Goodnight, Nurse.' Outside in the corridor he gave Sharon a quick, triumphant glance. 'There, what did I say? Come on, let's check up on our patient.'

Fortuna lay on her back with her head on one side. The saline/dextrose drip was adjusted properly and Vitale studied the chart and then scribbled on it.

'Fine. She's had diamorphine, she'll sleep now until morning.' He smoothed a wisp of pale hair away from Fortuna's eyes. 'Poor little cousin, and I was sure there was nothing the matter with her except a stomach upset!'

'I didn't know she was your cousin,' Sharon said as they walked out through the hospital once more. 'I thought she was just . . . just a friend.'

Vitale gave her an enigmatic glance, then steered her out through the front door and into his car.

'It isn't far, but when I leave you, I can drive straight home,' he remarked, climbing behind the wheel. 'Actually, she's more like a second cousin once removed, but there is a relationship. Let me see, my father and Fortuna's mother are first cousins. I think.'

She sat very upright in the car, aware suddenly how very tired she was and how easily, too, she could fall asleep, even on the short journey from the hospital to the flats. But when she got out of the car in the driveway, and began to climb the stairs, all her tiredness fell away and she realised that she was hungry for all her protestations.

'Here we are; got the key?' Vitale took it from her, unlocked her door, and ushered her inside. Standing in the small hallway, blinking in the light, he caught her shoulders and turned her to face him, smiling down at her.

'Look, little one, if you're really worn out go straight to bed, and I'll leave you to sleep. I can eat at home.'

'To tell you the truth, though I'm tired I'm not at all

sleepy,' Sharon admitted. 'And what's more, I'm famished! How about you?'

'I feel the same, it's the tension.' He preceded her into the tiny kitchen. 'Now I'll whip up an omelette because they're the things I cook best, and you can get us a nice big jug of coffee.'

After that, all her tiredness seemed to withdraw into the wings, so to speak, whilst the excitement of a midnight feast with Vitale took the stage. She fetched him eggs and cheese from the fridge and opened a tin of ham, and then she left him to his cooking whilst she made coffee and watched the eggs and milk being whipped, the cheese being grated, and the ham being sliced into thin curls.

'There's lovely new bread in the bin under the sink,' Sharon said. 'And butter. And a mango for afterwards, if you like them.'

'Love 'em. Heat the plates, there's a good girl, I can't abide being given hot food on cold plates.'

It was a good meal. The omelettes were excellent, the coffee just as she liked it, and by the time they had split the biggest of the mangoes between them and spooned out every last delicious, smooth mouthful, Sharon was replete. Her tiredness, however, had decided to make itself felt once more and when she stood up to clear the dishes she swayed and had to cling onto the table or she would have fallen. Immediately, Vitale was beside her.

'I've overstayed my welcome; you ought to be tucked up in bed. Leave those dishes until the morning, and I don't want to see your face on my ward until noon, Nurse. Is that clear?'

'I don't think I'll wake until noon, if I'm honest,' Sharon said ruefully, accompanying him to the door. 'Thank you, Signor, for making me that delicious omelette.'

They were in the hallway now, with the front door open. He took her hand.

'Thank *you*, Signorina, for my good supper! Sleep well, *cara mia*.'

'And you. And . . .' Sharon searched frantically through her mind for her small horde of Italian phrases. 'I know! *Grazie di tutta la sua gentillezza*.'

He raised a dark brow. Sharon could not help remembering the last time he had come to her flat and the passion his kiss had unleashed in her. He moved closer, lifting her hand as he did so.

'I should thank you for your kindness too—you did well tonight, my child, you have the makings of a first-rate nurse.' As he spoke he carried her hand to his lips, turned it over, and planted a kiss on the tender spot where wrist and palm join.

. Sharon gasped, she could not help it. Such a strange, old-fashioned gesture, and yet so sensuous!

It seemed, however, that he misinterpreted her gasp. He let her hand fall and smiled ruefully down at her.

'It's all right, I'm not going to grab you. Goodnight, Sharon. Sweet dreams.'

And Sharon, making her way to bed, thought that after such an encounter her dreams would be more than sweet, they would be downright wistful. But in fact she was so tired that she slept dreamlessly until morning.

The gastro-enteritis bug which had hit the hospital proved to be a nasty one. Nurse after nurse, doctor after doctor, and a good many of the patients, went down with it, though some, almost to their dismay, soldiered on, apparently immune—certainly untouched.

Julie and Sharon were fortunate, though, as Sharon remarked, there were occasions during the next fortnight when she almost wished that she could have been struck down just long enough to enjoy a day or two's recuperation afterwards.

'Day or night, you'll find me on Wisteria Ward,' she told Paolo, when he rang up hoping for a date. 'The trouble is, it isn't just a twenty-four-hour sickness.

People who get it can be really ill—some of them are off for ten days or more, and come back looking like death when they do return to work.'

'My poor Sharon,' Paolo said with real sympathy. 'Have you many patients?'

'Yes, we're nearly full. And what's worse, they aren't all nice, obliging people. One in particular is driving us all mad.'

The patient who drove Sharon maddest was Fortuna. Once she was off the drip and beginning to take solid food again, she began a positive campaign against everyone who annoyed her, starting at the top with Susan and Snowflake, who were only just ahead of Sharon herself.

'That cat is unhealthy, it should not be in a hospital, it should go,' she said twenty times a day to whoever would listen to her. 'And that child is spoilt and should be in the big *ospedale* in Sorrento with other brats, not here with sick adults.'

'*She* is the one who should not be here,' Carmella grumbled to Sharon after one particularly trying session with Fortuna. 'She makes more work than all the others put together.'

'What makes you say that now? Did she ring again?' Sharon and Carmella were laying up the drugs trolley, one checking off the drugs book and the other fetching the various medicaments. Normally, this would have been done by Sister, but there was no Sister available. Sharon was acting Sister until a more senior member of staff was able to take over.

'Yes, she rang again. Because she dropped her knitting needle, if you please, and cannot reach it from the bed.'

Sharon, counting tablets, stopped short to stare.

'From *bed*? But it's eleven o'clock, what on earth is she doing in bed still?'

'She won't get up. She lies there and rings for one of us to change the channel on her television set, or to pick up her knitting needle, or to tell Susan to be quiet, or . . . well, anything she can think of.'

'Yes, I know she did hate getting up, but yesterday she was out in her chair for a couple of hours . . .'

'A couple of minutes, I believe,' Carmella said crossly. 'We're all too busy to keep arguing with her, and she simply won't get out of bed! Didn't you wonder why she kept ringing all the time?'

'No, I didn't, and I should have,' Sharon said grimly. 'Signor Vitale would probably blame me if he knew! On the other hand, he could use his influence to see that she behaves herself, she won't get well if she lies in bed all day. And now she's eating normally and sleeping well and the wound's healing, there's no reason why she shouldn't go home. She'll be well looked after, I'm sure, once her parents get back, which will be very soon, I believe.'

She did not voice another thought—that once Fortuna went, Vitale would discontinue his frequent visits to the ward. For ever since his young relative had been in the second turret room, he had been in and out of Wisteria Ward on every possible excuse. Oh, he had been friendly and pleasant with Sharon, going out of his way to see how she was managing, but it had been Fortuna's presence which had made him such a constant visitor, there could be no doubt of that. Yet even though it was Fortuna he came to see, Sharon enjoyed knowing that he was often around, positively basked in the warmth of his mere presence. It might be silly—*was* silly—but she could not help it. It'll wear off, this stupid glow whenever he's near, she told herself constantly.

'How do you know he doesn't come to see you?' Julie asked her once, as they snatched a quick lasagne at the Caffé Rosso. 'I don't see how you can be so sure.'

'You would, if you were on the ward,' Sharon told her. 'The difference in his behaviour is so marked. He's businesslike and impersonal, even when he needn't be, when he's in Sister's office, checking admissions or records with me. Not a bit like he was in Herculaneum, or how he was when he made me the omelette. And not a bit like he is with Fortuna, either,' she added crossly. 'Laughing, teasing her, talking about mutual friends, and then rushing off without another word to me.'

'He's a conscientious man,' Julie reminded her. 'He's working all the hours God sends at the moment, just like we are, because of so much illness amongst the staff.'

It would have been nice to have believed this, but Sharon was a realist. If he had wanted to take her out, he had only to ask!

'Sharon . . .'

Carmella's voice shattered Sharon's gloomy thoughts. She blinked, then took one end of the drugs trolley.

'Right, we'll get this lot delivered and then I'll go and tackle Fortuna.'

As soon as all the patients had been dealt with, she hurried along to the second turret room. Fortuna was sitting up in bed staring sulkily at the television set and eating languidly, her hand going constantly into a huge box of chocolates.

'Morning, Signorina; why aren't you out of bed?' Sharon removed the box of chocolates to the windowsill, ignoring Fortuna's sharp protest. 'And if you carry on eating chocolates and not moving, you'll get horribly fat!'

'I shall never be fat!' It must have been a sore point, for Fortuna's cheeks mottled unbecomingly as she said the words. 'Bring those chocolates back at once, please, Nurse!'

'Sorry, I'm afraid I can't. You are supposed to be down in the day room, you know, or at least sitting out of bed in your chair. If you do that, you'll be able to fetch the chocolates for yourself. And anything else you require, of course, such as knitting needles or writing paper.' She whipped the covers off her reluctant patient, revealing the fact that Fortuna had seen fit to paint her toenails with gold lacquer. 'Gracious, how . . . how unusual!'

'That, Nurse, is none of your business,' Fortuna said waspishly. 'I'm not getting out of bed until after lunch, and then only if I feel like it. I know very well why you want me to, of course, but I'm not here just to make the nurses' lives easier.'

'That's the gospel truth at any rate.' Sharon caught Fortuna's legs and swung them round onto the floor, then sat her patient up with a swift and practised jerk. 'Come along, you must have sat up to lacquer your toenails, so you can sit up to oblige me, and don't tell me you don't want to oblige me, because you've made that painfully obvious!'

'I am *not* going to sit in that hard leather chair,' Fortuna said breathlessly. 'If you try to make me, I'll tell Vitale that you've got a personal spite against me.'

'He wouldn't believe you, because he is the person who insists that all his patients learn to become mobile speedily,' Sharon assured her, lugging her to her feet and guiding her over to the chair. She sat her down heavily, for Fortuna was a well-built young woman and had not helped in the least. 'There! Now, if you need to change channels you'll just have to get up and move about two steps and you can do it for yourself!'

'Give me my chocolates, then,' Fortuna said sulkily. 'And I shall not move from this chair!'

'No, leave the chocolates for a bit, you've eaten far too many already,' Sharon said. 'And if you don't move then you won't get much, because I'm going to put a notice over your bell saying that it is not to be answered except by the acting Sister—that's me—and I shan't answer it unless I think you really need something.'

Fortuna's face reddened still further and her eyes narrowed.

'I tell you to give me those chocolates. Vitale brought them for me last night, he cannot disapprove!'

Sharon's eyes went to the huge bouquet of hothouse flowers on the windowsill.

'That's right, the flowers too. *Now* will you pass me those chocolates?'

'No. If you want them, get up and fetch them.'

Sharon went out of the room, closing the door sharply behind her, and then leaned against the corridor wall to allow herself time to recover before seeing anyone else. So it was expensive presents now, was it? How could he be such a fool, unless it was true that he just wanted Fortuna for her expectations. Although . . .

Abruptly, the door of the first turret room opened and Ian Ridgeway appeared. He grinned at her.

'Hi, there, Sharon! I know you're desperately busy, leaning against that wall, but it is well after eleven and poor Sue is desperate for a glass of fresh lemon. Any chance?'

'I'm awfully sorry, Ian,' Sharon said, conscience-stricken. 'We are rushed, and Carmella knew I was seeing Fortuna so she probably thought I'd cope with their mid-morning drinks, especially since they're the only patients who don't go up to the day-room and help themselves off the trolley. Tell her to wait two minutes and she'll get her lemon. And some biscuits, the nicest I can find.'

'Great. By the time you bring them, I'll be gone, so thanks anyway. And how's my best girl this morning?'

He and Sharon had progressed to first-name terms ever since he had taken her and Julie out to dinner one night, as a thank-you for their care of his daughter. And it was very obvious that he was fond of Julie, though precisely what form this fondness would take was not yet clear.

'She's fine, thanks, though desperately busy.' Sharon turned away, to find herself confronting Vitale, who was standing in the middle of the corridor, staring from her to Ian. She smiled at him. 'I'm sorry, Signor, I didn't see you there. I'm just going to fetch Signorina Russano a

cup of coffee and Susan some fresh lemon, and then I'll
be with you.'

'Very well, I'll wait for you in Fortuna's room.'

Hurrying off down towards the day-room, it occurred
to Sharon that Vitale's voice had been cold, his eyes
somehow condemnatory. She sighed. Imagination, that
was what it was, he could not possibly be annoyed with
her so early in the morning, before he had even seen
Fortuna!

She hurried with the coffee, however, dumping
Susan's lemon unceremoniously on her tray and promising to come back as soon as she had dealt with whatever
awaited her in the second turret room.

'She's in a temper, and I got the impression that he
wasn't feeling too sunny, either,' she hissed at her young
patient. 'Cross your fingers for me.'

'I will, 'cos she's been telling him things about you, I
can hear through the wall,' Susan confided. 'Hurry back,
Craigie, and I'll reveal all, as they say in spy stories.'

So it was with some trepidation that Sharon entered
Fortuna's room, to find her patient looking so bright-
eyed and triumphant that her heart sank. Vitale started
quite mildly, however.

'Nurse Craig, Fortuna's been complaining about the
tardiness of the nursing this morning. Can you explain?'

As he spoke, he laid a light hand on Fortuna's
shoulder. A proprietorial hand. Sharon bristled. So she
was his cousin, was she, and possibly his mistress, who
might one day become his wife. But that gave her no
right to complain about the nursing on the ward, nor him
the right to take a well-known complainer seriously!

'We're short-handed, Signor, and what is more to the
point, Signorina Russano is supposed to be mobile, she
is not supposed to lie in bed and ring for the staff
whenever she wants the programme on her television set
changed.'

Vitale, she saw with satisfaction, looked a trifle taken
aback. No doubt Fortuna had not been quite so explicit!

'Well, it's true that I encourage my patients to get out of bed as soon as the operation is behind them, but I think the Signorina was complaining more because there never seems to be any lack of staff to attend to Susan, nor any attempt to prevent the child from keeping everyone wakeful with her video games.'

The video games had been brought in by Ian when it became clear that with the gastro-enteritis bug affecting more and more of the staff, Susan would necessarily have to amuse herself. They did make a noise, of course, playing a repetitive little tune interspersed with buzzings and the odd squeal as a character 'died', but Susan rarely played them after seven o'clock at night, though she did start, sometimes, rather early in the morning.

'We do our best to keep Susan amused, since she is literally unable to leave the room. If Signorina Russano was in a similar position she, too, would receive special treatment. Are you saying that you think the Signorina merits special treatment, Signor?'

There was a pregnant pause, then Fortuna spoke, her voice sharp with spite.

'I don't want special treatment, Nurse, but I do think it unfair that you have no time for me yet can spend time in Susan's room when her father's there, making light conversation, amusing him and being amused. Of course, I realise that he's a film producer and probably irresistible to a girl of your . . . type, but that you can pretend such behaviour is nursing seems not only unfair to your other patients, but unfair to your staff as well.'

'I'm very rarely in the room with Susan when she has any visitors,' Sharon said, but she felt her face warm as tell-tale blood rushed to her cheeks. She did exchange the odd, bantering remark with Ian, of course she did, because he was her flatmate's friend, but as for getting up a flirtation with him, nothing was further from her thoughts!

'Well, we'll leave it for now, Nurse,' Vitale said. 'But do try, in future, to remember that whilst your social life is your own, when you are nursing on my ward, I expect your patients to come first.'

Sharon turned and left the room. It was plainly useless to explain that Fortuna was simply telling lies in order to keep Vitale's sympathy. Vitale knew her, had worked with her for years. He wanted to believe ill of Sharon, that must be the answer. It hurt to tell herself this, but what else was she to think?

'Nurse!'

She turned, reluctantly. He had emerged from Fortuna's room and was closing the door behind him.

'Yes, Signor?'

'Come here a moment, I can't call up the corridor!'

She went towards him, stiff-backed, stiff-faced, wanting to say a thousand things and knowing that she could not say one of them.

'Yes, Signor? What did you want?'

'I know you dislike Fortuna, Nurse, and I know that she dislikes you, so I daresay there was a good deal of personal feeling in some of the things she said. I also heard you talking to Mr Ridgeway just now, however, so I know there was some truth in her remarks.' He hesitated, looking down at her as though no longer absolutely sure of himself. 'Any friendship between you and he should be kept in a low key during working hours. Or is this friendship, too, just the result of Fortuna's wishful thinking?'

Sharon stared at him. What on earth was he getting at now? Why should she pretend that there was no friendship between herself and Ian, for goodness' sake? Or did he mean something warmer than friendship? But he could not be so misguided as to believe she would flirt with her friend's man! If he did think it, then he must believe her to be a pretty despicable person anyway, so little harm could come of whatever she might say or do!

'I'm Ian's friend, and Susan's too for that matter,' she said crisply. 'However, I resent the implication that I am anything more, particularly in working hours.' She meant to go on, to explain that Julie would scarcely thank her for spreading such a rumour, but Vitale turned on his heel.

'I see. That's all, Nurse.'

Sharon stood still for a moment as he disappeared into Fortuna's room, half believing that he would emerge again and apologise for his curtness, but nothing of the sort happened. The door remained firmly closed and presently, from behind it, she heard a burst of laughter. Feminine and masculine laughter.

Sharon turned and made for Sister's office as fast as she could. Let them laugh, the two of them! They could do whatever they pleased, so long as they left her alone!

CHAPTER EIGHT

'Do you realise, Sister, that it won't be all that long before Susan leaves us? Which means that I've been here nearly three months? Time's flown.'

Sharon and Sister Young were in the second turret room, waiting for its new occupant to come up from theatre. It was another holidaymaker who had ignored stomach cramps and come on his holiday, only to find himself on the operating table having his gallstones removed instead of sunning himself on a beach.

'The summer always goes quickly, because if you're not on home leave you're slaving day and night,' Sister Young said, going over to the window. 'Look at that sea! It never fails to thrill me, the colour of it, not after all these years. We'll miss Susan though, won't we!'

'Yes, very much. And Ian, too. He's a nice chap, isn't he, Sister?'

'Charming.' Sister turned and fixed Sharon with an inquisitive eye. 'Rumour has it that he's in hot pursuit of one of my nurses.'

Sharon laughed. 'Well, rumour's got it a bit wrong. He's in hot pursuit of a nurse all right, but it isn't me, nor Carmella, nor any of the others on Wisteria. It's Julie Drummond, my flat-mate.'

Sister Young nodded in a satisfied manner.

'That was just what I thought. Some people are such fools!'

'Who, Ian or Julie?' Sharon shook her head. 'No, you couldn't mean that, because those two are made for each other, though perhaps they don't fully realise it yet. I'm hoping that when Susan goes and Ian can't visit here three or four times a day, he'll realise who he misses most.'

'He probably will. What's going to happen to Snowflake, though? And to Susan, for that matter?'

'Well, Ian says he's keeping Susan with him for a bit so that she gets some sun and sea and perhaps even a bit of that horseriding she's been on about. But later, where she lives, or rather with whom, has got to be faced. She really doesn't want to go back to Morena, you know—the woman's scarcely been here above four or five times since Ian started regular visits.'

'I've noticed. I've wondered whether it might be possible . . .'

But at this point the door swung open and two porters appeared, with the recumbent figure of Mr Harold Spigget on a trolley between them, and Sharon and Sister Young became too busy for idle chat.

In fact, it was not until tea-time, when Sharon took Susan a glass of milk and a piece of fruit-cake, that the vexed question of Susan's future came to her mind again, and that was because, when she walked through the doorway, she saw at once that Susan had been crying.

'Susan!' Sharon put the milk and cake down on Susan's bedside table and threw her arms around her patient. 'What on earth's the matter?'

'I-i-it's *her*,' Susan muttered, between gasps. 'Mummy came this afternoon, Craigie, the f-first time for ages. And she s-says I've got to go back to England with her. In t-two weeks, Craigie! And she w-won't hear of me taking Snowflake, she d-doesn't believe in quarantine, she says she'll think about buying me another k-kitten. Another one! As if any other kitten could be as dear to me as Snowflake!' She buried her head in Sharon's shoulder and wailed again, loudly. 'Oh, Craigie, I don't want to live!'

'Now come on, love,' Sharon said gently, cradling Susan lovingly and stroking her shaking shoulders. 'You don't mean that! And anyway, I don't believe your mother can whisk you off to England in a fortnight, the film won't have finished. Your father said . . .'

'The film's finishing for *her*,' Susan said, sniffing. 'She's been offered a plum part—that's what she said—in a film located in London, and so Daddy's putting all her remaining scenes into the next few days so that she'll be free to go whilst the rest of them finish off the work in the rest of the time. They often do films like that. And then . . . then . . .'

A fat tear slid down one thin cheek.

'Look, Daddy won't hear of it,' Sharon said firmly. 'He is allowed to have you to stay with him for weeks at a time, I know it, and he hasn't had you at all so far this year. I'm sure, when he hears, he'll just tell Mummy that she'll have to wait for you.'

'She always gets her own way,' Susan said bitterly. 'Daddy won't have a leg to stand on, he never does—he never even tried to get custody when they divorced, you see, because I was only a tiny baby and he thought my place was with my mother. And when it comes down to it, I expect he'll be happier without having me round his neck—that's what *she* said—and so he'll give in, like he always does, and promise to have me to stay when he can spare the time. And I'll just be a parcel at the left-luggage place again, pushed around and sent away to school and left.'

At this point her tears began again in earnest and Sharon kissed her, hugged her, and then jumped to her feet.

'You're my patient and I won't have you upset like this,' she declared. 'I'll speak to your Daddy and . . .' at this point the door opened and Vitale strode in. Their relationship of late had been both cool and distant but Sharon had never doubted his fondness for Susan nor his ability to use his influence for her good if he so wished. So she turned to him gladly. 'Ah, here's Dr Vitale, Susan, he'll tell you it's all nonsense.'

Vitale sat down on the bed and pulled Susan's hands down from her tear-wet face.

'What's all this? Who's been upsetting my favourite girl?'

'Oh, Signor!'

Susan flung her arms round him and proceeded to pour out her tale of woe. Sharon, standing by the bed, waited for the surgeon to reassure the child but instead he looked up at her.

'And you've said nothing, Nurse? Surely, in your privileged position as a—a family friend, you could tell her that her fears are groundless?'

There was a nasty gleam in his eye, though why, Sharon could not imagine. Presumably he had heard the rumours of an affair between Julie and Ian, but he could not think that she would try to placate real fears with rumours?

'I've told her she's got nothing to worry about, and that her father will see she stays here, for a while at least, but she seems to think her mother will treat her father's wishes as of little account.'

'And even if Daddy does insist that I stay here for another week or two, I'll have to go back then, and without Snowflake,' Susan pointed out. 'You don't know what it's like, Craigie—no one does. Boarding school's probably fun, if you can stay at the same one for a bit, but I get changed over two or three times a *year*! There's no point in trying to make friends when it's just for a little while, and Daddy doesn't come to see me at school because he's often not in the country and he never knows which school I'm at, half the time, until it's too late. And s-s-speech days and o-open days are *awful*, when you've no one of your own there at all, so you hide away and the other girls say you're a snob and the teachers say you're difficult, and . . .'

The two adults had been staring at each other with increasing horror, but now Vitale touched the child's shoulder, putting a stop to her stumbling recital.

'I see. I had no idea it was as bad as that, my child, but

rest assured, Nurse Craig and I will see that this comes to a stop. I'll speak to your mother myself—and your father too, if necessary. Tell me, where do you go during holidaytimes? Is there no kindly aunt, or perhaps a grandmother, who could take you in?'

Susan shook her head.

'No. There are the au pair girls, you know, Signor, foreign girls. Some of them are nice and some of them aren't, but they're never the *same*!' Susan rubbed her eyes. 'The nicest thing about being in hospital has been the *sameness*—the nurses don't suddenly go away, nor do you, Signor, and Daddy's been here almost all the time!'

Tears were obviously in the offing again. Vitale stood up and took Sharon's wrist in a grip of steel. He turned her to face the bed.

'I believe that Nurse Craig will confirm that there are plans afoot which will change things for the better, Susan! Nurse?'

He was looking at Sharon very nastily and she could only stare back, a suspicion slowly crystallising in her mind. Ian must have spoken to Vitale, told him of his intention to ask Julie to marry him, and the surgeon assumed that, since she was Julie's flat-mate, she was also in on the secret. Except, of course, that whatever Ian might mean to do, she was very sure that he had not yet said a word to Julie!

'I know that Mr Ridgeway is hoping to make changes,' Sharon said, her voice carefully vague. 'But that's all I do know.' She turned to Susan. 'Play with Snowflake for a bit, darling, whilst I phone Daddy. Then I'll either come back with a message from him, or I'll get him to come up himself. All right?'

Susan, no fool, was looking from one to the other of them, her eyes bright, her whole face beginning to look more cheerful.

'Changes? Oh, Craigie, if they're the sort of changes I've wondered about, wouldn't it be the most wonderful thing in the world? Oh, Craigie, go and ring him at once!'

Sharon hurried out, but before she had gone more than a few feet from the door, Vitale was beside her, catching her arm.

'Sharon, I must speak to you! I shouldn't have tried to force your hand in there, but the child was so forlorn— and what a fate, to have Morena treating you like an unwanted burden! Look, I take it from what you said that things aren't by any means as finalised as I was led to believe?'

'No, they aren't,' Sharon said stiffly. 'Please let me go, I want to telephone.'

'You won't do anything—anything drastic, just for the child's sake? It could hurt her more, in the end.'

'All I'm going to do, Signor, is to ring Ian and find out just what he's considering for Susan,' Sharon said with asperity. 'You can scarcely find fault with that!'

She wrenched herself free and began to jog-trot down the corridor, but he kept pace easily beside her.

'No. But just remember that Ridgeway's an experienced man of the world, and if he really wants his little girl to live with him then he can well afford a full-time housekeeper! No one has to sacrifice themselves for Susan's sake; I hope you realise that?'

'Sacrifice themselves?' Sharon's patience snapped. Why did everyone assume that Julie, if she did marry Ian, would do so for all the wrong reasons? Either because he was rich and glamorous, or because she was sorry for his daughter? Ridiculous, when one glance at Julie's face could tell you that the girl was head over heels in love with Ian! 'That's absurd, Signor!'

'Yes, it is absurd.' She glanced at him as they reached the head of the stairs and he was looking disproportionately relieved. 'Remember it, Nurse.'

'I will. She hesitated, three stairs down, then turned back. 'I hate to sound corny, Signor, but . . . well, there *is* a thing called love, you know!'

He was still staring after her when she reached the foyer, but even as she looked back, he swung on his heel and disappeared into the ward.

'Well, Julie, I rang your Ian and he was at the hospital in ten minutes, promising the kid the moon by the look on her face.'

It was lunchtime and Sharon and Julie were sitting on the terrace of the Caffé Rosso, with the breeze just cooling them enough to make the heat out there bearable and the wide green awning keeping them in the shade.

'I'd love to know what he said,' Julie remarked, taking a mouthful of spaghetti. 'He's sort of hinted sometimes that he might think of asking someone to come and nurse Susan privately for a bit . . . I wonder if he'd ask me?'

'What would you do if he did? Leave us all without a backward glance, I suppose.'

'We-ell, I'd be terribly tempted. I love Susan and I get on awfully well with Ian.'

'Julie, you once accused me of being in love with Vitale, and though I protested, I did accept that there was some truth in what you said, even though, as it turned out, it was only sort of calf-love,' Sharon reminded her. 'You don't just get on well with Ian, you're in love with him. And if that's so, do you think it would be wise to work for him?'

'No, it wouldn't be wise, but it would be great fun,' Julie said. 'I'm sick of being cautious and doing as I should. If he asks me, I'll go, though I may dither a bit at first.'

'Suppose he asks you . . .' began Sharon, but was abruptly cut short. Julie leaned across the table and put a firm hand over her mouth.

'No! Don't you dare even breathe it, Sharon Craig, or I'll duff you up! If there's one way to ensure that something marvellous doesn't happen, it's to talk about it. Now shut up and eat your nice dinner!'

'Lunch,' corrected Sharon. 'Can you catch Poppa's eye? If so, we'll order coffee and ices now, and then perhaps they'll be here by the time we finish our spaghetti, or we'll be late back and I've had one encounter with Vitale today, I don't fancy another.'

'Right.' Julie did as she was bidden and then sank back in her chair. 'Are you looking forward to tonight?'

That evening, they were going out in a foursome to the tiny village of Ravello, high in the mountains. Ian and Paolo were to be their escorts, and Ian was taking them all in his hired car. The plan was that they would go to see the opera which was playing that night in the grounds of the Palazzo Rufolo and then dine at a nearby trattoria in the village.

'Looking forward to it?' Sharon considered, her head on one side. 'Yes, I am,' she decided. 'Though as a rule I prefer pop to opera. But I love dressing up, eating good food, and putting on the style once in a while, and I gather we'll be doing all three tonight.'

'That's it. Anyway, it isn't a terribly highbrow opera, it's *Cavalleria Rusticana*, and there's some lovely singing in it.'

'Good. Did Ian scream and moan when you told him that I wanted to travel up there in his car?'

Julie sniggered. Sharon's steadily mounting conviction that Paolo was going to pounce again shortly never failed to amuse her.

'He was the perfect gentleman, once I'd told him why you wanted our company throughout the evening. He rather likes Paolo, and thinks he'd make you a good husband. Not that he's proposed yet—or has he?'

'Not marriage.' Sharon smiled at Julie's open-mouthed astonishment. 'No, I'm only kidding, Paolo is being the soul of discretion and the ideal escort, it's just that sometimes I catch him looking at me as if I were a cream cake, and I get a bit worried.'

'Why on earth? I thought you had an understanding.'

'Mm hmm, so we have. But whenever he's with me for

a whole evening I can sort of sense a mounting pressure. One day it's going to get too much for him and he'll blow off steam—or try to. Which is why I like foursomes just at present.'

'You make him sound just like a pressure cooker! Come on, drink up, and then we'll get back.'

It was a brilliant evening, with a sunset flaming across the western sky and outlining the savage shapes of the great mountains. The road led upwards through orange and lemon groves, past palm trees and cataracts, tiny streams and echoing gorges. Sharon leaned forward in her seat and drank it all in, conscious of a little ache that she was not seeing such beauty in the company of someone she cared about deeply, someone with whom she could share her feelings of awe, as she had once shared her feelings over the ancient city of Herculaneum. But it was no use wishing, and presently they reached Ravello, a tiny, picturesque village surrounded by trees and surrounding, in its turn, an open square from which tall gateposts and a crowd of elegantly dressed people announced the Palazzo Gardens.

Sharon and Julie got out of the car and made their way, beside their escorts, towards the crowd. Both girls, having been warned in advance, wore full-length evening gowns, Julie's was dark green with a slinky skirt and Sharon's was pale candy-pink. Neither girl owned a long dress so both were borrowed, which did not detract from the pleasure of preening themselves in such elegance, however.

'We'll be well-advised to go straight to our seats,' Paolo said as they displayed their tickets and walked along winding paths between lovely flower displays. 'The orchestra always starts promptly, and those who are late are unpopular both with the artistes and with the audience.'

They sat down, therefore, and the two girls were glancing round and admiring some of the really beautiful and obviously expensive dresses, when Ian leaned over and nudged Sharon.

'Look, my dear—your friends and mine!'

Sharon followed the direction of his eyes and there was Vitale, looking incredibly handsome and aristocratic in a dinner jacket, with Fortuna in a black sheath evening dress, smiling up at him.

'Wouldn't you just know it, when I was looking forward to an evening of relaxation and enjoyment? Never mind, perhaps they won't see us.'

'No reason why they should,' Ian pointed out. 'They're in front of us and if we move fairly quickly we can reach the bar and get our drinks in the interval before they've even got out of their seats.'

After that, the conversation became general, but Sharon found it almost impossible to concentrate on what the others were saying since her own thoughts were so chaotic. If there was one thing needed to convince her that Vitale was serious over Fortuna, this was it! Fortuna was at home now, with her parents, she had not yet started work at the Villa L'Arancia again, so Vitale must have made a point of booking seats and asking her to accompany him. Stupid fellow, Sharon thought savagely, when Fortuna would make anyone a perfectly awful wife!

During the interval, an annoying thing happened. Sharon had been determined to engineer an opportunity for Julie and Ian to wander off into the darkness of the garden where, beneath the palms and in the romantic moonlight, with the soft sounds of the orchestra tuning up in the background, Ian might propose to her friend. What he might propose she had no idea, she just hoped for the best.

But the best-laid plans frequently come to nought for the least suspected reasons, and this was one of them. Julie suddenly gave a squeak of 'Angela!' almost at the same moment as Paolo declared, 'Can it be . . . ?' in a deep, operatic voice. And the two of them rushed across the terrace to fall, with exclamations, upon a young woman in her mid-twenties with brassy blonde hair, a protuberant bosom, and a middle-aged man tucked, casually almost, in the shelter of her arm.

'By all that's wonderful,' Sharon said to Ian, who looked every bit as surprised as she felt. 'We've been stood up, Ian, in favour of that odd-looking woman who, I suspect, used to nurse at the Villa L'Arancia, only it was before my time.'

'Really? She certainly seems an old friend.' Ian's voice was a trifle sarcastic for Paolo was making a meal of Angela's hand whilst clutching enthusiastically at any other part of her which came within reach.

'Oh, she *is*! She's the reason why Paolo considered all English nurses, particularly blonde ones, fair game.' Sharon subjected her rival to a long scrutiny. She was wearing a cream silk dress which clung like a second skin and left almost nothing to the imagination, and it had a slit skirt which revealed that Angela was wearing black fishnet tights with a red garter, presumably for looks and not support.

Ian, too, was staring.

'Do you mean Paolo compared you to—to *that*? My dear child, if you're mortally insulted I'm not surprised. And who's that dreadful little man she's got in a stranglehold?'

Sharon shrugged. They were standing in a corner of the shrubbery which had been converted into a bar, sipping their drinks, and she saw, out of the corner of her eye, Vitale stroll past and saw, too, that he was looking at Paolo and Angela. Damn him! Now he would think she could not even hold the affection of a little pipsqueak like Paolo! To Ian's surprise, no doubt, she proceeded to talk to him with great animation, laughing frequently and generally behaving like someone having a good time.

'If you wonder why I'm acting like this,' she hissed, between taking a sip at her drink and looking archly up at him over the rim of her glass, 'that cow Fortuna is watching us, and I want her to think I'm quite happy to have Paolo drooling over Angela, because I've found something better to do. See?'

'More or less,' Ian said, looking happier. 'In fact, Sharon, I've been hoping to get a word alone with you. I want your advice.'

'If it's about . . .' Sharon hesitated. 'What is it about, Ian?'

'My future. And Susan's. And . . . look, when can we meet? Are you free tomorrow evening?'

'Well, I am. Look, Ian, rumour has it that you may be thinking of remarrying. Has it anything to do with that?'

'Yes, in a way. But I don't think that's quite what the rumours are about—it's Morena who's remarrying. Look, we can't talk here, it's too confidential. I'll pick you up tomorrow, at about eight-thirty, and we'll dine together and talk it over. Is that all right?'

'Fine. But . . . well, I don't want Julie getting hold of the wrong end of the stick and thinking I'm muscling in on her—her friendship with you.'

'It's all right, she's working nights tomorrow, that's why I suggested it. And anyway, I'm not too sure that she'd care what you muscled in on. That, dear Sharon, is the rub!' He took her empty glass. 'Careful, Paolo and Julie are coming back—until tomorrow, then!'

The following evening, promptly at eight-thirty as arranged, Sharon and Ian set off for a quiet restaurant he knew of where the food was good and the view breathtaking.

'But the prices are also breathtaking, so I don't expect we'll meet anyone we know,' he told her with a grin as his big car swooped up the mountain road. 'I've been going mad, you know, with so much on my mind and Morena at me every hour of the day to get Susan out of hospital in time to fly home with her when she goes.'

'If she doesn't care much for Susan, why this obsession

over having the kid with her?' Sharon asked curiously. 'And don't try to convince me she really loves her daughter, because it's as plain as the nose on your face that the only person Morena loves is Morena!'

'That, my love, is putting it in a nutshell,' Ian said. He swung the car into a broad driveway and drew up before a fairytale castle, moat, turrets and all. 'Well, here we are, we'll continue this fascinating discussion over dinner.'

'Well, fire ahead then,' Sharon said half an hour later, when they were settled cosily in an alcove with a tiny table between them, and their starters in two silver dishes before them. 'I've been longing for someone to ask my advice for years!'

'Right. Well, it's common knowledge that I would like Susan to live with me instead of with my ex-wife, right?'

'Yes, I know that. Oh, by the way, you still haven't explained why Morena pretends to want Susan when she doesn't have time for her.'

'Oh, that—it's obvious, really. It's too much like losing face. At first, you see, she did the little-woman-coping-with-child-alone act, and that was fine, and she probably meant it, too, when Susan was small and a bit like that white poodle she trailed round with her at one time; it focussed attention on her, not on itself. A small child did that too, people said how sweet Morena and her baby looked together, but now Susan's a person and it's all different. Now, if she let Susan come to me, people would say that it was laziness, indifference, all those things, because it isn't as if I've got a wife who can look after the child, there's just me.'

'I see. Then you don't think Morena will ever give her up?'

'Oh yes, if she can do so without losing face. And if I were married, or had some sort of resident housekeeper who could take care of Susan all the time and stop this dreadful business of changing schools and changing au pairs, that would suit Morena just fine. She could explain to all her friends that she was doing it for the child's sake though her heart was breaking, and it would do her credit. See?'

'I think so. Only . . . what do you want my advice on?' She hesitated, then spoke out. 'Look, you're fond of Julie, aren't you?'

'Fond? Well, I'm fonder of her than I ever thought I'd be of anyone again. Only, you see, I made such a hash of marriage with Morena—she told me I was the most difficult man to live with and I'm sure she was right. I wondered if Julie would come back to England with Susan and me and move in to the farmhouse I've bought as a sort of companion-housekeeper. I'd pay her a good salary of course . . . does it sound terribly cold-blooded?'

'No, not really. Let's be frank, Ian, you're paying her a good salary for what some fellows would expect her to do just for the sake of their charms. Unless, of course, a companion-housekeeper is just a euphemism for your mistress?'

'No, it isn't,' Ian said emphatically, though faint colour rose in his cheeks. 'Mind you, if we found it was working well and we wanted to change the arrangements . . . God, it sounds shabby put like that!'

'It does, a bit. But you wouldn't put it like that to Julie, would you?'

'No, of course not. What do you think she'd say? Would she turn me down flat?'

'No, I think for Susan's sake and because she likes you she'd agree to it,' Sharon said honestly. 'But I'm not sure that she'd be right to do it, even so. You see, Ian, suppose it didn't work out? Suppose you found you could manage rather well and didn't really need a— a housekeeper? What would happen to poor Julie then?'

'Well, it should be possible for her to go back to nursing.'

'That's true. But Julie's a gentle, loving girl, easily

hurt. She's very fond of Susan and she would be losing everything at one blow. Her new home, Susan, her job, and you. Even her reputation, Ian, because there aren't many people who would believe the pair of you had shared a house and not a bed.'

'Oh, that! But these days people live together without getting married all the time!'

'Sure they do, some people. People who can't take commitment, or who aren't either of them sure that they're doing the right thing. People who want an easy out. Personally, I've always thought that men who suggest living together are being cowardly and selfish. Cowardly because they're afraid of having to commit themselves to someone, though they're fond enough of that someone to want the good things of marriage, and selfish because men don't lose out as much as women when a relationship breaks up. They move on to the next thing in their lives—a woman has to rebuild from scratch. And in your case, Ian, it's worse, because of Susan. Julie will take the plunge almost as much for Susan's sake as anything.'

'I see.' Ian's face was very red but his eyes met Sharon's unflinchingly. 'You think I'm a swine to suggest it and you think she'll only accept because she's fond of Susan.'

'Look, are you in love with Julie, or just fond of her?'

'I'm not absolutely sure, that's the rub. I'm beginning to think life without Julie will be pretty dull and second-rate, but when I first fell for Morena that wasn't how I felt a bit, I can tell you that!'

'You probably felt lust and infatuation in equal proportions for Morena,' Sharon said placidly. 'You were a lot younger, remember.' She leaned across the table and patted his hand. 'Don't look so down, I think you're in love with Julie but haven't fully realised it yet. And if you are in love, then you should take the big, blind step out into the abyss. Damn it, Ian, you did it once for Morena, isn't what you feel for Julie every bit as important as what you felt for Morena all those years ago?'

Ian stared at her, his whole expression changing until a huge beam had spread across his face.

'Damn it, girl, why didn't you say that right at the start? Of course you're right, *that's* the secret! I thought I could fight dragons for Morena, but for Julie I'd step right out into space! I'll ask her tomorrow!'

'Ask her what?' Sharon said suspiciously. 'To be your housekeeper?'

'Of course not, it would be an insult! To marry me, of course!'

Next day, a telephone call during her coffee break confirmed that Ian had been as good as his word. Julie, wildly excited, would not say much, but asked Sharon to change her lunch-hour so that they could go to the Caffé Rosso together.

'And it's my treat,' she said mysteriously, before ringing off. 'I'm ringing Poppa presently to order us something special.'

If that doesn't mean that Ian was as good as his word I'll be very surprised, Sharon thought as she put the phone down. She turned to Sister, manfully plonking away on her typewriter.

'Sister, may I change my lunch-hour to the late-spot?'

'Certainly, if you don't mind being half starved,' Sister said cheerfully. 'I'll be around, unless Sister Brett asks me down for a drink then, and if she does, I'll be on call. Why? You look very bright-eyed!'

'I feel it. Not a word to a soul, but you know the rumour about Mr Ridgeway and one of our nurses?'

'I do. Has it now got substance? If so, I'm very pleased.'

'Well, Julie's rung and offered to buy me lunch, so I think we'll be celebrating something.'

'Like Sister Brett and myself, except that at Brett's age, another year is just another year.' It was Sister

Brett's fifty-fifth birthday. 'Right, my dear, as soon as
I've finished this report I'll change the lunch-rota.'

As soon as she could, Sharon hurried along to Susan's
room. She had no idea what Ian had told his daughter,
but she couldn't wait to find out, and one glance at
Susan's face told her that the little girl was in on the
secret.

'Hel*lo*, Craigie! Are you having lunch with Julie
today?'

'I am—how did you guess?'

'Didn't—I *knew*. Oh, Craigie, did you know I was the
happiest girl in the whole world?'

Sharon pretended to be mystified, and Susan hugged
herself and announced that she wasn't telling anyone
anything, except that all her friends must know at once
that Snowflake was no longer searching for a good home
and that she, Susan, looked like living happily ever after.
When Sharon pretended to press her for an answer she
just beamed, snatched up her drawing pad, and began to
draw furiously, announcing that she was designing a
bridesmaid's dress for a girl of about her age to wear.

By the time I get back from lunch there won't be a soul
in the hospital who hasn't been hinted into realisation,
Sharon thought merrily, hurrying down the stairs. Dear
little Susan, what a pet she was and how much she and
Julie would love playing at mother and daughter!

As soon as they were seated at their favourite table,
with a steak and side salad before them, Julie blurted out
her news.

'Ian's asked me to marry him, and I've said yes! We're
having the full business, though of course it'll be a
Register Office because Ian's been married before, but
I'm to wear white and Susan will be a bridesmaid; I feel
so happy, Sharon!'

'Congratulations, Julie,' Sharon said, kissing her
friend's cheek. 'He's a lovely fellow, I think you'll both
be very happy.'

'We shall! Oh, I never thought I'd marry someone so

. . . so lovely! It's different for you, Sharon, you're beautiful, but I'm so very ordinary and Ian's so . . . so . . .'

'Rich? Handsome? Successful? Or just plain old charming?' Sharon suggested, laughing. 'Tell you something, though, I've never told you that you were beautiful, but you are, now!'

And it was true. Julie's hair needed its twice weekly shampoo and she was wearing a very washed-out uniform dress with a faded ribbon tying back her hair. But happiness had given such a glow to her cheeks and a sparkle to her eyes that, thought Sharon, she could have competed successfully in a beauty contest against Morena Morasco today!

'Don't be silly. Ian is rich and handsome and all those other things, but he's special for me. I don't know quite how to put it, but if he was penniless and ill and had his face ruined in an accident, my heart would still turn over whenever he touched my hand.'

'Oh Julie, that's love for you,' sighed Sharon. 'When are you getting the ring?'

'I've got it, only it's gone to be made smaller. It was Ian's grandmother's, but Morena never cared for it. I love it, it's a cluster of sapphires. I'll be flaunting it in a day or so.'

'Marvellous. Dear Julie, I'll miss you like anything in the flat, but I'm terribly glad for you.'

And presently, making her way back to the hospital, she turned to Julie again.

'Won't Morena be mad to find Susan and Ian both prefer a mere nurse to her beautiful self? She was so beastly to me when she came to visit Susan, so off-hand and condescending. Ha ha!'

'She won't care at all, because she's marrying that fat man who came to visit Susan with her once—do you remember him? He had a huge cigar and Ian says he's the second richest man in Italy. That's all Morena cares about, money.'

'Crumbs,' Sharon said, remembering the fat man. 'It would need an awful lot of money to make me accept that—that slug! By the way, when will you be leaving?'

'Oh, when Susan does, I expect. We'll stay in Italy for a few weeks and then we'll go back to Ian's farmhouse in Dorset. Do you remember how I said I wanted to stay here for a good few years, when you first came? And now here I am, positively longing to be buried in Dorset, with Ian!'

'I can see you're hopelessly besotted.' Sharon waved and began to mount the stairs. 'See you later, love!'

At the top of the stairs she turned into the main corridor and headed for Sister's office, but even as her fingers closed round the doorknob it turned and Vitale erupted into the passage, almost knocking her over. When he saw who it was he stopped short, scowling blackly down at her.

'So! You are here at last!'

'Well, yes,' conceded Sharon, glancing quickly at her watch. To her relief it showed that she was five minutes early. 'Where else should I be?'

'Where indeed? And why should you not turn up here at this time, cool and smiling, when the whole ward has been searching for you for the past twenty minutes? It's about time, Staff, that you stopped using this hospital merely as a place where you come between your social engagements!'

The blatant unfairness of his remarks brought the words which crowded Sharon's mind out as croaks. What on earth was he talking about? She drew herself up to her full height and put some ice into her reply.

'I don't know what you mean, Signor. I've been having lunch—you know, lunch, the meal which divides the day into morning and afternoon?' She was speaking with insulting slowness and clarity. 'I took my break from one thirty today and since it is still not two o'clock you can scarcely accuse me of being late! And what did you mean by social engagements, anyway? I was having lunch with a friend, in my free time.'

He looked somewhat taken aback, she saw with relish, but he answered her briskly nonetheless.

'I've no time to quibble, Staff. If you intend to change the time of your lunch-break, as you obviously did, you should see to it that Sister knows. We've a new patient in the second turret room whose admittance I can lay fairly and squarely at your door! The least you could do in the circumstances is to be here to do the paperwork and make the telephone calls!'

'I think I'm going mad,' Sharon said, clasping her head with both hands. 'How on earth can I be responsible for a new patient's admittance?'

'Your friend Reynolds came calling and left Susan's door open,' Vitale said with assumed patience. 'The bloody cat—no, I make no apology for my language, Nurse—the bloody cat shot out of the room and down the corridor after the lunch trolley and dodged between Mr Sugden's legs. Mr Sugden fell down eight stairs, fracturing his thumb and sustaining bruising, besides opening his wound. He was, Nurse Craig, on his way back to his hotel when he was brought down. I had discharged him.'

'I see. Have you killed the cat?'

For the first time, Vitale looked less than sure of himself.

'Well, scarcely! I could not . . .'

'And has Mr Reynolds been sentenced to fifty lashes?'

Vitale blinked. '*Cosa intende dire?*'

Sharon smiled. It was the first time she had ever flustered the surgeon into addressing her in Italian. But despite her smile she was still coldly furious and hurt, as well. How could he treat her to such a display of prejudice and dislike?

'Well, why not? You obviously intend to crucify me for *not* being late back after lunch, for *not* being the one who let the cat out of the room, and for making very sure that Sister knew I was on late lunch today, so the least you can do is punish those who are more directly to blame! Although we both know, Signor, that a series of accidents such as those you describe can be blamed on no one and have to be accepted with as good a grace as we can muster!'

He was with her now. His face was icy with rage and contempt.

'You dare to speak to me like that! If Sister knew, why had she not changed the rota? From the very first moment I met you, Nurse Craig, you've been impertinent and . . . and generally impossible to work with. Now that you'll soon be leaving us, I daresay you think you can get away with it. Well, you can't! I'll speak to Sister as soon as she returns to the ward, and in the meantime, see to Mr Sugden!'

Sharon flew, tight-lipped, up the corridor to the second turret room where she sympathised with the unfortunate patient, saw to it that he was comfortable and assured him that he would only have to delay his departure by a couple of days whilst his wound healed up again.

'I daresay you feel you would like to kill the cat, and me for bringing her here in the first place,' she was beginning when Mr Sugden placidly interrupted her.

'It weren't no fault of the cat, Nurse! No, no, 'twere my suitcase what got tangled in me legs. The cat were ahead of me—nearly got hisself sat on, poor creature.'

This revelation brought Sharon up with a jolt, and started her thinking about the rest of that monumental telling off as well. He had deliberately told her that the fault was Snowflake's, subtly insinuating by so doing that it was also her fault, as the person who had brought the cat to the hospital in the first place, and throwing in poor Geoff, who was her friend, as a sort of make-weight. Why had he wanted so urgently to quarrel with her? And why had he made that strange remark about her leaving? *Now that you'll soon be leaving us*, that was what he had said. What on earth made him think she was leaving, when she had barely arrived? Unless he meant to try to sack her, which seemed unlikely since he had said only the other day how hard she worked and what a good nurse she was.

She went down to Sister's office when she had finished with Mr Sugden to do his readmittance papers, and found Sister Young at her desk. Sharon, who had intended to tell her with some humour about what had happened, smiled, began to speak, and promptly burst into tears. Thoroughly overwrought by the whole affair, she could not speak at all but merely continued to weep dolorously whilst Sister Young, baffled, could only pat her shoulder, advise her to sit down and, after a few moments, when Sharon's tears showed no signs of letting up, force her to take a few sips from a small glass of brandy.

'Medicinal, dear,' she said, as Sharon began to choke out a refusal to drink on duty. 'Just a drop, and then perhaps you'll tell me what's the matter.' She cocked a bright and knowing eye at her staff nurse. 'Not that you have to say much—it's Vitale again, I'll be bound, I've never known a man more apt to upset my staff more thoroughly, though you're his favourite. He should know better than to upset you.'

'Favourite! He says I'm impertinent and impossible to w-work with,' Sharon said, gulping back her tears. 'He said I took a late l-lunch just to be difficult and didn't tell anyone, he told me the cat had tripped Mr Sugden—I've just had to readmit him, Sister, with a fractured thumb and a wound re-opened—and he s-said since I was leaving I'd got above myself, or something like that.'

'Tell me the story right from the start, from the very first moment you got back on the ward,' Sister said kindly. 'Impertinent, indeed—my nurses are *never* impertinent!'

It took some time to tell the story, but when it was

done Sister Young's eyes were sharp as needles and there were high spots of colour on her cheekbones.

'This cannot be allowed to continue. I shall have a word with Dr Vitale this very afternoon! Oh, by the way, I popped in to Virginia Ward on my way back here and your friend Julie gave me a message for you—she said to tell you to give her news to Mrs Humphries, and see if that would do the trick.'

'Isn't that just like Julie, always thinking of other people,' Sharon said. 'She knows I've been worrying because several times Mrs Humphries has hinted about Signor Pappalardo and almost come out with a wish to see him, or so I've thought. I'll do that as soon as I get a chance.'

'Well, there's a good excuse for you—go and do obs. on Mrs Patten, she's come in with a cyst which will be operated on tomorrow—and then you can buttonhole Mrs Humphries afterwards. I'll ring down and see when Dr Vitale's free to see me, and I'll let you know when I get back.' She smiled at Sharon. 'I'll bring you his apologies, see if I don't!'

Sharon hurried down to Room 1, took Mrs Patten's b.p., checked her pulse and temperature and then, having reassured her as to the surgical procedure she would undergo on the following day, popped her head round the door of Room 2. She was in luck. Mrs Humphries was sitting in her chair by her bed, with a paper pattern spread out over her lap, marking it with a black pencil and frowning. She looked up when Sharon entered and her brow cleared.

'Hello, dear! I've decided to make myself something pretty—have you time to take a look at a few designs?'

'Well, I've got a moment.' Sharon walked over to her and sat down on the bed. 'Gracious, you design your own stuff, then?'

'Yes, I do. Well, I'm a difficult shape at the best of times, and I don't always suit conventional clothes, I'm too short and broad, to be honest with you, so I prefer to make my own things. I'm no artist, but I can draw clothes—odd, isn't it? What do you think of that?'

'It's lovely,' Sharon said truthfully. 'Almost . . . well, bridal! Which reminds me why I came to talk to you—guess who's getting married?'

'You are!' Mrs Humphries said, confounding Sharon somewhat. 'I'm very happy for you, dear!'

'No, it isn't me, it's Julie Drummond. She's marrying Ian Ridgeway, Susan's father.'

'Well, isn't that lovely? I'm not surprised, mind,' Mrs Humphries said hastily. She belonged to the large school of female thought that is never surprised by a love-affair. 'I thought they were going about together too steadily for anything but a marriage. Well! I bet young Susan's cock-a-hoop! She does love that Julie, and of course she fair worships her Daddy.'

'Yes, I'm sure they'll all be very happy, which is what we want for our friends.'

'Mm, true.' Mrs Humphries stared long and hard at her design, then added an extra flounce to the skirt. 'They said at one time it was you he was after—not that I ever believed that for a moment! You've had other fish to fry.'

'Yes, I suppose you could say that. But I think I'll pursue my career for a few more years, personally.'

Mrs Humphries looked up and laughed.

'Career! You're as bad as the rest—you'll be married come the year's end, I'd put money on it!'

Sharon laughed in her turn.

'You'd lose, Mrs H!' Highly daring, she continued, 'You approve of marriage, don't you? I'm the same myself, but I want my marriage to be perfect, or as near perfect as possible, which is why I'll do plenty of looking before I leap.'

'I do approve of marriage. A happy marriage is the best thing that can happen to a woman. Or a man, for that matter.' She glanced almost shyly at Sharon. 'I daresay you won't believe it, but I was to have been married in ten days—come to that, I don't actually know that all the arrangements have been cancelled, though I told him I'd changed my mind.'

'Why on earth did you do that? The poor man, he must have been frantic with worry, not knowing why you'd changed your mind. You really should change it back, Mrs Humphries—you're so well now you could easily be out of here in a couple of days. I know Dr Vitale was only hesitating because you would have to go home to an empty house.'

'Yes, I have been thinking about it,' Mrs Humphries said rather unexpectedly. 'Edvige knows why I changed my mind, though—because of the operation. I told him I didn't want to see him again, but I never thought, truth to tell, that he'd take me at my word and not come near nor by the hospital.' She sniffed rather forlornly. 'I've wondered how I might get in touch with him, many a time.'

'I see. But surely you could send him word—ring him up, perhaps, or write?'

'He isn't on the telephone. Hates the thing, though I told him all that would have to change once we were married. And he can't read English though he speaks it quite well and I can't write Eye-talian,' Mrs Humphries admitted. 'And tell my family I will not, for that would mean eating my words to them, which I'm too proud to do.'

'Yet you'd eat your words to Signor . . . what was his name? I call that true love, Mrs Humphries.'

'Ah well, Signor Pappalardo's a man it's difficult not to love,' Mrs Humphries said. 'He's a farmer, but he thinks he'd like to retire and so he's building a big villa down on the coast. That was where I was to go when we married. But now . . . well, I don't know.'

'Where does he live?' Sharon said craftily. 'I wouldn't mind popping round with a message. All I need do is ask him to visit you, after all.'

'Ah, but he lives miles from here, in the mountains at

the back of Amalfi,' Mrs Humphries disclosed. 'It would be different if you had a car, but public transport, and you not speaking the language—well, it would take you a month of Sundays I daresay.'

'Yes, but I've a good friend with a car, more than one, actually. What did you say Signor Pappalardo's address was?'

'I didn't, and I don't know as how he's got an address, exactly, not such as we have at home. But if you say the Pappalardo place, outside Amalfi, most folk up there know it. Still, don't you bother, dear, I've quite made up my mind to see Edvige again, so when I get out of here, if I can summon up the strength, I'll get a hire-car to take me.'

Sharon made reassuring noises and presently left to hurry along to Sister's office, feeling pleased with herself. It would be a relatively simple matter to get a message to Signor Pappalardo and when she had done that, she had little doubt that Mrs Humphries would find herself getting married, if not in ten days then as rapidly as her suitor could arrange it. She was such a nice, courageous little woman, and she would make her Edvige a wonderful wife. It was a pity that he seemed little more than a peasant farmer, with no telephone and probably no transport other than buses, but she was determined to do everything in her power to further the romance.

Sister, when she heard the story, was every bit as eager as Sharon for a happy ending.

'Wonderful, but what fools we've been not to see that she was hankering after her Edvige all this time,' she said enthusiastically. 'Now, how can we get you to Amalfi, my dear? Odd, I seem to recall someone telling me that they were going to Amalfi tonight . . . who on earth was it?'

'It doesn't matter, I'll ring Paolo and he'll take me over there if he's free,' Sharon said. 'May I use the phone now?'

But though she rang several times, the phone was not answered.

Sister, meanwhile, had gone hurrying out of the office so that Sharon could telephone Paolo in peace, as she put it, but she came back presently, looking very pleased with herself.

'No luck? Well, that doesn't matter, because I've got you a lift.'

'Oh? I hope whoever's been kind enough to offer does understand that I don't know the way and haven't managed to get a proper address?' Sharon said anxiously. 'I wouldn't want someone to take me on this wild goose chase not knowing it might be a wild goose chase.'

'He understands. It's Dr Vitale,' Sister disclosed. 'Don't look like that, my dear child, he's extremely sorry for the rude and silly way he behaved earlier and wants to apologise to you himself. And it's a long way to Amalfi, he'll have plenty of time to do the job properly.'

For a moment, all Sharon could do was to gape at Sister. Then she shook her head wildly.

'Oh, no! I couldn't, honestly, Sister. I don't understand Dr Vitale, and I don't want to, he's either nice as pie or unbearably horrible, and I've just had enough of it. I want to keep as much distance between us as I possibly can.'

'Don't be silly, Sharon,' Sister said calmly. 'Vitale's every bit as interested in Mrs Humphries as you are, and it will be a great help that he can speak Italian you know, should there be any doubt in Signor Pappalardo's mind. Also, Vitale can explain just why Mrs Humphries thought her operation debarred her from a normal, happy marriage, and that, my dear, is more than one of these uppity Italian males would *allow* you to do, even if you wanted to, which I doubt.'

'That's true. But Sister, I'm scared stiff of the man! What sort of drive will it be with the two of us silent and antagonistic for miles and miles?'

Sister laughed.

'My child, I have many reservations about Dr Vitale, but I am a realist. If he apologises and decides to charm you out of your silence, how long do you think you'd stand out against him? Five minutes? Ten? You'll be chattering away like a little canary long before you reach Amalfi.'

Sharon considered this, and laughed too, albeit reluctantly.

'You're right, of course. And I don't want to be bad friends with him, it's just that we seem fated to fight. All right, Sister, thank you very much for arranging it. When do we leave?'

'He'll pick you up at the flat at four,' Sister said. 'Now make sure you give Ivonne instructions as to what needs doing, and I'll tell Amaryllis what I want her to do, and then you'd better be off. You'll want to shower and change and do something to that pretty hair, I daresay.' She waited until Sharon was half out of the door and then added, 'Have a good time, Nurse!'

'Huh!' Sharon said bitterly, but she could not help laughing. Sister had sounded so smug, as though the whole thing had been her idea!

CHAPTER NINE

ONCE back at the flat, however, the calm which had gradually grown on her during the afternoon deserted her and wild thoughts of rushing down to the main road, thumbing a lift, and reaching Amalfi without having to face Vitale, assailed her mind. But she knew it was impossible. If Vitale was at his worst, if he spent the whole journey being sarcastic and biting or if he simply drove in total silence, it would be worthwhile if it also meant that Signor Pappalardo would come down to the hospital and see Mrs Humphries.

Accordingly she put on a thin blue cotton dress and sandals, tucked a lightweight cardigan into her straw basket, and ran downstairs as soon as she saw the long bonnet of the Lamborghini nose into the drive. She slipped out through the front door and there was Vitale, carrying an armful of fragile white roses, and looking surprised and a little put out by her unexpectedly prompt appearance.

'These are for you. Shall we take them back to your flat and put them in some water? Sister told me off, you see, said you were perfectly within your rights to take the late lunch hour, said it was she who had forgotten to change the rota. She told me I'd behaved like a boor, and would give you a very low opinion of Italian men. She said rude things about my lack of charm and machismo and reduced me to the level of a sulky five-year-old in two minutes flat.' He had been talking as they climbed the stairs and now he took the key from her fingers, unlocked the front door and ushered her into the flat as politely as though he were the host. 'Come on, let's get these in water and then go.' He went into the kitchen, shoved the flowers in the washing up bowl, ran some water on top of them and turned to Sharon once more. 'Really, Nurse, has no one ever taught you to accept an apology gracefully? Don't just stare with your mouth open!'

He was plainly in good form and almost irritatingly cheerful. Sharon felt quite battered by his bonhomie.

'I didn't hear you apologise, Signor,' she said, recovering from her surprise. 'All you did was quote Sister!'

'And who better?' He swung round, ushered her out of the flat and down the stairs and then, at the door of the car, turned her to face him, looking down into her eyes with a question in the dark depths of his own. 'I am sorry, Sharon, for a good many things. Are you going to forgive me and let us start again?'

'That's noble, if a trifle vague,' Sharon said. She climbed into the car, suddenly not wanting him to be serious. 'I forgive you! Do you know the way to Signor Pappalardo's by the way, and where do you have to go in Amalfi? I suppose you could leave me at the Pappalardo's place whilst you do your own visit, but I must admit I'd prefer it if you'd stay with me.'

'I know the way, and I have to see a patient in the town itself; it won't take long,' Vitale assured her. 'I thought, by the way, that a more concrete apology than a few roses might be that we should dine together on the way home, and then we can spend the rest of the evening as you wish.'

'Suppose Signor Pappalardo wants to come back to Sant' Agnello with us?' Sharon suggested hopefully. 'If he has no transport he might be glad of the lift.'

Vitale snatched a quick, mocking glance at her before his eyes returned to the ribbon of road unwinding ahead.

'Don't leap to conclusions just because a man lives on a farm and has a jolly little fat name. Pappalardo's a wealthy man and runs two or three cars.'

'Then why doesn't he have a phone, and why does he

live on a farm at the back of beyond?' Sharon said sceptically. 'You're having me on!'

'Really? When? And on what?'

There was a short, scandalised silence before Sharon began to giggle. Vitale was in good form tonight, determined to amuse as well as to 'start again' as he had put it. She was about to ask him what had suddenly caused him to change his sober and rather condemnatory attitude towards her when he answered the unspoken question.

'Sharon, I've a confession to make, I more or less engineered this trip to Amalfi. If Mrs Humphries hadn't suggested you visit Pappalardo, I intended to ask you to accompany me anyway. You see, I've been horrified by the way I've got off on the wrong foot with you almost from the word go, and I wanted a chance to put it right. I admire you work and your attitude to the patients, and I like you as a person. I'd like to take you out again and if we find we enjoy this trip as much as I, at any rate, enjoyed our outing to Herculaneum, then it will be the start of a long and pleasant friendship.'

'This is somewhat sudden, isn't it?' Sharon said suspiciously. 'You haven't seemed to be very fond of my company lately!'

'That was because . . .' he glanced sideways at her and slowed the car, drawing into a lay-by which overlooked the dazzling sea. 'Are you in a mood for frankness?'

'Yes; I always am. I hate half-truths and white lies.'

'I've noticed.' He grinned wryly, then slid an arm round her shoulders. 'I, too, prefer to have everything above-board. Fortuna, you see, managed to get the impression . . .'

'That you were going to marry her,' Sharon supplied. 'Yes, I knew *that*.'

'Well, there was that, but there were other things as well. And I would like, little one, to put right the bad impression you have received of me. According to Sister, of course.'

'It's improving every minute,' Sharon murmured as he pulled her closer. 'Oh, Signor, look at that vi . . .'

His mouth, gentle at first, cut her words off short. He held her quite loosely, his arms round her, one hand stroking the nape of her neck as his mouth explored hers. Sharon's hands crept across his shoulders and her mouth softened beneath his. Mounting excitement had her melting against him, until she tried to turn further towards him and caught her knee a crack against the gear lever.

The pain acted like a douche of cold water. Sharon yelped and drew back.

'Ouch! As I was saying, S-signor, look at that beautiful view!'

Vitale, breathing rather hard, shook his hair back off his forehead, straightened his tie, and started the engine.

'One should never try to make love in a car, it's far too cramped! I meant to ask you earlier, would you like to visit Positano? We pass directly above it and could walk down to it in a few minutes.'

'Positano? I seem to have heard the name.'

'It's a tenth-century Moorish village, very picturesque. A great tourist attraction, you can't see the beach for people.'

'No, I don't think so, not today, thank you. Today is for Pappalardo.' She would have liked to ask him just what he meant by making love in a car. Could it be that he simply meant kissing and cuddling? If so, she agreed that such things were more satisfactory when a gear lever did not suddenly leap up and crack one across the patella, but if he meant love-making in any other sense, then she really should tell him that she was not in the market for that sort of thing. But he was speaking again, obviously unaware of her dilemma.

'I agree that today is for our patients. But tomorrow . . . ?'

'Oh, let tomorrow take care of itself, Signor.'

He glanced at her, a brow rising.

'I think we'll help it along a little. When is your next day off? Would you like to come to my home and visit my parents?'

Sharon had an immediate and terrifying vision of a huge mansion inhabited by smooth and sophisticated Italians who spoke not a word of English and assumed that Vitale would marry Fortuna. She shuddered.

'No, thank you. My Italian isn't good enough.'

He grinned mockingly.

'You're a coward, Sharon Craig! I'll start giving you lessons in my language right now. Say after me: Rodrigo.'

'That isn't a language, that's a name.'

'That's clever of you. It's my name and I want you to use it instead of calling me Signor all the time. When you meet my parents what will they think of us if you don't use my given name?'

'I don't know that I'm going to meet your parents,' Sharon said with a flash of desperation. 'I know what you're like, Signor, by tomorrow you'll probably be disliking me intensely again!'

'Oho!' He shot her a glance which melted her bones. 'I think not! Now say my name, please—I call you Sharon, do I not?'

'All right then, for the sake of peace. Rodrigo.'

'Better. Now I'll teach you to admire the view in Italian, since you seem rather set on the scenery.' He indicated the sea, the sweep of the cliffs, the tiny villages, sugar cubes in the sun, clinging to the precipitous heights. 'Say *Questo è veramente bello.*'

'I would if I knew what it meant. You might be teaching me to say rude things!'

He flashed a grin at her which made her heart turn over. He could be so charming when he wanted to be; if only he always wanted to be!

'So I could, but in fact it only means *that is beautiful.*' He slowed to take a sharp bend and continued, in an ordinary, conversational tone, 'As beautiful as you, *mi amica.*'

'*Grazie,*' Sharon said coolly, but with thumping heart. 'Now let's be practical. Teach me some verbs, that ought to help.'

And if he can make that sound amorous I shall be very surprised, she told herself, as Vitale obediently began to tell her about Italian verbs.

Sharon's suspicion that Signor Pappalardo was just a well-to-do peasant farmer dissolved as soon as she saw the Pappalardo property. It was less of a farm than an estate, surrounded by well-tended fields and orchards, and as they drove up the long carriageway she became less and less anxious to confront the owner of all this splendour with her story. She had not realised he was a rich and important man, suppose he had got engaged to Mrs Humphries as a whim and the whim was now over? Or suppose he was as repulsed at the thought of the operation as Mrs Humphries herself had once been? As the car drew to a halt beside the front steps Sharon turned impulsively to her escort.

'Oh, Signor Vit . . . I mean Rodrigo, could you do the talking? I'm so afraid I might say the wrong thing and spoil it all.'

'*Sciocchezze!* That means nonsense, my child. You're thinking that Pappalardo may regret his impulse to marry Mrs Humphries and that this is an unwarrantable interference, aren't you?' He came round to her side of the car and helped her out, an indulgent, teasing look on his face. 'I won't let you make a fool of yourself, but you must show me that British girls have courage.'

Sharon squared her shoulders.

'Right!' She marched over to the front door and hammered on it with the big, ornate knocker. The noise it made seemed to boom hollowly throughout the entire house. 'Open, Sesa . . . Oh!'

The front door shot open and a wizened little man in a

dark suit with a shock of black hair and bright black eyes grinned at them.

'Signor, Signorina?'

Beside her, Vitale gripped her hand for a moment, then answered the manservant in English.

'Is Signor Pappalardo at home? We come from the Villa L'Arancia, in Sant' Agnello, and would like to see him.'

'Of course, Signor, at once, Signor, news from the hospital is always brought straight to my master.' He looked from face to face. 'It is good news, I hope?'

'Yes, indeed.'

'Follow me, then. Signor Pappalardo is on the terrace, I was about to take the drinks trolley out there.'

They crossed a very ornate dining room and gained the terrace through wide open glass doors. Signor Pappalardo rose from his chair and came across to them, a hand held out, a smile beginning to form. He was not small at all, but he was very fat and very jolly looking as well. He began to speak in Italian, but was cut off short by Vitale cutting in and saying something so rapid that Sharon could not catch even the gist of it. However, it plainly explained things to Signor Pappalardo, for he gestured to two chairs and then to the drinks trolley.

'The doctor and the nurse who take care of my Florrie—ah, then I feel I know you well. You will be Dottore Vitale and Nurse Craig.' He was at the drinks trolley, hand waving hospitably over its well-filled surface. 'Nothing is wrong? No? Good, good, then what would you like to drink?'

Vitale having settled for whisky and Sharon for a sherry, Signor Pappalardo helped himself to a brandy and then they sat down on the well-cushioned patio chairs. Signor Pappalardo turned enquiringly to Sharon.

'This message, Nurse Craig? Can I have it, please?'

'Mrs Humphries is fine and missing you very much,' Sharon said quickly. 'The truth is, Signor Pappalardo, that you took her too literally when she told you to go away, and she would love to see you again, but as you are not on the telephone and she can't write Italian, she could think of no way of getting in touch with you which would not make her lose face.'

'Aha, her friends the Marchese family said that it was so,' Signor Pappalardo said delightedly. He whisked a huge white handkerchief out of his pocket and fanned himself vigorously, then wiped his brow. 'I have longed to visit her, but dared not risk spoiling everything.'

'What could you have spoiled?' Sharon ventured. 'I should have thought you had more to gain than to lose by a visit.'

'Ah, yes, but you see Florrie has always been a little embarrassed by our marriage, she persisted that we were too old, that people would laugh. I was sure once she came out of hospital that I could persuade her to see the truth, but whilst she was in there, with other English people, I thought it would merely seem more and more absurd, to be marrying a fat old Italian. Ah, I have been unhappy!'

'Well, now you know the truth, you might tell us if the wedding preparations have been cancelled,' Vitale put in. 'If they have not, it might be as well to go down to the hospital tomorrow and sweep your lady love off her feet. Take it for granted that the marriage is to go ahead, and I don't think you'll be disappointed.'

'I will, believe me, I will!' Pappalardo surged to his feet with the obvious intention of kissing Vitale and Sharon on both cheeks. He swept Sharon up in a vast embrace, beaming and chuckling. 'You must dine with me, both of you, and we will talk of our wedding, and of Florrie—you must both come to the wedding, of course!'

'We'd be delighted,' Vitale said, taking Sharon's hand. 'But I'm afraid we've a table booked for dinner at Ricardo's, and I've a patient to see, so we must leave you now. But I assure you, your presence at the hospital is eagerly awaited.'

'Eager! My little Florrie is eager!' Pappalardo muttered. 'Ah, Dottore Vitale, Signorina Craig, you have brought me much happiness! And you dine at Ricardo's you say? A wonderful spot, perfection!' He kissed his fingertips. 'I would take my Florrie there, but she does not like to climb the . . . the . . . how do you say it?'

'The spiral staircase,' Vitale said, eyes twinkling. 'Well, Miss Craig will have to climb it or miss her dinner, and it's such a curious edifice that I daresay she'll mount it without too much difficulty.'

Pappalardo was effusive in his thanks and farewells and then Vitale drove back into Amalfi, parking the car just off the steep little street which sloped down to the harbour. But a disappointment awaited them. Sharon stayed in the car, but after only a few minutes Vitale joined her, a frown on his face.

'It's a nuisance, but we'll have to defer seeing Renato until after we've dined. His sister, with whom he was staying, says he moved back to Furore three days ago, despite her pleas. Young fool! Though the people of Furore are very independant and she says he was homesick for his own place, and for the sound of the sea on the shingle.'

'Would you rather visit your patient first?' Sharon suggested, though her inside felt quite hollow with hunger. 'I don't mind. In fact if you'd prefer it, we could eat back in Sant' Agnello.'

Vitale started the engine and drove out onto the roadway once more.

'It's all right, Ricardo's is on our way home and so is Furore, so it will be best if we dine first. Anyway, I've booked a table, and I'm pretty hungry.' He glanced at her in the deepening dusk. 'Knowing you, you could eat a horse by now.'

'Well, I could, though I'd prefer beefsteak, or spaghetti or something,' Sharon admitted. 'Is Furore the name of a village?'

'That's right. It's an extraordinary place, a cliff village

in which the houses are actually burrowed out of the cliff itself, are in fact, caves. Only six or seven families actually live there, and that's because it would be impossible to build on or build more houses. They are at the foot of gigantic cliffs, in a narrow gorge, with the sea just feet away from their doors. It's just as it must have been for many centuries, because it can only be reached by sea or by the extremely steep and dangerous cliff path, so they can't get quantities of food in, or people, or things.'

'I wonder why they chose to live there, in the first place,' Sharon said. 'Were they fleeing from justice, or from war? Would it have been easy to defend?'

'Yes, and almost impossible to attack, even if anyone wanted to bother for a mere handful of lives. But you'll see it for yourself, which is more than most people do, so you're lucky. And first, you'll see Ricardo's, which is also quite an experience.'

'Tell me about it,' Sharon said, settling back comfortably in her seat. 'It must be quite well known— Pappalardo had certainly heard of it.'

'Yes, it is. I won't tell you about it, though, I'll let it spring its own surprise.' A hand came out of the darkness and squeezed Sharon's fingers as they lay in her lap. 'I'm sure you'll like it, spiral staircase or no.'

She did. From the moment that he led her into the circular cave, brightly lit and with paintings and baskets of flowers hanging from the natural rock walls and the domed ceiling, she knew that this was somewhere special. At the foot of the staircase was a perfectly ordinary reception desk with a dark-haired girl sitting behind it and with the usual range of telephones and account books ranged out on it, and as soon as Vitale stepped in the girl smiled at them.

'Good evening, Signor—a drink before you go up?'

She spoke in Italian and Vitale translated in a whisper before refusing her offer and explaining that this guest had not been here before, so would prefer to take her aperitif upstairs.

'Take your time on the stairs,' he advised Sharon, guiding her up on to the cobwebby metal of the spiral staircase. 'Don't be nervous, I'm close behind you— I'm glad to see you've got sensible, flat-heeled shoes on.'

'Why? Oh, because I suppose high heels might stick in the metalwork. Shouldn't you have gone first though, up this sort of staircase?'

He caught her meaning and chuckled low in his throat.

'As if I'd look up a lady's skirt! But as you'll see, the stairs speedily become rock, and very solid, though still spiralling. Well? What do you think?'

They had emerged into the restaurant itself. It was really nothing more than a broad ledge cut in the cliff, surrounded by a bamboo balustrade and roofed with thick, golden straw. The balustrade was covered with climbing geraniums, scarlet, pink and white in the light of the only illumination, which was oil lamps which dangled from the thatch at intervals. The view, of course, was incomparable, and the breeze which blew into their faces from the darkness was scented with pine and cool with the salt sea.

'I'm speechless.' She glanced round again, seeing the tiny, pink-clothed tables, the silver vase on each containing one rose, the waiters moving unobtrusively around, neat, quiet, quick. 'It's like nothing I've ever seen before.'

He nodded, pleased with her reaction.

'True, it's unique.' A waiter glided over to them. 'Vitale, table for two.'

They were led over to the balustrade and seated at a small table with the perfume and presence of the geraniums almost taking over from the sea scent. But the blaze of the stars against the velvet dark and the lights of the ships out to sea dispelled, somehow, the scents of an English garden.

'Shall I order for us both? The menu is in Italian and I think I know your taste by now.'

She nodded.

'Please do.'

The soup was made with real tomatoes, garlic and cream, and eaten with crusty bread. The beefsteak was garnished with piazzola sauce, a sauce rich in mushrooms, peppers and aubergines. It was served with tiny crisp little chips and a big side salad. Next they had something called *fichi al cioccolato* which Vitale told her were chocolate covered figs with an almond and lemon filling. They were delicious, and Sharon ate several whilst she sipped the big cup of foamy coffee, topped with finely shredded bitter chocolate.

'That was fantastic,' Sharon said at last, when she had, regretfully, to refuse a platter of crumbly biscuits and white goat's cheese. 'I dare not risk another mouthful—imagine getting stuck halfway down those stairs!'

Vitale, too, decided that he had eaten quite enough, and presently they dared the stairs again, though Sharon felt obliged to leave her companion at the foot of them and visit the lady's, a nicely appointed little cave with pink-washed walls, which amused her. She saw her face in the mirror above the washbasin, aglow with good food and happiness, and dashed a comb through her soft, tangled hair until it was tidy again, then returned to her escort.

'That was an experience not many people have,' she said drowsily as she settled back into the passenger seat once more. 'I'm far too well-brought-up to comment on the prices but I couldn't help noticing them. It's not the sort of place nurses get taken often!'

'Nurses? What are they? I'm dining and spending the evening with a beautiful young woman, not with a nurse,' Vitale said, starting the engine. 'Alas that the evening is so nearly over! But there will be others.'

Content, drowsy, full of food, Sharon scarcely opened her mouth during the journey to Furore except once, when she commented on the size and brilliance of the stars. In fact, she was almost asleep when she felt someone draw a hand across her cheek.

'Sharon? Wake up, *cara mia*, we're the nearest we can get to Furore, and I dare not leave you up here, sleeping like an angel, in case you were to wake and find yourself alone and, perhaps, get out of the car and go over the cliff.'

'I wasn't really asleep, just dozing,' Sharon protested, rather spoiling the effect by adding, 'Where are we? Is this Sant' Agnello?'

'Foolish one, don't you remember that I have to visit a patient in Furore? Will you come down with me, or would you prefer to stay here and continue to . . . to close your eyes for a moment?' She could hear the smile in his voice though she could see nothing more than the shape of his head, outlined against the brilliant stars. 'You'll be safe here if you promise not to leave the car.'

Sharon sat up, then opened the passenger door and climbed, a little stiffly, out onto the short grass of what she knew must be a clearing just off the road. There were great trees all around her, though, and they made the darkness seem almost impenetrable, though she guessed that once her eyes were used to it, she would be able to see much better.

'I'll come with you, please,' she said. 'I'm not tired now and I'd love to see the village, if your patient wouldn't mind my accompanying you.'

'My patient will be delighted, as I am.' He took her hand in a firm grasp. 'I'll keep hold of you, little one, because the steps are steep and a bit frightening, even in daylight. At night they will probably be worse.'

They were not only frightening and steep, there were thousands of them. Long before they reached the bottom Sharon's knees were trembling and she was clinging to Vitale, but at last they reached the beach and crunched across the shingle towards the warmly lit windows of the nearest cave-house.

'Only a little way more and then you'll be able to sit down for a minute,' Vitale said encouragingly. 'My poor child, if I could promise to carry you up those steps on the way back I would, but it would be far too dangerous. I'm afraid it's self-propulsion in both directions when one visits Furore.'

'I'm quite all right, I was only a bit scared because I couldn't see too well,' Sharon said as Vitale knocked on the ancient wooden door. 'Going up again won't be nearly as bad because I shan't have to look down into nothing, so to speak. And we can rest halfway, can't we?'

'Of course. In fact . . .' the door opened and Vitale smiled at the elderly woman whose nutcracker face was applied to the crack in the door. He broke into Italian, and had barely said a dozen words before the door was thrown wide and they were ushered into a small living-room whose walls were of the natural rock, whitewashed over, and whose floor was hard-packed sand. The woman cackled something at Sharon and pressed her gently into a big chair with soft, well-worn cushions. Vitale touched her hair with his finger-tips.

'This is Signora Immacolata, Sharon. She speaks a difficult dialect so you won't understand much of what she says, but she says you must rest and that she will make you some hot chocolate whilst I see Renato. And then we'll climb back up to the car and I'll hurry you back to your own bed. It's been a long day for you.'

'But a nice one.' Sharon smiled and watched him leave the room, then yawned behind her hand, apologising in English as she saw her hostess watching her as she boiled a small pan over the fire. Presently, she brought a thick, white cup with the hot chocolate in it over to Sharon, and began to chatter to her as she drank. Sharon's few words of Italian came in useful here, since she could just about manage to agree warmly with whatever her hostess said to her, and she continued to do this without understanding a word until Vitale rejoined them.

'Renato's doing very well, though I've made him promise to come up to the hospital to see me in a week or two, whenever he can get a lift,' Vitale said. He spoke to the old woman in Italian, shook his head at her pantomimed offer of a drink and a sticky almond cake and then, after voluble goodbyes and thanks, he and Sharon set off once more across the dark, pebbly beach. Ahead of them the sea sighed on the shingle and a faint breath from the pines came to their nostrils. Sharon started on the long climb with a good heart, knowing where she was going and preferring to climb up with hands and feet engaged, rather than the frightening descent, where she had been, as she had put it, climbing into nothingness.

She reached the top in good order, with the help of Vitale's hand in the small of her back giving her the illusion, at least, of being assisted. They went over to the car and Vitale opened the passenger door, saw her safely settled, and then went round and slid behind the wheel. He turned the key in the ignition. The engine coughed, purred, and died!

'Good Lord, what's the matter?' Sharon said, as two more attempts ended in the same way. 'Oh Rodrigo, this isn't a good place for a breakdown, is it?'

Vitale chuckled grimly.

'No, it isn't. Pass me that torch, would you, and I'll go and take a look at the engine.'

But though he looked, fiddled, did things to plugs and connections, the result was the same. The starter whirred and then the engine coughed, purred—and died. The last time it didn't even do that. The key clicked, and then there was nothing. Vitale swore softly and clasped his forehead.

'Here is a go,' he said slowly. 'We're miles from civilisation and this car wasn't meant for sleeping in. I think, *cara mia*, we'd better go down into Furore again.'

'Oh, no!' Sharon wailed. 'Couldn't we . . . couldn't we . . .'

'It's the only place for miles where we might get help,'

Vitale said decisively. 'I hate to admit it, but I think I'm out of petrol, I must have switched onto the reserve tank without noticing and now it's run dry too. But it's possible that someone's got a tin of the stuff hidden away down there for a motor bike or something and that could get us to the nearest filling station.'

'Right.' Sharon accepted the inevitable with what courage she could muster. 'Off we go—and Signor, if I fall asleep at work tomorrow, we'll know who's to blame.'

'Fair enough.' He took her hand. 'No use saying I'm sorry, you know I hadn't planned this. Down we go!'

But back at the cave house once more, a disappointment awaited them.

'No one's got petrol, not a drop,' Vitale told her. 'And what's more, all the boats are out, that's why we didn't see any on the beach as we crossed it. They're night-fishing, otherwise I could have begged a lift and come back with fuel. So I'm afraid, *mia cara*, we'll just have to make the best of it. The Senora has offered us her marital bed, she says she can sleep on the couch as she always does when they have visitors, so I think we'll have to accept her kind offer.'

'Her marital bed? We couldn't possibly. I can't imagine what sort of a girl she thinks I am, do I look as if I . . .'

'No, of course not, but unfortunately in the course of your earlier conversation with Signora Immacolata you told her you were my wife. You can scarcely blame her, you see, for suggesting that we share a bed!'

'I never did, I wouldn't know how . . .' Sharon was beginning, then stopped short at the expression on his face. 'Rodrigo, you know very well what I mean, I wouldn't know how to tell her I was you wife in Italian, not I wouldn't know . . . well, not what you meant!'

'You told her you were my wife by replying "*Si*" when she asked if that was the case,' Vitale said blandly. 'Now be a good girl and stop fussing. After all, we're both fully clothed and can remain so, if that makes you feel more comfortable. I do believe I can share a bed with you and refrain from seducing you, if that's what you're afraid of.'

'Oh! Yes, but what will people think? They'll soon realise we aren't married!'

'These people? It won't occur to them to wonder, one way or the other. They rarely leave the village. As for others, I'll tell them I slept in the car—which I can do, if you'd prefer it.'

'No! I don't want to be left alone down here! I know, why don't we suggest that Signora Immacolata and I share her marital bed as you call it, and you can have the couch?'

'Yes, that's a solution. Only there's a good deal of inter-marrying amongst these people and they rarely see a doctor, they aren't the healthiest of mortals, but it's up to you, of course.' He contrived to look both noble and deeply hurt at the same time. 'I can assure you, however, that you'll be perfectly safe with me.'

Sharon looked doubtfully at Signora Immacolata. She was rather strange looking and her skin, in the lamplight, looked dark and wrinkled and somewhat prune-like. Sharon shut her eyes for a second, then made up her mind.

'*Grazie, Signora*,' she said earnestly. She turned back to Vitale. 'Come on, then!'

Vitale looped a casual arm round her shoulders and together they followed the old woman to the doorway of the main bedroom. It was clean and pleasant looking, with a large bed, a fly-spotted mirror on an ancient chest of drawers, and a marble-topped washstand with a basin and ewer on it.

'*Le sono tanto grato*,' Sharon said haltingly since Vitale had told her, earlier, that this was a polite way of saying thank you. '*Buona sera*, Signora.'

The old woman, after a stream of fast, clicking Italian, withdrew, shutting the door firmly behind her and leaving Sharon and Vitale standing side by side, whilst Sharon's eyes were unable to stare at anything but the big bed.

Vitale was first to move. He began to tug his shirt over his head, speaking as he did so.

'I hope it won't worry you, my child, if I remove my shirt and trousers? My shorts are perfectly respectable and I don't want to look untidier than I have to in the morning.' His shirt was tossed to one side, revealing a broad and hairy chest. Sharon's gaze fixed itself on this virile display with the fascination of horror.

'If I were you, I should slip off that dress—that is, if you're as respectable as I, beneath it,' Vitale went on, hanging his dark trousers neatly over the wash-stand. 'I suppose, since I am the man, that I ought to offer to sleep on a shakedown on the floor, but the bed looks extremely comfortable. However, if you insist . . .'

'I'll see how we get on,' Sharon said feebly. She stood there, fiddling with the buttons on her dress, trying to remember which bra and briefs she had put on that morning. Fervently, she prayed for sensible white cotton and not for frilly pink transparent nylon.

'Come on—want some help? Good God, girl, this is 1984 not 1884!'

He moved towards her and Sharon was galvanised into action by the thought of those long, strong fingers undoing her buttons. She was far too susceptible herself, that was the trouble!

'I won't be a moment. There!'

She unpopped the buttons with desperate haste and dragged the dress over her head, glancing apprehensively down at herself. Thank God! White cotton! However, respectable though they were, it was still underwear and she fairly bounced into the bed, eager to hide beneath the covers.

'That's right, no coyness.'

Presently she felt the springs give as he, too, climbed

into the bed. She closed her eyes and lay there, pretending to be asleep. He blew out the candle and at once she became convinced that he was not lying down, as she was, but was sitting up and staring down at her with wolflike longing. *Suppose he was about to pounce on her at this very moment?*

'Sharon?'

She was so surprised to hear him speak that she jumped and squeaked. He laughed. A laugh, she realised, could be a sinister sound.

'So you aren't going to pretend to be asleep. Good, because I want to talk to you.'

Sharon groaned and gave an artificial yawn.

'Talk away then, but don't blame me if I fall asleep.'

'You won't fall asleep.' There was amusement in his voice again. 'I want to make a confession.'

'I am *not* a priest,' Sharon said firmly, and heard him chuckle.

'I guessed you weren't. One rarely encounters priests dressed in white bras and tiny white briefs. I cannot understand,' he continued irrelevantly, 'why you women wear such tiny undergarments. What *use* are they?'

'They serve a purpose,' Sharon said tartly. 'They're better than nothing, as I'm sure you'll agree.'

'No, I wouldn't, but we'll let that pass.' Sharon, to her annoyance, had to stifle a giggle. 'I'm about to make a confession, remember?'

'Yes, vaguely, but wouldn't it do tomorrow?'

'It could wait, of course, but there's something about being in bed with a woman which makes confession much easier.' This time Sharon did not rise to the bait and after a short pause he continued: 'I wanted you right from the first, *cara mia*. I liked the look of you, the feel of you in my arms, even the smell of you.' Another pause. Sharon's heart was beating rather fast and she didn't trust her voice to stay indifferent and impersonal so she remained silent. 'I made my first move and we got on very well, and just as I was poised for the second move, the serpent entered Eden.'

'Are you referring to Fortuna?' Sharon said sweetly. 'Because if so, she was there from the start.'

'No, I wasn't. I was referring to jealousy, as I'm very sure you knew! Several people had said Ridgeway was starting an affair with one of the nurses, and it was Fortuna who told me that the nurse in question was you. I looked at Ridgeway and decided you'd come to your senses soon enough but in the meantime you were so at ease with him and so defensive and touchy with me! Fool that I was, it didn't occur to me that my attitude to you coloured your attitude to me!

'Then Fortuna told me Ridgeway was contemplating marriage, and I overheard a conversation between you and he in the corridor one afternoon which I thought clinched it. "How's my best girl?" he said to you, and you said that she was very well, but busy. Naturally, I thought you meant yourself, but even that didn't stop me hoping that you'd see he wasn't right for you. I encouraged Fortuna to hang around me, hoping to make you jealous, I did everything in my power to get your attention. And then, earlier today, Susan told me her father had proposed and been accepted. She took it for granted that I knew to whom and I thought she was right, I was sure it was you. So I completely lost my head and went for you with every insult I could think of, putting all the blame on you for that fellow falling down the stairs, telling myself I'd had a lucky escape when you stood up for yourself. But all the time I was in misery, because I'd mishandled the whole thing and it looked as though I'd lost you.

'Then along came Sister Young and gave me one hell of a telling-off and in the course of it, she also told me that it was Julie Drummond who was to marry Ridgeway, not you.'

'I'm glad you didn't just hate me the way you seemed to,' Sharon said shyly. 'If that's all, Rodrigo, I think we'd better settle down now and try to get some sleep.' She was devoutly hoping to be able to get to sleep before her over-active imagination got going again!

'I haven't finished—how rude you are, trying to stop me in mid-confession! When Sister's words sank in all the bitterness and jealousy drained away and I had to be with you, tell you what had happened. So I invented a reason for going to Amalfi, so that I could give you a lift. Oh, I did have a patient I had to see, but I needn't have seen him today or even this week. I had something I wanted to ask you.'

'Go ahead,' Sharon said in a muffled voice. She had decided that the safest place to be was under the covers, with her back to the other occupant of the bed.

'How can I ask you to marry me when you've got your head under the blankets and your back to me?' Vitale sounded understandably irascible. 'Come out of it, and look at me when I'm speaking to you!'

By now, Sharon was wide awake and extraordinarily alert. She sat up and turned towards Vitale, holding the sheet protectively up against her chest. He immediately caught hold of her, dragging her into his arms. With his mouth against her hair he muttered: 'Will you marry me, my love?' and then moved his mouth down the side of her face in small kisses until he reached her mouth, and then he kissed her with a depth and intimacy which had Sharon's heart pounding at twice its normal speed and all her pulses quickening to keep time with it.

'Yes, I will,' she said breathlessly, when her mouth was freed. 'And now, Rodrigo, I think it's high time that one of us got out of this bed, otherwise . . .'

His mouth was moving, burning across her throat and upper breasts and his hands were moving too, stimulating her by languorous and seductive touches until she was helpless to resist him, wanting him as much as he wanted her.

It was only when she felt his hands on the fastening at the back of her bra that she drew back, and then she did so pretty sharply. Heavens, what was she thinking of? Now that she came to think of it, he'd behaved disgracefully, and yet he expected to be able to propose to her and make love to her in someone else's bed when she was only wearing flimsy underclothing. Just why this was so disgraceful she could not have said, but every instinct was warning her to get out of the bed before she did something she might well regret!

Abruptly, she slithered out of his grasp, taking one of the blankets and her pillow with her. She saw his face in the moonlight, looking grim and yet a little amused, and smiled sardonically across at him.

'Yes, I know, you wouldn't touch me, you'd spend the whole night happily in the same bed and not seduce me! But all the same, I'd feel a good deal safer on the floor.' Her eyes softened as she took in his rumpled dark hair, the gleam in his eyes, his sensuous mouth which had just been giving her such pleasure. 'Don't be cross, Rodrigo, I know you think you mean it, but . . . well, it isn't just you, there's me too, and I'm afraid I'd make a fool of myself. I'll be quite all right on the floor, honestly.'

He was sitting up, staring broodingly down at her. In the dark, she could not quite read his expression, but she was sure he was not angry with her, which was as well, because she could not bear his anger!

'All right, *cara mia*, you're probably right, though I wouldn't do anything you didn't like. Are you warm enough? Sure you can sleep down there? Goodnight then, my love.'

She was a little disappointed that he did not insist that she had the bed and he the floor, but it was only fair, she had been the one to make the first move. She lay down slowly, wrapping the blanket securely round her, cuddling into the pillow. It was not too uncomfortable, especially when one was as tired as she!

She had actually fallen asleep, she must have done, or she could not have been awakened by the scratching noise. A tiny, almost infinitesimal sound which some people could have completely ignored. But not Sharon. She stiffened. What ever was it?

Scratch, scritch, scratch. Her blood ran cold. It might, of course, be a cat somewhere in the house, trying to gain admittance to the room. Or it might be a rat—and she was sleeping on the floor!

She had no idea, afterwards, how she attained the bed, she thought it quite possible that she had flown, casting off her blanket, kicking aside her pillow, and landing right in the middle of Vitale's chest, tearing the blanket off him, clutching his naked shoulders, screaming 'Rats! There's rats, huge, big rats!' In a hissing, terrified whisper.

He was obviously half asleep still, for he dragged her beneath the blanket with him, put both his arms round her, and began to kiss her. Not one word did he say about the rats, or her sudden appearance on his chest, or even the fact that she was trembling like a leaf. Instead, his hands comforted, soothed, caressed, whilst his mouth excited.

Presently, warm and glowing and feeling wonderfully safe, Sharon said against his neck, 'Did you hear the rats? Suppose they come onto the bed? Have you anything you can throw at them?'

'I'll find something.' He was kissing her again now, in a very strange and exciting fashion, and Sharon had almost forgotten the threatening rodents when he drew back his arm and threw. Wide-eyed, she saw her bra perform a parabola through the air and land against the door. She gasped. She had not even noticed that it was no longer where it should have been.

'Rodrigo, what did you do that for? I'll be cold without it.'

'My darling, you said to throw something at the rats, so I did. I daresay that'll be enough to keep them at bay, but if not, I'm sure I can lay my hands on something else. Don't worry about them any more, you're quite safe here with me.'

'I don't think I'm safe with you,' Sharon remarked breathlessly five minutes later. 'I think I'm in deadly peril. But do you know, Rodrigo, I don't mind at all?'

'That's good, because there's no safety, not in love. Did I tell you how desperately I loved you, *cara*?'

His voice was shaking a little.

'I think you tried to tell me, darling Rodrigo, but it doesn't really matter, does it? It's the loving that matters, not the telling.'

Later, they lay in each other's arms and watched, through the tiny window, the sunrise.

Soon, Sharon knew, the men of the village would return from their fishing, and they would have to go off in one of the boats to Amalfi in search of petrol, and then they would go back to Sant' Agnello, and the idyll would be over.

Or would it? She turned her head, to look into the dark face so near her own. Vitale had said they would marry soon, because he could not bear to be without her, and they would buy a pretty little villa in Sant' Agnello so that he could come home often, from his work at the hospital. Was not that, in its way, an idyll? To spend the rest of your life with the man you loved?

He saw her watching him, and moved, to kiss her mouth.

'What are you thinking about, my love? And why are you smiling?'

Sharon returned the kiss, then rolled over on her stomach so that she could watch his face.

'I'm thinking of the future. Shall we be happy, Rodrigo, once we're man and wife?'

She expected an immediate and positive affirmative, but instead, he put a finger on her lips and smiled before answering.

'Perhaps. Oh, there will be days when you spit and scratch and I growl and grumble, because that's all part of life. I daresay you'll throw a few more of my bottles of wine at my head, and I daresay I'll tell you what a little cat you are. Happiness, my child, has to be worked for.'

'Yes. But being in love helps, doesn't it?'

'It does.' He cocked his head on one side, listening. 'Hear that? It's the boats, being dragged up the shingle. I'm afraid our night of love is over.'

Sharon knew that she was going bright red, but she couldn't help it, not when he said *night of love* in that matter-of-fact way. She changed the subject quickly.

'You make it sound sinful, but if it hadn't been for those rats . . .'

He leaned up on one elbow and reached for the wooden headboard of the bed. *Scratch, scratch, scratch* went his fingernails on the rough wood. Then, whilst Sharon was still taking it in, his arms went round her in a tight hug, making nothing of her half-hearted struggles.

'No sin, *cara mia*, just a little trickery for a wonderful gift—from me to you, from you to me. Don't turn your face away, kiss me!'

Outside the window the fishermen's feet crunched across the shingle and Sharon pulled herself out of Vitale's arms.

'Fooled, bamboozled and thoroughly in love with a rat,' she remarked, hopping out of bed and collecting her clothing. 'Will I never learn?'

Vitale lay back against the pillows and watched her through half-closed eyes. He looked more relaxed and happier than she had ever seen him.

'I hope not, my love.'

Mills & Boon

4 Doctor Nurse Romances
FREE

Coping with the daily tragedies and ordeals of a busy hospital, and sharing the satisfaction of a difficult job well done, people find themselves unexpectedly drawn together. Mills & Boon Doctor Nurse Romances capture perfectly the excitement, the intrigue and the emotions of modern medicine, that so often lead to overwhelming and blissful love. By becoming a regular reader of Mills & Boon Doctor Nurse Romances you can enjoy EIGHT superb new titles every two months plus a whole range of special benefits: your very own personal membership card, a free newsletter packed with recipes, competitions, bargain book offers, plus big cash savings.

**AND an Introductory FREE GIFT for YOU.
Turn over the page for details.**

John Harma He has worked in ace industry in m America. In the early '80s he his own film production company which he sold a few years later in order to write full time. He now lives in a pretty village close to Cambridge with his wife Abigail, a professional photographer. They have five children.

Also by John Harman

Money for Nothing
The Bottom Line
Called to Account

Dangerous Assets

John Harman

First published in Great Britain in 1996 by
HEADLINE BOOK PUBLISHING

First published in paperback in 1997 by
HEADLINE BOOK PUBLISHING

A HEADLINE FEATURE paperback

10 9 8 7 6 5 4 3 2 1

ISBN 0 7472 4443 X

Typeset by Avon Dataset Ltd, Bidford-on-Avon, Warks

Printed and bound in Great Britain by
Cox & Wyman Ltd, Reading, Berks

HEADLINE BOOK PUBLISHING
A division of Hodder Headline PLC
338 Euston Road
London NW1 3BH

For
Linda and Peter Smith

Chapter One

The man in the shadows shifted his grip on the gun.

The slight movement swished his raincoat and his body stiffened. In his business a rustling coat could get a person killed.

The man was dressed entirely in black and in the shadowy alcoves of the tenement landing he was almost invisible. Undetectable . . . as long as he stood still.

The man was sweating. It was sweltering inside the dark, decaying building. Outside, the oppressive heat of the tropical night had been lightened by a few showers. Luckily for him and the girl it had been raining hard when the car had dropped them and they'd hurried along the murky street.

No one had seen them.

In a neighbourhood where stomachs were empty, faces thin and eyes as sharp as needles, strangers were noticed. And he was a stranger with a gun. Strangers were a threat . . . unless they were tourists who had foolishly wandered away from the city's glittering boulevards.

Then they were victims.

But the man and the girl had made it to the tenement door unnoticed. Now, with the AKR nestling in the crook of his arm, it seemed only the rats knew he was waiting.

It was raining again.

Raindrops, falling from the broken roof, slapped loud and flat onto the stone-flagged floor at the bottom of the inky black stairwell. The monotonous sound echoed up into the vaulted darkness.

The tenement had four floors. The man was deep in the shadows of the second landing. He'd been there for an hour . . . sweating in the torrid heat, breathing the damp, familiar smells of the slum, listening to the soft, scuttling sound of rats on the floors above.

1

His sight, like an alley cat's, had grown accustomed to the night. Even so, he could see no further than the landing's rotting wooden balustrade. Beyond that was a black void.

He leaned carefully against the wall, feeling its dampness through his lightweight coat. It was tiring, all this waiting. He wished the man he had come to kill would hurry. Vaguely he wondered why such a rich and educated man should come to a place like this . . . a place only cockroaches could call home.

The heavy wooden door to the street creaked slowly open.

Immediately he was alert.

A wan, silver light washed over the flagstones of the hall, silhouetting a figure in the doorway.

It was the girl.

Like him she was dressed in a long, dark raincoat and a soft, felt hat. Her shadowy figure looked like a man's. He saw the dark shape of her head shake. There was no sign of their quarry.

The street door closed quietly and she was gone . . . back to the shadows of the alley across the street where she waited to follow their victim into the building. That was how they always did it: one in front, one behind . . . bracketing the target.

The man stared into the blackness, readjusting his sight to the night.

Yet not quite like a man's, he thought. Through the gloom and the enveloping raincoat he had caught a hint of roundness about the girl's silhouetted hips, sensed the fullness of her breasts in the sweep of the loose-fitting coat.

The man's mind was hauled to thoughts of her body: the surge of her superb breasts; the greedy need in her grinding thighs; the feel of her young, succulent flesh beneath his.

Soon, he thought, he would be inside her and it would be frenzied. It always was. Afterwards. After a kill.

They would do it for hours . . . like savage, sweaty animals, their frantic passion reaffirming the fact that they were alive . . . effacing the awful knowledge that, because of them, someone else was not.

Outside, a dog yelped.

Instantly the man's mind switched back to the reason he was there. His body tightened and he listened. The dog yelped again. It was the girl's signal. The quarry was close.

He took up his firing position, waiting for his prey to climb the stairs and walk directly into the barrel of the AKR. It would be easy. The girl, following the target like a panther, would wait at the bottom of the staircase. Should the victim see him and run she would assassinate him as he ran back down the stairs. Trapped between them their quarry was as good as dead already.

The man heard the scuffling of the rats on the floors above and smiled grimly. They sensed the coming blood.

The door below creaked slowly open, the ghostly glow from the street subtly changing the nature of the light in the stairwell. The waiting man saw the outline of a short, stocky figure framed for a moment in the doorway before the measured click of heels on stone echoed up the stairwell.

The silent watcher tensed. He was ready.

A sudden, shrieking scream ripped apart the dark silence.

'Doctor, look out!'

The waiting man jerked in shock.

'Doctor, doctor, be careful!'

A woman's screams, coming from one of the landings above, filled the stairwell with terror.

'Get out, run!'

The screeching pierced the assassin's brain . . . like the scream of an eagle trapped in a cave. He glanced down. The figure below was rigid, pinned to the flagstones.

The assassin cursed. This wasn't meant to happen. It was going wrong.

Swiftly he moved to the edge of the landing and peered up, carelessly risking his weight against the rotten balustrade. The anaemic light from the open door scarcely reached the stairwell. Above him was as black as a bats' belfry. Yet . . . maybe . . . he could just make out a shape, darker than the rest, leaning out over the void.

'Get out, doctor! Run!'

The hysterical shrieking came from the vague shape. The man raised his gun and fired.

The noise was stunning.

The hammering detonations, exploding against the stone walls, crashed back onto his head like blows. He screamed, his mouth a yawning gap to counterbalance the eardrum-perforating effects of the sound waves.

He sprayed half a magazine at the dark contour then ceased firing . . . and screaming.

Instantly his ears were assaulted by a single roaring boom,

3

followed by another . . . the unmistakable roar of a .45 automatic.

It wasn't a sound he should have heard. The girl always used a Steyr.

The man faced upwards for another moment. From what little he could see through the blackness and the wreathing wisps of grey, acrid smoke, the shadowy form was gone.

He shifted his position and looked down.

Stretched across the threshold of the street door was a body wearing a long, dark coat. Beyond it, just visible on the pavement, was a hat. There was no sign of the man he had come to kill.

The echoes of gunfire faded. The stairwell was as silent as a grave. No sound above, no movement below.

The man waited. Nothing.

He took a small torch from his pocket. Holding it with his arm extended, he flicked it on. From the darkest corner of the hallway came a sudden stab of flame and the bark of the .45. A heavy bullet smacked into the porous stone wall less than three feet away.

The man sighted the AKR at the spot where the flame had pinpointed the darkness and emptied the rest of the clip, roaring maniacally as the stuttering explosions hammered inside his skull.

Immediately the clip was finished he drew a full magazine from inside his raincoat, locking it home with a smooth, practised movement. He waited, peering hard into the dark for any sign of life below . . . glancing up for any sign of life above.

It could be *he* who was trapped now, he thought. Should the woman above still be alive and armed, then . . .

But he couldn't think about that. He had to finish the job and get away. Quickly.

Catlike, he ran fast and light down the stairs, keeping his gun trained on the part of the darkness at which he'd fired. The hairs on the back of his neck bristled at the thought of a bullet in the back. None came. He reached the ground floor close to the door . . . to where the pale light of the street washed across the flagstones around him.

He was exposed.

Somewhere in the shadows his quarry lay concealed.

He ran crouching and crabwise away from the light and stumbled over something metallic. It was a .45. He lashed out with his foot and sent it rattling across the flagstones. The noise echoed eerily in the dark silence.

In a far corner of the floor was a shadowy bundle. The man flicked on his torch. This time there was no returned fire. He moved closer. The bundle was the body of a man and the man was dead. Most of the rounds from the AKR had caught him in the head and chest.

Switching off his torch, the assassin turned and hurried to the doorway where he crouched beside the girl.

There were two holes close together in the cloth of her coat. In the pallid street light he could see blood, scarcely visible against the coat's sombre colour. The girl's eyes were closed. She was wheezing gently. The man bent his head to her chest and heard the bubbling in her breath as the blood filled her lungs.

Gently he took hold of her hand and pressed it momentarily against his cheek. All his expectations of sex had gone . . . evaporated into fantasy. He knew he wasn't going to enjoy her that night. Or any other night. Soon her warm, lovely body would be cold and lifeless . . . the only creatures to enjoy her now, the worms. In the equatorial heat they would be wriggling inside her soon enough.

He told himself later that what he did next was an act of humanity . . . an isolated incident of kindness in a predatory life. But inside he knew it wasn't. Inside, he knew it for what it was . . . an act of self-preservation.

He didn't know how long she might live . . . couldn't know if there was not some clever doctor who might keep her alive just long enough for her to gasp a name. His was a name she had gasped often enough at the height of her frenzy.

The man stood up, took one last look at her lovely face and inserted the gun barrel into the girl's gaping mouth.

He squeezed the trigger.

He didn't stop to see what havoc he'd wreaked. She was beyond them all now and that was enough.

He stepped over the body and looked along the street. His heart surged in panic. The car wasn't there.

It had been no more than sixty seconds since the man who lay tumbled and lifeless in a corner of the hallway had walked into the tenement. Throughout those hectic seconds the assassin had maintained a deadly calm; adapting and reacting to the flickering shift of events with a cool, detached intent. But now he was afraid.

5

Without the car he wouldn't make it out of the neighbourhood . . . wouldn't get five blocks before the police, or the denizens of the mean streets, got him.

The warm rain drifted obliquely through the drab light of a street lamp a block away. The man peered into the charcoal gloom. The street was deserted.

It wouldn't stay that way for long.

Then he saw it . . . the dark, square shape of the car, sitting silently halfway along the next block. He couldn't understand it . . . it wasn't in the plan that he should have to run a hundred metres to the car. Like everything else that night, the getaway plan had gone to hell. He cursed quietly and started to run, making no attempt to hide the gun. There was a chance he might have to use it.

He reached the car, yanked open the door and threw himself in beside the driver.

'Where the hell have you been?' The driver was American.

'Drive.'

The driver snatched a glance over his shoulder. 'Where's the girl?'

'She didn't make it.' It was an appropriate epitaph. Short and brutal. Like her life.

The American was young but a good driver. He drove fast, though not so fast that the car's suspension might be damaged by the potholes in the street. They turned a corner. The bright lights of the city were eight blocks away. The assassin counted them off. He heard the wailing of the sirens just as they reached the swirling stream of vehicles on the boulevard.

The driver eased the car into the traffic, heading for the centre of the city.

The man took off his hat and placed the AKR carefully on the floor close to his feet. The presence of cars and people, the glow of bright lights and the sound of laughter from the pavement cafés, crowded despite the intermittent rain, brought him the comfort of anonymity.

'What happened?'

'There was a woman.' The man spoke softly and slowly. 'Waiting, hidden.' He shrugged and turned to stare through the rear window. The car circled the busy city square four times, the man watching for any headlights that might be following. Satisfied they were unaccompanied, the driver took the road leading towards the airport.

'Go on.'

'The woman warned him. She called him doctor.'

'Doctor?' the driver repeated. He was quiet for a moment. 'What did you do about her? The woman?'

'I did what I could,' the man said simply.

'What happened to the girl?'

'She was following him. Into the tenement. She was in the doorway with the light behind her. He had a gun . . .' His voice trailed off.

For a while they drove in silence. The driver turned on the windscreen wipers. Their metronomic beat had a tranquil, almost hypnotic effect on the man.

'I never knew him carry a gun before,' the driver said quietly.

The man stared out at the darkened buildings of the city's suburbs. 'In that neighbourhood he would need something. A gun would give him an edge. He was a stranger and he was not a big man.'

The driver shot him a penetrating glance.

'It went wrong,' the man continued in a sad voice. 'It was the woman. I did not think anyone would be watching out for him.' He turned and looked hard at the driver. 'You said he would not be expecting the hit . . . that he had no friends in that part of the city.'

'That's what we thought.' There was a pause. 'Is he dead?' the driver asked.

'He is dead.' The words were quietly dignified. Almost proud.

They came in sight of the airport, the bright terminal buildings like ocean liners on a calm, dark sea. The man pressed a button and his passenger window smoothly opened. The rain had stopped and the humid night air was tinged with the smell of oleander and aviation fuel.

'You have my money and passport?'

'Sure.' The driver turned the car into a car park and drove beyond the harsh glare of the sodium lamps towards a dark corner.

'Why stop here?' queried the man. 'It's a long way to walk back.'

'You don't want anyone seeing you, do you? Here.' The driver pulled an American passport and a bulky envelope out of a pocket and passed them to the man. 'You said he wasn't very big,' he continued: 'how tall was he?'

In the gloom of the car, the man was counting the banknotes

7

spilling out from the envelope. 'One metre, sixty-five maybe.'

The American shook his head impatiently. 'What the hell is that in feet and inches?'

The man was inspecting the passport. 'Maybe five and a half feet,' he murmured. The car was silent as he examined the passport. 'Why?' he asked.

There was no reply and after a moment the man looked up.

The object in the driver's hand was dark and solid. It had a long, bulky barrel. Pointing at him.

'You dumb bastard.'

The man heard the young American's voice from far away. 'You whacked the wrong guy.'

Something mechanical clicked in the assassin's brain and slowly the long-forgotten words began to turn. Words he'd not heard since he was a white-surpliced boy, standing perfectly still before the altar.

The ancient incantation echoing in his memory... *Santo Padre!, mi vida no ha servido para nada* ...

The gun moved up, level with his face. He stared at it. And at the eyes beyond. It had all gone wrong, he thought. If there was a hell, then he would be seeing the girl much sooner than he expected.

The silent recitation reached *absolutamente nada* before the .38 bullet from the silenced gun hit him above the left eyebrow and blew his confused brains out of the car window and into eternity.

Chapter Two

'I don't need this shit.'

'Sir?' The fresh-faced rookie sitting next to the driver turned at the sound of his voice.

Mullhane, hunched in the back of the car, glowered at him and grunted dismissively. The young man's face reddened and he turned back to his front.

Mullhane scowled at the lines of cars and black cabs going nowhere in the Strand. It was raining and the traffic was backed up as far as Hyde Park Corner. It had taken twenty minutes to crawl a mile from Grosvenor Square. At this rate, he figured, it would take more than an hour to reach the Bank.

In the old days, Mullhane thought darkly, a traffic jam – even a traffic jam in the heart of London – might have been a set-up. The elaborate ploy of an enemy, orchestrated to stage a kidnap or open up on the car with machine pistols.

In the old days a traffic jam meant danger. It made the heart race. Not any more. Now, all a traffic jam signified was that the system was completely screwed up . . . that the world was going to hell in a handbasket.

Barney Mullhane was thickset and medium height, with blue, Irish eyes and short, spiky grey hair. He was sixty and grizzled. Like an old buffalo, he thought.

An old buffalo whose world had changed and who didn't care too much for the changes. Even though he had played a major part in bringing them about. Even though he was one of the winners in the brave new order.

Barney Mullhane was a Cold War warrior. He had been fighting the Soviets and their allies ever since he'd joined the Agency, way back before the Kennedy Administration. Mullhane had been involved in every major initiative against the Communists from Cuba to Afghanistan. He had fought a forty-year war. And he, and the Agency, had won it.

Now, he reflected, the Eastern Europeans were independent, the old Soviet Union had collapsed and the KGB was disintegrating. Instead of spying, most of its best people were writing their memoirs. These days, to believe in Communism was as ludicrous as to avow the theory of a flat earth. Marx, Engels and the rest of them were in the dustbin of history.

Close to the end of a long and successful career, Senior Section Chief Mullhane should have been content. Yet often he thought of the old days with nostalgia. At least then, even in his shadowy world of espionage, he had known who the enemy was. Today's enemies were different. A motley bunch of Muslims, a whole slew of assorted raghead terrorists – he grunted with contempt, even organised criminals. He leaned back in his seat and shook his head. He hadn't joined the CIA to be a goddam policeman.

He stared out of the window as the car inched forward.

And even more bizarre than the new enemies, he reflected, were the new masters. The money men, the slick-suited lawyers and bankers, economists and accountants. They called the shots now. He hated them, with their economic models, their budgets and their cost calculations. To him they were a bunch of yelping mongrels . . . bean-counters endlessly debating whether Uncle Sam could afford to be a world power. He sighed as the car stopped yet again.

He was an old buffalo being led by yapping dogs.

Often there were times when he longed for the old days. Times like now.

Thirty minutes later the car drew into the kerb of Threadneedle Street. The rookie leapt out, glanced around for a moment then opened the rear door. Mullhane got out, gazed up at the massive curtain wall confronting him then marched across the narrow pavement, past the enormous bronze doors and towering Corinthian columns into the Bank of England.

Just inside the busy, high-ceilinged vestibule were a couple of gatekeepers in pink tailcoats and black top hats. Mullhane eyed them stonily, thinking how typical it was of the goddam Brits to have their Central Bank filled with flunkeys in fancy dress.

He gave one his name. The gatekeeper indicated a solidly built man standing to one side of the entrance hall. The man stepped forward. He wasn't a flunkey. He was wearing a suit and had the kind of hard, penetrating eyes that men in Mullhane's business had. Eyes which took in everything and gave away nothing.

The man asked Mullhane to follow him. They mounted a broad staircase and walked along a long, wood-panelled corridor into the heart of the massive building. The man stopped at a pair of polished mahogany doors. He knocked and, following a muffled summons, showed Mullhane inside and closed the door quietly behind him.

It was a large, elegant room with a high, ornately corniced ceiling and rococo mouldings on its pale green walls. A couple of dozen smart-suited men and women were standing around, talking quietly and drinking coffee. A tall, thin man with ice-blue eyes, fair hair and a face as sharp as a sabre, detached himself from the group. He marched across the room as if it were a parade ground.

'Mr Mullhane, I'm Steven Timmison.' The man had a clipped, public-school accent. He shook Mullhane's hand. 'I'm glad you could make it. Come into the parlour and have some coffee.'

'The what?'

Timmison laughed briefly. 'Ah, yes, I'm sorry, it's your first visit isn't it? Here in the Bank they call their meeting rooms parlours.' Mullhane noticed he said it in that faintly deprecating manner the Brits always used when alluding to their revered traditions.

He also noticed that Timmison had referred to the people at the Bank as *they*. As if he wasn't one of them. A frown scudded across Mullhane's face. If the guy wasn't a banker, he reflected, then what was he?

Timmison went off to organise coffee and Mullhane looked around. In the centre of the room was a long polished board table with namecards and papers placed down both sides, whilst along the length of the opposite wall were a succession of tall Georgian windows overlooking a sunless courtyard. The courtyard had a small, well-tended lawn. The grass, glistening in the late May rain, was virescent against the pale, grey stone blocks of the building.

Mullhane knew about half the people in the room. There was a guy from the FBI, another from the DEA, a guy and a young, good-looking woman from Justice, a woman he knew from the Criminal Investigation Division of the IRS; a couple of guys from Treasury, and a man from the Customs Service. He noticed that most of the Americans were, like him, Washington based and senior people in their agencies. They had flown in especially for the meeting.

He knew a couple of the Brits. One was a senior man from Scotland Yard's Special Branch. The other belonged to a security department the British did not acknowledge existed.

Two Americans to whom he was introduced were from the US Federal Reserve System, the American equivalent of the Bank of England. The rest of the people were Brits and, like the guys from the Fed, money men.

All told there were twenty-two of them, seventeen men and five women. Twenty years ago, he thought, there wouldn't have been any women. Some of them looked not much older than his granddaughter. Twenty years ago he would have been one of the youngest men in the room. Now, he was probably the oldest guy there. With one exception. John Kilbride.

Dressed in a dark, superbly cut three-piece suit, Kilbride was talking quietly to the good-looking woman from Justice. He must, thought Mullhane, be seventy at least. Yet standing tall and erect, with his patrician features and mane of white hair, he scarcely looked a day over fifty.

John Kilbride was a minor legend. A war hero from an old, though impoverished, Southern family, he had married into a family even older than his own and, after qualifying as an attorney, had moved to Washington. Within a short time he had graduated into the enchanted inner circle of power and become a counsellor to President Eisenhower.

Kilbride's speciality was advice in business and finance. He had proved himself to be one of those rare men who transcended party politics for, after Eisenhower, he had become an adviser to Kennedy and subsequently served on the staffs of Nixon, Ford and Reagan. He was an *eminence grise*, an attorney who for almost forty years had been a distinguished counsellor and confidant to a succession of presidents.

Kilbride's eldest boy, Philip, was the senior senator for his state and was being talked of as the Party's favourite son. A lot of people inside the loop reckoned Phil Kilbride could go all the way. He had the looks and the charisma and the tough, balls-out politics that seemed to go down well in middle America. Above all, Philip had the money to make it.

Mullhane glanced at Kilbride and, not for the first time, wondered if he was looking at the father of the next President.

He eyed the older man warily. Kilbride was a suit – a lawyer and close to the money men and the bean-counters. Yet Mullhane had good reason to know the guy was no mewling poodle.

Kilbride was tough . . . and very influential. He was also a friend of the CIA . . . one of the few suits who were. Kilbride had helped the Agency out on a number of occasions: he was trusted enough to know where a lot of the bodies were buried. And as an adviser to various Senate appropriations committees – including those that allocated and agreed CIA funds – the man was extremely powerful.

Mullhane smiled quietly to himself as he watched the old guy charming the shit out of the woman from Treasury. Kilbride wasn't his boss, he reflected. Hell, no, the crafty old fox went one better than that. Kilbride was the guy who *paid* his boss.

Mullhane's attention was drawn off the older man by the sound of Steven Timmison calling the meeting to order. Everyone in the room moved to their places at the long polished table. Next to each namecard was a slim file with the word 'Sensitive' stencilled across its manilla cover. They took their seats and started skimming the documents inside the files.

Timmison, sitting at the head of the table, began. His tone was incisive.

'This meeting is confidential. No recording is being made; there will be no minutes; no one is to take notes and the files in front of you must remain here.'

He paused, then continued in the same commanding tone. 'Tomorrow morning, regulators from the Bank of England, from the Federal Reserve System and from the Central Banks of Canada, Luxembourg, Italy, Hong Kong, France, and other countries will meet in this room to consider a report prepared under Section forty-one of the British Banking Act. At the end of that meeting they will vote to shut down the Exchange Bank of International Industry and Trade.'

There was a murmur from those around the table. A few of them had heard faint rumours but for most the sudden closure was a shock.

'The shutdown,' Timmison continued, 'has been agreed by the Governor of the Bank of England who has cleared it with the Chancellor of the Exchequer and the Prime Minister. The

13

President, along with the Chairman of the Federal Reserve System, has also been told.

'It will happen on Friday. It will be coordinated by all the countries concerned. We have agreed with the United States Federal Reserve to schedule it for 5 p.m. New York time. After the close of trading. That should lessen any disruption on the dollar markets and should allow us time over the weekend to prepare for the flak. The Official Receiver will move in first thing on Saturday morning. He will immediately put the Bank into liquidation.'

There was a moment's silence, punctuated by the sonorous ticking of a large case clock standing in a corner. Mullhane, sitting further down the opposite side of the table from John Kilbride, shot him a look. The older man's face was impassive.

'How do you know the regulators will vote to shut the bank down?' someone asked.

Timmison's faint smile reappeared. 'Bank regulators are not a democratic debating society. They'll have no choice. Not when they've seen the evidence. The papers before you are just a summary of the report prepared by the Exchange Bank's auditors. That runs to a hundred pages. It's a damning indictment of the bank.'

There was another pause as they considered Timmison's words.

'There's going to be a hell of a row about it,' one of the British bankers pointed out. 'The political fallout will be considerable.'

Timmison nodded seriously. 'I'm afraid that's true.'

'Then why pull the plug so suddenly?' The question came from John Kilbride. 'Wouldn't it be politically more expedient to take things slowly? Why not wind the bank down?'

'Definitely not.' Timmison was curt. 'To wind it down would give the people behind it warning. The Exchange Bank is holding billions of dollars' worth of demand deposits. If they knew our intentions, the organised criminals behind the Bank, as well as the crooks and fraudsters using it, would immediately move their assets upstream. They would withdraw their deposits and disappear.'

'Yeah, but this is helluva short notice,' Mullhane interjected. 'The Agency has a number of covert operations involving this bank. Right now we're using it to push funds through to some people we're working with. We need at least a month to clear out our operations . . . pull all the threads straight. Otherwise

14

we're gonna have some of our people left high and dry, with their dicks swinging in the wind.'

Some of the women frowned at his words. Mullhane ignored them. There had been a recent Federal directive instructing all CIA employees at Langley to avoid the use of sexist language. Mullhane had thrown it in the trash can. Old buffaloes, he thought, had much in common with old dogs. The politically correct crap was no more than a set of new tricks.

'I'm sympathetic but we cannot give you more notice. That's it. I'm sorry.'

'But that's not reasonable,' someone else protested. 'The CIA isn't the only agency using this bank for undercover work. The DEA needs time to pull out too.'

'Yes, it's a pity you are acting so suddenly.' It was one of the British intelligence men, his voice slow and measured. 'The Exchange Bank has been useful to us as well. A number of terrorist organisations have accounts there in the names of front men and nominees. We've been monitoring the IRA, Hamas, the Fatar Revolutionary Council and a few others through the movement of their money. We know what they're buying and where they're investing. That's prime intelligence. It'll be a blow to lose all that.'

'I'm aware the Exchange Bank has been useful to the intelligence agencies,' Timmison conceded. He nodded in Mullhane's direction. 'It's common knowledge the CIA was using it to make life hot for the Russians in Afghanistan.'

Mullhane saw the bankers around the table raise their eyebrows. Clearly it wasn't common knowledge to them.

He shrugged. 'They'd made it bad for us in Vietnam, we figured we'd do the same to them in Afghanistan. The Exchange Bank is thick on the ground in that part of the world. It was the perfect conduit to move money to the Mujahideen. To buy arms.'

'You mean secret money? Untraceable?' one of the bankers asked in a critical tone.

Mullhane nodded. 'Sure. That's what this bank is good at.' The money men looked disapproving.

'So the CIA cooperated with the Exchange Bank in breaking the law,' another said accusingly. Mullhane scowled. It was the kind of typical, half-assed remark he expected from a bean-counter.

'It was an approved covert operation against the Soviets,' he growled.

'We know all about the CIA's covert operations,' someone further down the table said maliciously. 'Frequently they're illegal. And you're not even good at moving the money.'

'The problem with the CIA,' observed one of the British bankers laconically, 'is that no one there can read a balance sheet.'

A laugh rippled around the table. Even the men from the Fed were amused. Mullhane felt himself reddening. Goddam money men. He opened his mouth to retaliate, then caught John Kilbride's eye. Kilbride shook his head imperceptibly. Mullhane subsided into his seat and gritted his teeth.

'Gentlemen, gentlemen,' Timmison brought the meeting to order sternly, 'we are not here to score points off each other.' He leaned forward. 'The point is, the Russians got out of Afghanistan in '89. Their espionage operations against the West have been scaled down. The KGB is a spent force . . . as are the other East European intelligence services. Whatever benefits the intelligence community once derived from the illegal skills of the Exchange Bank is beside the point. We have decided the bank must be shut down. And quickly. The threat it represents outweighs any benefit the security services may still be getting from it.'

'Threat? What kind of threat?' It was John Kilbride.

Timmison stared at him, then at the other faces along the table. 'Look at the map,' he said quietly.

'What?'

'You have a map of the Bank's branch network in your files. Look at it.'

There was a rustling as they retrieved the photocopied maps. On them were hundreds of little red dots, the Bank's major branches throughout the world. Everyone frowned at the maps for a few moments then, mystified, looked along the table to Timmison.

'So, what's this supposed to tell us?' asked the man from the Fed.

'Doesn't it strike you as odd,' Timmison said dryly, 'that the Exchange Bank, with branches in more than fifty-five countries, doesn't have one branch in the world's most powerful economy?'

'Hell,' retorted the man from the Fed triumphantly, 'that's because the US never rated this bank. It's registered in Luxembourg yet it's dollar denominated. The Fed isn't happy about a lot of US dollars swilling about in the hands of some

16

itty-bitty bank out of nowhere. We have a different attitude to you British about banks. We don't like offshore banking. You people here live off it. We like tight regulation . . . London is more deregulated. We never thought the Exchange Bank was solid. So we refused it a licence to set up in the States. We,' he said proudly, 'kept it out of America.'

'Actually,' said Timmison coldly, 'I was referring to Japan.'

The man's head jerked back as if his face had been slapped.

'In Switzerland,' Timmison continued impassively, 'it has just three branches. In fact, the bank's branches are mainly concentrated in South America, the Gulf, Pakistan, India and the Far East.'

'So what?' someone observed. 'It's a Third World bank. That's where you'd expect them to be.'

Timmison ignored the interruption. 'In Colombia, the Exchange Bank has twenty branches holding more than eleven billion dollars in customer deposits. The three branches in Switzerland hold less than a billion. That can only indicate one thing.'

There was a long silence.

'Drugs,' said the young woman from Justice.

'Exactly. We now have absolute proof that the Exchange Bank of International Industry and Trade was formed by organised criminals for the benefit of organised crime. It has become the primary conduit of Mafia money. The main route through which much of the world's drug money is laundered.'

There was another subdued murmur around the table.

'I don't need to tell you how serious that is,' Timmison continued. 'The influx of more than two hundred billion dollars a year from the proceeds of organised crime – mainly drug dealing – into the world's economies is causing dangerous distortions in our financial systems. Along with the rest of our economic problems, the distortions in global money flows caused by narco-dollars are endangering world economic stability. Frankly, the economic effects of organised crime, particularly narcotics, are devastating.

'What about the moral effects?' asked the girl from Justice quietly.

Timmison stared at her as if she were a child. 'The moral effects are irrelevant to this discussion,' he stated in a sharp, dry, voice. 'So,' he added, 'are the legal issues. Morals are for individuals, laws for nations. Economics apply universally. In the end, economic issues are the only ones that matter.'

Mullhane snorted loudly.

'It's vital,' Timmison went on, 'that we stop this invidious movement of criminal money. Even more so now that gangsters in Russia and Eastern Europe are organising themselves into their own Mafia. They're already laundering their proceeds through banks in the West. Closing the Exchange Bank will be a major step in reducing the effects of organised crime.'

'Arresting the criminals would be a better way,' commented one of the bankers.

'Easier said than done,' said Timmison. 'Especially when they're involved in drugs. Narcotics is like any other business. It's based on three things: manpower, materials and money. As far as manpower is concerned . . . well, most of you know how useless it is arresting dealers on the streets. There's always plenty more where they came from. Similarly with the product. Far more class A drugs get through customs than are seized.

'No,' he shook his head, 'it's the money where they're vulnerable. What do they do with it? How to hide it without it being traced? That's their problem. There isn't a big enough hole in the ground for them to hide two hundred billion dollars of profit every year. As an asset, all that money is useless unless its provenance – its origins – can be obscured. Unless it can be changed from illicit income to lawful resource.

'Asset redeployment,' he went on: 'the Mafia and their associates are the world's experts at it. What the economists call capital flight and the rest of us know as money laundering. And the Exchange Bank was set up to be a major player in the business. We estimate it has been washing more than fifty billion dollars every year for the last twenty-five years.'

He paused, then added quietly, 'The Exchange Bank is a trillion-dollar laundry.'

There was a long silence. The flat sound of the ticking clock filled the room. Barney Mullhane stirred in his seat. Something was bothering him. He couldn't put his finger on it. Why, he wondered, was he sitting in this room listening to this supercilious Brit giving him a lecture about money laundering?

'Is that what you intend telling the press?' someone asked. 'After the shut down? That it's a Mafia bank?'

'Definitely not,' Timmison responded sharply. 'That

information stays inside this room. We'll be announcing that the auditors have discovered malfeasance on a massive scale. Fraudulent conversion of deposits, fictitious loans, that kind of thing. All of which is perfectly true. The bank is going into liquidation for good reason. A lot of money is unaccounted for. By going the commercial route we can hide what we know about the money laundering. We can also use a firm of accountants to track the money. In a situation like this, they'll have considerably more power than the police. The Serious Fraud Office and other agencies will remain in the background.'

'What about the money the bank has already laundered? How will it be traced?' one of the British bankers asked.

'That will be the liquidators' job. The practice we are appointing are one of the biggest in the country. One of the best at following financial tracks. Moving money, even secret money, leaves a trail. Although it may take years, I'm convinced they'll trace most of it.

'Of course,' he added, 'a fallout from their work may be that we uncover evidence of money laundering, tax evasion and that kind of thing, against some of the big names in organised crime. It would be a nice bonus if we could put a few of them away.'

'Don't expect them to cooperate,' the man from the FBI said bleakly. 'Those guys play for keeps. They're not going to take kindly to a bunch of accountants trying to trace their money and prove it's laundered. Your liquidators will need protection. Otherwise, they could wind up finding themselves liquidated.'

'Naturally we shall be looking to the law enforcement agencies to give them protection.' Timmison replied.

'So what happens once you've shut the bank down?' asked the woman from the IRS.

'The Bank of England will apply to the court for a Winding Up Order. Once that's been granted, the bank's assets will be frozen by the liquidators and ultimately seized by the British Treasury.'

Suddenly, Mullhane realised. This was all domestic stuff – British – he thought. *That's* what was bothering him. Why the hell did he need to know all this? Why was he here?

Timmison caught the look on his face. 'Something wrong, Mr Mullhane?'

Mullhane shrugged. 'Yeah. I want to know why I'm here.'

A surprised look passed over Timmison's aristocratic features. 'Pardon?'

'Why am I here? Why are any of us here?' He indicated the other Americans seated around the long, polished table.

'I don't understand.'

'No? Then I'll explain. You've had a whole bunch of us fly across the pond to listen to what is basically a British matter. I don't get it. Why? There's gotta be more to it than closing this goddam bank. You could have told us all this by coded fax.'

Timmison's faintly superior smile reappeared. 'It does affect you in America, you know. It's already been pointed out that the Exchange Bank is dollar denominated. And a great deal of the laundered money has found a home in the United States.'

'Sure, I know that,' Mullhane replied. 'But you've got people here from pretty well every law enforcement and intelligence agency in the US. Why? I've got the feeling there's something you're not telling us.'

The room was quiet. Everyone stared at Timmison. His face was impenetrable. After a moment he nodded. 'Yes, you're right. There is something else.' His voice was slow and measured. 'The fact is, we have uncovered evidence that the Exchange Bank is operating in a big way in the US.'

'The hell it is,' responded the man from the Fed. 'I told you, we didn't grant the bank a licence.'

'That hasn't kept it out. The Exchange Bank, or more accurately the people behind it, has been buying into the American banking system for years. Hiding behind respectable names and nominees.'

Only the ticking case clock punctured the silence in the room.

'Go on,' said the man from the Fed quietly.

Timmison shrugged: 'Offshore branches of the Exchange Bank have been lending apparently legitimate individuals and organisations money to buy into selected American banks and S&Ls. In most cases the target banks and Saving and Loan Associations were in difficulties. Naturally they were delighted when these individuals or organisations said they were prepared to invest. Usually the investors bought convertible bonds, waited for the stock prices to rise then converted the bonds into stock.' Timmison smiled ruefully. 'Very neat.

'And,' he went on, 'so long as no single investor owned more than five per cent of the equity, it wasn't necessary to declare an interest to your SEC. So the Exchange Bank has built up big stakes – majority holdings in most cases – in a large number of

American banks through lots of separate investors. And there is no evidence that any of the loans it made to the legitimate investors have been retired.'

'What the hell does that mean?' someone asked.

It was the Fed man who replied, his voice low and intense. 'It means that if the loans have not been repaid, then the Exchange Bank can legally take possession of the stock in the banks and S&Ls that it's been holding as collateral. And it can pass that stock on as loan repayment to other people. People who have supposedly made loans to the bank.'

'Those other people being organised criminals,' someone ventured.

'Right.'

'Why not just take the shares back?' someone suggested.

'It's not that simple,' the man retorted. 'In the event of default the shares are legally owned by the individuals who hold them as collateral. It's a can of worms. The Fed can stop it by issuing "cease and desist" orders but, even so, it'll take years of motions and court orders to crowbar the stock away from those guys.

'And in the meantime, a bunch of crooks own a big piece of the American finance industry,' the man from Treasury moaned. 'I don't believe it,' he went on, 'I just don't believe it.'

From around the table came a series of loud, growling murmurs.

'I'm afraid it's true,' Timmison announced. 'We have absolute proof that the Mafia controls a large number of your banks and Saving and Loans.'

'If you're right,' the man continued, 'it could put the American economy into reverse for years. Think of the publicity . . . the media fallout. Jesus, if the American people think organised crime is controlling our finance industry it'll push hundreds of billions of dollars overseas. Money will be moving offshore like water off a rock. Wall Street and the bond market will be in terminal shock. The big institutions will be shovelling money into Eurobonds like there's no tomorrow.'

There was a loud murmur of assent from the group as Mullhane shot another glance along the table. John Kilbride's face was grave.

'Jeeesus,' the man wailed.

'Wait a minute. Just hold up a moment here.' It was John Kilbride, his voice dominating the room. He waited for the noise

21

around the table to subside. 'What I want to know is . . . how the hell do you know all this? What makes you so sure?'

Immediately the room fell silent.

Timmison looked along the table at a tunnel of startled faces. When he spoke his voice was flat but assured. 'The same way we know, after years of probing and getting nowhere, exactly where the auditors had to look to prove the Exchange Bank was corrupt. The same way we know so much about the money laundering. We have someone on the inside.'

Chapter Three

The train was pulling in.

Panting, she ran up the station stairs, over the bridge and onto a platform crowded with suits.

She struggled onto the train and threaded her way through the carriages to the first-class compartment. All the seats were taken. She sighed. The point of the first-class season ticket had been to ensure she got a seat. It had been a waste of money. More often than not she stood for the forty minutes that, on a good day, it took the train to get to London.

A man seated close to where she was rocking with the motion of the train and struggling with her paper, spent the journey peering round his *Telegraph* at her legs.

Jamie had made her late again. Sometimes he was fine. Then she could leave him playing happily with Astrid whilst, unobtrusively, she left the cottage. Other times, especially after a happy weekend, he would cling to her, crying and mumbling for her not to leave.

This Monday morning had been particularly difficult. Finally she'd been forced to gently disengage his grip and shepherd him into the outstretched arms of the smiling, anxious-eyed Astrid. Today was one of those days when she would arrive at Waterloo with aching legs and a heavy heart.

The train took almost an hour and, as usual, the short journey on the City Line was indescribable. She arrived at the magnificent entrance lobby of Rolay Richard's tower block on the corner of Eastcheap at nine fifty-five.

The uniformed men at the polished, limed-ash reception desk eyed her appreciatively as she hurried across the rose-coloured marble floor. The huge atrium, with its high glass panels and thirty-foot weeping fig trees, sprouting from their bulky, pink-granite rotundas, towered above her.

23

'Mr Hawick was asking for you, Miss Semmington,' one of the security men called. 'He wants you to go straight to his office.'

Melissa was fixing her ID to her lapel as she walked. She turned and caught the glint in the man's eyes as he stared at the fullness of her breasts beneath the dark fabric of the Louis Féraud suit.

At least, she thought, I've got some appeal left. Even if it is from some overweight gorilla who's into uniforms.

'Thanks.' She gave him a brief smile.

She took the lift to the fourteenth floor and stepped through the whispering doors into a vast, busy, open office area which, the designers said, had been ergonomically planned for optimum working conditions.

She made her way towards her office, past clusters of desks, cabinets and shelves called workstations. They were divided from each other by pastel-coloured partitions. Slotted between the partitions were small meeting and reception areas, little enclaves with low, vivid green easy chairs and white melamine coffee tables. Across the oatmeal-carpeted floor, tall, pale grey filing cabinets stood against the walls. Palms, in fat white pots, were everywhere. The vast office was filled with the subtle hum of word processors, the soft clicking of keyboards and the warbling of telephones.

Of the sixteen floors in the building fifteen were exactly the same. All artfully designed, expensively appointed and, in Melissa's opinion, completely without character.

As a partner, she had an office of her own. Despite Nigel Hawick's request she went there first. She needed to call home. Nigel was her boss but Jamie was her son.

She opened the door of the big, glass cubicle and heard the faint hiss of the air conditioning as the pressure inside the room changed. The office was set on an outside wall of the open-plan area. It faced east. From its huge smoky plate-glass windows she had a spectacular view of the river snaking away towards the Isle of Dogs and the buildings at Canary Wharf.

She dropped her briefcase onto the desk and punched the single button on the phone that automatically dialled home.

She was surrounded by glass. The office's inside wall looked out onto the open-plan area whilst its side walls abutted onto other expensively furnished fishtanks. In the one next door a

24

well-built man with a shock of dark hair stood up from his desk, walked across the office and rapped on the glass which partitioned them. Melissa looked up to see him gesturing to her to come into his office. She put on a bright, sickly smile and nodded vigorously, impatient for Astrid to pick up the phone.

'I'm sorry I'm late,' she said a few moments later as she closed his door. 'Jamie was a bit awkward this morning. It was difficult to get away.'

He waved her apologies aside. He wasn't concerned about her timekeeping . . . nor about Jamie.

'Did you see Sunday's papers?' His voice was eager.

She smiled to herself. Much of Nigel Hawick's Sundays were spent reading the business sections of the papers. He had a wife who stayed at home, took care of the house and cooked his meals. He also had two teenage children who were away at school much of the time. Two *normal* children. Hawick had time to read the papers.

As always, she had devoted her weekend to Jamie. To acceding to his every wish. Playing with him, taking him for walks across the fields, reading to him. So much of her life was spent away from him – twelve-hour days at the office . . . days, sometimes weeks, abroad. The weekend was sacred. It was dedicated to Jamie. It belonged to him.

Over that weekend she had managed a few minutes with Saturday's *Financial Times* and an hour late the previous evening with the *Observer*.

'You read about the shutdown of the Exchange Bank?'

This time she smiled openly. Even she, immersed as she was in her son, could hardly have missed the news of that. It had been the lead story everywhere. From Saturday morning onwards.

'Yes of course.'

'Did you see the article in the *Sunday Times*?'

'No.' She shook her head. Her hair moved like a gentle wave. It was shoulder-length, a rich, deep, copper colour. In the fluorescent lights the highlights shimmered like spun gold.

'It said there was a rumour that Rolay Richard is to be appointed liquidators.'

'Really?' Surprise widened her eyes and apprehension gripped her stomach. She could guess what was coming.

'Well, it's true.' He was quietly elated. 'We've been appointed by the Court. We'll make millions out of it. The job will go on

25

for ever. It'll take years to trace and liquidate all the bank's assets. It will keep the firm in profit for ages.'

She smiled wanly. 'That's great.'

'Some of our people are over at the Exchange Bank's head office now. Doing a few preliminaries. There's a briefing meeting at the Bank of England. At eleven. You need to be there.'

'Me? Why?'

He stared at her in surprise. 'Come on, Melissa, why do you think?' His voice was faintly condescending. Normally she would have said something but she let it pass.

'You're one of the team,' he went on. 'The Old Lady wants us because Rolay Richard are the best there is. We are the great liquidators.' He laughed briefly.

'Yes but why do you want *me* there? We've got hundreds of qualified people.' She waved her arm in the direction of the glass partition and the open office beyond. 'You don't need me on this one.'

Hawick stood up and walked out from behind his desk. He was in his shirtsleeves. Unlike most of the other senior partners in Rolay Richard, who sported bright, garish braces, he was wearing a Gucci belt – a style of dress retained from his years in the United States.

Early in his career, Hawick had gone to America and qualified there as a Certified Public Accountant. After working for a few practices, he had set up and managed Rolay Richard's North American business, buying up and developing accountancy practices from Florida to Toronto. Within ten years he had established the firm as a major player in American accounting.

Hawick was one of the men who had made Rolay Richard what it was: a multi-million-pound business – one of world's top six accountancy practices.

He perched himself on the edge of his desk. He looked serious. 'I *do* need you on this one, Melissa. You're better at doing what you do than anyone else in the business. So, you'd better start assigning your current workload to some of the others. You need your desk clear by this afternoon. After that, this job takes priority. Nothing else matters. Okay?'

She made a rueful face. 'Come on, Nigel, I've just got my workload organised for the whole of the next quarter. You could give this job to someone else. There are plenty of other people in FI who can handle it.'

He shook his head. 'No. I want *you* to manage it.'

'But . . .'

He waved aside her protest. 'Assign people as you see fit, but you personally must concentrate on the Exchange Bank. I'm counting on you, Melissa. You're one of the reasons why the Bank of England chose Rolay Richard.'

'Don't tell me that,' she moaned. 'I don't need that kind of responsibility.'

He laughed. 'Well, you've got it. Don't worry, everything will be fine.'

She could have argued. After all, she was a partner. She had control over her career and the kind of work she did. But it wasn't logical to kick against the decision. The Exchange Bank would be an enormous job. Prestigious. Important. And as the most experienced partner in Financial Investigations she was bound to get caught up in it. She sighed. It was too bad if the job had been dumped on her at short notice. That's the way things were in business. She knew that. At least her head knew it. Her heart yearned for Jamie.

She shrugged ruefully. 'Okay. If you say so.'

Debbie, her secretary, passed her a clutch of telephone messages as she walked back into her office. Inside, she closed the beige, narrow-slatted Venetian blinds hanging at the interior window panels and flopped into her chair.

She stared at the locked filing cabinets containing her current workload. Nigel was right, she thought. None of it was priority. It could all be assigned to members of her staff. Which was why she was so reluctant to give it up.

The work had, for once, guaranteed her an easy life. It had meant three months of normal hours. Three months of never leaving London, of not getting on aeroplanes, of never rushing off for meetings on the other side of the world. A summer of long evenings and regular weekends with Jamie. She had even been planning a holiday. Just for herself and her son.

Now all her plans were like Humpty Dumpty.

She swallowed hard, choking back the tears and the un-summoned lump in her throat, feeling the accustomed tugging of her divided heart. She loved Jamie. Yet she needed her career . . . needed her high salary to give Jamie the best possible life.

But with the career came the guilt . . . the schizophrenic affliction of the professional businesswoman who was also a single parent.

The job Hawick had handed her would swamp her with work. It would mean long hours in the office uncovering complicated paper trails followed by long days out of the country tracing where the trails might lead.

Once again she would be flying halfway round the world to talk to hard-eyed men with calculators in the company of hard-eyed men with guns.

Chapter Four

Shortly after twelve the group was escorted back along the wood-panelled corridor to the Bank's entrance lobby.

Mullhane hung back, waiting for Kilbride, who was at the back of the crowd. In the lobby he motioned to the rookie standing close to the wall. The young man straightened up and began talking quietly into a small radio transmitter. Mullhane turned to Kilbride: 'Can I give you a ride to the Embassy?'

Kilbride nodded. 'Thanks.'

The rain had stopped and a moist, glossy sun hung high in the midday sky. Raindrops like splinters of light glittered on the red paintwork of the buses trundling down Ludgate Hill.

'I love this town,' Kilbride murmured, staring out of the car window.

Mullhane pressed a button in the armrest of the seat and watched the thick glass partition slide smoothly up behind the two men in the front of the car. He sat silently for a moment, staring at the backs of their heads. Then he said, 'This is one helluva mess.' His voice was low and strained.

'First the Brits say they're pulling the plug on the Exchange Bank . . . then they tell us a big piece of our finance industry is compromised by a bunch of hoodlums. Jeeesus. If this guy Timmison is right and the Mob has gotten control of the banks . . .'

'There's no doubt he's right,' Kilbride interrupted quietly. He was still staring out of the window. 'He wouldn't say it unless he had proof.'

'Yeah, but who the hell *is* Timmison? I'm damn sure he's not with the Bank of England. And if he's not a bean-counter . . . then what? I don't know him . . . and I know most of their intelligence people. So, who is he? Do you know?'

'No.'

'Then why the hell should we believe what he's telling us? Why trust him?'

Kilbride turned from the window and gave Mullhane a faint smile. 'You don't trust him?'

'Jesus, John, are you kidding?'

Kilbride's smile broadened slightly. He knew Mullhane well enough to know the guy's history. Mullhane's grandparents had left Donegal at the turn of the century to emigrate to America. Mullhane was third-generation Irish . . . too Irish to trust the British.

'The whole thing stinks,' Mullhane continued. 'If they've got a man on the inside of the Exchange Bank then he's gotta be connected to the Mob. So, if he's Mafia, how come he's run to the British? To the Bank of England for Christ's sake? It doesn't make sense. There's something Timmison isn't telling us.'

'I think there's a whole lot he's not telling us.' Kilbride's voice was low and troubled. 'He knows a lot more than he's saying.' He paused, his face darkening into a worried frown. 'You figure he knows about . . .'

'I hope not. How could he?'

'Well . . . a guy on the inside of the Bank . . . maybe he could have . . .'

Mullhane shrugged lightly. He noticed the gesture did nothing to lighten the anxiety in Kilbride's eyes. 'Yeah, maybe. But it's a long shot.'

Kilbride erupted. 'Jesus, Barney,' he snarled. 'You said the Agency had covered its tracks. You said there was *no way* anyone could find out.'

'Sure, anyone on the *outside*. But someone on the *inside* . . . that's different. Someone on the inside . . . well, maybe, just maybe, if they knew what they were looking for they could put it all together . . .'

'Oh, Christ.' Kilbride stared hard at Mullhane. After a moment he went on. 'How likely is that?' His tone was more controlled.

Mullhane pulled a face as he thought about it. 'It would be a helluva long shot,' he intoned. 'Thousands to one. Even someone on the inside would have to be as sharp as a whip to figure it all out. They'd have to know where to look.'

'But there's a risk?'

Mullhane's shrugged again. 'Yeah, there's a risk. A small one. Damn,' he snarled loudly, 'if only we'd had more time. Four

30

weeks, even three, and we could have pulled everything through, fixed it so no one would have ever known.'

'You could try talking to Timmison. Asking him to delay.'

'Why would he do that? He's hell bent on closing the bank this week.'

'Maybe if you told him that shutting the bank down this quick means putting some of your people's lives in danger. He might hold off if you told him that.' Kilbride caught the look on Mullhane's face. 'He might,' he repeated. 'We're Americans aren't we? We're supposed to have a special relationship with the British.'

Mullhane let out a sharp laugh. 'Special relationship my ass. That's something the Brits invented to put the squeeze on Uncle Sam. It don't swing both ways, John. Hell, I've got a special relationship with my ex-wife. It don't stop me wishing the bitch was dead. No,' he continued, 'Timmison's a stuck-up Brit. He won't go for any delay. The bank is on the block and he's just itching to chop it.'

Kilbride stared at him for a moment then nodded. 'I guess you're right.' His voice was low and strained with worry. He turned before Mullhane could see the anxiety deepen in his eyes and stared morosely at the knots of early-summer tourists in Trafalgar Square.

For a while they were quiet, listening to the powerful hum of the car's engines.

Mullhane broke the silence, murmuring pensively. 'Yet, I guess if Timmison's deep throat *hadda* known anything . . . he'd have talked. And if he'd talked, we'd have heard. By now they'd have come for us. Knocking in the middle of the night. By now they'd have our nuts in a bucket.'

Killbride turned back to him. 'So if we haven't heard then it follows Timmison's man doesn't know.'

Mullhane shook his head. 'It means he hasn't talked. Maybe he doesn't know . . . or maybe he does know and he isn't saying.'

'Why would he do that? Not say?'

'Who knows? There could be a lot of reasons. Whatever, there's only one way to find out.'

'Which is?'

'Locate the guy. Track him down.'

Kilbride gazed at Mullhane for a moment then nodded. 'Yes, you're right. But you'll have to be quick. And careful. Every law enforcement and intelligence agency in America is going to go looking for this guy. Treasury, DEA, the Bureau, they'll all be wanting to find out what he knows. They've all got skeletons in the Exchange Bank cupboard. You'll need to get an early jump on it, Barney. Get to him first. Before the others.'

Mullhane nodded. 'Sure, I know that. But it won't be easy. The guy, if it is a guy, could be any nationality. And if he isn't holed up somewhere . . . or if the Brits haven't got him in a witness protection programme here in England . . . then he could be in any country in the world. The Exchange Bank is a Third World bank. The guy could be in Bangladesh or Bangkok or Bolivia.'

Kilbride frowned. 'Maybe. But whoever it is, he knows about organised crime infiltrating American banks. That suggests to me the guy is connected to the Mafia. Which means he's an American.'

'Or a Colombian . . . or an Italian . . . or a Canadian,' Mullhane said morosely.

'Yes, but more likely an American. In America.'

'That doesn't make my job any easier. The Agency isn't supposed to operate on the mainland.'

'You've done it before,' Kilbride growled. 'Do it again. The CIA Charter is the least of our worries. You need to find this person. Fast. Get him away from the British if you have to and find out what he knows.'

'And supposing he knows a lot? Then what?'

Mullhane watched the patrician face beside him. Beneath the mane of white hair he saw an eyebrow raise and then lower. The leonine head inclined slightly.

Mullhane grunted. 'You figure that's necessary? Turn him off?'

'It's him or us.' Kilbride's low voice grated harshly.

Mullhane gazed at him for another moment then turned back to the car window.

'Timmison's deep throat isn't the only thing we're going to have to worry about,' Kilbride went on.

'Yeah? What else am I gonna lose sleep over?'

'The liquidators. When the regulators pull the plug, every account in the bank will be frozen. Including those the Agency is operating for covert operations. The liquidators will start backtracking those accounts. Whatever happens, you'll probably lose the money. And if the liquidator is smart he could trace those accounts back to the Agency.'

'He's gonna have to be good to do that. We've got all those accounts well hidden. And anyway, the bean-counters will be looking for hot money . . . Mafia funds washing through the system.'

'Liquidators are clever, Barney. If they trace the money, even your legitimate operations could be compromised.'

Mullhane turned to him. 'I know. But don't worry about it, we'll be keeping close watch on whoever they've got tracking the money. And if they get lucky and start getting too close . . . well . . . maybe they'll have an accident.'

Kilbride looked startled. 'Look, Barney, we don't want a high body count in this thing. We may have to silence Timmison's deep throat, but you don't want to start terminating liquidators.'

'Don't worry. The Agency wouldn't need to. There are plenty of other people who'd do that. LCN . . . the Colombian cartels . . . the Turkish Horse traders . . . more than half the world's terrorist organisations . . . all of them are gonna be falling over each other to stop the accountants confiscating their money. A quiet word in the right ear – and the world could be minus another bean-counter.' He laughed quietly.

Kilbride's look of concern remained. 'Well, for Christ's sake be careful. Concentrate on finding the Exchange Bank's inside man. That will be hard enough with all the publicity this thing will attract.'

'Publicity?'

'Hell yes. The political fallout from closing the Exchange Bank will be enormous. Once the media get to hear that organised criminals have infiltrated US banks and S&Ls there'll be a helluva commotion. Like the man said, there'll be pressure on the dollar; a lot of money will be running for cover and congressional committees will be sprouting up like poppies in cotton.'

Mullhane grunted. That was all high finance. Not his problem.

'And don't forget, on the surface of it, the Exchange Bank is a legitimate financial institution. There are a lot of branches here in Britain and throughout Europe. Plenty of ordinary people use the bank. Legitimate businesses. When it goes down, there's going to be the mother and father of all rows. Everybody's going to be screaming for their money. And all the regulatory authorities will be covering their asses . . . blaming the other guy. If it gets known that the Agency was using it, some of the folks on the Hill are going to start asking questions. Why did the CIA use a corrupt bank? . . . Did the Agency keep the bank going for its own ends? Is the Agency laundering dirty money. You know the kind of thing.'

Mullhane grunted and slumped back in his seat. He knew the kind of thing all right. The bureaucrats and the bean-counters . . . the number-crunchers snapping at the Agency like yelping dogs, trying to bring it down.

He could feel one of his headaches coming on as he stared dolefully out of the window and brooded on Kilbride's words.

All that mattered these days was money. All ends were economic . . . the whole point of everything, pecuniary.

Within the Agency to which he had given his entire life, the only way to get ahead now was to comprehend the intricacies of earnings and assets. Fiscal literacy . . . that was the name of the game now. Intelligence, covert action, sticking it to the Soviets . . . the kind of action at which he had excelled was out of date. These days, it seemed to Mullhane, the only action the Agency endorsed was crunching numbers . . . the only people it recruited, dry, financial limp-dicks.

He stared at the streets as the car swung into Grosvenor Square.

Once, in the service of Uncle Sam, Barney Mullhane had been a snorting warhorse. Now, near the end of an illustrious career, all it appeared the men in Washington wanted was a goddam carthorse.

Chapter Five

The meeting at the Bank of England confirmed her fears.

The air of the large, classical room into which Melissa and six other partners of Rolay Richard were shown was redolent of authority; evocative of a room filled with wealthy, elegant women. The rich, sweet perfume of power was subtle and discreet yet it pervaded every corner.

They were briefed by three venerable and dignified officials from the Bank's supervisory department. Another man attended the briefing, sitting off to one side of the large room. He was tall and fair-haired, with a hawklike face. No one introduced him; nor did he take any part in the proceedings. Instead he sat silently for the ninety minutes, listening to the supervisors detail in dry, precise terms what was required.

Scores of Rolay Richard's accountants were to be employed in tracing, securing and selling off the Exchange Bank's assets in order to pay something back to its creditors. It would be years of work which in the early days, the supervisors pointed out sombrely, would be undertaken in a welter of publicity.

It was obvious to Melissa as she listened that the media didn't know the half of it. And they weren't going to. The ominous-voiced officials, silently supported by the intimidating presence of the sharp-faced man, made it clear that no one was to repeat what was being said behind the windowless walls of Threadneedle Street.

After the meeting, Melissa waited for Nigel Hawick who had been called to one side by the supervisors. She saw the tall stranger walk over to join the group.

Exiting the Bank a few minutes later they opted to walk back to the tower block in Eastcheap. It was a bright, buoyant day of blue skies and scudding clouds. Sunshine and shadows pursued each other along the crowded pavements of Lombard Street.

Hawick seemed bothered about the silent man at the meeting.

'There was a time,' he said grimly, 'when the Old Lady used moral 'suasion. Not any more. These days the Bank of England uses strongarm tactics. Whoever that man is, I'm pretty sure he's not with the BoE.'

'Weren't you introduced when you spoke to the supervisors after the meeting?'

'His name is Timmison and I noticed all the supervisors seemed to defer to him. As if he were the Deputy Governor or something. That's unusual. My guess is he's a spook.'

'Spook?' Melissa frowned at him.

'Some kind of secret policeman. Intelligence maybe. I don't know. Whatever, he isn't a BoE official and he's too high-powered to be from the Serious Fraud Office. He could be from the Treasury but I'm pretty certain he isn't. He's not a Treasury type. No,' he concluded, 'I think he's a spook.'

The pavements were crowded. Hawick and Melissa parted and merged as they weaved their way through the streams of office workers on their lunch break.

'Whoever Timmison is,' Hawick continued as they fell back into step beside each other, 'he told me we'll have to keep the SFO informed on progress. We have to tell them about all funds we think have been laundered. That's down to you, Melissa. You must stay close to the Fraud Office.'

'Well, they know where to find me,' she said firmly.

Hawick laughed as they turned into Gracechurch Street. 'What have you got against the SFO?'

She gave him a withering glance. 'I'm not spending my time trailing across London to be grilled by some bureaucrat in a grotty office on Elm Street. If the Serious Fraud people want to know what I'm doing, they can come to me.'

'Okay.' He shrugged and side-stepped a city-suited youth carrying a packet of plastic wrapped sandwiches. They walked in silence for a while. When Hawick spoke again his tone was sombre. 'They want you to sign the Official Secrets Act.'

'What?'

'Yes, I'm afraid so. That's partly why they called me over after the meeting.'

'Why?' Her voice was high-pitched and querulous. 'For God's sake, I'm a chartered accountant and a qualified insolvency practitioner. I'm already an Officer of the Court. What more do they want?'

He pulled a face. 'None of that cuts much ice from the supervisors' point of view, Melissa. Even less with the spook, Timmison. I'm afraid they were adamant. You have to sign. You heard what they said at the meeting. Politically, the Exchange Bank is a very hot potato. It has laundered billions. Now it's closed down, there's a lot of funny money swilling around in the system. God knows what you're going to find once you start tracking the cash. A lot of that money may belong to people it ought not to. Highly placed people. So, our masters want to ensure you're not tempted to talk to anyone you shouldn't. Signing the Official Secrets Act keeps people quiet, Melissa. It's very tough . . . makes you very vulnerable. It's prison if you blab.'

'Bloody marvellous,' Melissa wailed. 'They want me to do the job but they don't trust me not to talk about it. Anyway, who the hell do they think I'm going to talk to? Jamie?'

'Anybody. The press, somebody you meet at a party,' he paused, 'someone you're having a relationship with.'

'What do you mean? A lover?'

He shrugged. 'It happens.'

She laughed sharply and a passing woman turned at the sound. 'Chance would be a fine thing. For heaven's sake, what do they think I am?'

They had reached the corner of Eastcheap. In front of them the dark, glass-plated skin of the Rolay Richard tower rippled with the reflecting effects of the sun and scudding clouds.

Hawick stared at her. 'They already know that, Melissa. You're the best there is. The most able forensic accountant around. The most successful tracker of capital flight in London. If anybody can track the money that's moved through the Exchange Bank, you can. Why do you think Rolay Richard was appointed the liquidator?'

She looked at him and laughed. 'God, you're a smooth-talking bastard when you want to be. Don't give me all that rubbish.'

He laughed.

Melissa considered Hawick's words as they walked the rest of the way in silence. She ignored his bullshit and cajolery about being the best in the business. That was just masculine shine. She knew Hawick wanted her to take on the job, so, like most men who wanted something, he was rubbing her back with warm blandishments.

No, the flattery meant nothing. But she pondered his words

about tracking the money. Yes, she thought, he was probably right. She *could* track the money that had flowed through the bank.

Of course there were other forensic accountants working for the big six in London who could have done the job as well. But she was the one who had been given it. She'd been chosen. And though it was her biggest job yet . . . though it would stretch her to the limit . . . she knew . . . she was sure . . . she could handle it.

She caught herself. Damn. Already she was getting hooked . . . sucked in by the challenge.

And weighed down by the guilt.

She thought about Jamie.

Yet despite her love for Jamie . . . despite her remorse at being so long and so often away from him, she could feel the excitement humming in her blood.

Next to Jamie, the thing she loved most was her work.

Hunting the money.

Chapter Six

She put her key in the lock, turned it gently and pushed against the front door. As always, when it was late, it creaked like a graveyard gate.

A couple of table lamps glowed warmly in the low-beamed living room. In the kitchen a lonely salad, wrapped in clingfilm, sat on a polished pine work surface next to a note from Astrid concerning the day's calls and events. Astrid was from Dresden and although her spoken English was good, her writing was bizarre. It took Melissa a while to decipher the messages. There was nothing urgent.

Astrid had gone to bed. Melissa could hear the soft, constant thump of Hardcore Techno coming from her bedroom.

Sometimes, when the music was at full blast, Melissa feared the vibrations would bring the cottage's thatched roof crashing in. Yet she rarely objected . . . especially when the decibels were at a reasonable level. Jamie liked it.

During the day, when Astrid played her tapes, he swayed in time to the beat. And if for some reason he woke at night and heard the dull pulse through the cottage's uneven lath and plaster walls it gave him comfort.

Though, she reflected, exposure to the music seemed to have inured Jamie to noise. He could sleep through virtually anything.

She stared at the salad for a moment then put it in the fridge. She was too tired to eat. She had been in Luxembourg all day and the last flight out had been delayed.

She moved to the cabinet and fixed herself a vodka and tonic, reflecting as she took her first sip that she was doing more of that lately. Skipping supper and moving straight on to the alcohol. She'd probably have another one before the evening was out, she thought. Maybe two.

Sometimes it bothered her. Was she drinking too much? she

39

wondered. Was the job getting to her? She grimaced in irritation at herself. When she was tired she had a drink. Because she was tired she worried about it.

She kicked off her shoes and fell into an easy chair.

Luxembourg had been a waste of time. The creators of the Exchange Bank had been clever. They'd split the bank into two separate entities . . . the bank and its treasury operation. The bank itself had a Luxembourg holding company, subject to the control and inspection of the *Institut Monétaire Luxembourgeois*, the regulator of banks in the Grand Duchy.

The treasury operation, based in the Cayman Islands, also had a Luxembourg holding company. But, because the inventive men behind the Exchange Bank had made sure the holding company didn't have the word 'Bank' in its title . . . it hadn't been recognised as a bank. Or, more importantly, Melissa reflected, leaning back in her chair . . . *inspected* as one.

It was a classic case of financial fragmentation. She had come across plenty of similar schemes before. They were the standard tactics of the big corporations, of the rich tax evaders . . . and the money launderers.

Divide and confuse.

That was their motto. It meant there was always a legitimate reason why files and documents were unavailable for inspection by the authorities and auditors. It also meant that, after a long and tiring day, Melissa had got precisely nowhere.

She had flown out early that morning and been met at the airport by a couple of partners from the local practice of Rolay Richard. They had driven to the offices of the bank's holding companies in Luxembourg's financial district, close to the Boulevard Royal. The premises were distinguished by a couple of gleaming brass name plates on the wall of an impressive, ornately gabled, nineteenth-century town house. The street, Melissa noticed, getting out of the car, boasted scores of similar name plates.

She had spent most of the day in the expensive offices, sifting through piles of papers with her colleagues. A few supervisors from the *Institut Monétaire* had also turned up to inspect the documents. Melissa had eyed them impassively. She didn't think much of Luxembourg bank regulators. Not for nothing did the business district glitter with the brass name plaques of thousands of holding companies of banks and big corporations. The Grand

Duchy was one of the world's major staging posts in the movement of hot money. As far as Melissa could see, the supervisors were there to close the stable door.

At lunchtime she and the local partners had decided on lunch at the *Alsacien* in the rue du Cure. They had walked, skirting the deep, green slash of the Petrusse, the wooded gorge cutting the city in half. The weather had been warm, with a bright blue shimmering sky. The pavements and sidewalk cafés were crowded. As always in the continental capitals, Melissa had been impressed by the sartorial elegance of the people in the streets. Luxembourg was a small, rich city; its wealth reflected in the stylish and expensive clothes of its inhabitants. Here, she thought, she looked almost ordinary. In scruffy London she stood out like a super-model in a surplus store.

Over lunch the younger of the two partners had started coming on to her. He was a tall good-looking Belgian in his late twenties with a deep, sexy voice. Melissa's French had been good enough to acknowledge his compliments about her looks: her soft, feline face with its wide-set, blue-grey eyes, her firm jawline and full sensual lips and, most of all, her shining, copper-coloured hair.

She'd thought about it for a while. He was certainly very attractive. She could always find an excuse to stop over for a night. But . . . he wore a wedding ring. And there was Jamie.

She sighed. There was always Jamie.

Suddenly she felt very tired.

She finished her drink, switched off the lights and stole up the staircase. Softly she eased open his bedroom door. His big, moon face was in repose and there was a smile on his lips.

She stared at him for a moment, trying to imagine what was going on in his curious brain. Whatever it was, it made him happy. Even in his sleep Jamie liked to smile. Gently she straightened his covers. Bending over, she brushed her lips lightly over his forehead. He stirred contentedly as she crept from the room.

Debbie was holding up a wad of messages. Bustling past her workstation, Melissa shook her head. 'Coffee first,' she demanded. 'The journey was hell.'

She sat at her desk sipping the coffee as Debbie went through the messages. Mostly they were from people who wanted something. Information, help, cooperation . . . whatever it was,

41

she decided, if they wanted it badly enough . . . they'd call again.

Four messages were from people from whom *she* wanted something. She told Debbie to get the callers on the phone. That, she reflected, was how the system worked. Power was getting your calls returned.

Debbie finished with the messages and moved on to her schedule for the day. Melissa had a meeting with the SFO in Elm Street at eleven, a working lunch with Nigel Hawick, and in the afternoon a meeting with the former auditors of the Exchange Bank.

There was a heap of correspondence on her desk, a mass of memos to read and, inside the row of filing cabinets lining one of the glass walls of her office, piles of papers and files to examine. She sighed. It was to be another adrenalin-pumping day of pressure and deadlines.

At just before three, one of Rolay Richard's extensive fleet of BMWs drew up outside the firm's glass-fronted entrance. A few seconds later Melissa, accompanied by Nigel Hawick, emerged from a lift and clicked across the marble floor of the high, wide atrium. They climbed into the back seat.

The car took them less than a mile . . . to Broadgate, close to Liverpool Street Station, where they were dropped outside the offices of Berrenstein Lang, another of the world's top accountancy practices.

Inside the plush, cedar-panelled reception area they were issued with visitors' tags before being escorted into the lift by a security man.

The floor at which they emerged could have been in their own office block. The colours of the vast, open-plan office were slightly different, but the concept of nests of desks and screens and pot plants was the same. As the security man led them across the floor, Melissa noticed the familiar glow from the fluorescent lights and the same, all-pervading hum from the desktop computers. The man deposited them at the door of a large meeting room in a corner of the office area.

Three partners of Berrenstein Lang were waiting for them. Two were seated at a polished board table whilst a third was closing the Venetian blinds hanging at the internal glass partitions. After the introductions Melissa and Hawick were invited to sit down. Berrenstein Lang's senior partner, Kenneth McKinnie, a tall, balding Scotsman in his late fifties, began immediately.

'We have been asked by the Bank of England to give you our full cooperation,' he said. There was a note of irony in his dry, cultured, east-coast-of-Scotland voice. 'Of course, we would have done that anyway,' he continued, 'but the Bank's request was more in the nature of an order. The Bank also made the point . . . unnecessarily . . . that what we say here is confidential. The supervisors have made it very clear as to what we may tell you . . . and what we may not.'

McKinnie paused for a moment with an unhappy look on his face.

'We were auditors of the Exchange Bank for more than ten years,' he continued, 'and for almost all that time we were pretty sure things weren't right. But we could never prove it. We found numerous questionable procedures in their operations . . . loan churning . . . insufficient adequacy . . . overly exposed positions . . . no third-party confirmation of loans . . . but we never found sufficient proof.'

'Did you tell the BoE of your suspicions?' Hawick asked.

'Of course. And the BoE seemed concerned. But it said without proof it could do nothing. Part of the problem was the Exchange Bank had grossly inadequate paper trails. The other problem was language.'

'Language?' Hawick queried.

'Yes. The Exchange Bank's management was almost exclusively Third World nationals: South Americans, Pakistanis, Arabs, ex-pat Chinese. That meant the language inside the Bank was rarely English. In London, it was mainly Urdu or Arabic. Many of their important loan documents were in one or the other. Yet, whenever we put in one of our own Urdu-speaking accountants to audit the loans and check the documentation, the Exchange Bank's management found a reason to object. The management also had a large number of accounts which it said were classified and which no one, not even the auditors, were allowed to see. The entire bank operated in a culture of secrecy.

'Furthermore,' he added, 'although we audited the bank worldwide, we didn't audit the treasury operation in the Caymans. So we never saw both sides of the picture.'

'Divide and confuse,' Melissa murmured.

McKinnie looked at her sadly. 'Exactly. Well, that's all water under the bridge. As you know, a lot of people are now baying for our blood. Saying Berrenstein Lang was negligent. Naturally, we refuse to accept that.'

'Absolute nonsense,' one of the partners seated next to McKinnie agreed indignantly.

'But,' McKinnie continued in his dry tones, 'it's almost certain we'll be sued by someone. Quite likely by you.'

Melissa gave him a sympathetic look. Senior partners at Rolay Richard were already discussing whether the firm should institute legal proceedings against Berrenstein Lang. Everybody agreed it would make Rolay Richard appear to be doing its job.

'It happens,' Nigel Hawick said unsympathetically.

'It happens in America,' McKinnie said sharply. 'When I first came into this profession, chartered accountants would never have dreamt of suing each other. Now . . .' He shook his head.

'The point is,' he went on after a moment, 'we were not negligent. We were just slow to understand that the culture of this bank was completely criminal. It's very difficult for people like us to accept that a major financial institution was set up with the sole intention of perpetrating fraud on an international scale . . . of laundering vast amounts of money. The bank was one of the biggest privately owned banks in the world, yet it owed allegiance to no one. To get what they wanted, the men behind it were paying enormous bribes. Hundreds of officials and bank regulators in Third World countries were being paid off by it.' McKinnie hesitated and shook his head. 'I think this bank would have bribed God if that were possible. And yet it was all an illusion: much of the money on its balance sheet simply wasn't there.'

McKinnie paused once more. When he spoke again, his voice suddenly had a sharper edge. 'Then, a few weeks ago, we were told by Bank of England supervisors that they had conclusive proof of everything we had suspected for so long. What they showed us was almost unbelievable. They had chapter and verse. Misappropriation of depositors' funds to cover up losses on treasury trading . . . evidence of massive money laundering . . . using drug money to window-dress its balance sheet. The supervisors had copies of documents, names, dates, everything. God knows how they'd obtained all of it. They even had proof that the firm of accountants who'd been auditing the Exchange Bank's treasury operation in the Caymans was corrupt. Something we had suspected for a long time. The practice was in the pay of the bank. It had been supplying us and everybody else with false information for years.'

Nigel Hawick was leaning across the polished table, a frown of concentration on his face. 'How?' he asked. 'How did they know all this?'

McKinnie ignored the question. 'The strange thing is . . . the BoE didn't want to reveal what it knew. At least not directly. That's why they sent for us. They wanted evidence about the frauds to appear to be the result of our audit and subsequent investigations. What's even more curious, they didn't want any mention of capital flight. They didn't want it known that the Exchange Bank was laundering money. Our instructions were only to reveal the cover-ups and the misuse of depositors' funds. The supervisors gave us scores of documents and they told us exactly where to look to dig up the dirt.' He smiled wanly. 'Within a week we had seven hundred qualified accountants across the globe, from Bogotá to Bombay, working on thousands of transactions. Of course, once we knew where to look, it was easy to get the evidence.'

'Why didn't the bank want you to investigate the money laundering?' asked Melissa.

McKinnie shrugged. 'I gather a vast amount of money has been washed through the Exchange Bank. Hundreds of billions in fact. I don't suppose the authorities want that known. You have to admit, it casts rather a poor light on the world's banking industry.'

'I suppose it does,' Melissa conceded. McKinnie hadn't really answered her question. She had the impression he was holding something back.

'What I don't understand,' Hawick announced, 'is why the BoE didn't blow the whistle on the Exchange Bank itself. Why do it through you?'

Again McKinnie shrugged. 'To avoid getting the kind of flak this practice is getting I suppose. The Old Lady doesn't like criticism. She likes to be above all that. She won't get her skirts dirty if she can help it. So she's arranged for us to get it instead.'

It was a reasonable answer to the question. Yet, Melissa thought, it was somehow too glib for the dry, ironic Scotsman.

She stared at him. Much of Melissa's job was talking to people who didn't want to talk to her. Listening to people who weren't inclined to be entirely candid. She had become adept at listening

45

for signals . . . at filtering answers and assaying them for the truth. Now, her instincts told her that McKinnie's replies were not entirely complete.

'Is there some other reason, do you think?' she asked quietly.

McKinnie glanced at her sharply then smiled, acknowledging her perception. 'Yes, I believe there may be. I'm guessing, but . . . I think the BoE may have someone on the inside of the Exchange Bank. Someone very senior. And if I'm right, then I'm willing to wager that the person has been passing on inside information.'

'Do you know who it is?' Hawick asked.

McKinnie chuckled. He shook his head. 'No. And if I'm right, then I'd doubt that the supervisors who briefed you at the Bank know. Nor even *their* superiors. Whoever it is, I think we can safely assume the authorities will be anxious to protect him. Or her,' he added, glancing at Melissa. 'Which I suppose is why they want all the nasties in the woodwork to be exposed through you.'

They were silent for a while, the only noise in the room the subtle hum coming from the huge office outside.

'Now,' McKinnie's voice became businesslike, 'the BoE has asked us to hand over to you copies of all our papers. Sometime this afternoon, Berrenstein Lang will be delivering everything we've unearthed concerning the Exchange Bank to your offices.'

'Is there much?' asked Hawick.

McKinnie consulted with one of his colleagues. 'There will be four large security vans,' he replied. 'About five tons.'

Hawick glanced at Melissa and pulled a face. 'Our first problem will be where to put it all,' he moaned.

They left a few minutes later.

They were quiet during the short journey back to the office. Hawick, slumped in a corner of his seat, was deep in thought. As the car drew up outside the glass doors of the atrium on Eastcheap, Melissa turned to him.

'There's something not quite right about all this.'

'What do you mean?' he grunted.

'If the Old Lady has someone on the inside of the Exchange Bank . . . someone who knows about the bank's money laundering activities, then what do they need me for?'

He frowned at her. 'We don't know there *is* someone on the inside. McKinnie's only guessing. He said so himself.'

'Yes, but *if* there is, then presumably the authorities already know the schemes the bank was using to hide its illegal transactions. They probably know where the laundered money is and how it got there. So . . . why not tell me what they know? Why even use me in the first place?'

He had a puzzled, dubious look. 'I don't know.'

The chauffeur had got out and was standing by the car door, ready to open it as soon as one of them made a move.

Hawick was silent for a moment. When he spoke his voice was low and strained. 'There's more to all this than meets the eye.'

He eyed her for a moment. 'When things are going well, when the markets are strong, the type of people who were running the Exchange Bank cut corners. But when the tide goes out on them . . . then you get to see the wrecks. I've got a nasty feeling that a lot of things about this bank are dangerous, Melissa. I think you're going to have to be careful.'

She gave him a startled glance.

Chapter Seven

Big Vinny Harold slowly and methodically shifted the thick wad of gum from one side of his mouth to the other as he slightly – very slightly – shifted his position.

From where he was hunkered down beside a stunted tucuma, he could just make out Billy Bob on the other side of the narrow track of dull red earth.

Big Vinny eyed his younger brother with a professional eye and approved of what he saw. Billy Bob was well hidden, his camouflage combat uniform merging perfectly with the jungle undergrowth, his face beneath his bush hat smeared with black greasepaint.

Just like Big Vinny.

A few yards away the Kaplin boys and Carver Fylde were similarly well hidden, flanking the track in enfilade.

Chomping rhythmically on his gum, his small, hard eyes focused on the narrow, Sienna-coloured thread of track winding through the endless mass of green, Vinny thought about another jungle . . . about the other times he had lain hidden and waiting with the sweet stench of rotting vegetation in his nostrils and the sound of a million insects hissing in his ears.

In Nam, he thought, he would never have chewed gum when he was in country. Charlie would have smelled it. Hell, Charlie would have been able to tell what flavour it was from more than a mile away. Charlie was a great jungle fighter – in Big Vinny's opinion, the best there was . . . God damn him.

Charlie could move through the jungle quieter than mist moves over water. Charlie could have crawled up your ass and you'd have never heard him. Not, that is, until he blew your brains out.

It wasn't so with the men Big Vinny and his men were waiting patiently to kill. They were a bunch of dumb Mestizos who had

48

been painfully and noisily making their way down the track since first light.

For most of the morning Big Vinny and the boys had been listening to the sounds of their progress . . . their ceaseless cursing and beating of the mules, their raised voices, their sudden bursts of coarse laughter.

They were in high jungle, over six thousand feet, in the Eastern Cordillera and the men, most of whom were from the slums of Medellín, had been forced to stop every so often to rest and catch their breath. Their progress had been slow and Big Vinny and the boys had needed to be patient. Now the men were only a few hundred yards away, cautiously moving down the narrow, steeply sloping path.

Earlier Big Vinny had watched them through his field glasses.

The men were bunched up, as close to the mules as the path would allow. He had counted them. Seven mule-handlers, one to each mule, accompanied by an armed escort of ten . . . no . . . twelve men carrying an assortment of automatic weapons, mainly Kalashnikovs, slung over their shoulders. He could see the mules, sure-footed despite their heavy loads, were truculent and difficult. He had watched the muleteers beating them unmercifully.

Goddam stupid peons, he had thought. They had no idea how to treat critters. Mules were their lifeline; in this terrain the only practical form of transport there was.

It was the very inhospitability of the terrain that appealed to the men who employed the disorganised rabble struggling down the mountain.

Somewhere higher up was a complete processing plant to which the local farmers brought their dried coca leaves. The plant was secure and isolated: inaccessible except by way of a few days' struggle on foot through the mountainous jungle, and well hidden from the air. Every week millions of dollars' worth of uncut cocaine left the plant and was brought down from the mountains by armed men with mules.

It was a procedure that had been going on unhindered for years; unhampered by the law thanks to the application of enormous bribes and unthreatened by competitors or thieves through the certainty of awful and barbaric retribution. Even the DEA, in cooperation with the Colombian army, had not been able to pinpoint and interdict the supply line.

But Big Vinny wasn't the law nor the army nor the DEA. Big

Vinny and the boys were the Chicashaw Commando. And they had come to this Godforsaken hellhole to kick ass. And to steal over twenty million dollars' worth of cocaine.

When he had finished studying the slowly approaching group through his glasses, Big Vinny had issued his orders in a series of precise whispers. His last words to the men had been, 'Waste 'em all, but for Chrissakes, don't hit the mules.'

It was good tactical advice. Without the mules Vinny's men would be unable to transport the precious merchandise packed in large, heavy plastic cartons and strapped to the animals' backs.

Nevertheless, Billy Bob, the Kaplin boys and Carver Fylde had allowed themselves a small smile beneath the black streaks of greasepaint on their faces. Back home Big Vinny was well known as a guy who dearly loved critters. Any critters. Greasers, he hated . . . as much as he hated niggers and kikes. But critters he loved. Even dumbass mules.

The men and the mules were drawing closer.

Vinny had chosen the place for the ambush well. They were in a hollow. The path ran steeply down into it, levelled out for about thirty yards, then, just as steeply, ascended a small hill. Though the jungle pressed relentlessly in upon the pathway on both the descent and ascent, in the hollow it eased back a few yards. Here the path was slightly broader.

Big Vinny knew this was just the place where a bunch of shit-for-brains greasers would slow down and bunch up. It was the perfect killing ground.

The men and their mules were almost upon them. The man they had out front at point was about as useful as a dead gopher. The guy, short and dressed in jungle fatigues, was no more than twenty yards ahead of the main group and though his AK-47 was unslung he was carrying it at high port. He slipped down into the hollow, then glanced to the left and right of the path. Big Vinny watched him from his well-concealed position behind the palm fronds, a few feet inside the thick wall of jungle.

The point man would be no problem. Carver Fylde was toting, along with his M-16, a silenced version of the British Sterling sub-machine gun. The weapon was virtually noiseless, and at the range Carver Fylde would be firing . . . deadly. The man would start up the steep slope and then go down. For a couple of seconds the rest of the group would think he had tripped.

In those two seconds half of them would be dead.

The point man passed within a few feet of Big Vinny. Despite the fact that the man had just come down the hill, Vinny could hear his laboured breathing. The man slowed, waiting for the others to catch up. Big Vinny smiled wolfishly. He was right, the group was about to bunch up.

The main body dropped into the hollow, the mules slithering the last few feet down the steep path. Big Vinny could see the steam rising from beneath the heavy plastic cartons on their backs; could smell the rich earthy aroma of their sweat along with the more tangy acrid sweat of the men.

The men were talking loudly, waiting for the tail-enders to ease down the path and join them before ambling across the small open space. Slowly Big Vinny rose from his haunches.

His predatory eyes, glittering brightly against the smears of black greasepaint, were fixed on the men. He turned his head cautiously, watching the point man move across the hollow and begin the climb up the opposite slope. He raised his Colt Commando assault rifle to the firing position.

He was too far away to hear the soft popping sound but he saw the point man go over onto his face like a felled tree. Some fool in the main group laughed. The laughter died with the man as Billy Bob's M-16 carbine cracked and a Teflon-coated round tore out the man's throat.

Big Vinny opened fire.

Six or seven of the Mestizos had bunched up ahead of the column of mules. The Kaplin boys took them out with automatic fire. The sudden noise of the firing and the screeching of startled Macaws and Blue-Headed Parakeets was tremendous. The men went over like pins in a bowling alley.

Big Vinny took swift but careful aim. He and Billy Bob were switched to single shots. Their job was to hit the men close to the mules without injuring the animals. Most of the men were short, standing scarcely head and shoulders above the mules' rumps. They were difficult targets.

In anticipation, Vinny and the rest of the boys had loaded the clips of their weapons with soft-nosed slugs . . . the kind that would, on penetrating the men's bodies, shatter into small pieces of red hot shrapnel and shred their vital organs to ribbons. Such rounds would exit the bodies as small pieces of lead and steel alloy, their velocity diminished, their destruction done.

The men would be murdered but the mules preserved.

Big Vinny's first shot hit the man at the tail end of the column, the round exploding in the man's viscera and punching him backwards as if he had been hit by a speeding train. He drew a bead on a second man, watching as he did so some of the armed men desperately running the short length of the hollow... towards where the Kaplins were hidden.

Others, ducking and diving behind the shifting, kicking mules and the plastic panniers on their backs, were frantically tearing at the weapons slung across their shoulders, trying desperately to return fire. None of them got that far.

Big Vinny's next two rounds were clean headshots, easy at less than thirty feet for someone with his training. His forth shot hit a man in the pelvic area, fragmenting the man's small intestine and genitals and severing his femoral artery. The man bled to death beneath the stamping feet of the terrified mules.

Then, suddenly there were no more victims; nothing was standing on the jungle path but a bunch of leaping, bucking mules. Vinny bellowed the cease fire.

The noise of gunfire stopped immediately, the vicious, staccato sounds receding in a long rolling wave of diminishing echoes into the green-covered mountains.

Vinny pushed his way out of the foliage and quickly surveyed the scene as the others emerged onto the path. The action in which he and his men had taken out nineteen drug smugglers had lasted less than a minute.

'Billy Bob,' he snapped, 'help me get these damn critters calmed.'

The Kaplins and Carver Fylde joined them in grabbing the mules' halters and pacifying the terrified beasts. They were all country boys and knew how to talk reassuringly to frightened animals. Big Vinny had thought to bring some sugar lumps. He handed them to the others who, grinning, fed them to the mules. When the last of the animals was relatively peaceful and holding still, he ordered the Kaplins and Carver Fylde to check there were no survivors.

Holding a mule's halter he nodded at his younger brother. 'You did good there, boy.'

Billy Bob grinned at him. Big Vinny called his brother 'boy', even though Billy Bob was more than thirty years old and married.

But Billy Bob hadn't been in Nam like his twelve-year-older brother. And up to that moment he had never been in action in the jungle.

52

'Was no more'n a turkey shoot,' Billy Bob replied.

'That's 'cos we was well briefed, well armed and well trained,' Big Vinny said knowingly. 'These guys were a shit-heeled rabble. They weren't soldiers. They didn't know nothing and they didn't train hard like you do, boy. How many you hit?'

'Three, four maybe.'

'You did good.'

Secretly Big Vinny had been worried about his brother's first jungle firefight.

Billy Bob was the only one left.

Joe, Vinny's older brother, had been killed in the Mekong Delta in '69 and now Ma and Pa were gone Billy Bob was all he had. The boy was Vinny's entire family. His responsibility. He surely did love the boy, even though he was sometimes wayward and didn't pay enough attention to his training. Still, Big Vinny thought, he was young and didn't always understand and appreciate the great cause that he and thousands of others were embarked upon.

The sharp crack of a .45 automatic cut across his thoughts. He glanced at the line of fallen bodies and watched Zeke Kaplin shoot another wounded Mestizo in the head. Carver Fylde, bending over a quietly moaning body with a glittering Bowie knife, flicked open the man's carotid artery like he was cutting string. Not for nothing was he called Carver.

'Okay, move it up, move it up,' Big Vinny snapped. 'We ain't got all day. We got a rendezvous to keep.' The others finished off two more of the fallen before returning to the mules.

'All done?' inquired Big Vinny.

'Yeah they're all screamin' in hell by now,' Carver Fylde replied. He grinned, showing the black gaps in his teeth.

'What about those guys?' Billy Bob asked, nodding at the dead men. 'We gonna leave them there, out in the open, on the path?'

'Sure,' Big Vinny told him. 'Even if we hid the bodies, we couldn't hide the blood. An' we ain't got time to be movin' bodies. Okay,' his voice took on the tone of command: 'we're outa here. Carver, you take point. Let's get these mules into a string an' get going. We got six hours' hard marching if we wanna meet that chopper. An' we better make it, 'cos chopper jockeys don't wait for no one.'

The men moved into their assigned tasks with the smooth,

practised professionalism of well-trained soldiers. Big Vinny watched them with pride and satisfaction, noting the distinctive rectangular flashes of red, white and black on the shoulders of their uniforms . . . the insignia of the Chicashaw Commando.

They had done well, he thought. Done what they had been sent to do. Of course the quality of the intelligence they had been working with was a hundred per cent. The cocaine had been exactly where they had been told it would be. He marvelled at the accuracy of the information. Whoever was supplying it knew what was going on in the Colombian drug business better than the DEA and all the rest of the goddam federal agencies put together. Shit, if they'd had that quality of intelligence in Vietnam, they'd have won the war.

But, intelligence wasn't everything, Vinny decided as the unit moved out and he took up tail position, peering back along the trail every few seconds. In the end it was the guys on the ground who had to do the business.

And they had.

The Chicashaw Commando had relieved the greasers of twenty million dollars' worth of cocaine. Not that any of it was destined for use by the commando. Any man found using dope, in any unit anywhere in the country, would have been court-martialled and shot. No, the cocaine was a high-value commodity to trade. The millions of dollars from its sale to the niggers and spics and fags and rich Jewboys would buy a lot of ordnance – arms and ammunition that the army of which the Chicashaw Commando was a part, badly needed.

The proceeds from the sale of the captured cocaine would enhance the army's war chest and would eventually help it win the war that every man in the Chicashaw Commando knew was inevitably coming.

The war with the United States of America.

Chapter Eight

There were a couple of dozen of them parading outside the building in Finsbury Square. They were carrying placards and chanting.

Melissa did a double take. One of the signs read 'Rolay Richard are Robbers'. She had never seen the name of the firm on a picket's placard before.

Other signs brandished by the demonstrators accused the auditors, Berrenstein Lang, of negligence, of theft, and of being in cahoots with criminals. One, carried by a good-looking black girl, read 'The Old Lady is a mean old bitch.'

'What old lady?' queried the young driver as the taxi drew up at the kerb.

'The Bank of England,' Melissa said.

'Oh, right,' he nodded. 'The Old Lady of Threadneedle Street. What I don't get is why the hell they call it that?'

'I'm not entirely sure.'

The driver was eyeing the demonstrators. 'They're right about one thing,' he declared, 'bankers are all bastards.' He frowned at the picket line. 'You going in there?' He sounded concerned.

'I have to,' she told him. 'Anyway, they're peaceful enough. They've got a right to show how they feel. They've been thrown out of their jobs and it's not their fault.'

'It's always the little people,' the cabbie spat. 'Bleedin' banks. Bunch of crooks.'

Melissa got out and paid the fare, intensely conscious of two dozen pairs of resentful eyes needling into the back of her neck. Most of the small crowd on the pavement were young and either Asian, Oriental or African. As the cab moved off, Melissa turned and attempted a sympathetic smile. None of the demonstrators reciprocated.

Of course they wouldn't, she thought. They had nothing to

smile about . . . especially to her. They were on the outside . . . picketing the Finsbury Square head office of the Exchange Bank, where they had once worked as clerks and tellers. Melissa was on the inside. She was in work and clearly, from the way she dressed, well paid for it.

Andrew Bailey, one of her staff, was standing just inside the big banking hall. 'You all right?' he inquired.

Running the gauntlet of hostile looks had flared her face. She could feel her cheeks burning. 'I've just come past the people demonstrating outside.'

He frowned. 'I thought there was a policeman out there. Did they give you trouble?'

'No, they didn't give me any trouble. It's just that seeing them there makes me feel a little guilty.'

He looked at her blankly. Clearly it didn't do the same to him. She took a deep breath. 'Well, what have you got?'

Bailey followed her as she moved towards the polished mahogany front counter and stared through the toughened glass panels which rose to the high, yellowed ceiling of the old banking hall. Beyond the glass, about thirty people from Rolay Richard's Financial Investigations department were busily sifting through piles of papers.

'A mess, that's what we've got. They were operating a bank within a bank. We can't tell if London was running the treasury operation in the Caymans or if it was the other way round.'

She nodded. 'What about the computers?'

'They're working on them now.'

Fixing her ID tag to the lapel of her jacket, she followed Bailey through a security door and down a long corridor with offices off to one side. At the end of the corridor was a large, modern suite of air-conditioned rooms.

Inside, half a dozen of Rolay Richard's computer experts were working at terminals. Smiling, she crossed the room to the desk of Boris Redbourn, the computer division's manager.

Redbourn, in his late twenties, was tall and lanky with a pony tail and round, rimless spectacles. Unlike the formally dressed accountants, he and his team were in jeans and casual shirts.

He looked up from a screen shimmering with green numbers. 'Hi, Melissa.'

She hitched herself onto the side of his desk and smiled down at him. 'How's it going, Boris?'

He shook his head. 'I've never seen anything like it. These people were living on a knife edge. There are no back-ups to this system, no bureau transfers, no duplicate tapes. It's all in-house. What's in the computer room,' he nodded towards the mainframe in the room next door, 'is all there is.'

'Playing it close to their chest.'

'More than that. If we hadn't known what we were doing, we'd have wiped everything the minute we started getting into the system.'

'What do you mean?'

'They'd set it up so if there was any unauthorised entry, the system would crash. All the entries would have been wiped out. Completely lost. The last six months' transactions.'

She pulled a face. 'Nasty.' She peered down at the screen. 'So what are you doing?'

'Running a list of overseas wire transfers made from head office. When I've finished, I'll take it to the bank's International Section in Hammersmith. I'll integrate it with the overseas currency transfers made by all the other branches in the UK and then try and run it through the mainframe at their computer centre in Ruislip.'

Melissa nodded. 'Looking for a pattern?'

'Right. Regular movements, that kind of thing.' Redbourn looked up and grinned. 'Inventing my own computer games.'

She smiled back. 'What about forms 941 and printouts of past transactions?'

'They're in a security warehouse in Deptford. Tons of 'em. Copies of remittance forms going back ten years.'

She stood up. 'Good. I want them all. Also journal rolls, monthly statements, microfiches of cheques, everything. Keep me in touch.'

She wandered into one of the offices where members of her staff were analysing deposits and withdrawals. Frank Levinson, one of the qualified accountants in her department, was supervising them. He was in his shirtsleeves, wearing a brightly patterned tie.

'Hello Frank. Found anything yet?'

Levinson looked up and grinned. He was in his late twenties, about the same age as Andrew Bailey. 'You're joking,' he said. 'These people have never heard of Bankers' Association guidelines. We've uncovered scores of dodgy transactions. As

57

far as I can tell, none of them have been reported to the NCIS.'

'Show me.'

He turned to the desk, picked up a sheaf of papers and waved them. 'Deposits of between two and three hundred thousand pounds a month being made by an antiques business in Brighton. Every month for the last two years.'

'Do we know anything about the business?'

He nodded, retrieving more documents. 'The company hasn't filed any figures with Companies House for two years. Before that, it was showing a steady stream of losses. The money deposited stays in the account for a couple of days before it's wired to a branch of the Exchange Bank in Milan.'

'Good. That's the kind of thing I want. Find out who counter-signed the deposit slips. I need the name.'

'Yeah, but that's chickenfeed,' he went on: 'there's a guy importing Chinese ceramics from Hong Kong who's depositing over a million a month. The money is being wired to Florida.'

'Who authorised the account? Do we know?'

Levinson was scrabbling among the papers covering the desk when Andrew Bailey strode into the office. 'Melissa,' his voice was agitated. 'I hear you want copies of remittance forms for the last ten years. Along with journal rolls and all the other bumph.'

She straightened up. 'That's right.'

'Why that far back, for God's sake? Where the hell are we going to put all the paper?'

She shrugged. 'I've no idea. Nigel Hawick will have to sort that out. All I know is that I want everything I can get, going back as far back as I can get it. We have to pick up the paper trail. You know that.'

She saw him flicker a glance at Levinson. 'Yeah, I know that, Melissa. But ten years, for God's sake? Why can't we just get on with it? Start by tracking the cash for the last six months?'

She sighed quietly.

She wasn't old, she told herself. Only thirty-two. Yet sometimes there seemed to be an entire generation between her and her assistants. They were both good guys, she reflected, hardworking and loyal. They just seemed so young.

'People who launder money,' she began, 'build walls. Walls of paper . . . complicated bureaucratic barriers. They build them to stop people like us following the money. It's no good attacking

58

the walls with sledge hammers. It takes too long. And when the walls do, finally, fall over, they're in such a mess it's hard to piece together any evidence to prove laundering. And that's our job. We're forensic accountants. We're supposed to produce evidence that will stand up in court. The only way to do that is to trail the paper. Slowly and methodically. To pick out a brick – just one – and carefully chip it out of the wall. Then another brick . . . and another. The only way to get the wall down is . . .'

'. . . is one brick at a time,' Bailey intoned. His eyes had taken on a glazed look.

Melissa laughed. 'Have I said that before?'

'Only about a million times,' Levinson chuckled.

Bailey was slightly mollified. 'Okay, well, I suppose you're right,' he grumbled. 'But God, ten years!' He disappeared.

She turned to Levinson. 'Let me have the name of the manager who countersigned those deposits as soon as you can. And,' she added, 'any other dubious transactions you find.'

'Okay.'

She left the office, wandered along the corridor and found herself an empty room where she emptied the contents of her attaché case onto a desk. She sat down. Instead of starting work she stared out of the window.

Has she *really* made that speech so many times before? If so, it was no wonder Andrew Bailey had looked bored. *Everybody* must be thinking how deadly dull she was.

Melissa Semmington . . . thirty-two and boring. She could believe it. What else, she asked herself, had she got apart from the job and Jamie? She never went out . . . never went to the theatre or the cinema, never ate out with friends – in fact, hardly ever saw her friends. She didn't see much of her parents. They found it difficult coming to terms with Jamie. She didn't even have a man, for God's sake. Christ, when *was* the last time she had slept with a man . . . ?

She looked up with a start. Frank Levinson was standing in front of the desk. He frowned down at her. 'You okay?'

'What? Oh yes, yes I'm okay. I was thinking about something.'

Levinson grinned. 'Bad habit, Melissa.'

He was carrying a few of sheets of paper. 'This bank had a corporate tree like the Medicis',' he complained. 'But I've been able to narrow down who authorised those deposits. Most of the slips were countersigned by the General Manager, a man called Chalmodly.'

'Chalmodly?'

'Yeah, but he's done a runner like the others.'

Melissa pulled a face. More than half the senior managers of the Exchange Bank had skipped the country as soon as news of the bank shutdown had been announced. 'You said *most* of the slips were signed by Chalmodly.'

Levinson nodded. 'Yeah. A few were signed by his executive assistant, a guy called Akhtar Aziz. He's still here. On the payroll.'

'Good.'

Melissa knew that Rolay Richard as the liquidators had required certain employees of the bank to remain in their jobs to help sort out the administrative mess. She also knew that as soon as their use came to an end – as soon as they had been squeezed of their last few drops of value – they would be made redundant. Like the people parading outside, whose chanting she could faintly detect through the barred office window.

'Okay, get me his personal file. Then find him. Tell him I want to see him. In the General Manager's office.'

'Do you mean the big boss's room?' Levinson asked in surprise.

'Yes. Do you know where it is?'

'Yes.'

Levinson disappeared and returned a couple of minutes later carrying a collection of manilla files. Melissa took a few minutes to read through them before following Levinson along the corridor and up a broad staircase to a double set of polished, hardwood doors.

Beyond them was an office the size of a football stadium.

It looked like the dining room of the Ritz. Light from three enormous, gold-leaf chandeliers reflected faintly off twenty-foot walls of polished scagliola. Standing in solitary splendour in the middle of the room was a huge, excessively carved and gilded Louis Quinze desk. A vast, deep-pile, cream-coloured carpet stretched into the distance like a desert.

Melissa gaped at the place. She had seen the executive offices of some eminent bankers, but never one like this.

Levinson grinned at her surprise as he placed the files on the enormous rococo desk. 'The top dogs certainly knew how to look after themselves here,' he said. 'God knows what this room cost. A quarter of a million maybe?'

Melissa grunted disdainfully. As far as she was concerned the place was the ultimate triumph of money over good taste.

She pulled at an enormous, green leather chair tucked behind the desk. It was so heavy she could scarcely move it. Sitting in it was like being swallowed

A slim Asian, of medium height and in his early thirties, appeared at the open doorway. Levinson showed him in, introduced him and left. With a smile Melissa indicated the chair in front of her desk.

Aziz was agitated. Melissa watched him fidgeting in his seat. Although he must have visited the room often, he seemed intimidated by its overpowering opulence. Then she realised . . . it wasn't the room that was bothering him. It was the fact that a woman had taken it over . . . a female was sitting in the General Manager's chair. An unknown woman who seemed suddenly to have seized the power. The young man's eyes held a mixture of fear and defiance.

'Mr Aziz,' she began. Her voice was warm and friendly: 'my name is Melissa Semmington. I'm one of the liquidators with Rolay Richard. My particular job is tracking criminal capital flight. In other words, money laundering.'

He nodded, licking his lips.

'Mr Aziz, are you aware of the British Bankers' Association's guidelines on money laundering?'

'I may have read them,' he mumbled.

'They are pretty specific about suspicious transactions and what bankers should do about them. As you know, anything suspicious should be reported to the National Criminal Intelligence Service.'

He shrugged but said nothing.

'Well,' she continued quietly, 'my staff have come across dozens of transactions we consider dubious. None of them appear to have been reported.'

'I don't know about any dubious transactions,' he said defiantly.

'Really? You don't consider somebody walking in off the street and changing twenty thousand pounds into dollars at your Bureau de Change suspicious? Somebody doing it *every week*?'

'Mr Chalmodly authorised that.'

She shook her head. 'Not always.' She flipped through one of the manilla files. 'I see that sometimes the currency conversions were authorised by you.'

He stared at her silently as she continued in the same calm, gentle voice.

'Don't you consider it suspicious that this branch has accounts in the names of individuals that often contained millions of pounds? Yet none of that money was earning interest . . . none of it is on deposit or in the money markets? And that those accounts were constantly using wire transfers and letters of credit to move large sums abroad?'

Again he shrugged. 'Mr Chalmodly said it was okay.'

'You don't think it strange that an antiques shop in Brighton that had losses a couple of years ago has since deposited nearly five million pounds with you?'

'Mr Chalmodly said that was okay too.'

She nodded gently. 'Yes, but the point is Mr Aziz, Mr Chalmodly isn't here. You are. And as I need to know a lot more about these transactions . . . I'm asking you.'

He stared at her. The defiance in his eyes was in the ascendant. 'What right have you got to ask me questions?'

She smiled amiably. 'As a liquidator, Mr Aziz, I have a lot of rights. But I don't want to talk about my rights. I just think it would better for you if you answered *my* questions rather than be interviewed by the police.'

She saw him start at mention of the police.

'You see,' she went on, 'I'm not here to accuse anyone. I'm not concerned about arresting people. All I'm interested in is following the money. But, if some policeman were to investigate these transactions,' she nodded at the pile of files sitting at the side of the ornate desk, 'and he found that they were drug-related, well . . .'

'Drug-related?' Aziz blurted out. 'Why would he think they're drug-related? And, even if they are, what has that to do with me?'

'If the police thought you were helping drug traffickers retain the benefits of their proceeds, then . . .' she looked at him in concern, 'you could be liable to serve up to fourteen years in prison.'

Fear flared at the back of his eyes.

'What's more,' her tone remained serene, 'the police might even believe that you had financially benefited from helping criminals launder drug money. If they did, then the court might, conceivably, issue a confiscation order.'

'What do you mean?' His voice was croaky.

'It means the court could confiscate your property, Mr Aziz. *All* your property. Your house, your furniture, your car . . . everything. Anything it thought you might have bought with money paid to you for laundering the proceeds of drug dealing. In other words if the court thought you had helped to launder drug money, and that you *knew* it was drug money, it could lock you up for a very long time. And take away everything you own. Everything,' she repeated the word quietly but firmly.

Aziz's face had turned to the colour of dead meat.

Melissa felt sorry for him.

From his file she knew he had been an assistant manager in a bank in Allahabad. Then, because he was someone's relative and because he was clever he had been brought to England to work for the Exchange Bank. And because he was very clever and had worked hard and had done as he was told without asking questions, he had been made an executive assistant to the General Manager. The poor sod, she thought. He would have been thinking he had made the big time. Seventy thousand a year and a BMW.

Now it was all going down the toilet.

It must be a nightmare, she reflected. Watching the bright, shiny life turn to ashes. And on top of that, some woman was threatening him with the police.

'But I didn't know it was anything to do with drugs,' he whined. 'They couldn't prove that I knew.'

She shook her head. 'No, I'm afraid you don't understand the law, Mr Aziz. *They* don't have to prove that you knew. *You* have to prove that you didn't.'

There were flecks of white at the corners of his mouth. He was beginning to shake. 'Whatever happened to British justice?' he said venomously.

She thought about it for a moment. 'I don't know,' she said softly, shaking her head. 'It probably went the same way as honest bankers.'

He stared at her. The light of defiance had flickered out in his eyes. There was nothing in them now but fear.

'Of course, there is a way out of all this.' Her voice was warm and encouraging.

His eyes glimmered.

'Disclosure of suspicion that transactions might be related to drug trafficking is a defence in law.'

He didn't understand. All he knew was that she seemed to be offering him an exit.

'If you had told Mr Chalmodly that you thought these accounts and transactions were dubious, and if he had informed the Criminal Intelligence Service about them, then nobody could have accused either of you. But Mr Chalmodly didn't tell the NCIS. And now he's disappeared.'

Aziz was staring fixedly at her.

'Which leaves you in an awkward position. There's no proof that you said anything to Mr Chalmodly. What's more, many of the authorisations are signed by you. It really would have been better if you had told your boss of your suspicions. Wouldn't it?'

He was gazing at her like a dog. He nodded.

'Of course,' she said quietly, almost as if to herself, 'I suppose you still could. After all, I'm the liquidator and you work for me. I'm your boss now, aren't I?' She smiled at him. 'So, if you told me everything, and I mean everything, about what was going on in this bank . . . told me where all this funny money was coming from, and, more importantly, where it was going to, then nobody could accuse you of anything. Could they?'

He swallowed hard. 'Couldn't they?'

'No. You will have told me. I will have told the Criminal Intelligence Service. We will have done our duty as citizens. No arrests, no prison, no criminal record. Both of us will be in the clear. But,' suddenly her voice was stern and crisp, 'you must tell me everything. No secrets. Nothing held back. You understand.'

He was agitated. 'But if I tell you what I know the men I work for will be very angry.' His voice was low and scared. 'They may punish me . . . my family.'

'Mr Aziz, I told you. You work for me now. Mr Chalmodly and the other men you worked for . . . most of them have run away . . . left the country.'

'No, no, I don't mean Mr Chalmodly,' he murmured. 'I mean the others.'

She frowned. 'Others? What others?'

He wasn't listening. 'They are very powerful, very ruthless. I think they would not like me to talk to you.' He was almost mumbling. 'They are remorseless. They have much influence and long memories. They do not forget anyone who betrays them. No. I cannot tell you anything.'

64

She grimaced. What the hell was he was talking about? she wondered. She stared at the scared man across the rococo desk.

'Will these men come and visit you in prison, do you think? Will they buy you another house and new furniture? A new car? Because that's what you're facing if you *don't* talk to me.'

She gave him an encouraging smile. 'All you have to do is tell me what I want and I'll go away.'

He gazed at her with rheumy eyes. He was on the edge. She could tell. From experience she knew this was when he could go either way. Open out or close down completely. Now, she thought, was the time to give him a little room. A little time to consider the mess he was in.

Suddenly she stood up from the deep, leather armchair. Aziz started in his seat.

'Think about it,' she said. 'I'll be here tomorrow. Come and talk to me. If you tell me everything then, probably, you won't have to talk to the police. And no one else need ever know that we talked.'

He stood up. He was like an old man, slack-mouthed and shaking. She watched him shuffle across the enormous expanse of carpet towards the big double doors.

As soon as he had gone she picked up the phone. For a moment she stared at it . . . then put it down. She gazed unseeing at the room's polished marble-like walls, thinking hard about what she intended to do.

It was pretty mean and shitty. No, not *pretty* shitty, she corrected herself, it was *definitely* shitty – a mean and sleazy act. But what else could she do?

She had no desire to cause Aziz any more grief. She knew the poor sap was just a small player in a very big game. But now she had him on the run she had to do something to frighten him into going the distance . . . scare him enough to tip him over the edge. To tip him *her* way. She had, she told herself, no alternative.

She sighed and lifted the phone, got an outside line and punched up a number.

The phone at the other end was lifted and she asked for DCI Lankell. After a moment a voice grunted down the line. 'Dennis,' she announced, 'it's Melissa. Listen, I'm at the British head office of the Exchange Bank. There's an executive assistant here called Aziz who's right on the edge of telling me everything he knows. And I'm pretty sure he knows a lot. He's stalling right now, but what I think might push him over the edge is if some policeman turned up at his house asking for his passport.'

The deep voice at the other end of the line chuckled. 'Do we have any legal grounds for asking for this man's passport?'

She laughed lightly. 'Dennis, I'm an accountant, not a lawyer. I've no idea. But my guess is that it would induce Mr Aziz to tell me all he knows.'

'We could get into a lot of trouble seizing a passport without good reason.'

'I'm not suggesting you *seize* it. Just find some reason to politely take it away for a couple of days. When he's told me everything, you can give it back to him. Say it was a mistake.'

The voice chuckled louder. 'A mistake eh? So, is it going to be worth my while then? This mistake?'

'Yes, I think it is,' she answered quietly. 'On my desk right now is a pile of deposit slips and transfer receipts. It amounts to a lot of money. Millions. All of it laundered through this branch. And I'm pretty certain most of it's drug-related. Which is why I'm calling you and not the SFO.'

The voice snorted in derision. 'The SFO. That lot are about as much use as tits on a pilchard.'

She smiled. Nothing would get Dennis Lankell onside quicker than playing to the inter-departmental rivalry that existed within the forces of law and order. 'Maybe. But whilst it's still around, I'm supposed to report to it. Only pulling passports isn't really their thing. Nor are drugs.'

'So, like I said, what do I get out of scaring this bloke shitless?'

'God, Dennis, I don't want you scaring him to death. Just frighten him a little. He's got enough problems without you getting heavy. He'll be out of a job in a week.'

'Jesus,' the voice laughed sharply, 'you've got a soft heart. So, okay, what do I get out of being nice to Mr Aziz?'

'Do you know anything about an antiques shop in Brighton?'

There was a moment's silence. 'I might do.' The gently mocking voice was suddenly guarded and serious. 'Why?'

'A Brighton antiques shop, which not long ago was losing money, has deposited over five million in an account at this branch. I have chapter and verse of when those funds arrived and where the money has gone. Mr Aziz probably knows a lot more about the account than that.'

'You'd better give me his address,' the voice at the other end growled.

Aziz asked to see her early the following morning.

Melissa decided to interview him in an office close to where her people were working. She couldn't abide the ostentatious grandeur of the General Manager's room.

She motioned Aziz to a seat across the desk. He looked ghastly. His face was drained and muddy and the skin beneath his eyes black from lack of sleep.

'The police came to my house last night,' he croaked. 'They took away my passport.'

'I'm sorry.' Melissa was silent for a moment. 'Maybe I could help you get it back.'

Aziz's tired eyes slitted with suspicion. He stared at her. 'But only if I help you first,' he murmured.

Melissa shrugged. She felt uncomfortable. 'I'm afraid that's how the system works.'

He nodded. 'For you to help me, I must help you.' His tone was leaden.

'Yes.'

The leaden tone became anguished. 'What choice do I have?' She didn't answer.

After a while he seemed to come to a decision. 'Very well. I will tell you what I know. If you promise to help me get my passport back. And,' he added intensely, 'if you will not tell anyone that it was me who helped you.'

'I promise.'

He studied her for a few moments then pulled a number of folded papers from an inside pocket. 'This is a list of all the Managers' Ledger Accounts.'

'The what?'

'The codename accounts the bank was operating.'

Melissa frowned. 'Mr Aziz, we already know which accounts were numbered and had codenames. We are in the process of examining them. I need you to do better than that.'

'No, you don't understand. The Managers' Ledger Accounts are the accounts the auditors were not permitted to access. These were completely secret.'

Melissa's face puckered as she recalled the meeting with Kenneth McKinnie and the other auditors. 'The accounts the

Exchange Bank said were classified? The ones the bank wouldn't allow to be inspected?'

He nodded. 'Yes. There are some that the auditors did not even know existed.'

Melissa stared at him. 'The auditors didn't know about them? How the hell did the bank manage to keep them from the auditors?'

Aziz shrugged. 'We had ways.' He was clutching the sheaf of papers, holding them close to his body.

Melissa could feel the excitement bubbling in her blood. 'I see.' She was quiet for a moment, her eyes fixed on Aziz's face. 'Would you like to give me the list?' she said gently.

The face across the desk took on a hunted look. 'But if I give you this list, you must never say where you got it. Never. And you must help get me my passport back. The men behind the bank – I told you – these men are dangerous. If they knew I had given you this information . . .' His voice tailed off. Melissa watched his adam's apple slide up and down. 'They must not know I spoke to you . . . that I told you anything.'

Melissa smiled gently at him. 'And *I* told you, Mr Aziz, that most of the senior management of the bank has left the country. You have nothing to fear from them.'

He shook his head, irritated at her obtuseness. 'No, no, you still don't understand. The men *behind* the bank. The backers. The Americans . . . the Arab gentlemen. It is they who are dangerous.'

She stared at him. 'You know who these people are?'

'Yes.'

'How? How do you know about them?'

'I was the General Manager's assistant,' he replied proudly. 'It was my job to go with the driver of the limo to the airport. To greet our important visitors. To settle them in their hotels . . . accompany them back here. Some I met were not officers of the bank. Mr Chalmodly told me they were the bank's backers . . . investors. He said they were very powerful. Very discreet . . . but powerful. He said they were the ones who really ran the bank. He told me always to be careful around them. That they were . . .' his voice tailed off again, ' . . . extremely dangerous.'

She frowned once more. Aziz, she suddenly realised, had access to more information than she had thought . . . information that would be of great value to other people digging into the background of the bank.

She gazed at the young man across the desk, realising that, whatever she had promised him, she wasn't going to deliver. She would be unable to keep her promise. Other people, the police, the SFO, would have to know what Aziz knew. She would have to tell them.

Informing on Aziz was necessary . . . what he knew might be vital in investigating the bank's affairs. Blowing the whistle on him was the right thing to do. It was her job. But knowing that didn't make her feel any better.

She had promised to protect his anonymity. And she was going to betray him.

She shook her head, banishing her concern. Right now, the men behind the Exchange Bank were not her problem. What had happened to the millions washing through its secret accounts was.

'So, as the General Manager's assistant, you must have had a great deal of responsibility?' Her tone was encouraging, masking her treachery by massaging what little was left of his ego. 'You would have known a lot about the Managers' Ledger Accounts.'

'Of course,' he responded proudly. 'Here in this office, only Mr Chalmodly and I were allowed access to them. I inspected them often . . . monitored the movement of the funds.'

'I see. So you can help us decipher those accounts . . . tell us who or what the codewords represent . . . tell us where the money came from and was moved to?' She tried to keep the excitement out of her voice.

His face clouded over. 'Maybe,' he croaked. 'But only if you tell no one that I have helped you. And if you help me get my passport back.'

'Of course.' She nodded, looked directly at him . . . then averted her eyes. 'So,' she repeated, 'do you want to give me the list?'

He gazed at her like a frightened animal, then slowly, reluctantly passed the papers across the desk. Melissa saw his hand was shaking.

There were three sheets of paper. About fifty names were listed alphabetically. She skimmed the names swiftly. They looked like a long list of British and European place names. Melissa guessed they had been lifted from a gazetteer.

'And you had access to all these?'

'Yes. Well . . . all except the Austerlitz Account of course. No one had access to that. Not even Mr Chalmodly. Only Mr Kunzman had access to the Austerlitz Account.'

Melissa made a puzzled face and looked up. 'Who is Mr Kunzman?'

'He was one of the men I was telling you about. An American gentleman. Mr Chalmodly said he was *very* powerful; one of the most influential men behind the bank. I think Mr Chalmodly was extremely afraid of Mr Kunzman. He visited us often. He visited all the regional head offices.'

'You mean like some kind of bank regulator. A compliance officer?'

'Yes.'

'Was he an officer of the Bank?'

'I don't think so.'

Melissa shook her head in puzzlement. 'And you say only he had access to this Austerlitz Account?'

'Yes, only him. He operated it solely. It was very secret.'

Melissa stared at the young man across the desk for a moment longer then drew a bold blue ring around the name Austerlitz.

Chapter Nine

'This bank was a Frankenstein!' she exclaimed. 'A monster. Uncontrollable.'

Hawick was staring at Melissa's notes and the papers spread across his desk. He nodded in agreement.

'It was a bigger crook than the people using it,' she continued. 'It was losing millions on currency transactions and covering the losses with money taken over the counter. It was transferring funds to third-party banks, then bringing them back as fresh deposits. God, it was a hall of mirrors. It was breaking all the rules. It had to keep taking in more and more deposits to keep going. Vicious circle. It's obvious that billions of dollars of the laundered money I'm looking for were used by the Exchange Bank to cover its own losses.'

'So you think the Exchange Bank's senior managers were double-crossing the gangsters behind it?'

Melissa was standing in Hawick's office with her back to the glass partition and the busy office beyond. 'It certainly looks that way.'

Hawick's face was serious. 'Christ, you just don't cross people like that. Not and get away with it, you don't.'

Melissa shrugged. 'But I think the Exchange Bank *did* get away with it. Well, pretty much. As the men behind the bank weren't bankers, they wouldn't have been up to all the tricks. It must have been difficult for them to keep a check on what was going on.'

Hawick's forehead puckered in thought. 'You reckon that's why they employed this man Kunzman? To tour the bank's offices? Check up on them?'

'Maybe. It's possible. I've talked to Aziz four times in the last ten days, going through the codename accounts. Whenever the name Vito Kunzman has come up, he's gone pale. He said people in the bank were more frightened of him than anyone else who visited. The word is that Kunzman was more than some kind of bank inspector. It's rumoured that wherever he went, violence followed. If someone in the bank stepped out of line ... was found with their hand in the till, well ...'

Hawick made a deprecatory face. 'Bit dramatic isn't it?'

'Shady money attracts shady characters, Nigel.'

'Well, this bloke Kunzman is so shady I'm not sure he actually exists. He definitely wasn't an officer of the bank. His name isn't on any employee payroll anywhere in the world. In fact there's no record of him anywhere. We've only got Aziz's word about him. I've circulated all Rolay Richard's offices to see if *we* have a record of any dealings with him. Though I don't think it's likely. Not if the man was some kind of enforcer for the bank.'

'If the bank really did use people like that, it's no wonder Aziz was so frightened in handing over that list.'

'It also explains why so many of the top people have skipped Europe and disappeared back home. Well, at least,' he grinned at Melissa, 'we've got Aziz. He's not going anywhere.'

She grimaced. 'God, I feel bad about that, Nigel. I told him I'd help get his passport back.'

Hawick laughed and shook his head. 'He won't be getting that back for a while. He's too valuable. He can point to the people behind the bank. The *real* people.' He paused. 'I hear some officials from Washington are flying over to talk to him about the men he met at the airport.'

Melissa frowned, remembering Aziz's terror of being known as an informer ... his anxiety at helping with her inquiries. 'I promised I'd protect his identity,' she said in a leaden tone. 'I said I wouldn't tell anyone he was helping us.'

Hawick shrugged indifferently. 'You have to say what you have to say, Melissa. Make promises you know you can't keep. Sometimes it's the only way to get the job done.'

'He won't want to talk to them,' she stated firmly.

Hawick laughed harshly. 'He won't have any choice. The people coming across are heavyweights from the Fed and the US Justice Department.'

Melissa shook her head in despair and her shining, copper-coloured hair splayed an arc over her shoulders. 'Why can't they leave the poor man in peace?' she wailed.

'Because he knows things they want to know . . . that *we* want to know. Aziz may not like it but . . .' he shrugged dismissively, 'the silly bastard shouldn't have got mixed up with the bank in the first place.'

Melissa opened her mouth to remonstrate but Hawick waved her protest aside. 'Anyway, never mind him. What else have you got?'

Melissa grimaced. Right now Hawick was too gung ho to concern himself about Akhtar Aziz. Maybe later, she thought. She turned her mind to the papers on Hawick's desk.

'We've got deposit trails crossing and re-crossing each other all over the globe. The cash tracks go everywhere. I tried drawing them the other day, making a diagram to see if there was a pattern. After a while it looked like . . .' She stopped.

She was about to say one of Jamie's drawings . . . one of those stuck to the refrigerator on which scores of coloured lines whirled and looped aimlessly all across the paper.

She smiled wanly. 'Well, it looked like I'd split the atom. So I've got the computer boys working up a programme of asset hierarchies and corporate networks. When that's finished we might see some patterns . . . we may be ready to start unravelling a few strands.'

'Yeah, but have you got any definite leads right now?'

'Yes, I'm pretty sure I've found my first brick.'

Hawick smiled. He had heard her little homily.

'So far, Aziz has taken me through about a dozen of the codenamed accounts. All of them relate to dubious businesses which were shifting stacks of cash overseas. Some look like tax evasion . . . one of them I'm pretty sure is an enormous VAT scam. Four that I've referred to Dennis Lankell at the Drugs Squad definitely check out to be drugs-related. One of those is an antiques shop in Brighton. Actually, we picked up the fact that the business was making big deposits when we first started, but the information hidden in the codename accounts shows the total funds flows.' She grinned. 'Thanks to Aziz I've got a pretty good picture.'

'So, what is it?'

'Money from the antiques shop was being deposited at the London head office branch of the Exchange Bank and then wired from there to an account in the Milan branch. I've checked with our own Milan office and found out that the account belongs to a small Italian company whose parent company is incorporated in Canada. The Canadian company is owned by a corporation registered in Hong Kong. The interesting thing is that none of the money going into Milan was being remitted to the holding companies. Instead it was converted to dollars, bundled with other funds coming into the Milan account and then wired to the Exchange Bank in the Cayman Islands.'

Melissa could see Hawick was interested. 'So how much are we talking about?' he asked.

She leaned over to check a fact in a file on his desk and after a moment straightened up. 'The account in Milan was remitting about eighty million dollars a month to the Caymans.'

Hawick raised his eyebrows. 'Hell, that's a billion a year.'

'About half of that was being forwarded straight away from the Caymans to a branch of the Exchange Bank in Barranquilla. The rest . . . well,' she shrugged, 'we don't know. The trail goes cold in the Caymans. Maybe the money stayed in the Caymans. Maybe it moved on.'

Hawick turned in his seat and stared through the glass partitioning at the open-plan offices, silently deliberating. Finally he nodded. He had come to a decision. 'You'll have to go out there.' His tone was definite.

She was shocked. 'What? To hell with that. Forget it, Nigel. I'm not going anywhere near Colombia. It's too dangerous. I've got Jamie to think about.'

He shook his head. 'I don't mean Barranquilla. I'm not interested in the money going there. It's obvious what that's for. More drug deals. The narcotics boys can worry about that. But what about the rest? What's happened to it? That's what we need to know. Where's the forty million a month that wasn't moved out of the Caymans? Where's it gone? There's only one way to find out, Melissa. You'll have to go out there. See if you can get a lead on it.'

'For God's sake, Nigel. You can't ask me to leave Jamie to go swanning off to the Caribbean. Why can't Andrew go? Or Frank? Why not let the people out there handle it?'

He shook his head. 'Frank and Andrew are too junior. And the local people will need directing. By you. You need to go, Melissa.' His tone was definite.

'But I'll be gone at least a week,' she moaned.

'That's all right,' he said brightly, 'you've got a good nanny haven't you? She'll take care of your son. He'll never know you've gone. It'll be just like having his mother with him.'

'Nigel,' her voice was icy with outrage, 'it *won't* be just like having his mother. *I'm* his mother for Christ's sake.'

He stared at her in shocked silence. He couldn't figure out what had suddenly got her so upset.

She sighed.

'You look as unhappy to be leaving London as I am.'

She looked up from her seat in the departure lounge.

He was tall and dark and smiling down at her. She wondered if it was a line.

For a moment she thought of disdaining him. She could be good at that. Like any attractive woman who travelled widely, she'd learned to treat pick-ups with icy dismissal, But he *was* extremely good-looking and he *did* have a disarming smile. Most of all, she knew exactly what he meant. She had been frowning dourly at the floor, trying to remember if there was anything she'd forgotten to tell Astrid before she'd left the cottage.

'You look like you're trying to figure out if you've covered all the bases.'

'Bases?'

'I mean all the things that might possibly go wrong . . . all the nightmares that could happen whilst you're out of the office. You looked to be worrying about whether you'd thought of everything. Hell, I know the feeling.' Again the disarming smile.

She gave him a neutral took. 'As a matter of fact I wasn't thinking about work. I was thinking about my son.'

'Your son? I see.' He gazed down at her for a moment then smiled sympathetically. 'Life is pretty easy for us guys, isn't it? We can leave all the problems behind. Go off at a moment's notice with no more to worry about than whether we packed a spare pair of socks. But I guess it's much tougher for mothers. You gotta travel to do the business, yet there's nobody at home who can do the kind of job you can do.'

He sounded as if he understood. A rare man. She stared up at him. He was tanned and athletic and looked in his mid-thirties. Touches of grey were appearing in the dark hair at his temples.

'May I sit down?'

She nodded cautiously.

He took the seat next to her. 'I saw you from the check-in

desk. You looked so . . .' he searched for the word, 'sorrowful. I thought I just had to come over and say hello. Try to cheer you up.' He paused. 'No, no, not cheer you up. To commiserate. Yeah, that's it: to commiserate. I guess it's because you were looking the way I feel.'

She considered him with interest. 'Why should you be unhappy? You sound as if you're going home.'

He laughed. 'I'm sad because I love this country so much. I always hate to leave it. But, sure, I'm an American if that's what you mean. Though Miami isn't my home. I'm just there on business.'

His brown eyes were warm and friendly. Melissa relaxed a little. The eyes of aspiring one-night stands were usually filled with stony guile.

'So where is home?' she asked.

'Manhattan.'

She nodded. 'Exciting city.'

'Sure is. What about you? Where're you from?'

'I live in Hampshire. In the country.'

'I envy you,' he laughed. A steward called the flight and they both stood up. 'My name is Robert Briscoe by the way.'

'Melissa Semmington.' They shook hands.

'Maybe we'll get a chance to talk some more on the flight,' he said.

He was sitting three rows behind her in First Class. Halfway through the flight he wandered along to her seat and they talked casually. They had a lot in common.

He was in investment banking and, like her, travelled a lot. She liked him. He was easy and relaxed . . . amicable but not overpowering. He wasn't pushy; he didn't ask for her telephone number nor suggest a date when next he was in England. He said to call him Bob.

After a while he made ready to return to his seat. He told her he'd enjoyed the conversation and hoped they might meet again. She didn't see him when the flight landed at Miami. She was vaguely disappointed.

She made her connection at Miami International and just over an hour later heard the change in the monotonous tone of the Boeing's engines. The 727 was starting its approach to Robert Owens airport.

Melissa peered down. Beneath the wing was Grand Cayman, its low-lying terrain lushly covered in the vivid, sub-tropical green of the Caribbean. Circling the rim of the island was a narrow, glowing, almost pure white margin of sand beyond which an aquamarine sea shimmered into the horizon in a billion scintillas of dancing light.

She stared down at the island with mixed feelings. It wasn't her first trip to the Caribbean. She had been there before.

It had been on a holiday in Antigua, she reflected ruefully, that she'd met the man who had become Jamie's father. Her other trips to the area had been on business. None of them had turned out very well either.

Her last visit had been the previous year when she had spent a week in Barbados, kicking her heels in the Hilton on Needham's Point. She had been waiting for the outcome of a petition to the court to release records relating to the bank account of an English multi-millionaire businessman.

The businessman's company was in liquidation and he had been arrested on suspicion of embezzling millions out of the company and its pension funds. Melissa was sure that documents in the small Bridgetown bank would lead to the location of the missing money and prove the man's guilt.

The court had finally ruled there was insufficient proof that the man had committed any crime. Therefore it was not prepared to grant an order to release the requested documents. Melissa had retained a good local lawyer who'd pleaded that if there *had* been proof of the man's guilt, the liquidators would not have been asking for release of the papers. The proof, the lawyer told the court, hinged on the papers locked in the bank. The argument had cut no ice. The court announced that as no crime had been committed in Barbados, it wasn't prepared to grant the speculative requests of some multinational accountancy practice from London. It was tantamount to telling Melissa to sod off.

Colleagues in London had been envious. She had returned from the island looking wonderful. She'd got a lot of sun. But she hadn't got any satisfaction. Even now the case still rankled. It had taken her weeks of extra work to compile the evidence. In the end the SFO had dropped the case for lack of evidence and the businessman had walked away as free as a bird.

Staring at the Caribbean paradise from the window of the plane, Melissa hoped this trip would turn out to have a better result.

A tall black man in his early forties was standing at the barrier. He was dressed in a white short-sleeve shirt and dark cotton trousers, and he was holding a large white card. Her name was written on it. She saw him through the crush of tourists. 'Hello,' she smiled, 'you're looking for me.' He stared at her appreciatively for a moment then grinned.

His name, he told her, was Eugene Dacre and he was a partner from Rolay Richard's Miami office. He was heading the team of accountants shipped in from the firm's offices in Miami, Houston and New Orleans to work on the shutdown of the Exchange Bank's Georgetown Branch. He lifted her suitcase off the trolley and they walked outside.

The humidity hit her instantly, enveloping her like a hot flannel. It was the rainy season and a shower was imminent. A taxi driver, standing close to an old and dusty Volvo, gave Melissa an enormous grin. 'Welcome to Grand Cay-*mahn*,' he exclaimed. He took her case from Dacre before asking: 'Where you wanna go *mahn*?'

Dacre looked at her inquiringly. 'The Hyatt Regency,' she said. Suddenly, she was exhausted. She was desperate to call Astrid.

'You been to the island before?' Dacre asked as the driver crashed the gears and the Volvo shot away.

She nodded wearily. 'A few times. When you're hunting money, the first thing you do is raise your eyes to the havens.' He chuckled.

The hotel, set in broad acres of luxuriant landscaped gardens, was close to a wide strip of beach stretching miles into the distance. It was late afternoon and the azure sea was calm. A slight wind stirred the flaming red blooms of the flamboyant trees.

'It's paradise isn't it?' said Dacre as they followed the driver and her case into the hotel.

'So was the Garden of Eden,' Melissa observed in a tired, sardonic voice, 'and look what happened there.' Dacre gave her a peculiar look.

By the time she was shown into her room the sky had turned slate grey and the rain was rattling against the windows like a bootleggers' gun battle. She fixed a swift drink from the mini-bar then called England. Astrid answered immediately. Jamie was sleeping peacefully and everything was fine, she said.

After the call Melissa took a shower and put on a white

towelling bathrobe she found hanging behind the bathroom door. She lay on the bed and fell asleep.

The taxi ride from the hotel was short. The driver, when he wasn't cursing American tourists for looking the wrong way as they crossed the road, was cheerfully talkative.

It was eight thirty and already the temperature was in the seventies with the humidity building. The sky was a cloudless, cobalt blue and the radiant light to seaward so bright it was dazzling. Georgetown was busy. It was Saturday morning and the streets were already bustling with tourists and locals. Melissa eyed them enviously. None of them were forensic accountants she thought.

Forensic accountants worked weekends.

Melissa liked Georgetown. It was the size of a small English town, with palm trees instead of plane trees lining the pavements. The buildings were on a human scale, with nothing taller than five stories. Many were built of white-painted clapboard; the sun's glare bouncing off their surface hurt Melissa's eyes. Almost as painful on her optic nerves were the clashing colours of the tourists' shorts and shirts.

The Exchange Bank was a white, colonial-style building near Elgin Avenue. Dacre was waiting for her in its expensively appointed, subtly lit, air-conditioned interior. It was the start of a gloriously sunny weekend and his team were hard at work. After he had introduced everyone to Melissa he led her into a back office.

'I've got the general manager coming in every day to give us some help,' he said. 'Not that he's much use. I hear he tried to make a run for it but he couldn't get off the island. My guess is that he knows a lot more than he's saying. He was in charge of the branch here as well as the bank's treasury department.

Melissa nodded. Miguel Artevalo was a Panamanian who had been with the bank a long time. Akhtar Aziz had told her something about the man before she'd left London. 'I'll see if I can get him to cooperate,' she told Dacre.

He looked at her sceptically.

In his experience you needed to be hard-nosed and nasty when dealing with someone like Artevalo. Privately, he didn't think Melissa had what it would take to make the guy come across. It wasn't that she was a woman. He knew plenty of women who could shred a guy like Artevalo into a million bits. It was her nationality. He figured this beautiful English rose was far too polite and well-mannered to get anything out of that bastard.

Melissa caught his look but ignored it. 'I'm going to need you and your people to help me track every dollar of the money coming from Milan,' she told him levelly. 'I'll want details of all the accounts into which it's been deposited. If it's a company account, then I want everything we have on record about the company. Whether the Exchange Bank was acting as the company's agent . . . whether it was owned by a trust . . . anything and everything. Okay?'

'What if it's been moved to an account in another bank?'

'Depends which bank and where. If it's one of the Canadian or Swiss banks here in the Caymans, well . . .' She shrugged. 'You know what they're like. It'll be difficult to get them to open up.'

'Not as difficult as it used to be.' Dacre's voice was hard-edged. 'Uncle Sam has got pissed off with the banks down here. The Fed has been putting pressure on them . . . telling them to regulate their offshore branches – or else. The banks can't afford to get on the wrong side of the dollar so they're coming into line. They're more cooperative now. If you can show the money passing through their branches is drug- or terrorist-connected, they'll come across.'

Melissa raised her eyebrows. 'Really? That's useful to know.'

She went in search of Artevalo. He was a tall, heavy-set man in his mid-forties with dark hair and a full, fleshy face. His English accent was British rather than American. He affected the bonhomie he believed appropriate to an English country squire.

'My dear Miss Semmington,' he announced, 'do come in. Sit down. How nice to meet you, though how sad to do it under such unhappy circumstances. Who would have thought that the Exchange Bank would one day be in the hands of liquidators? It was such a force for good you know, a beloved bank in the Third World, a wonderful . . .'

She interrupted him. 'Mr Artevalo, I am going to need your full cooperation.'

'Naturally dear lady. And you will have it. Anything in my power.'

'Good. Firstly, I need you to help me track some funds that

80

have been arriving here regularly from Milan.'

His face changed slightly. 'Yes, but you realise I must protect the interests of the bank.'

She stared at him unblinking. 'Mr Artevalo, the liquidator *is* the bank.'

'Well, yes of course I realise that but . . .'

'So I will decide what's in the bank's interests.'

Melissa opened her attaché case, extracted a file of papers and laid it on the desk before her. 'I have information here which alleges you were helping to create the illusion that the Exchange Bank's treasury department was independent, when in fact it was being controlled by London. The British tax authorities might consider you were helping the bank evade UK tax on the treasury's profits.'

Artevalo smiled superciliously. 'The treasury department made more losses than profits. Anyway, it's hardly a crime.'

'These papers also contend that you were using depositors' funds to cover up those treasury department losses. That *is* a crime. The British police could decide to prosecute you for fraud. So might the local authorities.'

Artevalo's bonhomie was disappearing. His face had turned pale. 'Who told you all this?'

'I have a notarised statement signed by a senior person in the London head office. I also have information that this branch, under your instructions, was receiving millions of dollars in cash. Suitcases full, flown in by private jet from Canada, the United States and South America. Either you were not registering the deposits or you were falsifying them.'

Perspiration was beading Artevalo's forehead. 'Who in London would tell you such a thing. How would they know?' he croaked.

She shook her head. 'That is none of your business. Just take it from me that I have chapter and verse about the activities of this bank and of the treasury department.' Melissa stood up and picked up the file. 'Naturally, Mr Artevalo, in view of the seriousness of these allegations, I shall be expecting your complete cooperation with my colleagues.'

He stood up with her. He was trembling. 'I have to say,' he told her petulantly, 'that I find your manner a little brusque, Miss Semmington.'

She looked up from putting the file in her attaché case. 'I'm sorry if you find me brusque,' she told him, 'but I need to get this job done. I have responsibilities in England to get back to. Also,' she snapped the locks of the case shut, 'I don't care too much for people who collaborate with crooks.'

Ten minutes later Dacre found her in an empty office. 'What the hell did you say to Artevalo?' His voice held a note of admiration. 'The guy's out there busting his balls to be helpful.'

She gave him a wide, innocent smile. 'That's nice.'

For three days she worked with Dacre's people, sifting through the records. Carefully they tracked the funds as they moved in and out of accounts, inspecting every transaction slip, analysing every account statement, noting every signature on every mandate.

By the fourth day she had started to see some light through the mountains of paper. She sat down at a desk with Dacre.

'It looks like most of the accounts the Milan money disappeared into are owned by Swiss or Liechtenstein trusts,' she told him.

'Then it's gonna take us months to trace the people behind them,' Dacre said mournfully.

'If we ever do,' she agreed. 'Some accounts – those owned by Panamanian shell companies – we may *never* find out who the beneficial owners are. Still, we're getting there.'

'Yeah?' he sounded doubtful.

'Definitely.' She smiled encouragingly at him. Her face was lightly tanned from spending lunchtimes outside and the sun had sheened her hair to a lustrous gold. 'I think I've found my brick.'

Dacre frowned and gave her a puzzled look.

She shuffled a pile of papers and pushed a few towards him across the desk. 'Look. This account is owned by a Cayman-registered company called Pemblin. The account was receiving between three and seven million dollars a month from Milan. Now, Pemblin owns a Californian company called . . .' she shuffled the papers some more, 'Piagini, which has a loan from a company registered in the Bahamas called Cyclix. The loan is for forty-five million dollars. But I don't see anything about collateral for the loan. It's unsecured. And anyway, why borrow from a third party when Piagini's own parent company, Pemblin, is stuffed with money? And why is Pemblin receiving all this cash from Italy?'

He looked up and nodded. 'It doesn't make sense. Not unless

the three companies are owned by the same people.'

'Exactly.' She was triumphant. 'Piagini is moving money out of America. It's transferring it to Milan then washing it back into the Caymans. Then it rehabilitates the money into the States by apparently borrowing it. It goes out dirty and comes in clean. One clean dollar for every dirty dollar. It looks legitimate . . . looks like a genuine loan. Piagini will even be getting tax relief on the interest which, in reality, it's paying to itself. The company is making itself a series of back-to-back loans . . . borrowing its own money.'

'It's a classic laundering operation,' observed Dacre dryly.

She nodded. 'I've phoned the San Francisco office and asked them to fax me what they can on Piagini.'

Dacre sifted through the papers then glanced up at the lovely face smiling quietly across the desk.

He had misjudged her in the beginning, he thought. It was a simple mistake to make. She was English and easy to underestimate. But it hadn't taken him long to discover that behind the lovely face was a mind as tough as whipcord. Melissa could hunt the money through the most tortuous routes. She didn't give up.

She could also, Dacre reflected, turn an arrogant, uncooperative bastard like Artevalo into an eager, kiss-ass toady. She was as tough as any professional he knew. The only difference was . . . she didn't show it. Not unless she had to.

'There's one piece missing,' she continued. 'Pemblin is also receiving payments of five million dollars a month from the local branch of the Royal Bank of St John's. If that money is being transferred by Cyclix, then we've got the full picture. We've tracked the cash all the way home.'

'How're you gonna find out?'

'I have an appointment with the manager of the St John's Bank this afternoon. I'm hoping he's going to tell me.'

Dacre pulled a face. 'The guy may not be too happy to oblige.'

Her eyes narrowed slightly. 'You don't think he'll cooperate?'

He stared at her for a moment, then his face broke into a broad grin. 'Are you kidding? Hell, my money's on you, Melissa. All the way.'

The Caymans branch of the Royal Bank of St John's was just off Edward Street. It was a modern, three-storey building, with brick stonework and smoked-glass windows.

Melissa was shown into an office with a bakelite sign on the desk. It announced to anyone who might be interested that the manager's name was Ian Forbes Paston, a thin, nervy man of medium height with sandy hair and rimless glasses. He was from Ottawa, he told her as they exchanged business cards. He invited her to sit down.

'So, what can I do for you, Melissa?' he drawled.

'I need details of who has been paying these sums from your bank into that account at the Exchange Bank.' She pushed a sheet of paper across his desk.

He glanced at the paper then looked up. 'Details?'

'Who controls the account in the Royal Bank of St John's? In whose name is it operated?'

He gave her a condescending smile. 'Hell, Melissa, I can't reveal that kind of information. Not to an outsider. This is the Caymans.'

'What do you mean, an outsider?'

He shrugged. 'A person who has no legal right to the information.'

'Any bank has a legal right to know who is depositing money with it.'

'Sure, the bank's entitled, but . . .'

She sighed. 'Mr Paston,' she interrupted, 'Rolay Richard is liquidating the Exchange Bank. That means we *are* the Exchange Bank. I'm not an outsider. I'm an insider. I'm also an officer of the court. I want what my bank is legally entitled to.' Her voice was calm and controlled but with a cold, steely edge. 'And by the way,' she added, 'I would prefer it if you didn't call me Melissa.'

He flushed. 'Look, you can't come out here and start demanding information about other people's bank accounts. Maybe you don't know it, but here in the Caymans you can go to jail for making inquiries into the financial affairs of a bank's customers.'

'You can also go to jail for laundering drug money.'

His face changed. 'If it can be proved,' he said cautiously.

'It can. I'm currently tracking the transfer of a billion dollars a year from Europe into the Exchange Bank here in Georgetown. If necessary, I can obtain a signed affidavit from Detective Chief Inspector Lankell of the Metropolitan Police Drugs Squad stating that more than five million dollars of that money is known to be from the sale of drugs.'

'That's hardly a significant proportion,' Paston sneered.

Melissa shook her head. 'One bad apple in the barrel isn't a significant proportion either. One drop of prussic acid in your tea wouldn't be significant. But it would be enough to do the business. If even a small amount of drug money is involved, *everything* is tainted.'

'I don't see how the information you want,' Paston waved a hand at the paper she had passed him, 'relates to any of that.'

'It completes my investigations.'

'Well, I'm sorry,' he said defiantly, 'I'm not going to divulge this information. Not without a court order.'

Melissa took a deep breath. 'Mr Paston, Rolay Richard will soon be knocking on the doors of the Fort Street Courts and applying for production orders. We both know the firm will succeed in getting them. The thing is . . . I'm not prepared to wait.'

Paston shrugged insouciantly.

'I don't need to,' she continued. 'I'm liquidating the Exchange Bank under the direct supervision of the Bank of England.'

'So?'

She gave him a bleak smile. Her voice remained steady and hard-edged.

'The Cayman Islands are a British colony, Mr Paston. And the Cayman Islands Currency Board is advised by the Bank of England. *Closely* advised,' she emphasised. 'The Bank of Canada also works closely with the Bank of England. All these central bankers and regulatory authorities . . . well, you know how they are. They're very close. They're a club.'

Paston was frowning at her. 'Yeah. So what?'

'What I'm saying is that I'm working for one of the biggest members of that club. Which gives me a lot of leverage on this island. Far more than any agent from the United States. If someone from the FBI or the DEA were to walk in here waving a warrant, you could ignore them. Well, you can't ignore me. If I don't get what I want . . . now . . . this afternoon, I'm going to call a man at the Bank of England and scream blue bloody murder. That man will make two phone calls. One to the Bank of Canada and one to the Currency Board here. And twenty-four hours from now, you'll be en route to your next posting. As assistant manager of your bank's Moosejaw branch, north of the Arctic Circle. Now, I hope I've made myself clear.'

Melissa paused and gave him an angelic smile. 'Just give me what I want,' she said sweetly, 'and I'll go away.'

It was less than a mile back to the Exchange Bank. The rain was holding off and Melissa strolled through the hot afternoon sun.

'Well?' inquired Dacre as she walked into a wall of cool air in the lobby. 'Did you get it?'

She nodded. 'I was right. The owner of the account at the Bank of St John's is the Cyclix Corporation of Nassau.'

'The manager at the St John's Bank told you that?' Dacre's voice was incredulous.

She grinned. 'Yes. In fact he's given me everything about *all* of Cyclix's accounts. Which was more than I asked for.'

Dacre threw back his head and laughed. 'Goddam. You just made me forty dollars, Melissa.'

She frowned. 'I did? How?'

'The guys here were making book on whether you could screw anything out of the manager at St John's. I had my money on you.'

She laughed. 'You did, did you? Well, it wasn't easy. I hate having to bully people. Anyway, now you're in the money, you can buy me a drink. I earned it.'

It was still early when Dacre and the others left the beach club bar. Melissa wasn't hungry, so instead of crossing the road back to the hotel, she took off her shoes and wandered a little way along the broad strip of Seven Mile Beach.

The sand was damp and as soft and pale as powdered milk. She dug her toes in as she walked, staring out over the dark, softly washing sea to where a huge, gibbous moon was slowly rising. To her right, a myriad lights were sparkling on West Bay road. The restaurants and hamburger joints, set in among the hotels and low blocks of condominiums, were doing good business. The rhythm of Caribbean music and the sounds of laughter and tinkling glasses came muted on the velvet night.

She felt the tears stinging her eyes.

She wished Jamie could be there to enjoy in his own private way what she was enjoying. Even more, she wished she could be there with a man. A man she could love. A man who would love her. And Jamie. She blinked back her tears. She was being silly, she told herself. The magic of the place was arousing the impossible . . . conjuring up absurd fantasies.

High above the emerging moon she noticed a single, solitary star. She stopped and stared at it, feeling an instant affinity. She and the star had a lot in common. They were both alone.

A couple of young men, islanders, strolled past on the sand. One called to her. 'Hey, *mahn*, you wanna come for a beer?' She looked around, smiled and shook her head. She turned back towards the hotel.

Two faxes, one from London, the other from San Francisco, were waiting for her the following morning.

'Oh, no,' she moaned as she read the one from London.

'What's wrong?' Dacre inquired.

'Nigel Hawick wants me to go on to California.'

'Why?'

'The San Francisco office has a lead on Piagini. They've faxed me the details. But,' she wailed, 'I want to get back to Jamie.'

She called Hawick who was adamant she make the trip. 'Barry Wagstaff will explain,' he told her. 'You must go, Melissa. I'm sorry.'

She put the phone down and checked her watch. It was nine thirty. She would have to wait five hours before she could call Wagstaff. She sighed and stared out of the window. An American tourist wearing a gaudy pair of yellow and purple shorts was climbing into a van parked in the street outside.

She went in search of Artevalo. She wanted to get him alone and was pleased to find him shuffling papers in a small office. She closed the door behind her and sat down without being invited. 'I have some more questions,' she announced.

Artevalo stared at her across the desk and a hunted look appeared in his eyes.

'Did Mr Kunzman visit the bank often?' she asked.

The hunted look turned to fear. 'You know about Vito Kunzman?'

'Please answer my question.' There was a long pause, the silence of the office broken only by the faint hiss of the air conditioning.

'About every four months,' he croaked after a moment.

'What was the purpose of his visits?'

Artevalo shrugged. 'To check up on branch operations. And the treasury department.'

'Why? What was he? A bank supervisor? Some kind of compliance officer?'

'You could say that.'

She wondered what he meant. 'Well, was he or wasn't he?' she snapped. Artevalo said nothing. She considered him irritably. God, it was so bloody annoying when she had to drag the information out of them, she thought. When she had to prod them into answering every damn question.

She leaned forward in her seat, her voice soft but insistent. 'Look, just give me what I want and I'll go away.'

Artevalo took out a large, red, polka-dot handkerchief and, despite the air conditioning, began wiping the perspiration off his forehead and the back of his neck. 'Very well,' he said reluctantly.

The look on Melissa's face softened. 'Now . . . Mr Kunzman. What did he do? Was his job to ensure the Exchange Bank complied with the law? That things were done properly?'

'Yes, that was mainly what he did. He represented the owners . . . the investors behind the bank.'

'But there's no note of his name anywhere on any of the bank's employment rolls. So he wasn't employed by the bank.'

'No. I think he was employed by the owners. You see, the bank's backers didn't really understand banking. I mean, they had invested their money, but, well, modern banking is very complex and they couldn't always understand what was happening.'

'So Mr Kunzman's job was to protect the owners' interests.'

'Yes. Vito Kunzman knew more about what went on in the Exchange Bank than anyone else in the world. Excepting of course the bank's founder, Dr Campeche.'

Melissa screwed up her face. 'Campeche? Wasn't he killed?'

Artevalo looked mournful. 'Yes. An awful thing. He was shot dead in a tenement slum in Caracas three months ago. No one knows why. Dreadful business, simply dreadful. In my opinion Hidalgo Campeche was one of the greatest men of the twentieth century. He founded this bank to be a force for good, you know. To help the little people of the Third World. Perhaps it's as well he didn't live to see its demise . . . to see it being picked over by liquidators.' Artevalo shot her a baleful look. 'He was a truly great man. I met him on several occasions you know and . . .'

Melissa wasn't interested in Artevalo's stories of rubbing

shoulders with the rich and the famous. She watched him closely. 'Do you know anything about an account codenamed Austerlitz?' she asked. 'It was a Manager's Ledger account. Operated solely by Mr Kunzman.'

Artevalo thought for a moment then shook his head. 'Austerlitz. No I've never heard of it.'

She was disappointed. She stared at the big man across the small desk, certain he was telling the truth. 'Was it usual for people who weren't even officers of the bank to be operating codename accounts solely on their own? Without bank officials knowing what was going on in them?'

Artevalo shrugged. 'We did not always do things conventionally,' he said proudly. 'After all, it was not considered conventional wisdom in the first place to set up a bank for the benefit of the citizens of the Third World.'

'Many of whom have now lost a lot of money,' Melissa pointed out acidly.

'Only because regulatory officials in the West decided to close the bank down,' Artevalo responded sourly.

Melissa made a face. She wasn't about to get into some pointless economic argument about the rich nations versus the poor. Nor could she be bothered to point out how corrupt the Exchange Bank had been. That was not what she was there for. 'You said Mr Kunzman's *main* job was as a kind of compliance officer,' she said. 'What else did he do?'

Artevalo's voice lost its edge. 'Bad practice,' he said quickly. 'He was concerned about any misfeasance in the branches.'

'Checking to ensure no one was defrauding the bank?'

'Defrauding the bank meant defrauding the owners,' Artevalo said bleakly.

'Did he discover many incidents?'

Artevalo nodded 'A few,' he muttered.

'Were the individuals prosecuted?'

The big man across the desk dabbed at his throat with the polka-dot handkerchief and pulled a wry, pained face which Melissa couldn't interpret. 'Were the people involved prosecuted by the authorities for fraud?' she repeated.

'They died,' he mumbled.

She wasn't sure if she had heard him aright. 'Pardon?'

'They had accidents. Or they were murdered. Or they disappeared. Sometimes their families as well.'

Melissa felt something cold crawling up her legs and into her belly. She hoped Artevalo could not sense her discomfort. 'What do you mean?'

He looked sick. 'Occasionally Mr Kunzman would say that a manager or a clerk in a branch somewhere had been caught defrauding the bank. That's all. He would merely make a point of mentioning it.'

'He didn't say the branch had reported the matter to the local police?'

He shook his head. 'The bank had a policy not to involve the police. But, always a few weeks afterwards we would hear on the grapevine that the person Mr Kunzman had mentioned was dead. Or had disappeared.'

Artevalo paused. 'The death was always violent,' he went on in a strained voice. 'One man in Karachi was burnt to death in his home. He and his whole family. Another, in Brazil, was found in his car which had run off the road into a swamp. Some managers were shot dead . . . murdered in front of their families. Supposedly by robbers. Invariably it was the people Kunzman had said were suspected of stealing from the bank.'

'Are you suggesting he was involved in the deaths of these people?'

'Personally, no. Vito Kunzman is an extremely sophisticated and urbane businessman. He would never be involved in anything like that personally.'

'But he could arrange them. He could order these . . .' she paused, seeking the word '. . . murders.'

Artevalo stared at her. 'He is a very powerful man,' he said.

Melissa gazed back at him numbly. 'Do you realise what you're saying?'

A glimmer of a smile passed over his face. 'Yes, I do realise what I'm saying, Miss Semmington. Though I fear it is not what you wanted to hear.'

At just after two thirty local time she rang Rolay Richard's San Francisco office and asked for Barry Wagstaff. Wagstaff was the senior partner in the office. She had met him a few times at some of the firm's international seminars.

'Melissa, you got the fax?'

'Yes. But I don't see why you want me out there. Not if the FBI is involved.'

'Because, all of a sudden, you're the one driving the bus,

Melissa. The Bureau says it's been watching Piagini for over a year yet you've come up with a lot of stuff about the company the Feds didn't know about. If you're onto tracking Piagini's money, the boys in the Bureau would like to talk to you.'

'But you know the FBI,' she grumbled. 'They're more concerned with arresting people than following the money. Though of course,' she added acidly, 'if I do manage to track Piagini's funds and get a court order to have them confiscated then, all of a sudden, the Bureau will be interested. Whereupon there'll be an almighty bloody row about who gets to keep the money. I don't need it, Barry. I'm not working for the American Justice Department. I'm working for the Bank of England.'

She heard Wagstaff's chuckle down the line. 'Don't worry, that's all taken care of, Melissa. The senior man in their field office here has cleared it through Washington. Someone there has spoken to your Serious Fraud people and to a guy at the Bank of England. It's all set. The deal is that the FBI gets the indictments and the bodies and the British get the money. A search warrant is being executed tomorrow morning. The Fibbies want you in on it.'

'What?' she yelped.

'Yeah, that's right, Melissa. They want you here. There may be papers and such relating to the money.'

'For God's sake!' she moaned. 'Tomorrow morning? I haven't booked any flights. I'll be travelling half the night. I wanted to get back to my son.'

'Yeah, I'm sorry. It's a tough break.' He sounded sympathetic. 'Still it's only for a couple of days.'

She wasn't mollified. 'This is ridiculous. It's too much to ask.'

'There is something else,' Wagstaff said enticingly.

Her voice was bad-tempered. 'Oh yes? And what the hell is that?'

'The raid tomorrow. It's on a house.'

'So?'

'The house is registered in the name of a guy Nigel Hawick says you dug up in London.'

'Guy? What guy?' she snapped.

'Kunzman. Vito Kunzman.'

91

Chapter Ten

The man with the gaudy shorts of mauve and yellow dolphins took the flight out of Grand Cayman to Miami International where, in the men's room, he changed into a medium grey Brooks Brothers suit. He was just in time to catch the seven fifteen flight to Washington.

The man wasn't important enough to rate a chopper. The unmarked car waiting for him at the National Airport whisked him rapidly through the light traffic on the George Washington Memorial Freeway, following the west bank of the dark Potomac.

Security at Langley checked him through quickly. They had been told to expect him. He took the elevator to the third floor and walked the length of a dark-blue carpeted corridor to an office in which, even though it was late, a bulky, middle-aged man with short grey hair and blue eyes was seated behind a desk. Waiting.

'Well?' demanded Mullhane.

The man shrugged and slumped into a heavy leather chair in front of the desk. 'It isn't good. The liquidators have got some hot-shot forensic accountant bitch called Semmington tracking down a flood of Mob money going through California.'

'To hell with the Mob,' growled Mullhane. He was chewing on a half-smoked cigar. Wisps of smoke hung in the still, golden lamp light of the large room. 'Are the bean-counters going to trace the Agency funds?'

The man made a face. 'Right now they have people working in every branch of the Exchange Bank throughout the world. They're looking at transactions going back years. In London they're analysing the bank's computer records and matching them to the wire transfers. These liquidator guys are thorough. I figure sooner or later they're bound to uncover something.'

Mullhane grunted. 'Yeah, but it depends on *what* they uncover.

If they get inside our accounts, are they gonna know they belong to us? Will they figure out what the funds were for?'

The man shook his head. 'I don't see how they can. They're too deep, too well protected. No one's gonna figure what they were for.'

'If they do, years of work will be compromised,' Mullhane growled. 'And even if they don't, we're still gonna lose the money. None of the front companies will stand up to scrutiny. The liquidators will assume they're criminal and confiscate the cash.'

He chomped on his cigar. 'It's a mother of a mess. Either way we lose. Shit.' He stood up, paced around the desk and leaned against its edge. 'If only we could find this deep throat the Brits have gotten hold of. Know where they're holding him . . . what he's told them. We need to know how much this guy knows.'

'Who's to say he knows anything?' responded the man. 'The Agency didn't advertise it was using the Exchange Bank.'

'Yeah, but somebody smart on the inside could maybe have figured it. It's just possible. It didn't take us long to know the IRA, Hamas and the rest were using the bank. If we knew about them, then it's possible this guy could've known about us. The only way we'll know for sure is if we find him.'

The man looked doubtful. 'Sure, but first we have to know who he is.'

'So, when's that gonna be?' Mullhane spat viciously.

The man looked up, spreading his hands. 'We're working on it. It could be one of dozens of guys. We're following through on all of them.'

'Any leads?'

'Maybe.' The man was cautious. 'We've got a couple of things to work on. They could amount to something or nothing. We don't know.'

'Well, for Chrissakes get on with it. And this woman, Semmington. She's good you say?'

The other man nodded. 'Yeah, I'd say.'

'Still, she's gonna be stuck on Grand Cayman for a while, eh? They're not well known for cooperating with investigators.'

The man shook his head. 'Don't count on it. We ran audio surveillance on a meet she had with a bank manager yesterday. She had the guy running scared. Told him the money she was tracking was narcotics-related. That got him worried. Things have changed. If the banks down there think they're handling

93

drug money, they roll over easy. This dame and the rest of her people have got a lot of clout in that part of the world. More than our people.'

'Yeah, how's that?'

'She's working for the Bank of England. That counts for something on Cayman.'

'For Chrissakes,' Mullhane wailed, 'you mean to say some bean-counting broad working for a bank with nancy bouncers in pink frock-coats has more leverage than we have?'

'That's about the size of it.'

'Judas priest,' he groaned. He turned, went back to his seat and threw himself into it. He drew long and hard on his cigar and shook his head slowly at the ceiling. 'What kinda fucking world is this?' he murmured.

Suddenly he sat bolt upright. 'Shit, maybe that's why this guy went to the Bank of England. Why he blew the whistle to the Brits and not Uncle Sam. He went to them because he knew they'd have the muscle to dig things up. Yet, at the same time, it would be harder for everyone: us . . . the Mob . . . the mad mullahs . . . to know what was happening. Hell, this guy is really smart.'

'But why not go to the Fed?'

Mullhane shrugged. 'Who knows? Maybe the Mob has friends in the Fed. It's pretty certain the Bank of England doesn't have any connection to the Mafia. Gay Liberation maybe. Not the Mob.'

The man across the desk looked doubtful. 'Somehow, I don't see the Mafia having friends in the Federal Reserve. There's got to be some other reason why the guy ran to the Brits.'

'Such as what?' Mullhane shook his head. 'No, my guess is it's the Mafia. The guy's worried about LCN getting to him.' He paused and frowned. 'Did you say the accountant broad was tracking a stack of Mob money in California?'

'Yeah. And she's got details of all the Cyclix accounts.'

'The Mob accounts in Nassau we've been using?' The man nodded. 'Damn.' Mullhane stared up at him. 'That's bad. How the hell did she get onto them so fast?'

'This dame is good. Very good.'

Mullhane looked perturbed. 'It's serious if she digs into those accounts.'

'Maybe,' the man began in a cautious voice, 'if the bitch gets any closer, we should think about doing something to slow her up.' He gave Mullhane a calculating look.

Mullhane was guarded. 'Yeah? What did you have in mind?'

'Well, if we're worried about her, then you can bet your balls that so are some of our Colombian and Arab friends. We could always get word to them. Tell them the person who's looking to walk off with their frozen funds is some hoity-toity English broad. Those guys don't mess around. If they thought the bitch was gonna grab their cash, they'd put her out of business. Permanently. She may be shit on wheels in Grand Cayman, but she wouldn't be so hot lying on a slab in a morgue.'

Mullhane chomped on his cigar and stared at the man.

'Melissa.'

She heard the raised voice and turned. The concourse at Miami International was crowded with departing passengers and at first she didn't see him. Then he emerged, weaving his way through a group of diminutive Japanese tourists shuffling towards a check-in desk like a bunch of myopic moles.

'Hey, whaddaya know.' He grinned at her boyishly.

'Bob, what are you doing here?' Her face lit up as they shook hands. She was amazed yet delighted at the coincidence.

He laughed. 'Catching a flight. Just like you I guess.' He was carrying a foldover flight bag and a bulky attaché case. 'I'm done with my business in Miami so now I'm flying out to the coast. To San Francisco. I guess you're going back home huh?'

'No, no. I'm going to San Francisco too.'

He stared at her. 'Gettoutahere!' His smile was tinged with doubt. 'Come on, you're putting me on!'

'It's true,' she protested, laughing at his look.

'Hey, isn't that something. But we can't both be on the same flight.'

They compared tickets. Melissa was booked on a later flight. She felt a pang of regret.

'Hell, that's a shame.' He looked disappointed.

'Well, at least it gives me the chance to say goodbye to you properly,' she said. 'I missed you when we got off the flight from Gatwick.'

'Yeah, I had to hurry. I was . . .' He stopped, his face brightening. 'But wait up. Where are you staying in San Francisco?'

She frowned. 'I can't remember where they booked me in.'

She put her suitcase down, opened her attaché case and began searching for a scrap of paper.

'They?'

'Colleagues of mine in San Francisco. Ah, here it is. The Pacific Plaza.'

'How long will you be there?'

'Just a couple of days. I want to get home to my son.'

She closed the case and put it down on the polished flooring of the concourse next to her suitcase. She was standing close to Briscoe. Bubbling streams of people eddied around them like a river around a rock.

'Sure. Of course. But look, as I'm staying in the city too, why don't I call you? We could have lunch or drinks or maybe even dinner.'

She studied his tanned, handsome, animated face. 'Wouldn't you prefer,' she asked quietly, 'to get your business in San Francisco over with and get back to Manhattan and your wife? Rather than have dinner with me?'

His face changed and became serious. 'Melissa, you're absolutely right.' He paused. 'If I had a wife, that's exactly what I would do. Finish my business and get right back to her. But, I don't have a wife. Nor even an ex-wife. Honest.'

She kept her eyes on his face for a few seconds longer. Then she smiled. 'Then, yes, I'd like it if you called me. Though I really don't know what my plans will be.'

'That's okay,' he grinned. 'I'll call tomorrow. Early. If you're not there, I'll leave a message. It'll be good to see you again. Even if we only have time for a coffee. And speaking of time,' he went on, 'I must check in or I'll miss my flight.'

'Yes of course. Well, I'm so glad we met again.'

'Me too. I'll call you. Have a good flight.' Again they shook hands.

She had only moved a few yards when he called after her. 'Hey, Melissa.' She turned. 'I don't know where you've been but you've caught a little sun. You look terrific.'

His words kept a smile on her face for the duration of the long, tedious flight.

The phone by the bed warbled insistently. When it finally occurred to her that it wasn't going to go away, she reached out from under the covers and picked it up.

96

'Hi, Melissa, morning!' It was Barry Wagstaff.

'What time is it?' she mumbled.

'Six fourteen,' he replied in a bright voice. 'It's a beautiful day and I thought I'd call and tell you what the plans are.'

'My plan was to sleep a little later than six fourteen, Barry,' she said caustically. He exploded in a loud guffaw. With a wince she pulled the phone away from her ear.

They met in the local offices of Rolay Richard which occupied the twenty-seventh to the thirtieth floors of one of the financial towers on Jackson, north of the Square. Melissa was captivated by the view eastward over the sunlit waters of the Bay to the distant shoreline of Oakland and Berkeley. Nobody else in the crowded office paid any attention to it.

'Melissa,' said Barry, 'this is Sam Barber.'

She shook hands with a tall man in his mid-forties with sharp blue eyes and grey hair. He was wearing a well cut, lightweight suit and had a look about him of tough intellegence – a reliable, steady man with a reliable, steady handshake.

'Sam,' Wagstaff continued, 'is special-agent-in-charge of the Agency's West Coast Enterprise Crime Unit.'

Melissa smiled quietly to herself. She had never yet met an FBI man who wasn't a *special* agent. Maybe, she thought, because of the nature of her work, the men she worked with from the Bureau and from its Enterprise Crime Units had to be 'special'. But the title always made her think of little boys' adventure stories.

Like all the others Barber smiled with his mouth but not with his eyes. Like all the others, she reflected, he was undoubtedly carrying a loaded gun.

'Sam is the coordinator on this investigation with the other agencies,' Barry explained.

'Other agencies?'

'That's right, Mizz Semmington. There are people here from the Agency, from the DEA, the IRS and the DA's office.' Barber swept a hand around the crowded room. Melissa's gaze followed the gesture. She noted four or five women in among the dozen or so men. Everyone was talking quietly and drinking coffee out of styrofoam cups. 'A lot of folks are interested in Piagini and its activities.'

She frowned. 'I hope this won't turn into a bureaucratic battle over who gets what.'

'No way,' Barber assured her. 'The lines are very clearly drawn. You fill us in on what you've discovered in the Caymans and give us copies of any documents. Though of course you keep the originals for any application you make to the court. Any papers we find today that you think might help your application,' he gestured expansively and almost spilled his coffee, 'we'll let you have.'

She was surprised. 'It's not normally so cut and dried.'

'There's a lot of cooperation on this one,' he told her, 'from both sides of the pond. We intend to nail this outfit. We want to put a lot of bodies away for a long time. But we figure a liquidator like you has the best chance of winning an application to confiscate the money. And money is the lifeblood of these people. We wanna see 'em bleed to death. We don't care too much about who gets to keep the blood. Just so long as they don't.'

'Well, that's fine.' She smiled at him.

He smiled in return and his eyes softened slightly. 'I also want to say thank you for coming so far out of your way to be a part of this morning's team.'

She nodded in acknowledgement. 'I have to admit I was torn,' she told him, 'but when Barry said your warrant was for a house I was hooked. It's hard to give up the chance of a house search. Businessmen's homes are like goldmines to a forensic accountant.'

He laughed loudly. A young man came up to him and whispered in his ear. He listened, then nodded. The young man retreated as he called the room to order.

'Okay, listen up everybody.' There was instant quiet. 'The place we're going to is a private residence. It's supposed to be the address of some stockholders of Piagini and its associate companies. We've had it under surveillance for a couple of days and now we've got a warrant we intend to hit it. A team from the DA's office and officers from Marin County went out there earlier this morning to secure the place. We've just heard they're set and everything is fine.'

There was a murmur around the room. Barber paused for it to subside.

'Now . . . we're taking some people from Rolay Richard with us. That's why we're meeting here. These people are part of the team liquidating the Exchange Bank . . . which, as I guess you know, is almost as much in the news in Britain as it is over here. The accountants have a high sight on Piagini's money laundering.

So if we find anything relating to the business, or the money, we let them know. Okay? Right, the time is now eight fifty-two. Let's move out.'

A score of them filed out of the room. Melissa noticed the light from the fluorescent tubes reflecting off the plastic of their ID tags as they moved along the corridor. She allowed herself another little grin. Everyone was labelled . . . like a line of luggage on legs.

In the lobby Barber lightly touched her arm to hold her back. The others, with the exception of Barry Wagstaff, went on through the automatic glass doors and onto the sunlit sidewalk. A long line of cars drew smoothly into the kerb. 'We take the third car,' murmured Barber.

It was a Lincoln. A young man holding a mobile radio got in beside the driver as Melissa, Barber and Wagstaff climbed into the back. The convoy moved off immediately.

'How did you find out about Piagini and the house?' Melissa asked as the driver made a left turn.

'Piagini is in the leisure business,' Barber told her. 'Theme parks, movie theatres, night clubs, that kind of stuff. Perfect for moving dirty money. We figured some time ago it was a laundering enterprise for organised crime. We started surveillance proceedings . . . monitoring the company and its affiliates. We discovered the corporation has a lot of associated and subsidiary companies, one of which is buying up chunks of real estate in Alberta.' He stopped to issue some instructions to the young man riding shotgun who immediately started speaking into his radio.

'One of the vice presidents of that company had put down as his address this place we're going to. Someone in the Bureau thought they recognised it. We checked. The address had been used several times before. Seven names associated with Piagini, all supposed to be major stockholders, had it listed as their residence. We started to wonder if it was a branch of the Y, or some high-class flophouse. Then we checked some more . . . and found that none of those stockholders existed.'

Melissa nodded. 'Standard practice for setting up crooked or dummy companies. Real person, false address. Real address, non-existent person.'

He gave her a penetrating look. 'You've come across it before?'

'Oh, yes. It gives bent businessmen a measure of protection.

Because one or two names on the register of shareholders are real, the natural assumption is that they're all real. Because a couple of the addresses actually exist . . . then it follows they all exist. Corporate crooks and laundrymen do it all the time. Who can possibly check everything?'

Barber laughed sharply. 'You're right.' He was silent for a while, studying her. 'By the way,' he asked, 'where are you staying?'

'The Pacific Plaza. Why?'

His face was impassive. 'I'm assigning one of my people to keep an eye on you. While you're in the city.' He saw Melissa frown. 'It's probably not necessary but . . . well, I like to play it safe.'

Barry Wagstaff leaned forward in his seat. 'You think there could be a problem, Sam?' His voice was serious.

He shook his head. 'No. The people from Piagini don't know what we're doing.' He glanced at Melissa. 'They certainly don't know you're in town. But, the fact is that right now over one hundred million dollars of their money is frozen in accounts in the Exchange Bank. That has to be hurting. And they must know that sooner or later someone's going to start investigating those accounts. What they don't know . . . yet . . . is that we're on to them this quick. But searching this place today is gonna alert them.'

'And you think that could make them . . .' Wagstaff chose his words with care ' . . .interested in Melissa?'

Barber chuckled. 'Hell, Barry, everybody involved with the Exchange Bank is interested in Miss Semmington.' He switched his gaze to her. 'The guys behind the bank would give their right arms to know what you're doing . . . where your investigations have gotten to . . . what kind of progress you're making.'

'Yes, I'm conscious of that,' she said quietly.

'But why are you babysitting Melissa? You think these Piagini people might want to take things further?' The anxiety lingered in Wagstaff's voice.

'I can't believe they would, Barry. They're businessmen. They know there's not much they can do about their money without coming out into the open . . . going through the courts. I don't think they would try to . . .' it was his turn to hesitate, searching for the right word ' . . . intimidate anybody. They know they're facing major institutions – the central banks – big firms of

100

accountants. There's no point in using force on people like that. The institutions would just keep on coming.'

'But . . . ?' Melissa said heavily.

'But you never know,' Barber continued. 'Liquidators have been attacked before. You never know whether there's some screwball out there who doesn't understand how it works. I don't want to take that chance.'

Melissa was quiet for a few moments. 'Well,' she said finally, 'if you're going to have someone watching over me, I hope he gives me some elbow room. I'm hoping to have dinner with someone this evening.'

Barber smiled. 'There's no way we would interfere with your social life, Mizz Semmington. Anyway, who said anything about a he? If I assign a guy to the job, he might be too busy looking at you to be looking at the people around you.'

He grinned at her and she laughed appreciatively.

She glanced past his shoulder and noticed they were on an elevated section of the freeway over the Presidio. Seated between the two men Melissa had not taken much notice of where the car was heading.

Suddenly, she caught sight of one of the world's most familiar sights, its towering, red-leaded stanchions bracketing an endless span of gently curving highway strung beneath steel suspension cables which, at that distance, seemed no thicker than harp strings.

The structure, soaring above the green-grey waters, glowed in the sea-washed light sweeping in over the Bay. The cars crossing the bridge glittered in the sunshine of the fine, early June morning.

'Golden Gate?' she exclaimed. 'Where are we going?'

'Didn't I tell you?' Wagstaff sounded surprised.

'Tell me what?'

'The house is across the bridge. In Marin County.'

'Oh.'

The driver slowed the car long enough to throw some coins into a hopper at the tollbooth and then they were on the bridge, following the leading cars and heading for the haze of Marin County.

Across the bridge the convoy came off the freeway and drove into Sausalito through sunlit avenues lined with palms. The streets by the waterfront were filled with tourists scrutinising the chic clothes and expensive jewellery in the windows of the little shops. Bobbing on the water was a forest of yacht masts. 'This place seems familiar,' Melissa said, gazing along the waterfront at some gaily coloured houseboats.

'Oh yeah? You been to Sausalito before?' Wagstaff inquired.

She shook his head. 'No. It's just that it seems . . . feels . . . European. It reminds me of Montreux. You'd scarcely think this was America.'

Barber laughed. 'Well, it is. You'd better believe it.'

The lead car made a turn and the convoy headed west, away from the centre of the town and up a series of steep, pine-lined avenues. The street they levelled out on was broad and straight, with an occasional glimpse of the sparkling, silvery Bay through the Cypresses and Monterey Pines lining its edge. The houses on it were large and rustic and set well back from the road.

The driver reduced his speed to a crawl. Melissa noticed a couple of police cars parked outside a house up ahead.

The driver swung the Lincoln through a broad, stone-pillared entrance and onto the drive. Melissa studied the house. It was big, built sometime in the twenties, of stone and shingle with a three-storey turret at one end. She got out of the car, noticing the tarmac drive was ribbed and pitted and that, on closer inspection, the house needed a lot of attention.

'This is Vito Kunzman's house?' Her voice was slightly incredulous.

Wagstaff nodded. 'The place is in his name.'

'I'm surprised. I'd have thought someone like him would have lived in the East. New York, or Washington perhaps. Not here.'

'Why, what's wrong with here?' Wagstaff inquired grinning. 'Sausalito is a nice spot.'

'Oh, yes, I'm not saying it isn't. It's just . . . well . . . it's out of the way. And the house looks a little run down. Why would he choose to live here?'

Wagstaff chuckled. 'I'll tell you what, Melissa. When we get inside, let's ask him.'

Chapter Eleven

His final act was to give the mules the last of the sugar and to remove their halters. When the chopper's rotors whirred into an awful cacophony of noise and motion they set off at an ungainly gallop and disappeared into the jungle.

The chopper flew them south and east, crossing the border into Venezuela and finally arriving over a clearing high in the jungle south of San Cristobal.

Big Vinny stared out of a window as the helicopter hovered at treetop height. The clearing had two big prefabricated hangars and a small barracks. All the buildings were well camouflaged from the air and looked as if they had been there some time.

Maybe, Vinny conjectured, the base had once been part of some strategic support command for the Nicaraguan Contras; the prefabs filled with Claymore mines and M-16s, the barracks peopled by mercenaries who had spent their days teaching teenage students how to ambush Government patrols.

Now, he thought, all of that was long gone. The students and the Government troops had long ago died crying in the mud and the mercenaries had grown old and gone home to dream of blood and battles and whatever old mercenaries dreamed of. Since when the command had lain empty and deserted and the jungle had silently crept up on it.

Until Big Vinny's people had quietly commandeered the place. He wondered how they had managed it. Small and unauthorised as the base was, someone had to have a lot of pull to take it over.

Connections, he decided. It had to be connections. It always surprised Big Vinny just how well connected the Movement was . . . how well connected and how well supplied.

There were a couple of hundred armed units like the Chicashaw Commando scattered throughout every state in

America, and someone, somewhere, was providing them with a steady supply of money – money to buy modern arms and ammunition.

Someone, some man or group of men, was powerful enough and rich enough to do that. Someone had the strategic vision to be coordinating the units, meshing their command structures, integrating their training, overseeing their recruitment.

Soon, Big Vinny reflected as he watched the jungle at the edge of the clearing bend and shimmer beneath the beat of the rotors, the Manifest Militia would be big enough and strong enough to form its own party. A party ready to threaten the fatcat Republican and Democratic placemen who lined their pockets on Capitol Hill whilst they sold the country down the river.

And soon after that – no matter what happened, no matter whether the party won or lost – the Militia would take over.

And then the cleansing would begin. The niggers and the spics, the greasers and the beaners, the fags and the Catholics and the Jews – all the vermin would be exterminated. It was what the people really wanted. They just didn't know they wanted it. Not yet. But they would.

When they could see, when they could finally accept that America had a chance to go back to the way it once was . . . when they realised that the country could fulfil its Manifest Destiny . . . the destiny that the Almighty had given to the American people alone . . . then the people would welcome the militia and rejoice to see vermin's blood washing in the streets . . . washing the country clean.

It all came down to vision. To seeing the future and grabbing it by the balls. And to connections, he decided. Whoever had known about the cocaine coming down off that mountain had been party to first-rate intelligence. They had known the time and the location to within a few hours. All Big Vinny and the boys had needed to do was waste a few greasers and lift the stuff. Easy. As sweet as a nut.

The mission, he concluded, had turned out to be the smoothest he had ever been on. And the most important. Its success would help shape the destiny of America.

He grinned at Billy Bob sitting in the metal bucket seat opposite as the chopper touched down close to one of the hangars. Billy Bob grinned back. He too seemed happy in the knowledge that the Chicashaw Commando had played its part in bringing their country's destiny a little closer. Twenty million from the sale of the dope securely tied down in the rear of the cabin would buy a lot of ordnance.

One of the chopper crew swung open the loading door as the rotors slowed. Vinny moved out of his seat and stood at the gap in the fuselage, blinking in the bright light bursting into the gloomy cabin. A man was standing in the clearing a little way outside the downdraught of the blades. Vinny recognised him. He was an ordnance officer from one of the other commandos: a Vietnam vet with black polished boots, pressed uniform and a maroon military beret placed precisely on his close-cropped head. The man waited until the rotors had slowed to a listless circling before moving to the opened door.

'How'd it go?' he inquired, staring up at Vinny.

Big Vinny kept his face straight. 'Jake. One hundred per cent success.' The man allowed the shadow of a smile to sweep over his predatory face. 'In fact,' Vinny added with a grin, 'it was fuckin' ace.' The man laughed sharply.

'Okay,' he said. 'I got orders to get you guys on your way fast.'

He turned and gestured to a file of men in combat suits who ran across the clearing and began unloading the plastic containers of cocaine. Vinny recognised their shoulder flashes as belonging to a commando unit from New Mexico. He and the others leapt down from the chopper's deck and followed the ordnance officer at a trot into the barracks where an orderly checked their assault rifles and grenades before packing them into metal weapons carriers.

Vinny and his men stripped off their uniforms and took a hot shower, rubbing vigorously to remove the black and green greasepaint from their faces. When they returned from the showers their own clothes were neatly laid out on benches. Once more Vinny marvelled at the logistics and organisation of the Manifest Militia. The last time he had seen his clothes was two days earlier in a small shack close to the airport at Maracaibo.

Quickly they pulled on their jeans and their check shirts, laced up their high tie, heavy duty Caterpillars and picked up their soft roll sportsbags. The ordnance officer handed them their IDs, which showed them to be roustabouts working for a US civil engineering contractor building a road way down in the swampy south near San Fernando de Apure.

Within ten minutes they were back outside in the hot baking brilliance of the clearing. The distinct smell of aviation fuel hung sweet and heavy in the sweaty, sultry air. A team from the New Mexico commando had just finished refuelling the chopper from a small fuel truck. At a sharp order from Vinny, Billy Bob and the others doubled over towards the chopper.

Vinny looked around the clearing. There was no sign of the cocaine. He guessed it had been carted off into one of the hangars. The ordnance officer caught him staring curiously at the hangar's closed doors. 'Don't worry about it,' he said as they marched towards the helicopter. 'The stuff is going back by a different route.'

'Yeah, well I hope it makes it,' Vinny replied gruffly. 'Me and my guys risked our goddam asses gettin' it.'

'It'll make it,' the other man declared quietly. 'It'll be there almost as soon as you are.'

They reached the helicopter and turned to face each other. 'You did a good job, Vinny. The brass and the boys upstairs are gonna be pleased. They won't forget it.' Vinny grunted. 'Well, so long big guy. Have a safe one.' They shook hands.

Big Vinny climbed aboard the chopper as its rotors whirred into a high-pitched whine and the blades began lazily to move. The ordnance officer moved back out of the downdraught and stood watching as the machine lumbered into the air. He waved. Big Vinny, staring out of the window, acknowledged the wave with a brief motion of his hand before slipping a wad of gum into his mouth.

They flew northeast, across country towards Caracas, and landed at a tiny airstrip about thirty miles from the city. They walked a couple of miles into a small nearby town where they had been told they would find a flophouse.

They stayed the night, and although they had a couple of beers in a local bar they didn't get drunk. Nor did they go looking for whores. Their orders were to stay out of trouble.

The next morning they caught a bus which took them into the centre of Caracas from where they caught a cab to the airport. There they split up. After a final, celebratory beer in the bar, Carver Fylde and the Kaplin boys moved off, making for the flight to Miami from where they were ticketed to Atlanta. Big Vinny and Billy Bob were booked on a flight direct to Houston.

After they cleared customs in Houston they made their way towards the car rental desks.

They had just reached the Avis counter when Big Vinny heard someone call his name. He whirled, lightning fast – a shockingly quick movement in a man of six two and weighing two hundred and fifty pounds.

A smartly dressed man in a dark casual jacket and grey slacks was standing a few yards away. It took Vinny a second to realise who it was. Then it came to him. The last time he had seen the man, he had been wearing a uniform . . . a uniform similar to the one Big Vinny had recently taken off.

The man was a general . . . the Militia Area Commander for the whole of the south-eastern States.

Big Vinny clamped his jaws together to hide the fact he was chewing gum. Jeeesus, the guy was Militia top brass. And he was calling him by name. For a moment Big Vinny stared at the man in disbelief. Beside him, Billy Bob, slack-mouthed at the best of times, was gawping.

Though Big Vinny was familiar with the tall, heavy-set figure with the prison-gate face and the short, salt and pepper hair, it was only from a great distance. He and the rest of the Chicasaw Commando had stood to attention as the Commander had inspected them in their training camps . . . had saluted him as they had marched past. But Big Vinny had never spoken to the man, much less been aware that the Commander knew his name.

The man was almost as far up the command structure as it was possible to go. He was one of the five members of central command, one step down from the Commander in Chief whom Big Vinny and the Chicasaw Commando had seen only once.

The Area Commander was also a confidant of the Supreme Executive, the triumvirate who provided the driving force behind the Manifest Movement and about whom neither Big Vinny, nor anyone else of his acquaintance, knew anything at all.

Big Vinny gulped and swallowed his gum, resisting the urge to salute as the Commander moved towards him.

'Vinny, Billy Bob.' The Area Commander nodded at them. His voice was deep and distinct with a strong southern inflection.

'Sir,' they mumbled in unison.

The Commander smiled. 'I guess you boys are surprised to see me, huh?'

'Yessir,' Vinny responded.

107

'Well, I'm here to welcome you both home. And to say well done to all you guys for a fine job. We got word by radio yesterday. I want you to know that the Movement truly appreciates what you've done. Right now my second in command is in Atlanta, saying the same thing to the Kaplin boys and Carver Fylde.'

Big Vinny felt his face reddening at the Commander's words. 'Hell, sir,' he said, his voice low and emotional, 'we was just doing our duty. But we're glad it was a good mission and that we secured it right. And we sure do appreciate you coming all this way to say what you just said.'

The Commander nodded and smiled. 'Hell, boys it was the least I could do. Now Billy Bob, I got a big red Cherokee waiting outside and my driver is ready to drive you two heroes all the way home. It's a long drive so you get along there and tell him to be ready to move out as soon as we get there. Me and your brother are just on our way.'

'Yessir.' Billy Bob picked his roll bag from off the polished floor of the arrivals hall and hurried away.

The Commander watched him for a moment before turning to Big Vinny. 'Vinny, I want to tell you that the Movement is mighty grateful for what you and your men did down there in the jungle. That merchandise you secured is going to buy us a lot of firepower. We've already got it pre-sold to a bunch of lowlife middlemen. The money will go into the Movement's bank and then, when we're ready, we'll start procuring some high-performance ordnance. The kind of stuff we're going to need for the future. And because of you, we're going to get it.'

The Commander smiled at him then turned and began ambling across the floor of the concourse. Vinny, grabbing his roll bag, fell into step beside him.

Vinny stared at the man, flushed with pleasure and embarrassment. The Area Commander, like most of the officers in the Militia, was nothing like the senior officers he had known in Nam.

Those guys had been bastards. Uncaring, incompetent, motherfucking bastards, who had never acknowledged a lowly marine unless it was to intone a few words of fatuous crap about winning the war before sliding as quick as shit out of the war zone and back to their high-class brothels and bars.

Vinny and millions like him had fought a war without honour for a cause that none of the top brass had cared a fuck about. It was no wonder, he thought, that they had lost.

The Manifest Movement on the other hand was a cause for which Big Vinny had decided he would willingly die. If he had to make the big leap then he would. All he hoped was that when his time came he could take a whole lot of the Movement's enemies with him.

He had found a cause. The Movement, and the Militia, had regained the honour that America had lost in the mud of Southeast Asia. And Big Vinny felt as proud as a game rooster to be a part of it.

The Area Commander was saying something as they walked towards the doors of the concourse. Big Vinny pulled his attention back to his Commander.

'I gotta tell you Vinny that you have been noticed. Yessir, all the way to the top . . . to the very top . . . you have been noticed. The Chicashaw Commando is one of the best commands in the whole Militia and your unit the best in the commando. That's not just my opinion, that's the opinion of the whole fucking command.' He noticed Vinny's reddening face and smiled. 'You think I'm bullshitting you?'

Vinny shook his head. 'No sir.'

'Good. 'Cos I ain't. Even the guys in the Supreme Executive have heard of you. You're the kind of man we need in this movement. You've shown you can get things done, that you're not afraid of kicking ass and taking down a few lowlifes. So, I'm here to tell you that the next time a really important job comes up, one that has to be done just right, well the whole command is gonna think of you Vinny. We are going to think of you first.' The Commander smiled again. 'Think you can handle that, big guy?'

They had reached the plate glass doors of the hall. Vinny, his eyes suddenly misty, saw a bright red Jeep Cherokee standing at the kerb with its engine running. Vinny stared at it, almost as if in a trance, then looked beyond the vehicle to where he could see America.

He turned to the Area Commander. 'Yeah, I can handle it.' His voice was low and hoarse with emotion. 'Me and my boys can handle anything. Anything at all. Whatever it is, all you gotta do is say the word. We'll do it.'

Chapter Twelve

The house was empty. Vito Kunzman wasn't there.

The local cops sent to secure the property had already made inquiries in the neighbourhood and discovered that Kunzman was unknown. Even though the house was registered in his name, no one knew him or what he looked like. None of the neighbours, to their knowledge, had ever set eyes on him. As far as they were aware the house had been rented to a variety of tenants . . . and always, it seemed, on a short lease. They believed the rental business was handled by an agency in San Francisco.

Although Kunzman was not her concern, Melissa felt vaguely let down when one of the deputies from the Sheriff's office told her the news. She mentioned her disappointment to Barry Wagstaff. 'I might not have come if I'd known he wasn't going to be here,' she said petulantly. 'I'd have gone home to Jamie.'

Wagstaff laughed. 'Who are you kidding, Melissa? Since when did you pass up on a house search? Anyway, Kunzman isn't important. Who the hell is he anyway? He isn't an officer of the Exchange Bank, he's not a director or officer of Pemblin or Piagini or Cyclix. The guy is outside the loop. Forget him. He's not our concern. If anybody is going to be interested in the guy it'll be the cops or the FBI. Not Rolay Richard.'

Melissa pulled a wry face. 'I suppose you're right.'

She could hear officers from the federal agencies and the District Attorney's office noisily moving about upstairs. She told Wagstaff she would see him later and went in search of Sam Barber.

The house had a lot of rooms and as she moved through them Melissa noticed how much the place had suffered from its years of inconsistent ownership.

The sparse furniture was cheap and unkempt; the interior decorations, dating mainly from the seventies, shabby and stained.

She imagined the house as it once might have been: comfortable and affluent, its rooms vibrant and filled with life. Not any more, she thought. Now the place was flat and as characterless as a hostel for the homeless. It reeked of disappointment.

Sam Barber caught her in one of the rooms staring at an expanse of grubby wallpaper, the backdrop to a cheap, uncomfortable-looking sofa. 'Shame, eh?' he said smiling gently at her. 'The place could use some love.'

She nodded. 'All houses need love. Especially one like this.'

'Sure. It was built when they really knew how to build a house. You seen the woodwork on the balustrade? That's teak, for Chrissakes. God knows what that would cost now.'

'But why?' she asked. 'Why abandon such a nice place? Why let it deteriorate . . . get into this state?'

He shrugged. 'I assume no one was responsible for it. My guess is that it was used as a kind of safe house by LCN.'

She was surprised. '*La Cosa Nostra*?'

'Sure. I don't know whether this guy Kunzman is Mafia or if he's just associated. We know scarcely anything about him. What we do know is that, according to the records, he purchased this place in the early sixties. Maybe it was bought with Mob money . . . maybe with the deliberate intention of using it as a post office box for dummy corporations.' His brow furrowed. 'What do you guys call that over there?'

Melissa shrugged. 'We call it the same . . . a post office box.'

'Yeah? I thought you had some fancy title for it.'

'Do you mean *poste restante*?'

'Yeah, that's it.'

She laughed. 'You have some romantic notions of the British, Sam. We don't all wander around using scholarly foreign expressions you know.'

'No? Well, anyway, I expect the local Mob sent some minion out here every few days to pick up the mail . . . share certificates and proxy forms and the like. If I'm right, then all they had to do was keep the place habitable. Just good enough for the times when LCN wanted it to hide out someone who was hot.'

'Hot? You mean wanted? Like a murderer? One of their paid assassins?'

It was Barber's turn to laugh. 'Now who's got the romantic notions. If anyone connected to the Mob was on the run for a hit, especially a Mob-related hit, there's no way the boys would

111

hide the shooter here. Hell, no. They'd hide the guy at the bottom of San Francisco Bay. The Mafia wouldn't jeopardise a sweet little location like this by sheltering some low-life hitman. This place was for guys in the front office . . . important people . . . the accountants and lawyers. People we in the Enterprise Crime Unit wanted to talk to. Businessmen who'd been served subpoenas . . . guys like that.'

'And what would have happened to them?'

'Some would have been smuggled abroad for a new identity and expensive plastic surgery. Others,' he smiled as if at some secret joke, 'well, they probably got to be close neighbours of the hitmen. Standing around in concrete at the bottom of the Bay.'

Melissa shuddered slightly. 'I'm sorry,' Barber added quickly. 'I didn't mean to upset you.'

She shook her head. 'It's okay. I'm not upset. Sometimes I forget that so much of the money I'm hunting is blood money.'

Barber looked serious. 'Yeah, it's worth remembering, Melissa.'

She brightened as the noise level of people moving furniture above their heads intensified. 'And talking of hunting money,' she said lightly, 'I ought to get to work.'

Every room in the house was crowded with forensic officers wearing surgical gloves and dusting the furniture, doors and window frames for fingerprints. Melissa moved from room to room carrying a small tape recorder. She spoke into it in a low, soft tone, recording for any future court appearance where, when and exactly what papers had been found.

Over the first couple of hours the best the agents and DA's people could came up with were a lot of old utilities bills, a stack of circulars, a few ten-year-old copies of *Esquire*. *Time* and *Business Week* – and a cache of Danish pornography.

A couple of the women officers chided their male colleagues for poring over the lurid photographs, though Melissa noticed most of the women spent as much time scanning the pictures as the men. She would have liked to have taken a look too, but by the time she had surreptitiously squeezed her way into the wisecracking knot of agents and officers, the material was being bagged by a black female DA's assistant.

The woman, her white surgical gloves contrasting with the skin of her arms, was about to seal the bag when she noticed

Melissa. 'You wanna take a look, honey?' she inquired with a warm smile. 'Get you horny.'

Melissa felt herself colouring. 'No no. Thanks all the same. Thank you.'

She turned quickly, hoping to hide her embarrassment from a group of people who clearly thought horny was normal.

Silently she cursed her tyrannical middle-class education and her awful, tight-arsed British inhibition. She would dearly have liked to feel horny. Even in company.

It was a long time since she had felt that way.

The best find of the morning came just after midday, in a small bedroom at the back of the house. On top of a wardrobe pitted with woodworm was a brown paper supermarket bag, containing a sheaf of documents. Melissa dictated a brief description as a gloved agent flipped through them.

The papers covered a two-year period in the late seventies and were mainly contracts, loan documents and draft accounts. Melissa noticed the names Piagini, Cyclix and Pemblin occurring frequently. The agent bagged the find ready for fingerprinting.

Sam Barber suggested lunch and after locating Barry Wagstaff, he had his driver drive them to the waterfront in Sausalito. The agent dropped them near the Plaza where they found a fake fisherman's bar with a friendly atmosphere. They had clam chowder and sea bass and Melissa had a vodka and tonic.

Afterwards, they strolled along Bridgeway and looked at the waterfront. Glancing back, Melissa saw the Lincoln quietly following a few yards behind. She turned to her front and lifted her face to the sun. The day was warm and bright; the sun sparkling the gently stirring waters, the air filled with the soft sound of halyards slapping the metal masts of the yachts.

She thought about Jamie.

'How long before I can get my hands on the papers we found and go home, Sam?' she asked earnestly.

'Twenty-four hours tops,' he told her. 'Once we've dusted and catalogued them, then all we have to do is make photocopies. After that, they're yours.'

'Hey, Melissa,' Wagstaff volunteered, 'if you want to leave sooner I can take notarised possession of the papers from Sam and have them couriered over to you. That means you could fly out tonight.'

Melissa shook her head. 'Thanks, Barry, but no. Any other

time I would have jumped at the offer but not this evening. I told you, I've been asked out to dinner. It's my first date in ages so . . .' She grinned

'Do you know where you're going?' Barber's voice was serious.

'No, I've no idea,' she said lightly. 'Somewhere nice I hope.' She caught his expression. 'Why?'

'Like I said. The Bureau needs to keep an eye on you whilst you're in town.'

Deliberately she kept the smile on her face and her voice light. 'Well I hope you can do it a little more subtly than at present.' She nodded at the Lincoln, its engine idling at the kerb thirty yards away.

'We'll try to be a bit less obvious,' Barber said quietly. He smiled at her. She noticed the smile didn't reach his eyes.

They were silent for a while, looking out over the water. 'Did you notice the papers we found were all dated '78 and '79?' Melissa said, changing the subject. 'They're almost twenty years old. Kunzman must have forgotten them.'

'Maybe the guy is dead,' Wagstaff volunteered.

Barber frowned. 'I don't think so. If he was, the house would have gone to probate. The fact that it's still in his name is almost certain proof that he's alive.'

'We know he was alive a few months ago,' Melissa added, 'when he was visiting London and the Caymans and other branches of the Exchange Bank. It's just a bit strange that we can't get any kind of lead on him now.'

Wagstaff chuckled loudly. 'What is it with you and this guy Kunzman, Melissa? How come you're so interested? The guy is gonna turn out to be nothing more than some Mafia bagman who owns what was once a nice house in Sausalito.'

She wondered if she should mention the account that Akhtar Aziz had said Kunzman operated on his own. Would the name, Austerlitz, mean anything to either of them? she wondered. She doubted it. She decided to keep quiet. Barber suggested they get back to the house.

Their stroll in the sun had taken them as far as the ferry slipway at El Portal. As they turned towards the car a sudden movement close to a collection of black garbage bags caught Melissa's eye. She glanced down in time to see two big grey rats scurrying along the waterline. They disappeared behind the bags. A cold frisson ran up her backbone. She hated rats. Rats and

114

affluence, she thought as they moved towards the car. It seemed appropriate.

The Mafia owned nice old houses in Sausalito and rats gambolled in the sunshine.

That afternoon they found another bundle of papers rolled up and wedged at the back of a bureau. Most of them had dates in the early nineties.

In the car on the way to her hotel, Barber asked her if she was pleased with the day's haul.

'I told you, businessmen's houses can be goldmines,' she said.

'So it was worth making the detour?'

She nodded. 'Oh, yes.'

Her voice was definite, though what she failed to add was that, right then, she was thinking less about what they had discovered at the house in Sausalito and more about her dinner date with Bob Briscoe.

Chapter Thirteen

The day's heat had trickled down into the cool of a San Francisco night, with smoky grey tongues of sea-mist hanging around the shadows of the sloping streets like muggers' ghosts.

Melissa had done the best she could with the clothes she had with her. When setting out from home almost a week earlier she hadn't planned on being asked out to dinner by a good-looking man. And since Briscoe's call early that morning she'd been too busy to go shopping for something new and suitable. Yet by the time the front desk rang to say Mr Briscoe was in the lobby, she was reasonably satisfied she had done the best she could with her face and hair and the clothes she had.

She stared into the dressing-table mirror, giving herself the final once-over.

Behind her the United States Senator and hotly tipped pesidential candidate, Philip Kilbride, was being interviewed on a cable TV current affairs programme about the hijacking of the American financial system by organised criminals. Though Melissa had been following the story in the *Wall Street Journal* about panic in the markets and billions of dollars moving offshore, right now she was in no mood for stories of monetary shock and fiscal calamity.

She ignored the droning voice, concentrating instead on her hair sheening in the soft glow of the lamps and on her eyes which, in the subtle light, appeared a much deeper shade of blue. She was wearing her favourite lipstick: the one which, in her opinion, made her generous mouth look sexy.

She straightened up and eyed her figure. She was, she thought, still in good shape . . . could still look desirable when the chance – the rare chance – occurred.

He took her to Amelio's. It was expensive but not ostentatious. He chose a couple of bottles of Sauvigny-les-Beaune and recommended the pasta, which was delicious. Briscoe, she discovered within a few minutes of sitting down in the restaurant, was good company. He told her something about himself and his work but mainly they talked about her.

'A forensic accountant,' he exclaimed in wonder. 'Hell, I don't get to meet many of them. Much less have dinner with one. Tell me about it. What exactly do you do?'

She told him about economic crime and the devious ways enterprise criminals worked. He was fascinated. 'It's not a part of the financial world I know much about,' he told her. 'It's got its own language, hasn't it? I mean placement and layering. What the hell does it all mean?'

She smiled at him. He looked like an eager schoolboy. An exceedingly handsome schoolboy.

'Criminals need to conceal the real source of their illicit wealth,' she began. 'As their assets, which are usually vast quantities of money, come from crime, they need to convert the money to something which gives the illusion of legitimacy. So, after they manage to get the cash deposited in a bank or some other financial institution, they convert it to another currency and then move it around the world. Wire transfers from one tax haven to another. Vanuatu to Liberia to the Caymans to Nauru . . . there are plenty of shelters. The trick is to keep it moving.'

'I didn't realise there were so many places where gangsters could hide their money.'

She nodded. 'There are dozens of tax havens. They're my Antilles heel.' He laughed.

'Anyway,' she continued, 'the point is to keep the funds moving in and out of all these havens at great speed. It's high velocity money. It has to be moved around the world as fast and as many times as possible.'

'And that's what they call layering?'

She nodded. 'Creating layers upon layers of transactions that someone like me has to cut through before we can even start to find the first brick.'

'Brick?' He gave her a puzzled look.

She shook her head. 'It doesn't matter.

'Eventually the launderers either own millions of dollars' worth of certificates of deposit and borrow against the CDs to fund more drugs deals . . . or they invest the money in whatever business enterprises they own – though usually their beneficial

117

ownership is concealed. Businesses like construction or property development or real estate, or haulage. You name it, they own it.'

'So, it's called laundering because it goes in dirty, spins around the world a few times and then comes out sanitised?'

'That's right.'

He smiled. 'The world turns and whirls out clean money.'

'It may be clean money,' she said quietly, 'but it's a dirty world.'

He gave her a penetrating look. 'Yes, you're right. So how do you go about it? Preventing this money laundering?'

She shook her head. 'I don't prevent it. My job is to investigate it. Other people dream up measures to inhibit laundering.'

'Yeah?'

'A while ago the Group of Ten devised a set of rulings called the Basel Principles. They're meant to prevent the criminal use of the banking system for money laundering.'

'And do they work? These principles?'

She shrugged. 'I'm still in work. Still chasing laundered money.'

'So how do you do it?'

She told him. Without naming names she told him about her investigation in the Caymans and described how she had tracked the companies' loans and persuaded the banks to part with information.

'A liquidator and an officer of the court,' he exclaimed. 'Hell, I need to watch my step. I'm having dinner with a *very* powerful lady.' She laughed. 'No I mean it. Liquidators scare the living daylights out of people like me. All that authority and influence . . . all those D forms on the conduct of directors. It's scary.' He gazed at her in admiration. 'So much power in someone so beautiful. It's helluva impressive.'

For the second time that day she felt herself colouring. She lowered her eyes and looked away.

Fleetingly she wondered if Sam Barber had made good on his promise to have someone watch over her. She glanced around the warm, genial restaurant. If he had, then whoever it was had merged perfectly into the background. She thought about what the cost of babysitting her in Amelio's was doing to the FBI's budget and smiled.

Briscoe asked what had brought her to San Francisco.

'I took part in a house search. In Sausalito. With the FBI and some other agencies.'

She saw his eyes widen in amazement. 'What, guys bursting in with guns and stuff?'

She chuckled – a low, rich, warm sound. 'No nothing like that. The local District Attorney's office had a warrant, but the place was empty anyway.'

'What were you looking for?'

'Treasure.' He laughed and raised his eyebrows. 'Businessmen's houses are little goldmines.'

'They are? Why?'

'No matter how bright the bent businessmen and the fraudsters and insider traders and money launderers are . . . they have a weak spot. Almost always it's their house. For some reason crooks seem to think that any damning evidence they take home will be perfectly safe. Like nobody is ever going to think of looking there. You'd be amazed at the incredibly incriminating papers I've found stuffed inside shoe boxes hidden in wardrobes.'

Briscoe laughed again. 'And did you find any treasure in Sausalito?'

'Oh, yes, quite a lot.'

He was smiling at her. 'So, if I'm ever involved in anything shady I need to remember not to take any papers home.'

'Yes. And also remember to check up on your secretary. Never tell her anything you don't want somebody else to know.'

He shook his head. 'My secretary is the soul of discretion,' he said slightly pompously. 'Absolutely tight-lipped about my business.'

'She wouldn't be if she were being interviewed by a liquidator. Or the Fraud Squad. Or the FBI. The point is . . . a secretary remembers things. That's what she's paid for. And the things she remembers are often the things her boss said in an unguarded moment. And secretaries keep things: files and documents and diaries . . . items their bosses told them to throw away. Some secretaries keep papers on file going back years. Of course the boss doesn't know she's still got them until . . .'

'. . . until a forensic accountant comes calling . . .'

'Absolutely. And with all those papers the man thought were destroyed, we can build a case for the courts.'

'It's impressive stuff, Melissa.' He sounded as if he meant it.

After coffee and liqueurs they caught a cab going south on Powell towards her hotel.

In the lobby she asked if he would like a nightcap at the bar. She was surprised when he declined. He had an early start next day, he told her. She wondered if her disappointment showed, because he took out a small notepad and wrote down a number. He tore out the sheet of paper and gave it to her. On it was a number with a Manhattan area code.

'Why don't you call me when you're next in New York?' he said. 'We could have dinner again. Or maybe I could take you to a show.'

'I might take you up on that,' she said smiling at him.

She took a business card out of her small handbag and wrote the number of the cottage on the back. 'The same goes for me when you're next in London.'

He glanced at the card then at Melissa. 'As a matter of fact,' he told her, 'I'm scheduled to be back in London in the next few days. I'd like to call you. If that's okay.' She saw the earnest look on his tanned, handsome face.

'Yes,' she told him quietly. 'I'd like that very much.'

He grinned. 'Great. Well, I guess it's time to say goodnight. I gotta tell you, Melissa, I had a really good time this evening.'

Melissa stared in surprise at the hand he was holding out to her. She shook it, wondering if he could sense her frustration.

He said goodnight once more then strode purposefully out of the lobby. Melissa watched him get as far as the cab rank before turning to the elevators. She glanced at her watch. It was just past twelve.

She let out a small sigh. It was gone midnight, the ball was over, the handsome prince had gone and she was on her way back to a lonely bed. There wasn't even an ugly frog to kiss. It was the Cinderella syndrome all over again. The story of her life.

She sighed again and pressed the button to summon the elevator.

She knew caution was the better part of amour . . . she even believed that, sometimes, reticence could be sexy. But, she brooded, she really wouldn't have objected if he'd planted one fleeting, tender, goodnight kiss on her lips.

The following morning she took a taxi to the offices of the

120

FBI's Economic Crime Unit in Golden Gate, close to the Civic Centre. Barber was waiting for her. Stacked on his desk were the documents they had found at the house in Sausalito. His staff had catalogued them. Melissa ran her eye down the items listed on the pages as Barber organised a mug of coffee.

When he returned she signed the affidavit which affirmed under oath that she had taken receipt of the documents as inventoried.

'We've taken copies,' Barber told her. 'We figure with these documents and with what you've given us from the Caymans, we've got sufficient to start making arrests. What about you? Have you got enough to apply to the Court to confiscate those funds?'

She nodded. 'Almost certainly. I think with the loss of a hundred million dollars we can safely say the Pemblin and Piagini corporations are out of business. Along with their money laundering operations.'

'It won't hurt if we can put their senior corporate officers away for a few years either,' Barber added tersely. He frowned. 'What about the other outfit? Cyclix? The Mafia storefront corporation in Nassau? You got enough to put them in the tank too?'

'Cyclix? Oh yes. Cyclix is definitely tied in. But there are a couple of things about the company's operation I want to follow up. There's something not quite right about what they were doing with their funds.'

'Yeah? You wanna tell me about it?'

Melissa shrugged. 'I can't. It's only a feeling at the moment.' She smiled at Barber. 'Anyway, it's nothing to do with what was going on with Piagini or Pemblin. Those two are definitely dead in the water.'

'I'll drink to that.' Barber raised his coffee mug.

Melissa smiled, sipped her coffee then fixed Barber with a look. 'What do you know about this man, Kunzman?'

'We're checking him out now. We know he's an attorney and a longtime bagman for the Mob. He's been working for LCN since the sixties, though as far as we can tell, he, personally, is clean. Kunzman was the Mob's chief contact with the Exchange Bank. Anyway,' he cocked his head to one side, 'what's so special about him? Why do you wanna know?'

She told him what she had learned about Kunzman from

121

Akhtar Aziz and Miguel Artevalo. 'I think he could help me get to the bottom of what was happening at Cyclix. His name appears mainly on the documents connected with Cyclix.'

'Yeah? I hadn't noticed that.'

She nodded. 'I think it could be very useful to talk to him.'

Barber smiled. 'You and me both. But first we gotta find him. He disappeared before the bank went down.'

'*Before* the bank went down?' Melissa was surprised. 'Are you sure?

'Yes.'

'Do you think he knew? Got wind that the bank was about to be closed?'

Barber shook his head. 'No. I doubt if he knew any more than anyone else what was going to happen. We figure he went on the run because his life was in danger.' He saw Melissa frown in confusion. 'Someone tried to whack him out,' he explained.

'Tried to kill him?'

'Sure. Only they got the wrong guy.'

'I don't understand.'

'You heard about the Exchange Bank's chairman, Hidalgo Campeche?

'The one who was murdered?'

'Right. Dr Campeche was assassinated in a tenement in Caracas about three months ago. The strange thing was that at the time no one knew why. I mean, the guy was a big Third World financier and larger than life and it was well known he'd made enemies, but . . .'

'But what?'

'But there wasn't any reason why someone should want to kill him. Then, not long after the murder, rumours started coming out.'

'What rumours?'

'That the hit was a bust. The button men had whacked the wrong guy. The *real* target had been this guy Vito Kunzman.'

'Kunzman? Why him?'

Barber shrugged 'Who knows? Maybe he'd crossed the Mob . . . had his hand in their pockets. Maybe they found out he was robbing them.'

Melissa shook her head. 'That doesn't sound very likely. He, more than anyone, knew what happened to people associated with the Exchange Bank who got caught with their fingers in the till.'

'Okay, but that's the only explanation we can come up with. Kunzman and Dr Campeche were close business associates. We figure that as soon as he heard that his buddy had been clipped Kunzman got jittery. Then when he heard the stories that Campeche had got it instead of him – he beat it.'

'How would he have known he was the intended target?'

Again Barber shrugged. 'Maybe Campeche's girlfriend told him. She's disappeared too.'

'Who?'

'Campeche had a longtime girlfriend. Egyptian. From some high-class family in Cairo. Been with him twenty years or more. She was also his secretary and personal assistant. From what we've been able to piece together, we know she was in the tenement when Campeche got hit. Now she's evaporated.'

'That's a pity,' Melissa observed dryly. 'In my business secretaries can be a mother-lode of information.'

'Yeah, especially in a situation like this, where the boss was humping the help. That broad would definitely know where all the bodies are buried. But,' he spread his hands in a gesture of resignation, 'she's gone. She hasn't been seen since the night of Campeche's murder.'

'Do you think she and Kunzman have disappeared together?'

'Melissa, I don't know what to think. When something as big and rich and powerful as the Exchange Bank goes down, there are bound to be a helluva lot of pieces of the jigsaw that you never get to find . . . never get to fit together. Maybe Vito Kunzman and Campeche's secretary are two of those pieces. Maybe we'll never find them . . . never get to know what they knew. All I know is, thanks to you, we're going to nail a bunch of local money launderers to the wall. I'm just grateful for that.'

'But when you get some information about Kunzman will you share it? I mean can you tell me what you find out?'

'Sure. I'll keep you in touch. Why not? Rolay Richard are a major player in the marketplace. You never know, you might find this guy before we do.'

She smiled at him. 'I think that's highly unlikely.'

Chapter Fourteen

She flew home the following day.

Her flight was delayed and she arrived at the cottage after midnight. The following day, Sunday, she spent playing with Jamie and catching up on domestic events with Astrid. Jamie was delighted to see her and even more delighted with the enormous, cuddly Garfield she had brought back from San Francisco.

She slipped out of the cottage early on Monday morning, quietly leaving before Jamie was awake. For once the journey was painless – she even got a seat. She arrived at her office before everyone else and started shuffling through the stack of messages Debbie had accumulated for her.

As soon as Debbie arrived, Melissa got down to planning and rescheduling her workload, ruthlessly disposing of the unimportant stuff and delegating much of what was left. Even so, there was an enormous amount for her to do. She stared at her crowded diary and the piles of files and felt the familiar queasy feeling in the pit of her stomach.

'Nigel Hawick wants to see you,' Debbie told her.

'When?'

'As soon as you're free.'

Melissa made a face. 'Tell him I should make it by the middle of next year.' Debbie chuckled.

She went to see him in his office later that morning.

'Did the search in Sausalito turn anything up?' he asked.

'Yes, a bit. Mainly papers relating to Piagini.'

Hawick frowned and grunted. He seemed irritated. 'Are you all right?' she asked him.

'What? Oh, yes, I'm fine. It's just all this bloody paper. There's tons of it. And more coming.'

Melissa glanced at the big open office through the glass

partitioning. Lining the walls from floor to ceiling were hundreds of brown, cardboard banker's boxes. Most of the staff in the department were at their workstations, trawling through the boxes' contents.

'FI is having to examine every document,' he moaned. 'The Old Lady is certainly making us sweat for our money.'

Melissa couldn't understand why he was bothered. Tons of paper arriving in the offices was nothing new.

'Did you get anything on this fellow Kunzman?' Hawick went on.

She shook her head. 'No. The house is registered in his name but he hasn't lived there for years. And there's no up-to-date address for him. The place was being rented out by an agency. The FBI thinks the people who occasionally lived there were involved in enterprise crime. There's no doubt it's been used for years as a dummy address by directors and shareholders of funny companies.'

'Well, if you didn't get anything on Kunzman, what *did* you get?' Hawick's tone was peevish.

She glowered at him. She could do without Nigel having a Monday morning moody. Especially, she thought angrily, as *he* hadn't spent over a week away from his son and half his weekend on a plane trying to get back home to him.

'Apart from being a damn sight closer to tracking a billion dollars a year going into Grand Cayman,' she snapped, 'it looks like the papers from the house in Sausalito may well prove that the hundred million Piagini has in its accounts at the Exchange Bank is from organised crime. For once, even the bloody FBI are pleased. And I've also got some material on an associate company of Piagini called Cyclix. Registered in Nassau.'

'Cyclix,' he repeated. 'Never heard of it. So what's the story?'

'I don't know yet. I chiselled a lot of detail about the company out of a bank manager on Cayman. There's something not right about its accounts.'

'Such as what?'

She shook her head. 'Too soon to say. It's just a feeling I have.'

Hawick nodded. Melissa's reputation for feelings was well known. More often than not her instincts turned out to be right. It was one of the things that made her so good at her job. 'Okay. Well, let me have your report as soon as you can. And keep me up to speed on everything you're doing. All right.'

She grunted something and left, stalking irritably back to her office. Hawick had called her into a meeting merely to tell her to do what she intended doing anyway. It was typical of a bloody man, she thought. She *always* kept him up to date on her work. Only bad managers issued unnecessary instructions. Hawick was not usually so naïve.

She dropped into her seat then glanced out of the plate-glass windows. Through the faintly smoked glass she could see the sun glittering on the graceful curve of the river at Shadwell. She sighed and turned back to the papers on her desk.

Later that day she picked up a set of manilla files and took the lift four stories down to the computer department.

Boris Redbourn had one of the biggest offices in the building. Its size was less a reflection of his status and more to do with the fact that he had two banks of big, twenty-inch monitors sitting on computer desks all around the office walls. Melissa noticed his tall lanky frame hunched over a keyboard surrounded by more than a dozen blinking screens as she strolled through the main office which housed at least fifty more computer terminals, all shimmering with pixellated graphics.

She strolled into his office. The place hummed with the soft sound of cooling fans. 'Hello, Boris.'

Redbourn looked up. He was dressed in jeans and a faded granddad shirt, hair pulled back off his face in a pony tail. Melissa noticed he was wearing an earring. She gave him a grin.

Boris Redbourn's appearance was not the norm at Rolay Richard. But if the senior partners in the practice disapproved, she reflected, they kept it to themselves. When it came to electronic data processing, Redbourn was in a class of his own. And even in a large, traditional and conservative accountancy practice like Rolay Richard, someone that clever – and valuable – got to dress how he pleased.

'Hi, Melissa. What's happening?' He blinked at her through his rimless glasses.

She pulled a face. 'The usual. Too much work, not enough time. I've just got back from the States.'

'Lucky lady.'

'Oh, sure. Tell me about it.' He laughed. 'Can you show me what you've got on a company called Piagini?'

'One of the accounts at the Exchange Bank?'

126

She nodded. 'I'm finishing up an investigation and I want to see what you've got on them.'

Redbourn turned to his keyboard, wristed the mouse and clicked on a pulldown menu. Instantly every screen in the big office was filled with a series of brightly coloured, three-dimensional boxes. The boxes were connected by arrows and separated by small icons. Inside each box was a list of names, some of which Melissa recognised. Emblazoned at the top of the screens was the title, Piagini.

He looked up at Melissa. 'I've constructed an electronic flow chart of the Exchange Bank's money movements,' he explained, 'and from the flow chart, a diagram of the routes the money followed. I'm also assembling asset hierachies of the separate companies and net worth analyses of the corporations and their individual officers.'

He swivelled to the screen. 'Okay, this is Piagini's corporate structure. The graphics show the relationship of its subsidiaries and associate companies . . . all the minority stakes and cross-collateral deals. The names are those of the directors and officers of each of the companies.' He peered at the screen. 'Piagini is owned by a company called Pemblin, registered in the Caymans.'

'That's right.'

'I can show you Pemblin's connections if you want.'

'Go ahead.' The screen changed and more coloured boxes, arrows and icons appeared.

'I've got the names of all the companies' officers cross-referenced to show which companies they controlled.' The screens' multi-coloured graphics disappeared, to be replaced by others. 'Some of these characters were directors of hundreds of companies. But,' he looked up and grinned, 'I got 'em sussed. Once they're in the programme there's no way I can't track them. I can stick closer to those blokes than shit on a shoe.'

Melissa screwed up her face and snorted good-naturedly at the analogy. 'What are these?' she asked, pointing to small red and blue icons.

'The branches of the Exchange Bank that Piagini and its associate companies were using to move the laundered money.'

Redbourn clicked the mouse on the icon and the screen resolved into a larger coloured box, filled with names and dates. 'All the companies using that particular branch, the amounts moved and the dates,' he explained. 'We've got data on every branch. Throughout the world. We're updating it daily from the stuff your department sends down to us.'

'Boris, that's really impressive!' Melissa exclaimed.

'Shit, that's nothing.' Redbourn gave her a wide grin. 'Look at this.' He clicked the mouse once more and every screen in the room resolved itself into a moving kaleidoscope of colour. Melissa stared, entranced. Broad, computer-graphic arrows were actually moving between the coloured boxes. Some arrows were larger than others and some moved more rapidly across the screens as they continuously crossed and re-crossed each other.

'Very pretty,' she murmured. 'What is it?'

'The arrows represent the movement of money between branches of the Exchange Bank. Along with deposits and withdrawals from other banks. The size of the arrows represents the amounts moved. The speed is the frequency of movement.' He glanced up. His face was serious. 'If you look at this long enough you can see there's a definite pattern. Once the people in the bank got a system worked out, they never varied it. Added to it perhaps, but never varied it. Everything FI is sending down confirms it.'

'So you can tell who was moving money into a branch of the bank and who was moving money out?'

Redbourn laughed. 'Easily. All the movements, all over the world. I can even show you on a map.' He clicked the mouse on a button at the top of the screen. A simple graphic map of the world appeared. Arrows began sliding across its surface. 'That's where Piagini was moving its money,' he said quietly. 'First they accumulated a stack of cash in Milan then wired it across to the Caymans . . .'

Melissa watched an arrow ripple across the screen, moving from northern Italy across the Atlantic to disappear somewhere in the Caribbean.

'. . . then they moved some of it to Canada and some to Hong Kong.' More arrows appeared.

Melissa was mesmerised as she watched the silent movements. She listened intently to Redbourn's quiet, authoritative voice.

'From Hong Kong some went to Nauru.' An arrow silently shimmered southeast across the Coral Sea. 'And some to Liberia.' A broader arrow moved westwards across the Indian Ocean to the west coast of Africa. Instantly, more arrows appeared, moving in new directions. 'From Nauru,' Redbourn continued, 'the money moved to Zurich and then to Los Angeles. And from Liberia it went straight to Los Angeles.'

He leaned back and grinned. 'Neat, isn't it? The trouble is, so far I've got eleven hundred companies involved in the money laundering and I can only show movements on the map one company at a time. At the beginning I tried putting all the movements on at the same time, but I got so many bleeding arrows going everywhere, it looked like Custer's last stand.'

Melissa chuckled as he laughed loudly at his own joke.

'Do you have anything on a company called Cyclix? Registered in Nassau?' she asked.

He clicked the screen and another series of boxes appeared. 'Not much.' He switched to the screen with the moving arrows. There were only a few of them. 'That's all I've got.' He sounded disappointed.

Melissa dropped the files she had been holding onto his desk. 'Well, I've got more data on Cyclix here. I'd like you to feed it into the system. There's also stuff there,' she nodded at the files, 'on Piagini and Pemblin. Some of it's almost twenty years old but it might prove useful. But it's Cyclix I'm particularly interested in. There's something different about it. Something not quite right about its accounts.'

'Like what?'

Melissa shook her head and frowned. 'I don't know. And if I knew I wouldn't want to say. I just want to see what you and your computer games come up with.'

Redbourn laughed. 'A mystery, eh? Okay, Melissa, I'll input the data and see what comes out.'

'That's great. Thanks, Boris.' She moved towards the door then stopped. 'Oh, there's one more thing. Have you come across the name Kunzman anywhere in your database?

'Kunzman?'

'Yes. Vito Kunzman.'

Redbourn turned to the screen, pressed a key and called up a find text dialogue box. 'How do you spell it?' She told him. He input the name, clicked the mouse and they waited. After a few seconds a large red box appeared in the middle of the screen announcing the name was not found. Redbourn caught the disappointed look on her face. 'Is he important?'

She shrugged. 'I really can't say. I think so, but so far no one has been able to get a handle on him. Can you try Vito?'

Redbourn did a search on Vito and on various permutations of the name Kunzman. Each time the same stark response flashed up on the unfeeling screen.

'Whoever he is,' Redbourn observed, 'he was either using a different name or he had nothing to do with the bank.'

'Or maybe he was just very careful,' Melissa said softly. 'Oh, well, thanks anyway, Boris.'

'Any time, Melissa.' He gave her a big grin.

Debbie was waiting for her in her office. She was agitated, her face strained. 'What's wrong?' Melissa asked.

'Mr Hawick has just had a phone call. He wants to see you straight away.'

Something in Debbie's look made Melissa's stomach tighten in apprehension. She stared at her secretary. 'Why? What is it?'

Debbie shook her head. 'I dunno but *something*'s happened.'

Melissa glanced through the glass partition separating the offices. Hawick was slumped in the chair behind his desk. His face was drained. He looked ghastly.

She burst through the door of his office. 'What's wrong? What's happened?'

'Close the door,' he murmured.

She shut the door and stood in front of his desk. 'What is it?' she pleaded.

Hawick stared up at her. His eyes were glaucomatous, bulging like a frightened horse's. There was something behind them . . . fear . . . dread . . . anxiety? . . . Melissa couldn't figure out what.

'For God's sake, Nigel. What's wrong?' she cried.

'It's your man. Akhtar Aziz.' Hawick's voice was flat and lifeless, like ashes in a dead fire. 'He went missing last night. Along with his wife and his kids.'

The dread in the pit of Melissa's stomach reached up and snatched at her heart. 'Oh, no.'

'They found them this morning,' Hawick rasped. 'In their car. In Epping Forest.' He stopped. His face was so strained he was scarcely recognisable. He touched his hair with a shaking hand. 'They were . . .' He stopped again.

Melissa closed her eyes. She knew what was coming.

'Dead,' Hawick intoned. 'Him, his wife, the two children. They've been shot. All of them.' He shook his head and stared down at his desk. 'All of them,' he repeated.

Chapter Fifteen

She left the office before six. Her staff were surprised. It was unheard of for her to leave so early but she was desperate to get back to Jamie. The appalling news about Aziz and his family made her sick to her soul.

As the train clattered south and west through a pale sunlit evening, visions of the awful massacre spooled through her brain in a closed, hideously lurid loop. Guilt knawed at her. She felt so responsible. She trudged across the station car park, telling herself Aziz's death was her fault.

It was she who had manoeuvred him into divulging the codenamed accounts . . . into telling her about Vito Kunzman. It was her fault he had been forced to talk to the people from the Fed and the US Justice department.

She had got him killed.

But why kill his wife? And his *children*? Dear God, she wailed silently, what kind of people would do such a thing? Mindlessly she buttoned the control of the BMW and climbed in. She gunned the engine and exited the car park, driving as fast as she dared through the narrow Hampshire lanes.

She'd heard on the grapevine that Aziz had asked his wife to take the children back to Allahabad but she had refused to go without him. *He* hadn't been able to go because Melissa had contrived to have his passport seized. If she hadn't done that, she agonised, he and his family would still be alive.

Her eyes filled with tears. It was all her fault. She'd promised to help him out of the mess she'd got him into. Only she hadn't kept her promise. She'd been too busy.

Astrid was surprised to hear the car tyres scrunching on the broad gravel drive at the front of the cottage. She had just got Jamie ready for bed. He was sitting in front of the television in a bright pair of Mickey Mouse pyjamas, watching a Flintstones

131

video. Melissa hurried into the cottage, threw her attaché case onto a sofa and swept him up in her arms.

She grunted at his weight. 'God, you're getting big,' she gasped. She kissed him fervently, on his cheeks and forehead. Jamie laughed and threw his arms around her neck.

Melissa hugged him tightly, but within seconds he was fidgeting to get down and get back to the Flintstones. She put him down, moved to the clump of bottles on top of the carved walnut sideboard and fixed herself a large malt.

Astrid was eyeing her speculatively. 'It was a bad day?'

Melissa threw herself into an armchair. 'A bloody bad day,' she intoned. 'The worst.'

She allowed Jamie to stay up until he fell asleep in her arms. Earlier she'd watched him playing with his Lego, smiling at the intense look of concentration on his face as he fitted the bricks together with his short, stubby fingers. She stared at his fine, downy hair and the curve of his neck and trembled at how innocent and defenceless he was . . . at how vulnerable they both were.

There were men out there . . . men whose money she was hunting who massacred women and children.

In a surge of guilt and love she had asked him if he would like a present – a new toy, or teddy bear, something like that.

'A puppy . . . a puppy,' he had said eagerly.

He had been asking for a puppy for some time and she had been resisting, knowing that though Jamie might love the animal, it would be she and Astrid who would be stuck with the extra work. A puppy meant more responsibility. Now it didn't seem to matter.

'You really want a puppy?'

'Yes, yes.'

'And you'll look after it? Properly?'

'Yes, yes.'

'Then we'll get you a puppy.'

His smile had been like the sun bursting within the oak-beamed room.

After she had taken him upstairs, she settled down with half a bottle of the Macallan. She finished it and went to bed in the early hours with a Nembutal.

Hawick called her into his office as soon as she arrived in the building. He looked the way she felt.

132

'I think we have to take you off the Exchange Bank job,' he croaked. 'Assign it to one of the others.'

'Because of what happened to Aziz?'

He nodded. 'Yes.'

She sat down heavily in the chair opposite his desk. 'I've got to admit I've been thinking about it. For most of last night as a matter of fact. About asking for a transfer.'

'Yes, that would be best. Get you away . . . back to your old workload.'

She nodded. 'I thought about it a lot,' she repeated. 'But, in the end, I've decided I want to stick with it, Nigel. I don't want to be taken off the job. Not yet, anyway.'

'But these people are crazy,' he protested. 'You know what they've done. You've got a kid, Melissa. A sick kid.'

Her voice was high and hard-edged. '*Jamie isn't sick*, Nigel!'

'Okay, okay, but you know what I mean. It's just become bloody obvious that the people behind this damn bank will stop at nothing to protect their interests. And I mean *nothing*. They know Rolay Richard is liquidating the bank's assets and they must know you are chasing down the laundered money. That makes you a potential target. And your son,' he added ominously.

'God, don't say that about Jamie,' she wailed. 'Don't say that.'

'Christ, what else can I say? This job is *dangerous*.'

'I *know* it's dangerous. I don't need you to tell me it's dangerous.' She could hear the shrillness rising in her voice. '*You* were the one who assigned me. You said *I* was one of the reasons the Bank of England gave this job to Rolay Richard.'

'I know, I know. But this is different. You can't carry on after this.'

'But the Bank won't want me to give it up. The Bank will want me to carry on.'

'Well the Old Lady can just go fuck herself.'

He stared at her, bug-eyed. Melissa stared back. Hawick's nerves were even more ragged than her own. The silence settled in the room. She took a long, deep breath and settled herself firmly in her seat.

'Look Nigel.' Her tone was a stiffer, more controlled. 'I've thought a lot about this since last night. God, I haven't thought about anything else. What happened to Akhtar Aziz . . . what they did to him and . . .' she stopped and shook her head, '. . . what they did was because, in their eyes, he betrayed them. I mean, it's awful, but they think of him as a traitor. But me . . . I'm just a person doing a job. And they know if I don't do it, someone else will. I honestly don't think anybody is going to come after me. If I did, if I actually thought someone was going to attack Jamie or me, I'd ask to be taken off the job right now. Christ, I'd resign from the firm, rather than jeopardise Jamie.'

'But you don't know these people. What they're like.'

She shrugged. 'Nor do you. No one does. But even if they do come after me, I think they'd give me a warning first. Warn me off with a telephone call . . . something like that. If that happens,' her hand sliced through the air in an arc, 'then I am definitely out. Off the job. But until then, I'm going to stick with it. I've found a few threads which could go somewhere. I want to find out where.'

'But I can get one of the others to do that. Someone else can take over and follow through on what you've got.' Hawick's protests were weakening.

'Who? Frank's wife has just had their first baby, Andrew lives with his elderly parents, you've got a family. We're *all* vulnerable. The difference is that I've got a head start. Right now, I'm the best person to track this money down *quickly*.'

She left his office a few minutes later. He wasn't happy, but she'd made him see it her way. Walking back to her own office she prayed she had done the right thing.

She threw herself into her chair and stared out over the river, wondering if she was taking the British stiff-upper-lip thing too far. Was she exhibiting a determined fortitude in the face of menace . . . or was it merely enormous folly?

She wasn't sure. Jamie's safety and security were involved too. What kind of bloody mother was she? Maybe, she thought, years of working with men had affected her mind. Maybe some of their childish machismo had rubbed off onto her.

Debbie followed her into the office with the usual clutch of messages. One was a nice surprise. Robert Briscoe had called. He was staying at Grosvenor House. He wanted her to call him. She asked Debbie to get the number.

'Hello,' she said when she was put through to his room. 'I didn't expect to hear from you quite so soon. How long have you been in town? What are you doing here?'

'Hi, Melissa.' He sounded pleased to hear from her. 'I just got in. A couple of hours ago. Flew in from the Coast. I have some business to take care of in London then I fly to Europe.'

She laughed. 'You're already in Europe.'

He chuckled. 'Okay, I'm here till I cross the Channel. I was hoping we might have dinner. Tonight maybe. Or tomorrow. Whenever you can make it.'

'I'd love to. Tomorrow would be fine.'

'Great. Where? You wanna eat here? At Chez Nico?'

'No. This is my town, so I'm the host. Okay? It'll be my treat. Let me choose a place. I'll get my secretary to fix it. She'll call and tell you where.'

His chuckle was louder. 'Sounds good to me, Melissa.'

She put the phone down and again stared out at the snaking river through the plate-glass windows.

Chez Nico was the hotel's restaurant. It was one of the best in town. She had nothing against it, except that it *was* the hotel's restaurant and therefore in close proximity to the hotel's bedrooms. She wasn't sure she was ready for bedrooms yet.

She liked Bob Briscoe. A lot. There was something about him. Maybe, she thought, it was his manner – smooth and easy but not unctuous. Maybe it was his sophistication; maybe it was because, like her, he was right at the centre of the world's business.

Or maybe, she smiled quietly, it was simply because he was so damned good-looking.

She wondered what he was like in bed. Probably fantastic, she decided. The thought sent a warm pulse shimmying into her belly and down to her loins. How long was it since she'd had a man? God, she could do with a screw. A week of ceaseless, incessant, unending sex was what she . . . She shook her head and looked away from the window.

No. She had to be cautious. She didn't want to be in the position of being asked up to his room for a nightcap. To refuse could seem churlish and naïve, to accept might precipitate her into something for which she wasn't ready. At least, not yet. One more time, she thought. Another candlelight dinner and then, maybe . . .

She buzzed Debbie. 'Book a table at La Tante Claire for tomorrow evening. For two.'

'Oooh, nice.'

'Then I want you to call Mr Briscoe.'

She did her best to ignore Debbie's warm, salacious chuckle.

Later that morning Boris Redbourn called on her internal phone.

'You know those papers you gave me yesterday? About the company in Nassau? Cyclix?'

'Yes.'

'Well, I've input the data and something interesting has come up. You want to come down and take a look?'

'I'm on my way.'

Redbourn, hunched as usual over his keyboard, was staring at a set of monitors filled with brightly coloured icons and moving arrows.

Melissa perched herself on the edge of his desk. 'Okay, Boris, what have you got?' she said brightly.

Redbourn grunted and ignored her, intent on the screen.

Melissa watched him for a few moments. Computer freaks were all the same, she thought, more interested in RAM and ROM than the real world.

'Boris,' she called quietly, 'Cyclix.'

He looked up and stared at her blankly through his spectacles. Then it came back to him. 'Cyclix. Oh yeah. You were right about them, Melissa.'

'I was?'

He turned back to the monitor, moved the mouse and clicked on a pulldown. The screen resolved into a graphic map and a succession of shimmering arrows emanating from the Caribbean.

'At first I thought Cyclix was like all the others,' he began. 'The company had a system for moving money and never varied it. Its account in the Exchange Bank in Nassau received large, regular payments from a correspondent bank in New Orleans, along with even bigger payments from a branch of the Exchange Bank in Honduras. And every month it moved five million dollars to an account in the Caymans.'

'That was to Pemblin,' Melissa told him.

'Right. The rest, always between twenty-five and thirty million a month, went out to various banks in Switzerland, mostly in Basel. *But,* here's the thing. Every so often the company's account in Nassau received an injection of funds from a bank in Houston. Not a lot . . . not in comparison anyway. About sixty million over a period of a couple of years. That money was telegraphed to a bank in Basel, where it stayed for about a week before being recycled back into America, to a bank in Atlanta.'

Melissa had been watching the movements on the screen. 'Okay,' she said cautiously, 'so what are you telling me?'

'Well, when you watch the monitor you'll see there's no consistency in the timing. And the amount of money Cyclix received from Houston was never the same twice. It's curious. Half a million . . . a million and a half . . . inconsistent amounts just turned up. The only thing that stayed the same was the destination of the funds. Now that's unusual.'

Melissa watched the movement of the arrows across the monitor. 'I knew it,' she said triumphantly. 'Cyclix was piggy-backing.'

He glanced up at her. 'It was what?'

'Carrying funds for somebody else. For a fee, Cyclix was bundling other people's money with its own.'

Redbourn frowned. 'I don't get it.'

'It's simple. Cyclix had a set-up, a mechanism for regularly moving money to Switzerland, right?' Redbourn nodded. 'So anyone who wanted to move money to those locations, but who wanted to hide the fact, could put their money with Cyclix . . . who would move it for them. Who could possibly know it wasn't Cyclix's money? None of the receiving banks would be surprised if the amounts deposited with them were occasionally different. Cyclix was a good account.'

'But why would someone want to hide movement of their money?'

Melissa gave him a pitying look. 'Come on, Boris, get real. Some rich, international fatcat salting tax-evaded cash overseas. Maybe some big company shifting cash for bribes. Far better for them to use an existing set-up for secretly moving the money. Rather than invent one of their own.'

He laughed. 'Okay, so you're telling me it was bent.'

'Everything to do with the Exchange Bank is bent. I'm pretty certain Cyclix is crooked. The company is tied in with Piagini, which we know was laundering drug money. Right now Piagini has a hundred million dollars frozen in Exchange Bank accounts. But, the question is: does Piagini have funds we don't know about? Was Cyclix piggy-backing Piagini cash? And if it was . . . why? Why hide it?'

Redbourn had turned back to his bank of screens. 'Search me,' he said dolefully.

'What we need to know,' Melissa went on, 'is whether the people behind Piagini are still doing it . . . still laundering dirty money.'

'They can't be. At least not through the Exchange Bank they can't.'

'Yes, but supposing they're still doing it using another route. One we don't know about? I mean, no one knew about this piggy-backing until you and your little box of micro-chip tricks exposed it, Boris.'

Redbourn smiled. 'That's not all I've come up with.'

'No? What else have you got?'

'The bank in Atlanta, the one receiving the cash from Basel, is on the list of American banks infiltrated by the Mafia. The list the Fed gave us.'

'That doesn't surprise me.'

'Okay, but what is surprising is that the recycled money coming out of Basel didn't stay in Atlanta. It didn't even stay in America. The Atlanta bank only ever kept the cash for a few days. Then it was moved offshore. The whole lot went out to the Exchange Bank in the Netherlands Antilles. Along with a whole lot of other funds. Nearly two hundred million appearing out of nowhere. After that . . .'

'None of that is surprising, Boris,' she interrupted. 'Funds never stay put for long. Not until they end up as an investment. The first law of laundering . . . keep the funds moving.'

'They do that all right,' Redbourn said, staring at the multitude of arrows shimmering across the screens. 'Shit, Melissa, I don't envy you having to follow up on all of this. It'll take years. How the hell are you ever going to make sense of it for a courtroom?'

'The main thing is patience,' she said gently.

He chuckled. 'Yeah, I suppose. So what are you going to do about this Cyclix thing? You going to pursue the piggy-backing?'

Melissa was gazing at the screens. 'Oh yes,' she assured him quietly. 'I'm going to pursue it.'

Redbourn shook his head as he contemplated the colourful moving graphics in front of him. 'Christ, I wouldn't know where to start.'

'I'll start in Basel,' she intoned. 'Arrange a few meetings as soon as possible. I've got the feeling I've found another brick. A big one.'

Redbourn looked up at her and frowned.

Chapter Sixteen

The internal phone bleeped. It was Andrew Bailey. 'Have you got a moment?'

'When?'

'Now.'

'Is it important?' Melissa snapped. As soon as she said it she regretted it. Andrew knew the score. He wouldn't have phoned and asked for her time if it wasn't important.

'Yes.' He sounded serious.

'Okay,' she sighed. 'Give me five minutes.'

She glanced at her watch. It wasn't even nine thirty. She had been in the office less than an hour and already the day was going pear-shaped.

Debbie had handed her a pile of urgent messages; Nigel Hawick had rescheduled a couple of important meetings, and she had a stack of files to plough through before flying to Basel the next day. It was damned annoying.

Today, of all days, she wanted things to go smoothly.

She had a date.

Whatever happened, she thought, she didn't want a bloody bad day spoiling her evening. She didn't want to be upset or get irritable. She didn't want to turn up at the Grosvenor House with the skin of her neck blotchy with tension.

She gritted her teeth. She wished, she told herself, to remain serene. Cool, calm and even-tempered. To be beautiful and poised and at her best for Briscoe.

Bailey appeared in her office on time. Frank Levinson was with him. She waved them into a couple of seats on the opposite side of her desk. They looked sombre. 'We've constructed a draft balance sheet for the bank,' Bailey announced.

'And . . . ?'

'It doesn't look good, Melissa. There's a bloody big hole in it,' Levinson said.

'So, tell me,' she said irritably.

'Half a billion dollars has gone missing,' he went on.

'What?'

Bailey nodded. 'It's true. We've checked and double-checked. Five hundred million . . . gone . . . moved out of the Exchange Bank.'

'What do you mean, moved out?' she demanded. She could feel herself getting tense.

'Disappeared. Gone with the wind. There's no trace of where it's gone.'

'There must be. There'll be journal entries, remittance forms, computer records.'

Levinson shook his head. 'Everything was done through the secret, codename accounts. The ones the auditors weren't allowed to see.'

'The Managers' Ledger Accounts,' Bailey piped up. 'An awful lot of the bank's hot money flowed through them.'

Melissa tried hard to restrain her impatience. 'Yes, I know,' she said sweetly.

'Okay, well, four of the biggest accounts . . . in London, Bogotá, Panama City and Karachi were systematically milked over a period of about a week.'

'When?'

'About ten weeks ago,' Bailey replied. 'The person who did it must have been very senior. He knew the right passwords and coordinates to trigger the money flows.'

'But half a billion!' Melissa protested fretfully. 'Some of it must have gone through New York. And if the amount was denominated in dollars, it would have been reported.'

Levinson shook his head. 'The amounts moved were always under the US Treasury reporting requirements. They weren't picked up as significant.'

'And at least half the money was switched into other currencies,' Bailey added. 'Swiss Francs, German Marks, Japanese . . .'

'I can guess the currencies, Andrew.' Her voice was acid. The two men opposite glanced at each other. 'Where was it moved to?' she snapped.

'Well, there was an awful lot of layering, but it looks like it went into nominee accounts in Nauru, Liberia and Liechtenstein. As soon as the funds were received, the accounts were closed out and the funds converted.'

'Into what?'

'The usual stuff . . . bank drafts, cashiers' cheques, money orders, certificated cheques, certificates of deposit.'

'For God's sake, not half a billion dollars. Surely it can't all be in negotiable instruments?'

'No,' Levinson cut in, 'we think most of it has gone into bearer bonds. Eurobonds most probably.'

'Which will be hell to trace.' Melissa snarled.

Bailey shrugged. 'Well, we will eventually.' He tried to sound optimistic.

Melissa glowered at him. 'In a few years.' Her voice was caustic. 'In the meantime, the bank's creditors will have to wait. Damn. Damn.'

She caught herself. For God's sake, she was agitated, already.

Oh no, not today. It was not what she wanted today. Calm down, she told herself. Today there must be no hurry . . . no worry. She took a deep breath. Serene. That was the order of the day.

'You say the money came out of the Managers' Ledger Accounts?' Her voice was sugary.

Again the men across the desk glanced at each other. 'Yes.'

A thought occurred to her. 'Was the Austerlitz Account one of them?'

Levinson consulted a document in a file. 'No.'

'The Austerlitz Account is a locked box, Melissa,' Bailey moaned. 'That is, if it exists at all. So far, the only record of it is on the list Aziz gave you. There's no reference to it anywhere else. No document or printout that anyone has come across makes any mention of an Austerlitz Account.'

The sound of Aziz's name brought a pained expression to Melissa's face. She made an effort to get her mind back on the business.

'Well,' she announced, 'we know the money in those accounts was criminal. So my guess is someone got wind that the bank was to be shut down and moved a large chunk of illicit funds out of our reach. Do we know who? If we knew who, it might give us a clue as to where.'

Bailey shook his head. 'No. But whoever it was, he knew the

141

Exchange Bank inside out. It looks like he had carte blanche to move funds around whenever he wanted. He knew the codenames of the Managers' Ledger Accounts and, like I say, he knew all the passwords and the coordinates to move the money. Here's a list.'

He handed her a slim file with a list of names inside. Melissa glanced at it. As far as she could see it looked like a list of foreign place names. She pulled a face. 'This bloody bank,' she moaned. 'Everything inside was codenames and passwords. The place must have been like MI5.'

'I expect that's because no one trusted anyone else.'

'With good bloody reason,' she said bitterly. She took a deep breath. 'Okay, well, you had better leave me what you've got and I'll take a look.' She stared darkly at the thick sheaf of documents Levinson dropped onto her desk.

'So, in the meantime, what do we do?' Bailey inquired.

She fixed him with a malevolent look. 'You do what you're paid to do, Andrew. Start hunting the money.'

Bailey made a face. 'Like you say, that could take years.'

'You got any better bloody suggestions?' Melissa snarled.

They looked startled.

At precisely five thirty that afternoon, having done her best to remain an island of serenity in a sea of increasing hysteria, insistent phones and instant meetings, she took the small executive lift up to the top floor of the Eastcheap tower block where she showered, changed and applied her make-up in one of the partners' marble-tiled restrooms.

She picked Briscoe up at seven.

'You look fantastic,' he said appreciatively as she drifted elegantly across the floor of Grosvenor House to join him at the bar. She smiled demurely. With plenty of notice to do the business, she had pulled out all the stops.

The dress was Gianni Versace, a chiffon and silk number in the perfect shade of midnight blue to complement her burnished, shining hair. It was strapless and cut on the bias, subtly accentuating her breasts and clinging softly at her hips before flaring at the knee. Her tailored jacket was a misty grey-blue crêpe, her heels high, with ankle straps and pointed toecaps, and her tights ultrasheer black opaque. She had taken a long time over her make-up, wearing a bright glossy lipstick which lit up her face. Her grey-blue eyes, accentuated by the attention she had given them, were deep and liquid.

She looked good. She knew she looked good.

Briscoe looked good too. The pale blue silk shirt beneath his charcoal grey Armani suit showed off his natural tan. But he looked tired. Too many flights across the Atlantic, she thought.

After a drink at the bar they took a cab to Chelsea. Melissa recommended the terrine of foie gras with marinated aubergine, followed by the red mullet. She ordered a couple of bottles of *Poligny Montrachet Grand Cru*. Briscoe was impressed. He told her so.

She laughed and tossed her hair. 'I thought I'd show you I know almost as much about French food as you know about Italian. Silly really. It's just showing off.'

Again she found herself talking about herself and her work. She wanted to tell Briscoe about the murder of Akhtar Aziz and his family... to confess to him, an outsider, how responsible she felt about their terrible deaths.

She wished for absolution... and knew she couldn't get it.

She couldn't talk to Briscoe about Aziz. Maybe, she thought, when she knew him better.

Instead she told him more about the work she had done in San Francisco, though she was careful not to be specific with details, nor to mention names. It was so wonderful, she reflected, to have an attractive man sitting across a table from her. A man who was happy to listen to her talk about herself and her career. She couldn't remember when that had last happened. Briscoe seemed fascinated by her stories.

'Actually, I probably shouldn't be telling you all this,' she announced, taking another sip of her wine. 'I could get into serious trouble.'

He held up a hand, palm facing her. 'Hey, Melissa, don't tell me anything you shouldn't. Hell, we're both in the same line of business. I understand confidentiality. We all have to keep our lips buttoned about stuff. I would hate for you to get into any trouble on my account. Anyway, don't worry about it. I wouldn't tell anybody anything you've told me.'

She smiled and nodded. 'Thank you. I'm afraid I have to be very careful. Especially now.'

'Yeah? Why now?'

'They've made me sign the Official Secrets Act.' She giggled. The wine was going to her head. 'I've probably already infringed it.' He looked at her inquiringly. 'By telling you I've signed it,' she explained. She giggled louder. 'Spooks and bureaucrats, who needs 'em?' She waved her hand, as if shooing them away. 'I don't want to talk about them.'

He asked her about Jamie.

Melissa described her son in detail and told Briscoe how much she adored him. She was silent for a moment, before saying, quietly: 'Jamie has Down's Syndrome.'

'Oh.' He seemed unsure about how to react. 'I'm sorry,' he said lamely.

She felt an irrational sense of disappointment at his reaction. It wasn't what she had expected. What had she expected? she asked herself. She didn't know. Suddenly she didn't want to talk about herself or Jamie any more.

'Anyway,' she said brightly, 'what brings you back here so soon?'

Briscoe launched into an amusing story about some enormous financial investment which was going disastrously wrong. He had been asked to try and save it. Soon he had her laughing loudly at his graphic descriptions of inept executives and frightened bankers.

This time he kissed her.

She had told him her last train home left soon after midnight. Just before twelve they hailed a cab outside the restaurant and he rode with her to Waterloo. He didn't ask her back to Grosvenor House for a drink. She was grateful to him for that.

He stood close to her at the platform barrier, close enough for her to sense the warmth of his body and detect a lingering whiff of his musky aftershave. 'I can't tell you how much I enjoyed this evening,' he told her. 'Dinner was great. Thanks a lot.'

He paused and stared down at her. 'I want to see you again, Melissa.' His voice was low and husky. 'I mean soon.'

'I want that too.' Her throat was suddenly very dry.

He nodded then bent his head and kissed her full on her lips. It was a deep, rich, powerful sensation. She let herself be taken by it, returning the kiss ardently. She felt his arms drawing her body into his.

After a moment he raised his head, reluctantly drawing his lips away from hers. 'Don't miss your train,' he whispered. 'I'll call you. Soon.'

She waved to him from the other side of the barrier before boarding the train.

She travelled home in a state of slightly stunned amazement. Her legs felt as flimsy as the chiffon of her dress and there was a flickering fire somewhere deep inside her belly.

With a sudden shock she realised she was wet . . . there. God, she hadn't felt like this in years. It was as if she was a teenager again. She looked at her reflection in the darkened windows of the carriage and grinned.

The train stopped at every station on its long, tedious journey into Hampshire but she didn't notice.

Chapter Seventeen

The first flight out of Heathrow landed early at Mulhouse Freiburg. She caught a cab outside the terminal of the Euro Airport and made the short journey across the border into Switzerland.

Of all the big Swiss cities Melissa liked Basel the least. The city, though right at the fulcrum of France and Germany, seemed to her to exhibit a blithe indifference to history.

Earth-shattering events had happened all around it. World wars had been staged just beyond its lush parks. Bitter enemies had faced each other across its northern suburbs. And throughout everything Basel had remained resolutely insouciant.

She checked her case at the Hilton on Aeschengraben before making her way to her first appointment close to St Alban-Graben. It was a beautiful day, with a blue, elevated European sky streaked by long filaments of high, white cirrus.

Melissa gazed around her, recalling the confrontations she'd had in the city, as she walked through the warm sunshine of Elizabethenstrasse. For Melissa, Switzerland was a battlefield.

On every one of the frequent trips she'd made to the country, she had found herself clashing with lawyers and bankers. This trip, she thought, was unlikely to be different.

She had arranged a hectic schedule . . . two busy days of battles with a bunch of Swiss bankers.

In her early years she had won a few . . . and lost a lot.

These days she reckoned the scoreline was more in her favour. Much of her recent success was due to getting to know the system. She had made a careful study of the law relating to bank secrecy in Switzerland and had discovered that Swiss banking was like Swiss cheese . . . full of holes.

Melissa had become a wise mouse.

Through a thorough understanding of the rules she had been

able, legitimately, to prise a lot of vital information out of the banks.

What had helped her immensely had been the number of embarrassing, high-level scandals involving prominent Swiss citizens suspected of international money laundering and shady financial dealings with organised criminals. Melissa grinned as she moved through the crowds of shoppers.

The scandals had forced the Swiss financial authorities to adopt a Diligence Convention, requiring bankers to inquire into the source of cash deposits over a hundred thousand Swiss Francs, as well as to enact new financial legislation allowing outsiders – especially the American federal law-enforcement agencies – greater access to information.

A new spirit of cooperation was developing, in which the strict secrecy of the Swiss banks was slowly eroding. The hugger-mugger mentality of the bankers of Basel was changing.

A bit.

Even so, it still wasn't easy.

Most Swiss lawyers, bankers and businessmen were deeply conservative. They were suspicious of outsiders, even officially appointed outsiders, trying to pry into their affairs . . . resentfully suspicious when the outsiders were foreigners . . . and totally bloody hostile when the foreigners were women.

Right now, she ruminated, Rolay Richard's lawyers, supported by letters rogatory, were in the process of seeking judicial attachment orders to block more than sixty accounts in various Swiss banks. Millions of dollars from branches of the Exchange Bank had been deposited into those accounts.

Melissa's job as the firm's forensic accountant was to chase down the money . . . to glean as much information as she could about the accounts. Who owned them? What had they been used for? Where had the money in them been moved to? She expected it to be a long and tough process.

Despite the new spirit of cooperation, blood out of stones was easy in comparison to information from a Swiss banker.

The bank manager at her first appointment was typical of the species. She was shown into an austere, characterless office where a slightly nervous man in his mid-thirties repetitiously quoted Article 273 of the Penal Code at her.

Melissa assured him there was no possibility of either of them being guilty of economic espionage. Legal orders were in force on the accounts in question. She, as the liquidator and an officer of the High Court, albeit the English High Court, was well within her rights to make the inquiries she was making.

Her assurances seemed to mollify the man. Melissa gave him a list of the documents she wished to see. The list ran to seven pages. The bank manager glanced at it. 'This will take hours to retrieve from our files!' he yelped. 'And they will be costly to photocopy.'

Melissa nodded. 'I appreciate that. And my firm will pay for the photocopying. In the meantime, there are a few documents I'd like to see now. They relate to a couple of the accounts named on the list. It would be helpful if I could see the papers whilst I'm here.'

'Why especially those two?' the manager asked suspiciously.

Melissa stared at him innocently. She had to be careful. The accounts had been used by Cyclix to deposit the piggy-backed funds coming from America. If the manager suspected her inquiries were not directly related to the liquidation of the Exchange Bank, he would scream *Spécialité* and terminate the meeting.

Melissa knew the information she gained from her inquiries was only supposed to be used in connection with the investigation for which the information was being sought. She couldn't use incidental facts or intelligence she picked up in the course of her investigations for any other offence.

Liquidators, she reflected ruefully, were not allowed to go fishing.

'The corporation depositing money into those two accounts,' she replied, 'is part of an organisation currently under investigation by federal authorities in the United States. Officers of the corporation may soon be facing charges for narcotics smuggling and money laundering.'

The manager looked disdainful. 'Ah, but that is in America,' he commented.

'They are both crimes under Swiss law,' Melissa replied sweetly. 'And as Switzerland has agreed to render assistance on matters of international organised crime through its Mutual Assistance Laws, I expect you will want to cooperate.'

The bank manager scowled. 'You are very well informed about our Penal Code and our international treaties.'

She gave him a honeyed smile. 'Yes I am. I also know the authorities here in Switzerland are as anxious as the rest of us to eliminate enterprise crime. That's why I've come to you for help. And, as this bank has signed the Observance of Care Agreement, I'm sure I can count on your assistance. So, perhaps I can see those documents now?' She smiled at him sweetly. 'Just give me what I want and I'll go away.'

The manager's scowl deepened. He rose irritably from behind his desk.

The documents didn't tell her much. Melissa hadn't expected them to. The accounts had been opened by nominees, Swiss and Liechtenstein lawyers, acting as front men. The beneficial owners of the accounts would be corporations, which in turn would be fronted by business agents. Yet more lawyers, she thought. There would be layers upon layers of tight-lipped attorneys for her to cut through before she finally got to the people who owned the accounts.

She sighed as she sifted through the papers. The owners had assigned general powers of attorney to the lawyers. They'd also signed Code Name Agreements, which allowed them to run numbered accounts at the bank.

Melissa smiled grimly. The infamous Swiss numbered bank accounts. In fact, she reflected, the accounts, like those in the Exchange Bank, were more often designated by codenames than numbers.

But, whichever way they were designated, she thought ruefully, it would take months, maybe years, of legal argument, wrangling and submissions, along with a whole slew of court orders, to prise out the names of the people behind the accounts.

She took a note of the lawyers' names and asked the bank manager if she could see the latest statements. At least, she reasoned, if she couldn't find out who owned the accounts, she could learn what they had been doing with the money.

The rest of Melissa's day was spent in meetings with similarly recalcitrant bankers. By late afternoon she was exhausted. It was tiring, picking away at the bricks in the wall.

She got her break at her last meeting of the day. The bank was another into which some of the piggy-backed funds had been deposited by Cyclix. The manager was marginally less tight-lipped than his counterparts. He was younger and not quite as bloodless and Melissa had an idea he was getting the hots for her. She allowed the skirt of her suit to ride up a little past her knees.

The manager showed her what information he could on the accounts she was investigating. As usual they were fronted by nominees and as difficult to penetrate as the bank's vault. Melissa noted the names of the nominees and took down the details of where funds from the accounts had been moved to. None of the information was of any use to her right then. But, maybe one day . . . she thought.

'All the accounts have refused to submit to the stipulations of Agreement Sixteen,' the manager told her.

Melissa grunted. She was in the middle of writing her notes, a pad on her knee, her shining hair draping forward and framing her face.

Not signing Agreement Sixteen was par for the course. The agreement related to any dealings done through the accounts on the US securities markets. Submitting to the agreement's stipulations would have allowed an investigator like Melissa a lot more information about the account.

'Except one,' the manager continued.

She looked up sharply. 'What?'

'One of these accounts has signed Agreement Sixteen. It was the first one opened in 1973.'

Somehow Melissa managed to keep her face straight. Someone had screwed up. If the men behind the accounts had signed the agreement, it meant names were available . . . names of the people behind the account. 'May I see?' It was hard to keep the excitement out of her voice.

The manager passed a clutch of documents across the desk. There were two names on the agreement. One meant nothing to her. The other was one she knew. The signature of Vito Kunzman was appended to the bottom of the agreement in a tight, controlled hand.

She kept the excitement out of her voice. 'Anyone signing Agreement Sixteen,' she said, 'must also supply an address. May I see the address provided by this man Kunzman?'

The manager frowned. 'I don't know if I am permitted to do that.'

Melissa gestured and moved in her seat. Her skirt rode up a little further. 'As an officer of the court,' she said in a neutral tone, 'I am allowed to see the signed agreement you have shown me. The address constitutes part of the agreement, so it follows I should be permitted to see it.' She smiled warmly.

The young manager gazed at her for a moment then, with a sigh, pushed another document across his desk.

The address was in White Plains, New York.

She arrived back in her room at the Hilton tired but elated. For once the breaks had gone her way.

She called Astrid who said Jamie was fine. As she was about to take a shower the room phone buzzed. It took her a moment to realise who it was.

'Melissa? Hi, it's me.'

'Robert? Is that you?'

'Sure is. Howya doing?'

She was delighted to hear from him. 'I'm fine. How did you know I was here?'

'I called your office. They said you were in Basel.'

Melissa frowned. Briscoe, she thought, must have been enormously compelling to persuade Debbie to reveal where she was. It was standard security in the firm not to tell unknown callers the location of partners when they were abroad.

'Where are you?' she asked.

'You're not going to believe this,' he laughed, 'but I'm in Switzerland.'

She couldn't believe it, though now she understood what might have made him put pressure on Debbie to tell him where she was.

'In Basel?' she asked incredulously.

'Hell, no, I'm not *that* lucky. I'm in Geneva. But listen, why don't I catch the shuttle and come see you. We could have dinner again.'

Melissa was shocked. 'You mean tonight?'

'Sure. It's less than an hour's flight.' His voice grew deeper, more intense. 'I told you I wanted to see you again real soon.'

'Yes, but I didn't think you meant in the next couple of days.'

'I didn't either. But then I didn't know you were coming to Switzerland.'

She laughed. 'No, I didn't tell you.' She was silent for a moment, trying to think. It was all happening so fast. 'There may not be a seat on the shuttle,' she said lamely.

'There is. I checked.'

'But where will you stay? There's a big convention here. I had a hell of a time getting a room.'

Briscoe laughed. 'Hell, Melissa, there's *always* a big

151

convention in Basel. I called the Three Kings on the Rhine. They're holding a room for me.'

'God, you were lucky. I tried to get in there but they were full.'

'They had a cancellation. Maybe it's fate, huh? Maybe we're *meant* to have dinner tonight.'

Melissa was beginning to think the same thing . . . and it bothered her.

What was worrying her was what could happen *after* their dinner. If Briscoe was to fly over the Jura to be with her, would he expect to sleep with her? No, she decided, he wasn't like that. He wouldn't *expect* to sleep with her. He might *want* to, but the decision would be down to her. She grimaced at the walls of her room.

It was make-your-mind-up time.

Did she want to go to bed with Robert Briscoe? Could she in all conscience say yes to him flying over the mountains if all she intended was merely to have dinner with him? If she encouraged him to come, would she feel obliged to sleep with him? she wondered.

She stared into space and thought about Briscoe. Memories of the kiss on Waterloo Station came back to her.

Shit, who was she kidding?

If she was obliged to sleep with Robert Briscoe it wasn't through any action of his. The compulsion would come from the delicious buzzing sensation she could suddenly feel somewhere below her navel.

Wanted to sleep with him?

Hell, she was *desperate* to sleep with him.

Why, she asked herself, should she pass up the opportunity? What the hell was she saving herself for? This was the perfect time and place. It was anonymous . . . she was miles away from anyone she knew . . . there was no Jamie to rush back to. It was the best chance she'd had in years.

His voice brought her back to the present. 'Hello, Melissa, you there?'

'Yes, I'm here. I think you're right.'

'Right?'

'Yes. Maybe it *is* fate. What time will you be here?'

They dined in the Rotisserie des Rois, the Three Kings' expensive and exclusive restaurant. Melissa ate sparingly and drank only enough wine to take the edge off her nervousness. She didn't want to spoil anything by being tipsy.

Briscoe told her that he'd flown to Geneva in connection with the financial deal he was trying to salvage. Melissa chuckled at the stories of his day in the city. He asked her what had brought her to Basel. She told him something about the day's frustrations and of the difficulties she had in getting Swiss bankers to part with information.

He nodded. He understood, he said.

Yes. That was one of the many things she liked about Bob Briscoe. He was in her line of business. She didn't need to explain things. He understood the jargon of money.

Even so, she found it difficult to concentrate on their conversation. She scarcely tasted her food, and the restaurant's elegant ambience was entirely lost on her. Her attention was completely centred on the lubricious quivering somewhere in the region of her clitoris. God, she was hot.

She thought about the DA's assistant in Sausalito bagging the pornographic literature.

Now she *was* horny.

She said yes to coffee and no to Courvoisier. Later, after what seemed an age, Briscoe asked, 'Would you like a nightcap? At the bar?'

'Yes, I'd like a nightcap,' she said softly, 'but I'd prefer one in your room.'

She had to admit that Briscoe was the ultimate in cool aplomb. Propositioned across the snowy white tablecloth of a chic, expensive restaurant by a beautiful woman with shining, sexy eyes and glossy, coppery hair, he didn't miss a beat. His dark eyes were deep and mysterious. 'I'd like that too,' he said quietly.

They travelled up in the lift with an elderly couple. Melissa caught the woman giving her the hard eye and smiled sweetly at her. It was as well the pair were there, she thought, otherwise she would have started proceedings in the lift. As it was, as soon as Briscoe closed the room door she reached up, put her arms around his neck and pulled his mouth down onto hers.

She clung to him for a long time, gorging herself on his mouth, on his lips, taking his tongue into her mouth. She was abandoned and unrestrained . . . and loving it.

She started pulling at his clothes, yanking his jacket down

his back, tugging at his shirt. In no time she had his upper torso stripped. She was surprised. His body was hard and wonderfully muscled, the muscle definition underscored by the subtle, raking, ambient glow of the room's sidelights.

For an international financier, she thought, he took amazingly good care of his physique. To get that way he had to work out a hell of a lot. She crushed herself against the solid wall of his abdomen. It was like a washboard. She began pulling at the belt of his trousers.

'No,' he whispered, grasping her wrists, 'it's my turn.'

Gently he turned her around and slowly drew down the zip at the back of her dress. The dress dropped softly to her ankles. Melissa stepped out of it. She felt Briscoe unclasping the strap of her brassière. His hands on her back were warm and sensuously gentle. He moved them lightly down her ribcage to the top of her panties. Slowly he drew the French silk over her hips, the tips of his fingers gently caressing her thighs as they moved down.

Melissa moaned.

She slipped out of her shoes and was perfectly naked. She tried to turn and face him. 'Not yet,' he whispered.

Melissa stood in the middle of the room like the statue of Venus as Robert Briscoe gently moved his hands over her back. With one hand she supported her breast, her thumb lightly teasing her nipple, whilst with the other she clutched at her vagina.

She threw her head back in ecstasy as she felt his hands softly caressing her buttocks. His thumbs moved up the inside of her thighs towards the little bush of soaking hair between her legs.

Then she felt the tip of his tongue on her backbone. Slowly it began to move down. One hand tenderly massaged her buttocks as the fingers of the other lightly stroked the soft flesh inside her thighs. The sweet, sensitive microvilli at the tip of Briscoe's tongue reached the sweet, sexually sensitive area just below Melissa's coccyx.

'*Ohhhhhhhhhhh.*'

She shivered in delirium. It was too much. She was going to come.

Briscoe sensed from her shudder she was close to a climax. His tongue moved off her body. He held her steadily with one hand. Melissa heard a faint rustling behind her and a moment later felt something against her thigh.

Though it had been a long time she knew immediately what it was. A solid shaft of muscle . . . hard and hot and throbbing. Briscoe was moving it up between her legs.

He was going to have her from behind.

She pulled out of his grip and spun around. 'No,' she croaked. 'Not that way. Not first time. Later. Not now. Now I want to feel everything. See it all.'

Briscoe was naked. She looked down at his penis . . . and groaned in pleasure. God, it was so beautiful. Big and rigid, like the barrel of a cannon . . . like a pikestaff, the glans swollen purple and red. Melissa grabbed at it with both hands. It was heavy and hot with wanting. Just like her. She groaned again.

She began reversing towards the bed, gently guiding him by his penis. She fell backward onto the counterpane. 'Come on,' she whispered urgently. 'Come on. Do it. Now.' She felt the slippery tip of his glans moving over the silken surface of her vulva. 'Oh, yes,' she urged, 'yes.'

'Wait,' he whispered, straightening up. 'I need to get something.'

'Oh, Jesus,' she wailed. 'Not now. Christ.'

He padded swiftly across the room to where his jacket lay crumpled on the carpet. He was back in seconds, half-kneeling on the bed, expertly slipping on the condom. He leaned over her and grinned. 'Now, where were we?'

Melissa's breath was coming in staccato rasps. She was clutching her vagina as if trying to hold something back. Which, in a manner of speaking, she was.

She reached up with her other hand and grabbed at the taut flesh over his ribcage. She twisted it cruelly. 'For God's sake, do it,' she snarled. 'Come inside me.'

Briscoe moved on top of her. He lowered himself down and into her. As Melissa felt the gorgeous pole moving into her vagina, she let out a long, low, animal moan. Clutching savagely at his back she pulled his delicious heaviness hard onto her breasts. His body, so solid, so immovable, was crushing her into the bed. It was heaven.

For the first time in ages she had a man between her legs. She was engorged, crammed, stuffed, packed, chock-a-block . . . and somewhere at the back of her head, in a small pinpoint behind her pituitary gland, as well as in the tingling place in her clitoris, her climax was building.

Gathering . . . like a hurricane . . . like a typhoon. And, like a typhoon, when it came it was going to blow them both out of their minds . . .

Later, Briscoe had her on the floor . . . and in a chair . . . and standing up . . . and in the bathroom . . . and from behind.

For most of the night they jerked and shuddered, whinnied and moaned, probing and sucking, filling their mouths with each other's flesh, until, long after first light had come creeping over the Rhine, they fell asleep.

Exhausted.

Chapter Eighteen

They woke before seven and made love again.

Afterwards he ordered breakfast, apparently in no hurry to check out and catch his flight back to Geneva.

Melissa took a shower and examined herself in the bathroom mirror.

She moaned.

God, she looked ravaged. Her skin, drawn tight over her cheekbones, was roughly the colour of the bathroom tiles. Her eyes were like bomb craters. Yet she noticed a softness about them that hadn't been there before. For all its pillaged appearance, her face was that of a woman who had been well-pleasured.

She tried to recall how often she had come. Had she climaxed many times, she wondered, or had the night been one long, multiple orgasm? In the unremitting light of a Swiss summer morning she couldn't remember.

Room service arrived with breakfast. She sipped a cup of black coffee. It was all she could manage. She told Briscoe she had to get back to the Hilton. She needed a change of clothes and was due to check out.

'I'm flying back to London later,' he told her. 'I've got the early flight to New York tomorrow morning, so I've booked into the Holiday Inn at the airport. But I could see you this evening.'

Her heart leapt. Then she thought of Jamie. 'I don't know how we can manage it,' she said wistfully. 'I have to go back to the office and after that I want to get home to see my son.'

He nodded. 'Sure. I understand. Look, why don't I call you when I get in. Maybe we can meet for a drink in London or I can rent a car and come see you in Hampshire.'

She said that would be marvellous. They kissed once more before she left.

The morning passed in a kind of dream. The bankers she met

157

were as coy and evasive as those of the day before but she scarcely cared. She was operating on auto-pilot: going through the motions; asking the questions she had to ask; listening to the replies the men gave her, jotting down her notes . . . and hardly noticing. She knew it was unprofessional . . . but for once it didn't matter.

She was dog-tired, her back ached, she could barely put her legs together and her pubic bone was sore. But there was languor in her loins and the small, sharp, itchy sensation inside her head had gone. She felt marvellous.

She caught the late afternoon flight and landed at Heathrow a little after five. Unlike Basel, which had been warm and sunny, the sky over London was overcast. Melissa noticed a slight chill in the air as she joined the queue for a cab. It looked like rain. She grimaced. The weather had all the makings of a British June weekend.

Waiting in line, she could feel the effects of the previous night's fun and frolics catching up with her. She reflected on how much she would have loved to go straight home . . . back to the cottage for a hot bath . . . back in time to spend a couple of hours with Jamie.

She remembered she had said she would take him to get his puppy the following morning. They could have gone that evening, she thought, if she had opted to go straight home. Instead, she'd promised Nigel Hawick to return to the office and report on progress.

Sitting in the back of a cab and watching the Friday afternoon traffic streaming out of London through the drizzling rain, it was a promise she regretted. What was so important, she wondered, that it couldn't wait until Monday morning?

She arrived at the office at a little after six. Except for a couple of uniformed security guards at the desk, the magnificent atrium on Eastcheap was silent and empty. Melissa checked her suitcase with one of the men who put it behind the desk. She fixed her ID to the lapel of her suit and took the lift to the fourteenth floor. Hawick was waiting for her in his office.

'How did it go?' he asked.

Melissa shrugged. 'The usual. Everyone trying to hide behind Article 47. All scared to talk, frightened of giving anything away in case someone jumps on them from a great height for divulging secrets.'

Hawick shrugged. 'Nothing ever changes. Certainly the Swiss don't. At least, not much. What progress with the bank accounts?'

'They're Form B accounts. Lawyers fronting for the beneficial owners. It'll take months to discover who's behind them. But at least our legal people have done a good job. All the accounts into which the Exchange Bank was moving money are now completely blocked. Frozen solid. There's no way whoever owns them can move the assets upstream.'

Hawick pulled a face. 'Well, I suppose that's something.'

Melissa was surprised at the laconic response. 'It's a helluva good start, Nigel. We wouldn't have got this far this quick with the Swiss authorities a few years ago. And,' she added dramatically, 'I got a breakthrough on the Cyclix funds.'

'Oh yes?'

From the start Hawick had made it apparent he thought her interest in the funds Cyclix had piggy-backed to Switzerland was irrelevant. He had never said as much, but Melissa knew it all the same. She hadn't told him that her main reason for going to Basel had been to pursue the funds. Now, she felt a small glow of justification.

'Well, not exactly a breakthrough on the funds themselves,' she admitted. 'But I wouldn't have found out what I discovered if I hadn't been checking on them.'

'Okay, okay. So what *did* you find out?'

'I got a lead on Kunzman.'

Hawick sat up in his seat. Suddenly he was interested. 'Yes?'

'He'd endorsed an Agreement Sixteen. It was back in the seventies, when the Swiss banks were really tight. Probably someone insisted. And I don't suppose he realised the implications. By now I expect he's forgotten he signed it. There was an address on the authorisation.'

'You took a note of it?'

'What do you think? Of course.'

'Great,' he said eagerly. 'Where is it?'

'In my attaché case. Why, what's the rush?'

Hawick leaned back in his seat. 'I've got a meeting with the supervisors at the BoE on Monday morning. I'm supposed to report on progress . . . bring them up to date on where we are with the liquidation. Which means I need a detailed report from you. Everything you've been working on: the Caymans, San Francisco, Basel . . . everything. I'm going to need it by Sunday morning. So I can go over it in detail.'

He saw her face and shrugged. 'I'm sorry, Melissa. That's how it is. When you've written it, have it biked over to my place. Include what you've found out about Kunzman.'

Her face darkened. Now, even more, she regretted her promise to return to the office. She had been hoping for a clear weekend. The paperwork would take her at least a couple of hours. 'For heaven's sake, Nigel,' she moaned, 'is that really necessary? Surely you don't need to give the Bank my report on Monday morning? Can't it wait a day?'

'No. I want to show the BoE that the firm is making progress. That we're getting closer to tracking down some of this bloody money.'

'But they already know that. They don't need me to tell them.'

'Well, you know how it is, Melissa. He who pays the piper and all that . . .'

She could see he was adamant.

She left his office a few moments later and walked into her own. Angrily, she emptied the contents of her attaché case onto her desk and fired up her PC.

She would write the report straight away. It was, she reasoned, too late to get home before Jamie went to bed, and whatever happened she meant to keep her promise to buy him his puppy in the morning. Doing the work now would leave her weekend free. She took off her jacket and sat down at her desk.

Forty minutes later Hawick poked his head round her door to say goodnight. By then she was well into the work. It took her another two hours. Halfway through she called Astrid to let her know what was happening.

Though she had given Bob Briscoe her night-line number, he didn't call. She wondered vaguely if his business had kept him in Geneva or if his flight had been delayed.

After she finished she stood next to the small inkjet in the corner of her office, watching the report's printed sheets whispering easily onto the paper tray. Idly, she looked out of the big smoky windows and watched raindrops spattering against them. It was past nine o'clock, and although it was practically midsummer, the view beyond the windows was grey and gloomy. The river was scarcely visible in the mist.

When the printer finished, she clipped the papers of the report together, sealed them in a strong internal-security envelope, collected up her things and took the lift to the ground floor.

'This needs biking to Mr Hawick's home first thing tomorrow.'

The security man was a sergeant-major type in his early fifties. 'Very good, miss. I'll make sure it's done.'

'Thank you.' She collected her suitcase from behind the desk.

'You want me to call you a cab, miss?' The sergeant raised his eyes to the roof of the atrium forty feet above them. The noise of the rain on the glass panels was noticeable.

She shook her head as she detached her ID from her lapel. She was anxious to get away, to get out of the building, to escape the air conditioning and get out into at least partially fresh air. 'No, thanks. I'll get one outside.'

The sergeant deactivated the alarm, accompanied her to the big, plate-glass doors, unlocked them and let her out of the building. It was raining steadily. Melissa put up the umbrella she had picked up from a collection she kept in the office. Frequently glancing behind, she hurried to the end of Eastcheap.

There wasn't a cab in sight.

'Shit,' she hissed.

The rain was heavier than she had thought and she was beginning to get wet. It was obvious by the time she walked up King William Street that she was going to be a lot wetter. She turned left and made for the steps leading down to Monument tube station. She would take the underground escalator link to Bank.

She grimaced as she trotted down the steps, thinking irritably what a stupid bitch she was.

She hadn't had the patience to wait for the security man to call a cab. Oh no. She'd been too anxious to get away from the office. So she had swapped a short wait in a light, airy atrium for a long walk down a tunnel deep beneath the streets.

A long walk lugging an overnight case, an umbrella, her shoulder bag and her attaché case.

'Serves you right, you impatient cow,' she muttered to herself.

The station booking hall was practically deserted. A solitary cleaner was morosely mopping the floor. He looked up as she walked past. Melissa started down the gently sloping undershaft towards the escalators. There was nobody about and the click of her heels echoed in the long empty tunnel. She had never known it so deserted. She felt a little shiver run up her spine. At this time of night the place was slightly creepy.

For God's sake, why hadn't she waited for a cab? she asked herself angrily. All that screwing last night must have affected her brain.

She reached the top of the first of the long, steep escalators and put her case down beside her on the moving step, watching her distorted reflection sliding past in the broad, stainless steel frames of the advertising panels.

She didn't know why, but she felt nervous and edgy. Lack of sleep, she thought. She grabbed her case as the treads flattened out at the bottom of the escalator.

The click of her heels seemed even louder on the polished, marbled floor of the lower level. The noise, bouncing off the curved, shiny walls, came back to her like a ghostly tattoo.

A solitary man was walking towards her. He glanced at her furtively as he passed.

Melissa listened to the sound of his footsteps disappearing down the tunnel behind her. They stopped. She glanced over her shoulder.

The man was on the up escalator, his back to her, staring at the advertisements.

Her gaze switched to the other escalator. Two men were riding down, standing together and staring into space. She watched them for a moment.

She wasn't sure . . . there was something in the way they ignored her . . .

She turned her head and hurried on. The problem was, she told herself, she had spent all last night reaching orgasms. Now she was paying for her pleasure. Exhaustion was betraying her. It made her jittery.

She reached the top of the next escalator. There was no one in sight: no one descending in front of her; no one ascending the up-escalator.

The broad shaft, plunging diagonally into the earth, was deserted. Hard, bright lights and the raucous, mechanical clanking of chains and electric motors bounced off its polished walls.

She gazed at the ads as she rode deeper into the bowels of the earth. Out of the corner of her eye she saw the two men appear at the top of the escalator. Neither paid her any attention. She reached the bottom, picked up her case and headed towards Bank Station.

She was in a broad, well lit tunnel in the deepest part of the link. On either side of the tunnel's shining, marble-tiled walls were the platforms of the Docklands Light Railway, connected to the tunnel by high, arched walkways.

Melissa glanced uneasily down each of the wide entrances as she walked quickly past. Somebody waiting in one could easily leap out on her.

For God's sake, she chided herself, she was turning into a neurotic.

A man passed her, striding quickly. The suddenness startled her. It was one of the men who had been behind her on the escalator. She watched him, wondering what his hurry was all of a sudden.

The man stopped dead ten yards ahead. He swung round to face her.

Melissa halted abruptly.

For a moment she and the man stared at each other. She noticed he was short and heavily built. Like a wrestler. There was some-thing about his eyes. Something cold and hard and malevolent. He started towards her.

Melissa dropped her overnight case and turned to run.

A man was standing silently behind her. He had a smirk on his face.

Melissa smacked into him.

She opened her mouth to scream.

A hand whipped up and slapped across her mouth, the force jarring her head backwards. She felt an arm, as strong and sinuous as a python, whip around her waist, dragging her close in to the man's solid mass, close enough to smell the sour, acid odour of his body.

'Shaddup, bitch.'

Other hands grabbed her from behind, shoving her skirt halfway up her thighs.

Dear God, they meant to rape her.

She stared, bug-eyed, beyond the leering face of the man clamping her mouth. The bright, shining tunnel was empty.

Nobody.

There was nobody to save her. She was on her own. She struggled for breath.

'Get the case,' the man holding her barked in a low tone. His voice was rough. East London.

She tried to shout from beneath the man's hand. 'Take the

case. Just leave me.' Her words came out a muffled gabble.

'I told you. Shut the fuck up,' the man snarled.

The hand clamping her mouth shoved her head backwards in another vicious jolt. The force twanged the muscles at the back of her neck, half-scrambling her brains.

The man behind put an arm around her hips and lifted her off her feet. Melissa tried kicking him, but sandwiched so tightly between the men her efforts were useless. They bundled her easily through one of the archways and onto the west track platform of the DLR.

The place was deserted.

They dropped her on her feet a few yards along the empty platform.

The man with the grubby hand over Melissa's mouth took it away.

She took a gulp of air and made to scream. The man grabbed her by her shoulders and hurled her brutally against the platform wall. The back of her head cracked against its marbled surface. Bright, glittering lights burst inside her brain.

From somewhere beyond the zinging in her head she heard the man's voice.

'Okay, bitch. This is it.'

He planted the flat of a big hand in the middle of her chest and pressed her mercilessly into the wall. His eyes glittered with malice. Dazedly, Melissa gazed at his face. It was grey and pitted like a pineapple, with a deep scar running from the corner of the mouth right along the jawbone.

The lights inside her head, spiralling in a tight, glittering vortex, were surrounded by a black, woolly fog. Somehow she managed to find breath. 'Please leave me alone,' she pleaded. 'Take my bag, my purse. Take the cases.'

The one built like a wrestler cackled. 'We'll have them, anyway.'

'But first we're gonna have *you*, bitch.' The man pressing her chest moved his hand onto her breast. He squeezed it cruelly. Melissa let out a cry.

'She ain't bad-looking,' his companion said.

Melissa felt her blood turn to ice. Her stomach heaved. She wanted to vomit.

'Please. Let me go,' she croaked. 'I have a little boy.'

'You should have thought about that before you started sticking your nose into other people's business,' the man twisting her breast snarled. 'Now you're going to find out what happens to busybody bitches who go looking for other people's money.'

The man holding her overnight case let it drop. It hit the floor with a smack. He laughed again; a frightening, obscene chuckle. 'Yeah. What happens is you lose your nose. It gets sliced off your face.'

It was the other man's turn to laugh.

Out of the corner of her eye, Melissa saw him dig a hand into a pocket of his leather jacket. It came out holding something. She couldn't make out what. The man brought it up close to her face. She still couldn't make it out. There was a sharp click.

The blade snapped up, bright and glittering, two inches from her face. Now she knew.

The platform lights glinted on its stark, merciless edge.

The man's hand came off her breast and grabbed at her throat. She was too petrified to move. From somewhere beyond the numbing, nightmarish fog she heard his voice.

'Now, bitch, let's see how good you look without a face.'

The knife's razor edge sliced down towards her cheek.

Chapter Nineteen

The phone on his desk bleeped. He picked it up.

'Barney?'

'Yeah.'

'There's a sub-committee of FINCEN called FATCAT. You know it?'

'Yeah, I know it,' Mullhane answered guardedly. The caller was John Kilbride.

'It meets this afternoon. It would be a good idea if you were there.'

'Yeah? Why?'

'Because there's an item on the agenda about the Bank of England's deep throat the guy Timmison has got hidden somewhere.'

Suddenly Mullhane was interested. 'Oh yeah?'

'Like I told you, Barney, the CIA isn't the only agency anxious to find this guy. Bearing in mind that you . . .' Kilbride paused, his voice low and conspiratorial, ' . . . we . . . need to find him before the others, I figured you ought to know about the meeting.'

'You going to be there?'

'Yes. I'm cleared for both FINCEN and FATCAT. I asked Jack Paulden if I could go along. And I told him you might be there too.'

Mullhane grunted. 'I bet that surprised him. The Agency usually sends some low-level gopher from Financial Crimes Division to put in face time at that kind of meet.'

'I know. But on this occasion I think it's important for you to be there.'

'But I'll see the minutes,' Mullhane complained. 'Why do I need to go? I'm not gonna find Timmison's snitch sitting around flapping my jaw with a bunch of guys from other agencies.'

'Because someone from one of the other agencies has a line on who the snitch is.'

'Shit. Is that right?' Mullhane was suddenly anxious. 'Okay, I'll see you there.'

Mullhane replaced the receiver and screwed his lined, grey face into a deep scowl. Despite the sudden importance of the imminent meet, he wasn't anxious to go to FATCAT. He hated meetings and committees. Most of all he hated meetings of financial committees.

Whenever the money men met, he brooded, the CIA was mandated to be there. The World Bank, the IMF, the Basel Committee, G7 . . . the Agency was involved with all of them. And they were all, in Mullhane's opinion, a goddam waste of Agency time, effort and resources . . . the biggest waste being FINCEN.

It was Barney Mullhane's considered opinion that the meetings of the Financial Crimes Enforcement Network were attended by everybody . . . including Joe Blow and his dog.

Apart from the Agency, which Mullhane figured had no business being there, FINCEN's meetings involved the Justice Department . . . which included the FBI and the DEA; and Treasury . . . which fielded the IRS and the Customs Service. Also in on the act was the Postal Inspection Service, the Bureau of Alcohol, Tobacco and Firearms, the Secret Service, the Coast Guard, the Federal Aviation Service, the US Marshalls' Service, senior intelligence people from all the armed services . . . even, Mullhane reflected, the Federal Reserve Board, for God's sake.

Mullhane knew of a dozen Federal detection and enforcement agencies with a finger stuck somewhere in FINCEN's pie. Its meetings were like those of the College of Cardinals, congregating for the election of a Pope. On the few occasions he had reluctantly shown up at one, Mullhane had half-expected to see the Scouts, the Salvation Army and the Daughters of the American Revolution represented.

Like the College of Cardinals, FINCEN had spawned a myriad cliques, factions and cabals. One of them was FATCAT which, with the community's love of acronyms, stood for Financial Acts and Transfers by Criminals and their Associates Taskforce.

FATCAT was a creature of the FBI and normally Mullhane wouldn't have touched it – not even with the other guy's barge pole.

But, he reflected darkly, with the Exchange Bank in the tank, the CIA's own financial acts and transfers were sitting high out of the water. Whatever moves the Agency had been making to covertly transfer funds were in danger of becoming the subject of a great deal of attention.

Furthermore, Mullhane knew that, like the cardinals, there was no love lost between members of the community. Whenever the Agencies were forced to work together, cooperating in FINCEN, ODETF or FATCAT, most of their energy and attention invariably went into jockeying for position.

Lead Agency status – that was the name of the game. In any task force it was which Agency got to drive the bus, which one was top dog, that was the first and most important consideration.

The only thing all other Agencies had in common was their jealousy and dislike of the CIA. If one of the other organisations could expose it, could accuse it of malfeasance, then, Mullhane thought ruefully, the CIA's standing would be diminished and the accuser's enhanced.

For an agency to succeed another had to fail . . . for someone to win, someone else must lose. It was the zero numbers game and in Washington's tight-knit federal community it was the only game in town. Arlington hardball.

Mullhane's scowl turned into a grimace as he considered the imminent meeting. He could do without it. He had other things to occupy him . . . other worries to aggravate his ulcers.

His major preoccupation right now was with preventing that pain-in-the-ass English accountant getting any closer to the CIA's affairs. The goddam woman had already dug deep into Agency business. Mullhane wondered if she actually realised *how* deep . . . whether she had the faintest idea of what she was digging up. A lot depended, he thought darkly, on whether she could be stopped before she *did* realise.

The official car dropped him at the corner of Tenth and Pennsylvania. He was escorted in the elevator up to the sixth floor of the J. Edgar Hoover Building, to a large meeting room looking south over Pennsylvania Avenue.

'Barney, good to see you. Though I got to admit I'm surprised. You're not usually interested in what gangsters do with their money.' Jack Paulden, FATCAT's chairman, was a tall, smartly dressed, FBI man of about Mullhane's age.

He smiled and shook Mullhane's hand warmly. 'Anyway, come

on in. Grab a coffee. I guess you know everybody here, huh?'

Mullhane looked around and grunted. He viewed the room with a jaundiced eye.

By Washington standards it was a small meeting: maybe eighteen or twenty of them. Apart from the FBI, there were people from all the other agencies, including the inevitable couple of money men from the Fed, though he noticed the Secret Service agent recently seconded to the Fed's Criminal Investigations Division wasn't around. He grabbed a coffee and made his way towards the tall man with the mane of white hair drinking coffee in a corner of the room.

'Barney.' Kilbride inclined his leonine head. 'Good to see you.'

Mullhane nodded. 'Thanks for telling me about this,' he murmured.

'We need to keep ahead of this one, Barney. It's our ass in a sling if we don't.' Kilbride gave him a tight smile.

Mullhane nodded. Kilbride was as desperate to get to Timmison's deep throat before the others as he was. He glanced at him. In a room full of potential adversaries, the old guy was a useful ally. A friend to the Agency.

Paulden called the room to order and started the meeting by asking one of the men from the Fed to speak.

The man got up out of his seat. 'I'll be short and to the point,' he began.

'That'll be a first, for a bean-counter,' Mullhane muttered to the woman from the IRS next to him.

The man spoke for a few minutes about the media fallout following the news that organised crime was controlling a significant portion of the American financial industry.

'The fact that the Mafia is deep into the banks and S&Ls,' he announced, 'has caused hundreds of billions of dollars to move out of America. Mostly to London. Great for the Brits . . . bad for us. A lot of money is moving offshore. Even Wall Street is getting jittery. The bond market is in shock and the big institutions are shovelling money overseas like there's no tomorrow.'

Mullhane grunted dismissively, listening with no more than half an ear. Bankers and gangsters . . . who the hell cared about either? Money men were always bitching about the economy.

For an hour he shifted uncomfortably in his seat, listening to agents from the various agencies report on the international war

169

against dirty money. At last Paulden came to the only item he was interested in. The Exchange Bank mole.

'I guess we're all agreed it's vital we discover who this guy is,' Paulden said by way of introduction, 'and, if possible, interrogate him for ourselves. We need to find out what he knows first hand, rather than have the British tell us stuff piecemeal.'

'Why the hell don't the British simply tell us who he is?' Mullhane asked indignantly.

'I think it's pretty obvious,' Paulden replied, 'that the deal they made with the guy included preserving his anonymity. They'll have guaranteed not to tell anyone who he is.'

'Who the hell is *anyone*?' Mullhane barked. 'We're not anyone. We're supposed to be their buddies. What do the Brits think we're gonna do? Tell the *New York Times*? Put the guy's name up in lights on Broadway?'

Paulden shrugged. 'You know the Brits. They don't trust anyone.'

'They don't trust us, that's for sure,' Mullhane growled. 'Smug, double-crossing bastards. You can bet your pecker that they're playing some devious game of their own.'

'The British usually do,' John Kilbride observed dryly. 'It's obvious that whatever this man is telling them, they're not telling us. At least not everything. That's why I agree it's important for us to get a handle on him ourselves.'

'Okay, well, we may have got a jump on that,' Paulden said. He nodded to a man seated halfway along the table. The man stood up.

'This is special agent Sam Barber,' Paulden announced, 'who heads the Bureau's Economic Crime Unit on the West Coast. Sam.'

Like everyone else in the room, Mullhane eyed the special agent. Barber was tall and well set, with grey hair and blue eyes. He was wearing a neat, two-piece navy suit. The guy had FBI written all over him.

'When it's necessary, the ECU works closely with the local offices of Rolay Richard, the London firm of accountants who are liquidating the Exchange Bank,' Barber began. 'Last week we heard that one of their forensic accountants, a Miss Semmington, had traced the movement of a lot of money laundered by some LCN front companies we're investigating. Miss Semmington was in the Caymans but she kindly came to

San Francisco to share with us what she'd found. The following day the ECU hit a house in Sausalito. The reasons aren't important: the house was being used by the front companies as a registration address for non-existent officers. As they'd been using the Exchange Bank to launder their money, Miss Semmington was in on the search. The house belongs to a man called Vito Kunzman. We found papers at the house which indicated that Kunzman was loosely connected with the companies we are investigating and also with a company in Nassau called Cyclix.'

Mullhane shot a cautious look along the table at John Kilbride. The man's face was impassive.

'Miss Semmington,' Barber continued, 'had already dug up some information about this guy Kunzman which she was happy to give us. We now know that Kunzman was the main contact between the godfathers who originally funded the Exchange Bank . . . and the bank's management, particularly Dr Hidalgo Campeche.'

'The guy who got wasted in Caracas?' someone asked.

'Right. And that's where it gets interesting. Because word got out on the street after the hit that the target should have been this guy Kunzman. The hit went wrong. In fact Campeche shot one of the assassins himself.'

'Some bank president,' someone commented wryly. There was a subdued laugh around the table.

Paulden joined in the laughter. 'Hell, these days it's not the Mob who robs the banks. It's the banks that rob the Mob. The bankers are the guys who drive the getaway cars.'

Barber smiled quietly. 'Because he was who he was,' he went on, 'and because of his lifestyle, Campeche had gotten a licence to carry a gun. Anyway, the other hitman was found in a car at the airport with his brains blown out. Which I guess is what happens in his business if you whack the wrong target. The assassins were locals but we think the people who put the hit together were an independent, freelance outfit operating out of Chicago. They could have been hired by anyone.'

'But we have to presume it was the Mafia who wanted Kunzman dead,' someone observed.

'Why?' asked a voice. 'Why would they want to kill him?'

'We don't know. Kunzman was their version of a bank inspector. As far as we know he was doing a good job, so on the surface of it there doesn't seem to have been any reason for LCN to kill him. Anyway, as soon as word got out that he'd been the target, Kunzman disappeared.'

'And you think this is the man who ran to the British? You think Kunzman is Timmison's deep throat?' Kilbride inquired.

Barber shrugged. 'I don't know for certain but it looks that way. We can't find him, that's for sure.'

'But why the British? Mullhane protested. 'Why not run to you in the Bureau? Or to any of us? Why to them?'

'There can only be one reason,' Jack Paulden interrupted. 'He trusts the Brits more than he trusts us.'

It was John Kilbride's turn to shoot a swift glance down the table at Mullhane.

'What about this woman Semmington. She's British. Would she know if they've got Kunzman?' someone queried

Barber smiled. 'She doesn't know any more about the guy's whereabouts than we do. But she and I have agreed to share information . . . to fax any details we discover about the guy to each other.'

'Is that a good idea?' There was a critical note in Kilbride's voice.

'Sure. Why not? These big accountancy practices cover a lot of ground. They've got almost as many resources as we have and they get where most of us don't go. There's a good chance Miss Semmington could locate Kunzman before we do. If she does, she's promised to let me know.'

'And you believe her?' Mullhane growled.

Barber gave him a level stare. 'Yeah, I believe her.'

'What do we know about this guy Kunzman anyway?' someone asked.

Barber pulled a sheaf of monochrome ten-by-eights from a file on the table in front of him and passed them around.

'These were taken three or four years ago,' he explained. 'Kunzman came here with his parents shortly after the War. From what was Czechoslovakia. His father was Czech but his mother was Italian. They settled in San Francisco and took US citizenship. Kunzman graduated law school and now he's a New York lawyer. The Bureau has received a lot of skinny on him from the NYPD. Their Organised Crime Bureau have known about him for years. It seems he started working as a lawyer for some of the West Coast families way back in the fifties . . . when the Mob was called the Combo. He started out in San Francisco, which is why he bought the house in Sausalito, though he hasn't lived in the place since the sixties.'

Everybody around the table was studying the photographs. They showed a man in his late fifties with receding grey hair, dark, intelligent eyes and a prominent nose.

'When LCN began forming itself into a national organisation,' Barber continued, 'they moved Kunzman to New York to work for the families there, although sometimes they subcontracted him out to Chicago or Vegas or wherever. The guy has worked for *La Cosa Nostra* for years, yet, as far as OCB can tell, everything he's done has been strictly legit. Corporate work, real estate, investments, takeovers, that kinda stuff. Although Kunzman doesn't appear to be one of your sharp, downtown lawyers, it's clear he's very smart and, in his own way, pretty ruthless. When the Mob got behind the Exchange Bank he was the obvious front man to look after their interests. He has been spotted by OCB a number of times in the company of Hidalgo Campeche and some of the other Third World financiers who helped establish the bank. We figure Kunzman's job was to check the books, run a few special accounts and, if someone had their mitts in the till, point the finger. OCB has a file on him but it doesn't amount to much.'

'He sounds like a guy who could know where the bodies are buried,' someone observed laconically.

'Which would explain why he's made a run for it,' said someone else.

'But it don't explain why he's run to the British,' Barney Mullhane growled.

'He's disappeared somewhere, that's for sure,' Barber continued. 'He hasn't been seen in almost three months. Not at his offices, not at the family home on Long Island, not at an apartment he keeps on the East Side. Nowhere.'

There was a murmur around the table. 'So you think he's not around because the British have got him in a protection programme somewhere,' someone suggested.

Barber shrugged again. 'I don't know what to think. What the hell, Kunzman may not even be our man. There's no proof he's the Exchange Bank mole. All I know is that we're running the guy down as hard as we can but there's no sign of him.'

After the meeting Mullhane and Kilbride shared an elevator

and left the building together, walking north on 10th to the junction with E Street.

'It sounds like this guy Kunzman is our man,' Mullhane said.

'But if he is, why go to the British?' Kilbride's voice was strained. 'There can only be one reason. He knows about our deal.'

'Maybe.' Mullhane stared darkly at the passing traffic. 'And then again, maybe not. I don't think anybody knows what we were doing. And even if Kunzman *did* know and has gone to Timmison, he hasn't talked. If he had,' he shrugged, 'we'd have heard.'

'So what do we do?'

'We keep looking. At least now we know who we're looking for.' He glanced at Kilbride. 'You're close to the Bureau, aren't you?'

Kilbride nodded. 'Sure. I'm close to everyone at Justice.'

'Okay. You keep tabs on what moves they're making to locate the guy. That's important. The Bureau ain't gonna broadcast what they're doing to find him. No one in that meeting is gonna tell anyone else diddly squat. Everybody wants Kunzman for themselves. You stick with the guys in Justice and in the meantime I'll put some people to work on tracking him down.'

'People? What people?

'Freelancers. Ex-Agency people. We've used them before.'

'And if they find Kunzman?'

Mullhane could hear the viciousness in Kilbride's voice. He stared at him. 'Then we talk about our options,' he said quietly.

'We've only got one option,' Kilbride hissed. 'You know that.' Mullhane didn't reply. 'And you'd better get your people to do something about that goddam woman as well.' Kilbride's tone was stiff with malice.

'Semmington?'

'Yes. She's getting too damn close. And now she's cooperating with the FBI she could get closer. She's as dangerous as Kunzman. We need to do something about her, Barney. She has to be stopped. You'd better get your people to stop her.'

Mullhane gazed at the man next to him for a moment longer then went back to surveying the traffic. Again he didn't reply.

Chapter Twenty

Out of the corner of one bright, terrified eye she saw the glittering blade come arcing down.

It stopped a millimetre from her face. The man squeezing her throat laid it across her cheekbone. The metal was pitilessly cold.

The man was grinning. Playing with her. Choking her. Waiting for her hammering heart to burst. Her body was tense. As rigid as a poker. Anticipating the dreadful pain . . . the slicing apart of her flesh . . . the destruction of her face.

'*Stop.*'

The shout came from somewhere to her left . . . somewhere back along the deserted platform.

The man turned towards the noise and the knife blade sliced her cheek.

Melissa yelped as she felt the hot, searing bite of pain. Then, as the man fractionally slackened his grip, the blade moved off her face She turned her head slightly towards the sound of running feet.

A figure moved into her peripheral vision. Dark . . . moving fast . . . a *familiar* figure.

Melissa watched the short, heavily built man turn to face the intruder.

The figure ran at him. As they closed, the dark, fast-moving shape dropped and turned, pivoting on one leg. In a flickering blur Melissa saw a foot lash out at the squat man's kneecap.

There was a sharp crack, made louder by the arching, marbled walls of the empty platform.

'*Aaaeeeeiiiiiiii!*'

The man's scream of agony echoed off the curved surfaces and reverberated into the empty tunnels. He dropped onto the platform and rolled onto his back, clutching his knee. He screamed again.

'Aaaaeeeeeeeee!'

The high-pitched shrieking unnerved the man holding Melissa. He released her throat and turned to face the attacker, his body crouched, his knife arm extended. The figure whirled to face him.

It was Bob Briscoe.

Melissa clutched at her aching throat and pressed her fingers to her face to stem the blood pouring down it. She stared at Briscoe stupidly.

She couldn't believe what she was seeing.

The last two minutes had been beyond belief. A nightmare. Her brain, unable to acknowledge the horror, had virtually seized up. She couldn't grasp what was going on . . . couldn't accept what had been about to happen to her. Her mind had refused to admit that any of it was happening to *her*.

Now, into the nightmare, had come Sir Galahad storming to her rescue. That was even *more* unbelievable. It was all too fast, too much for her to handle.

It was impossible to grasp that an unknown man had been about to slash her face to ribbons . . . and impossible now to believe that it might not happen.

She gawked stupidly at the action on the platform.

Almost without breaking his stride Briscoe reached down and grabbed Melissa's overnight case. Holding it square in front of his body he ran at the man with the knife. The man slashed at his hands. He missed, puncturing the soft hide of the case. Suddenly the knife was entangled with the clothes inside. Briscoe pushed the case hard against the man's body.

For a moment the man's knife hand was trapped. A moment was all Briscoe needed. He let go of the case, leaned forward and, with a flashing upward movement, chopped beneath the man's nose with the edge of his hand. The man's head snapped back like a squash ball off a wall. He staggered and fell, the knife shooting out of his grasp and bouncing off the edge of the platform onto the rails.

Briscoe stepped past the fallen case and with a cold, savage precision kicked the man twice on the side of his head. The man grunted and lay still.

Swiftly he crossed the platform to Melissa who was slowly sliding down the wall. His eyes took in the blood flowing between her fingers and dripping off her chin. He grasped her arm and eased her up. 'Come on,' he said gently, 'we've got to get you out of here.'

He extracted a large, snowy-white handkerchief from an inside pocket of his dark suit and, tenderly prising her fingers away from her cheek, made her press it against the wound.

Melissa stared over his shoulder at the two men. The wrestler was sobbing and trying to stand up; his scar-faced crony moving his head from side to side and groaning.

Briscoe glanced behind. 'Forget them,' he told her. 'They're out of it. They won't harm you now.'

He picked up her cases, umbrella and handbag, somehow managing to stuff them under one arm as he supported her with the other. He eased her gently along the platform, past the sobbing man and out into the broad pedestrian tunnel leading to Bank Station. The people in the ticket hall stared as they shuffled through and up the stairs to Prince's Street.

In the darkness outside the rain had turned to a drizzle.

Briscoe craned his neck, looking for a taxi. 'What about those men?' Melissa croaked. It was the first time she had spoken. 'We should report it to the police.'

'First things first,' Briscoe said. 'Let me take a look at that.' Gently he eased the handkerchief off her cheek.

'Is it bad?' she whispered. 'Am I going to be scarred?'

'I don't know. I can't see in this light. We have to get it treated. Quickly.'

'Oh God, please don't say I'll be scarred,' she whimpered. She took a deep breath and tried to pull herself together. 'I think the nearest casualty is at Barts. If it's still there,' she told him miserably.

He shook his head. 'To hell with hospitals. I've got some connections in this town. Now I'm gonna use them.'

He propped her against the wall, reached inside his jacket, pulled out a mobile phone, punched up a number and spoke quietly and rapidly for a few moments. He listened closely to whoever was at the other end, then disconnected the call and rapidly pressed out another number. Melissa couldn't hear what he was saying, but his tone was stern and authoritative. The two calls took less than a minute.

He finished and slotted the mobile back inside his jacket. 'Okay, Melissa, all we have to do now is find a cab.'

They were lucky. Within seconds they saw through the drizzle the bright yellow sign of an empty cab rolling down Prince's Street. Briscoe hailed it.

'Harley Street,' he told the driver.

'What's wrong with her?' the cabbie asked suspiciously, nodding at the blood seeping beneath the handkerchief and dripping onto the pavement.

'Forty pounds if you get us there fast,' Briscoe replied.

It was a modern, prestigious block at the south end of the street, not far from Cavendish Square. A uniformed security guard unlocked the front door and helped Melissa into the lobby. Briscoe dumped the cases with the guard and eased Melissa up a flight of stairs and along a richly carpeted corridor to a large, well-appointed, brightly lit room with an antique desk in the centre and a medical couch against one wall.

A big, middle-aged man, dressed in a dinner jacket, was waiting.

'I came straight away,' he said. Briscoe nodded noncommittally.

The man moved to Melissa and took her gently by her arm. 'I'm Doctor Lubitsch,' he told her in a plummy voice, 'and you are?' She mumbled her name. 'Please sit down, Miss Semmington.'

He helped her into a seat, knelt at her side and gently eased the handkerchief off her wound. 'I have to clean it up,' he announced. 'Whilst I do so, perhaps you can tell me how this occurred.'

Despite the pain and her spasmodic bouts of uncontrollable shuddering, Melissa recounted what had happened. In a low, halting voice she told him about the attack, gritting her teeth as the antiseptic bit deep into the open wound. Briscoe, his arms folded and half-sitting on the edge of the doctor's desk, listened intently.

Lubitsch nodded and made sympathetic noises as she talked. Even though seized by the after-effects of trauma, Melissa couldn't help noticing that Dr Lubitsch had the smooth, well-practised manner of a typical Harley Street physician.

He finished cleaning the wound, then examined it minutely. 'Well, Miss Semmington,' he announced finally, 'it's a nasty cut. It may leave a scar. I don't know. It's too soon to say.'

He gave her a professional smile. It was too shallow to be reassuring.

'You don't know?' her voice filled with anxiety.

He pulled a face. 'No. But if you do sustain a scar, it will only be a little one. A minor piece of plastic surgery should eliminate it entirely. The incision, though quite deep, is only about two centimetres long. The knife that cut you was extremely sharp. Curious as it may seem, in many ways the sharper the knife the less chance of scarring. If it is possible to be lucky in such circumstances, you were lucky.'

Slumped in her seat, Melissa stared at him numbly.

'Now,' the doctor went on, 'I'm going to put some butterfly tape on your cheek. It will look a little strange for a few days but it will ensure that the wound heals properly.'

He gave her another shallow smile, a fleeting beam of medical reassurance. To Melissa it was as comforting as a blast of radiation.

He moved across the room to a cabinet. When he returned he carefully positioned a strip of clear tape over the wound. Afterwards, he inspected her throat and the back of her head before staring into her pupils with an ophthalmascope. Melissa blinked at the bright light. Finally he gently probed the trapezius muscles at the back of her neck.

'Physically you've come out of this ordeal in good shape,' he said when he had finished. 'Your neck and throat will feel sore for a couple of days and you're getting a lump on the back of your head. But there's no serious physical damage. However, what's far more important in a situation like this is the emotional trauma. It's vital that you go home and rest. Sleep for the weekend. The more you sleep, the more you distance yourself from what happened.'

He moved to a wall cabinet, extracted a handful of pills from a pot and trickled them into a small plastic bottle. 'Take one of these as soon as you get home,' he instructed, 'and one every six hours thereafter. In the meantime I'll give you something that will keep you calm. Steady your nerves.' He produced a single pill and a plastic cup of water which he handed to Melissa.

'What is it?' she croaked. She had a horror of unknown pills.

'Just a mild sedative. It should make your journey home a little easier.'

Melissa swallowed the pill. 'Come and see me again first thing Monday morning,' he instructed. 'By then the wound should have started to heal.'

Shakily, Melissa stood up. Her legs were too weak to support her and she began to topple. Lubitsch held her by the shoulders as Briscoe rushed forward. She felt a strong, solid arm encircle her waist.

'You've been very kind,' she said to Lubitsch. 'What do I owe you?'

'Forget it,' Briscoe growled. 'It's all taken care of.'

'But . . .'

'Forget it, Melissa,' he growled again.

'Monday morning, first thing,' Lubitsch repeated, flashing his professional smile.

Melissa smiled wanly at him. 'Thank you very much for taking care of me. And for turning out on a wet night.' She looked at his dinner jacket. 'I'm sorry if I spoiled your evening.'

'Not at all. I live nearby, just off the Park. And anyway, it was a boring dinner party. Now, I recommend you go straight home and get to bed.'

'But I have to report the assault to the police.'

The doctor shrugged. 'Of course, if you think any good will come from it. If you think there is a chance of catching the men.' He looked at Briscoe. 'Is there?'

Briscoe made a noncommittal face. 'They're both hurt, but not so bad that they couldn't get the hell out of there. They'll be long gone by now.'

'I should have reported it straight away,' Melissa moaned.

'You were in no state to do that,' Briscoe told her gently. 'You were half bleeding to death. We had to get you treated first. It wouldn't have made any difference, anyway. If the cops know who those guys are, they'll pull them in as soon as you give them a description. If not . . . well . . . I doubt if they'll ever catch them. Not unless the cops in this town are a helluva lot smarter than in New York.'

Melissa stared at Lubitsch who nodded in confirmation. 'I'm afraid he's right. You may as well report it first thing tomorrow. After you've had a good night's sleep. You're in no fit condition to talk to the police at the moment.'

Melissa swayed unsteadily and felt Briscoe's arm tighten around her. She was too tired to argue . . . which, she thought dully, only went to show that the others were right.

Briscoe helped her down the stairs, collected her bags and stood at the edge of the pavement, looking for a cab. 'I'm going to see you home,' he said.

She nodded gratefully. 'Thank you. I'm not sure I could make it on my own. We need a cab to Waterloo.'

'To hell with that,' he grunted. He saw an empty taxi and hailed it. 'Where exactly do you live?' he asked her as the cab drew up at the kerb.

'What?'

'Where do you live?'

She told him. 'It's a small village, between Alton and Petersfield,' she explained. 'In Hampshire.'

Briscoe turned to the driver. 'You got that?'

'I'm not bleeding well going out to Hampshire,' the cabbie protested. 'This is a London cab.'

'You'll be well paid for it,' Briscoe snapped.

'Oh yeah? How much?'

Briscoe took out his wallet. 'I've got two hundred pounds in English money. One hundred now; the other hundred after you've taken us to Hampshire and then dropped me at Heathrow.'

'Get in.'

Sitting in the back of the cab Briscoe gently pulled Melissa close to him. She laid her head on his chest. The warmth of his body brought her comfort, infusing her with a hesitant sense of security.

She looked up at him as they were crossing Putney Bridge. 'How did you find me?' Her voice was croaky from the pain in her throat. 'How on earth did you manage to be on that platform just when I needed you? I couldn't believe it. Not when I saw it was you.'

'It was helluva lucky,' he nodded. 'I could so easily have missed you. Christ, what would have happened if I had?' He clutched her tighter. 'It doesn't bear thinking about.' His voice was intense. He made it sound as if she meant something to him . . . as if she was precious. She smiled up at him weakly. He was silent for a while.

'So how did you find me?' she asked again.

'I got delayed in Geneva. My business took longer than I thought. When I got back to Heathrow I called your home. Your housemaid said you'd called from the office to say you were working late. I dropped my cases at the Holiday Inn and took a cab into town. I figured we might have a drink or dinner or something.'

'But how did you know where I was? That I'd taken the underground link to Bank Station?'

'I saw you on the sidewalk. I'd given the taxi driver the address on your card and he had just said we were close to your offices when I saw you. It was real lucky because you were hurrying and holding an umbrella. But I knew it was you.'

Melissa gazed up at his face, illuminated by the passing lights of Wimbledon.

'I yelled at the driver to stop but by the time I'd paid him, you'd disappeared into a subway station. I followed you down. There was a cleaner in the booking hall. I asked if he'd seen you. He showed me which way you had gone.'

'But how did you know those men had dragged me onto the platform? Could you see me?'

'No, but I could see them. They were way ahead of me and I figured you must be a little ahead of them When I got to the top of the moving staircase they were at the bottom. All of a sudden they started hurrying. I don't know why, but it made me suspicious. Why start hurrying there? But by the time I got to the bottom of the staircase, no one was around. I was hurrying along the walkway when I heard a sound. From somewhere on my right. Like something dropping. So I took a look and saw that bastard with the knife holding you by the throat.'

'God, I've never been so pleased to see anyone in my life,' she murmured. She was getting sleepy: Dr Lubitsch's pill was kicking in. 'Did you get a good look at the men?' she asked.

He shook his head. 'No. Not really. They were just a couple of bodies. A couple of lowlifes I had to take down quickly.'

She stared at him, her eyes glazing with the effects of the sedative. 'You did it very efficiently,' she murmured. 'You seem pretty competent at that kind of thing.'

Briscoe shrugged. 'I was in the Service. You don't forget what they teach you. And I work out a lot.'

'Yes, I noticed.' She giggled. She was quiet for a while. 'Well, all I can say is thank you. I know it's not much to say after you've saved me from . . .' She shuddered and her voice tailed off. 'Thank you anyway,' she whispered.

'You're welcome.' He smiled at her warmly. 'Now, try and get some rest.'

She nodded. 'Yes.'

The cab had reached the A3 and was doing a steady fifty on the Esher Bypass. She was silent for a while and Briscoe thought she had fallen asleep. Then she said, 'I still think I should have reported it to the police. Before leaving London.'

'Do it tomorrow,' he murmured. 'When you feel up to it.'

'But won't they be angry that I didn't tell them straight away?'

'What right have they got to be angry? It's you who got attacked. Don't worry about it. In your job you must have contacts in the police. Call one tomorrow. Explain what happened. Chances are those guys are a couple of muggers who saw you going into the subway and figured you for an easy mark. When it's a random attack like that, there's not much for the cops to go on. If they don't have those guys on record already, there's no way they're gonna catch them. Either way, twelve hours won't make much difference.'

Melissa frowned, her tired, wrung-out brain remembering the scarred man's words as he clutched her breast.

'But it *wasn't* a random attack,' she croaked. She struggled to ease herself up off Briscoe's chest. 'Those men were after *me*. Specifically me.'

'What?'

'The man with the knife. He said I was a busybody bitch, who shouldn't have gone looking for other people's money. How could he have known that? How would he have known what I do for a job if I was only a random victim?'

Briscoe was staring at her with a deep puzzled frown. 'You sure you heard him right? Hell, the guy had a knife, Melissa. He had a hand round your throat. You must have been petrified. You sure that's what he said?'

A tremor shuddered through her as she recalled the deserted platform and the man with the bright gleaming knife. 'Yes I'm sure,' her voice rasped. 'That's what he said. I'm never going to forget it.'

He stared at her a while longer. The deep, somnolent sound of tyres drumming on the road filled the inside of the warm cab. 'That makes a difference,' he said finally. 'You'll have to tell the police that. It may make it easier to catch the guys.'

'Easier?' she murmured. Despite her anxiety it was getting harder and harder for her to keep her eyes open.

'If those guys are professionals, guys hired to beat up on women, they may have a record. Can you remember exactly what they looked like?'

'Yes,' she mumbled. 'I told you. I'm not likely to forget.' She described the men in detail to him.

'Well, it'll still have to keep until tomorrow morning,' he said. 'You're in no state to start providing descriptions of a couple of lowlifes to the police. You need to sleep. To recover from all this.'

'Yes.' She yawned deeply.

Sleep was bearing her away like a warm, gentle avalanche. There was nothing she could do to resist it. The narcotic effects of the sedative Lubitsch had given her were overwhelming. She couldn't resist the pill, she thought wearily. The pill . . . and her bone-weary exhaustion.

She fell back against Briscoe's chest, snuggling into his strong body, secure in the knowledge she was safe. The nightmare was over and a soft, dark curtain was falling across her mind. The steady drumming of the taxi's tyres was like a lullaby.

She slept.

Chapter Twenty-One

She awoke as the taxi scrunched to a halt on the gravel outside the cottage.

Briscoe told the driver to wait as he collected Melissa's bags and helped her to the front door. She fumbled for her keys and opened it. As always, it creaked painfully. Inside Astrid had left a few sidelights burning. From upstairs came the dull thumping of the stereo.

'Are you going to be okay?' Briscoe asked.

Melissa slumped onto a sofa and nodded drowsily. 'Yes, I think so.' She looked up at him. 'Can I get you anything?' Her tone was dog-tired.

He laughed quietly. 'Hell, Melissa, you're in no state to get anybody anything. Take your pill and go to bed.'

'I don't think I need another pill.'

'It's what the doctor ordered,' he insisted.

He fetched a glass of water from the kitchen as she retrieved the small bottle from her bag. He stood over her as she swallowed the pill. 'Go to bed now,' he told her. 'Try to forget everything. Remember what the doctor said: rest as much as you can.' He kissed her lightly on her undamaged cheek. 'I'll call you over the weekend.'

'But what about the police?'

'Talk to them tomorrow.'

'Yes, but won't you be there?'

'Me? No. I told you, I have to fly out first thing. I've got urgent business in the States. Anyway, I didn't really get much of a look at the guys.' He noticed her strained, anxious face. 'Look,' he said softly: 'don't worry about it. If they need to talk to me, you've got my number. If they want a statement, I'll give them one when I'm next in London. Okay.'

He moved towards the door, glancing at the dark oak beams

in the ceiling and the big, brickwork fireplace as he went. 'Nice place, Melissa,' he commented. 'I'll call you.'

He closed the creaking door firmly behind him. A few seconds later she heard the cab drive away. She eased herself up off the sofa and crawled upstairs, leaving the sidelights on and her cases where they were, the clothes in her overnight case bulging out of the slashed hide lid. She put her head round the door of Jamie's room for a moment before shuffling wearily into her own room, dragging off her clothes and falling into bed.

She was out for ten hours. The combination of the sedative and the sleeping pill put her down so deep that, when she awoke, if she had bad dreams, she recalled nothing of them.

She felt terrible. Her tongue was arid, like the Great Salt Lake, and the inside of her mouth tasted like a Moroccan drain. She had trouble thinking. It was as if her brain was encased in a great dollop of dough. She felt less as if she had been asleep, more as if she had been dead.

Like a narcoleptic she wandered into the bathroom where she took a long look in the mirror. The butterfly tape stuck high on her left cheek was as obvious as an aircraft carrier.

She studied her face. Her hair was lank and stringy and her finely boned features pale and as drawn as a corpse. She noticed the corners of her wide mouth. They were turned down, sharp and tight. Her eyes were like bomb craters.

There was a constant buzzing throughout her body, as though a low-intensity electrical current was passing through it. She thought of the assault and the voltage inside her shot up. The buzzing became a shudder and the hand holding her toothbrush begin to shake.

She screwed up her face and forced her mind off the attack, hanging on to the bathroom basin until the shakes were under control.

She showered and washed her hair and did her best to look presentable. Her efforts were not especially successful. She caught Astrid giving her some intense, Teutonic looks. Melissa told her nothing about the attack, instead saying that she had cut her cheek on a filing cabinet in the office. Astrid obviously didn't believe the story, but with her customary Germanic reserve, decided it was not her place to inquire.

Jamie was excited. It was Saturday morning and Melissa had promised to take him into Winchester to pick up the puppy. She had forgotten about that. Oh, God. She wanted to scream. She couldn't do it. She wasn't in any condition to punch her way through Saturday morning traffic to pick up a puppy. Not with half the National Grid coursing through her nervous system. Not with porridge inside her head and sticking plaster on her face. She couldn't do it. She had to report the assault to the police, for God's sake.

She gazed at Jamie's happy, animated face and decided her son came first. Telling the police would have to wait another couple of hours. She took a deep breath and made an effort to get a grip on herself. She must not give in, she told herself. If she gave in, then the bastards who'd attacked her would have won.

And she wasn't going to let them win.

She wasn't.

They bundled into the car and she drove as best she could through light showers to a pet shop where a Springer Spaniel bitch had recently delivered six puppies. Jamie sat on the threadbare carpet in a room which smelled of dogs and made cooing noises at a churning bundle of puppies in a big wicker basket. Melissa watched a small, fat ball of white and tan fur detach itself from the bundle and struggle across the floor on four stumpy, unsteady legs to lay its head on Jamie's knee.

Jamie's puppy had chosen him.

Driving home, Astrid and Jamie sat on the back seat, taking turns to nurse the puppy which was wrapped in an old shawl. They were trying to think of a name. Halfway back to the cottage Astrid giggled. The puppy had peed in her lap. Melissa heard a sudden strange sound. With a shock she realised it came from her. She was laughing. It wasn't her usual laugh, it was too high and harsh and sharp to be her usual laugh. But it was a laugh all the same. It surprised her.

After lunch she began to feel better. It was time for her next pill. She took the bottle off the bathroom shelf, stared at it and then put it back. She didn't want to be dependent on pills, she decided. She would take her chances with not sleeping . . . with having nightmares. She would fix herself a drink instead.

She wandered into the oak-beamed lounge, poured a vodka and tonic and sat down. The weather had cleared and Jamie was outside in the cottage garden playing with the puppy. She could hear Astrid through the open, lead-mullioned windows telling him not to tire the little ball of eager fat.

The everyday domesticity of it — the pale sunshine dappling the lath and plaster walls, Jamie's laughter and Astrid's voice — helped calm her. For the first time she found herself able to think about the events of last night without breaking out into uncontrollable shakes.

Her most serious omission was in not reporting the attack to the police. She had to get on with it, she told herself. She could feel the shakes juddering just below the surface as she contemplated telling them. Would they understand why she hadn't told them immediately? Would they insist she went over the details time and time again? The thought of sitting in some awful interview room reliving the attack filled her with horror. She recalled Briscoe's words from the night before. She had contacts in the police. Now was the time to use them.

She reached for the phone sitting on an occasional table and punched out a number. 'DCI Lankell please.'

'It's his day off.'

She said thanks and killed the call. She looked up Lankell's home number in her book and pressed out the digits. A deep, stony voice answered.

'Dennis, it's Melissa,' she blurted. 'Listen, I was attacked last night by two men.'

There was a pause on the other end of the line. 'Attacked?' he repeated.

'Yes.'

'You hurt?'

'No. Well, not really. Thank God.'

'What happened?'

She told him briefly. 'The thing is,' she went on, 'I haven't reported it yet. I know I should have done, but . . .'

'You can report it to me.'

'I was hoping you'd say that.'

'You at home?'

'Yes.'

'Stay there. I'll drive down and you can tell me about it.'

Lankell lived in Chislehurst. It was an hour's drive. 'There's no need to do that.'

'Yes, there is. I'm bored shitless here. There's no football on TV and my wife's out shopping. I've got the choice of staring at the bleeding wallpaper or mowing the bleeding lawn. I'm on my way.'

He arrived less than an hour later. Melissa heard the tyres on the gravel and opened the front door.

Lankell filled the doorframe. He was middle-aged and big, with grey hair, hands the size of oven mitts and a face as craggy as the cliffs of Moher.

Melissa sat him down and offered him a drink. He asked for a beer. He glanced at the tape on her cheek but said nothing. She fixed herself another vodka, sat herself opposite and told him the story up to the time Briscoe had brought her home. She gave Lankell the best description she could of the two men. He listened with scarcely a word until she had finished.

'This friend of yours, Briscoe,' he observed coldly: 'he's pretty casual about cooperating with the police.'

'He's an international financier, Dennis. Billion-dollar deals depend on him being in the right place at the right time. He *had* to be in the States this weekend. Anyway, without him, I wouldn't be sitting here talking to you.'

Lankell grunted.

Astrid popped her head around the door to say that the puppy was sleeping in its new basket next to the Aga and that she was taking Jamie for a walk to the village. 'Jamie wants to call the dog George,' she added.

'George? Why George?' Melissa asked in surprise.

Astrid shrugged. 'He says that is his name.' She closed the lounge door behind her.

Melissa turned back to Lankell and apologised for the interruption. She stared at the drug cop's hard grey face and thought about a sleeping ball of puppy fat called George. For some unaccountable reason her eyes filled with tears. Suddenly she was shaking uncontrollably. 'I'm sorry,' she stuttered. 'You must think I'm an absolute wimp.'

'No, I don't.' Lankell watched her for a moment, then moved across the room and sat beside her on the sofa. He put an arm around her. 'Come on girly,' he said softly: 'let it all come out.'

She did.

She buried her face in his huge chest and howled as her body shuddered like a leaf in a storm. Tears of fear and insecurity streamed onto Lankell's creased summer shirt. She clutched him tightly. His clothes had a warm, lived-in smell of beer and cigarettes. The smell brought her comfort.

She didn't know how long she held onto Lankell, sobbing

and crying. She thought it was probably a long time. At last the shakes began to wane and the tears to cease. Lankell released his hold on her and she straightened up.

'Oh, God, I'm so sorry.' She gave him a wan, tearful smile. 'Look at your shirt. It's soaked. I'm sorry. You probably think I'm a complete idiot.'

He shook his head. 'No, I don't. And stop apologising. It's the best thing. Cry it out.'

She excused herself and tottered to the bathroom on unsteady legs. She washed her face and did her best to repair the damage. In the lounge, Lankell had moved back to his own seat. He acted as if nothing had happened. Melissa fixed them both another drink.

'I'll make sure the City police are told about the assault,' Lankell said, 'and that they're given the descriptions. But what worries me is that these blokes came after *you*. You weren't just anybody, you were a specific target.'

'Because of my job,' she added hesitantly.

'Yes.' His voice was deep and serious. 'If you heard the bastard with the knife right . . .'

'Yes I did,' she insisted. 'I know I did. I know I was terrified but I'm sure that's what he said.'

'Yeah, I believe it. But what that means is someone wants to stop you tracking their money. And those two bastards were hired to do the stopping. The assault has to be connected to your work at the Exchange Bank.'

'That's what I think.' She put her drink down and crossed her arms over the front of her body, clutching herself.

'So,' he stared at her pensively, 'who was laundering money through the bank who might want to stop you tracking it?'

She let out a hollow, caustic laugh. 'Christ, Dennis, the list is endless. Practically every legal organisation and criminal enterprise you've ever heard of, plus a few you haven't, was using the Exchange Bank. They *all* want to protect their funds.'

'Yeah,' he frowned, 'but which ones are prepared to have you attacked and slashed to ribbons to stop you tracking their cash?' He saw the sick look on her face. 'Sorry, I didn't mean to remind you,' he mumbled.

'Any one of them,' she answered in a soft, frightened voice.

He was quiet for a while. 'Are you chasing down anything specific at the moment? Could the attack be related to something you're working on right now?'

She thought about it. 'I've been tracking drug money in and out of the Caymans,' she said tentatively. 'But you already know about some of that. And I've cottoned on to a big money-laundering operation run by organised criminals in California. But,' she frowned, 'I've pretty well finished with all that.'

'Organised ciminals,' he repeated. 'Mafia?' She nodded. He pulled a face. 'I suppose the assault could have been sponsored by the Mafia,' he mused. 'But it doesn't sound like them. Too crude.' He frowned and shook his head. 'The only way we're going to know who was behind it is if we find those two bastards and get them to talk . . . tell us who they were working for. *If*,' he emphasised heavily. 'I don't suppose finding them will be easy.'

'One of them may have a broken kneecap,' Melissa volunteered.

Lankell nodded. 'Could help, maybe.' He thought for a moment then focused on her. 'So what are you going to do? Are you going to carry on with the job?'

She shook her head. 'I don't know, Dennis. I never want to go through what I went through last night. Definitely never. Next time I may not be so lucky. Bob Briscoe got to me just in the nick of time, you know.' She stared at the patterned Axminster on the floor. 'The thing is, I'm all Jamie's got. If I'm at risk, he's at risk. You understand that, don't you?'

'Sure.'

'There's plenty of other work I could be doing in the firm,' she went on. '*Safe* work. I don't *have* to work on the Exchange Bank liquidation.'

'Yeah. It sounds to me like it would be safer for you if you didn't,' Lankell agreed darkly. He left a few minutes later.

She wasn't hungry, though she sat with Jamie through his tea. Afterwards she soaked some bread in milk and together they fed George. They played with the puppy until it fell asleep then watched television together. Jamie fell asleep and she carried him up. She fixed a drink and watched some more television. She scarcely noticed what was on.

Astrid had taken the night off. Melissa heard her come in soon after she had gone to bed. She finally fell asleep without the benefit of one of Dr Lubitsch's pills. Her dreams were horrific: she was running through long, dark tunnels and screaming without making any sound.

Twice she awoke in the small hours to find herself covered in sweat. By the morning she was exhausted. Even so, she decided, it was better than the drugging effects of the pill.

Sunday was breezy, with occasional light rain but in between the showers the brassy sun looked warm and inviting. Jamie wanted to take George for their usual Sunday walk but Melissa insisted the dog was too little. She got Jamie togged up and together they walked across the Downs near the cottage.

Not long after they got back the phone in the lounge warbled. It was Nigel Hawick. He had some questions about her report. It took Melissa a few seconds to comprehend what he was talking about.

Of course, she had written him a report. She had the curious feeling that everything that had happened to her in the days and hours leading up to the assault had occurred in another lifetime.

She told him about the attack. He was horrified.

'For God's sake,' he said in a strangled voice: 'you think these men attacked you because of the liquidation?'

'Yes. So does Dennis Lankell.'

'You've reported it to the police?'

'Of course.'

'Good.' He was silent for a moment. 'I'll have to tell the BoE supervisors tomorrow morning. They'll be extremely upset that a liquidator working on their behalf has been assaulted.'

'I wasn't too happy about it myself,' Melissa said darkly.

He grunted. 'Well, look, take as much time off as you want. Don't come back to the office until you are completely recovered.'

'Yes, I was going to do that anyway. I'll call you in the middle of the week and let you know how I feel. And when I come in, I want to talk to you about the Exchange Bank liquidation, Nigel. I don't think I want to carry on with it. Not after what's happened.'

'Yes, of course. I understand.'

Later that day Bob Briscoe phoned to check on how she was. Merely hearing his voice made her feel better. She told him she was resting a lot and making a good recovery. He said he would call again in a few days.

Sunday night her sleep was less disturbed and by Monday morning she was beginning to look a little better, though she was acutely conscious of the butterfly tape stuck to her cheek on the crowded train journey up to town.

She arrived at the surgery in Harley Street at a little after nine thirty. It looked different in the daylight. Giving her his customary shallow smile, Dr Lubitsch sat her down, took off the tape and carefully examined the wound. 'It's doing very well,' he told her. 'You're young. You heal very quickly.'

'But will there be a scar?' she asked again.

He shook his head. 'I don't know. It is difficult at this stage to tell. But, as I said, minor plastic surgery will eliminate it if there is one. In the meantime I can put on a smaller dressing. Now,' he asked when he had finished, 'how are you feeling . . . in yourself?'

'Better.'

'Good. Remember, plenty of rest and no excitement.'

She smiled and rose to go. 'Thank you again for looking after me. It was good of you to come out at such short notice on Friday night. Mr Briscoe must have quite a lot of influence to get you to do that.'

Lubitsch smiled. 'He does.'

'Have you known him long?'

'A while.'

Melissa was puzzled. 'How did you meet?'

Lubitsch shrugged. 'Oh, I cannot recall now. It was some time ago.' Curiously, Melissa had the impression that Lubitsch didn't want to talk about Bob Briscoe. Professional etiquette, she decided.

Outside, Harley Street was bathed in bright sunshine. Melissa caught a cab back to Waterloo, decided against the *Economist* and *Business Week* and bought *Marie Claire* and *Vogue* instead.

Chapter Twenty-Two

It was heaven to be at home during the day and with nothing to do.

Jamie was at his school in Petersfield and Astrid was cleaning up around the cottage. George was skidding about on the polished, hexagonal tiles in the kitchen. He seemed pleased to see her, his little stump of a tail wagging furiously.

After making herself and Astrid a pot of coffee she went out into the sunshine to do some gardening. She took George with her and staked him out nearby. He spent most of his time tangling himself up in his thin leather lead.

At lunchtime she heard the phone in the lounge. She eased herself up from pruning roses and ran in to pick it up before the answering machine cut in.

'Miss Semmington?'

The voice was clipped and precise. She didn't recognise it.

'This is Steven Timmison. You may recall I was present when Rolay Richard was first instructed by the Bank of England.'

She recalled the tall, fair-haired man with a hawkish face who had sat silently and ominously off to one side as she and the other partners had been briefed by the supervisors.

She said something about vaguely remembering him.

'I've just heard about the appalling attack on you last Friday night. I am most distressed to hear you were injured. I cannot tell you how upset I am.'

Melissa mumbled her thanks at his concern.

'I wonder, Miss Semmington,' he continued in his clipped tones, 'if you could spare me a few minutes of your time. Here in my office. You see, I sat in on the meeting this morning when your colleague, Mr Hawick, reported to the Bank of England supervisors. There was some mention in his report of your work in tracking large amounts of money laundered by a company in California. Piagini, I believe it's called.'

Melissa frowned at the wall opposite. What was this stranger getting at? She recalled Nigel Hawick's opinion that he was a spook. Her response was noncommittal. 'Oh, yes?'

'Yes. The thing is, Miss Semmington, I happen to know the attack on you was connected with your work in tracking those funds.'

Melissa was startled. 'You know that for sure?'

'Absolutely. There's no doubt. You've uncovered a hornets' nest. That's why I think we must meet.'

Melissa felt the hairs rising at the back of her neck. Despite the warmth of the day, she shivered. 'You think I was attacked because of my work in California?'

'Yes.'

'But how can you be sure? How do you know?' Her voice was insistent.

'Perhaps I can tell you that when we meet,' Timmison said calmly.

'You want me to meet you?'

'Yes.'

'Where?'

'In my office.'

'When?'

'This afternoon.'

She grimaced. The last thing she wanted was to get on a train and travel back to London. 'I'm not sure how long it would take me to get to London,' she said flatly. 'Trains aren't very frequent at this time of day.'

He laughed sharply. It was a distant, glassy sound. 'Please don't worry about trains, Miss Semmington. There's a car on its way to you. It will be with you in under an hour. Naturally it will take you home after our meeting. I'll look forward to seeing you later.'

Timmison hung up. Bemused, Melissa stared at the dead, faintly buzzing phone she was holding.

She had just finished changing when the car arrived. It was a Daimler. A dark green, glossily polished Daimler. The young, uniformed driver ushered her into the back seat and set off for the M3.

On the motorway he kept the car at a steady hundred and ten. It was obvious to Melissa he wasn't bothered about traffic police.

195

Probably, she thought, because driving that particular car they weren't going to bother about him.

The driver stayed south of the Thames, heading east towards Vauxhall. Melissa guessed he was making for the City. She was surprised when he turned north at Vauxhall Cross and crossed the bridge.

She was even more surprised when he turned off Whitehall into King Charles Street, and drew the Daimler smoothly to a halt between the dignified George Gilbert Scott façades of Her Majesty's Treasury and the Foreign and Commonwealth Office.

He accompanied Melissa to a nearby entrance of the Foreign Office where he left her in a small office with a security guard. The guard made a telephone call and asked her to write her details in an official-looking ledger. Not long after she had fixed her visitor's badge to the lapel of her lightweight, cream-coloured jacket, a young man appeared. He was well-dressed and wearing a Harrow tie.

The young man led her around a large, richly decorated, glass-enclosed courtyard. Melissa gazed at the three stories of high-arched windows staring down on the courtyard's marble floor. The windows were fronted by columns and piers of polished red granite and decorated with ornate friezes.

She remarked on the splendid square, saying it wasn't what she had expected to find in the Foreign Office. Actually, the young man explained in the clipped, easy idiom of his old school, they were in the India Office.

Leaving the courtyard, they mounted a magnificent, pale-marble staircase. Melissa looked about her as she strode beside the man along a broad corridor replete with yet more high-arching columns.

The building, with its marvellous classical decoration and its plethora of marble and polished wood had a nineteenth-century feel to it . . . redolent of lapsed affluence, lost Empires and the solemn obligation of the white man's burden.

The man stopped halfway along the corridor and knocked at a pair of polished walnut doors. A sharp, crisp voice beyond the doors called out. The young man ushered Melissa into a big, square office with high ceilings, long windows and an empty fireplace.

The tall figure of Steven Timmison rose from behind a large Victorian partner's desk. Melissa noticed the expanse of green leather inlaid on the desktop. Polished to a genteel sheen, it was pitted and marked by generations of scratches. Scarred by history, she thought.

Behind him, the windows allowed a marvellous view of the great square of Horse Guards Parade.

'Miss Semmington.' Timmison extended an arm. His grasp on her hand was tough and bony. 'Please do sit down. Thank you so much for agreeing to see me.'

Melissa, as far as she could remember, *hadn't* agreed to see him, well at least not willingly. She had been bounced into the meeting. For a moment she thought of pointing that out, but decided to let it go. Timmison, she guessed, was the type who chose to believe his commands were everyone else's desires. She put him down as a Fascist.

She gazed around the solid, imposing office. 'I didn't expect to meet you here,' she said. 'I take it you're not actually with the Bank of England.'

'I am and I'm not,' he replied enigmatically. 'I work closely with the Bank. I also work closely with the Treasury, just across the street. Basically, Miss Semmington, my job is to protect the economic interests of this country. Just as there are people who protect our military and diplomatic interests, I endeavour to preserve our business interests. As much of my work is in cooperation with the Foreign Office, they allow me a little space here.' He waved an arm around the big room.

'I see,' Melissa nodded. Nigel Hawick was right. Timmison was some kind of economic spook.

'Naturally, what I've just told you is confidential. Still,' he appraised her, 'you've signed the Official Secrets Act haven't you.' It was a reminder rather than a question.

'Yes.'

He attempted a smile. It didn't work. 'Would you like tea?'

'Thank you.'

He pressed a button on an intercom and a secretary appeared through a side door carrying a tea set on a silver salver. Melissa noticed the crockery was Spode.

Timmison looked up from pouring the tea and nodded at the dressing on her face. 'Did you sustain that in the assault?'

The question came as a surprise. For a few moments Melissa had forgotten the wound on her cheek. She felt herself colouring. 'Yes.'

'Is it serious?'

'I'm told not. I'm hoping there won't be a scar.'

'If there is, I will make sure any surgery you have is paid for out of State funds.'

'Thank you.'

'It's the least we can do. Sugar?' She shook her head. 'Now,' he passed a cup to her across the desk, 'please tell me exactly what happened.'

This time Melissa was able to recount the facts of the attack with less emotion. Her voice faltered on a couple of occasions, but the cathartic effect of her tearful, sobbing paroxysm with Lankell and the healing nature of time had already given Friday night's events a sense of distance. It was almost as if they had happened to someone else.

Timmison listened attentively but said nothing. 'I have reported the matter to the police,' she said in conclusion, 'to a Met Drugs Squad officer with whom I occasionally have dealings.'

Timmison nodded. 'Yes, I've seen a copy of Chief Inspector Lankell's report.'

Melissa was surprised. The hawk-faced man opposite could move quickly. 'I have also been in touch with both the City of London and the Metropolitan police forces,' he continued, 'who assure me they are doing everything they can to find these two men.'

He could, she thought, also pull strings.

'DCI Lankell believes,' Timmison continued, 'that the men were hired to stop you investigating something related to the Exchange Bank. He thinks you were getting close to something important.'

'You mentioned my work in California.'

'Yes. I'm afraid the attack was connected with your investigation into the funds that Piagini and Pemblin were washing between them.'

Melissa frowned. 'But what makes you think that? Why? Why that part of my work? There are plenty of other financial threads running through the Exchange Bank. I'm following through on many of them. What makes you think it was Piagini?'

'The company is a front for a nasty bunch of organised criminals who have over a hundred million dollars frozen in accounts at the Exchange Bank. Furthermore, you have provided evidence of how that money got there . . . how they laundered the cash from drug deals.'

'But I've done that before,' she protested. 'Admittedly, not to the tune of a hundred million, but I've uncovered Mafia money laundering in the past and haven't been attacked. Why should the people behind Piagini attack me? What's so special about them?'

Timmison's face was blank. 'I'm afraid I can't tell you that, Miss Semmington. You must accept my word that your recent work in California was the reason for the assault. But what I *can* tell you is this. Because of the excellence of that work, you have penetrated far deeper into the movement and whereabouts of the laundered money than the criminals behind the funds thought possible. That's why they had you attacked. And that's why I wish you to cease all work related to that particular aspect of the investigation.'

'You want me to stop chasing down the cash moving between Piagini and Pemblin?'

'Absolutely. There's no way we wish to have your personal safety jeopardised, Miss Semmington. Your reports on the investigation are extremely detailed. They clearly show where the money came from and where it's gone. It will be easy enough for some of my own people, along with the FBI, to carry on the investigation. Once they take over it will become obvious to the men behind the money that you have stopped working on the case.'

Melissa stared at the sharp, sabre-like face across the desk in silence. He struck her as a cold, arrogant bastard. But powerful, she thought. *Very* powerful.

After a moment she shrugged. 'Well, as a matter of fact I'd pretty well done all I could do in connection with Piagini. And I certainly don't want to be attacked again. So, if you don't want me working on anything to do with the company, that's fine by me. I take it you'll tell Rolay Richard and my boss of your decision.'

'Instructions have already been passed by the Bank of England that you are not to take any further part in that investigation.'

Melissa shrugged. 'You're the boss,' she said, adding, *sotto voce,* 'apparently.'

She paused. 'As a matter of fact,' she went on, 'I'm going to ask to be taken off the Exchange Bank liquidation altogether.'

Timmison raised his eyebrows. 'Really? I'm sorry to hear that. Why?'

'I would have thought it was obvious.' Her voice was cutting. 'I don't want any more assaults. I was very lucky to escape the last one with no more than this.' She touched her cheek. 'I have a small son. He needs me. I'm all he has.'

'So I understand.' From the way he said it, Melissa could tell Timmison knew about Jamie and her single status. She wondered what else he knew about her private life.

'And anyway, you can't be absolutely certain that the reason those men attacked me was the Piagini cash washing. It could be something else. Almost all the laundered money I'm tracking belongs to professional criminals, drug dealers or terrorists. Most of them wouldn't hesitate to have me beaten up and maimed. Or worse,' she added darkly. 'A man and his family have already been murdered.'

Timmison nodded. 'I know. But in this case it was definitely your work in California that prompted the assault.'

'But how can you be so sure?' she insisted.

'I'm sorry, I'm afraid you'll just have to take my word. That's all I can tell you.' She heard the note of finality in his voice.

Timmison was sure and that was it. End of discussion.

'But of course,' he went on in a heartfelt tone, 'I do appreciate your position, Miss Semmington. Naturally you have no wish to put either yourself or your son at risk.'

'Naturally,' she repeated coldly.

Timmison studied her for a moment then rose from his seat, walked around the massive desk and hitched himself onto an edge close to Melissa's chair. He gazed down at her with concern. 'However, I would ask you to think most seriously about transferring off the Exchange Bank liquidation. You've done a superb job up to now. The FBI are delighted with the work you did on Grand Cayman. And some of your other investigations are showing signs of progress. But there is still an awful lot left to do. As you know, half a billion dollars has gone missing. I'm extremely anxious that we find that money, Miss Semmington.'

'I'm sure you are. But you'll have to do it without me. If I stayed with the job I'd be constantly worried about another attack.'

He nodded seriously. 'Yes, I appreciate that. I understand your position. Believe me. But, if you decided to stick with it . . . if you agreed to carry on with your work tracing the

Exchange Bank's dirty money, I would ensure you were given total protection. Twenty-four hours a day.'

'Protection?'

'Yes. Guaranteed.'

She pulled a face, trying to make sense of what she was hearing. 'But why should I need protection if I'm not working on Piagini?'

'Purely for your peace of mind, Miss Semmington. You, your son and your home, would be kept under discreet observation at all times by a team of police officers. And when you were actually working, physically engaged in tracing the bank's money, you would be accompanied by an armed police officer.'

Melissa stared at him. 'Well, I suppose that's all right here, in this country,' she said slightly flustered, 'but a lot of my work is abroad.'

'The same conditions would apply when you were out of the country,' he stated.

She continued to stare at him. It seemed Timmison meant what he said about her work. He really wanted her to continue.

'Can you do that?' she asked in an incredulous voice. '*Guarantee* me police protection. Even when I'm out of the country. In America for instance?'

He nodded. 'Yes, I can. I'm not without influence, you know. Even in America.'

'It sounds expensive, all the same. All that protection.'

Timmison shrugged. The shoulders of his Savile Row suit moved then settled softly back into place. 'In comparison to the amounts of laundered money you're tracing, it's negligible. In comparison to your peace of mind, Miss Semmington, not to mention your safety and that of your son, it's nothing.'

He stood up from his perch on the corner of the desk. 'Will you think about it? Please? Give it some serious thought?' He looked down at her. 'We would be most loath to lose you from the Exchange Bank liquidation, Miss Semmington. Frankly, one of the reasons we chose Rolay Richard as the bank liquidators was because of your reputation in tracing laundered money. So, please, do think about it.'

She gazed up at him. After a moment she said quietly. 'All right, I'll think about it.'

'Good. And please be assured that I personally shall do

whatever is in my power to ensure your protection.' He gave her an intense look and did his best to smile.

The meeting was at an end.

The young, well-dressed man accompanied her back through the ornate interior of the building to the entrance on King Charles Street. The Daimler was parked nearby, its engine running, the driver waiting by the rear door, ready to whisk her back to Hampshire.

As the car turned south off Westminster Bridge and onto Lambeth Palace Road, Melissa pondered the meeting. She was uneasy. She felt as if she had been conned. It seemed to her that Timmison had got her to his office under false pretences. She had expected him to tell her how he knew her assault was connected with her work on Piagini. But he hadn't. He hadn't told her.

Instead, he had ordered her off anything to do with investigating the company. Yet, she reflected, he had tried to persuade her to stick with the rest of the job. She frowned. She couldn't understand it.

What was so different or special about Piagini? Her work in relation to the company was virtually complete anyway. So why wouldn't Timmison tell her why the company had ordered the attack on her? He obviously knew . . . knew a lot more than he was saying. But he wouldn't tell. Maybe, because of his job – and because of his peremptory personality – he was used to withholding information. But, she told herself, there was more to it than that. She could feel it.

She thought about his offer of protection if she carried on with the job. Did she want to stay with it if she had protection? she asked herself. She remembered the two men and the cold numbing fear she had felt on Friday night. She couldn't go through that again. But she wouldn't have to – not if she had protection.

She caught the thought. For God's sake, she was seriously considering the offer.

She thought of Jamie. No, she wasn't going to risk Jamie, not even with protection. In her heart of hearts she knew if she had been on her own she would have said yes to Timmison's offer. She would have continued with the job. But she couldn't risk Jamie. Not with men like those two still at large. Even if she wanted to continue she couldn't do it. For Jamie's sake.

Suddenly she felt very tired. She let herself sink back into the soft leather of the seat. She had travelled a long way for very little. Even if it was in the exhilarating luxury of a Daimler doing a hundred and ten on the M3.

At the cottage, Astrid had a message for her. It was from Dennis Lankell. 'He wishes you to telephone him as soon as you return,' she said. 'He says it is very important.'

She dialled his number at the Drugs Squad. 'Dennis, it's Melissa. What is it? Have you found those men?'

'Thanks for calling back,' he said in his deep, stony voice. 'Listen, you said one of the blokes had a pockmarked face. And a scar along his left jaw. Is that right?'

'Yes, that's right.' Her heart hammered as she recalled the awful face.

'And the other looked like a wrestler. Built like brick shit-house?'

Despite her panic she let out a faint, silvery laugh. 'I didn't describe him quite like that.'

'But that's what you meant. Yes?' Something in Lankell's voice took the smile off her face. 'And you thought he could have a damaged knee?'

'Did I? I don't know. I can't remember. But why? Why do you want to know?'

''Cos we've got them. The boys in Three Area found them this afternoon. Out on Walthamstow Marshes. The bloke with the scar had your name on a piece of paper in his pocket.'

Melissa's heart surged again. 'You've caught them.' She was exultant. 'God, Dennis, that's marvellous. Have they said why they attacked me? Who was behind it?'

'No.'

Her elation turned to fury. 'Well, can't you *make* them? Force them to tell you?'

'No. We can't.'

'For Christ's sake, Dennis,' her voice went up an octave: 'those bastards attacked me! They were going to slash my face. They *did* slash my face. They frightened me. I'm having nightmares. And now you've got them you're telling me they refuse to say why. Well that's not bloody good enough. Why won't they tell you?'

Lankell's voice was dry and laconic. 'Because they can't. We found them lying face-down in six inches of water.'

Her angry face puckered. She didn't understand. 'What do

you mean, six inches of water? Are they drowned?'

'No. Not drowned. Both men have got a couple of bullets in the back of the head.'

Chapter Twenty-Three

The smell of the formaldehyde caught the back of her throat. She felt nauseous. Partly it was the smell, but mainly it was the thought of what she had to do. It was her first time in a mortuary.

Dennis Lankell was waiting.

He glanced at her strained face. 'You're going to be fine.' His voice was reassuring . . . surprisingly soft and gentle. 'It won't take a moment. All you have to do is nod if these are the blokes. Okay? Look only as long as it takes for you to be sure. There's nothing to worry about. They don't look bad.'

Melissa wondered how well a man could look with a couple of bullets in his head.

Lankell took her arm and gently steered her into a large room walled from floor to ceiling in glazed white tiles. At one end were a couple of marble slabs, with running water softly washing over them. Melissa looked away. She had a good idea what the slabs were for.

Motionless in the middle of the room were two stainless steel trolleys. Dark green shrouds covered whatever lay beneath them. Lankell eased her towards them. An attendant in green fatigues was standing close by.

'Ready?' Lankell asked.

She gulped quietly. 'Let's get on with it.'

Lankell nodded at the attendant who pulled back one of the green covers. Beneath it was a face. The skin was the colour of candle grease and the eyes were closed. Melissa stared. It wasn't what she had expected. The man looked ill. Ill and asleep. There was no sign of any damage from bullets.

She had expected the process of identifying the men to be horrible. A sickening experience. But this . . . this she could handle. Just about.

'Well?' she heard Lankell inquire.

She frowned. 'I'm not sure,' she said in a low voice. 'I think that may be the other one. All I remember about him is his eyes. And his build.'

'Could this be him?'

She peered almost unselfconsciously at the body.

'Yes, I think so.'

Lankell nodded and the attendant let the cover fall over the face. They moved to the other trolley. The attendant pulled back the cover.

'Oh!' Melissa cried out and recoiled.

The features of the still, set face with its chin jutting up at the ceiling were stamped onto her brain. The skin was pockmarked and there was a long scar along the jawline. The face, though motionless in death, held terrors for her. 'Yes, yes,' she gabbled: 'that's him.'

She reached out for Lankell. He took hold of her hand and enveloped it in an enormous, warm fist. 'That's the one who had the knife,' she gasped. Lankell nodded and the attendant let the cover drop.

Lankell led her from the room and along a corridor out of the mortuary. Outside, Melissa leaned against a wall of the building, took a couple of deep breaths of scarcely fresh Walthamstow air, and waited for the smell of the formaldehyde to fade from her nostrils.

Lankell lit a cigarette and watched her.

She straightened up off the wall. 'Who are . . . were they?'

'A couple of local thugs. Nasty pair. They've got a string of convictions as long as a supermarket queue . . . attempted murder, GBH, assault with a deadly weapon, that kind of stuff.'

She shuddered. 'But why did they attack me?'

'Because they were paid to. We know they hired themselves out.'

'Hired themselves? Who to?'

Lankell shrugged. 'To whoever needed their particular job skills. They had a special brand of brutality. Anybody who wanted some poor bastard beaten up as a punishment; anyone who wanted someone maimed in a revenge attack, could call them in. At a price.'

'So who hired them to attack me?'

'That,' said Lankell, 'is what we have to find out. We can't ask them, that's for sure. Which,' he added ruminatively, 'is probably the reason they were executed.'

'Executed?'

'Yeah. Two small-calibre bullets in the back of the head. Not much noise, not much mess, just two very dead bodies. It was an execution all right. Classic.'

She gazed at Lankell, suddenly conscious that she was in an alien environment.

A couple of minutes earlier she had identified two murdered men; now she was standing outside a mortuary talking about executions. This was not a jungle she was used to. Though it was about money... connected ... it was different. This was another jungle, where the assets were dangerous and the ultimate liability could be a small-calibre bullet.

Despite the sun she shivered. 'But who would execute them?' she queried in a low voice.

He took a long drag on his cigarette. 'The people who hired them in the first place. That's usually the way it goes.'

'Is that the way the Mafia execute people? A bullet in the head?'

He nodded. 'Yes.'

'Well, I suppose that makes sense. I was told yesterday that the people behind my attack were Mafia money launderers running a bunch of front companies in California.' She told him of her meeting with Timmison. Lankell listened, his eyes, screwed in concentration, never leaving her face.

When she had finished, Lankell dropped the butt of his cigarette and ground it out with the sole of his shoe. He shook his head. 'It's hard to believe,' he said, 'but I suppose this bloke Timmison knows what he's talking about.'

'Why is it hard to believe?'

'It's difficult to believe that people as organised as a bunch of Yank money launderers would think about contracting an attack on you. They're too clever for it. They know there's no point. If anything happened to you, you'd be replaced And even if they did, they wouldn't have hired a couple of shit-for-brains hoodlums like those two,' he nodded at the mortuary wall. 'They'd have got real professionals.'

'Still,' he made a wry face, 'the killings have the hallmarks of a Mafia hit. And who am I to argue with a bloke with a big office in Whitehall? One thing is for sure, though.' He grinned at her. 'Those two aren't going to bother you any more, Melissa. It's all behind you now.'

'Do you really think so?'

'Yeah. Unless they come back from the dead. From now on it's down to the police. We have to find who killed them.'

'And who was behind them,' she added.

'Same thing,' he pronounced. There was a note of finality in his voice. 'So,' he grinned again, 'can I give you a lift?'

'Yes. Could you drop me at Eastcheap? At the office.'

'You going in to work?' He sounded surprised.

She nodded. 'Yes. I didn't think I would when I got here this morning. But now . . . now I've seen them – those men – well, as you say, it seems like it's all over. Everything is behind me. If I go home I'll probably start thinking about it again. I'm better off going into the office. Even with this.' She touched the tape on her cheek.

'Good girl,' he exclaimed. 'That's the spirit. Anyway,' he nodded at her cheek, 'that's nothing. I can scarcely notice it. It'll soon clear up.'

'It may be nothing to you, Dennis, but it's a lot to me,' she said stiffly.

'Naw, don't worry about it. It's nothing. I've got nicks like that all over me.'

'Yes, but you're an ugly brute.'

He laughed all the way from Walthamstow into the City.

Nigel Hawick was at Elm Street, at a meeting with the SFO, but everyone in Financial Investigations was pleased to see her. They had heard about her experience and were filled with sympathy and support. She told them she didn't want to talk about the attack. They said they understood. Even the tape on her cheek was quickly accepted. After a first glance no one paid it any attention.

Debbie had a thick wad of messages.

Melissa had been out of the office for three days: two in Basel and one at home. The work, meanwhile, had kept on coming. There was a backlog. She began to regret her decision to come into the office. Except, she thought, the longer she stayed away, the more the work piled up.

'Oh, and while you were away, we got a fax from someone called Barber in the American Federal Bureau of Investigation,' Debbie told her.

Melissa recalled the tall, grey-haired man in San Francisco who had led the raid on the house in Sausalito. She had quite liked him . . . for an FBI agent. He had appreciated her making the trip to be in on the raid.

'What does it say?'

Debbie handed her the fax.

She read it quickly. 'Well, that's nice of him to tell us what he has on Vito Kunzman. But, as usual with the FBI,' she added tartly, 'nothing is for nothing. He wants anything *we've* got on Kunzman. Okay,' she looked up at Debbie, 'ask Boris Redbourn to let me know if he's come up with any background on Kunzman. But nothing is to go out until I've seen it first. Okay?'

'Yes.'

Hawick returned from his meeting and banged on the glass partition dividing their fish tanks. She walked into his office. 'I didn't expect to see you back so soon.' His voice was concerned. 'Are you sure you should be here?'

'I'm better off here than moping at home.'

He nodded. 'I hear they found the bodies of the men who attacked you. So, what happened?'

'I don't want to talk about it, Nigel.'

He grunted. 'Okay.' He was silent for a moment. 'What are you going to do now?' he asked.

'Do?'

'Will you stick with the Exchange Bank? Or do you want to transfer to something else?'

'I don't know,' she said gloomily. 'Up to a couple of hours ago I thought I wanted out. But now . . .' She stared out of the glass partition at the big, busy office beyond. 'That man, Timmison . . . he wants me to stick with it. I met him yesterday.'

'I know. He called me.'

'I told him I wanted off the job. He said if I stayed he'd provide Jamie and me with twenty-four-hour police protection.'

Hawick smiled grimly. 'They don't do that for everyone, Melissa.'

She pouted, unimpressed.

'The thing is, what do *you* want to do? After Aziz and his family were murdered, you said if you were threatened you'd stop working on the Exchange Bank. Well, you've been more than threatened. You've been attacked.'

'I don't need bloody reminding, Nigel!' Her tone was high, sharp, and shrewish. After a moment she said, 'I'm sorry. I'm still on edge.'

He shrugged. 'It was my fault. You're right, you don't need reminding. It was stupid of me. I'm sorry.' He paused. 'So what do you want to do?'

She shook her head impatiently. 'I don't know. Now I'm not tracking the Piagini cash, Timmison is convinced the danger is past. And if he's providing police protection, there seems no reason not to carry on. But . . . I'm not sure.'

'Why don't you have a couple of easy days in the office?' Hawick suggested. 'Come in late, go early . . . see how you feel. Take it slowly. Just do desk work. If there's field work, send one of the others.'

'I wasn't attacked doing field work, Nigel,' she said bitterly. 'I wasn't in America or the Caymans or Basel. I was attacked here, within half a mile of the office. After I had written a report for you.'

He made a face.

She moderated her tone. 'But you're right. That's what I'll do. I'll take it easy. See how I feel in a couple of days.'

She left the office at five. Downstairs, in the atrium, a young woman was waiting for her by the limed-ash reception desk. She introduced herself. Her name was Liz. She was a plainclothes policewoman . . . Melissa's escort home. Timmison, it seemed, had decided to provide the protection anyway. They chatted pleasantly on the way to Waterloo where they boarded the train together.

In the car, Melissa asked Liz if she was armed. The policewoman, who looked no older than twenty-five, gave her a Gioconda smile and declined to answer.

A dark blue Mondeo was parked close to the entrance of the cottage driveway. Melissa stared at it as she drove past. Liz told her not to be alarmed. The men in the car were colleagues.

Her escort the following morning was Simon. He too was in plain clothes. Melissa was shocked, he seemed even younger than Liz, though she did think he was rather dishy. And he was good company. For once the journey up to town was bearable.

By the middle of the morning life in the office was the normal whirling circus of non-stop deadlines and frantic phone calls. The condolences and sympathy that had greeted her the day before had evaporated. Things were back to normal. Melissa was glad.

She went into the ladies' room and carefully peeled away the tape over her wound. The thin, vivid line on her cheek was forming a crust. The tape, she thought, looked worse and more obvious than the mark. She decided it would heal faster with the air to it.

Back in her office, Boris Redbourn called her on the internal. 'This bloke Kunzman you're interested in,' he drawled. 'I've dug up some stuff about him. If you're interested.'

'I'm on my way down,' she said.

Chapter Twenty-Four

Around the walls of Redbourn's office computer screens were silently shimmying arrows across the globe.

Melissa grinned as she walked in. Redbourn was sitting at a console wearing a bright yellow teeshirt beneath a denim waistcoat. His trousers were army surplus, tucked into black, high-leg Dr Martens. Compared to the rest of Rolay Richard's employees, Redbourn looked like a lama.

'Hi, Boris,' she greeted. 'What have you got?'

'The address you picked up in Basel. For this bloke Kunzman.'

'White Plains?'

'That's it.'

'What about it?'

'It's not residential. It's a small bank . . . a correspondent of the Exchange Bank. I've checked with the New York office. It's one of the banks the American crime syndicates took over. Vito Kunzman was using it as an address.'

'Yes, but that was twenty years ago, Boris.'

'Okay. But I cross-checked the address through the computer and . . . bingo . . . it came up with the names of about thirty corporations who'd been using it as their registered address back in the seventies and early eighties. So, I did some more digging and discovered the address was that of a small legal firm. It probably had a suite of offices above the bank. Anyway, you'll never guess the name of the firm.'

'Vito Kunzman and Associates,' Melissa said.

Redbourn's grin of triumph faded. 'You know.'

'I'm sorry, Boris. The FBI sent me a fax. They've found out about him. They know he's a lawyer. They've even found out where he lives.'

Redbourn looked disappointed. 'Shit, there's no pleasing you people,' he moaned.

She smiled sympathetically. 'It's my fault, Boris. I should have sent you a copy of the fax as soon as it came in. I wasn't here on Monday... it's down to me... I'm sorry.'

Redbourn glanced up at the vivid line on her left cheek. 'No, it's okay,' he said quietly. 'It's not your fault, Melissa.' He shrugged, then gave her a smile. 'Well, at least now you've found this bloke Kunzman.'

She shook her head. 'No, we haven't. The FBI say he's disappeared. There's no trace of him. He has a wife out on Long Island but she doesn't know where he is – or at least she's not saying. He's got a couple of married daughters, but they don't know where he is either.'

Redbourn nodded. 'That makes sense, I suppose. A lot of the top dogs hopped it when the bank was closed.'

Melissa made a puzzled face. 'According to the FBI, Kunzman went missing some time *before* the bank went down.'

'Maybe he knew.'

'I don't think so. If he'd known, he would have told a lot of other people.'

'So, what spooked him? Why did he disappear?'

Melissa stared down at Redbourn, her eyes distant and unseeing. 'I'm not sure,' she murmured. She stood for a moment longer, unconscious of Redbourn or the silent images moving across the screens around her.

She shook her head, yanking herself free from her distraction. 'Well,' she smiled at Redbourn: 'let me have details of the companies registered at Kunzman's address. I'll fax them to the FBI. They may not be aware of them.'

'Here.' He passed her a printed sheet of names. 'I've listed the company officers as well. Where I've been able to find them.' He nodded at the shimmering terminals. 'A lot are names we know.' He stood up and peered at the list over Melissa's shoulder. 'You see Kunzman was a director of all the companies.'

She nodded. 'Yes.'

'There's another name that appears regularly. There.'

Melissa gazed at the name above Redbourn's index finger. 'Imola Varese,' she read aloud. She frowned. For some unknown reason the name seemed familiar. She looked up at Redbourn, her gaze questioning.

'Mrs Imola Varese,' he explained. 'I think she was the vice president or treasurer or whatever the American equivalent is.

213

My guess is she was Kunzman's secretary and he made her an officer of some of the companies to make up the numbers. It didn't mean much. They were all shell corporations anyway.'

'It's done a lot. There's nothing illegal about it.' Melissa's voice was distant, her face contorted in thought. She was still trying to work out why the hell she seemed to know the name. 'Do we know anything about her?'

Redbourn bent to the keyboard and pressed a couple of keys. An orange cube appeared on the screen with a list of names inside. He highlighted one, Imola Varese, then he pressed another key. A further list appeared. It was identical to the one Melissa was holding. Redbourn shook his head. 'What you've got is what there is.'

He pressed a key and the highlighted name reappeared. Melissa stared at the screen in disappointment. She had seen that name somewhere before. She knew she had. 'She's not connected with Cyclix and the piggy-backed funds is she?' she asked intently.

'No. If she was the data would connect. It would show up.'

'Are you sure?' Her tone was persistent.

'Sure I'm bloody sure, Melissa. Cyclix is a complete crock of crap.' Redbourn's voice was suddenly whining and defensive. He slumped back into his chair and scowled at the monitor through his glasses.

'I've traced that sodding cash out of Houston to Grand Cayman, then across the Atlantic to Basel, then back to Atlanta, then over to the Netherlands Antilles. But after that,' he looked up at her, 'nothing. Complete bugger all. The money went into the Exchange Bank on Curaçao . . . and disappeared. Into a total, bloody black hole. We've got the account number it went into, but there's no trace of that number in the branch or in any branch of the bank anywhere. The damn number must be linked to a codename. We've tried the codenames Aziz told you about, but,' he made a waspish face, 'absolutely sod all. We need the codename to open the account and gain access. Without it I've got no details of transactions or anything.'

'All right, Boris, all right,' Melissa tried to placate him. She knew how much he hated to be beaten. 'I know you're doing your best. You've done wonders with everything else. Cyclix probably isn't that important anyway.'

'The problem with this business,' Redbourn went on petulantly, 'is that it's like one of those Russian dolls. Every time you get inside something, you find it's hiding something else you have to get inside. To get into an account you need the codeword. But then, to follow the transactions, you need a whole bunch of bleeding passwords. It's a total pain in the arse.'

Melissa was fond of Boris but she was in no mood to listen to his complaints. She'd heard them all before. She tried heading him off at the pass. 'Boris, do you have an address for this woman, Varese?'

He glowered at her, turned back to the keyboard and punched a number of keys. An address appeared. 'Greenville,' he grunted. 'Where the hell is that?'

Melissa stared at the screen. 'Somewhere near New York by the look of it.' She took a note of the address. 'Boris, that's great,' she said encouragingly. 'You've been a lot of help. Thanks for the stuff on Kunzman.'

'You knew it all already,' he growled.

'Well, thanks anyway.' She gave him a warm, bright smile. After a moment he chuckled and smiled in return. 'Yeah.'

She took the lift, ascending to her own floor deep in thought.

Instead of making for her office she knocked on Hawick's door and walked in. Hawick was on the phone. He waved her to a seat and quickly finished his call. 'Hi,' he said: 'what can I do for you.'

'Do you remember our meeting with Berrenstein Lang? Kenneth McKinnie said he thought the BoE had someone on the inside of the Exchange Bank? Someone passing on the bank's secrets . . . telling the Old Lady where the bodies were buried.'

Hawick looked puzzled. 'Yes, I remember.'

'I think that person is Vito Kunzman.'

Hawick's face changed. 'Kunzman? Why?'

'The FBI faxed me some data on him. They say he is an attorney, a front man for the Mafia who's handled a lot of their investments and corporate work. He had a legal practice in New York. He's legitimate apparently. Never been in any trouble himself but from what we know he was the link man with the Exchange Bank. The Mafia's compliance officer if you like.'

'So what makes you think he's the Old Lady's snoop?'

'He disappeared some time before the Exchange Bank was shut down. No reason apparently. Just,' she waved an elegant hand in the air, 'vanished.'

'That could mean anything,' Hawick pointed out darkly. 'With

215

the Mafia as friends he wouldn't need any enemies. He may have upset someone . . . someone who decided he was surplus to staff requirements.'

'Yes, that's possible,' she conceded, 'but if he was murdered his body has never been found. And another thing. He disappeared shortly after Dr Campeche was shot to death in Caracas. Kunzman was close to Campeche. He was the link, remember. The FBI think Campeche was shot in mistake for Kunzman. So, if Kunzman thought he was next it would account for why he went on the run.'

'And ran to the Bank of England? That doesn't make sense. If he was going to run to the authorities it would be to the Americans. He wouldn't come to us.'

Melissa made a face. 'Yes I know that's difficult to understand. But perhaps there's a reason. Wait,' her voice changed gear, 'suppose he went to that man Steven Timmison. And suppose Timmison is hiding Kunzman because he's playing some devious game. A game we know nothing about. Suppose Timmison's using us for his own ends.'

Hawick laughed. 'There's no doubt he's using us. He's a spook, remember.'

'That's what worries me. I don't trust him. Timmison tangos to a different tune to the rest of us. He's got some hidden agenda. I'm sure of it.'

Hawick shrugged. 'It wouldn't be the first time a government department has used a firm like Rolay Richard to do its dirty work. You'll notice the Old Lady is standing well behind the touchline and letting Berrenstein Lang take the flak for the Exchange Bank going down.'

Melissa grunted. 'Timmison isn't behind the touchline, Nigel. He's a player. And it's his game. I'm sure of it. He's pulling our strings.'

Hawick let out a sharp laugh. 'Come on, Melissa, this is the world of high finance. Everybody is pulling everybody else's strings.'

'But usually it's easy to see. And easy to know why. It's always about money. But not with Timmison. He's not about money. He's about something else. And it bothers me.' She gazed silently at Hawick's face. 'A lot of things about this job bother me,' she added quietly. She touched the hardening crust on her cheek. 'Things that don't add up.'

'Yeah?'

She nodded. 'Those Cyclix piggy-backed funds for one thing. Boris Redbourn has just been bitching about how he's traced the money to Curaçao and then seen it disappear into the void. A big, black hole.'

'What's so different about that?'

'Nothing, I suppose. Except there's something about the money Cyclix is moving that doesn't make sense. The numbers don't add up.'

'What do you mean?'

'I'm not sure.' She dismissed the matter with a shake of her head. 'It doesn't matter.'

'And you think finding Kunzman will clear up the mystery?'

'About Cyclix?' She shrugged. 'I don't know. Maybe. He knows a hell of a lot about this bank: maybe he knows about Cyclix. Anyway, the man's a mystery in himself. Why did he disappear well before the bank went under? And what's this locked-box account he was operating? The Austerlitz Account? No one can even locate it. Maybe Aziz made it up. I don't know.'

She stood up. 'I just don't know.' Her voice was edgy with frustration. 'I don't know anything. There's a lot about this damn bank that doesn't add up. I just think Kunzman is important.'

'Well, at least you've got a handle on him now.' Hawick grinned up at her. 'All you've got to do is find him.'

Melissa gave him a withering look.

Andrew Bailey came to see her later that afternoon with an update on the search for the missing half billion. It was a brief meeting. They were making progress, he told her, but it was slow. It was going to take his team a long time to sift through the piles of forms relating to cashier's cheques, money orders and other negotiable instruments and to pick up the paper trail of the millions that had been transmuted into Eurobonds.

Bailey passed a sheaf of papers across her desk. Melissa skimmed them briefly. Lying close to her elbow was the slim file of passwords used by whoever had lifted the money out of the Managers' Ledger Accounts. From time to time, as Bailey was speaking, she glanced at the file. Something in it kept catching her eye. Puzzled she stared at the list of names, looking but not seeing.

What the hell was it about the list of names? She stared hard at the list.

'Oh my God!' she yelped.

Bailey jerked violently in his seat across the desk. 'What?'

Melissa grabbed the file and shoved it under Bailey's nose. 'These two passwords,' she rapped, jabbing at a couple of names: 'were they used to trigger funds out of the codenamed accounts?'

Bailey gazed at her in shock then peered at the names she was impatiently pointing to. 'Yes. Those two were used to move two hundred and twenty million dollars out of a Managers' Ledger Account in Bogotá.'

'Then I know who lifted the half billion,' she screeched excitedly.

The look of shock deepened on Bailey's face. 'You do? Who?'

'Vito Kunzman, that's who. I thought these passwords were a list of place names. But they're not . . . at least not all of them. These two, Imola and Varese. Together they're the name of the woman who was Kunzman's secretary in the seventies. I knew I'd seen the name before. But I hadn't seen the *complete* name. Only parts of it. Separated. Kunzman turned Imola and Varese into *passwords*.'

'But that doesn't prove he took the money.'

Melissa gave him an indulgent look. 'Come on, Andrew. I think it's pretty conclusive. Imola Varese worked for Kunzman for at least fifteen years. Her name meant enough for him to use it as passwords in an account he raided. If she was his secretary, then she must know a lot about him.' She tapped the file. 'This has to mean something. I've got a feeling this woman is significant.'

Bailey chuckled. 'Your famous instinct, eh?'

After he left, Melissa moved to the plate-glass windows to stare out over the snaking river. Ordinarily, with the strength of feeling she was getting about Imola Varese, she would have got Debbie to book her a flight to New York immediately.

But not this time. This time she wasn't sure if she wanted to go to New York.

Though memories of her attack were fading, diminished by the habitual urgency of her work and the lengthening vapour trail of time, the events of Friday night were still coming often and unsummoned into her mind. Usually they came at night, but – waking or sleeping – whenever she thought of the assault she found her hands shaking and her forehead beading in perspiration.

Was going to America a good idea? she asked herself. Here, with police protection, she was beginning to feel safe again. Would she feel the same in America?

And what about Jamie? If she was any kind of mother, how could she leave Jamie so soon after she had been attacked? If she was any kind of mother, she reviled herself, how could she continue with what she was doing? For Christ's sake, if she was a *real* mother she would get herself transferred off the Exchange Bank job. Maybe even resign.

She stared out of the smoky glass windows for a long time, feeling the tears pricking her eyes, unsure if they were tears of guilt or frustration.

Finally she decided. The best way to make the decision was to postpone it. She called Debbie on the internal. 'Debbie can you come in. I want to send a fax to Sam Barber of the FBI.'

Debbie dropped Barber's faxed response on her desk late the following afternoon.

After thanking her for the information on the companies registered at Kunzman's White Plains address, the fax went on to say that the Bureau had run a check on Imola Varese.

She had been Kunzman's secretary from the late sixties until the early eighties when he had moved his firm to Manhattan. As the work Kunzman had done for the Mob was legitimate, the Bureau was convinced Mrs Varese was straight. It was most unlikely she knew Kunzman undertook legal work for the Mafia. Recently widowed, she lived modestly in Greenville.

Melissa read the short, terse sentences in the fax twice. It was time to make up her mind. She couldn't postpone it any longer.

Was she going to carry on with the biggest job of her career or pass it up? Was she going to face up to her fear and go back out into the world or stay safely in the office doing desk work? She glanced up at the busy office beyond her windows.

After a moment she reached for her phone. 'Debbie, can you get me Steven Timmison, please. His number will be in your Rotadex.'

Timmison was on the line in seconds. 'Miss Semmington,' he said in his sharp, military voice. 'What can I do for you?'

'I have a possible lead in New York. On Vito Kunzman. And also, perhaps, the missing money. I think it may be important.'

'Really?' He sounded pleased.

'I can't be sure. It's just . . . well, I have a feeling.'

'That's why I'm so anxious you stay on this case, Miss Semmington. You have an excellent instinct for these things.' Melissa grimaced at Timmison's unctuous idea of a compliment.

'But I'm worried about leaving my son if I go to New York. And about getting protection over there.'

'Please be assured that both will be provided in the fullest measure,' Timmison barked 'A policewoman will live in with your son and his nanny whilst you are away. She will accompany your son and the nanny everywhere. The car outside your cottage will remain. I further guarantee that the American authorities will provide twenty-four-hour protection whilst you are in the United States. When are you going?'

'I'm not sure I *am* going. Not yet. I'm only thinking about it.' Melissa said brusquely. She said goodbye and put the phone down.

Within minutes Debbie announced a call from Nigel Hawick. 'Timmison tells me you've got a lead on Kunzman in New York.'

'Hell that was quick,' she responded. 'Are you two living together or something.'

He laughed. 'No. I was in a meeting at the Bank of England. He had me called out. What's the lead?'

'It's just a hunch. I think it might be important. Only . . . well . . . I don't want to say too much at this stage.'

'Okay. I understand. Anyway, Timmison asked me to speak to you. He wants me to assure you he'll provide complete security.'

'He's already told me that.'

'I know, but he's anxious I persuade you to follow up on your lead.' She heard him take a deep breath at the other end of the line. 'But I'm not going to do that, Melissa. I'm sure you and Jamie will get good protection, but, as far as I'm concerned, it's up to you whether you go to the States or not. I don't mind if you don't go. I can always send someone else. Or go myself. I don't want you to feel pressurised. Okay?'

She told him she appreciated that.

What finally persuaded her was the call which came in as she was about to leave the office. It was Bob Briscoe.

'Hi, I just called your home.' His voice, bouncing down off the satellite, echoed slightly. 'Your housemaid said you were at the office. Should you be back at work this quick?'

She laughed. 'I came back to the office a couple of days ago.'

He sounded serious. 'Is that wise?'

'I'm okay.'

He grunted noncommittally. 'I phoned to see how you were.'

'That's kind of you. I'm doing well. Honestly. Making a full recovery, as they say.'

'Well, that's good. I'm afraid I also phoned to say I can't see you for a while.'

Her heart dropped like a brick. 'Why not?'

'I'm all jammed up here. It looks like the deal I'm doing may go belly-up. Getting it straight will tie me up for weeks. I'm gonna be stuck here. I won't make it to London for a while.'

'But listen,' she said excitedly. 'I was thinking of going to New York. Following something up.'

'What, in connection with your work?'

'Yes.'

'Should you be doing that? This quick after what happened?'

'I'll be all right. There'll be people looking after me. And looking out for Jamie too, whilst I'm gone. Anyway, I'll only be away a couple of days.'

His voice was cautious. 'It sounds too soon to me.'

'But don't you see,' she went on enthusiastically, 'it's a good opportunity. If you can't come to me . . . I'll come to you. At least we can see each other for dinner. Or . . .' she felt her face suddenly colouring, 'or . . . well . . .'

He chuckled: a rich, deep, sexy sound. 'Okay, if you're sure. When will you be here?'

'I don't know yet.'

'Okay. You have my number. Call me when you get here. Leave a message on my machine and tell me where you're staying. Even if I'm out of town, I'll be picking up my messages. I'll fly back to New York. We can at least have one night together.'

Melissa felt the wonderful, sensuous buzzing in her loins. 'Marvellous,' she gasped. 'I'll see you soon.'

It was only after she cleared the line she remembered the livid mark on her cheek. She took a mirror from her bag and examined it. Suddenly it looked ten times worse. For a moment she stared in dismay at the ugly crusting, then muttered. 'To hell with it.'

She had the chance of another night of wonderful fucking. Of completely abandoned grabbing, sucking, thrusting, pumping copulation. She wasn't going to pass that up because she had a healing scar on her cheek. If she could put up with it, then so could Bob Briscoe, she decided. Besides, she'd make sure his attention was on other parts of her anatomy. He wouldn't see much of her scar if his face was between her legs for most of the night.

She moved to the glass partition and banged on the glass. Debbie, who was putting on her jacket ready to leave, looked up. Melissa waved her into the office.

'I'm sorry,' she said, 'but before you go can you fix me a flight to New York. I want to fly out the day after tomorrow. Then see if international DQs can get me the number of a Mrs Imola Varese in Greenville, New York. I need to talk to her.'

Chapter Twenty-Five

Big Vinny stood in the doorway of the cool, dark bar.

The scarce daylight squeezing past his huge, blockading frame flowed across the polished wooden floor and for an instant limned the sepia prints of hunched boxers on the walls close to the door. Motes of dust danced in the bright, stunted looms, though the light did little to alleviate the darkness further inside the long, narrow bar room.

Vinny moved quickly. Stepping to one side, out of the backlight from the open door he blinked rapidly to adjust his sight to the gloom.

His actions were instinctive. He was pretty sure he had nothing to fear in this place but it was not his natural milieu. He was in a city – a northern city, and a long way from home. And whether close to home or a long ways from it, the propensity for self-preservation ran deep in Big Vinny Harold. Which, he reckoned, was why he had survived so long in his dangerous profession.

He loped past the long wooden bar with its dull glowing brasswork towards the back of the saloon. He had been told the last booth but one. He wiped his hands on his jeans as he went. His palms were sweaty. He would have died sooner than admit it . . . but he was nervous.

He was due to meet the Area Commander.

He reached the booth. A young, military-looking guy – tall, lean and mean – stood up and nodded to the place he had vacated. Vinny slid into the seat and the young guy vanished without a word. The Area Commander was seated opposite, across the table.

'Sir,' Vinny murmured.

'Vinny. Good to see you. Hey, put it there, big guy.'

The Area Commander extended a hand and in shock Big Vinny shook it. He had never shaken hands with top brass before.

The Commander read the dazed look on his face. 'We ain't in uniform, Vinny,' he said pleasantly. 'We're just a couple of guys having a drink. An' hell, I'm pleased to see you.'

Vinny felt his ears and neck grow suddenly hot.

'What'll you have?' the Commander asked.

Vinny blinked in surprise. He was in a bar and he hadn't thought about what he was going to drink. 'Beer,' he muttered. 'Sir.'

The young man appeared from nowhere. 'Get the man a beer,' the Commander ordered. 'And a chaser. What is it you favour, Vinny? Rebel Yell? Is that right?'

Vinny's eyes widened in surprise. The Commander even knew his favourite bourbon. He nodded. 'Yessir.'

Vinny watched the aide walk the length of the bar to the waitress – a young, skinny blonde – and give her the order. He wondered why he hadn't waited for the woman to come down to their booth.

The Commander was saying something. Vinny jerked himself to attention and focused on his words. 'How many operations you been involved in for the Militia, Vinny?' he asked lightly.

Big Vinny considered. 'I guess it's seven sir.'

The Commander shook his head. 'It's nine, big guy.'

'Nine?' He was surprised.

'Sure, nine, including the tour you just completed down south.' The Commander gave him a broad smile. 'Hell, that action you and your boys pulled off in the Cordillera . . . that was really something. The best yet. We're getting close to twenty million for that merchandise. Thanks to you and the Chicashaw Commando.'

Vinny grunted. He was feeling uncomfortably warm under the collar of his check shirt.

'You know, counting the last operation, you've brought more than forty-five million dollars into the Movement?'

Vinny was surprised. 'Shit, no kidding!' he exclaimed. 'Sir.'

He stared at the Commander. Yeah, he probably had collared that much for the Militia's war chest, now he thought about it. Before the last action in Colombia he had led the commando on ambushes of narcotics smugglers in Mexico, Venezuela and Florida. In Chile they had robbed a warehouse of gold bullion and in Los Angeles intercepted a diamond shipment. Then there had been the armoured truck in Vancouver . . . that was the first action he had let Billy Bob in on . . . and the banks in Maine and Oklahoma. Shit, he *had* seen a lot of action.

It all added up to a lot of booty . . . and a lot of blood.

The aide approached the booth followed by the skinny waitress who was carrying a couple of beers plus a glass of bourbon on a tray. Vinny noticed the aide was holding a full glass of beer. The waitress put the drinks on the table and left without a word. The aide watched her go then disappeared somewhere behind Vinny.

Vinny sipped his beer, cautiously watching the Commander over the rim of his glass.

Watching and waiting.

He knew there had to be more to the meeting than a sociable drink with the brass. He hadn't been ordered to travel all the way to Baltimore just to buddy up with the Area Commander. He figured he was there to be briefed on a mission, though it surely had to be a helluva important one.

A mission with a difference.

In every other action he had led, orders had come down through the chain of command and he had been briefed by the Major. For the Area Commander to short-circuit that chain it had to be something real special.

Vinny lowered his beer and took a slug of bourbon, feeling the hot, smoky, satisfying sensation of the liquid hitting the soft palate at the back of his throat before sliding down his oesophagus to burst like a benevolent incendiary in his stomach. He took another slug.

A man moved swiftly and easily into the seat opposite, positioning himself alongside the Area Commander.

Still sipping his drink, Big Vinny started in shock at the man. For an instant he stared wide-eyed at the newcomer. Then he choked on his bourbon. Jesus Christ. He crashed his glass to the tabletop, the bourbon billowing up and spilling over its surface.

'Fer Chrissakes,' he choked, desperately trying to control his coughing.

The newcomer was the Commander in Chief.

Big Vinny stared dazedly at the man, tears brimming in his eyes and his heaving chest erupting in a series of short, sharp, dry coughs. Jeeesus, the man sat opposite him was the supreme fucking commander of the entire Manifest Militia. And he was choking fit to rip.

The Commander in Chief sat watching him, waiting patiently.

Vinny gazed stupidly back, his eyes protruding as his coughing spasm continued. He took in the the man's lined, grey face . . . almost as grey as his crew-cut hair; his high, prominent cheekbones and his jawline as stark as a destroyer's prow. The man was over sixty, yet he looked as tough as the roots of a savannah oak.

The veins on Vinny's thick red neck stood out like knotted ropes as he fought to bring his coughing fit under control. 'Goddam,' he snarled beneath his breath. He gazed at the Chief not knowing what to do. The man was in civilian clothes, yet Vinny was tempted to leap to his feet and salute.

'Take your time, Big Vinny,' the Chief said. His voice, though low, was stark and harsh – like gravel turning in a barrel. At last Vinny regained control of his lungs and was silent.

'You know who I am?' the Chief asked.

'Yessir,' Vinny barked softly.

'That's good, because I assuredly know who you are, Big Vinny. You're an exemplary soldier, and you have a magnificent reputation in the Militia. A well-earned reputation.'

'Thank you, sir.' Vinny coughed once more to clear his lungs. The choking fit had inured him to praise . . . the fiery red of his face and neck was now nothing to do with embarrassment and everything to do with his recent fit of coughing.

'That's why I'm here personally to talk to you. We have a mission for you.'

Big Vinny's eyes widened in anticipation.

'It's classified . . . priority one. You understand that?'

'Yessir.'

'It's outside the loop. It's something we have to get done and done quick.'

The Chief leaned back in the padded seat of the booth, his hands clasped loosely on the table in front of him. Vinny noticed strong fingers and short, square-cut nails. A few liver spots . . . though not many. The Chief was relaxed, completely in control. His composure communicated itself and Vinny felt some of his tension ebbing away. Calmer now, he risked a sip of his beer, his eyes fixed on the Chief's face.

'Your last operation, in Colombia: that was a very dangerous mission for us,' the Chief stated.

Vinny was surprised. He shook his head. 'Hell, it weren't

226

that dangerous, sir. There was a few more of them than us, but we had 'em down cold. I don't guess any of them ever knew what hit them.'

The Commander in Chief shook his head. 'No, no, I don't mean dangerous for you, Big Vinny. What the hell . . . an outstanding soldier like yourself, with a squad of well-trained men. Damn, I'd put you up against twice that number of stupid peons and still lay my life on you coming out on top. But,' he added hastily, 'don't misunderstand me. You and your men still put your asses on the line and we appreciate it.' Sitting next to the Chief the Area Commander nodded in agreement.

'But the real danger was to the Militia. To the Manifest Movement.'

Vinny frowned. 'It was? How?'

'Because if it became known it was the Militia who intercepted that dope shipment, it might expose the source of our intelligence. The authorities could begin putting two and two together and start coming up with some answers . . . right answers, for a change. Obviously we don't want that. We don't want the enemy to know what we know.'

'No sir.' Vinny's frown deepened. 'But if it was dangerous to the Movement . . .'

' . . . why the hell did we do it?' The Chief completed Vinny's question.

'Yeah. Sure. I mean . . . well . . . maybe it's not for me to ask . . .'

'No, no, it's a good question,' the Area Commander interjected.

The Chief nodded. 'The reason we did it was because the Militia needed the money.'

Vinny's face lightened a little, though his eyes remained puzzled. 'Oh, sure. I understand.'

'No, I don't think you do understand, Vinny. How could you?'

Vinny grunted. The Chief was right. He didn't understand.

'You see, we need the money because pretty well every penny we had . . . all the millions of dollars you and other commando units have liberated on behalf of the Movement . . . that's all gone.'

'Gone?' Vinny yelped. 'Whaddaya mean gone? You mean stolen?' He remembered himself. 'Sir,' he added.

'Yes, you could say it's been stolen,' the Chief conceded. He turned to the Area Commander. 'Wouldn't you say?'

'Right,' the Area Commander agreed. 'I'd say it's definitely been stolen.'

Vinny glanced from one to other in confusion.

'It's all related to what's been going on in the country over the past few weeks,' the Chief explained. His grating voice was low and modulated . . . as if he were talking to a child. 'You know, all this stuff about the financial crises . . . about organised crime taking over a lot of banks and Wall Street going into trauma. You been following any of that, Vinny?'

Big Vinny grunted. 'Yeah, sure, uh huh.'

Following it was maybe overstating the case. He hadn't exactly been riveted by the newscasts. Stories of the Mafia taking over half the American banking industry didn't surprise him . . . fucking wop goombahs got themselves everywhere. As for the crisis on Wall Street . . . well, it was great to hear the frigging Jews were *losing* money for once. Sure as shit made a change.

No, the truth was the headlines and newscasts had not seemed relevant to him. In common with most of the American people, news about the economy, high finance, and the rest of that shit left him cold. Anyway, what the fuck *was* the bond market?

'Well . . . not a lot I guess.' Vinny confessed. He shrugged and gave the Chief an apologetic smile.

The Chief appraised him. 'Okay, well, the details don't matter, but everything that's been going on . . . all the things you've been seeing on the news . . . have happened because a big, Third World bank with headquarters in Europe went down the tubes. It went bust. Now, our problem is, Vinny, that the Movement had all its money in that bank. And now the money is locked in . . . frozen. We can't get it out.'

Suddenly Big Vinny's eyes sharpened in understanding.

Now he could see where all this was going. Okay, so he wasn't so hot on high finance and Wall Street and all that crap. But that was all right: sharp, clever guys like the Commander in Chief and the Area Commander and the men on the Supreme Executive . . . the powerful, unknown men who were shaping his destiny . . . *they* understood all about that stuff. He didn't need to know about it. He knew what he was good at – and now he understood what they wanted him for.

In that instant he saw the light.

'Okay,' he cried, 'and you want me and the guys to hit the bank. Go get our money back.' He grinned wolfishly.

An Arctic smile moved across the Chief's face. 'If only it were that simple.'

'Hey, we done it before . . . sir.'

'Sure, I know you have Vinny. And if that was the way we could solve our problem, I'd be happy to have you to do it again. But this bank is in what's called liquidation. So, in a way, it's as if it doesn't exist . . . like there is no bank to hit. And there's no money either . . . no actual cash to grab. Once our money was deposited, it became a whole bunch of figures on account statements. We moved it around to various locations to keep it hidden by what's called wire transfer. Everything was done electronically. So it's not like you can lay your hands on anything.'

Vinny grunted. He didn't get it. Any of it. It sounded to him like the whole thing was done with smoke and mirrors.

'So what we have to do now is to start again,' the Area Commander interjected. 'Rebuild our finances. And although your action in Colombia was risky for the Movement, at least it was a good start.'

Vinny grunted again, and eased back into his seat. Money he didn't understand; military briefings he did.

So far the two men opposite had divided their time between blowing smoke up his ass and telling him stuff he didn't understand. There had to be more to his being there than that. He hadn't been ordered all the way to Baltimore to be briefed by the top brass about a problem he couldn't do anything about. They wanted him for *something*, that was for sure. He wondered what. Whatever, he guessed they would tell him in their own good time. He took a long sip of beer. 'How much did we lose in this bank?' he asked quietly.

The Chief glanced briefly at the Area Commander, who said: 'About a hundred and ninety million.

Vinny almost choked again. 'A hundred and ninety million?' he yelped.

'You can't fight a war without money, Vinny.' The Chief's voice was back to its usual stark, grating timbre. 'We need that kind of money for training and recruitment, for the weekend camps, for weapons. Especially for weapons,' he added.

'But we lost *a hundred and ninety million*? And we can't get any of it back? Jeeesus.'

'We can't get it back without going through the courts and having to prove the money is ours. Having to explain who we are,' the Chief told him. 'That's too risky.'

In one swift motion Vinny threw the rest of his bourbon down his throat. 'It seems to me,' he growled, 'this goddam bank going broke ain't done us no favours at all. The Movement is at risk every which way.'

The Chief nodded. 'It gets worse.'

'Yeah?' Vinny's small, hard eyes narrowed. He could feel the muscles at the back of his neck tightening. His head was beginning to hurt and he would dearly have liked another four fingers of Rebel Yell to ease the ache.

Banks and high finance were not the stuff of Big Vinny and the Chicashaw Commando. All he wanted was for his Commander in Chief to tell him which way to point his M-16 . . . tell him who he had to kill.

'The people who closed the bank are called liquidators,' the Chief explained. 'They have a special kind of operative called a forensic accountant whose job it is to trace the money which passed through the bank. This operative gets inside bank accounts and finds out where the money came from and where it's gone to. The forensic accountant also tracks back to find out who owns the account.'

The Chief paused and stared across the table, deep into Vinny's eyes. 'We can't let that happen, Vinny. It's bad enough to have lost all that money . . . but to have those accounts traced back to the Movement . . . hell, that could destroy us.'

'The authorities would want to know how we came by all that cash . . . what we wanted it for,' the Area Commander added.

'Everything we've worked for, everything we believe in . . . *you* believe in, would be threatened,' the Chief continued.

'And this forensic whatever,' Vinny growled: 'there's one dogging our trail right now?'

'Yes.'

'And you want me and the boys to stop him?'

The Chief bowed his head in acknowledgement. 'You catch on quick, Vinny. This person represents maximum danger to the Movement. And anyone who is a danger to our great cause has to be stopped. We need time to cover our tracks. It's priority one.'

Vinny was leaning across the table. He knew the importance of making sure he understood his orders. 'You're ordering me to stop the guy,' he repeated distinctly.

'Terminate, Vinny,' the Chief amended softly. 'Terminate. We need time to clear everything out, erect a few barriers between us and those damn accounts. A dead liquidator will buy us that time. And we also need to discourage anyone else from following up on the work already done. So you must terminate WEP.'

Vinny leaned back. The Chief was ordering him to butcher this accountant, to blow his guts all over the walls, to spill his blood in a messy, sickening massacre – to use whatever extreme prejudice was necessary to deter anyone else who might be tempted to follow up on his work. 'Sure,' he said calmly. 'So where do we find this guy?'

The Chief nodded at the Area Commander who produced a Kodachrome print from an inside pocket of his cotton blouson. He pushed it across the table.

Vinny gawked in surprise. The guy he had been ordered to hit was a woman.

And a real good-looking woman too, he decided. She looked like one of the anchors on the TV news shows. No, she was better than that . . . better looking than those stuck-up bitches . . . not as false. Her glossy hair looked natural . . . ungelled and unlacquered. It reminded Vinny of beech leaves in fall.

He looked closer at the picture. The woman's eyes were an interesting shade of blue and her mouth was wide and generous. She had been snapped on a sunny street somewhere: Vinny couldn't tell where. The clandestine photographer had caught the top half of her body.

'Great tits,' he remarked.

'It's not her tits we're worried about,' the Chief grated roughly. 'She is the target,' he tapped the print with his finger. 'She's the one you have to take out. At all costs. This woman is a threat to us all. If she finds what she's looking for, then . . .' he paused, ' . . . then we could lose everything. Do you understand?'

'Yessir. I understand, sir. You want me to turn her off,' he jerked his head at the coloured snapshot, 'with extreme prejudice. It'll be done, sir.'

'Good, I knew we could count on you, Big Vinny.' The Chief allowed him another icy smile. 'Okay, now here are her details.'

The Area Commander pushed a folded piece of paper at Vinny. 'Who she works for; where she lives: it's all in there,' he said in a low voice.

Vinny unfolded the paper and glanced at it. 'England!' he

yelped. 'The bitch is English?' He looked up. 'You want me to go to England?'

The Chief's icy smile grew teeth. 'We would have done, but our information is she's on her way over here. To America. She's coming to New York. So you can get it over with real quick and get down home straight after.'

'When?'

'Next few days. You'll be told where and when. She'll have a bodyguard, but only one. Either the New York police or the FBI. Kill the bodyguard too. Understand?'

'Yessir.'

The Chief stared across the table. 'I want this hit splashed all over, Vinny. You know what they say in the media: "if it bleeds it leads." Right? Well, we want enough blood to have this story leading all the networks. Lots of blood. That's showbusiness. Right?'

Vinny had already decided that for the hit all weapons would be loaded with splat softnose metal mix rounds. Two or three of those at short range and the bodies of the woman and her bodyguard would be so shredded as to be indistinguishable.

The Chief was still speaking. 'I figure that you plus a couple of men from the commando should be able to handle it. What do you think?'

Vinny considered. 'Two of them and only one armed,' he pondered in a low voice: 'yeah, three's more'an enough.'

'Okay, well you get back and choose your men and be ready on three-hour standby until further orders. Understood?'

'Yessir.'

Once more Vinny felt the compulsion to stand to attention and salute the Chief. Out of the corner of his eye he became aware of the presence of the young, tough-looking aide standing at his side, close to the edge of the table. The briefing with his Commander in Chief was at an end.

'Oh and Vinny,' the Chief continued, 'good luck.' He extended a hand across the table and Vinny shook it before shaking the Area Commander's hand once more. He scarcely blushed. Shaking hands with the top brass was becoming a habit.

'Remember, Vinny,' the Chief's harsh voice growled, 'this is a vital mission. More important than anything you've done before. For the sake of the Movement this woman has to be stopped. Don't forget it.'

'I won't, sir.' He drained his beer and stood up smartly. The aide stepped back a couple of paces. 'Thank you, sir. And don't worry, the Chicashaw Commando ain't about to let you down.'

The Chief looked solemnly up at him 'Yeah, I know that Big Vinny. That's why you were chosen. Good luck.'

Vinny's eyes lingered on his Chief's face for a moment then flipped to the picture of the good-looking woman lying on the table.

Shit, it may have been the most important mission he had been on since he had joined the Militia, but it looked like it was also going to be the easiest. If he and four other guys could take down almost a score of armed drug runners, what chance had one number-crunching bitch and her limp-dick bodyguard got?

She was as good as dead already.

He stared at the photograph for a moment longer before turning smartly. Followed by the aide, he marched rapidly away.

Chapter Twenty-Six

She was driven to Heathrow in an unmarked police car and seen onto the plane by Simon.

She smiled queasily when the young policeman announced he was not authorised to accompany her on the flight. As anxious as Timmison was to ensure her safety, his budget apparently did not run to flying a police officer across the Atlantic first class.

As it turned out she felt safe enough in the plane and slept for much of the way. Debbie had booked an afternoon flight which deposited her at Kennedy in the middle of the evening.

A young, olive-skinned woman with a good figure, well-chiselled features and deep, knowing eyes, was waiting for her on the air bridge. 'Miss Semmington?'

'Yes?'

The woman flashed a badge. 'Detective Morton, New York Police Department. I'm assigned to accompany you whilst you're in New York.'

Melissa felt the detective's eyes examining her. She smiled and proffered her hand. 'How do you do?'

Morton shook Melissa's hand briefly. 'Yeah, I'm doing okay. How're you doing? Was it a good flight?'

'Fine, thank you.'

Morton appraised her some more, then said, 'Okay, so you wanna come with me?'

She walked rapidly, leading Melissa along a deserted corridor, down a flight of stairs and out into immigration control where she had a rapid conversation with an immigration officer who took a long look at Melissa and a quick look at her passport. He waved her through.

After retrieving her case from the carousel, Melissa followed the detective to a battered Dodge Diplomat parked in a tow-away zone outside the busy terminal. A uniformed policeman was eyeing the car and its leather jacketed driver speculatively. Melissa dropped her case in the trunk and climbed into the back with Morton

The driver drove as fast as the traffic would allow, ferrying them north and west. Crossing Queensboro Bridge, Melissa saw the big, sooty orange ball of the carbon-monoxide sun dipping gracefully behind the skyscrapers of Central Park South. The skyline of mid-town Manhattan looked as if it was on fire.

The driver pulled the Dodge to a halt at Fifth and Sixty-first. Melissa got out and stared up through the gathering dusk at the high, imposing edifice of the Pierre. She turned, gazed across the busy traffic towards Central Park then smiled at Morton. 'I suppose you're used to all this?' she said above the roar of the traffic.

The detective shrugged. 'Yeah, I guess.'

'I love this town. I don't think I could ever get used to it.'

Morton gave her a sardonic look. 'If you did, this sure is the right side of town to get used to.'

They were shown up to Melissa's room, which was big, plushly furnished and overlooking Fifth Avenue. After Melissa tipped the bellhop, Morton said: 'I've got the room next door. There's an interconnecting door. Leave it unlocked.'

Melissa was impressed. 'New York City police have booked a room here? How long for?'

'For as long as you stay I guess.'

'That might be expensive.'

Morton allowed herself a tight smile. 'What the hell. We're billing everything to England. Some department in your government.'

'Really?' Melissa was intrigued. 'Which one?'

Morton laughed briefly. 'If I knew, I don't suppose I'd be authorised to tell you.'

Melissa laughed too. 'Shame. By the way, what's your Christian name?'

Morton stared at her and again Melissa felt the probing sensation of the detective's brown, perceptive eyes. 'Chauncey,' she said finally.

'Chauncey,' she repeated. 'Interesting name. Chauncey Morton,' Melissa articulated it slowly, nodding her head. 'It's a good name. Strong.'

'You think so, huh? So what's yours . . . your name?'

'Melissa,' she said with a smile. 'Please call me that.'

Morton shook her head. 'I can't. It's not department policy to get close to sitters.'

'Sitters?'

'People we gotta take care of . . . protect. Officers are not supposed to be on first-name terms. The department don't like us getting familiar. It could affect our judgement.'

Melissa smiled. 'They have the same policy at Scotland Yard but I've got my two guardian angels calling me Melissa. I hope you'll do the same. I hate being called Miss Semmington. It makes me think you're a tax inspector.'

Chauncey Morton laughed again. 'Okay. Melissa, if that's the way you want it. Fine by me. Now, I gotta check in.' She crossed the room and opened the interconnecting door. 'Don't forget to leave this unlocked,' she commanded.

As soon as she was gone, Melissa called Bob Briscoe's number. His answering machine switched in immediately. The message was typically New York. Brief and anonymous.

'Thanks for calling,' it said. 'Leave your name and number and time of calling and I'll get straight back to you.' The tone was precise and businesslike. It was Bob Briscoe's voice all right, but without the warmth.

'Bob,' she blurted excitedly, 'it's Melissa. It's gone nine and I've just got in. I'm staying at the Pierre.' She told the machine her room number. 'Call me as soon as you can. Please. I can't wait to see you.'

She replaced the receiver. A moment later she screwed up her eyes in embarrassment. 'Oh God,' she moaned softly. 'Damn, damn, damn.' The excitement in her voice had made her sound like a schoolgirl with a gigantic crush. 'Shit,' she said loudly. She might have tried to be a little less obvious in her eagerness to screw the man's brains out.

'Something wrong?' It was Chauncey, standing at the interconnecting door.

'What? Oh, no it's nothing really. I phoned someone and made myself sound like I was just into my first bra.'

'A man?'

'Yes.'

'Listen, Melissa, you wanna tell me if you're making any more calls? I have to know. You tell this man where you're staying?'

She felt herself blushing. 'Yes, I'm afraid I did. I was hoping he might call me.'

'You dating this guy?'

Melissa knew enough American to know what she meant. She shrugged. 'Just started. Once, as a matter of fact.'

'So he's a pretty fresh date and you told him where you're staying? Not a good idea.' Melissa's mouth turned down in contrition. 'And you figure on seeing him with that on your face?'

Before her flight she had covered the crusting incision on her cheek with a length of clear surgical tape. With the exception of the shock she had received glancing in the mirror of the aircraft's cramped toilet, she'd forgotten about it.

Instinctively, the fingers of her left hand flew to her cheekbone. She turned and surveyed the tape in the room's large, gilt-framed wall mirror.

She sighed. 'I'm afraid I have to. It's the only opportunity I'm going to get to see him. At least for a while.'

'Men usually don't like women with marks on their faces,' Chauncey observed dryly.

'Oh, he knows about it.' She ran her fingers lightly over the tape. 'If it hadn't been for Bob, I'd have looked a lot worse than this. He saved me. Without him I probably wouldn't be here.'

She felt the familiar tightening in her stomach as she recalled the attack. Seeing Chauncey's eyebrows raised she told her the story.

She was slightly mortified at Chauncey's reaction. 'Okay, well you had better give me what you've got on this guy,' she commented laconically. The detective seemed considerably underwhelmed at the account of her salvation at the hands of Bob Briscoe.

Melissa put it down to her profession. Tough New York cops had heard it all before . . . heard it all, seen it all, and done most of it. Nothing moved them, nothing surprised them. It was to be expected the story of her escape would leave Chauncey unimpressed. She retrieved a notepad from her bag and wrote down Briscoe's name and Manhattan number.

'This is all you have?'

Melissa reacted defensively. 'I told you, he's a new date. Anyway, why do you want to know about him? What's he done?'

Chauncey shrugged. 'I don't suppose he's done anything. But

the guy knows where you're staying. We'd better check him out. Just to be sure.' She half-turned towards her room then nodded at the tape on Melissa's cheek. 'You wanna let the air get to that. It'll heal faster. I'll see you tomorrow. Okay?'

When she had gone, Melissa peeled the tape away and examined the wound in the mirror. It seemed the way it was healing it was likely to leave a small scar.

Mournfully, she stared at her reflection in the mirror, studying her face, checking the eyes for anxiety. The eyes were all right, she decided, but the face was wan and drawn. She was tired . . . too tired to worry about how she looked. She turned from the mirror, undressed, took a long hot bath and crawled into bed. The phone didn't ring.

She slept well and called Hampshire early the next morning. Everything was fine and Jamie was in fine form, Astrid told her. And so was George. The two were inseparable: the puppy forever wagging its tail and peeing on the scullery floor. Astrid was doing her best to get it housetrained. The small dog was already part of the family. Liz, the policewoman, was staying in the guest bedroom and was having fun playing with Jamie. The dark blue Mondeo was in constant attendance close to the cottage driveway.

By the time she got off the phone Melissa was relaxed and happy and ready to face the day.

Chauncey joined her for breakfast in her room. 'So, when do we get to see this Imola Varese?' she asked.

'When I called from London she said she'd be happy to see me any time.'

Chauncey stared at her over the rim of her coffee cup. 'It's a helluva way to come just to talk to a secretary. What's to stop her changing her mind and refusing to see you?'

Melissa shrugged. 'Nothing. 'I can't *make* her see me. But secretaries are important in my business. Like untapped oil deposits. It's worth the money and effort to get them gushing.'

'Yeah? So what exactly is your business? What are you?'

'I'm a forensic accountant.' Chauncey's finely sculptured face remained deadpan and unimpressed. 'Right now my job is tracking down a few hundred billion dollars laundered through the Exchange Bank.'

'Hundred *billion?* Shit!' For once Chauncey was moved.

Melissa grinned at her. 'I don't normally get involved with

238

anything below double digit billions. Though I have to admit the Exchange Bank is the biggest job I've ever handled. Still, anything less than ten figures just doesn't mean very much.'

'Maybe not to you it doesn't,' Chauncey observed dourly. She frowned across the snow-white cloth draping the trolley table. 'So what's this Imola Varese done? Heisted a couple of million for herself?'

'No. She was secretary to a man called Vito Kunzman, an attorney here in New York. Kunzman was the primary link between the organised criminals backing the Exchange Bank and the bank itself. He was a kind of bank inspector.'

Chauncey nodded wisely. 'So this guy is likely to have the real skinny on the bank.'

'In more ways than one,' Melissa murmured.

'You said was. He's not around any more?'

'He disappeared before the bank was closed down. I'm pretty sure he also stole half a billion dollars and took it with him.'

'Half a billion. How the hell do you rip off half a billion?'

'If you know the system it's not that difficult. A few phone call . . . a few coded wire transfers.' She shrugged. 'It's clean, neat, no violence, no one gets shot . . . often no one gets caught. And if they do, it's . . .'

'Easy time. Sure. A couple of years in a low-security joint. Hell, the way to rob banks is with a computer. Definitely. Only dumbasses rob them with guns. But, if there's no violence, how come you got that?' Chauncey nodded at the slash on Melissa's cheek which she had left uncovered. 'And what am I doing here? Looking after you?'

'These people don't need violence to *launder* the money. But they'll use violence to *hang onto* it.' Melissa touched her left cheek. 'Anyone trying to track down and confiscate contaminated money flowing through the Exchange Bank is bound to make themselves an awful lot of enemies.'

Chauncey gazed at her cheek. 'Yeah. It figures.'

'People who launder billions of dollars don't care for people like me who are employed to track it down.'

'For that kinda money, you can see why,' Chauncey commented laconically. 'Anyway,' she fixed Melissa with a lopsided smile, 'what the hell are you doing chasing down half a billion – that's only nine digits.'

Melissa glanced around the expensively appointed room. 'I know, but times are hard.'

Chauncey chuckled.

'But this time it's more than the money,' she continued seriously. 'Kunzman was operating a number of codename accounts in the Exchange Bank. One of them was a locked box.'

'A what?'

'A locked-box account. Most codename accounts you can unpick, little by little and follow the transactions. Of course you need passwords once you're inside the account, but the computer boys are brilliant at decoding passwords. But a locked box -- well, that's different. First, you have to find it. The one Kunzman was operating was called the Austerlitz Account. So far we haven't found any trace of an account called Austerlitz in any branch of the Exchange Bank anywhere in the world.'

'So how do you know it exists?'

'We don't. Not absolutely. Not for certain. I was told about it, with a lot of other stuff, by a man who worked for the bank. Everything else he told me has checked out. And,' her voice suddenly caught in the back of her throat as if her pharynx was lined with Velcro, 'not long afterwards he and his wife and both his children were murdered. Shot dead.'

Chauncey's dark eyebrows raised a fraction. 'These people don't fool around. So you think he and his family got whacked because he told you about this Austerlitz thing.'

Melissa stared sombrely at Chauncey for a few seconds. 'I think it's possible.' Her voice was still hoarse. 'He gave me a list of Managers' Ledger Accounts, secret accounts which the bank's auditors hadn't been allowed to inspect. The thing is, we would have uncovered most of those ourselves. Sooner or later. But the Austerlitz Account . . . well, we might never have found out about that.'

Chauncey looked pensive. 'Yeah, they could have iced him because of that. Or, maybe it was a Mob hit. Your man and his family could have gotten hit as a warning to everyone else.'

Melissa nodded. 'I was told that happened inside the Exchange Bank. Still, I have a sense the Austerlitz Account is important.'

'You got a gut feeling?'

She grinned. 'Yes. Billions of dollars moving through the Exchange Bank have disappeared into thin air. Black holes. My feeling is that some of that money has gone into that account.'

She paused again and frowned. Something she had just said had just rung a bell. Her words resonated . . . someone, somewhere had recently said something similar. She screwed up her face. She couldn't think who or what.

'What's wrong?'

Chauncey's voice cut across her thoughts. She blinked, unscrewed her face and smiled blandly. 'Nothing. I was trying to remember something. It'll come to me.'

Chauncey grunted. 'And you think this secretary, Imola Varese, might know about the Austerlitz Account?'

Melissa smiled across the table. 'I think that's too much to hope for. But there's no doubt she'll know a lot about her ex-boss Kunzman . . . and whatever she knows might lead me to him.'

'Well,' Chauncey's eyes were suddenly playful, 'whatever she knows, you ain't going to find out about it sitting here.'

There were three of them, all big and dressed alike . . . brown, high-sided engineer boots, faded jeans, check shirts and light, cotton windcheaters. One of them, the youngest, wore a Dodgers cap. They were carrying roll bags. The biggest, who was very big, was at the front as they loped across the parking lot towards a brown, battered Mitsubishi Shogun.

Two men were seated in the front of the Shogun. The driver, with his elbow on the window sill, was smoking a cigar. The large man fronting the trio approached the driver's side of the vehicle. The driver stared at the man with a stony, malevolent gaze and blew smoke in his direction. 'What the fuck do you want?' he growled.

The big man's face was fixed. 'Mongoose,' he said simply.

'Mongoose,' the driver snarled, 'whaddaya mean Mongoose? What are you boy, sick in the head?'

'Mongoose,' the big man repeated in a monotone. 'You're Mongoose.'

'Yeah? Well, if I'm Mongoose then maybe you're Red Beach? Eh?'

The big man's face broke into a smile. 'Damn right. Against a deep green sea.'

'Yes,' the driver whooped. He and his companion leapt out of the vehicle and shook hands with the three men. 'Okay, get in,' the driver instructed when they had finished.

The three men piled into the back of the Shogun. The driver turned in his seat. 'You're Big Vinny Harold, right?' he inquired.

'Yeah, and this is my baby brother, Billy Bob, and this here is Carver Fylde.'

'I'm Stu, he's Chet.' The driver indicated his companion. 'You have a good flight?'

Vinny shrugged. 'Was okay. So,' his voice was suddenly incisive, 'what are our orders? Where're the weapons?'

'There's a steel box welded to the floor at the back. Here's the key. Inside is a holdall. In it are three disassembled M-16s, plus a twelve-gauge pump-action Ithaca. There's two twenty-round box clips per carbine and two eight-shot magazines for the shotgun.' The man grinned. 'Oughta be enough.'

'What's the load?'

'Softnose, metal mix.' Stu the driver grinned. 'You're sure gonna ruin someone's day.'

Vinny grunted. 'Okay, what's the orders?'

Stu passed him a scrap of paper. 'That's the name of a motel in Jersey City. You're to check in there . . . separate rooms . . . and wait. And take the weapons bag with you.'

Big Vinny gave him an Arctic look. 'Whaddaya think we are . . . stupid?'

'Hey, big guy, I'm only tellin' you what I was told to tell you.'

Vinny grunted. 'What are our orders?' he repeated.

'Go to the motel and stay there.'

'That's it?'

'That's it. The bitch you gotta hit is staying at some ritzy hotel over there.' Stu nodded at the windscreen of the Mitsubishi. The men in the rear peered.

Across the Hudson, a few miles distant, the skyline of Manhattan, glittering in the morning sun, soared like a diamond barbican.

Billy Bob gawped at the battlements of affluence. 'We gonna go there?' he asked excitedly. Big Vinny silenced him with a look.

'What protection she got?' he asked.

Stu shrugged. 'Another bitch . . . ball-breaker from the police department. They pack Glock semi-automatics. Seventeen rounds, nine-millimetre.'

'Shit, she ain't even gonna get time to draw it,' Carver Fylde growled.

242

Stu grinned briefly. 'Yeah. Two dames. One with a pop gun. Ain't much of a match for you guys. Not from what I hear anyway.'

'When do we hit them?'

Stu shrugged. 'I dunno. You're to go to the motel and wait for a call. The caller will be Sidewinder. Your code stays the same. Sidewinder will tell you where and when. Okay?'

'Sure.'

Stu nodded out of the window. 'Jersey City is that way. The motel is on route 501.' With a jerk he yanked the keys from the ignition and handed them over to Big Vinny. 'She's all yours. Okay, we're outa here.'

He and Chet opened their doors simultaneously and got out.

Big Vinny and Billy Bob alighted from the rear and climbed into the front seats. Stu leaned in the driver's window and shook Vinny's hand. 'Good luck,' he grinned maliciously. 'Not that I figure you're gonna need it. For the Chicashaw Commando this hit is a cinch.'

Chapter Twenty-Seven

Chauncey left her in the room with instructions to lock the door whilst she went to collect her car. Melissa punched out Imola Varese's number in Greenville and told her she was on her way. Afterwards she pressed the number for the hotel switchboard. There were no calls.

In accordance with Chauncey's instructions she took the service stairs two flights down, then rode the elevator to the street. A dusty, well-worn Buick Regal was waiting for her at the front of the hotel. Melissa slipped quickly into the passenger seat.

Chauncey turned the car onto Madison and went north to 79th where she headed west. Across the Park she got onto the Henry Hudson Freeway, joining the endless streams of fast-moving metal following the river north past Washington Heights. In Westchester County she switched to the State Throughway, which she left a few miles further north to turn onto Central Park Avenue.

The address in Greenville was just off the Avenue. It was a neat, brick and timber built two-storey house, in a line of neat, brick and timber two-storey houses. The gardens were well kept and filled with mature foliage. It was the kind of house, Chauncey murmured, that middle-ranking Scarsdale executives lived in.

Melissa asked her if she would mind waiting in the car. 'It's easier,' she said slightly apologetically, 'if the people I talk to don't think the police are involved. At least, not unless they refuse to talk to me.'

Chauncey's face clouded. 'No can do,' she said. 'I'm supposed to be protecting you.' She stared at Melissa across the car. 'I need to stay close to you. Really close.' Her voice was low and powerful.

The sudden penetrating intensity of the look caught Melissa

unawares. It disturbed her. She laughed nervously, feeling prickles of heat rising on her breasts beneath the cool silk of her blouse.

Chauncey's look evaporated and she smiled. Melissa wondered if the detective sensed her discomfort. Her tone was light. 'There's no need for this broad, Varese, to know I'm a cop. Why don't you introduce me as a colleague? I'll sit in a corner and keep my mouth shut.'

Melissa made a face. 'I like to work alone.' She glanced out of the car window. 'It should be safe enough here. It *looks* safe enough.'

'That's when you have to be most careful,' Chauncey growled. 'This woman knows you're coming to see her. That's gotta be a perfect opportunity for anyone who wants to . . .'

She saw Melissa's sudden look of fear. Reaching over, she laid her hand on Melissa's and squeezed it gently. 'Don't worry, it'll be okay. I'm here.' Her hand lingered a moment longer and the heat rash got hotter.

Melissa got out of the car, feeling the bright sunshine on her face. It was mid-morning and the temperature was already in the high seventies. Yet the air was cool in comparison to the heat of her body.

They started towards the house. Chauncey glanced at her and chuckled. 'So, these people you interview. If they refuse to talk to you . . . then you tell 'em they're gonna have to talk to the cops. Right?'

'Yes, something like that.'

'Does it work? Can you get them to open up?'

She nodded. 'Yes, usually. I tell them to give me what I want and I'll go away. That's what gets results in the end. Persistence.'

'Damn right.'

Mrs Imola Varese was a shock. And a disappointment. She was an affable, plump lady in her late fifties, of Italian extraction and with some evident, white-collar affluence. In Britain, Melissa thought, she would have been considered middle-class. She was delighted by Melissa and her English accent and made no sign of noticing the clear strip of plaster attached to Melissa's cheek.

She offered them coffee on the back porch overlooking her well-kept garden. The garden had a small pool.

She had worked as Mr Kunzman's secretary for a lot of years, she told them. Since the mid-sixties. But she gave up the job when her husband was taken ill. 'When was that?' Melissa asked.

'Oh, that was almost fifteen years ago,' Mrs Varese replied. Her husband had died and left her a good pension and she had decided not to return to work. No, she didn't see anything of Mr Kunzman now, she said, although he always sent her a card at Christmas.

Melissa asked what Kunzman had been like. Mrs Varese painted a picture of a quiet family man; well-mannered, if slightly distant, a competent lawyer and a good employer.

She inquired about the companies registered at the address in White Plains.

Mrs Varese confirmed that Kunzman's small suite of offices had been over a bank. Yes, she was aware he had made her an officer of a lot of the companies. They were only shell companies and he had assured her it was perfectly legal. No, she had no idea why Mr Kunzman had set the companies up, but as most of his work had been corporate it wasn't surprising, or unusual. He'd had a lot of dealings with corporations. And with banks, she added. All she had been required to do was to file the statutory returns of the companies.

Melissa talked about what had happened to the Exchange Bank.

Mrs Varese said she had no idea why her name might have been used as passwords in some of the bank's financial transactions. Certainly she had never used the Exchange Bank and she had absolutely no idea what could have happened to any missing half billion dollars. In her opinion that seemed an awful lot of money to lose.

Anyway, wasn't the Exchange Bank foreign? she inquired. Melissa said it was, whereupon Mrs Varese observed tartly that it wasn't surprising that the money had gone missing. She personally wouldn't even consider using a bank which wasn't one hundred per cent American. But, she prattled, wasn't the news terrible that so many banks had been infiltrated by gangsters? You didn't know who to trust these days. You didn't know who was the Government and who were crooks. It hadn't been like that when . . .

Melissa headed her off at the pass and switched her line of questioning back to Vito Kunzman. What exactly had been his work? she inquired.

Mrs Varese shrugged. It was difficult to say. Much of it, like all lawyers' work, had been confidential. To do with companies and money and tax and such. No, she couldn't remember the details now, it was too long ago.

But why, she inquired, was Melissa asking so many questions about Mr Kunzman?

Melissa explained that Kunzman had disappeared.

From the look on her face it was obvious his disappearance was news to Mrs Varese.

Melissa explained that, whilst the authorities were looking into Kunzman's disappearance, she needed answers to some questions about his connections with the Exchange Bank. She asked Mrs Varese what she remembered about Kunzman's work for the bank.

Mrs Varese said she could scarcely remember anything. All she knew was that he had started working with people in the bank soon after it had been set up in the early seventies and that his work had increased until it had taken up almost all his time. That was what had prompted him to move his offices to Manhattan. At about the same time her husband had been taken ill and she had left the firm.

She asked Melissa and the silent Chauncey if they would like more coffee. They said yes.

As Mrs Varese blathered happily about the old days, Melissa sipped her coffee and stared morosely at the flashing blue water of the pool and the radiant colours of the sunlit garden. Had her famous instinct deserted her? she wondered.

So far, Mrs Varese had been unable to tell her a thing about Kunzman and it was obvious she knew nothing about any missing half billion dollars. It was clear she was getting nowhere.

What was worse, her inability to elicit anything useful from Mrs Varese was being played out under the intent and watchful gaze of detective Chauncey Morton. Not that Chauncey's presence should have mattered, she told herself. Only it did, though why she couldn't quite work out. Whatever . . . the bottom line was – it looked like she had come a long way for nothing.

She took a slim file from her attaché case, opened it and placed it gently in Mrs Varese's ample lap. 'This is a list of passwords, Mrs Varese. They were used to prompt the movement of large amounts of money out of and into accounts in the Exchange Bank.'

Mrs Varese gave her a startled glance. Melissa smiled gently. 'Don't be alarmed. In themselves, passwords mean nothing. Lots of banks use them. What I want to know is . . . apart from your own names . . . do any other names here mean anything to you? Are there any names of people you know . . . any name that strikes you as different or out of the ordinary?'

Mrs Varese put on her spectacles and surveyed the list. She shook her head. 'No,' she said slowly. 'Except there's my first name and there's my married name, of course.' She jabbed at them with a stubby finger.

Suddenly, she exclaimed. 'Oh yes, look!'

Instantly, Melissa leaned forward in her seat. She noticed Chauncey doing the same.

Mrs Varese looked up and grinned at her. 'That was my name before I got married. See, Vergoli.'

'Is that significant, do you think?' Melissa asked eagerly.

The woman stared at her and shrugged. 'How would I know?'

Melissa checked her records. Vergoli was one of the passwords used to trigger seventy-five million out of the Exchange Bank's branch in Karachi. She stared at Mrs Varese blankly, trying to decide if the woman's maiden name held any other significance.

'Are there any other names you think might be important,' she queried. Her tone was harder.

Mrs Varese surveyed the list again then shook her head. 'No.'

Melissa felt the muscles at the back of her neck twisting in tension like steel rope. For God's sake, what a waste of bloody time, she thought. Mrs Varese had turned out to be a red herring. She could have stayed home with Jamie. 'I thought Vergoli was a place,' she snapped irritably.

'It is. It's also the name of my father's family.'

Melissa glanced peevishly at Chauncey. The detective's well-defined features might have been cast in stone. Her eyes were immobile . . . unreadable.

'I thought *all* of these were place names,' she went on bitterly.

Mrs Varese cast a cool eye down the list. 'I think most of them are. But then I guess they would be.'

'Would be?' It was Chauncey. Melissa shot her a thunderous look. The bloody woman had promised to keep quiet. Chauncey ignored the Gorgon glance. 'Why is that?'

Mrs Varese shrugged. 'Mr Kunzman travelled a lot. He knew many places. When I worked for him he had a big globe in his office. One of those old ones . . . you know . . . with yellow maps. I think it was quite valuable. He liked maps. And,' she paused and smiled, 'he was not what you might say . . . imaginative. If he needed these special code words he would have used the names of places and people he knew.'

Melissa retrieved the file off Mrs Varese's lap, closed it and deposited it in her attaché case. Her eye caught another file. It was the list of codenamed accounts Aziz had given her. She pulled it from the case. 'This is a list of account names,' she explained. 'They're codenames. I think most of these are places, too. But maybe not. Maybe some are names of people. Please take a look. Tell me if any of them mean anything to you.'

Mrs Varese took the manilla file and smiled at her. 'This business. Full of codenames and passwords . . . it seems very secretive.'

'The word is secure,' Melissa announced. Her tone was more abrupt than she had intended. She forced herself to smile. 'People like their money protected. A lot of banks use numbers and codes and passwords.'

Mrs Varese studied the file, turning the pages and running a finger down the names. 'No,' she said definitely. She closed the file. 'Nothing there means anything to me.' She passed the file back to Melissa

'I see.' Melissa's voice was heavy with disappointment. She put the file back in her attaché case.

'Except Austerlitz of course.'

'Pardon?'

'Austerlitz. Austerlitz was one of the words on your list. Someone has drawn a ring around it.'

'Yes,' Melissa said quickly, 'that was me.'

'Oh well, you know then.'

'Know, know what?' Her voice was feverish.

'That's where Mr Kunzman had his cabin. Perhaps he still has. He used to go there sometimes. For a rest. To get away from everything. Though,' she paused reflectively, 'sometimes he went there to work. If he had something important to do and wanted peace. I don't think anyone knew about the place. I don't think even his family knew.'

'Austerlitz? But isn't that somewhere in Europe?'

The woman smiled. 'Europe? No, no it's upstate. In the Catskills. Somewheres around there.'

Melissa could feel the excitement vibrating in her blood. The hairs on the back of her neck were lifting as if they had a life of their own. 'No one knew about this place, you say?'

'No.'

'Then how did you know about it?' It was Chauncey again. A quiet authoritative voice. Not pushy, just determined.

'Oh, Mr Kunzman had me take care of it. Pay the utilities, fix for any repairs and such. I took care of everything. From home. He didn't want any record of it kept in the office. When I left he took everything over. But . . . that was a long time ago. Maybe he doesn't have the place any more.'

'Utilities,' Chauncey repeated. 'So you paid the phone bill.'

Mrs Varese shook her head. 'No, there was no phone. I told you, Mr Kunzman went there to get some peace.'

Melissa was almost afraid to ask her next question. 'Can you remember the address?'

The short, plump woman frowned. 'No, I can't recall it. Not now.'

'Is Austerlitz a very big place?'

She shrugged 'I don't know. I've never been there. I did everything by phone. But wait,' she paused, 'I may have some old utility bills.' She smiled. 'I'm afraid I don't throw much away.'

Melissa shot a triumphant glance at Chauncey as Mrs Varese eased herself out of her chair. 'Secretaries rarely do,' she said softly. The detective gave her a quiet smile.

Mrs Varese was away a few minutes, returning with a yellowing power company bill. Melissa had to prevent herself from snatching it out of her hand.

The address in Austerlitz was on the bill.

'Great,' Melissa exclaimed loudly. 'Fantastic.'

They had said thank you and goodbye to Mrs Varese and were walking back to the car. 'Bloody marvellous.'

Chauncey nodded. 'Yeah, it's pretty good. If no one knows about the place, it's possible this guy Kunzman could he hiding there.'

'Absolutely. See, I told you secretaries know a lot of secrets.'

'Sure. You were right.' They reached the car and Chauncey smiled at Melissa across the roof. 'Though it was looking a tad iffy for a while back there. You looked pretty pissed off when the old lady wasn't coming across.'

'Me? Pissed off? Not at all.' Melissa gave her an innocent smile and Chauncey laughed loudly. 'Where is this place,

Austerlitz?' she asked as she got into the car.

Chauncey shrugged and gunned the engine. 'Search me. I've never heard of it. Upstate somewhere.'

'Is it far? Could we go now?' Her voice was filled with excitement.

Chauncey shot her a dark glance as she swung the car onto the Avenue. 'That isn't a very good idea.'

'Why not?'

'Because if Kunzman *is* there, you don't know who else might be there with him. Looking after him. You wouldn't know what you're walking into. These guys play for keeps Melissa. You know that.'

Her face darkened. 'So what should we do then?'

Chauncey was silent for a while, the car filled with the humming of tyres on asphalt. 'Well, you can't ask the State Troopers to turn up at Austerlitz and arrest the guy. As far as we know he isn't wanted by any police force. Though maybe the Feds might want to talk to him. I guess the best thing is to contact your boss in England. The guy seems to have a lot of pull over here. See what he can do to line you up some extra protection. Maybe get a couple of Fibbies to go up there with you.'

'What about you?'

Chauncey pulled a face. 'Upstate is outside my jurisdiction. The NYPD can't accompany you up there. The guys in Loudonville are pretty protective about their territory. That'll be a job for the State police.'

'Oh.' For some unaccountable reason, Melissa felt disappointed.

'But,' Chauncey continued, 'you could ask your boss to swing me a section seventy-two. That's an inter-jurisdiction permit. It would allow me to accompany you upstate. To Austerlitz. A section seventy-two would mean we can stay together.'

For an instant Chauncey's expression flickered with the same intensity as before. Then she smiled, and went back to concentrating on her driving.

Melissa bought a New York State map from the kiosk in the lobby of the Pierre. Back in her room she and Chauncey pored over it until they found Austerlitz. 'Yeah,' the detective commented dryly, 'just inside the State line. Maybe four hours' drive up the Taconic. That's bear country all right. You're gonna need the State Troopers.'

Melissa put a call through to Nigel Hawick to tell him what she had discovered. She was excited. Afterwards she called Steven Timmison. She told him about the cabin in Austerlitz and asked if he could arrange a section seventy-two for Detective Chauncey Morton.

His clipped tones, made eerie by the echoes of deep space, told her it would be done immediately.

The phone warbled an hour later. Melissa, calmly watched by Chauncey, leapt at it. The morning's success had electrified her. Now there was just one final thing to make her day complete. A call from Bob Briscoe.

It took her a few moments to recognise the voice. It was Sam Barber.

'Sam,' she said in surprise, 'how did you know I was here?'

She heard him chuckle. 'The Bureau got a call from some guy in England who seems to have a lot of pull hereabouts. He told us about what you'd found upstate. Luckily I was in Washington for some meetings and I got to hear about it. I've switched my schedule. I'm coming to New York this afternoon. I'll see you in a couple of hours.'

A few minutes later the phone warbled again. Melissa dived across the bed to take the call. It was for Chauncey. She handed her the handset with ill-concealed disappointment.

Chauncey was wanted at her precinct. A bemused lieutenant had been instructed to issue a section seventy-two to allow her to accompany her sitter upstate. The request for the seventy-two had come from England and was endorsed by the FBI. The irate lieutenant wanted Chauncey to explain exactly what the frigging hell was going on.

'I gotta go and sort this out,' Chauncey explained. She looked bothered. 'I'm gonna have to leave you here. On your own. We don't have anyone else to cover you. But you should be okay, so long as you stay put in the room and don't answer the door to anyone. I mean anyone. You got it?'

'Yes, I understand,' Melissa assured her. She was still euphoric from the morning's discovery.

'Good girl.' Chauncey grasped Melissa's forearm lightly and squeezed it. It was a warm, reassuring gesture. 'Okay, lock the door behind me.'

She left the room.

Chapter Twenty-Eight

She came to with a start. Something had woken her.

She stared up at the ceiling. She had lain down on the big bed for a rest . . . it seemed only a few seconds ago. She blinked. Damn, she must have dozed off. Now something had woken her.

A strange noise.

There it was again. It took her another second to realise it was the phone. The muted, intermittent warbling filled the room. She stretched out and picked it up wearily.

'Hello,' she mumbled

'Melissa? Is that you?' It was Bob Briscoe.

She sat up. 'Bob?' Instantly her voice was melodious with delight. 'You got my message?'

'Yeah, I just checked in with my machine.'

'Checked in? Why, where are you?'

'New Orleans.'

Her heart dropped. 'When are you coming back?'

'Not until tomorrow, I'm afraid. But I can make it back early. We could meet for lunch.'

Her heart dropped further. 'I have to go out of town tomorrow.'

'Oh, okay. Well, where're you going? We can maybe meet for lunch there.'

'I don't think that will be possible. I'm going upstate. Somewhere near Albany.'

'Albany? Okay, I guess I can get a flight there.'

'No, I can't see you for lunch. I'll be too busy. But I'll be back in New York by evening.'

'You will? Well, that's fine. Okay, as soon as I get in I'll leave a message at your hotel. You call me as soon as you get back. Okay?'

She told him she would and said goodbye. She caught sight

of herself in the mirror. Her smile was angelic.

Sometime afterwards Chauncey tapped on the door. Melissa let her in. She decided to keep quiet about Briscoe's call.

Chauncey apologised for being away so long. She'd a few things to take care of, she said enigmatically. She looked quietly pleased with herself. She had placated her irate lieutenant and sorted out the paperwork concerning the section seventy-two. She would definitely be accompanying Melissa to Austerlitz. She said it with a broad smile. 'So that's okay, huh?' She reached out and touched Melissa's arm.

There was a knock at the door. Both their heads jerked in the direction of the sound. It came again.

Rap, rap rap. A strong, assertive knuckling.

'Stay there,' Chauncey ordered. She moved swiftly, unbuttoning her linen jacket as she crossed the room. For the first time Melissa saw the holstered automatic at the belt of her skirt.

She stood close to one side of the doorframe, close to the door. 'Who is it?' she demanded.

The answer was muffled. 'Sam Barber, FBI.'

'You got any proof of that?' Chauncey called.

'I have if you open the goddam door.'

'Slip your ID under the door.'

'Shit, I'm not slipping anything under the door,' the muffled voice announced irately. 'My guess is you're Detective Chauncey Morton. If you are, then a couple of hours ago I recommended a section seventy-two for you. Now . . . open this damn door.'

With a swift glance at Melissa, Chauncey unchained and opened the door to reveal the tall, grey-haired special agent. He stepped into the room and scowled at Chauncey. 'Where's the ID?' she demanded.

'It's all right, Chauncey,' Melissa called from across the room. 'It's Sam. I know him.'

Barber crossed the room and shook her hand. 'It's good to see you again, Melissa,' he said warmly. His steely blue eyes appraised the tape on her cheek. 'You get that working on the Exchange Bank?' he asked quietly.

She nodded. 'I'm afraid so.' She told him briefly about the attack in London and the two dead men.

'Well I guarantee it won't happen here. Nobody's going to get near you. Not while you're in America.'

'Damn right,' Chauncey murmured behind him.

Melissa introduced Barber to the detective and they shook hands, eyeballing each other professionally. Barber gave Melissa another smile as she invited him to sit down in one of the room's small easy chairs. Chauncey sat in the other one as Melissa hitched herself onto the edge of the bed.

'Apparently the cabin is some way back in the hills, close to this place Austerlitz,' he began. 'At first the State Police weren't particularly helpful. They said if an official visit had to be made, then they were the ones to make it. By themselves. They didn't see any reason to provide protection to an English forensic accountant chasing money missing from a bunch of big city banks.'

Chauncey shook her head. 'Bunch of shit kickers,' she said quietly.

Barber smiled at her. 'Since then they've had a call from Washington. From an office that had gotten a call from London. Now they've changed their tune. They say they're happy to cooperate with the Bureau and the Bank of England and *even* the NYPD.' Chauncey snorted. 'They've even agreed your section seventy-two,' he went on playfully.

She stared stony-faced at Barber. Slowly she allowed a smile to creep over her features. 'Yeah, okay. So what happens now?'

'I'm flying to Albany in a couple of hours. Meanwhile the State Troopers are going to put the cabin under surveillance. If the place checks out . . . if there's no one there . . . or . . . if we get *real* lucky and it looks like this guy Kunzman is there on his own, without protection, I'll call. You two can fly up first thing tomorrow. Or drive. It's a straight run three, maybe four, hours. We'll take him quietly. No fuss, no hassle. We won't hit the place until you arrive.' He fixed Melissa with a look. 'Okay?'

She glanced inquiringly at Chauncey who nodded. 'Yeah, that sounds okay,' she acknowledged.

'Good.' Barber stood up to go.

Melissa looked up in surprise. 'Oh, do you have to go straight away? Wouldn't you like to stay for some tea? I can ring down.'

Barber looked down at her and chuckled. 'Jeez, you English. Everything stops for tea.' His smile broadened. 'Sure. Why the hell not? I've got time.'

When he had gone, Melissa phoned home. Afterwards she went into the bathroom and carefully peeled the tape off her

255

cheek. The crusting had gone, leaving a thin purple line. She gazed at it for a while then turned from the mirror.

She told Chauncey she was going to take a nap and slept solidly for more than an hour. Later she showered and washed her hair and put on a favourite kaftan; a swirling mass of soft blues and greens which contrasted perfectly with the deep tones of her hair.

She called room service and ordered a large malt. She was feeling good . . . refreshed and satisfied. It was probably too much to hope that Kunzman would be at the cabin, but at least, she thought, swirling the golden liquid in the heavy crystal glass, if she hadn't tracked *him* down, she was pretty sure she had tracked down his lair.

She was looking forward to tomorrow. She had a notion the search of the cabin would be rewarding.

Chauncey joined her in her room and she ordered dinner for both of them. She asked for a bottle of good Pouilly-Fuissé to be sent up. 'The bank's creditors can afford it,' she told Chauncey exultantly. 'We're on the way to finding half a billion of their money.'

'Sure, if you say so.'

Over dinner Chauncey told her something about herself. Her father's parents had escaped from the Ukraine at the end of the Second World War and managed somehow to make their way to America. The family name then had been Moracheveski which Chauncey's grandfather had transmuted into the easily pronounceable, all-American name of Morton.

Her father had worked for the City. She was the first in the family, she told Melissa, to go into law enforcement. Her mother's people were from Armenia.

After the meal Melissa sent down for another couple of malts. She was feeling expansive. She flopped into one of the easy chairs and looked at the dappled patterns on the walls made by the crimson shafts of the setting sun streaming through the big windows.

When the drinks arrived Chauncey poured half of hers into Melissa's glass. 'I gotta be careful,' she said. 'I'm supposed to be on duty. Looking after you.'

Melissa sighed contentedly. 'That's nice. Someone looking after me. It makes a change.'

'You don't have a lot of guys lining up to take care of you?'

Chauncey inquired with a faint incredulity.

She shook her head. 'This man, here in New York. He's the first date I've had in more than a year. The first man I've slept with since . . .' she paused, screwing up her face '. . . God knows. I can't remember.' She caught the look on Chauncey's face. 'It's true.'

'How come?' Chauncey asked quietly.

Melissa shrugged. 'I dunno. I suppose it's because I'm all work and no play. I'm dull . . . boring. And the men who do get interested, well, when they find out about Jamie . . .' she shrugged again '. . . they disappear. Very rapidly.'

'Why?'

'My son has Down's Syndrome.'

'I'm sorry.'

'Nothing to be sorry about, really. He's an exceptionally happy little boy.'

'What about his father? What happened to him?'

'He's become rich and successful, that's what happened to him. He doesn't even acknowledge he has a son.'

'Sounds a pretty shitty kind of guy.'

'A complete bastard. I just can't believe I was in love with him. He's a barrister, a QC.'

'A what?'

'A Queen's Counsel. A top lawyer. He's become quite famous . . . often in the papers, sometimes even on television. I expect they'll make him a judge in a few years.'

Chauncey smiled sardonically. 'At least you can hit him for a whole heap of alimony.'

Melissa shook her head. 'I've never taken a penny off him. We weren't married and even if we had been, well, I'd rather raise my son by myself. I've done okay so far.'

Chauncey watched her take a large gulp of whisky. 'How old is he?'

'Jamie?'

'Yes.'

'Five.' She shook her head, wondering at the passing of the years. 'Five years,' she repeated softly. She gazed at Chauncey in the chair opposite. 'Jamie's father and I met eight years ago. I suppose we'd been together about eighteen months when I found out I was pregnant. It was an accident, but after I'd got over the shock, I was delighted. I mean, we'd talked about marriage but – you know how it is – we hadn't got around to it. Too busy I suppose. Anyway, I thought the baby would seal it. Jamie's father would be as happy as me and we'd get married and . . .'

Her voice tailed off, and for a while she gazed sightlessly over Chauncey's shoulder at the peculiar pattern of her capricious history. It was like shining a light on the wake of a boat at night.

'And?'

She came to with a small snap of her head. 'Jamie's father was adamant. He didn't want any baby. He said he didn't mind getting married, but a baby . . . that was something else. A baby would hold up our careers. He said I should get rid of it.'

She paused, and Chauncey watched a cold, savage expression cross her face. 'I wasn't going to get rid of my baby. So I got rid of him instead. The bastard.'

She took another gulp of whisky. 'The thing is, sometimes when I look at Jamie . . . when I think how it might be for him when he's older . . . *if* he gets older . . . I wonder if his father . . .' The words turned to acid at the back of her throat and her voice tailed off. Tears welled in her eyes.

' . . . if his father was right?' Chauncey had got her drift. She shook her head. 'No,' she intoned softly, 'he wasn't right. He was wrong. And for the wrong reason. Which makes him a two-time loser. And a selfish shit. Like a lot of guys.'

Melissa smiled gratefully at her, sniffed and dabbed her eyes with a small handkerchief. 'Yes,' she said more resolutely. 'But Jamie is growing up without a father and I wish that wasn't so. It would be so nice to find someone.'

'And in the meantime?'

She smiled wanly. 'In the meantime I think it would be good to have a few more dates.'

'Like with this guy in New York? Robert Briscoe?'

She nodded. 'He's made me realise how sick I am of celibacy. It's not all it's cracked up to be.' Chauncey laughed. 'I'd like to see a lot more of him. Maybe other men too. The thing is . . . I need to get on with it. I'm not getting any younger. The mileage is starting to show.'

'You look pretty good to me.'

Melissa stood up. Far beyond the park, a thin incandescent band of vanilla and pink, like a squashed slab of ice cream, was stretched across the top of a darkening sky. Shadows of dusk,

258

like spectres from the twilight zone, were rising out of the street below. The room was gloomy. She moved about, switching on sidelights and bathing the room in a subtle, golden glow.

She caught her reflection in the big, gilt-framed mirror and stopped, putting her fingers lightly to the thin, purplish mark on her cheek. 'This doesn't help,' she said dolefully. 'I think it's going to scar.'

She stared at her reflection, watching Chauncey move into the frame of the mirror and stand close behind her. She turned and gave her a rueful smile. 'Well, there's one consolation. I've been promised free plastic surgery if it does scar.'

Chauncey raised her hand and gently touched the mark with the tips of her fingers. Melissa quivered. For some curious reason a frisson shimmered through her body.

'You don't want to do that,' she said softly. Her eyes moved back and forth between Melissa's and the mark on her cheekbone. 'The colour will fade. Then it'll be no more than a thin, white line. Leave it. It'll give your face character.'

Silkily she slid her fingers down Melissa's cheek and along her jawbone. 'More character,' she whispered, staring intently into Melissa's widening pupils. Delicately she pulled her face towards her own. Melissa was powerless, her legs like straws, her insides a mass of warm, quivering jelly.

Slowly, carefully, Chauncey put her lips on Melissa's.

Her kiss was sweet and sensuous, full of subtle hunger and gigantic passion. Melissa could feel Chauncey's tongue, warm and firm and tasting a little of good malt whisky, flicking exquisitely along her own. She was like a butterfly, pinned by strange, unexpected sensations. They stared at each as they kissed, Melissa wide-eyed and shocked, Chauncey intense and deliberate.

Chauncey's right hand slipped to her breast. Gently she began to tease Melissa's nipple through the material of her kaftan. Her other hand, moving slowly and deliciously along the outside of her thigh, pressed delicately on her hip bone before moving down and across . . .

'*Ohhhhhhhhhhh.*'

Despite herself, despite her shock and disorientation, Melissa could not suppress a long, soft groan. She was aroused, could feel herself getting wet, could feel her whole body trembling at the thrilling touch . . . the thrilling, illicit touch . . . of this strangely attractive woman.

Delicately, Chauncey drew her lips away, though her hands remained where they were, teasing and caressing . . . melting Melissa's flesh.

Melissa leaned back against the mirror, gasping for air. Treasonable blood pounded in her head. She could scarcely bear the pleasure that Chauncey's fingertips were bringing to her body.

'We can't do this,' she groaned.

The wet place between her legs was buzzing with a wonderful sensation, so acute it was almost painful. She needed to hold herself – there – to ease the vibration. Or was it Chauncey she wanted to hold her? Chauncey to hold her and to . . .

'No,' she gasped, 'we can't do this. It isn't right.'

Chauncey's fingers kept up their wonderful work. 'Who says it isn't right?' Her voice was low and husky . . . heavy with passion. 'You decide what's right for your body. You did it when you had your son. You decided that's what you wanted. It was right for you. If you want this . . . then this is right. And you do want it . . . don't you? Tell me you want it,' she growled. Her left hand glided across the front of Melissa's kaftan and her fingers brushed that hot, throbbing secret place in her body which had become the centre of her soul.

'*Ohhhhhhhhhhhhh,*' she moaned.

She couldn't help herself. It was a long, loud moan of wanting . . . of not wanting . . . an entreaty for mercy.

'*Ohhhhhhhhhh,*' she moaned again.

Then the room was filled with another noise.

A familiar sound which came to Melissa through a thick fog of physical longing. There it was again. Chauncey had heard it too. She looked angry. Her fingers stopped their teasing. 'Shit,' she hissed. Melissa stared at her stupidly. Again the sound.

It was the phone.

It warbled once more.

'I have to answer it,' Melissa panted.

'Yeah, I know.' Chauncey's words belied her expression. Her face was stamped with the pain of frustration and sudden denial.

Awkwardly Melissa stumbled past her and tottered across the room to the phone. She picked it up. 'Hello,' she mumbled.

'Melissa?' It was Sam Barber.

'Oh, hello, Sam.'

'Melissa, you okay?'

'Yes, yes, I'm fine.' Her voice was strained.

'You don't sound okay.'

'I'm fine.' She took a deep breath and did her best to gather her composure. 'I was resting on the bed.'

'Hey, I'm sorry. But I got good news. The best. The local cops have had the cabin in Austerlitz under observation all afternoon. And guess what. There's someone living there. One guy . . . early sixties. They got some pictures. They're long-range and a bit blurry but there's no doubt who it is. It's Vito Kunzman. We've found Kunzman.'

Chapter Twenty-Nine

Big Vinny lay on the bed, waiting. The motel room was dark, the television screen blank and silent. From the outside it looked as if the place was empty.

Earlier he had inspected the contents of the sports bag, entranced by the beauty of the weapons . . . assembling them; examining them minutely; checking the action and then, slowly and lovingly, taking them apart and replacing them in the bag.

Now there was nothing to do but wait.

Through the darkness he could hear the soft whooshing of traffic on route 501. He stared up at the ceiling and thought of Nam.

Not that he ever stopped thinking about Nam.

Not for long anyway. It was the country of his mind.

But at times like this, in the dark and the quiet, in what could have been called peace, the noises dinned unceasingly inside his head . . . the deafening whomping of the choppers, the fatal whoosh of incoming fire and the symphonic *bap, bap, bap* of countless assault rifles.

There on the bed he could smell the sweet, dead smell of the jungle and the unmistakable gut-rushing odour of corpses in open graves . . . could see in the darkness the big, bursting orange balls of napalm.

And he could hear the voices. Always, below the noise of war he heard the voices. Men . . . howling and screaming and crying and coughing blood. Men. Theirs . . . ours . . . he never knew. What the fuck did it matter anyway? he thought. The language of death was the same everywhere. For the first and only time men understood each other.

When they died.

Then they all spoke the same language.

Drrrrriiiing.

He started at the sudden trilling of the phone. His mind slipped the horror of Vietnam and homed in on his here and now. The phone trilled again. He stared at the outline of the instrument in the darkness. Goddam motel was so tacky they hadn't even gotten themselves modern phones.

He sat up on the edge of the bed, moving in one swift, disciplined movement. The phone was on the bedside table. He let it trill once more then stood up. He took a deep breath and lifted it.

The voice was not one he recognised. It was clear and precise and used to giving orders. That much he could tell. 'Who is this?' inquired the voice.

'This ain't nobody,' Big Vinny growled. 'Who is *this*?'

'This is Sidewinder. Who is this?'

'Beach Red,' Vinny responded, his tone softening.

'And?'

'Against a deep, green sea.'

'The target is travelling up-country tomorrow,' the voice intoned immediately. 'With one female escort. The general location is a place called Austerlitz, approximately twenty miles east of Albany. I have a map reference.'

A pencil and paper were on the bedside table. 'Go ahead.' Vinny copied the reference.

'Dispatch will be easier outside the city. It should happen when the target reaches the precise location.'

'The precise location,' Vinny repeated. 'Which is where?'

'Unknown at this time. It's a cabin somewhere back in the hills. You'll know when we know.'

Vinny grunted. 'How is the target travelling?'

'Also unknown. You'll be told.'

'Okay.'

'There's one more thing. It's possible there will now be *two* targets.'

'Two?'

'Affirmative. The second is a white male, early sixties, five feet ten, weighing close to two hundred pounds. His name is Kunzman. Vito Kunzman. Our information is that he may be located at the cabin. If so, it is essential he is also dispatched. Absolutely essential. Do you understand?'

'Yeah, I got it.'

'The priorities are the man and the woman. Dispatch the

263

protectors as necessary but get the man and woman.'

'Protectors?' Vinny queried. 'We was told there was only one.'

'There may be more when you get to the cabin.'

'How many more?'

'Likely just one. One more.'

'Carrying?'

'Sidearms only.' The caller paused, then continued rapidly: 'You are to remain on immediate standby. The next call will be final orders. When we have the location of the cabin.' The phone went dead.

Big Vinny replaced the receiver, switched on the bedside light and checked the reference on his AAA map. The location was in the western foothills of the Taconic Range, close to the Massachusetts state line, between the Catskills and the Berkshires. The map delineated it as well-wooded and hilly.

A tight, wolfish smile crossed his face. It looked like good killing country. Much better than the city. He had never been happy about wasting the woman in the city. It wasn't his natural hunting ground . . . not a place he knew or understood. The city was another jungle.

He turned off the light and lay back down on the creaking bed, putting his hands behind his head and staring once more at the darkened ceiling.

The picture was different now. Things had changed. But not by much, he reflected. Now there were two targets. Two sitting ducks. Along with two protectors. In a rural terrain.

Rural terrain suited the Chicashaw Commando.

It would be a turkey shoot.

It took her a few moments to understand what he was telling her.

'What? Are you sure?' she mumbled.

'Sure I'm sure.' Barber's voice was animated. 'The guy is very cautious, doesn't go out of the cabin, scarcely goes close to the windows. But the police photographer got one long-lens shot of him through a window. It's Kunzman. Definitely.'

She tried hard to comprehend what the FBI man was telling her. Like her body, her brain seemed to have become a trembling blob of jelly.

'Hey, Melissa, you there?'

'Yes, I'm here, Sam. Listen, can you just hang on a moment?'

'Sure.'

She put the phone down and walked shakily towards the bathroom. Chauncey had turned her back and was staring through the darkened windows at the lights of Manhattan.

The bathroom's pink and pale avocado tiles were cool. She leaned against them for a few seconds, seeking desperately to steady herself . . . to get her body and brain under control. Afterwards she ran the cold tap and splashed water on her face. Slowly she stepped out of the bathroom and moved cautiously and deliberately to the phone.

'I'm sorry to have kept you waiting, Sam.' Her voice was more incisive. 'So now you've found Kunzman, what do we do?'

'Right now we're fixing for you and Detective Morton to fly up. The first flight out tomorrow is at seven thirty. Turn up at the United Desk at Newark no later than seven. I won't make a move until you get here.'

'What about the local police?'

'Kunzman isn't someone they're interested in. They're happy to cooperate with the Bureau.'

'And you're prepared to wait until I get there?'

'Sure. You know the questions to ask, Melissa. We surprise him, he may give you a few useful answers before he thinks to start screaming for his attorney.'

'He *is* an attorney.'

'Yeah, but we get the jump on him and the surprise may shake a few things loose. You talk his language Melissa. You start talking funds flows and asset redeployment and all the rest of it and he could open up. No. We'll wait until you get here.'

'Sam, that's great. Thanks.'

'Okay. See you tomorrow.'

She replaced the receiver and turned to Chauncey. 'Did you hear that? Kunzman is at the cabin. He's actually there.'

Chauncey turned from the window. 'Yeah, that's good news,' she said. Her voice was flat. She didn't make it sound like good news.

Melissa stared at her across the room. There was a long silence. 'Look,' she began, 'I'm . . . I'm sorry about what happened just now. It was my fault.'

Chauncey raised her eyebrows. 'Fault'? she queried softly. 'Whaddaya mean fault? What's fault got to do with anything?

Nobody did anything wrong here, Melissa. What we did wasn't because of some defect in our character.'

'Well . . . yes . . . all right . . .' she stumbled. 'But maybe you thought I was . . .' She stopped. 'Oh, I don't know. I'm sorry. All I'm saying is that it was probably my fault.'

Chauncey moved towards her across the room. Almost involuntarily Melissa eased back. Chauncey stopped. 'We did what we did because we wanted to,' she said boldly. 'We had the hots for each other. What's wrong with that?'

'Well . . . eh . . . I don't really know . . .' Melissa could hear herself. She was almost inarticulate. Christ, she wished she wasn't so damn English . . . so painfully polite and hung up.

'You ever done it with a woman?' Chauncey asked. A half-smile played around her lips.

'No, no. Well, no not really. At school there was this girl and we . . .'

Chauncey chuckled. 'Yeah, there's always a girl at school. And did you like it . . . what you did together? This schoolgirl and you?'

Melissa felt herself blushing as she remembered what they had done. It had been one of her first sexual encounters. It had been thrilling. Wild and exciting and illicit. But then, so also had stealing apples from a nearby orchard. And she had grown out of stealing apples.

Chauncey watched her face colouring up. 'You liked it, eh? It's still a good memory.'

'Yes, I do remember it. Fondly as it happens. And I don't feel guilty. I suppose we were young and in a way, quite innocent. But the thing is, I don't think I'm lesbian.'

Again Chauncey raised her eyebrows. 'Nor am I.'

'You're not?' Melissa was confused.

'Not if by lesbian you mean I do it exclusively with women. Hell, no. I like men. I like to make love with men. But I like women too. Why not? And I like you a lot. You're beautiful. Really beautiful.' Melissa noticed once more her voice had grown husky.

'But couldn't you get into trouble?' she said hurriedly. 'I mean doing it with someone you're supposed to be protecting. Trying to seduce a sitter.'

'Sure. I could if you told them. I could get kicked off the force. The very least I'd get is a disciplinary hearing. Why,' she asked smiling, 'are you gonna tell the department?'

'No, of course not. Don't be silly.'

'Well, that's okay then.'

They were silent, staring at each other across the room.

'I really want you,' Chauncey said quietly. 'I wanna make love to you all night.'

Melissa felt herself getting hotter. 'Yes, but I'm afraid it's . . . what I mean is . . .'

'Sure,' Chauncey interrupted. 'It's gone cold. The mood has gone. But think about it, okay? Just think about it. We've got tomorrow night at least. Think about what was happening back there and how much you were wanting me. Wanting *it*. How you were feeling. We could both be feeling that tomorrow night. And more. A lot more. I could make you feel like you've never felt before. You could be moaning all night. Just think about it. Okay?'

Melissa nodded, gulping slightly.

Chauncey moved towards the interconnecting door. 'Okay. Well I guess I'd better say goodnight. Don't forget to leave this door unlocked.' She caught Melissa's look. 'Don't worry,' she laughed. 'I ain't gonna jump your bones in the middle of the night. That's not my style. It only works if you want me as much as I want you. And I think you do, Melissa. I think you do. Goodnight.'

She closed the door softly behind her.

The call came through after midnight. Big Vinny grabbed the phone.

'The target is flying to Albany first flight tomorrow. She'll be arriving with her protection at Albany airport shortly before nine. Be there.'

'Okay. Do we know where this cabin is?'

'Negative. We haven't gotten the precise location. Which means you must follow them from the airport.'

'Shit. That ain't gonna be easy.'

'No one said anything about easy,' the voice snarled. 'Just get it done. Don't lose them and when you get to the cabin make dead certain you prejudice the man and the woman. Without fail. Got it?'

'Yeah,' Vinny intoned. 'I got it.' The phone went dead.

A minute later he was outside Billy Bob's room with the

sports bag and his roll bag in one meaty hand. Twice he knocked softly on the door. Billy Bob finally opened up. He was tousle-haired and sleepy.

'Come on fer Chrissake's,' Big Vinny barked quietly. 'We're heading north. We got a long drive.'

Chapter Thirty

Melissa did think about it. For most of the night she tossed and turned – hot, bothered and sleepless. She was glad when five thirty came around and it was time to get up.

She called home. Jamie was fine. So was George. Astrid told her Liz, the young policewoman, had spent hours playing with them.

Melissa felt a pang. Some stranger was laughing and playing with her son whilst she was an ocean away, in pursuit of an elderly lawyer and a lot of hot money.

She showered and put on a chartreuse green silk blouse and her light grey suit. If Kunzman was at the cabin, she wanted to look her best. Chauncey, she noticed, had also dressed seriously, in a severely cut navy suit and a pale blue blouse.

They spoke little on the journey and Chauncey made no mention of the night before.

At the airport they were taken aside by a plainclothes security guard and processed through a different channel. The security man took a quick look in Melissa's attaché case before requesting Chauncey to unholster her gun which he checked and registered. She was permitted to keep it with her on the flight.

Melissa bought a copy of the *Wall Street Journal* and tried to occupy herself with the plight of financial markets and the current traumas of the American banking system, but she was conscious of Chauncey's presence on the aircraft: acutely aware of the proximity of her flesh in the narrow seats; sensitive to the sweetness of her perfume.

Halfway through the short flight, Chauncey half-turned and gave her a silent, enigmatic smile. Melissa wondered if the detective knew just how much her presence was disturbing her.

A big, New York State Police Chevy Caprice was waiting for them at the front of the airport terminal building. Sam Barber

269

was standing beside it. He gave them a broad smile.

'Melissa, Detective Morton, hi. Welcome to Albany.'

A uniformed trooper in his late twenties with a young face and short dark hair was waiting by the driver's door. His name tag read Mazello. Barber introduced them. Mazello grinned, gave them a half-salute and shook their hands.

'The Trooper will run us up to the cabin right away,' Barber said. 'If you're ready.'

'Absolutely. Let's get on with it,' Melissa said. 'We don't want Kunzman disappearing.'

'Don't worry, he won't do that,' Barber assured her. 'A couple of state troopers have been staking the place out. We'll meet with them first. Before we hit the place.'

'Just three troopers and you and me,' observed Chauncey dryly. 'Is that enough for a hit on this cabin? Supposing he's got company. Someone babysitting him.'

Barber shook his head. 'He hasn't. We've kept the place under close observation for more than twelve hours. He's there by himself. Definitely.' He grinned. 'Five armed officers to take one old lawyer. Yeah, we oughta be able to handle that.'

Melissa saw Chauncey make a small *moue*.

They climbed into the back of the police car, which had a steel prisoner grille separating the front from the rear seats. Barber turned and spoke through it. 'The journey's about half an hour.' He caught sight of Chauncey's pout and grinned at her. 'Not used to riding at the back, eh, detective?' Chauncey grunted and said nothing.

Mazello fired up the car and they moved away from the front of the building.

A moment later a brown, dusty Mitsubishi Shogun moved out of the parking lot and slotted itself a few vehicles behind the Chevy.

Mazello headed south and east on the busy Throughway then took Route 90, the road rising gently into the Taconics towards the state line. Almost at the line he made a right, turning the car due south onto a minor road.

They were cruising between steep, well-wooded hills, some of which, Melissa estimated, were a couple of thousand feet high. Mainly they were covered in spruce and fir, but she noticed a fair sprinkling of oak and birch and maple. The Taconic Range reminded her of the Trossachs.

They passed through Austerlitz, a small collection of stone and timber buildings, before turning off onto what amounted to little more than a track with a dense mass of pine trees over-hanging both sides. Mazello drove cautiously for another ten minutes, the endless switchback track ascending and descending the shoulders of the steep hills. Finally he rounded a bend and pulled the Chevy to a stop at the entrance to a track on their left, narrower and even more deeply rutted than the one they were on.

Barber got out of the car and let Melissa and Chauncey out of the rear as a uniformed trooper emerged from the trees. Melissa noticed another police Chevy parked on a steep slope well back in the timber opposite the track.

Chauncey, Barber and Mazello joined the trooper, who began briefing them in a low, animated voice. Melissa hung back, turning her face up to the warm sun. She knew better than to get involved in the plans and strategies of house raids. The job of the police was to get her in safely. She let them get on with it.

After a while Chauncey and Sam Barber returned. 'He's still there,' Barber said with a smile. 'In fact he's only just got up. The cabin has a rear entrance and there's a trooper covering it from a wooded ridge a little ways back. He's in radio contact with the man in the car. Our best plan is the simplest one. We'll drive up to the front door and ask ourselves in. The troopers have a warrant.'

'Will that be safe?' Melissa's question was half directed at Chauncey.

Chauncey shrugged, her face set and unreadable. 'So long as there ain't anyone around with guns . . . sure.'

'This man is an ageing corporate lawyer with no history of violence,' Barber said lightly. 'And he's there on his own. It'll be safe. Believe me. Let's get going.' They climbed back into the car, the trooper who had been watching the cabin piling into the front.

Mazello eased the Chevy around and drove cautiously along the narrow track, its deep ruts iron-hard from the summer sun. They bounced slowly for a quarter of a mile until, rounding a slight curve, they came in sight of the cabin. The track broadened into a wide semi-circle in front of a large, stone-built cabin. A Toyota four-by-four was standing in the clearing, close to the cabin door.

Mazello accelerated into the clearing and slewed to a halt in a cloud of billowing dust. The three men in the front leapt out and immediately began banging on the door of the cabin.

Chauncey tried the handle of the car door. It was locked. 'Jesus,' she spat, 'they've left us here. Locked in their frigging police car. We're sitting ducks.'

She rattled crazily at the door handle. Barber turned and saw their dilemma. He ran back to the car and opened the door. 'Sorry,' he grinned. 'Got so anxious we forgot about you.'

'Fucking Fibbies,' she hissed.

The cabin door was opened. Mazello and the other big trooper barged inside. Barber hurried after them. Melissa made towards the door before feeling Chauncey's hand on her arm.

'Not so fast,' the detective ordered. 'Let them do it. Wait till everything's straight.' Melissa noticed her open jacket, the holstered gun in full view.

They waited in the sunshine, Melissa admiring the solid, rural stonework of the cabin, Chauncey staring darkly at the dense timber surrounding them. The nearest trees were less than fifty yards away. Melissa caught the look on her face. 'What's wrong?'

'I ain't crazy about this,' she replied morosely.

'Why what's wrong with it? It's beautiful.'

'I like sidewalks under my feet. There ain't a sidewalk in miles. All this goddam country. It's creepy. I don't like it. I'm a city girl.'

Melissa laughed. Barber came to the door of the cabin. 'It's okay,' he called softly. 'You can come in.'

Inside was a large rectangular room with tongued and grooved boarding from floor to ceiling, bright scatter rugs on a wooden floor, a few comfortable chairs and a lot of books. At the far end of the room was a small open kitchen with a breakfast bar. Opposite the door Melissa had walked through was a fireplace built of local stone. The chimney breast reached to the ceiling. Close to the fireplace was the rear door of the cabin. Through an archway on her right was a short corridor, leading, she presumed, to the bedroom and bathroom. It was obvious the cabin had been designed for a person to get away from it all. By themselves.

A heavy-set man with grey wispy hair was sitting in one of the chairs. He looked more stunned than frightened. Barber was standing close to the seated man. As Melissa crossed the floor

272

she could hear Trooper Mazello moving about in the bedroom. The trooper they had picked up down the track was standing guard, close to the open door.

'Melissa,' Barber announced, 'this is Vito Kunzman.'

Melissa stood in front of the seated man. 'Mr Kunzman,' she began, 'my name is Melissa Semmington. I'm a forensic accountant with Rolay Richard. We are the accountants appointed by the Bank of England to liquidate the Exchange Bank of International Industry and Trade.'

The man looked down at the floor. Melissa frowned. 'Do you understand?'

He looked up at her with brown, rheumy eyes but said nothing. She gave him a small smile. 'Do you mind if I sit down?' Across the room she heard Chauncey snort at her English civility. The man shrugged lightly. She sat down opposite, arranging herself elegantly in the chair. 'I would like to ask you some questions,' she said softly. 'About the Exchange Bank.'

The man stared at her and she saw his eyes harden. Sam Barber moved closer to the seated man. He was holding a small sheaf of documents. 'We only just found Vito in time,' he said in a brittle, light-hearted voice. He waved the documents which Melissa could see were flight tickets. 'Two more days and he'd have been in South Africa.'

Melissa's eyes cut to Kunzman. 'Well, perhaps you would like to answer my questions before you go to South Africa?'

Kunzman let out a hollow laugh. 'I don't figure I'm going to make it. Not now.' His voice was low and smoky, like sticks crackling in a fire. 'I guess you ain't gonna let me.'

Melissa gave him a sweet smile. 'I'm not in a position to stop you, Mr Kunzman. I'm not the police. I'm just a simple, boring accountant. But I would be very grateful if you could answer a few questions. Before you go.'

Kunzman cackled again. 'You got a helluva weird sense of humour. What are you? English?'

Melissa smiled and ignored the question. 'I need to know about an amount of five hundred million dollars that was moved out of various codename accounts shortly before the Exchange Bank was shut down,' she began.

His stare was strong. 'What makes you think I know about that?'

'Quite a lot of things actually. And,' she paused, 'I need to know about one account in particular.'

'Yeah?'

'Yes.'

'What account is that?'

'I think you know. After all, you named it after this place. The Austerlitz Account.'

She saw Kunzman's eyes flicker. For a moment she thought she saw fear. 'I don't know anything about it,' he said.

'I think you do.'

'Yeah? Well, you're wrong.'

A strange, electric silence filled the room as Melissa surveyed the elderly man. Mazello had stopped banging about in the bedroom and had come back into the room. She was conscious that, like everyone else, he was watching her intently.

The air inside the cabin was still, hanging like an indrawn breath. Melissa felt the hairs rising on the back of her neck.

'If you talk to me,' she said softly, 'then maybe you won't have to talk to the police. You see, I'm not here to accuse anyone. I'm not concerned about arresting people. All I'm interested in is following the money. But if some policeman were to start asking you questions . . .'

'What kinda questions?'

'About all those Exchange Bank managers who died shortly after they had been suspected of fraud . . . about their deaths and the deaths of their families.'

'I didn't have anything to do with that. And you can't prove that I did.'

'I'm not trying to. That's not what I'm here for, Mr Kunzman.'

Again the electric silence filled the room. 'Look,' she leaned forward in her seat, her voice even softer, 'just tell me what I want and I'll go away.'

Kunzman gazed at her then laughed loudly. The noise startled her. 'You may go away . . . but they won't.' He nodded at Barber and at Chauncey who had moved closer behind Melissa's chair. 'They never go away.'

His eyes flicked to Barber. 'Anyway, how the hell did you find me?' he demanded.

Barber gave him an icy smile. 'We didn't. Miss Semmington did.'

Kunzman's eyes cut back to Melissa. He stared at her. 'You've killed me, you bitch,' he hissed.

The venom of the expression startled her. The old man meant

274

it. She did her best to hide the shock on her face.

'Watch your mouth, bagman,' Chauncey snapped.

For a moment Kunzman gazed up at her before staring at Melissa. A slow, secret smile grew around the corners of his mouth. 'So that's it,' he whispered. 'I'd never have figured it.'

Melissa had no idea what he meant. It didn't matter. She had found her quarry. Now her mind was fixed on tracking the money... on opening up the secret of the Austerlitz Account. Nothing else mattered.

'I found you because I needed you to answer a few questions. That's all you have to do... answer a few questions. If you answer my questions, I'll go away.' Her tone was soft yet filled with quiet persistence.

The dark rheumy eyes gazed at her in the silence. She saw them weaken, then, gradually, accede. 'I'm dead anyway,' he intoned. 'Whaddaya want to know?' His voice had turned to ashes.

The room let out its breath.

'Firstly, I want to know about the missing money,' she went on in the same gentle tone. 'I have a few papers here which track the cash up to a point, but I need you to tell me...' She reached for her attaché case. It wasn't there. She looked down.

For Christ's sake.

She had left her case in the car. She had left her damn, bloody, sodding attaché case in the car.

What an idiot. What a complete incompetent fool. She had Kunzman right on the edge... ready to talk... and she didn't have the facts. To stop now could ruin everything. The old man could clam up. Yet all her files, all the hundreds of hours' work by her staff were sitting in the big Chevy parked outside. She shot a pained, appealing glance up at Sam Barber and saw his puzzled look.

'I'm sorry,' she said weakly: 'I've left my case in the car. I need to get it.' She stood up quickly. 'I'm sorry.'

She walked quickly towards the open door of the cabin and the trooper who stood guard. He had been staring out across the clearing but turned at her approach. She gave him a pathetic smile. She saw him return the smile... and then, in surprise, watched his hat fly off his head and shoot across the room.

From somewhere outside she heard a loud crack.

The trooper's head exploded in a billowing burst of blood and brains.

From beyond the cabin's walls came the sound of more sharp cracks . . . from inside the crash and splintering of breaking glass and the dull, awful thud of the trooper's corpse crashing to the ground.

Chapter Thirty-One

Melissa screamed. Behind her she heard Chauncey and Sam Barber bellow with shock.

From outside came the renewed rattle of gunfire. A burst of bullets flew through the open door, splatting into the wooden panelling and shattering against the stonework of the large fireplace. Red hot slivers of steel hissed across the cabin, perforating the walls and floor. Melissa felt strong hands pulling her away from the door.

'Down,' Chauncey snarled. 'Geddown, for Christ's sake.'

She dropped to the floor, Chauncey half on top of her. Sam Barber, his head and body low to the ground, crabbed past them on all fours, heading towards the door. Trooper Mazello was crouched at the entrance to the bedroom corridor, gun in hand.

A small, solid green-leather chesterfield stood against the wall near the door.

In a swift, gymnastic movement Barber rolled across the open gap of the doorway. A solitary shot rang out and a portion of the panelling low down on the opposite wall exploded into fragments. For a moment Barber crouched beneath the chesterfield's leather arm. Then he began pushing . . . inching the sofa lengthways towards the door. Mazello crawled across to help.

With their arms extended and wriggling on their bellies they shoved at the sofa. It was heavy, but the slight patina of polish on the floorboards helped. Grunting and shoving they edged it forward, past the body of the dead trooper and towards the open door.

Flat on the floor, Melissa watched, expecting at any second an armed assailant to burst through the door and kill them all. The weight of Chauncey's body pressed her into the floorboards. She was aware of outstretched arms above her, the detective's pistol held in a double grip, trained on the doorway.

After what seemed an age, Barber and Mazello managed to get an arm of the chesterfield touching the back of the door. Both men eased gingerly onto their haunches and with a sudden crouching rush shoved the sofa hard against the door. It closed with a crash.

A furious burst of fire hit the cabin, splintering windows and smashing crockery in the kitchen. Everyone cowered.

'Thanks,' Barber panted to Mazello. He surveyed the cabin. Chauncey had dragged Melissa closer into the lee of the wall; Vito Kunzman was crouching behind an armchair, his face the colour of parchment.

Another burst of fire shattered the remaining windows. Arms cradling their heads, they shielded their faces from the flying glass.

'You figure that'll stop them?' Chauncey growled when the firing stopped. She jerked her head at the sofa hard against the door.

'Not if they rush us. But it may slow them down.'

'Them?'

He nodded. 'I count two weapons. Assault rifles.' He looked at Melissa. 'You okay?'

She eased herself out of Chauncey's protective embrace and moved to sit with her back against the wall. 'Absolutely, bloody marvellous,' she said bitterly.

A hail of bullets hit the cabin. Small, jagged splinters of wood ripped off the back of the door that Barber and Mazello had managed to close, leaving slivers of exposed timber.

Barber gazed at them and frowned.

Despite herself, Melissa stared at the body of the fallen trooper. A pool of dark blood was seeping from under the bloody mess which had once been his head. Barber caught the direction of her gaze. 'Don't look,' he said quietly.

He crawled to the trooper's body, retrieved his gun from the holster and checked the clip. It was full . . . seventeen 9mm rounds. He weighed the gun in his hand and glanced at Melissa. 'Can you use one of these things?'

She shook her head angrily. 'No. Of course not.'

Another couple of rounds came through the glassless windows and smacked into the rear wall. Barber pocketed the gun and pulled his own from inside his jacket. He eased to his feet, edged close to a window and took a swift glance outside. He turned back to the room. 'Anybody got a mobile radio?' he demanded.

Chauncey pulled a face as she moved up into a crouch. 'Sure, back in the precinct. My set wouldn't have been any good out here.'

Barber grunted and looked at Mazello. 'You?'

The trooper scowled. 'Shit, I left it in the goddam car.'

'I have a mobile phone,' Melissa volunteered.

Barber's face lightened. 'Great. We need to call Loundonville. Now.'

Melissa looked around. Her face fell. 'Oh, but it's in my attaché case. In the car.'

Barber cursed softly. 'You got a phone here?' he snapped at Kunzman.

The elderly man was on all fours behind the green leather wingback chair. He raised his face. 'What the hell's the use?' he croaked. 'The bitch has killed us all. She led whoever's out there to this place. They're gonna kill me. And you. All of you.'

'Do you have a phone?' Barber repeated flatly.

Kunzman stared at him for a moment. His eyes were glazed ... lifeless. He looked like a sick dog. 'No,' he mumbled.

'Shit,' Barber exploded. 'Damn and shit.'

'Jesus,' Chauncey howled: 'the only house in the whole goddam country without a phone and we're inside getting shot at.'

'Hey, wait!' Mazello cried. 'There's Bif. He's got a radio.'

'Bif? Who the hell is Bif?' Barber snapped.

'The guy covering the back. He has a short-wave. He was in touch with Jack in the car.' Mazello nodded at the body of the trooper.

'Well, where the hell is he?' Chauncey demanded. 'He sure ain't doing much to get us outa here.'

'Hey, Bif's okay,' Mazello responded. His baby face was animated, his voice excited by sudden relief. 'He'll have radioed for help. You can bet on it. My guess is right now he's working his way through the brush so he can draw a line on those bastards.'

Barber stared at the excited trooper then shot a glance at Chauncey. Melissa saw her eyes narrow in doubt.

'Well,' Barber said, 'let's just hope this Bif has got a call out and back-up is on the way. In the meantime, you'd better keep your eyes on those windows at the back. Just in case.'

'Shit, it's dangerous on that side of the room,' Mazello

protested. He nodded at the savage pockmarks that had ripped and scoured the panelling on the rear wall of the cabin.

'I know that for Chrissakes!' Barber exploded. 'But we have to watch our backs.'

Tentatively Mazello moved to the window next to the cabin's rear door. He crouched down, moving up every few seconds to cast a quick look outside.

'Okay.' Barber's voice was lighter as he glanced around the cabin. 'Well, we're not exactly defenceless here. The good thing is these old stone shacks were built like fortresses. The walls must be at least a foot thick and even the woodwork is solid. What's more, my guess is they're packing the wrong load.'

'Wrong load?' Melissa was seated on the floor with her back to the front wall. She was hugging her knees tightly to her chest.

'I think whoever's out there is using splat.'

Melissa's looked puzzled. 'What?'

'Splat loads,' Chauncey said glancing down at her from a place close to a window. 'They shred on impact. Spray out bunches of red hot lead and steel alloy. At close range . . . in here . . . devastating. They get inside this place,' she waved her pistol around the cabin, 'and our ass is grass. We'll get shredded.'

'Jeeesus,' Vito Kunzman moaned.

'Yes, but out there, against this kind of defensive position, splat loads are not so hot,' Barber added. 'Nothing short of a tank shell is going to pierce these walls. So, whoever those guys are, they're not going to get inside here. And they can't dig us out so easily. We're armed and we've got sufficient ammunition. Best of all, time is on our side. If Bif *has* put out a call, then help will be on its way.'

'And if he hasn't . . . ?' Melissa queried softly.

'Hey, you don't know Bif,' Mazello announced from his crouched position behind the door.

Barber gave Melissa a tight smile and shrugged. 'Sooner or later someone is bound to hear the firing. Even out here.'

The assault rifles opened up again, bullets flying through the broken windows and loudly puncturing the wooden walls. Mazello threw himself to the floor.

Chauncey waited until the firing ceased then eased herself cautiously around the window frame and took a peek out. Barber did the same from a window close to the front door. Mazello resumed his crouch and took a swift glance out of a rear window.

'I can see one of them,' Chauncey said quietly. 'The bastard is squatting down by the trunk of our car. I dunno, maybe he's reloading.'

'I see him,' Barber responded. 'There has to be another one somewhere. There are two of them. At least.'

After a moment Chauncey said, 'I see him. Big mother. Jeans, check shirt, windcheater. At the edge of the tree line. A little over to the right.'

'Got him,' Barber murmured. 'Do you recognise either of them?'

'No.'

'You ain't gonna recognise them,' Kunzman intoned in a flat, resigned voice. 'They're hitmen. Professionals. From out of town. Hired for the day. Here to make the hit and disappear.'

Barber glanced over his shoulder. 'You seem to know a lot about it, Vito.'

Kunzman grunted. Barber turned to Chauncey. 'Can you loose off a couple of shots at the guy by the car? He's in range. You never know, you could get lucky. And we gotta make those bastards understand we've got teeth.'

'Sure.'

Chauncey shucked off the jacket of her suit, letting it drop to the floor. With the Glock in a two-handed grip, the barrel pointing at the cabin's ceiling, she pressed her back against the boarded wall and took a deep breath. She held it for a moment, then, releasing the air in an explosive grunt, spun around into the window frame, aimed and loosed off two shots in one single flowing movement before pirouetting back behind the protection of the wall.

It seemed to Melissa, watching from her place on the floor, that the entire sequence took less than a second.

The man behind the car ducked at the sound of the shots. Spotting from his window Barber waited until the man peered back over the car then fired a further two rounds at him. One struck the trunk close to the man's face. He dived behind the car.

'You hit him?' Chauncey asked.

'No, I don't think so. But now they know we can take care of ourselves.'

Another fusillade of shots hit the stonework and flew through the empty window frames, exploding into the rear wall. Again

Mazello flattened himself to the floor as everyone cowered.

'They can do that all day,' Chauncey observed, 'and the worst they're gonna do is wound a couple of us.'

Barber shot a frown at her standing further along the wall. 'Yeah, but they must know that. So, why bother? They have to make a move soon or quit.'

Chauncey, peeking out of her window, made a face. 'They're dumb. They don't know what else to do.'

Barber's jaw tightened, making the masseter muscle above it pulse rhythmically. He didn't look convinced. He turned back to the window.

The silence was eerie. After a moment Melissa moved away from her place against the wall and crawled towards the kneeling Kunzman.

Crouched behind the rear door, Mazello watched her ungainly progress across the floor. Kunzman was gripping the back of the easy chair. Melissa noticed the knuckles of his gnarled, liver-spotted hands were deadly white.

'Mr Kunzman,' she said softly, 'why don't you come over to where I am. Against the front wall. I think it's much safer on that side of the room.'

He stared at her with his rheumy eyes. 'Why, what the hell difference will it make? Sooner or later they're gonna get us.'

'No way,' countered Mazello, glaring at the old man.

'I don't think they are,' Melissa murmured encouragingly. 'I know it's very frightening, but we've got three very experienced police officers protecting us. Plus another one, outside, who's undoubtedly already sent for help. As Agent Barber says, there's no way those men are going to get in here. I'm sure we're going to be fine.' She put out a hand and touched his arm. 'Help is on the way. But please come over to the wall. You'll be much safer.'

Kunzman gazed at her. 'If those guys out there don't get me,' he croaked, 'your friends in here will. Either way, it's your fault. You're the one who found me.'

She compressed her lips into a thin line of regret. 'I'm sorry,' she murmured, 'I really am. But I was only doing my job. And it's not only you, you know. I've been attacked too.'

Kunzman's eyes moved to the thinning scar on her cheek. 'Only doing your job!' he said in his rasping voice. A thin smile spread across his face. 'You were only doing your job,' he repeated.

'You wanna listen to the lady,' Mazello called to him. 'That ain't a good place to be. Look.'

They both looked up in the direction of the young trooper's gaze. A few centimetres above Kunzman's head a spreading ricochet had punched a jagged hole through the back of the wingback chair. Stuffing spilled out of shredded green leather like ruptured guts.

The elderly man blinked in horror. 'Christ,' he hissed. He let go of the chair as if it were on fire and stared aghast at Melissa.

'Come back with me.'

'Yeah, okay,' he croaked, 'I'll come. Thanks.'

She held his arm and helped him out from behind the chair. 'You go first. In front of me,' she instructed. Slowly Kunzman began crawling across the wooden floor. Melissa watched him for a moment then shot a backward glance at Mazello. He gave her a broad grin.

BOOM!

With a tremendous crash half the wooden door beside the crouching trooper blew apart. The door burst open with enormous force, hitting Mazello and sending him crashing across the cabin floor.

With a yelp, Melissa twisted around on her haunches and fell backwards against the wingback chair.

A man leapt into the room.

A man with a gun.

Pointing at her.

The scene in the cabin slowed to freeze-frame.

Lying with her head propped against the chair, Melissa saw Mazello prone upon the floor, holding the side of his head. Blood was seeping between his fingers. He was bellowing in pain.

Melissa stared down the big, black barrel of the man's gun.

From the corner of her eye she could see Barber and Chauncey turning in shock from the windows. Barber's view of the man was half-obscured by the open back door. Chauncey was dropping into the classic firing position.

There was a sharp crack, like the sound of a ruler slapping a table. Two more followed, instantly obliterated by an enormous explosion.

BOOM!

Orange fire leapt from the gun barrel. Melissa screamed and shut her eyes.

A moment later she opened them. In shock. She was deafened by the gun blast but she wasn't dead.

It came as a surprise.

She wasn't dead; she wasn't blinded; she didn't think she was even hurt.

From somewhere beneath the ringing in her ears she heard more shots – an uninterrupted succession of sharp reports.

She watched the man with the gun staggering against the back wall, as if repeatedly punched by a powerful, unseen fist. She saw his head jerk backwards. A large hole appeared in his throat. He clutched at it, the gun slipping from his nerveless fingers. He pitched forward, falling heavily. Like a tree. A dead tree.

The gun slid across the floor.

The cabin was filled with the sound of pain . . . loud, hoarse cries of agony.

Stunned and bemused, Melissa watched Trooper Mazello clambering to his feet. He was pressing a hand to the bloody side of a face pierced by splinters. But he was no longer bellowing. The agonised shouts were coming from the other direction.

She sat up and turned.

Vito Kunzman, his legs shattered to bloody tatters by the shotgun blast, was screaming and writhing on the floor.

'Oh, shit.' Sam Barber wailed in despair. He was schizo-phrenically torn between watching the front window for assailants and staring at the blood seeping from Kunzman's legs.

The sight and sounds of Kunzman's pain helped clear Melissa's head. She crawled towards the elderly man.

'Can you do anything for him?' Barber appealed.

She knelt beside Kunzman and looked up. 'I don't know,' she mumbled. 'I know some first aid, but I didn't learn about this kind of thing.' Her hands hovered over the man's legs. 'God, it's a mess.'

'Try to stop the bleeding.'

'I'll try.'

Barber glowered at Mazello. 'For Christ's sake secure that goddam door,' he snarled. 'You were supposed to be watching our backs. How the hell did you let that bastard get in here?'

Bent low and holding the side of his face, Mazello shoved the wingback chair up against what was left of the cabin's rear door. Barber eyed it acidly. With half the door blown to splinters, the arrangement didn't offer much protection.

'Our security is compromised,' he said seriously. 'Anybody can get past that.'

'But Bif is gonna be watching out for us,' Mazello said.

Chauncey moved from her window and bent to retrieve the dead attacker's shotgun. 'You can forget Bif,' she said in a matter-of-fact tone.'

The young trooper's face looked startled. 'What?'

'Bif's out of it.' She pumped the action of the Ithaca and shucked out an empty shell. 'Hey, now we got some real firepower,' she announced.

'Whaddaya mean, he's out of it?'

Barber nodded at the fallen man. 'If he got to us, that means he got to your buddy, Bif. Probably with the knife.' He nodded at a large bowie knife sheathed at the man's belt. Mazello stared at it with a sick look. Barber's eyes cut from the dead man to Chauncey who was holstering her pistol. 'Thanks,' he said grimly. 'You saved all our asses.'

Chauncey shrugged and crouched down beside Melissa. Kunzman's yelling had subsided into low moans. 'You reckon you can stop the bleeding?'

'God knows. If I can't, he's going to bleed to death. I need to get rid of all this,' she touched the tattered trouser legs, 'fix a tourniquet and bandage as much as I can. But I don't have anything,' she wailed.

Chauncey crabbed across the floor to the dead man. Sam Barber turned from the window and watched her pull the big bowie knife from its sheath. His face darkened and he shot a glance at Mazello. The knife's blade was bloody.

Chauncey scuttled back to Melissa. 'Cut the cloth away with this. Use your blouse for bandages.'

'My blouse?'

The detective gave her a grim smile. 'Sure. This ain't no time for modesty. Anyway, what the hell you got to be ashamed of? You got a great pair of tits.'

Melissa started to grin when something caught her eye. She looked up.

A man was at the window . . . aiming a gun into the cabin.

'Look out,' she yelled.

Chauncey came up off the floor as if she was spring-loaded, the shotgun coming up into position fast. She fired from the hip, the Ithaca detonating at the same time as the man's assault rifle erupted.

Instinctively, Melissa threw herself across Vito Kunzman. His mouth opened and she supposed he screamed but she heard nothing. Her eardrums were pummelled and her brain bounced inside her skull by the incredible cacophony of sound inside the cabin.

The blast from the shotgun blew away most of the wooded window frame. The man's head and chest shattered in a shower of blood. He went over backwards.

A single round from the M-16 blew Chauncey across the room and smashed her into the rear wall.

Melissa screamed once. 'Chauncey.'

She was across the room in an instant.

'Oh God! Chauncey, Chauncey!' She cradled the detective's head in her arms, staring in dread at the blood spreading red and implacably over the pale blue blouse.

'Chauncey, listen.' Her voice was thick with emotion. 'I need to turn you on your side. Get the wound above your heart.'

Chauncey's eyes were closed. Melissa saw her head shift imperceptibly. She croaked something unintelligible. Melissa bent her head close to the detective's mouth.

'No . . .' there was a long pause ' . . . use.'

Chauncey's eyes opened and stared unfocused at Melissa. Weakly she raised a trembling and bloodied hand and placed it on Melissa's breast. She mouthed something. Melissa bent closer and heard a single whispered word.

'Shame.'

For a moment Chauncey Morton's eyes stayed hazily fixed upon Melissa's face then, slowly, they rolled up into their sockets. She coughed once, and died.

'Chauncey,' Melissa's agonised wail reverberated around the cabin.

A man's shoe appeared beside her and she looked up. Sam Barber crouched beside her and took a quick look at the body. 'She's dead, Melissa,' he said softly.

'Oh, no! Oh no! Say it isn't true! Please! She's not dead! No!'

'It's true. I'm sorry.' He half stood up.

'Oh, no, no!'

'Melissa, Detective Morton is dead.' Barber's voice was soft but insistent. 'I know the pain is hard to take, but you're gonna have to take it. There's things to do.' He reached down, took hold of her arm and pulled her gently but insistently to her feet.

'Vito Kunzman is still alive,' he went on. 'But he won't be for much longer. Not if we don't get him outa here. And I need you to help me do that.'

Slowly Melissa became aware of the shambles in the cabin. Every window was blown out, the walls and furniture holed and shattered by gunfire and there were three dead bodies on the floor. The place was like a slaughterhouse. Blood floated across the polished floor like oil slicks, soaking the scatter rugs.

Kunzman moaned loudly and rocked on his back in agony.

Trooper Mazello was standing by one of the front windows, his Glock at the ready. Melissa did a double take when she saw the trooper's face. It wasn't young any more. It was never going to be young again. In what she realised with a shock had been less than five minutes, Trooper Mazello had aged twenty years.

Barber was pressing something into her hand. She looked down. It was the dead trooper's gun. 'When I tell you,' he instructed, 'I want you to fire this out of that window.' He pointed at the smashed, gaping frame next to Mazello.

'But I don't know how.'

'You pull the trigger,' he snapped. 'That's how.'

Melissa took hold of the Glock as if it were a live snake. 'It's quite safe until you pull the trigger,' Barber continued. Melissa looked sick. 'All you have to do is keep your head down, stick the weapon out of the window and keep firing.'

She frowned. 'But why?'

'Morton nailed the guy at the window. That means there's just one of the bastards left. I want him to know we still have firepower. If he knows that, my guess is he'll give it up and split.'

'You don't know there's only one left. Not for sure,' Mazello yapped anxiously from his place by the window.

'Sure I do. If there had have been more of them, they'd *all* have come piling through the goddam door you were supposed to be watching. The guy out there is the last one. He's no idea what damage his people have done to us. All he knows is that

287

his ambush is all screwed up and that two of his men are dead. But while the bastard stays out there we're stuck in here. With Vito Kunzman bleeding to death. So we have to persuade him to go. We gotta get rid of him. Quick.'

Chapter Thirty-Two

It was Vietnam all over again.

The mission had turned into a total fuck-up. Just like in Nam the enemy had been in greater strength than they'd been told. And just like in Nam, they'd been well dug in.

It could have gone all right. Big Vinny was convinced of it.

But Billy Bob had screwed everything up. It *would* have gone all right, he thought, if only Billy Bob hadn't opened fire when he had. It had been too soon. A horrible mistake.

And horribly had Billy Bob paid for it.

Billy Bob was dead.

The salt tears coursed down Big Vinny's cheeks as he sheltered behind a tree on the edge of the timber and stared at the twisted, ruined body of his baby brother. He had no doubt Billy Bob was dead. He had watched him take the full blast of a twelve-gauge carbide cartridge at close range. The Ithaca had blown him a dozen feet from the window. Now he lay abandoned in front of the cabin; face up and lifeless; inert as a fallen log.

Billy Bob was all he had left . . . had been Big Vinny's entire family. And now he was gone.

Vinny let out a small sob, raised his M-16 and sent a couple of rounds through the windows of the cabin. It was an empty gesture and he knew it. But it was the only thing he could do.

He stood at the edge of the timber, shattered in grief and maddened by impotence, staring at the dead body of his brother and cursing the consequences of a crapped-out mission.

Yet it had started well enough.

They had held well back in the traffic, finding the big Chevy Caprice easy to follow up into the Taconics. When it had turned off the road onto the track, the three men in the Shogun had given each other a tight grin. Killers' grins. This was their kind of country. Here they knew they would be at home. The mission would be a turkey shoot.

They had given the Chevy a mile start along the track then quietly eased the Mitsubishi after it. Topping a timbered crest they had seen the police car drawn to a stop in a wooded valley a few hundred yards ahead.

Through his field glasses Vinny had watched the state trooper and the two plainclothes cops emerge and talk to another trooper close to the edge of thick timber. Pivoting slightly, he'd focused on a figure leaning against the car. She was turning her face up to the sun. Even at that distance he could admire her looks. Too bad, he'd thought, that soon she'd be dead.

When the second trooper piled into the car, Vinny had watched it turn off onto another track hidden by the forest. Quickly he had driven the Shogun close to where the Chevy had stopped and reversed it as far back into the timber as he could.

'I reckon that trooper they picked up was watching the front of the cabin,' he said as they leapt out of the vehicle. 'Which means it's located somewhere down that track.' Swiftly they checked their weapons.

'So, if there's a guy watching the front,' Carver Fylde grunted, 'there's gotta be one watching the back.'

'Right. He's your job. See if you can make him talk. Find out how many are already in the place. Take the Ithaca, but no noise.'

Fylde grinned, exposing the gaps in his teeth. 'There won't be. Then what?'

'Check out the rear of the cabin. See what you can see. After that, report back. We'll be a little ways back in the timber, watching the front.'

Fylde set off at a loping run through the pinewoods. Jogging softly close to the edge of the forest, Vinny and Billy Bob followed the track.

Coming in sight of the cabin they saw the state police Chevy parked close to a Toyota. Two women were standing a little way beyond the vehicles, talking.

One of them was the target.

Vinny and Billy Bob hunkered down in the undergrowth, watching the women and eyeing the cabin's solid stone construction. The front door was wide open. After a moment a man came to the door and the women followed him inside. The door stayed open, a trooper standing in plain sight just inside the doorway.

'Hey, why don't we hit them now? Straight off.' Billy Bob whispered excitedly.

Big Vinny shook his head. 'We need to know how many there are,' he murmured. 'There may be more cops inside the place There's already five we know about. That's more than I was told. We ain't making a move till we know what we're up against.'

'Yeah, but we get inside that cabin and we could finish it real quick,' Billy Bob said eagerly.

Big Vinny grinned at him 'Ain't that the truth. But we'll wait for Carver to report. Getting inside may not be so easy.' He surveyed the clearing in front of the cabin. 'It might be better to hit them when they come out,' he murmured.

Billy Bob scowled impatiently.

Carver Fylde returned, moving through the woods like a shadow. 'Well?' Vinny demanded.

'The guy watching the back ain't watching nothing now. He's staring up at the sky but he ain't seeing it.'

Billy Bob sniggered.

'You make him talk?' Vinny demanded.

Fylde nodded. 'The only person in the place was the old man.'

'Okay, so now they're down to four,' Billy Bob whispered excitedly. 'We can take 'em easy.'

Big Vinny shot him a brutal look. 'What's it look like at the back?'

Fylde eyed the stone-built cabin from his low squatting position in the undergrowth. 'Like it looks at the front. The place has got thicker walls than the Alamo. There's a rear door though, right alongside the chimney. Just about opposite the window there.' He pointed.

Vinny nodded and silently surveyed the cabin and the clearing. 'If we'd had a coupla grenades,' he intoned, 'we could have done it real easy. As it is, we're gonna have to get in close, lay down heavy fire and bust in. And we have to do it fast. They'll have radios in there. We can't give 'em time to call for help.'

'Why not wait till they come out?' ventured Fylde.

Big Vinny shook his head. 'I thought about it but I figure it's too risky. We dunno how long they're gonna be in there. And suppose they go out back looking for the guy you iced. Or call up some of their buddies to come out. The Shogun ain't that well hidden. Some cop sees it and we could have to hightail it outa here on foot.'

He shook his head. 'No, we can't wait. You go around the back. When you're ready, make like a meadowlark. Count off thirty seconds to give us time, then bust in the back. We'll hit the front.'

Carver Fylde disappeared like the mist.

'You cover the front,' Big Vinny told Billy Bob. 'Get close but don't be seen. When the time comes, take out the guy in the doorway. Then we'll crash the place together.' He started to move away.

'Where are you going?' Billy Bob asked.

Vinny nodded towards a small knoll about seventy metres around the edge of the encircling timber. 'Over there. I wanna see if it gives me some elevation. Enough to hit a target inside the cabin.'

Reaching the knoll, Vinny discovered the elevation provided no advantage. The windows of the stone-built cabin were too small to allow much light into the place. From where he was concealed the interior looked dim . . . the people inside either sitting down or standing still.

A movement caught his eye. He turned his head and his heart lurched. His brother was snaking across the clearing towards the police car. Alarmed, he watched him reach the car and ease himself onto his haunches.

Hell, he'd told Billy Bob to get close . . . but that was too damn close. He could be seen.

As swiftly as possible he began slipping through the pines, heading back towards his original position opposite the front door.

He'd gone less than thirty metres when he saw Billy Bob raise his M-16. He stopped in shock. Jeeesus. He watched impotently. The stupid kid was about to . . .

The sound of the single shot rang through the pine forest.

Right then Big Vinny knew the mission was going belly-up.

He turned and opened fire on the windows of the cabin, hearing the *crack, crack, crack* of Billy Bob's assault rifle from beside the police car. The windows imploded, showering the people inside the cabin with glass.

It was a lot of noise but Vinny wasn't impressed.

Firing at the windows was useless. They could do that all day and achieve nothing. But they didn't have all day. The people in the cabin would already be on their police radios screaming for help.

Christ. Why the hell had Billy Bob opened up? Had the cop at the door seen him?

Right now, Vinny thought, there was one vital question. Was the cabin door still open? If so, maybe they could charge it. He was too far over to the side to see. He started moving swiftly around the edge of the timber, stopping once to fire at the windows.

He assessed the situation. The cop in the doorway was dead. That was for sure. Billy Bob was a crack shot. So, the defenders were down to three. Better odds. He wondered if they could charge the door before those inside got organised.

Halfway around the clearing he heard the sharp crack of wood on wood and saw the door slam shut. Billy Bob poured half a clip into it. Vinny yelled above the noise to get him to quit but he didn't hear.

'Goddam,' he moaned. Next thing, they would be running out of ammunition.

Now everything depended on Carver Fylde. No doubt he was wondering what the hell was happening out front. Was he in position? Vinny wondered. Had he already given the signal, which they hadn't heard because of the firing? Christ, what a mess.

Billy Bob was reloading by the car. Two shots rang out from a cabin window, followed quickly by two more. One hit the car close to Billy Bob's head. Vinny stared in fear. Hell, Billy Bob was exposed. The police car was well in range of the nine-millimetre pistols inside the cabin. If Billy Bob had to move back, it would be difficult. Shit. Vinny loosed off more shots at the cabin.

He ceased firing and glanced at Billy Bob who grinned at him. For God's sake the stupid kid was *enjoying* it.

The hit on the cabin had turned dick-shitty; they were in danger of getting their own asses burned . . . and Billy Bob was smiling about it!

Suddenly, from the direction of the cabin, came the loud blast of the Ithaca, followed almost instantly by a second twelve-gauge explosion, this time more muffled and booming.

Carver Fylde had made his move. He was inside the cabin. Inside without them.

His M-16 ready, Big Vinny left the protection of the timber, running towards the cabin. From inside he heard the sound of a handgun . . . three, four, five shots. He stopped, waiting for the next explosion of the Ithaca which would tell him Fylde was still alive.

It didn't come. The handgun fell silent.

Big Vinny scuttled back to the protection of the timber.

Carver Fylde was dead.

He was sure of that. But had he hit the woman and the old man before he had gone down? Shit, there was no way of knowing. All he knew for certain was that Fylde was dead.

Jeeesus. Carver Fylde dead. He had seemed indestructible.

Vinny bent his head to check his ammunition clip. He was almost out. He whipped out the fresh clip and slammed it home.

He looked up and his heart stopped.

Billy Bob had left the safety of the car and was running swiftly across the few yards of clearing towards one of the smashed windows of the cabin.

Vinny had tried to shout but his throat was suddenly seized up. He'd watched his brother reach the window and aim his M-16 inside.

He knew Billy Bob had fired because he heard the sharp *crackarackrackrack* of automatic fire at the same time as he heard the single booming eruption of the Ithaca.

The blast from the shotgun had lifted Billy Bob and thrown him back from the cabin wall as if he was tied to the end of a bungee rope. Arms and legs splayed, he'd flown through the air in the shape of a star. A falling star.

Billy Bob had hit the ground in a large puff of dust and lain still.

Big Vinny stared at the body of his brother.

Suddenly he wondered how long he had he been standing there, with the grieving tears trickling down his cheeks and the tight, bitter feeling at the back of his throat. It could have been a minute . . . it could have been ten. He didn't know. All he knew was the mission was a fuck-up and Billy Bob was dead. He didn't even know if the two targets had been eliminated.

He cleared his throat and wiped his face on his sleeve before firing a few more useless rounds at the cabin. Almost immediately fire was returned from three of its windows. Two of the weapons were handguns . . . the third the Ithaca. Steel shot chewed up branches of the trees in front of him.

Big Vinny got the message. There was little chance he would

have been hit by the returned fire, but he knew that wasn't why they had all opened up on him.

He was being told that inside the cabin were three law enforcement officers capable of handling guns . . . officers who, having killed one of their assailants, were better armed than before.

Whatever else had happened, whatever damage Carver Fylde or Billy Bob might have inflicted, the people inside could still defend themselves.

There was no way Big Vinny was going to get inside that goddam stone-wall cabin.

He fired two more rounds to keep their heads down and turned away.

He had to get moving.

By now, he figured, help for those inside the cabin was well on its way. He would need to stay deep in the forest. He knew he couldn't use the Shogun; with only a single track leading to the road he was bound to meet cops coming the other way. He had to stay well away from the track.

Yet, he thought, if he paralleled the track there was a chance he could ambush the Chevy. Maybe the cops and whoever was left in the cabin might decide to pull out before help arrived. He thought of Billy Bob. Christ, how he wanted to slaughter those bastards.

His heart yearned to attack them . . . no matter what.

His head told him to keep well inside deep timber, head east and make the road where he could hijack a car and escape south.

He started away from the clearing, loping through the woods with the M-16 across his chest, ready for instant use.

Soon he felt the acid feeling at the back of his throat and the sensation of salt tears rolling down his face.

Despite all the firepower they had brought to bear on the cabin, despite all the experience and training of the Chickashaw Commando, the people in the cabin had held out and defeated them. And in the process inflicted terrible, awful casualties.

Billy Bob was dead.

And now Big Vinny was running away through the woods.

The pride of the Chickashaw Commando in humiliating retreat.

He wept as he ran.

It was a fuck-up. It was Vietnam all over again.

Chapter Thirty-Three

'Now,' Barber commanded.

Melissa, her left shoulder pressed tight into the wooden wall, hooked both arms around the window frame and pulled the trigger. Sam Barber had shown her how to hold the gun with two hands. The moment she fired she knew why. The Glock recoiled as if it had a life of its own, kicking back like a stalling car.

She fired again . . . and again . . . her eyes shut tight against the loud reports of her own and Mazello's pistols and the booming of the pump-action shotgun Barber was firing from the next window.

She didn't need her eyes open anyway, she reasoned. She wasn't expected to hit anything. And if she did, she would rather not know about it.

'Stop,' Barber ordered loudly.

The mind-rupturing noise ceased. Gratefully, Melissa sank to the floor beneath the window and put the pistol down. Two rounds from outside exploded against the far wall as she crawled towards Vito Kunzman. She cowered slightly but kept going.

It was remarkable, she thought, how quickly she was adapting to life under fire. Fleetingly she recalled her grandmother's stories of life in the Blitz and how civilians had learnt to cope with the bombing.

Kunzman had stopped rocking on his back and was lying still, with only the occasional low moan of pain. Melissa was surprised he was still conscious, though she noticed he was fading in and out. She knelt beside him and picked up the big bowie knife.

It was, she guessed, probably no more than two or three minutes since Chauncey had handed her the weapon. It seemed a lifetime ago. It *was* a lifetime, she thought with an agonised heart: Chauncey's lifetime. Within those few, short, transient moments, Chauncey Morton's life had run right to the buffers and been snuffed out.

Melissa glanced across the room at the body, lying grim and still like a discarded doll upon the bloody floor.

After a moment she turned her head away. It seemed somehow obscene to look – almost as if she were watching Chauncey on the toilet. She directed her attention to Kunzman.

'Mr Kunzman,' she murmured, 'Mr Kunzman.'

His face was even more deathly pale and his eyes were screwed tight shut. Slowly they opened.

'Mr Kunzman,' she continued, 'I'm going to try to bandage some of your wounds. I'm afraid it may hurt, but I have to do it. Otherwise . . .' Her voice tailed off. She didn't want to enlarge on what the word 'otherwise' implied.

She grasped the knife firmly and cut away at the ragged material around the old man's legs. The blade was terrifyingly sharp, cutting through the blood-soaked material like a chainsaw through cheese.

Kunzman's legs were horribly mutilated by the shotgun blast and he had lost a lot of blood. Melissa marvelled at how tough the old man was to have survived semi-conscious for so long. She checked his femoral artery. Miraculously, it hadn't been severed, as far as she could tell. If it had, she supposed, he would have bled to death by now.

Not that bleeding to death wasn't still a probability, she thought darkly. She stared down at him. His dull, pain-filled eyes stared back up at her.

She pulled off her jacket. Like her skirt, it was heavily streaked with blood. She dragged off her green silk blouse, heedless of the popping buttons, and sliced it into makeshift bandages, all the time aware of Kunzman's eyes staring at her bare shoulders and at the full, rich roundness of her breasts filling her brassière.

Deftly she created two tourniquets, one close to the top of each of his thighs. She used what was left of the blouse to bandage some of the larger wounds. Immediately the green silk was soaked with blood.

Swiftly she looked around the furniture in the cabin, half conscious that Sam Barber and Trooper Mazello were holding a muted council of war close to one of the windows. She spied what she needed and crabbed across the floor to get it. Returning with the footstool, she placed it by Kunzman's legs.

'Mr Kunzman.' She kneeled close and leaned down so he could hear. 'I have to raise your legs. To reduce the bleeding. It may hurt. Do you understand?'

He nodded imperceptibly and she saw his lips move. She bent closer.

'Do it,' he croaked weakly.

He moaned loudly as she lifted his legs. They were light and flabby, with no muscle tension. It felt as if she was picking up cold spaghetti. She was no expert, but she was pretty sure the bones of both legs had been smashed by the shotgun blast.

Sam Barber squatted down beside her and glanced at Kunzman. 'That's a good job,' he told her.

'It won't keep him alive long,' she whispered. 'He needs to be in hospital.'

Barber nodded. 'We're pretty sure the last of the bad guys has lit out. Mazello and I are going out to the car.'

Melissa glanced behind her at Trooper Mazello. He was staring at her naked back. She caught his glance. He reddened and swung around to the window. She turned back to Barber who, she noticed, never took his eyes off her face. 'Are you sure he's gone?'

Barber grimaced. 'Sure? No, I'm not sure. But it's my best guess. We've been looking hard but we can't see the bastard. Mazello will put out a call on the car radio, if it's still working. I'm going to cover him. You'll be alone here with Kunzman.'

He placed the pistol she had been firing on the floor beside her. 'We won't be long. Okay?'

She watched them shove the Chesterfield out of the way before hunkering down beside the splintered door. They waited a moment, then, in a sudden, swift move, yanked it open and set off at a crouching run towards the car.

Melissa held Vito Kunzman's hand and tried to smile reassuringly at him. Suddenly she was afraid. Except for three dead bodies and the old wounded man, she was alone . . . waiting as tight and taut as a gallows rope for the sound of gunfire.

She thought about Jamie.

With a start she realised it was the first time she had thought of him since she had entered the cabin. She had been so busy coping with destruction and violent death . . . so preoccupied with trying to stay alive . . . she hadn't given her son a single thought.

What would happen to him if she were killed? she wondered. Where would he go? How would he cope? She shook her head, banishing her bleak thoughts. This was not the time to be thinking like that, she told herself. She was going to survive all this. She was going to make it.

She shot a swift glance at Chauncey's body. She felt something awful and ugly move through her. It was a bizarre, distressing sensation . . . a sickening mixture of complete relief and crushing guilt. She felt sick.

Crash.

Barber and Mazello smashed back into the cabin. Melissa jumped in alarm and let out a small, frightened cry.

Immediately she noticed that, though they were both still edgy and alert, for the first time in what seemed an age they were standing upright.

'We got through,' Barber announced. 'Back-up is on the way. We're gonna be safe.'

She didn't know whether to laugh or cry . . . whether to hug Sam Barber or scream hysterically. In the end she did none of them. She gave Barber a beatific smile and said, 'I'm so glad.'

Barber stared at her and let out a sharp, crazy cackle.

Like her, he seemed on the edge of hysteria. Melissa squeezed Kunzman's hand. 'Do you hear that, Mr Kunzman? We're safe. We're going to get you to a hospital.'

'Loudonville says the quickest way to get him there is to start off in the car,' Barber told her quietly. 'They're calling up an air ambulance but they say it's likely to be a while. And they're not sure about landing a chopper here. The best thing is to take him outa here in the car. They're sending out an escort. The chopper will spot us on the road.'

'But he may not survive a car journey,' Melissa whispered hoarsely.

Barber shrugged. 'What else can we do?'

Kunzman was mouthing something at her. She bent close. 'Get me outa here,' he gasped. She didn't know whether he had heard what they were saying or merely guessed.

'Water. Get me water,' he moaned.

She got up and hurried to the bathroom. She caught sight of herself in the mirror and stopped in shock. Her face, like that of some Sioux warrior, was streaked in blood. Her hair was matted by it. She dragged her eyes away from the nightmare vision, filled a glass from the cold tap, grabbed a set of clean towels and hurried back into the cabin's main room.

Barber and Mazello were using one of the bloodied scatter rugs as a makeshift hammock for Kunzman. The old man moaned horrifically as they moved him onto it and carried him out to the car. Melissa followed, staring nervously at the encircling woods. She poured a few drops of water into his mouth before they eased him into the back seat of the big Chevy.

'Do what you can for him,' Barber said, holding the rear door open for Melissa.

She looked back at the cabin. 'But what about . . . what about . . . them? We can't leave them there.'

Barber's face softened. 'People are coming to take care of them.'

'But . . .'

'They're dead, Melissa,' he said gently. 'The dead must take care of the dead. We have to take care of the living.'

She stared at him. 'Wait,' she said suddenly. She ran back into the cabin, found a bedroom and dragged a couple of blankets off the bed. Bundling them in her arms she ran back to the car. She didn't look at the bodies.

'He's in shock,' she said, clambering into the back of the Caprice. 'I have to keep him warm.' Barber slammed the door behind her and ran around to the front of the car.

Squatting in the back she did her best to tuck the blankets around Kunzman. Already thin streams of blood were running off the plastic covering of the seat and dripping into the matting of the car floor. Melissa pressed the towels as hard as she dared onto his wounds. He moaned pathetically.

The interior of the Chevy was filled with radio static and the voice of the police dispatcher checking on their progress. The car bounced wildly over the ruts in the track and Kunzman cried out in agony.

'Slow down,' Melissa yelled through the grille at Mazello. 'He can't take any shaking up.'

'But that bastard is still out there,' Mazello protested. 'Maybe figuring to take another whack at us. We go slow, we're sitting ducks.'

Beside him, Sam Barber was rubbernecking, his head constantly swivelling through a hundred and eighty degrees, checking the dark, menacing pine forest rushing past the sides of the car. He was holding the shotgun at the ready. He glanced swiftly at Mazello. 'Do as she says,' he ordered. Mazello slowed the car.

Melissa put her mouth close to Kunzman's ear and whispered. 'It won't be long, Mr Kunzman.'

He reached up a hand. She thought for a moment his bloodied fingers were seeking her breast but he grasped her bare upper arm. His grip was weak and flabby; the hand deathly cold.

'Listen . . .' he croaked.

She bent her head close to his. 'Mr Kunzman, you mustn't talk. You have to conserve your strength.'

'Listen,' he insisted. The flaccid hand tried squeezing her arm. It was completely devoid of power, as weak as a baby's. It dropped away.

'Listen, you wanted me to talk to you.' His voice was strained and weak, yet imbued with a kind of manic insistence . . . as if every last fibre of his strength was going into getting the words out. 'So now listen. Listen good. If you wanna know the answers to your questions.'

'But . . .'

'Listen.'

Half-sitting on the Chevy's bloody floor, Melissa listened.

With an ear close to Kunzman's mouth, her eyes screwed shut and her brow tightly furrowed, she concentrated on his every word. It was like a confessional.

Nearby was her attaché case. Inside was a small Pearlcorder. She thought for a moment of retrieving it, then abandoned the idea. Scrabbling about trying to get at it was too much of a risk. Whatever happened, she didn't want to interrupt the old man's flow.

Straining hard to catch the weak, wheezing voice, she did her best to block out the distracting static of radio traffic between Mazello and the state troopers racing to the rescue. Dimly, she was aware of the car slowing down and making a sharp right turn onto the track leading to the road. Here the ruts were less deep and Mazello edged up the speed. Flinging it too fast into a bend, the car fishtailed, bucking crazily.

Kunzman cried out weakly.

'For Christ's sake, slow down,' Melissa screamed at the back of Mazello's neck. She turned back to Kunzman. 'Go on,' she whispered. She pressed the sodden towels onto his wounds.

301

He went on.

Minutes later the car suddenly made a sweeping left turn and Melissa felt metalled road beneath the wheels. 'Not long now, Mr Kunzman,' she murmured encouragingly. 'We'll soon be there.'

He stared up at her from beneath the blankets and nodded weakly. She gave him an optimistic smile. His eyes, as unfocused as a baby's, closed, and Melissa watched him slip back into unconsciousness.

She gazed at the elderly man.

Kunzman had told her a lot. Yet there was so much he *hadn't* told her. She had a million questions to put to the old man. If only he had been able to say . . .

She caught her thoughts.

For God's sake. The man was close to bleeding to death and she was bothered about what more he might have told her? She was appalled at her own callousness. How could she be thinking of her job at a time like this?

She pressed the towels against his wounds to stem the blood and listened to his chest. It was hard to tell: she thought he was still breathing. She tugged the bloody blankets tighter about his body and held him close.

There was nothing more she could do.

Above the noise of the radio and the Chevy's engine, she heard the whooping of police sirens. Almost at once there was a louder, deeper, more regular beat. Sam Barber looked back through the grille. 'The chopper's here, Melissa. It's going to land on the road just ahead.'

She eased herself up as the car slowed and took a peek out of the windows.

The car was in the middle of a convoy, with three police cars leading them and a similar number behind. All had sirens wailing and red lights flashing. As the Chevy drew to a halt, Melissa watched a couple of the lead cars race ahead and swerve across the road to form a barrier. Two of the cars following them dropped back, blocking off the road to their rear.

Ahead, the air ambulance hovered noisily over the road before easing itself down in a billowing cloud of dust. Instantly three green-suited paramedics were out and running towards the car.

She looked down at Kunzman and saw his eyes flicker. 'The ambulance is here, Mr Kunzman,' she said. 'You're going to be all right.'

He gazed up at her and mouthed something. She bent to hear him. 'You get what I told you?' he croaked.

She nodded. 'Yes.'

'Good.' He lapsed back into unconsciousness.

The car door was yanked open and a young woman's face appeared. 'Okay, you wanna let us get to him?'

Strong hands helped her out of the rear seat.

She staggered out into the strong sunshine of the road and gazed dazedly at the timbered hills around her. Her legs began to buckle and someone grabbed her. 'It's okay,' Barber said. 'It's okay. It's all over.'

The blocked-off section of the two-lane country road was filled with cars and teeming with police. Red and blue lights flashed like morse code in the bright light and radios crackled in the dry summer heat.

Leaning against Barber, Melissa watched Kunzman being lifted out of the car onto the paramedics' gurney. One of them was holding a bottle of saline connected by a tube to his arm. The medics trundled him swiftly towards the helicopter.

A young trooper hurried past them towards the air ambulance, staring at Melissa as he went. Held up by Barber's strong grip, she was suddenly aware of her appearance. She looked down.

The front of her body and the delicate white lace of her brassière were daubed in great smears of blood. Her arms, all the way up to her elbows, were covered in it and her dove grey skirt had turned a rusty brown. She frowned stupidly at herself. She looked like a refugee from an abattoir.

Looking up, she was suddenly conscious of the stares of the troopers. She crossed her arms over her chest.

A policewoman approached her holding a state trooper's cotton blouson. 'Here you go, honey. You wanna put this on?' she said. Melissa gave her a grateful look.

Barber helped her on with the blouson, then eased her back until she was leaning against the warm metal of the Chevy. 'You going to be okay for a minute?' he said. 'I have to have words with the captain.' He nodded at a big, middle-aged trooper relentlessly questioning Mazello in the middle of the roadway. 'Only for a moment. Then we'll get you the hell out of here. Okay?'

She nodded. 'I'll be okay,' she mumbled.

She watched him hurry towards Mazello and the captain then

turned to peer inside the car. Her attaché case was still on the floor. She clambered onto the back seat.

When Barber returned, he found Melissa sitting on top of the bloodstained blankets in the back of the car. She was talking into her tape recorder in a strained, rapid voice. He stared at her in surprise. 'What are you doing?'

She gave him a manic stare. 'Doing what I came out here to do.' Her voice was harsh and bleak. 'My job. Whatever happens now, I'm going to finish what I started.'

Chapter Thirty-Four

'Frankly, Miss Semmington, we didn't realise you were being pursued by organised criminals. We weren't told there were people after you prepared to use deadly force . . . guys with assault rifles.'

The voice was rough, hard-edged . . . laden with blame for what had happened. Berating her.

'No one told us anything about any of that. If they had, we'd have been prepared. We'd have sent a coupla SWAT teams out there. But we weren't told diddly squat. So now we got two of our best men dead. Two good troopers . . . murdered. Not to mention a detective from the New York Police Department. What I want to know is: why the hell weren't we told?'

Melissa glanced around the squad room. It was crowded with detectives and uniformed troopers, all of them big and ominous, and glaring at her with accusing, granite-chip eyes.

Sam Barber came to her rescue. 'You weren't told because Miss Semmington didn't know. None of us knew.'

Barber was seated across the desk from her. Both of them had their seats turned out and were facing into a large room furnished with metal desks and filing cabinets. The place was untidy, piled with papers and reports and sprinkled with styrofoam coffee cups. Melissa heard someone call it the squad room.

Barber gazed evenly up at the big man in the crumpled suit, unfazed by his angry demeanour. Melissa hadn't caught the detective's name, captain something or other – she couldn't remember. She'd been too numbed when they arrived at the building in Loudonville to take any notice of names.

Soon after arriving, a female officer had shown her to the showers where she had spent twenty minutes under the hot water, washing the blood out of her hair and off her body. With cash from Melissa, the officer had gone to the local Wal-Mart and returned with fresh clothes . . . moccasins and white socks, jeans and a blue denim shirt.

After dressing Melissa had dumped her blood-soaked clothes in a plastic garbage bag, thinking it ironic that the entire ensemble she was wearing had cost her less than the blouse she'd used to bandage Vito Kunzman's wounds. Never had she been so glad to dispose of expensive clothes in favour of simple blue denim. Unbloodied denim.

She took a sip of the coffee someone had brought her.

The big detective, who was leaning against the edge of a desk across the gangway, bent forward.

Melissa wasn't wearing a brassière . . . that had gone into the garbage along with the rest of her blood-stained clothing. For a moment she wondered if the man was taking a peek down her open denim shirt. She killed the conjecture instantly.

It wasn't lust that prompted the stony-faced captain to surge forward . . . it was anger. Anger and grief. He had lost two colleagues. People he had known well. Two friends. Well, she could understand that. She had lost a friend too.

'Whaddaya mean she didn't know?' he demanded fiercely. 'If she didn't know, how come she had you and Detective Morton with her.'

The man was talking about her as if she wasn't there. For once she didn't care about misogyny. She was too numb and disorientated to get involved in any confrontation with the policeman.

'Miss Semmington was attacked in London,' Barber replied in an even tone. 'Following that, the authorities there arranged for her to have protection. Permanent protection. To last as long as she's running down hot money from the Exchange Bank. That protection extends to the States.'

'Attacked in London,' the detective repeated.

'By two men,' Melissa said dully. 'One of them had a knife.'

The captain's eyes moved to the fresh scar on her cheekbone. 'Jeeesus. If a coupla guys went after you in London – with knives . . . did you never think it possible that other guys would come after you over here – with guns?' His voice was bitter and sarcastic.

'We don't know that these people were after Miss Semmington,' Barber said coolly. 'It's more likely they were there to kill Vito Kunzman.'

'Right,' the big detective spat, 'a goddam bagman for the Mob. On the run after robbing them of a hell of a lot of money. And you didn't think the mob would send a hit team after him? Guys with machine guns?'

'He was in hiding. The FBI, along with a few other federal agencies had been looking for the guy for some time. If we couldn't find him, it figures LCN would be having trouble finding him too. In fact it was Miss Semmington who tracked him down.'

The detective's angry eyes cut to Melissa.

'So the Mob had you followed, and then sent in a team to take out Kunzman. And you didn't think to tell us that was likely.'

'What makes you think it was . . .?' Melissa began.

Sam Barber cut across her. His voice was suddenly metallic. 'Look, we don't know that Miss Semmington was followed. I think it's probably coincidence those guys showed up when they did. They arrived at the cabin, saw your trooper and opened up. That's the way it looks to me, anyway.'

'But we should have been told that could happen, for Christ's sake.'

'You knew all we knew. I briefed your people yesterday and told them everything. Everything. *You* provided the level of protection you thought was adequate. That we *all* thought was adequate. None of us, not Miss Semmington, not the Bureau, not the NYPD and not the New York State Police thought LCN would send in an assault team. We thought we were dealing with one frightened old man. We got it wrong. All of us.'

Barber paused, took a deep breath and exhaled a sigh. 'You gave us great cooperation,' he went on, 'and we're grateful for that. And I'm sorry about your two guys. Really sorry. I'm also sorry about Detective Morton.' He cast a swift glance at Melissa. 'But shit, bad shit, happens sometimes. Like here. But . . . we didn't expect it any more than you did. You have to understand that.'

The big detective grunted angrily. A man walked into the squad room and handed him a slip of paper. He glanced at it then fixed Barber with a bitter, piercing look. His grey rocky face was a mask of pain and rage. 'This whole thing has turned into a rat's ass,' he snarled. 'You haven't even got what you came for. Vito Kunzman died in hospital ten minutes ago. He never regained consciousness.'

They took the early evening flight out of Albany, Barber in

307

his crumpled suit, Melissa in her denims and carrying her attaché case. The case was streaked by a number of ugly, repulsive stains running from top to bottom, dark against the polished, claret-coloured leather.

They spoke no more than half a dozen words throughout the flight. Barber had somehow procured five milligrammes of diazepam for Melissa. Swaddled by its narcotic effects, she noticed nothing of the journey.

Waiting outside airport arrivals was a Bureau car which whisked them in the direction of downtown Manhattan. Slowly it occurred to Melissa that they were not making for her hotel. 'Where are we going?' she asked dully.

Barber turned in the front passenger seat. 'We're relocating you. This time you'll be under the protection of the Bureau.'

The hotel was quiet and unassuming, somewhere in the mid-twenties off Park. The room was smaller than the one she had left in the Pierre, but all her things had been moved and were neatly laid out or hung up. There were interconnecting doors on both sides of the room. They were open.

'There are Bureau teams on either side of you,' Barber told her. 'And I'm just across the hall. You need to eat, so order dinner. Then go to bed. Tomorrow we can talk. Okay?'

Someone sent down for dinner and a couple of women agents sat with her as she picked at the food. Melissa scarcely spoke to them. She didn't want to get acquainted with her minders. She had done that once. She wasn't going to do it again.

The short, intense friendship had confused and excited her. Now, after its sudden and sickening end, all she could feel was the crushing burden of guilt.

She was eating dinner and Chauncey Morton was in the morgue.

She stared around the plain, anonymous room with listless eyes. She was grateful to be there. To have returned to the room in the Pierre with its memories of Chauncey would have been unbearable.

After the meal, she emptied the contents of her attaché case into a plastic carrier bag and asked one of the agents to get rid of the case. The agent looked surprised. 'Hell, this is expensive,' she murmured. 'You sure that's what you want?'

'Please do it,' Melissa entreated.

It was too late to call England so she took a hot bath, washed her hair again and crawled into bed. Sam Barber had procured a small bottle of Temazepan. She took two. Just before she fell into a deep, dark, dreamless sleep, she remembered she was supposed to have called Bob Briscoe. He would be wondering where she was.

She woke early and for a moment stared at the ceiling in half-drugged puzzlement before where she was – and the reasons why – came flooding back. She groaned and felt the palms of her hands and the soles of her feet turn suddenly sweaty.

She lay still for a while, fighting the raw, naked fear.

She wanted to scream. Hysterically. To scream and scream and keep on screaming. She could feel her body trembling. She tried controlling it by telling herself repeatedly that it was all over . . . that she was safe.

After a time, the shaking subsided. She got out of bed.

She called home. Everything was normal, Astrid told her. Melissa insisted on speaking to Jamie as well as checking with Liz that all was safe and secure. She made no mention of what had happened. The young policewoman assured her that things were fine. The blue Mondeo was in permanent attendance and every one was well and happy. Jamie especially. He and George had been playing in the garden and the puppy had peed on the policewoman's shoes.

The call helped settle Melissa's nerves. She pictured the scene at the cottage, so far removed from the terror and violence of the day before. That, she told herself, was reality. That was the real world . . . her real world.

What had happened in the cabin, she reasoned, was an isolated incident of horror and violence. It had been a nightmare but, like all nightmares, when the morning came it was over. She had survived. It was the past and – whatever else it could do – the past couldn't hurt her.

She kept telling herself that as she showered and put on a knee-length cotton skirt and a navy blue teeshirt.

She called Bob Briscoe's number. He picked up almost immediately.

'Hi, what happened to you?' he quizzed. 'I called your hotel a few times last evening, but first they said you weren't there and then they said you had checked out. What happened?'

'I'm afraid something came up,' she replied as brightly as

she could. Though it was shallow and meaningless, it was the best description she could put on the previous day's events.

'But you're still in town?' Briscoe inquired.

'Yes. I had to change my hotel.'

'Yeah? So what happened?'

'I can't talk about it right now, I'm afraid. It was quite serious.'
He caught the change in her voice.

'Serious. I see. Well, no, I don't see, but if you can't talk about it . . . well.' He paused. 'Look, am I gonna be able to see you?'

'I don't know. I don't know what my plans are for the next day or so. I'm sorry. It's all very vague. I'm sorry.'

'Okay, well, can I call you?'

She frowned at the wallpaper. She wasn't sure if it was a good idea to give him her number. 'I don't know,' she stuttered. 'Perhaps it's best if I call you.'

It was his turn for a change of voice. 'Oh, okay. Well, I guess I'll have to wait to hear from you then.'

'Actually, Bob, it isn't like that. It's just . . .' She didn't know what to say or how to say it. She gave up trying. 'Look,' she said hurriedly. 'I'm sorry but I have to go. I'll call you again soon. I promise. Promise.'

She put the phone down and sat on the edge of the bed. Scarcely thirty-six hours earlier she had been impatient to see Bob Briscoe . . . desperate to get into his bed, even more desperate to get him into her. But now . . . !

Well, what now? she asked herself. Was she different? Had something changed?

She thought about it, staring at the wallpaper and hearing the sounds of the city a dozen floors below.

No, she concluded, nothing had changed. Whatever had happened to her since coming to America, she was still the same person she was before. Maybe she had learned more about herself: maybe Chauncey Morton, along with the terror of being shot at and surviving, had taught her things about herself she hadn't known before. But despite all that, she was still the same person.

What was different now was her feeling of numbness. Her experiences had desensitised her. Yet she knew herself well enough to know that when the paralysis wore off, she would be wanting Bob Briscoe as hot and fervently as she had before. Right now wasn't the time for lust. Her libido was as flat as a punctured tyre. But the time would come. She knew it.

In the meantime, though she didn't want to screw him, she didn't want to screw him up. She wasn't prepared to jeopadise what they had going.

She picked up the phone and pressed redial. Briscoe's voice came on the line immediately.

'Bob, it's me. Look . . .' she began.

' . . . your name and number and time of calling . . .' the voice continued.

Surprised, Melissa held the receiver away from her ear. She was talking to Briscoe's answering machine. In the short time since they had spoken, he had gone out.

She allowed herself a fleeting smile . . . the first since the shootings at the cabin. She guessed his rush was due to some urgent meeting. Urgent was the only kind of meeting bankers and financiers ever had.

'Look,' she repeated when the message finished, 'I didn't mean to sound so short with you. I really do want to see you. It's just that . . . well . . . I've had a bad experience. I'll tell you about it when we meet. And I'll give you my number.' She read the number off the phone. 'Call me when you get back and we'll see each other as soon as we can. I do want to see you. Really I do.'

Afterwards it occurred to her that, again, she had made herself sound like a schoolgirl with a crush.

The difference was that this time she didn't care.

She wondered fleetingly if she should have given him her number and decided it was okay. Bob Briscoe was part of her private life. And her private life was her business. She needed to see Bob. Seeing him would be good for her. Even though right now she didn't want sex, she could certainly use some comfort.

There was a knock at one of the interconnecting doors. Melissa's heart jumped, its beat suddenly supercharged.

'Melissa, it's me.' It was Sam Barber. The banging inside her chest eased off. 'Can I come in?' She told him he could.

Barber had on a fresh suit and his grey hair was perfectly combed. On the surface he looked as smart as when she had first met him, but Melissa noticed the skin beneath his eyes was dark and that the lines around his mouth were deeper than they had been twenty-four hours earlier. The blue of his eyes seemed washed out, their sharpness blunted by trouble.

Barber's evident reaction to the horrors of the shootings brought Melissa some comfort. If he, a professional, could suffer adverse effects from someone trying to kill him then it was all right for her to do the same. Their shared pain made her feel close to him. Together they had experienced the awful events at Austerlitz. Together they were suffering its after effects.

She grasped his arm warmly. He was surprised. 'How are you?'

He gazed at her and decided against bullshit or false nonchalance. 'I'll be okay,' he told her quietly. 'But I don't want to go through anything like that again. I'm getting too old. Nerves can't take it. What about you?'

'The same.' They smiled weakly at each other.

'We have to put it behind us,' he said soberly.

'I know. I'm working on it.'

He nodded 'Good.' His face fell.

'What's wrong?'

'I have to ask you to go through it again. With me. Everything that happened at the cabin. We need a statement from you. Somehow we have to try to make sense of it all. I appreciate talking about it will be painful . . . that it won't help you get over it.'

She felt sick. 'Is it really necessary?'

'Yes. I'm sorry. Three law-enforcement officers are dead, and their agencies want to know why. They want details . . . statements. The Bureau has said we'll handle it. If you do it once with me you don't have to do it twice over with NYPD and the State Police.'

'Yes, I see.'

'We can do it here if you like. Rather than at the Bureau's offices.'

Her eyes moved around the room. Already she was getting used to it. The sun was glowing through the windows, giving the place a warm, soft ambience. She visualised the local offices of the FBI and nodded. 'Yes, I'd prefer to stay here.'

Barber pulled up a chair and took out a notebook and silver ballpen as Melissa seated herself on the edge of the bed. She stared at him meditatively. 'Sam?'

He looked up and caught her expression. 'What is it?'

312

'Why do the State Police think the Mafia sent those men to kill Vito Kunzman?'

Barber was puzzled at the naïveté of her question. 'Well, it's pretty obvious really. Kunzman had stolen their money. You rob the Mob, they're gonna come after you.'

'Why? Why would they come after you?'

Barber's puzzlement deepened. 'Vengeance. Nobody stiffs the Mob. Not and gets away with it they don't. They go after you. *Pour encourager les autres.* Isn't that how you say it?'

She allowed herself another smile. 'Yes, something like that. But okay, I understand they'd do that if it were five hundred dollars. But Kunzman had embezzled five hundred million. Surely the Mafia isn't stupid.'

'No,' he said slowly, 'they're not stupid.'

'So why try and kill him? I imagine the Mafia are like bankers. The more you owe them, the nicer they are to you. If Kunzman had half a billion dollars of Mafia money, they would want him alive. To tell them where he'd hidden it. With Kunzman dead they could kiss the money goodbye.'

Barber's puzzled expression gave way to a pensive gaze. 'Yeah,' he ruminated: 'that makes sense. You could have a point, Melissa. But if those guys weren't from the Mob, then who the hell were they from?'

His face lightened. 'We may get some idea in a day or so. At least on the two Detective Morton shot. We've lifted their prints and we're running them through the Bureau's computer files. If their prints are in there, we'll have a handle on those bastards.'

Melissa felt her stomach churn at the mention of Chauncey's name. She did her best to ignore it. 'And another thing,' she pressed on: 'who says the five hundred million was Mafia money?'

Barber shrugged. 'Didn't you say it was lifted out of various accounts at the Exchange Bank? The bank was established by LCN for the benefit of LCN.'

'Yes, but they weren't the only people using the bank. The money could have belonged to any number of criminal or terrorist organisations. It could even be legitimate. Or, it could be from various sources: some criminal, some legitimate.'

Barber frowned. 'What makes you think that?'

'Because Vito Kunzman talked to me before he died. When we were in the car.'

Sam Barber straightened up in his seat. 'He did?'

'Yes. And at no time did he say the money he had stolen was Mafia cash. And,' she paused, thinking back to the scene in the cabin, 'what's more he never said those men shooting at us were from the Mafia.'

Barber reflected. 'Yeah, that's right,' he said carefully, 'he didn't.' He was quiet for a moment. 'So what else did Kunzman tell you?'

She shrugged. 'It was difficult to make sense of everything. And I'm not sure I heard it properly, not with the noise in the car and his being so weak. But mainly he told me how he'd lifted the half billion. He transferred it into Eurobonds, which he deposited in an account at the Exchange Bank a few weeks before it was shut down. Then he switched the bonds back into dollars and moved the funds out.'

She smiled quietly. 'Right now the money is sitting in a nominee account in a bank in the Channel Islands.'

'Kunzman told you all this?' Barber was impressed.

'Yes.'

'Jeeez, Melissa, you traced the money! That's great! Well done.'

'Thanks. Of course, I'm assuming what he's told me is the truth.'

'Do you think it is?'

She thought about it for a second, then: 'Yes, I'm pretty sure of it. Actually, he also told me something about an account I've been trying to locate. A locked-box account.'

'A what?'

'Locked-box. It's what we call an account we're not able to get into. This one is hidden somewhere in an invisible file in the Exchange Bank's computer system. So far even our best computer people haven't been able to find it.'

'And Kunzman told you about this account?'

'Well no, not exactly. He wasn't very coherent and he passed out before he could say much. But he told me a couple of things.' She shrugged. 'They may help.'

'And you got all this out of him in the back of the car?'

'He might have told me more if he hadn't lost consciousness. I think he wanted to. You remember just before the shooting started he said he'd answer my questions?'

'Yeah, that's right. You asked him about a bank account.'

She nodded. 'That's it. That's the one he moved the half billion into. The locked box. It's called the Austerlitz Account.'

Chapter Thirty-Five

'Well,' she asked, 'is it what you want?'

Sam Barber clicked his ball pen and slipped it inside his jacket. He flicked through the pages of longhand he'd written in his notebook. 'Yeah, I'd say so.' He looked up at her. 'Thanks. I'm sorry to have put you through it.'

She nodded. 'That's okay. It had to be done I suppose.' She glanced at her watch. The statement had taken almost an hour. 'So what happens now?'

'I'll have this typed and then you'll need to sign it.'

'No, I didn't mean that. I meant can I go home now? Back to England. After I've signed the statement. Can I go?'

He gave her an odd look. 'Well sure. If you have to.'

She was surprised. 'Have to? No, I don't have to. I want to. Frankly, Sam, right now I want to get the hell out of America. I'm sorry if that sounds rude but . . .'

'No, no, sure, I understand. But the thing is . . . I was wondering if you could stay for another day or so.'

'What? Are you mad? I want to go home. I want to see Jamie.'

'Of course. I understand.' He shrugged apologetically. 'Look, I'm sorry if it seems I'm the guy who's always in the way of you getting back to your son. But the fact is, it might be useful if you were around. Like the last time. In San Francisco.'

'Why?'

He seemed embarrassed. 'As I say, it's like San Francisco. What I mean is, we've got a forensic team from the ECU going in today to do a search on Kunzman's cabin. And I thought . . .'

'Jesus Christ, Sam,' she screeched. 'If you think I'm ever going back to that awful place . . .'

'No, no, wait,' he protested. 'I didn't mean that. There's no way I'd ask you to go back there. No . . . what I meant was . . . if you stayed here we would bring you any papers we found.

Anything we figured might be interesting. That's all. You stay here and I'll bring you what we uncover.'

'You? Does that mean you're going back there?'

'Yes.'

She shuddered and stared at him, appalled. 'God, you're brave,' she said quietly. 'How can you do that?'

His face was lugubrious. 'I'm not looking forward to it. That's for sure. But . . . it's the job.'

'So you want me to stay here and wait for you to bring back any documents you discover.' He nodded. 'But why? Why can't your Economic Crime Unit inspect them?'

'The deal still stands, Melissa. Washington and London are cooperating on this Exchange Bank thing at the highest level. Anything we find that the liquidators can use . . . you get to keep.'

She frowned. 'How long?'

'Two days, tops. The state troopers are at the place already. Picking up shell casings, digging spent rounds out of the woodwork, that kind of stuff.' He glanced at his watch. 'My people are going in about now. They'll be taking the place apart. I'm flying up midday. Whatever there is to find we'll have found it this time tomorrow. Maybe, another day for you to examine what we got . . . maybe less. You could be outa here tomorrow. At most, two days.'

'Thanks a lot,' she murmured.

'Well, what do you say, Melissa?'

She stared at Barber, examining his worn, tired face. She already knew the answer. Recent history had given her an affinity to the special agent. If he had the grit to go back into the nightmare, then, she concluded, the least she could do was to stay and examine whatever he brought back.

And Vito Kunzman was important, she thought. She had come to America in the hope of tracking the man down, of questioning him and thereby adding a few missing pieces to the jigsaw.

She was sure what he had told her as he lay dying in the back of the police car would prove vital. It could be the missing link. *Could be,* she repeated to herself.

But, she had no way of knowing. Not yet. Not for sure. And if it wasn't . . . if what he had told her was wrong or a pack of lies . . . if she couldn't make the connections between what he'd said and what she knew . . . then any papers Barber and his team found at Kunzman's cabin might be even more critical to her investigations.

'All right. Two days. After that I'm going home. No matter what.'

He smiled. 'Sure. You bet. Two days, max.' He stood up, pocketing his notebook. It was his turn to touch her arm affectionately. 'Thanks,' he said warmly. 'I appreciate it.'

'Will I be all right here?' she asked him. 'Safe?'

He gave her a direct look, his eyes locking onto hers. 'Absolutely.' His tone was definite. Reassuring.

'The teams will remain here to look after you. Eight agents, Melissa. Nobody's going to get to you this time. Though, I figure any danger is over for you. Whoever those guys were, it's Kunzman they were after.'

She stared back at him, praying he was right.

He moved away to the door. 'I'll see you tomorrow,' he said. He had reached the door when she called him.

'Sam.' He turned. 'What should I do about Chauncey?' Her voice was plaintive.

'What?' He didn't understand.

'Should I go and see her family? Go to her funeral? Talk to her lieutenant at the Precinct?'

He moved back towards her, crossing the room hesitantly, his expression combining bewilderment and alarm. 'Why?'

Her face twisted. 'Well . . . you know. She's dead because of me. It's my fault. Don't you think I ought to go and say sorry to someone?'

A loud, spontaneous sob caught at the back of her throat.

'Jesus, Melissa, no. No I don't. And Detective Morton isn't dead because of you. Her death wasn't your fault. Don't ever think that. You didn't shoot her, for Christ's sake. It was that bastard at the window.'

Without warning, all the emotions Melissa had sought to control, all the pain and guilt she had been attempting to suppress, blew up. Her eyes erupted with tears.

'Yes, but she wouldn't be dead now if it wasn't for me,' she cried out. 'She'd still be alive if she hadn't been looking after me.' Her voice rose to a wail.

'She was a detective. There was always a chance she'd be killed in the line of duty. She knew that. You could say she wouldn't be dead if she hadn't chosen to be a detective. Or she

318

wouldn't have died if I'd figured we might be attacked. Her death is a tragedy, Melissa, but it's no one's fault. No one's. And definitely not yours.'

'But I feel so guilty.' Her shoulders sagged and her hands flew to her face as the tears flooded. Loud, racking sobs convulsed her body.

Barber put both arms around her and led her to the edge of the bed. Sitting down beside her he pulled her head into his chest, stroking her hair like a father.

For a while she clung to him. When she pulled away she whispered 'I'm sorry.' Her eyes were curtained by tears. She tried a pathetic smile. 'I seem to be making a habit of weeping on policemen's shirts.'

'It's okay. Don't apologise,' he said gently.

She found a hankie in the pocket of her skirt and blew her nose. The tears rolled down her cheeks unchecked. 'What can I do, Sam?' she sobbed.

'Nothing. You can't do anything, Melissa. She's dead. You can't bring her back. You can't do anything.'

'But I ought to apologise to someone. Make amends. Her family . . . her friends on the force.'

'No. Definitely not.'

'Why not? Because they'd blame me? Think I was responsible for her death?' Her tone was shrill and bitter. 'That's it isn't it? And they'd be right. I *am* responsible.'

'For Chrissake no, you're not! I keep telling you that. But . . .'

' . . . but if I went to see them, they'd blame me.'

'Hell, you saw how it was at Loudonville, Melissa. Sure they'd blame you. People are like that, for Chrissakes. We're all like that when it comes to family. But them *thinking* it was your fault doesn't mean it *is* your fault. It *wasn't* your fault. It's just better not to go pushing into people's sensitivities right now.'

'So what should I do?' she howled. 'Walk away? Forget all about it?'

'Yes.' His tone was definite, assertive. 'Absolutely. It's the best thing. Shit, Melissa you knew Detective Morton for less than forty-eight hours. No matter what kind of impression she made on you, it was not a lifelong friendship. And you weren't responsible for her death. So cry if you want and then forget about her. Let it go. When you leave here, leave it all behind. Go home to your son and forget Chauncey Morton and all this.'

She stared at him with anguished eyes.

He shrugged. 'That's all you can do, Melissa. Weep some, then let it go. Think about Jamie.'

She sniffed hard and blew her nose once more. He saw her give a barely perceptible nod.

He stood up. 'I gotta go.'

Melissa stood up with him, wiping her eyes on her sodden handkerchief.

Barber took her gently by the shoulders and peered at her. 'You going to be all right?' She snuffled and nodded. 'Good girl.' He moved away then suddenly turned. 'You had breakfast yet?' She shook her head. 'Coffee?'

She shook her head again. 'Nothing.'

'For God's sake, Melissa. You gotta eat. I'll have someone order you something up.'

'Coffee would be fine,' she sniffed. 'I'm not very hungry.'

He jabbed a finger at her. 'You need to eat. Okay?'

She shrugged and gave him a wan smile. 'Okay.' She watched him walk to the door and open it. 'Sam.' He looked back. 'Thanks.'

He smiled and nodded. 'You really want to thank me? Eat your breakfast.'

He must have told one of the agents in the adjoining room to order her the works. Juice, waffles and syrup, eggs, bacon, hash browns, rye toast . . . it was all there, the great American breakfast, complete with a big pot of coffee. Curiously, as soon as the white-coated waiter wheeled in the breakfast trolley, she discovered she was hungry. She ate more than half and afterwards felt much better.

She glanced at her watch. It was mid-morning in Manhattan; mid-afternoon in London. Time enough yet to call the office. She dug into the plastic carrier bag, found her tape recorder and transcribed into a notebook the text she had dictated the day before. The voice emanating from the tiny speaker was rapid and flat. Below its dull intonation she could hear the hysteria trying to break through.

For a while she frowned at her notes. Some of what she'd written she had told Sam Barber in her statement. A lot more she hadn't. She wasn't sure Sam would have made any sense of it. She wasn't sure she could. She tried to remember what else Kunzman had said.

320

It wasn't easy.

As half her mind tried to recall the things Kunzman had told her on the bloody back seat of the car, the other half was pulling back like a frightened horse, desperate to distance itself from memories of the day's sickening incidents.

A few more things he had murmured came back to her and she jotted them down, screwing her eyes up at her notes, endeavouring to fit what she had been told into what she already knew.

Slowly, her mind came to grips with the challenge, her hunter's instincts in the jungle of money taking over. Gradually the vivid technicolor images of the attack at the cabin began to fade into dull, grainy monochrome.

After about an hour she lifted the room phone, dialled the office on Eastcheap and asked for Andrew Bailey.

'Melissa, hi. How's America?' His voice was chirpy.

'It's fine,' she replied evenly. 'Andrew, how far have you got with tracking the Exchange Bank's missing half billion?'

The chirpiness disappeared. 'Well,' he said sombrely, 'we're still itemising the conversion of the negotiable instruments into Eurobonds. It's a long job. And so far we haven't been able to trace the account where the bonds were deposited. But we're getting there, Melissa. It's tough but we'll get there.'

'You can save yourselves the trouble, Andrew. The money is sitting in an account in Jersey.'

'What? Really? Christ, Melissa how did you find out? Did you find that bloke Kunzman?'

'Yes, I found him,' she said grimly.

Three thousand miles away, Bailey was too excited to catch the nuance in her voice. 'And he told you? That's fantastic,' he exclaimed. 'Bloody hell, how on earth . . . ?'

She closed down his euphoria. 'Andrew, get the mill grinding will you. We need to apply to the Court to get a restraining order on that account. Today, if possible.'

'It may be a bit late today, Melissa.'

'Try.' Her voice was steely.

This time Bailey registered her tone. 'Okay, we'll have a go.' She gave him details of the account. Afterwards he asked: 'But how on earth did Kunzman manage to get the money into Jersey?'

'It's a long story. He used the locked box.'

'The Austerlitz Account?'

'That's right. It was a clever set-up. Of course, in a few months' time we'd have traced the funds as far as the account. But after that . . . well, it would have been a black hole. We'd never have known where the money went. Not once it disappeared inside . . .'

She paused. Something vibrated in her brain. A resonance. Something she had just said. She screwed up her face, trying to get a handle on the wispy, immaterial notion floating somewhere inside her head. It wouldn't come. She couldn't make it solid . . . tangible.

She shook her head in irritation. 'Anyway,' she went on, 'now we know where it went and where it was finally deposited.'

'So Kunzman set up the Austerlitz Account as a kind of cutout. So we couldn't get beyond it to where the money was.'

'Yes, it looks that way.'

'Yet, as soon as you find him, he tells you the full story. Jesus, Melissa, what the hell did you say to him? You must have scared the shit out of him.'

She grunted and said nothing, closing her eyes to shut out the images.

'Can we get into the Austerlitz Account now?' Bailey's voice, bouncing off the satellite, brought her back to the present.

'No. Kunzman didn't tell me about that.'

'So we still don't know where it is. Or how to get into it. Oh well,' he sounded dismissive, 'I expect we'll find it one day. At least we now know what the account was for. And why Kunzman was the only one to operate it. He used it to embezzle funds from the bank.'

'Yes, but all the same, I'd still like to find it. Get inside it.'

'Well, why don't you go back and talk to Kunzman some more?'

She gritted her teeth. 'You haven't found anything out about it have you? Since I've been away?' she asked hurriedly

'No, nothing. As you say, it's a black hole. We know it's out there somewhere – but where?' Bailey laughed. 'Even Boris Redbourn with all his computer networks and the Internet can't locate it. It really irritates him.'

'Boris gets annoyed when he can't . . .' Her head came up with a jerk. 'Oh my God!'

Startled by her yelp, Bailey responded urgently. 'Melissa? What is it?'

In that instant the phantom oscillating in her brain crystallised

322

into shape. The notion was as solid as a block of concrete . . . or a brick.

'Andrew, put me through to Boris will you,' she demanded.

'What?'

'Put me through to Boris. It's urgent.'

Chapter Thirty-Six

She waited impatiently, drumming the fingers of her right hand on the bedside table. Boris Redbourn's voice came on the line. 'Hello.'

'Boris, it's me, Melissa.' She stopped drumming her fingers.

'Oh, hi, Melissa. How's things?'

'Fine . . . thanks. Listen, Boris . . .'

'You sound a long way off. Where are you?'

'New York. Look, Boris . . .'

'Hell, you certainly do get around, Melissa. What's it like in New York? It's pissing down here. I tell you I wouldn't mind being in . . .'

'Boris!' she screeched. 'For God's sake, listen.'

The wounded voice floated down off the satellite. 'Okay, okay. I'm only being friendly for Chrissake. Surely Rolay Richard can afford a few seconds' social chat on the phone? It doesn't have to be *all* business, does it?'

She ignored his whinging. 'Boris, you remember you told me about the Cyclix piggy-backed funds moving from Atlanta to the Exchange Bank on Curaçao? You said the account the money went into was a black hole.'

'Did I? I don't remember.'

'Yes you did. You couldn't get into it.'

'Still can't.' The doleful comment came through as she was speaking.

'You said you'd got the number of the account the funds went into, but there was no trace of that number in the branch on Curaçao or anywhere else.'

'That's right. Someone must have got into the computer and hidden the file. Which means there's a bank account out there somewhere. Floating around. I know it's there, but I can't bloody find it. All I've got is a random number which doesn't fit or

324

match anything. I need a password to trigger it open. Without that, the sodding thing is a black hole.'

'Did you try getting into it using the codenames Aziz gave me?'

'Yes, of course. I told you that.'

She frowned. 'You did?'

'Yes.'

'Have you tried triggering it with the codename "Austerlitz"?'

'Austerlitz? Hang on, let me see.' The phone went down heavily on the desk beside him.

There was a long pause. At a distance of three thousand miles Melissa heard him tapping keys on his keyboard. She gazed at the wallpaper then noticed she had gone back to drumming her fingers on the bedside table. She forced herself to stop, dropping her hand to rest loosely in her lap. She straightened up her back and squared her shoulders, making a conscious effort to sit prim and properly on the edge of the bed. The way her grandmother had taught her.

'Yes.'

'What?'

'Yes, I tried opening the account using the name Austerlitz as a password.'

'What happened?

'Nothing.'

'Nothing?' she cried.

'That's right.'

'Shit.' Her back collapsed and she slumped untidily. She began rapping her knuckles on the bedside table. 'Shit . . . shit . . . shit.'

'Melissa, are you okay?'

'What? Oh yes. Damn. It's just . . . well . . . I thought I'd cracked it. I was sure I'd found the Austerlitz Account.'

'Yeah?'

'Yes. You see, the man who stole half a billion from the Exchange Bank used the Austerlitz Account to launder the money. But the same man, Vito Kunzman, was also loosely connected with Cyclix. Which means he could have been involved somehow with those piggy-backed funds.'

'Which means he might have used the same account for both the funds and the stolen money,' Redbourn added.

'Right. I thought the account on Curaçao might be the Austerlitz.'

'But,' Redbourn pointed out, 'the Austerlitz Account was listed here. In London.'

'The account was listed in London but it wasn't necessarily located there. Actually, it wasn't officially listed anywhere. Only Akhtar Aziz and Mr Chalmodly, the general manager of the London head office, even knew about it. And they couldn't get into it. Anyway, a lot of those codename accounts listed in London were actually operated elsewhere. Out of the tax havens. So why not the Austerlitz Account? It didn't have to be operational in London. There's no reason why it shouldn't be located in the Netherlands Antilles.'

'And you assumed you'd made a connection. Thought Austerlitz was the account on Curaçao?'

'Yes. I thought two and two might make four.'

'Two and two always does. That's the great thing about numbers. They're consistent.' She grunted sulkily. 'Anyway, I'm sorry, Melissa. It's no go with Austerlitz in Curaçao, I'm afraid.'

'Damn.'

'So when are you coming back?' She didn't reply. 'Melissa?'

She hadn't heard him. A sudden thought struck her. 'Boris, what's the number of that account on Curaçao?'

She waited as he searched the computer, hearing him tapping his way to the data. Moments later he was back on the line and reading off a number. She wrote it on her pad.

'No,' she announced, staring at the number: 'that can't be right.'

'What do you mean?'

'That's seven digits.'

'So?'

'Hang on.' She put the phone down and leafed through the notes in her notebook. She found what she was looking for and stared at it. She lifted the phone. 'Vito Kunzman said the Austerlitz Account had an eight-digit code.'

'Eight digits . . . Well, that's it then. Obviously it's not this bloody account in Curaçao.'

'No, wait. Austerlitz is a codename account . . . what they called in the Exchange Bank a Manager's Ledger Account. Now, we know most of the MLAs are umbrella accounts . . . operating separate deposits in different branches of the Exchange Bank all over the world. So maybe the account on Curaçao is just a part of the Austerlitz. And to open it we need the codename,

Austerlitz, plus its own unique eight-digit number.'

There was silence at the other end. She could almost hear Redbourn mulling over her words. 'So what you're saying is that this account could have both a codename and a code number.'

'Yes.' She was excited. 'Not could have. It *does* have.'

'Yeah, okay. It makes sense. If you're a security freak. So, what's the number?'

'I don't know. Mr Kunzman didn't say.'

'Well, why don't you go back and ask him?'

She breathed deeply. 'I can't. Believe me, Boris, I would if I could but . . . it's just not possible.'

'Well, I suppose I can get the . . .'

'Wait,' she interrupted, whooping into the phone. 'Just wait a minute, Boris.' She went back to her notebook, feverishly riffling through the pages. She found what she was looking for and lifted the handset. 'Kunzman said the number had a connection with Austerlitz. It was connected somehow.'

'Connected? What the hell does he mean by that?'

'I don't know. That's what he said. It had a connection.'

'Can't you ask him what he meant?'

'No. I've told you. I can't.'

'What the hell was this bloke Kunzman doing? Playing games with you? An unknown eight-digit code *connected* with Austerlitz. What's that supposed to mean for Christ's sake?'

'I don't know. Mr Kunzman wasn't very . . .' she searched for the word . . . 'coherent at the time. But I'm sure that's what he said. Connected.'

'What the hell. Was he pissed or something?'

'Come on, Boris.' Melissa rose urgently from her seat on the edge of the bed, seeking to take control of the conversation. 'Connected means just that. Connected. Connected to a place. Right? Or . . . or . . . an event.'

'An event?'

'Yes. Wasn't Austerlitz a battle?'

'Was it?' he queried peevishly. 'Buggered if I know.'

'Yes. Definitely. During the Napoleonic Wars. I'm sure of it. Don't you remember?'

'Shit, don't be silly. I wasn't even alive then.'

She laughed. 'No, you idiot. I meant at school.'

'I dunno. I wasn't interested in history. Never took any notice.'

327

'Well, take my word for it. Austerlitz was a battle. So you need to find out all you can about it.'

'What?'

She ignored his pained yelp. 'And the place. There's a place here in New York State called Austerlitz. Find out what you can about both the place and the battle. We're looking for any sequence of numbers connected with either.'

'Jesus, Melissa, what's got into you? Where the hell am I going to find out that kind of stuff? Who the hell knows about ancient battles? Who cares? It's impossible.'

'No it's not.' She lifted the phone off the bedside table and, carrying it with her, began marching up and down beside the bed. 'All the answers are sitting right in front of you, Boris. It's there. Whatever you want to know.'

'What do you mean?'

'The Internet. You're always raving about it. I bet you can find something out about the Battle of Austerlitz on the Internet.'

There was a short silence at the other end of the line. 'Well . . . maybe. Yeah, you could be right.'

'I am right. The thing is, Boris, I need you to get onto it now.'

'Now!' he yelped. 'Come on, Melissa. I've got a full workload here. I can't drop everything to go cybersurfing. Looking for some old bloody battle.'

'Boris, this is important. Really important. I need it done now. If we can find the number to open that account, I'm pretty sure I'll have found another brick. A bloody big brick. The whole wall could come down.'

'Jesus Christ, Melissa,' Redbourn's voice was alarmed, 'what's happening to you? Is America doing your head in? You caught Mad Accountant's Disease, or what? Bricks . . . battles . . . what the hell is all this?'

She stopped in the middle of her pacing. When she answered, her voice was firm and level. 'There's nothing wrong with me, Boris. I've got a feeling that's all. I think we could be close to getting inside the Austerlitz Account.'

'Well, all right. But what's the panic? What's so special about this particular account?'

Melissa knitted her brows. 'I don't know,' she answered haltingly. 'There's something not right about it. Something that doesn't add up.'

328

'Yeah, such as what?'

She smiled into the phone. 'Boris, I'll tell you when you've cracked it. So come on. What do you say? Say you'll do it. Now.'

Reluctantly, he agreed. He told her he would call her back within a couple of hours . . . sooner if he came up with the right number.

He was back on the line in less than a hour. She grabbed the handset at the phone's first warble.

'Boris? What's happened? How have you got on?'

His tone was heavy with frustration. 'Drawn a blank,' he said ponderously. 'A complete bloody blank. I've tried everything. Anything I could think that's connected, plus a few crazy things that aren't.'

She picked up the phone and carried it to the window where she gazed down on the spreading green branches of the plane trees in the street below. 'Damn,' she groaned.

'I've tried it all. First I looked up a gazetteer and keyed in the map reference for Austerlitz.'

'That's a good idea,' she told him. 'Kunzman's secretary said he was into maps and that kind of thing.'

'Well, it didn't bloody work,' Redbourn moaned. 'I tried it including the north and east references and then without. I even tried it backwards. No go.'

'So what else?'

'I checked up on the battle, like you suggested. I tried the date, second of December eighteen hundred and five. Nothing. I tried it backwards. Nothing. Then I tried more wacky stuff like . . .'

'Wait a minute,' Melissa interrupted, 'did you try the date the American way? Putting the month before the day? That might work.'

'Done it.' His voice coming out of space was dry and laconic. 'Tried that backwards too. No go. So I went for anything that would give me an eight-digit number. Napoleon's birthday, the birthdays of some of the generals who fought there . . . stuff like that.'

'It's a bit far-fetched, Boris,' she grumbled.

'Hell, it's connected isn't it?' he snapped. 'I mean, what was this bloke Kunzman trying to say when he said the code number was connected? How connected is connected for Chrissake?'

Redbourn was making no effort to hide his irritation; it came winging down out of space loud and clear and bitter. 'I think he's pissing you about, Melissa.'

She leaned against the wall close to the window and watched the traffic. She sighed.

'Why the hell can't you talk to him again?' Redbourn complained.

'I can't, Boris,' she muttered. 'I just can't.'

'Well in that case we're fucked,' he said savagely. 'I can't find the bloody code number. Nothing's connected that I can see.'

She sighed again. 'It's beginning to look that way.' Suddenly she felt tired. Resignation dogged her voice. 'What about the other Austerlitz?' she asked wearily.

'What other Austerlitz?'

'Come on, Boris. I told you. There's an Austerlitz here, in New York State.'

'That's the one I got out of the gazetteer.'

'But what about the other one?'

'What other one? There's only one Austerlitz. The place near you.'

She came up off the wall, suddenly animated. 'Boris, that's bullshit. There's an Austerlitz in Europe.'

'No there's not.'

'For Christ's sake, Boris.' Her voice was high and intense. 'Of course there is. The Battle of Austerlitz got its name from a place. What? You think Napoleon fought a battle and then decided to make up a name? Why don't we call it Austerlitz, guys?' she mimicked sarcastically. 'That's a nice name? Is that how you think battles get their names? Get real, Boris. They take their names from places . . . places close by. Hastings . . . Blenheim . . . Arnhem. You think the battle of Waterloo was called after the station?'

'Bloody hell, Melissa, what is *wrong* with you?' he wailed. 'How the hell would I know how battles get their names? Who gives a shit anyway? I thought the bloody thing was fought at the place near you. In New York.'

'Napoleon in America?' she howled. 'For God's sake, Boris!'

'Well I don't bloody know!' he bellowed.

'All right, all right.' She straightened up and took a deep breath, willing herself to be serene. 'Boris, I'm sorry,' she said

330

after a moment. 'I didn't mean to shout at you. Or be bitchy.'

He grunted in that special, dejected, sorry-for-himself way she noticed men used when they had as much to apologise for as her . . . only she had said sorry first. 'It's all right,' he said glumly.

'Look there has to be a place in Europe called Austerlitz. It will be the place they named the battle after. It's probably quite small but it's there. Definitely. Poland, Germany, Hungary, somewhere around there.'

'But it wasn't listed in the gazetteer I looked in.'

'But it must be.'

'It isn't,' he insisted. 'The only Austerlitz listed is in New York State. So, if this second one doesn't exist, this bloke Kunzman wouldn't know about it, would he? Which means he couldn't have used it as a code number for the account. So why are we bothering?'

Melissa wasn't listening. Something Sam Barber had told her, way back in what now seemed like centuries ago, was coming back. 'Wait. Kunzman's family originally came from Czechoslovakia. Maybe that's where Austerlitz is.'

'Well that explains it.' Redbourn's tone was acid. 'There's no such place as Czechoslovakia any more. Which probably explains why there's no such place as Austerlitz. There's the Czech Republic and there's Slovakia. Even I know that. So which one is this place supposed to be in?'

'Boris, I don't know. It's somewhere in Central Europe. I know it is. You have to find it.'

'How, for God's sake?'

'There's a copy of *The Times Atlas of the World* in the senior partners' library on the fifteenth floor. Go and get it. It's bound to be in there.'

'You want me to go up to the fifteenth floor? The holy of holies?'

'Yes. I'll hang on.'

'Bloody hell, Melissa, how much is this phone call costing?'

'To hell with the cost. We're talking billions here. Just go and get the Atlas and look in the gazetteer at the back. I'll wait.'

For the next ten minutes she counted the yellow cabs streaming through the street below.

Redbourn returned. 'Hello, Melissa, you there?' His voice was subdued.

331

'Yes.'

'I've checked the Atlas. There's no such place as Austerlitz.'
She caught her breath. 'But there must . . .'

'For some reason it's been renamed. Austerlitz is now called Slavkov. It's in the Czech Republic. You were right.'

'Do you have the map reference?'

'Yes.'

'Key it in. Without the compass directions.'

'Okay, I'll call you back.'

'No, don't call me back. Do it now. I'll hang on.'

'Jeeesus, this call must be costing a fortune.'

'Boris,' she commanded, 'just do it.' She heard the clunk as he put the phone down.

She screwed her eyes tight shut, knowing that all she could do now was hope. As far as she could see this was her last chance.

With her eyes still closed she pictured the scene in Redbourn's office. Surrounded by the silent screens with their shimmering multi-colour images, he would be hunched over his keyboard, clicking on the icon to connect his modem to the Exchange Bank computer in the Netherlands Antilles.

She heard the keyboard rattle as he typed in the word Austerlitz, and listened intently as he muttered the numbers: '49101653.'

There was a long, grim silence. She couldn't stand it.

'Boris,' she yelled, 'Boris. Talk to me. Pick up the bloody phone.'

'Shit,' she heard him say. The phone rattled as he picked it up.

'What? What's happened.'

There was another silence. Then his voice came through. Quiet, evenly modulated, filled with restrained astonishment.

'Congratulations, Melissa. It's your birthday. You've just opened the locked box. We're inside the Austerlitz Account.'

Chapter Thirty-Seven

Her instructions were clear and explicit, her tone resolute and decisive. Don't do anything until she got back to the office, she told him. Relock the locked box . . . Don't go near the Austerlitz Account until she was there.

'I'll be back, probably the day after tomorrow. Don't do anything until you see me. You understand?'

'Yeah, yeah, Melissa, I've got the message,' he laughed. 'First you want me to drop everything for this bloody account. Now you don't want me to go near it. Well, don't worry. I've got plenty other things to do. I'll see you when you get back.'

'Oh, and one other thing, Boris. Don't tell anybody we've cracked it. Okay? As far as anybody else is concerned, the Austerlitz Account is still a locked box. You got that?'

'Sure.'

'Good. I'll see you soon. Goodbye, Boris. And thanks.'

She replaced the receiver and stood close to the window holding the phone at her side. Sightlessly she stared at the buildings opposite, deep in thought.

'Hey, get away from the window.'

Melissa looked up sharply. One of the agents had come through the open door connecting the next room and was hurrying towards her. Melissa gazed stupidly at the man. He grabbed her arm and steered her into the middle of the room.

'Look, don't go near the windows, okay?' he said gruffly.

The knocking started up in her chest. 'Why?' She glanced anxiously back at the big rectangle of early afternoon light. 'You don't think someone is still out there, do you?'

He gave her a tight smile. 'No, I don't. But don't let's take any chances, huh? Windows are not the best things to stand close to right now. So stay away from them. Just in case.'

'Just in case what?'

He shrugged. 'Just in case.'

She glowered at him. 'I thought I was supposed to be safe.'

'You are safe. We aim to keep it that way.'

'By treating me like a prisoner? Supposing I want to go out? See a friend?'

Again the tight, guarded smile. 'You can forget about going out, Miss Semmington. Our orders are to keep you safe here until you fly back to Britain. Here means in this room. A lot of important people want you well protected.'

'You mean I'm stuck in this place? I *am* a prisoner?'

'Hey, you want some tea?' he asked, changing the subject.

'No.'

The phone warbled and Melissa realised she was still holding it. Giving the agent a dark look, she walked slowly and conspicuously to the bed, put the phone down on the bedside table and picked up the handset.

'Miss Semmington?' It was Steven Timmison. His voice was urgent and solicitous. 'I've just been informed about the attempt on your life. Dear God, what can I say? I am so sorry. Are you all right? I understand you weren't hurt but . . . well, it must have been traumatic for you. How are you?'

She sat heavily on the bed and closed her eyes. What she didn't need right now was to be reminded of what had happened at the cabin. Especially by Timmison. After a moment she opened them. It was no use acting like a child, she told herself. She couldn't shut out the past by closing her eyes. She watched the FBI agent leave the room.

'Miss Semmington, are you there? Miss Semmington?'

'As a matter of fact, the FBI believe the attempt was on Vito Kunzman's life. Which,' she added darkly, 'succeeded. The rest of us just happened to be there. We got in the way. It wasn't very pleasant but I think I'm going to be all right. I'm trying to put it behind me.'

The heavy emphasis on her last words was lost on Timmison.

'But how did these people find Kunzman? Were they following you?'

'I don't know. No one knows. Sam Barber, the FBI's SAC, thinks it was coincidence. The men who killed Mr Kunzman turned up just after we did.'

'Yes, but in view of the attack on you in London . . .'

The knocking in her chest moved up a gear. 'But . . . *you*

334

said that was related to Piagini.' Her voice was suddenly agitated.

'Yes, that's right.'

'But I'm not working on that now. You took me off that aspect of the investigation. Surely you don't think the two attacks are connected?'

'Please don't distress yourself, Miss Semmington. I don't for a moment think they're connected. I'm sure the FBI, who are the people most likely to know the truth, are quite right in believing the timing of the attack was a coincidence. My sole concern is that you have been attacked twice. I must admit to feeling partly responsible. To make amends I have contacted some people in Washington and emphasised that you must have much better protection whilst you are over there.'

Melissa grunted but said nothing.

'When are you coming back?'

'The day after tomorrow. I'm waiting to find out if Mr Kunzman had any papers that could be useful to my investigations. A man from the FBI is bringing them to my hotel room.'

Timmison sounded genuinely surprised. 'I must say, Miss Semmington, I admire your dedication to duty.'

Again she said nothing. For a man who appeared so ascetic, almost bloodless, his compliments were curiously unctuous. She would rather he didn't bother.

'Please phone me as soon as you return,' he told her. 'I think we should meet. I would like to get an update on your progress and naturally I am very concerned about your personal safety.'

'You can get an update from Rolay Richard,' she told him stiffly. 'They'll tell you that I've managed to track down the half billion dollars missing from the Exchange Bank's accounts.'

'Really?' His voice was elated. 'Well that's . . .'

'As to my personal safety,' she cut across him, 'that's my affair. But I must tell you that, when I get back, I'm going to ask to be removed from the Exchange Bank liquidation as soon as possible. Now, I'm sorry but I have to go. Goodbye.'

She put the phone down before Timmison could respond, kicked off her pumps and lay down on the bed.

She was jittery. The knocking inside had revved up into a kind of shuddering, so hard and palpable that it was as if she were standing stark naked on the polar ice cap. At the same time she felt depleted. Weary to her bones.

Her nervous system was being overloaded she thought. Too

many events piling one upon another. Being shot at . . . watching people die . . . finding half a billion dollars of missing money . . . getting inside the Austerlitz Account . . . things were happening too fast for her system to cope.

She caught sight of the bottle of Temazepam Barber had given her. Should she take one? In the middle of the day? Yes, definitely, she told herself. She had to rest . . . to sleep. Her system was close to blowing a fuse. She was staring down a black hole called breakdown. She reached out for the bottle.

The phone warbled. She groaned and picked it up.

'Hello?'

'Melissa, it's Nigel.'

'Oh, hi, Nigel.' she sighed. She glanced at her watch. It was an effort to lift her arm. 'You still in the office?'

He laughed sharply. 'Of course. Where else would I be at seven in the evening? Listen, Andrew has just told me you've traced the five hundred million. Melissa, that's marvellous. Great. Well done.'

'Thanks.' Her tone was dog-tired.

There was a short silence. 'So when are you coming back?' he asked.

'Soon. Tomorrow, day after maybe. I don't know.' She frowned at the phone. 'You haven't spoken to Timmison yet?'

'Timmison? No. Why? Funny enough, he put a call in for me earlier. I haven't had time to call him back. Why do you ask?'

'It doesn't matter. Look, Nigel, I'm sorry but I have to go right now. I'll see you in a couple of days. Okay?'

She replaced the receiver before he could ask what was wrong. Exhaustion pressed her down onto the bed like a pile of bricks.

After a moment she reached out to the Temazepam, shook a pill into her palm and swallowed it with a little water left in an overnight glass. She shucked off her skirt but was too weary to pull her teeshirt off. She crawled under the bed covers.

It was the phone that woke her. She blinked dopily, her mind coming up out of a deep, dark place in her subconscious. The room was dim. Someone had drawn the curtains. The phone warbled again and she reached for it.

'Melissa, hi, it's Bob. I got your message. I'm sorry I wasn't here to take it. I had to go straight out to a meeting. Anyway, we gonna get together this evening?'

She eased herself onto an elbow, a narcotic fog swirling in

her brain. She suppressed a groan. 'Bob, hello.' Her voice was thick and groggy.

'You okay?'

She waited a moment, getting her head together. 'Fine,' she croaked, 'Actually I was asleep.'

'Oh, hell, I'm sorry. I woke you.'

'No, no,' she yawned, 'that's all right. What time is it?'

'Just after nine. Are you okay?'

'Yes I'm fine. I was just tired that's all.'

'Oh, okay. Well, we gonna see each other tonight?'

She closed her eyes and shook her head, trying to rid her brain of the anaesthetic mist and, at the same time, lamenting how badly her affair with Bob Briscoe was going.

Much of the reason for coming to America had been to see him. It hadn't happened. It wasn't going to happen. Each time he called for a date, she was forced to put him off. It was not the way to keep a lover.

'Oh, God, Bob, I can't. I can't leave . . .' She stopped herself. She couldn't tell him the FBI had her incarcerated in her own hotel room. 'I can't go out this evening,' she went on falteringly, 'I have too much to do. I have an enormous amount of work to catch up on.'

'Oh.' He sounded disappointed. 'Sounds to me like you're overdoing it, Melissa.' His tone held a hint of chagrin. 'Well,' his voice took on a brighter note, 'how about I come over to you? We could have dinner at your hotel. And you could tell me the story of what happened upcountry yesterday. From what you said this morning, it sounds pretty intriguing.'

Dear God, that was the *last* thing she wanted. To talk about Austerlitz to Bob Briscoe.

'Bob, I can't do that either. Look, I just can't see you this evening. I really want to but I can't. In fact I'm not going to be able to see you whilst I'm over here. Something has come up and it's just not possible. It's a complete pain and I'm disappointed. I was really looking forward to being with you but . . . there it is, I'm afraid.' She grimaced. It all sounded so pathetic. Feeble excuses. Like she didn't *want* to see him.

There was a heavy silence at the other end of the line.

'Bob, please don't take offence,' she pleaded. 'It's not that I don't *want* to see you. Really I do. It's just that things have changed and it's not possible right now.'

'Okay, Melissa, well I can't pretend to understand but . . . I want to see you too. So I guess I'm gonna have to accept it.' The disappointment in his voice had given way to dull resignation.

'As a matter of fact my own plans have changed,' he went on. 'I have to fly to London in a couple of days. Do you think we can meet when I'm there?'

'What, you're coming to London? But that's marvellous. Yes of course. Wonderful. And by then everything will be straight . . . back to normal. I promise. We'll have dinner and . . .' She stopped herself. Exhausted as she was she wanted to avoid her usual impression of a gushing schoolgirl.

'Okay,' his voice was lighter. She could detect his smile behind it. 'We'll get together in a couple of days. In London. I'll call you as soon as I get in.'

'Please do. I'm so sorry about not seeing you tonight.'

'Okay. No problem.'

'In fact I'm really sorry we haven't been able to see each other since I flew over. But, believe me, it's been a difficult trip.'

'Tell me all about it when we meet,' he said gently. 'Goodbye, Melissa.'

She put the phone down and stared at the dark shadows on the ceiling for a while before dragging herself out of bed and padding to the bathroom in her teeshirt and panties.

The doors at each end of the room were open, casting long rectangles of yellow lamp-light into the dim interior. She could hear the sound of muted televisions from both of the adjoining rooms.

She cleaned her teeth, poured herself a fresh glass of water and shuffled back to her bed where she took another Temazepam. Almost immediately she fell back into the deep dark place in her unconscious.

Again it was the phone that woke her. Light was streaming through a gap in the curtains. She lay still for a moment, letting the phone warble before wearily reaching out to lift it.

'Melissa. It's Sam Barber.'

She tried rubbing the sleep from her eyes with her free hand. 'Lo, Sam,' she mumbled.

'Look, I'm sorry to wake you but we need a little time together before you fly back. I've left it as late as I could.'

Her forehead furrowed as she peered at her watch with eyes

scarcely focusing. It was after eight. She had slept for almost twelve hours.

'Okay, Sam,' she said groggily. 'But you'll have to give me a few minutes to get ready.'

'Sure. I'll see you in half an hour. I'll bring your breakfast in.'

'Where are you?' she asked.

He chuckled. 'In the room next door.'

Instead of a white-coated waiter it was Sam who wheeled in the trolley. The breakfast selection was the same as the day before, with an extra coffee cup for Barber.

He was attentive, moving a small round table away from the window and getting her seated, setting out the food and cutlery, draping her napkin in her lap and pouring her coffee. She smiled up at him. 'God, Sam, I can't eat all this. I left half of it yesterday.'

'Which means you ate half of it,' he countered. 'Drink your juice and then see how you feel.'

She surprised herself and finished most of it. The food, along with the long shower she had taken – first hot and then cold – made her feel a whole lot better. The mind-threatening exhaustion of the night before seemed to have gone.

For the moment, her demons were sleeping.

Barber began clearing the breakfast things, moving them off the table and back onto the trolley. Melissa stood up to help. He noticed she was wearing the same skirt as the day before, along with a fresh, moss-green teeshirt. An agent from one of the adjoining rooms wheeled the trolley away.

Melissa leaned back in her seat and sipped her coffee. 'Well, what did you find at the cabin?'

Barber shook his head. 'Not a lot. And nothing that makes any immediate sense. Some of the papers look like Kunzman's personal finances. Stuff relating to his legal practice and his investments, that kind of thing. The rest look like they're maybe old accounts at the Exchange Bank. But nothing we've found ties in with anything we know about.'

'Were any of the papers hidden?'

He nodded. 'One small set of documents. Three sheets of paper with nothing but lists of company names. None that we recognise. They were wrapped in plastic and stuffed into an unused drain at the side of the cabin.'

'Nothing else?'

'No.' He smiled. 'Nothing sewn into the curtains; nothing hidden in hollowed out doors or walls; nothing in the plumbing. There are no documents in that cabin that we haven't found, Melissa. Definitely. We've taken the place apart.'

She shrugged. 'Okay. Well let's take a look at what you've got.'

Barber called one of his agents who carried a file into the room and placed it on the small, round table. The file contained about fifty documents, all photocopies. The originals, Barber said, had been shipped to Quantico for fingerprinting.

It was a poor haul. At least half the documents related to Kunzman's personal finances. The rest were as Barber had described, old Exchange Bank accounts. Together they sifted through them, looking for connections . . . for familiar names . . . for anything that might ring bells. There was nothing.

'Which were the ones you found hidden?' Melissa asked.

Barber pointed them out. Melissa ran her eyes down the lists of company names. Some British, some French and German, some even Japanese. One she guessed was American. None meant anything to her.

She shook her head. 'I'm sorry you had to go back to that awful place just for this.' She nodded at the paper-strewn table. 'It doesn't appear to amount to much.'

Barber shrugged. 'I'm sorry I asked you to hang around. It doesn't look like it was worth it.'

'I'd like copies all the same. Something in here may tie in with something in London.'

'Sure. You can have these. We've made an inventory and prepared a notarised statement for you to sign.'

Melissa stood up. 'Good. So I can go now?'

Barber grinned. 'We've got you booked on a late morning flight. Get packed and we can move out straight away.'

'Thank God.'

She was reminded of the drive from San Francisco to Sausalito. It seemed a long time ago. They had been in convoy then and they were in convoy now . . . she and Barber in the middle car, with one car full of agents ahead and two behind.

The difference was that then she'd scarcely been conscious of the convoy . . . had hardly thought it necessary.

Now she was glad of it.

Emerging from the roar of the Midtown Tunnel, Melissa said, 'Sam, there's something I want to ask you about Chauncey Morton.'

'Hey, come on Melissa,' he chided her gently, 'what did I tell you about that? Forget it. You're leaving it all behind.'

'I know, I know, Sam but this is important. I want you to do something for me.'

'Concerning Detective Morton?'

'Yes.'

He made a face. 'You sure?' She nodded. 'Okay, what is it?'

She told him and he promised to do what she asked. They sat silently for a while, watching the streams of traffic on the Long Island Expressway.

'Oh, by the way,' Barber said, 'we got a make on the two guys detective Morton shot at the cabin.'

'You know who they were?'

'Sure. One was a guy called Fylde, Carver Fylde. The other one was Billy Bob Harold. We got a cross-match on their prints. We had them on file. So did their local state police.'

'Why? What had they done?'

Barber looked serious. 'Done? Nothing. Nothing that we could prove anyway. But both guys were real deep-river fundamentalists.'

'What?'

'Extremists. Ultra-hardline right-wingers belonging to some cockamamie, screwball outfit called Manifest. We don't know too much about it . . . except we think it's dangerous. It's tough to penetrate. But what we do know is the whole organisation is based on hate. Hatred of the government, the Jews, the Catholics, African-Americans, the FBI . . . especially the FBI. You name it. Those guys hate everything. Except patriotism of course. They've stitched themselves inside the flag and now they figure they own it.'

'But why would people like that attack and kill Vito Kunzman?'

Barber made a face. 'It's hard to say. It's certainly tough to see any Mafia connection. Neither of those guys was your typical LCN hitman.'

'Then why?' she insisted.

'Big business maybe. The right-wingers hate Wall Street. They think it's owned by the Jews.'

'But I don't think Mr Kunzman was Jewish. And the Exchange Bank certainly wasn't Wall Street.'

Barber shrugged. 'I'm not sure mouth-breathers like Fylde and Harold would have appreciated the difference. Most of these Manifest people are not very bright.'

She frowned. 'But there has to be some reason why they killed him.'

Barber gave her a fleeting smile. 'Sure there is. And I guess we'll find it sometime. But I wouldn't worry about it, Melissa. You're leaving it behind. The Manifest Movement is a uniquely American institution. I don't think you have anything quite the same in Britain. Mainly it comes out of the war in Vietnam. A lot of Manifest people are vets. Carver Fylde was one. In fact, he served in Nam with Billy Bob's older brother, Vinny. That's who we think may have been the third gunman at the cabin. Vinny Harold. We're looking for him now.'

'I hope you catch him.'

'So do I. Going on what we've gotten from his war record and the little we've found out since, I'd say Vinny Harold is a truly dangerous man. We were lucky, Melissa.'

Her eyes widened. 'You think so?'

'Definitely. My guess is Big Vinny Harold is probably like all the others and as thick as molasses pie . . . except for one very important particular.'

'What's that?'

'He's an expert at killing people.'

Melissa leaned back in her seat and shuddered.

Chapter Thirty-Eight

The car was a dark Pontiac. It drew smoothly into the kerb alongside him and a voice from the open rear window said, 'Get in.' The voice was used to giving orders.

Big Vinny moved towards the rear door. 'Up front,' the voice ordered sharply.

He climbed into the front passenger seat and looked across at the driver. It was the tough young aide from the bar in Baltimore. The man didn't look at him.

'Go,' said the voice. The car pulled away effortlessly, merging into the late evening traffic. Big Vinny turned towards the darkened rear of the car.

'Don't turn around.' The voice was harsh. 'Keep your eyes to the front.'

Vinny swivelled frontwards in his seat, again glancing at the driver. The man's hard, hawk-like face, briefly illuminated by the lights of the oncoming vehicles, was rigid and expressionless.

Now Vinny knew who owned the voice. It was the Commander in Chief. He hadn't been sure at first. The last time he'd heard those gravelly tones he had been seated across a table from the man in a bar and the Commander's intonation had been low and well-modulated. Friendly. As if he was talking to a child.

This time was different. The voice was hard and stark and as pitiless as stone.

'What the fuck happened back there?' it demanded. 'You were meant to take out two targets. You didn't do it. Why not? I thought you guys in the Chicashaw Commando were supposed to be the best.'

Vinny squirmed. What could he say? Billy Bob had got it wrong . . . had moved too soon and screwed up the hit. But he couldn't blame Billy Bob. Billy Bob was his brother.

Wrong. Billy Bob had been his brother. Now he was dead. He would not speak ill of the dead.

'It went wrong,' he mumbled. 'There was more of them than we was told. And they were ready for us.'

'Jesus,' another voice whispered.

Vinny started in his seat. He hadn't figured on two of them in the back. The presence of another man behind him in the darkness was unnerving. He wanted desperately to turn round.

'Went wrong,' the Commander repeated bitterly. 'For Chrissakes, you can say that again. It sure as shit went wrong. You may have wasted three cops, but you only got one of the targets.'

That was news to Big Vinny. Over the past thirty-six hours the reports he had seen on TV and in the papers about the action had said there were fatalities, but they hadn't been specific. He wondered how the Commander could know so much about what had happened at the cabin.

'You were supposed to get *both* targets,' the Commander's bleak, disembodied voice continued. 'Those were your orders. Goddam, I was the one who gave you those orders. I told you it was vital you kill them both.'

'Yessir. We tried, sir. But . . . it got all bitched up. When we got to the cabin I sent . . .'

'Don't give me excuses,' the Commander snarled. 'I already know what happened. I've had Sidewinder's report. You screwed up. That's what happened.'

'Yessir.' Shame and dishonour were crushing Big Vinny's chest, shoving him down into his seat. 'But you gotta know, sir, we took some bad casualties. I lost two good men.'

'Casualties are a part of war,' the Commander stated dismissively. 'You know that. As it is, your men have died for nothing. One of the targets is still out there. Still breathing. You didn't kill her.'

Big Vinny lowered his head still further and stared at the hands gripped together in his lap. His grip was so tight it hurt. Jesus, that was hard to take. The Commander was telling him Billy Bob had died for nothing.

He felt the familiar acid lump in the back of his throat as the awful sequence of images came to mind. He was never going to forget how Billy Bob had died.

Surely the Commander must know that one of the men who

died at the cabin was his brother? Surely he couldn't dismiss Billy Bob's death as a pointless waste. He didn't mean it . . . he couldn't mean it.

Big Vinny yearned to turn in his seat and to plead with his Commander in Chief . . . to beg him to say that Billy Bob's death wasn't a waste.

'You were supposed to get them both. Those were your orders,' the second voice snarled. Like the Commander's, the voice was used to authority . . . to issuing orders. Unlike the Commander's, Vinny noticed, it didn't have the timbre of the military.

Yessir,' he replied. He didn't know what else to say.

Miserably he glanced out of the windscreen as the car made a left off K Street and headed towards the Lincoln Memorial. He glowered at the illuminated edifice. Why the hell had they told him to come here? he wondered. Why not conduct the debriefing back home? In the South? He wanted badly to get back home. Why did they have to do it here, driving around Washington of all places? Aimlessly in the night, in yet another northern city?

And why in a car? Why seated with eyes facing front whilst two men, one of whom he didn't know, squatted close behind him in the darkness?

Why the hell was he here?

Shit, he ought to be glad he was anywhere, he thought. For a while it had been touch and go.

Moving through the deep timber eastward as far as the outskirts of Austerlitz he had found the country road swarming with state troopers. Troopers with dogs. Immediately he had reversed direction, travelling rapidly west through the pine forest with somewhere not far behind him the sound of baying dogs and somewhere not far above him the beating of low-flying choppers. He had made it to the Taconic Parkway where he had been lucky enough to hijack a car almost immediately.

He had left the car in a parking lot at Albany airport. In the trunk was his M-16 and the body of the driver, a middle-aged woman. Stabbed through the heart. Back at the motel in Newark he had called the contact number for Sidewinder and reported the action at the cabin. Sidewinder had phoned him back later with orders to take the bus to Washington.

'I was counting on you, Vinny,' the Commander said cruelly. 'I'd figured the Chicashaw Commando was the one outfit in the

Militia I could count on to do this job right. But you let me down, boy. You got out alive . . . but you didn't kill the woman. You failed me. You . . .'

'For God's sake get on with it,' the other voice interjected. 'We haven't got all night. I have to go.'

Big Vinny's head jerked in shock at the words. The Commander in Chief was the nearest thing to God he knew. The most powerful man in the Militia. Yet, here he was being spoken to as if he were a hired hand. The Commander was being given orders. Whoever the other guy in the darkness was, he was even more powerful.

With a jolt, Vinny realised who else was in the car with him. The unknown voice belonged to one of the men on the Supreme Executive. It had to, he thought. Nobody else could talk to the Commander in Chief like that.

Rumour had it there were only three of them on the Executive. And one of them was in the car with him. Jeeesus. He stiffened in his seat and brought his head up.

He was in the presence of the most powerful men in the Manifest Movement.

'Okay. Now look.' Suddenly he could feel the Commander's breath on the back of his neck. 'We're not lost yet. There's a way you can put this right, Vinny. You and the Chicashaw screwed up back there in the woods. But there's a way you can retrieve the honour of the commando.'

'How?' His voice was croaky but eager.

'Waste the woman. She's still out there. And she's dangerous. We have to kill her.'

'She's even more dangerous now,' the other voice cut in. 'Kunzman talked to her before he died. God knows what he said. She has to be killed before . . .' the voice stopped, suddenly conscious that it might say too much ' . . . before any more time goes by.'

'That's right, Vinny. You have to eliminate her quickly.' He noticed the Commander's voice was slightly softer. More conciliatory.

'Sure,' he said eagerly. 'Just gimme a weapon and tell me where.'

'England. You'll have to kill her in England.'

'England?' Vinny yelped. 'Why England?'

'Because right now she's in a New York hotel guarded by an

entire company of Fibbies. Well-armed and alert. There's no way you could get near her there. No way you can get to her as long as she's in the States. She's too well guarded. But tomorrow she flies back home. And once she's in England she's gonna feel safe.'

'But England. I ain't never been to England before. I ain't never been anywhere 'cept Nam and South America. And that time in Canada.'

'For Christ's sake, what's your problem?' the other voice snapped impatiently. 'They speak English in England. You won't have a problem.'

'That's right, Vinny. It's not a problem. You're the guy to handle this. It shouldn't be difficult. Not for you. We know the bitch has got protection in England although we don't know what it is. Whatever, it won't amount to diddly squat. That's for sure. English cops don't carry guns. You can get to her, Vinny.'

'Yeah, but . . .' He squirmed in his seat and made to turn around.

'Eyes front, soldier,' the Commander ordered.

Vinny snapped to his front.

They were cruising along Constitution Avenue, past the large darkened mass of the Justice Department building.

The Commander leaned forward until his mouth was close to Big Vinny's left ear. 'One of the guys you lost at the cabin was your little brother, wasn't it?' he said softly.

The feeling welled in Vinny's throat. 'Yessir. Billy Bob.'

'Well, you don't want his death to be for nothing now, do you?'

'No sir. No. No.'

'Of course you don't. You want to know that he died for a purpose . . . that Billy Bob died heroically for the cause. Isn't that right?'

Big Vinny nodded. He wasn't sure he could speak.

'Well, Vinny, the only way you're gonna be able to give his death any kind of meaning is to waste the Englishwoman. Billy Bob died trying to kill her. Did you know that? Now what you gotta do is finish the job. That way, Billy Bob won't have died in vain.'

'How do you know that?' Vinny croaked. 'How do you know Billy Bob was trying to take out the bitch?'

'Because the guy, Kunzman, died of gunshot wounds. Who

was carrying the Ithaca? Was it Carver Fylde?'

Vinny nodded. 'Yes.'

'So Carver wasted the man. Which means that when Billy Bob rushed the cabin, he was trying to take out the woman. Whoever shot him did it to protect the bitch. Right?'

Something was gagging in Big Vinny's throat. Rage. He managed to nod.

'So kill her . . . and you avenge your baby brother.'

The Commander sat back in his seat. For a few moments there was no sound in the car except the hum of the tyres.

'How do I get there?' Vinny whispered. 'To England?'

The Commander leaned forward and Vinny felt the man's solid, fraternal hand on his shoulder. 'Good man.'

The silent, stone-faced driver took a hand off the steering wheel and produced a manilla docket from somewhere down by his side. He passed the docket to Vinny, who examined it, turning it over in his big hands.

'Everything you need is in there,' the Commander explained. 'We've fixed you up with a new identity. Inside is a passport in your new name. You can use the same cover as you did after the action in the Corderilla. You're a roustabout, going to a job in the North Sea.'

'New identity?' Vinny queried.

'Yeah, it's necessary, big guy.'

'Why?'

'Because by now the cops in New York will have dusted the shell casings for prints. They could be looking for you already. Even if they're not, pretty soon they gonna make Billy Bob and Carver Fylde. It's more than likely they'll figure the third man at the cabin was Billy Bob's older brother.'

Vinny grunted and toyed with the docket some more.

'You'll find money and flight tickets in there, as well as what we know about the woman. Where she lives, where she works . . . everything we could find out. It's enough.'

'Enough for you to get on with it. Quickly,' the other voice broke in.

The car was slowing down. Vinny looked up. They were drawing up outside a Holiday Inn close to Scot Circle. 'You're booked in here for tonight,' the Commander explained. 'There's a bag in your room with a change of clothes inside. Your flight to London is first thing tomorrow morning.'

Vinny stared straight ahead at the Inn's neon sign. 'What about a weapon? he asked.

'You can't take a weapon on a plane, Vinny. You're gonna have to improvise. When you get there.'

'Kill her with your bare hands if you have to.' The voice of the unknown man in the back was cold and malignant. 'Just do it. Get it done quickly, for God's sake.'

The car had smoothed to a halt. 'Okay, Vinny, get out now,' the Commander ordered. 'Don't close the door after you, the driver will do that. And don't look back. Understand.'

'Yessir.'

'Okay, Big Vinny. Good luck. Don't screw up this time. All right? Kill the bitch quick and get the next flight back. Remember Billy Bob.'

'Yeah, I'll remember,' he said quietly.

He opened the door, got out and walked away from the car without a backward glance. He heard the door slam behind him and the car move off. It swished past him. He noticed sunblinds had been pulled down at the rear window, preventing him seeing anything of the two men in the back.

Not that he was bothered. The identity of the mysterious man who had sat in the darkness alongside the Commander in Chief didn't matter to Vinny. The guy was a member of the Supreme Executive. That was enough.

And whatever reasons the guy had for wanting him to kill the Englishwoman didn't matter to Vinny either.

Big Vinny had his own reasons for wanting the bitch dead.

Clutching the manilla docket, he made for the entrance of the hotel.

Chapter Thirty-Nine

She got in late, went straight to bed, slept surprisingly well and woke early the following morning.

It was joyous to be home.

Jamie was beside himself at her return, hugging her tightly and smothering her with kisses. Astrid was her usual practical, quietly happy self and Liz reserved but smiling.

If Timmison or any of her superiors on the force had told the policewoman what had happened to Melissa in America, she gave no sign of it.

George the puppy was pleased to see her too, sliding across the polished tile floor of the kitchen, wagging his tail and yapping madly. Melissa was surprised at how much he had grown, though a little vexed that, whenever she bent to fondle him, he scampered back to hide behind Jamie or Astrid or Liz. The damn dog had forgotten her. She put it down to his youth . . . and his gender.

She called the office and told them she was talking the day off to be with Jamie. It was a perfect summer's day and for once she broke her own rule and kept him off school. They spent most of the day playing with George. The normality of it helped settle her mind . . . to forget events in America.

By mid-afternoon she noticed the strain in her face was lifting, the lines of tension around her eyes and mouth all but disappeared. Even the scar on her face had receded, metamorphosing into a needle-thin, two-centimetre line running diagonally over her left cheekbone, pure white against the slight tan of her skin.

The only note that jarred was the presence of her protectors. Liz was pleasant and unobtrusive – but she was there. And so was the slightly sinister blue Mondeo at the end of the drive. She couldn't get used to the feeling of being in custody in her own home. She wasn't a prisoner, but she was under guard.

The following morning Melissa left for the office accompanied by Simon, the young, good-looking, plainclothes policeman. Liz had orders to stay with Jamie and Astrid. She was driven to the station in the blue Mondeo.

The journey was the usual hell but for once she appreciated it. She felt a sense of security in the British tradition of discomfort.

Nigel Hawick was seated at his desk in his shirt sleeves when she arrived at the office. She walked straight in to see him. 'For God's sake, Melissa,' he began, 'Timmison told me what happened to you in America. Jesus, it must have been hell. Why didn't you tell me . . .'

She interrupted him. 'Nigel, I want out . . . off the Exchange Bank liquidation as soon as possible.' His jaw dropped. 'No arguments. I've already told Steven Timmison. So now I want you to tell the firm's senior partners. Today. They can tell the Bank of England. If they or the BoE refuse to take me off it, then I'll resign from Rolay Richard. That's it. The job's not worth getting killed over. And I'm sick of having police protection. I want my life back, Nigel. I want to be a normal human being again.'

'But . . .'

'That's it, Nigel. There's no more to be said.' She flounced out of his office.

The work had piled up in her absence and Debbie's wad of messages was as thick as a brick. Melissa instructed her to get them both a cup of coffee.

Whilst waiting she closed the blinds on the office's three internal partitions and switched her line through to the answering machine on Debbie's phone. As soon as the secretary returned they settled down to arrange the workload into some order of priority. It took more than an hour.

Afterwards Debbie told her who had called whilst they had been closeted together.

'Three of the senior partners,' she announced, 'all of whom want you to call them back urgently. Mr Timmison, he called twice, can you call him, and also Mr Hawick. Can you see him. So, who do you want me to get first?'

'None of them,' Melissa said grimly. 'I know what they want. Don't worry, they'll call again.'

Hawick was the first to get to her. As soon as he saw Melissa draw up the blinds and Debbie return to her workstation, he came bursting through her door. 'Melissa, I have to talk to you,' he said sternly.

'If it's about the Exchange Bank, forget it. I told you, I want off the job.'

'All right, all right.' He held up his hands. 'I understand. Everybody in the firm understands. All the senior partners support your decision.'

She stared at him in surprise. 'They do?'

'Of course. We've just had a meeting. They agree you should be taken off the Exchange Bank liquidation. So do I. I was the one who said you should give it up after Aziz was killed. Remember?'

She frowned at him for a moment. 'All right, yes, but that man Timmison: he doesn't want me to give up.'

'It doesn't matter what Timmison wants. The Bank of England is more than pleased with the fact you've found the half billion Kunzman appropriated. We all know there's a lot more to be done on the Exchange Bank – years of work probably – but the firm can make other arrangements. After what you've been through, no one expects you to carry on.'

'They don't?'

'No, they don't. God, Melissa, you've had a terrible shock. You're not thinking straight. You probably shouldn't even be in the office.'

She gazed at him for a few moments longer. She was beginning to feel a great weight lifting off her. 'No, I want to be here,' she told him quietly. 'If I run away from work now, I may never come back. I need to be here.'

He nodded. 'Okay, if you say so. So what do you want to do? About handing over the job?'

She indicated her desk. 'This is all Exchange Bank stuff. It'll take me at least three or four days to tie up the loose ends. After that I'll write a report on progress to date.'

'Okay. That's fine,' he said lightly.

'But understand, Nigel,' her voice was brittle once more, 'no new investigations. No travelling, no chasing down any new leads, no more following hot money from the bank. That's all over for me. All I'm doing now is tidying up. Boring desk work. Okay.'

'Right.'

She spent the next half-hour with solicitous senior partners on the fifteenth floor. They told her they understood perfectly her wish to pull out of the Exchange Bank liquidation and agreed with her decision absolutely. She could tell from their eyes they were desperate to know the details of what had happened in America. She refused to talk about it.

Back in her office she emptied her briefcase. It was an old, battered, brown leather flaptop she had used when she was an articled clerk. For an instant she remembered the expensive attaché case she had asked the FBI agent to dispose of, recalling the brownish streaks of blood tainting the leather.

She grimaced and moved to the big windows to gaze at the distant silver river snaking past Shadwell. It helped settle her. The view, familiar yet always spectacular, took her mind off the past.

She spent half an hour examining the papers she had emptied onto her desk. The most interesting were those Sam Barber had found hidden at Vito Kunzman's cabin.

Interesting, she reflected, because they were mysterious. What was the significance of a long list of unknown names in Europe and Southeast Asia? What connection did they have with the Exchange Bank? She had no idea. Maybe, she thought, they weren't connected at all.

She furrowed her brow, studying the names for a while, then rose from her desk and left the office. Debbie was at her work-station, her fingers flashing over the word-processor keyboard. 'I'm going down to see Boris,' Melissa told her.

Redbourn was wearing trainers, jeans and a loud Hawaiian shirt, its garish greens, blues and reds reflecting the coloured icons and images silently shimmering across the screens around his office walls. As always he was hunched over his keyboard.

'Boris,' she announced loudly.

He started and looked up, blinking at her through his spectacles. He seemed surprised to see her. 'Melissa, hi.' He fixed her with a long look. 'I didn't expect to see you today.' He paused and added darkly, 'I heard about America.'

'So did the Pilgrim Fathers, Boris.' Her tone was firm and dismissive.

He understood immediately. 'So what brings you down here?' he asked lightly.

She thrust the papers at him. 'These were found hidden at a house in New York State. Three sheets of names. Some are companies. You can tell. But the rest . . . well, they look like individuals or maybe different types of organisations. I don't know what they are. I want you to find out. Run them through the Exchange Bank data files and see what you come up with.'

He took the papers and glanced through them. 'The Exchange Bank? I heard you were pulling out of that.'

'For God's sake. News travels like lightning in this place,' she snapped.

He grinned. 'If you want everybody to know something in Rolay Richard, put it on the grapevine. It's much more efficient than normal channels.'

She laughed. 'That's true. Anyway, you may as well know I've asked to be taken off the Exchange Bank liquidation. All I'm doing now is tying up the loose ends.'

'Loose ends. Okay.' He dropped the papers next to his keyboard. 'I'll let you know what matches with the data.' He gazed up at her with an expectant grin. 'So what do you want to do about the Austerlitz Account?'

Two vertical furrows appeared between her eyebrows. She considered the question. 'Nothing. Not right now. Key those names in first and let me know what you come up with. Then call me. Okay?'

He was shocked. 'What? After that bloody pantomime on the phone, you don't want to see what's inside Austerlitz? You're going to leave it for someone else?'

She shook her head. 'Someone else? Definitely not. The Austerlitz Account is one loose end I'm tying up myself. But I want to wait. I need to see what comes up with that list.'

He looked at her suspiciously. 'Why? You think they're connected?

'Maybe. I don't know. I hope so.'

Redbourn's suspicious look translated itself into a grin. 'You sure you're giving up on the Exchange Bank, Melissa? It sounds to me like you're as involved as ever.'

'Don't even think that, Boris. I'm off the job. Definitely. But,' she paused reflectively, 'like I said, I think Austerlitz may be a big brick. Prise it out and the whole wall could come down. After that . . . well, someone else can clear up the mess.'

Redbourn watched her walk out of his office.

Boris liked Melissa. She was smart, great-looking, always ready for a laugh and, unlike most of the other partners, never pompous. Irritable . . . yes . . . often . . . but never condescending. Yeah, he liked her a lot. But half the time he didn't know what the hell she was talking about. What, he wondered, *was* all this talk about bricks?

He grinned and turned back to his keyboard. In his opinion Melissa was as flaky as a box of Kellog's. Which, he supposed, was the main reason he liked her.

He called her early that afternoon. 'That list you gave me,' he began. 'Bad news I'm afraid. Not one name checks out in our files. Nothing in it has any connection with the Exchange Bank.'

'Damn,' she muttered. 'You sure, Boris?'

'What do you think?'

She made a face. Boris Redbourn got to dress and behave the way he did because he knew his job backwards. If he said there was no connection then . . . 'I'm sorry, Boris.' She was contrite. 'It's just that . . . well . . . I was pretty certain there was some kind of connection.'

'Not that we can find.'

'What about the other names?' she asked hopefully. 'The ones that aren't companies?'

'We're still running a match against data. Some are individuals . . . ordinary private people, but none are names we have in the computer. No connection that we can see with the Exchange Bank.'

'Names of people?' she repeated, surprised. 'What about the others? What are they?'

'A collection of odds and sods. Trade associations, research organisations, a couple of technical journals. Just a random collection, no connection with the Exchange Bank or with each other that we can see.'

Melissa stared out of the window, not seeing the distant, glistening buildings of Canary Wharf.

Redbourn's voice cut in on her thoughts. 'Melissa, you there?'

'Yes, I'm here,' she growled.

'So what happens now?'

'Now?' Her voice was suddenly decisive. 'Now I want you to do a search on the companies on that list. And on the trade associations, research companies, even on the individuals, if you can. The best, most thorough search your department can put together. Lock onto the computers in Companies House in

Cardiff and at the Tokisho in Tokyo and in the provincial registries in Germany and France. I want to know everything, as much as possible, about every single name on that list.'

'Hey, wait a minute, Melissa,' he protested: 'I'm supposed to give top priority to the Exchange Bank. This bunch of names isn't connected. We've just established that. What am I going to tell Nigel Hawick when he asks me what I'm doing?'

'Don't worry about Nigel, he's a pussy cat. I'll handle him. Just do it, Boris. If you get any flak, push it on to me.'

'It'll be a big search,' he moaned.

'So you had better start straight away. Get your people onto it now. In the meantime, you and I are going to take a look inside the Austerlitz Account. I'll be down immediately.'

A couple of minutes later she drew up a chair and seated herself beside Redbourn at his keyboard.

Behind her, through the open doorway of the office a score or more of his people were busily tapping keyboards, downloading financial data from the companies registration offices of the world's leading economies.

He glanced over his shoulder at his staff as she made herself comfortable. 'This is one hell of a bloody search you've got us on,' he said seriously. 'The company data is easy enough, but background on the other organisations – and especially the individuals – is going to be difficult. You realise all this time is going down against your department? I hope your budget can stand it.'

'Don't worry about my budget, Boris. Let's get inside Austerlitz.' He glanced at her, catching the excitement in her voice. She was staring at the big, twenty-one-inch computer screen on the desk in front of them.

He tapped the keyboard and an icon appeared telling him he was being connected with the Exchange Bank computer in the Caribbean. When the terminals were linked and a green-dotted request line appeared centre screen, he keyed in the number of the account on Curaçao, followed by the word Austerlitz.

Nothing happened. Except for the number and the name, the screen stayed blank.

'Now watch this,' Redbourn announced. He punched in the second number, 49101653. The screen remained blank for a second, then shimmered and dissolved into a pulldown menu. At the top, in bold red letters, was the title, Austerlitz.

'Shazaan,' he cried; 'open sesame.' He grinned at Melissa.

She smiled and said quietly, 'Let's look at the accounts.'

Redbourn moved the mouse and arrowed a box on the pulldown. A ledger appeared on screen, showing movement of dollars into and out of an account. Melissa studied it, saying nothing.

Suddenly Boris yelped. 'Jesus. Hey, look. The name at the top of the screen. It's one of those on your bloody list. Look.'

Melissa stared. 'It *is* connected,' she said softly. 'I knew it. I just *knew* it.'

She gazed at the screen a moment longer before turning to Redbourn. 'I bet we find every name on that list had transactions inside this account.'

He frowned. 'I don't understand.'

'I think the Austerlitz Account was a bank inside a bank, Boris. Once money had been moved into it, it couldn't be traced. It could be moved about inside and emerge anywhere else in the world and nobody would be any the wiser.'

He stared wide-eyed at the screen. 'The perfect money-laundering set-up.'

'That's right,' she murmured. 'Which makes it all the more curious . . .'

'What? What's curious?'

She glanced at him. 'Nothing. It doesn't matter. See if you can find Kunzman's transactions.'

Redbourn buttoned a search on any dollar amount with nine digits and immediately found a data page entitled 'WhitePlains'. They stared at the screen.

'He sold the Eurobonds for dollars and immediately moved them into the Austerlitz,' Melissa intoned. 'Then he transferred the funds to the Channel Islands. Under cover of one of the other companies using the account.'

'He didn't keep it in for long,' Redbourn pointed out. 'Just two days. Did he know the Exchange Bank was going down?'

'I don't see how he could,' she murmured.

'But if he'd left the money there, he'd have lost it. Like all those other poor bastards,' Redbourn chuckled.

'Bastards, certainly. Poor . . . probably not. Okay.' Her tone was suddenly animated. 'How many pages are there in this account, Boris?'

He ran a search. 'A hundred and ten.'

'I want them all. A hard copy of the entire Austerlitz Account on my desk in twenty minutes. Okay?'

'Shit, Melissa . . .'

'. . . and as your people complete their searches on the names on that list I want them delivered to my office.'

'What, piecemeal?'

'Yes.'

'Bloody hell, I'm going to have my staff running up and down in the lift for the next couple of days.'

'Not the next couple of days, Boris. The next couple of hours. I want that information immediately. Come on, Boris, I want it *now*.'

He stared at her and started to laugh. 'Jesus, Melissa, you sure you're giving up this Exchange Bank thing?'

She was moving towards the door. 'Yes of course I am. Absolutely. I told you.'

'My mother told me about fairies, but I didn't believe her either.'

She stopped at the door. 'I'm not your mother, Boris,' she announced. 'If I were, I wouldn't allow you out in that shirt. Twenty minutes, right.'

She could hear his laughter all the way to the lift.

Debbie waylaid her on her way back into the fishtank. 'Mr Timmison called again. Twice. He said it was important.'

'Important for him. Not for me.'

'And a Mr Barber called from the FBI. He said he'd call again in a few minutes.'

Inside her office she cleared her desk in advance of the avalanche of paper she expected from four floors below.

Redbourn had just delivered the hard copy of the Austerlitz Account and the first of the searches, when her phone bleeped.

'Mr Barber's on the line,' Debbie announced.

'Sam, how are you?' Melissa's voice was guarded. She wanted to talk to Barber but she didn't want to think about him. Thinking about Sam . . . picturing him . . . would bring back memories she would much rather not have. The terror of America was beginning to fade. She didn't want it coming back.

'I guess I'm okay, Melissa. You?' She guessed she was okay too. 'Listen, that thing you asked me to do? About Detective Morton?'

'Yes?' Her voice was guarded and flat.

'Okay, well I did it.'

She listened intently as he told her what he had done. When he finished she said, 'Thank you, Sam. I'm glad I asked you.'

'Yeah, well, I hope you're going to be okay. Stay in touch.'

She said she would and put the phone down. She crossed to the window and stared sightlessly out of it. The tears in her eyes glistened like the river.

After a while one of Boris Redbourn's people arrived with more copies of the searches. Melissa blew her nose and turned away from the window. Standing at her desk, she lifted the phone and punched the number for security control, fourteen floors below in the atrium. She asked for Simon.

The young policeman came on the line. 'Simon, just to let you know I'm working late tonight. Maybe you ought to go out and get yourself something to eat. Rather than wait until later.'

He said thanks for letting him know and that he would make arrangements. She didn't know what that meant but she let it pass. She was too preoccupied gazing at the pile of papers on her desk.

Somewhere inside she could feel a faint frisson of excitement. Perhaps, hidden in the untidy heap of documents was the answer to the questions that had been puzzling her since almost the first day of her investigation into the Exchange Bank.

She cleared the line, called Debbie and requested coffee before sitting down and arranging the documents . . . the Austerlitz Account immediately in front of her, the company searches within easy reach.

She opened a big, blank notepad.

She worked for hours, reading and rereading, checking and cross-referencing; constantly making notes, occasionally crunching numbers . . . her long, strong fingers whizzing over the keypad of her calculator. Every so often one of Boris Redbourn's staff arrived with more of the searches. Without looking up, she indicated the pile at the corner of her desk.

She was only faintly conscious of the noises outside her office . . . the gently warbling phones, the hum of the computer terminals, the subdued chatter. She didn't notice when the ambient sounds began to fade.

By six the chatter and hum were gone, replaced by the sound of vacuum cleaners intruding at the outer edges of her consciousness. The cleaners arrived at her office but she told them not to bother. They left her door open.

Somewhere at the back of her mind she was aware of other people working late. Now and then a phone would warble and be lifted and she would hear from a far distance a muffled voice and the occasional sharp laugh.

Then that too ceased. An unanswered phone warbled for minutes, the solitary, plaintive sound finally penetrating her brain like a plastic dagger. Melissa raised her head and gazed out over well-lit acres of deserted office. The caller gave up. She guessed it was a wrong number.

Suddenly, a man appeared in the open doorway of the office. Melissa looked up in shock, her heart surging.

It was one of Redbourn's people with another bundle of searches. They were the last for today, he told her. He was going home. Everyone else had already gone. She grunted her thanks and worked on, shuffling papers and making rapid notes.

As the light faded the smoky windows facing the river evolved into dark mirrors, reflecting the vast area of open office and the single, solitary figure tapping a calculator.

Fourteen floors below on the opposite side of Eastcheap the big, heavy-set watcher stood in the dark doorway of a tailor's shop and stared up unblinking at the glass-plated building.

He watched as the lights went out, floor by floor.

Chapter Forty

It was almost ten before she realised the time. Her lumbar region ached from the hours of inelegant crouching and the back of her neck was locked in spasm.

She leaned back in her seat and gently rotated her head. The cracking sounds as the cricks released were alarming – like small explosions. She lowered her head, raised both hands and gently began to massage the back of her neck.

She heard a noise and looked up.

From somewhere across the floor of the office came a soft, sibilant hiss. In the silence of the deserted office it sounded sinister. Like a malignant whisper.

The lift doors had opened.

She peered through the glass walls of her office, waiting for a night security guard to emerge from behind one of the far partitions. From where she was seated she couldn't see the lift. She heard the doors hiss shut.

Someone was out there.

Someone had used the lift to get out on her floor.

She sat fixed in her seat, staring intently, waiting for whoever it was to appear. Across the vast empty office nothing moved.

Something cold and fearful crawled up her backbone.

Suddenly, terror was clawing at her throat and the beat of her heart had accelerated into its now familiar supercharge. Above the drumming in her chest she heard her scared, quavering voice call out.

'Who's there?'

There was no answer.

Cautiously she stood up and moved to the open door of the office. She looked to her left and right. There was no one. She glanced back at her phone. Should she call security? Instinct told her not to go back inside the office. Inside was a trap.

She called out again. 'Who's there?'

This time she heard something. A soft noise: a body brushing against a desk or a chair. Her eyes slewed in the direction of the sound. 'For God's sake, who's there?' she screeched.

No answer.

She made a sudden rush towards Debbie's workstation. From there she knew she would have a good view of the whole floor. She reached Debbie's desk, her eyes darting fearfully around the deserted workstations nearby. She grabbed the phone off the desk, her paralysed brain struggling to remember the number for security.

Something shuffled behind her.

She whirled around, the handset lifted like a small club. A man was standing there. Right behind her.

She screamed.

The man's hand shot out and grabbed her by the arm.

'Hey, Melissa, Miss Semmington, it's okay. It's okay.'

'Simon,' she screeched. 'Oh Simon. Jeeeesus, you scared me. You *scared* me. You silly bastard. I damn near peed myself. You frightened me to death.'

The concerned look on his young, handsome face gave way to an apologetic smile. 'Oh, hell! I'm sorry. I came out of the lift and went the wrong way. I forgot where your office was.'

'Didn't you hear me calling out?' she squawked. 'You dumb bloody fool. Why didn't you answer me? I nearly died of fright. You could have killed me, you idiot.' She wanted to hit him, to smash his face in. Instead she pulled her arm roughly out of his grasp.

As soon as she was released she felt her legs turn to jelly. Suddenly she no longer had the strength to murder the young policeman. He saw her swaying. 'You okay?'

She replaced the phone with a shaking hand and took a deep breath, summoning up whatever mettle had not been shredded by her sudden fright. 'Yes I'm all right,' she breathed. 'You gave me a hell of a scare. I feel a bit weak.'

He reached out a hand to steady her. She lifted both hands abruptly, signalling him to keep off. 'I'm fine,' she repeated bitterly. 'Just . . . just . . . bloody well answer me next time. Okay?'

He nodded sheepishly.

They stood silently for a moment as Melissa sought to gain

control. Simon looked embarrassed. 'Anyway,' she said when she felt the rubber in her legs turn back to muscle, 'what did you want?' She gave him a penetrating look.

'I came to see how you were getting on,' he said lamely.

'I was getting on absolutely bloody fine until you came along and scared the shit out of me,' she snarled.

She saw his face fall. He looked like a schoolboy. Jesus, she wondered, why did she always feel so much older than the young men who surrounded her? She guessed she was less than five years older than Simon, and yet . . .

She forced herself to relax, allowing her shoulders to ease down and the outraged tension in her face to be replaced by something she hoped was a bit more amiable. 'No, that's not true,' she added in a saner tone. 'As a matter of fact I'd just about had it. I think I've done enough for tonight.'

He brightened up. 'Okay. I've got a car downstairs.'

'A car? You mean a car to take us all the way home?'

He nodded. 'Yes. I thought if you were working late it would be better than getting the last train.'

'Simon, what a lovely idea.' Now she felt guilty for screaming at him.

He shrugged and spoiled it by saying, 'Why not? It's all going against some other bugger's budget. Some big dick in Whitehall.'

She cleared her papers and locked them away before descending with Simon to the atrium where a couple of security men were on duty. One of them unlocked the big glass doors. They stepped onto the pavement, Melissa breathing deeply the soft, magic air of a summer night in London.

A grey Cavalier was waiting at the kerb. Melissa crawled into the back as Simon slid in beside the driver. Immediately the car accelerated away.

By the time it reached Waterloo Bridge she was asleep.

As always, the cottage door creaked when she opened it. From upstairs came the dull, vibrating thump of Astrid's music. The low-beamed lounge was bathed in the soft golden glow of the sidelights.

Melissa wandered into the kitchen and automatically put the clingfilm-wrapped salad back into the fridge. Messages from Astrid were scrawled on a piece of paper lying on the breakfast bar. She was too tired to bother with them. She returned to the lounge and poured herself a large MacAllan.

Curled up on the comfortable sofa she sipped it slowly and ruminatively, watching the light fracture and glint in the leaded crystal of the heavy glass. She thought of the day's events, slowly turning them over in her mind like a gardener turning mulch. She finished her drink and poured herself another, too deeply immersed in her thoughts to feel any of her usual guilt.

On her way to bed she checked on Jamie, planting a kiss on his soft, slightly damp forehead.

Lying in the darkness in the still of the night, she listened to the slow, rhythmic pulse of her heart and thought of Chauncey Morton. She thought too of her son, and of her past, and tried to make sense of all the events she knew were senseless. So much of her life had fallen out on the road and she hadn't noticed. She lay like a corpse with her head and her heart fighting for possession over her and the tears sliding down her cheeks like rain on a window pane.

She fell asleep sometime after two.

She was up again at five and out of the house at six. She had bullied Simon into having the Cavalier take her to the office.

'If I can have a car when I'm working late, then I can have one when I'm starting early,' she'd said crossly. 'And anyway, the big dick in Whitehall would have me driven to work in a Bentley if he thought it might keep me doing this bloody job.'

She was in the office shortly after seven. By the time Debbie arrived the blinds were down and papers were spread all across her desk.

'Coffee,' Melissa said more peremptorily than she intended; 'no interruptions, except for anything from Boris Redbourn's department. And absolutely no calls.' She turned back to the documents, her brow furrowed in concentration as she wrote rapidly in her notepad.

Halfway through the morning the phone bleeped. She grabbed it.

'For God's sake Debbie, I said no calls!'

'I know, but it's that Mr Timmison. He insists on talking to you.'

'Tell him I'm not here. I'm out of the office.'

'I did. He doesn't believe me. He says he knows you're here and it's vital he talks to you.'

'Shit,' she hissed savagely, 'shit.'

Debbie's voice was calm. 'Well, do I put him through or tell him to piss off?'

Melissa chuckled. 'No, best not say that. Damn. All right, put him through.'

His voice was as sharp and precise as a regimental sword. 'Miss Semmington, I appreciate you are busy, but in view of your remarks on the phone the other day, we really need to talk.'

'Why? I've traced half a billion dollars for you and now I'm coming off the job. What's to talk about?'

'I need an update on the rest of your investigations. How far have you got with them?'

She frowned. 'Who says I'm anywhere with them? And anyway, I'll be preparing a report in a few days. You can read that.'

'I would rather hear it from you. Face to face.'

'Look, there's no point in our meeting. No way are you going to persuade me to stay with this job. Not a second time, you're not. I've made up my mind. I'm finishing with the Exchange Bank.'

He sighed. 'Miss Semmington, I appreciate that. I really do. If you wish to be relieved of the Exchange Bank assignment, then obviously there's nothing I can do about it. Nothing I would *want* to do about it. But I do need debriefing.'

Melissa smiled at the thought of his white, skinny legs. 'Debriefing,' she repeated.

'Yes. Urgently. Today.'

'But why? I report to a senior partner here in Rolay Richard. Why should I have to report to you? Why do I need to debrief you?'

'Your senior partners have agreed that I may communicate directly with you, Miss Semmington. Please try to understand. There's no sinister motive. It's important in my business that I talk to people face to face . . . get a feel for what has been going on.'

Melissa swore savagely but silently. The man was as unrelenting as a Scud missile. 'Very well,' she groaned. 'If you're so keen to be debriefed then I'll talk to you. But you'll have to come here. I'm in the middle of something and I haven't got time to go traipsing halfway across London.'

She was surprised at his instant response. 'Certainly. When?'

She glanced at her watch. 'Now,' she responded coolly. 'If

you want to talk to me then you had best come over right now. I'll see you in half an hour.'

'I'm on my way. And thank you for agreeing to see me.' She grunted ungraciously. The phone went dead.

Debbie came back on the line. 'There's another call. He's hanging on.'

'For God's sake,' Melissa cried, 'I told you, no calls.'

'I thought you might want to take this one.' Debbie let out a low, lecherous laugh. 'It's your Mr Briscoe. You want to take it?'

'Yes. Definitely.'

His voice – dark, warm and affectionate – came on the line a moment later. 'Melissa, hi. I'm in town. Got in this morning.'

'Hello, Bob.'

'You okay now? You straight after all your problems in New York?'

'Yes, I suppose so. Anyway, I'm a lot straighter than I was.'

'Great. Well, when are we gonna get together? Can you make dinner this evening?'

She frowned. 'This evening. I'm not sure.' She considered. 'Look, why don't we have lunch? Can you make lunch? Today?'

'Lunch?' He sounded surprised. 'Sure. Why not? Then we can fix our schedules, right? Okay, where and when?'

She thought about it for a moment. 'I have a meeting due to start in a few minutes. It should be over by one. Whatever, I'll make sure it's over by then. So come to the office and I'll meet you in reception. One o'clock.'

'You got a date,' he told her. 'See you at one.' He rang off.

Debbie tapped on the door and walked in. 'What is it now?' she railed. 'Jesus, Debbie. How the hell can I get anything done if you keep bothering me?'

The secretary took no notice of her bad temper. 'Boris Redbourn is here.'

'Oh,' her anger evaporated. 'Okay, send him in.'

Boris dropped a small pile of papers on her desk. 'More company searches and the first into the trade organisations and research companies. We're getting on to the individuals now.'

'Great.'

'Don't go overboard, Melissa. It's much harder doing background checks on individuals overseas. We're not coming up with much. None of the people listed are tied in with the

366

Exchange Bank. None of them are bankrupts or have judgments for debt against them. In fact none of them even appear to be company officers. From what little we can find, they all seem perfectly ordinary, upright citizens.'

'But they do exist?'

He was surprised at the question. He shrugged. 'Yes. At least those that we've checked so far. They've got credit cards and bank accounts.'

'Rich?'

He shook his head. 'No, not fabulously. Well off, certainly, but not filthy rich.'

She stared at Redbourn, a perplexed look on her face. 'This whole thing . . . this Austerlitz Account,' she intoned almost to herself: 'it's all wrong somehow. It doesn't make sense.'

He turned towards the door. 'Well, maybe it will when you get the rest of the searches. I'll have more with you this afternoon.'

He was at the door when she called him. 'Boris.'

He turned. 'The funds coming out of Cyclix? The money going to Basel, then to Atlanta and then disappearing inside the Austerlitz? Have you got one of your graphics programs up and running yet? Showing where the money was going inside the account?'

'Shit, give me a chance, Melissa. I've got most of my people doing this bloody search for you. I'll get around to the program in a couple of days.'

'Okay. I'm just trying to get a notion of how the money was distributed.'

He thought about it. 'From what I remember the cash was pretty well disseminated, with about a quarter of it credited to the account of just one organisation. A company in America. In fact it's the only American company on the list. And the biggest account inside Austerlitz.' He shrugged again. 'I guess the money has to be bent, but the company certainly looks legit. We're doing a search on it at the moment.'

'And this American company has no other connection with the Exchange Bank?'

'None. Apart from the Austerlitz, it doesn't cross-check with anything else in the data.'

She shook her head. 'I don't get it.'

He gave her a sympathetic look and disappeared.

She called Debbie. 'Bring your pad in. I've made a stack of

367

notes. I need you to help me get them into some sort of order. For my report.'

A few minutes later reception called to say Mr Timmison had arrived.

Chapter Forty-One

Debbie helped her clear all the papers off her desk. They piled them onto a table in the corner of the office.

She made Timmison wait five minutes before calling reception and having him accompanied to her office by a security man. They shook hands. She asked if he wanted coffee. He said no.

'Your security is very good,' he said, settling himself in the seat on the opposite side of her desk. A plastic visitor's tab hung from the lapel of his Savile Row suit. He adjusted the sharp creases of his trousers.

She eased down into her seat, watching him cautiously. 'It needs to be,' she said in a loaded tone.

He glanced at her and his thin mouth tightened. 'Quite.'

'Please understand I'm not going talk about what happened to me in America,' she said aggressively.

'I'm not going to ask you.' His response was cool.

'And you're not going to try to change my mind about giving up the Exchange Bank?'

'No, I'm not Miss Semmington. I'm here to get an update on what progress you have made. That's all. Now, tell me, how did you trace the half billion dollars?'

She told him, closing off from her mind the scene in the back of the Chevrolet.

He asked how she had got a lead on Kunzman.

After she had told him about Imola Varese, she went on to describe the other lines of inquiry she had undertaken into the Exchange Bank.

After twenty minutes she was aware how intelligent and quick on the uptake Timmison was. Though she had in no way warmed to him, she had to admit he was easy to brief. What few questions he asked were incisive and to the point. She never had to repeat herself . . . never explain.

'And that's it,' she said finally. 'But frankly, you could have saved yourself the journey. It will all be in my report.'

'As I told you. I like to hear these things first-hand. I must say, Miss Semmington, you have accomplished a great deal in the liquidation of the Exchange Bank. We shall be sorry to lose you.'

She opened her mouth to protest. Before she could speak he raised his hands in a signal of surrender. 'No, no, don't misunderstand me. I'm not trying to persuade you to stay. I was merely complimenting you. You have done an excellent job. Really first-class.'

What was it she disliked about tributes from Timmison? She couldn't put her finger on it. She shrugged dismissively. 'I'd have done more. Only I've allowed myself to be sidetracked.'

'Sidetracked?'

She nodded. 'Early in the investigation I was told about an account called the Austerlitz. By Akhtar Aziz. You remember,' she gave Timmison a hard look: 'the man who was murdered. With his family. It was one of those the Exchange Bank called Managers' Ledger Accounts. The auditors couldn't get into them. In fact the auditors didn't even know about this one.'

'What was so special about it?'

She smiled. 'Mainly the fact that we couldn't get into it either. I mean, our computer people are pretty good, but they couldn't crack it. It was a locked box.'

'So you investigated it.'

She shook her head. 'Not really. There was too much else to do. But then I picked up on something else. Cyclix, one of the companies associated with the Mafia money launderers in California, was piggy-backing cash out of America into an account in Basel. Later it came back into America and disappeared into an Exchange Bank account on Curaçao. Something about the piggy-backing bothered me.'

'Really? What?'

'Two things. Firstly, it was irregular. Most money-laundering transactions in the Exchange Bank took on a pretty consistent pattern. This one never did. The money appeared and got pushed through with Cyclix's other funds at irregular intervals. It was against the pattern somehow.'

'And the other thing?'

'The other thing was far more of a puzzle.'

He was silent, waiting for her to continue. 'Yes,' he prompted. 'What was it?'

'The amounts. The amounts being piggy-backed by Cyclix.'

'Really? Why? Were they significantly higher than the norm?'

'No. Quite the reverse.'

He frowned. 'The reverse?' he repeated.

She nodded. 'I mean, if you're going to piggy-back funds, why do it for peanuts? The amounts moved were only a few million. Usually between ten and twenty million dollars. Never more than twenty-five. A drop in the ocean. Yet the layering involved in its movement was exceptional.'

Timmison smiled tightly. 'You don't think they're substantial sums? Most people would think twenty-five million dollars is a lot of money.'

'Most people, maybe. Not people in my profession. And certainly not people working on the Exchange Bank liquidation. In comparison to what the Exchange bank was moving, the funds were Mickey Mouse. The Bank moved hundreds of millions in one transaction. Cyclix was piggy-backing small change. So I began to wonder. Why? Why bother?'

Timmison gave her a tight smile. 'Your celebrated instinct.'

'If you like. The problem was . . . the account the money went into on Curaçao . . . well, we couldn't get into that one either. Just like the Austerlitz.'

'So you connected the two.'

She shook her head. 'Stupidly, no. At least, not at first. Not until Vito Kunzman was bleeding to death in my arms. He told me he'd washed the half billion he'd stolen through the Austerlitz Account. As Kunzman was loosely associated with Piagini and Pemblin and therefore Cyclix, I made the connection. And from something else Kunzman said, we finally cracked our way inside the account.'

Timmison raised a pair of fair eyebrows. The action made him look even more disdainful. 'None of this sounds like being sidetracked to me, Miss Semmington.'

She shook her head. 'But it is. You see, inside this account are transactions relating to about a hundred and twenty companies, organisations and individuals, none of whom otherwise has anything whatsoever to do with the Exchange Bank. None of them come up anywhere else on the databank. Not that we can see, anyway. This Austerlitz Account is like a

371

bank within a bank. It's bizarre. Like nothing I've ever seen before. It doesn't make sense.'

Timmison frowned. 'Why not?'

'Because it's one of the tightest, most secure set-ups I've ever encountered. It's a total cutout. Without the codename and number, nothing inside the account could be traced. Without the codename and number you would be hard put to know it even existed. It was a black hole. Absolutely secure. So secure in fact that Vito Kunzman used it to hide the trail of half a billion dollars.'

For the first time in the meeting Timmison looked blank. 'But what's so different about this Austerlitz Account? What makes it bizarre?'

Melissa was animated. She spread her arms expansively. 'The amounts,' she said emphatically. 'The sums. The amount of money inside the Austerlitz. Except for Kunzman's five hundred million which was a one-off and, anyway, was only there for a couple of days, pretty well all the money in the account had come from the Cyclix piggy-backed funds and . . .'

'. . . that's not a lot of money,' Timmison interrupted.

'Exactly. The Austerlitz has a total of about four hundred and thirty million dollars. That doesn't make sense. All that security for so little. It's like having a big bank vault for your Granny's pension book.'

Timmison nodded. 'I see. You would normally expect an account with that level of security to contain billions of laundered drugs dollars?'

'Yes.'

'So.' He was staring directly at her, his voice low and deliberate. 'If the amount of money inside the Austerlitz Account is such small beer, then . . .'

It was Melissa's turn to interrupt '. . . something inside the account is more valuable than money.'

Timmison's eyes widened. He gazed at her in appreciation. 'Quite.'

She shrugged. 'Now you see why it's a diversion. My job is hunting money. The Austerlitz isn't about money. I thought the account would contain vital information about the Exchange Bank. As it turns out, although it's inside the bank it's really nothing to do with it. Whatever the Austerlitz is about . . . it isn't about mainstream money laundering. So, it's a side issue.

At least that's what I'm going to say in my report.'

Timmison was silent. After a while he said: 'It would be most interesting to know what it *is* all about though.'

Melissa laughed. 'Not my problem, Mr Timmison. I'll report how far I've got, but it'll be up to some other poor sod to make sense of it. One thing is for sure: they're going to have their work cut out.' She jerked her head in the direction of the pile of papers on the corner table.

Timmison turned and stared. 'That's it? The Austerlitz Account?'

She nodded. 'That's it.'

He turned back to her. 'One question. When was the account created?'

Melissa checked her notes and the papers on her desk. What she was looking for wasn't there. She rose to her feet and moved across the office to the table in the corner. Timmison watched her riffling through the piles of documents. She found what she was looking for and turned to him. '1990,' she announced. 'By Vito Kunzman.'

Timmison considered her through narrowed eyes. '1990. I wonder if that's significant.'

She stared back at him. Slowly her face changed into a beautiful smile.

'I haven't the faintest idea,' she announced jauntily. In a faintly theatrical gesture she allowed the document she was holding to flutter down onto the pile beside her. 'Nor do I intend to find out. It'll go in my report, but someone else will have to work out the significance. I'm not going to let myself get dragged back into this thing, Mr Timmison.'

She returned and dropped lightly into her seat. She made a show of looking at her watch.

Timmison allowed himself another tight smile. 'One last question. What about movement of funds in and out of the Austerlitz? There must be signatories.'

'There are. Two I've come across so far. One called Mr Black, the other Mr White.' She saw his quizzical look and laughed lightly. 'The Exchange Bank allowed that kind of stuff to go on in its offshore accounts. Black was the prime mover. Whoever he – or she – is, they disseminated the funds to the companies and institutions inside Austerlitz. The organisations in turn would draw down the cash as and when they needed it.'

'How would the companies account for the sudden influx of money?'

She shrugged. 'Issuing false invoices to someone else inside Austerlitz probably. That's what's so disappointing about all this. Instead of a massive money-laundering operation, the Austerlitz Account turns out to be what looks like an enormous, sordid, inter-company scam.'

'If it was a fraud, would it have it worked?'

'Oh yes. Foolproof really. Until the bank was closed down.'

Timmison grunted and looked thoughtful. 'So,' he gave her his full attention, 'when can I hope to see your report?'

'That depends on when Nigel Hawick, my senior partner, sends it to you,' she replied evenly. 'I should get it to him within the next three or four days. Then I'm going to take a few days off. Have a holiday with my son.'

Timmison nodded. 'I think you've earned it.'

Melissa phoned for a security guard to accompany him down in the lift. When the guard arrived she and Timmison shook hands. As he turned away she saw his sharp blue eyes linger a moment on the pile of papers in the corner.

After he had gone she went to the ladies' restroom where she renewed her make-up and did her best with her hair. She returned to the office, put on her suit jacket and sat quietly staring out of the window.

Debbie called within minutes. 'Mr Briscoe's here,' she chuckled. 'Can I come down with you and have a look?'

'No, certainly not,' Melissa flashed. 'You stay away.'

Debbie laughed.

She walked slowly and sedately across the floor of the busy open-plan office and rode the lift down to the high, marble-floored atrium. Bob Briscoe was standing beside the reception desk. He was, she thought, looking particularly good in a clerical grey suit and pale blue shirt.

'Melissa, hi.' He took her lightly by the arm and kissed her on her cheek. Melissa smiled up at him weakly, conscious of the watching eyes of the security men. 'Okay, where are we going?'

'Let's go over here.' Melissa led him away from the reception desk towards one of the tall weeping fig trees, well out of earshot of the security men. She stopped by one of the big, earth-filled, pink-granite rotundas.

'Hey, we gonna have a picnic?' Briscoe laughed.

She shook her head. 'No, we won't have a picnic. In fact we're not going to have lunch.'

He frowned in disappointment. 'We're not? Why, has something come up again?'

She stared at him. 'You lied to me.'

'What?'

'You lied to me,' she repeated quietly. 'You're not who you say you are.'

'Hey,' he looked confused. 'What is this Melissa?'

'Please don't insult my intelligence by acting the innocent.' Her voice was frozen, as cold and pitiless as an iceberg. 'I know that my intelligence, when it comes to you, has been sadly lacking. Like my judgement and self-control and every other bloody facet of my personality. But not any more. That's past.'

'Look, Melissa . . .' He tried putting his arm around her. She twisted violently, raising her arm and slipping his embrace.

'Don't touch me,' she hissed. Her body was rigid, as if her anger had rusted her joints.

His face was shocked. 'I don't get it,' he protested softly.

'It's simple. I'm telling you to leave me alone, to go away, to sod off, to . . . go. You took advantage of me. Which I suppose wasn't all that hard to do. Easy for someone like you with someone like me.'

Memories of his treason made her tone as bitter as bile. 'You feigned affection for me. You insinuated yourself into my life.' She stopped, feeling the tears spring in her eyes. 'And into me. You used me.'

'Hell, Melissa, I didn't use you.'

'Yes, you did,' she spat at him. 'You lied to me. Lied about everything. You're not who you say you are. You don't work for who you say you work for; you don't live where you say you live. Jesus, I don't even know if your name is Bob Briscoe.'

'Listen, Melissa it's . . .'

'Why? That's what I want to know. Why? Why couldn't you have left me alone? Why latch on to me?'

A movement over Briscoe's right shoulder caught her eye. In among the streams of employees hurrying across the marble floor on their way to lunch, she saw Simon, her policeman. He had rushed out of the security office next door to the lifts and was glancing anxiously around the atrium.

It was the expression on his face that momentarily transfixed her. He looked terrified. Like a hunted animal.

She forgot about Simon and switched her arctic look back to Briscoe. He was gazing at her dolefully. Like a whipped dog.

'Why?' she repeated. 'Why? No, no,' she shook her head vigorously. 'I don't want to know. It doesn't matter. Who cares? You used me. You made a fool of me and that's all there is to it. It doesn't matter why. Just go. That's all. Just go.'

'Melissa.'

She turned.

Simon was by her side. In her cold fury she hadn't seen him approach.

'Not now, Simon,' she snarled.

'Melissa, it's important.' He glanced quickly at Briscoe before fixing her with his fearful look.

'Jesus, not now.' Her screech bounced off the massive window panes of the atrium forty feet above them. A few lunchgoers stopped in their tracks. 'Not now,' she said more softly.

'Melissa, it's Jamie. There's been a break-in at the cottage. Someone's got Jamie.'

Chapter Forty-Two

He hated England. He hated it almost as much as he had come to hate Vietnam. And for some of the same reasons.

Not that anyone in England was trying to blow him away. There were no VC waiting in their tunnels, preparing to ambush him. He felt safe enough here. But, as in Nam, he stood out. He was obvious. He felt obvious. Like an elephant in a greenhouse.

England was small, with narrow streets and tiny houses and small buildings and little fields and rinky-dink little cars which drove on the wrong side of the goddam road. The people were small, and grey, and spoke in a way he could scarcely understand.

There were no bars. Not proper bars. The places where they served beer were like something out of Disneyland. And they closed early. In England, everything died after eleven. It was a land for munchkins. The place gave him claustrophobia.

His size and the way he was dressed and the way he spoke all made the little grey-faced English people notice him. Some smiled, but their anaemic smiles looked to him like sneers. Others registered his presence and then looked right through him. Like he wasn't there.

Big Vinny was an alien. In an alien land.

He'd taken a taxi from the airport and had told the driver to drop him off at the only place he knew about in London . . . Buckingham Palace. He didn't want the cab taking him to where the bitch worked. Even in a big city, Big Vinny knew better than to leave a trail that could be followed. After he had paid off the driver he figured the ride had cost him over a hundred bucks.

He had asked the way and walked through the strange, unfamiliar streets, past the strange buildings and curious landmarks to the modern office block in Eastcheap. He'd scouted around the outside, as unobtrusively as he could, for a couple of hours.

The place had good security. There was no way he figured

377

he could get in unobserved. Storming the place would take at least six guys with automatic weapons. And he was one guy. Without a gun.

He wondered how he might get hold of one.

Kill a cop and take his gun? Except for the armed police at the airport, the few policemen he had seen in their peculiar uniforms and loony-tunes helmets were unarmed.

There were no gun shops that he could see. And even if there were, he figured there would have to be some sort of registration to buy a gun. Even in America an alien couldn't walk in off the street and buy a gun.

It was getting late. Vinny gave up the prowling and found a small commercial hotel off the Whitechapel Road. He bought a bottle of scotch and finished it in his room.

The following morning he returned early to the offices on Eastcheap and watched from across the road as the workers arrived. Then he saw her. It was shortly after nine and the bitch was striding along the sidewalk, straight-backed and sassy.

She was in company with a fresh faced young guy who had rookie detective written all over him.

Shit, if only he had a gun, he thought. With a gun it would have been a clean hit and home free. He could have wasted them both in the street and beat it back to the airport before anybody knew where to start looking.

He watched, his eyes glittering with hate, as she disappeared through the big, plate-glass doors of the giant atrium fronting the street.

He gazed up at the tower block. It was like a fortress. He couldn't get to her in there. It had to be outside. Going in or coming out, or . . . or at her home.

He had a few hours before she would re-emerge, he figured. Maybe enough time to do a reconnaissance of where she lived. He bought a road map, checked her address and found the place on the map, some way south of a town called Alton.

He passed a small shop selling cooking utensils, walked in and bought a six-inch kitchen knife, broad-bladed and with a real keen edge. Now, he thought, he had a weapon. Things were looking up.

He took a cab to Victoria, where he tried to rent a car at the rental booths on the station concourse. He was refused. His new identity had not been supplied with a credit card and despite cash and an American driving licence, he couldn't rent a car. Not without some other form of identification, the sniffy bitches behind the counters told him.

They kept calling it car hire and told him they would need to check that he was who he said he was and that he lived at the address shown on his licence.

He needed a drink, but the only goddam bar he found was closed. He bought himself a coffee and settled down to think. After a while he finished his coffee and walked out onto the sidewalk where he hailed a cab. 'The Hilton,' he said.

He noticed there were a number of smart hotels close to the Hilton. He chose the likeliest and walked through its busy lobby and down to the hotel's underground car park. No one paid him any attention.

He waited in the shadows behind a pillar until a metallic grey Mercedes 500 SEL smoothed its way into a nearby parking bay. The driver got out. He was short and middle aged. He unlocked the car trunk and lifted out a suitcase.

It was the sign Big Vinny had been waiting for. Silently he moved up behind the man and slipped a powerful arm around his neck. With a savage jerk he pulled the man's chin around and shoved hard at the back of his head. The man's cervical vertebrae snapped with a loud crack. The sound smacked against the low concrete roof of the car park like the crack of a whip.

With a grunt Big Vinny hefted the limp, dead body into the open trunk and threw the suitcase in after it. He waited a while, until at least a score of cars had driven in or out of the car park, then started the Mercedes and drove it up the ramp. The car park attendant didn't give him a second glance.

Driving was a nightmare.

He couldn't get used to being on the wrong side of the street and the traffic in London moved much faster than he was used to. He had a number of near misses, with drivers hooting at him and waving their fists. He ignored them. A mad munchkin was still a munchkin. He concentrated on the strange-looking direction indicators and headed cautiously southwest towards his destination.

He found his way onto a freeway called the M3 where he became slightly more accustomed to the car's right-hand drive. At junction 5 he turned south, driving between pint-sized cornfields. He kept going, through a series of low hills and the town of Alton, until he finally found the village.

It took him a while to figure out which was her house. In the end he decided it was the one with the dark blue car parked close to the gate. It was set off by itself on the outskirts of the village, at least a hundred yards from its nearest neighbour. The place was a two-storey timbered cottage with roses around the door and a low thatched roof. Big Vinny had never seen anything like it. He drove past it twice.

He parked the Mercedes in a lane and moved like a shadow through a small spinney. He hunkered down near its edge. From here he had a good view of the cottage and the blue guard car. There were two men inside.

Police . . . he had no doubt of it. He wondered if they were armed. If they were, then his problems about getting hold of a gun were solved. Two men in a car would be easy meat. Now that he had the knife.

But . . . were they armed? Shit, there was no way of knowing. This was munchkinland and it was possible they weren't. Vinny screwed up his face. It could go either way.

If they didn't have guns, then killing them would be more trouble than it was worth. And supposing they were in regular radio contact with their control? No, he decided, hitting the guys in the car could raise all sorts of hell.

Get inside the cottage without them seeing him. That was a better plan. Inside the cottage was the killing ground. That was the place to kill the bitch.

He switched his attention to the dark, mullioned windows.

It was difficult to see but after a while he was sure someone was there. A woman. Maybe even two women. He thought about it. Yeah, that would make sense. The bitch had a small kid. One of the women would be there to take care of it. The other, well, she could be the daily maid.

He thought about it. Two women to kill. Three, if the maid stayed over. Yeah, he could do that. Silently. At night. Sneak in and . . . A loud insistent yapping came from somewhere inside the cottage.

Shit. A dog. A young dog by the sound of it. Vinny swore quietly and violently. Sneaking in at night was no longer an option.

He leaned against the thin trunk of a grey alder and thought about it some more.

To kill the bitch inside the cottage would mean sneaking in during the day, when the dog's barking wouldn't be noticed. It would mean killing the other two and waiting for her to come home.

It wasn't a great plan. Too many things could go wrong. Still, it was a plan . . . and if all else failed, then that's what he would have to do.

It was beginning to look, he thought, as if killing her in the street was the better option. With the knife. From behind. Grab her by the neck, pull her back, two quick thrusts to the heart . . . she would be dying before the young cop had turned around. Then him. In the throat. And then away.

He glanced at his watch. He had a couple of hours before he needed to start back to the tower block on Eastcheap. He made himself comfortable and waited, staring unwaveringly at the cottage and the car.

After about an hour he saw the plainclothes cops get out of the vehicle and stretch their legs. They didn't approach the cottage. That's what he had needed to know. The guys in the car didn't communicate with the people in the cottage. If he had to sneak in, he could lie in wait inside the cottage undisturbed.

He edged cautiously back through the spinney and reached the Mercedes.

He found an underground car park close to the Rolay Richard building. Like everything else in the goddam country it was chickenshit, with piddly, narrow-gauge parking bays and close supporting beams. Cursing, Vinny manoeuvred the Mercedes as best he could. Twice he nearly sideswiped it.

He got to the tower block just before five and found a spot from which to watch the big glass doors. He figured it wouldn't be a long wait. Pretty soon she would appear with her boy protector. He was ready for them both. Inside the pocket of his windcheater he grasped the knife tightly.

He watched and waited for five hours, moving his location from time to time, so as not to appear obviously loitering.

It turned into a hard, troublesome vigil, the most difficult he could remember.

In the jungle it would have been easy, but here . . . here in this strange, alien city with traffic and noise and people passing by . . . he was uncomfortable. He felt obvious and out of place.

The bitch didn't appear. Was she still there? he wondered. There was no way of knowing. He had to stick it out until he was sure the building was empty.

Night came down and the lights went up. Exposing him. He moved to the deepest shadows he could find. Even here he felt uncovered. He was the one lying in wait, yet he felt vulnerable . . . almost at risk.

He watched the lights on the floors of the tower block above him go out one by one. Finally, just one floor remained lit up . . . the fourteenth.

A car pulled up in front of the building. Seconds later a security man was unlocking the atrium doors. Suddenly she was there. The bitch was there. Along with her novice cop.

Almost before Vinny could move she had climbed into the back of the car. It drove away.

He cursed long and unmercifully. For Chrissake, the bitch had fixed a car to take her home. Jesus Christ, he had waited all those hours for goddam nothing. He glanced up. The fourteenth floor was in darkness.

He made his way on foot back to his small hotel. En route he bought another bottle of scotch. Lying on the bed in his sparsely furnished room, he drank the whisky and considered his options for the next day. After he finished the bottle he let it drop to the threadbare carpet. He fell asleep on top of the bedcovers fully clothed.

He was outside the tower block in plenty of time to see the first of the office workers arrive. He waited on the same side of the street that the bitch and the cop had used the day before. This time he was really ready for them. The knife was instantly to hand, hidden by his windcheater in the belt of his jeans.

The goddam bitch didn't show. By ten he had figured she wasn't coming.

He found a phone and got the operator to give him the number of Rolay Richard. He punched it out and asked for a Miss Semmington. He was put through to a secretary who told him that Miss Semmington wasn't taking calls right now. When she asked who was calling, he put the phone down.

Shit, the bitch already was up there. She had been there all along . . . secure on the fourteenth floor. She had got to the office before he had.

None of the rinky-dink bars were open so again he found a

coffee shop and sat at an empty table with his coffee. He breathed deeply, making an effort to calm himself.

He was agitated. He could feel it. Like the worst times in Nam, this operation was going seriously out of whack. What was it about this woman? He should have been able to kill her by now. What little protection she had wasn't worth diddly squat. Snuffing her out should have been no more than a moment's work. But he hadn't been able to reach her.

She had proved elusive. If only he could get to her. So far he hadn't even gotten close. And he had a schedule to keep. He recalled the words spoken to him in the back of the dark Pontiac. Kill her quickly. That's what he had been told. There had been urgency in the unknown voice . . . maybe even panic.

He had to get it done. Today. Which meant only one option. Driving down to the cottage. He couldn't take the risk of waiting another whole day to kill her outside the office. Supposing she was driven home again? No, he told himself, surprising her in the cottage would guarantee her dead.

He made his way to the car park. The Mercedes was still there. He reckoned he had perhaps another twenty-four hours before the car and its driver were reported missing. He manoeuvred it out of the car park and took the same route as the previous day, parking in the same place.

This time he moved diagonally across the spinney to a point at its edge furthest away from the guard car. From here he could see the back of the cottage.

It wasn't going to be easy getting inside. There was a couple of hundred yards of open ground between him and the small hedge that marked the cottage's back garden. For at least the first hundred and fifty yards he would be in clear view of the cops in the car.

He frowned, carefully studying the terrain. Further over he thought he could detect a small fold in the ground. Maybe he could use that. If he kept low . . . crawled on his belly . . . maybe the cops wouldn't see him. So long as no one in the cottage decided to look out of a back window, he might make it undetected.

There was a noise. He swivelled in its direction. A small car was pulling into the drive. It stopped and a young, fair-haired woman got out, followed by a small boy and a dog. Big Vinny smiled. The dog was a Springer Spaniel puppy.

Another woman got out of the car on the far side. The car prevented him getting a good view of her. He could see she was young and dark-haired. The group entered the cottage, the pup yapping happily.

Shit. There were two of them. He would have to waste two women. And probably the kid as well. And fast. He'd have to do it quick. Before anyone started screaming.

He glanced up. The sun was high and beaming directly down onto the windscreen of the car at the entrance to the drive. For the next hour or so it would be directly in the men's eyes. He turned back to the cottage, peering at the rear windows.

He heard the clunk of a closing door. One of the cops had got out of the car. Vinny watched him bend down at the open window and have a quick word with his partner before setting off at an easy pace in the direction of the village. It would be hot inside the car. The guy was probably on his way to the store to buy a can of Coke.

Vinny stared at the cop who remained in the car. His head was lolling forward. The heat was making him drowsy.

'Now,' he told himself softly. Now was the time to get inside the cottage.

He moved further around the edge of the spinney. Yes, he was right, there was a fold. Deeper than he had suspected. He dropped to his belly, wriggled across the open ground to the crease in the field and eased up to his haunches. The cop's head was still lolling forward.

Deftly, Big Vinny bellied his way over the ground. It was something he had learned to do in Vietnam and in training with the Chickashaw Commando. Despite his size he did it expertly. Usually he had an assault rifle in the crook of his arms. Jesus, what he would have given to feel an M-16 in his arms right now. He missed it. Missed it far more than he ever missed a woman.

He reached the point where the cottage obscured the view from the guard car and got to his feet. He ran the remaining few yards and scrambled over the hedge. From inside the cottage he could hear the puppy yapping madly. Swiftly he ran up the garden and pressed himself against the white plaster wall. It was warm from the sun.

He waited a second to collect his breath, then raised his hand and gently turned the handle of the back door. The door was unlocked.

384

He took out his knife, waited another second then shoved the door open wide and burst inside the cottage.

The room was a big farmhouse kitchen with dark beams on the ceiling. It was empty. The puppy's yapping was coming from beyond an open door opposite. He cocked his head, listening for the sound of voices above the noise of the dog. He heard one. It was a man's.

He stiffened, then relaxed. The voice he was hearing came from a television. He heard a woman scolding the puppy. 'George, be quiet. George, what on earth is the matter with you?'

Treading carefully he followed the sound of the voice, moving out of the open door and along a short passage. On the right were stairs, on the left a closed door. The sounds of the television, the yapping spaniel and woman upbraiding it were coming from the other side.

Big Vinny placed one hand gently on the door handle, grasped the knife firmly in the other and took a short, sharp breath.

He thrust the door wide open and exploded through it.

The young, dark-haired woman was standing by a television on the opposite side of the room. Her startled look turned to ghastly fear as Vinny's massive frame rushed at her.

He moved at lightning speed, the knife coming up for the deep, driving thrust to her larynx which would sever her vocal cords. He saw she was holding an open shoulder bag, futilely raising it to protect herself as he closed on her. Stupid. That wasn't going to save her. Nothing was.

Then he stumbled.

Something caught in his feet and for a moment he lost his balance, tripping forwards and to one side. It was the dog. The goddam puppy, filling the sunny, low-beamed room with its falsetto barking, had got itself tangled up in his feet.

Vinny half-fell, bouncing against an easy chair. Immediately he corrected himself, coming up quickly from the stumble to move in on the woman.

She had dragged something out of her shoulder bag. Something dark and bulky. He was too close to see it properly. He was on her.

There was a bang and a flash of bright yellow flame beneath Big Vinny's chin. A solid wall of sound exploded against his eardrums and something like a runaway bus hit him on the left shoulder, spinning him around. He lashed out at the woman

385

with his knife hand and felt the blade slice into her body. She went over backwards with a cry, the gun flying out of her hand.

'Sheeeet.' Big Vinny bent double with the pain and clasped his shoulder. The bullet had shattered his clavicle. 'Jeeeesus.'

He scampered across the room in a crouch and retrieved the gun. It was a SIG-Sauer, a neat little shoulderbag weapon with probably fourteen rounds left. He didn't have time to check. He moved fast, scampering back across the room to the front window.

The cop in the car had heard the shot. He was outside the vehicle and sheltering beside the open driver's door. He saw Vinny and raised a pistol. There was a bang and a round crashed through one of the tiny leaded window panes close to his ear.

'Fuck.' The limey cops had been armed after all. He loosed off a round at the crouching cop and saw it whack into the metal of the car door. The cop dived behind the door.

Behind the car Vinny saw the other cop running diagonally across the garden towards the side of the house. 'Shit.' The guy was making for the back. He fired at the fast-moving figure twice but the guy kept on running.

He swivelled from the window and moaned loudly at the agony of his shattered collarbone. He had to get out of the back before the cop got it covered. Otherwise . . .

He ran across the room, pressing his shattered shoulder with his gun hand. Standing mute and rigid with shock in the short passageway was the young, blond-haired woman he had seen get out of the car. He barged into her, bouncing her cruelly out of his way. 'Bitch,' he bellowed.

He made it through the kitchen, the puppy yapping hysterically at his heels. He surged through the open door and stumbled into the sun.

A heavy bullet smacked into the plaster above his head, sending up a cloud of white plaster dust. Another whacked into a dark wall beam by his side. Vinny stopped and stumbled backwards, firing once in the direction of the shots.

He half-fell into the kitchen and pushed at the door with his good arm. The puppy scampered through the fast-closing gap. Vinny crashed the door shut and locked it.

He leaned against the kitchen wall, breathing noisily, his shoulder and the left side of his head roaring with pain. He couldn't make it out the back. Not now. The cop out there had the cover of the cottage wall and the hedge. All he had was a lot of open ground.

It was the same at the front. His shoulder made him slow. He wasn't going to make it across the front. It was exposed all the way to the spinney. These guys could shoot well enough to bring him down in open ground. Goddam munchkins.

He put the SIG down and, moaning loudly, shucked his windcheater off as gently as he could. He moved to the sink and with one hand splashed cold water in his face. He had to think . . . had to determine a way out of this mess.

He picked up the pistol. What had he got? He slid the magazine out of the pistol grip. Ten rounds. Ten 9mm Parabellum rounds . . . and . . . his small eyes slitted as he figured the situation . . . and . . . hostages.

He shuffled quickly into the front room.

The blonde girl was kneeling beside the body of the fallen woman, trying to stem the blood seeping from a wound in her side. The woman was moaning softly.

Vinny crabbed across to the front window, checked it, then moved to the blonde girl. Shoving the pistol into his belt he reached down, twisted her hair in his thick fingers and yanked her cruelly to her feet. She cried out in pain.

'Listen, bitch,' he hissed: 'where's the kid?'

The girl stared at him stupidly.

'The kid!' he exploded. 'Where's the kid?'

Chapter Forty-Three

Briscoe eased her down onto the rough, cold edge of the pink-granite rotunda. Melissa sat, gripping his arm tightly, afraid she might faint out and slip off. She was having trouble breathing . . . having trouble seeing. She seemed to be surrounded by security men and office staff.

Simon disappeared for a short time and then came back. 'The car's on its way over,' he told her in the most comforting tone he could. He sat down beside her.

Briscoe loosened her grip on his arm and for some unaccountable reason moved away. In a daze she watched him take out his mobile phone, punch up a number and start quietly talking.

She grabbed Simon with both hands. 'What did they say about Jamie?' she pleaded.

He frowned. 'They said someone has him.'

'But what does that mean? Are they hurting him? Oh God, what does it mean?'

The young detective stared at her, his eyes lambent with pity. 'Melissa, that's all I know. It was a transmission from the local cops. Someone is inside the cottage.' He paused. 'He's got a gun.'

'Oh no,' she wailed. 'Oh no.'

'Melissa, they're doing all they can. There's a siege team already on its way. They've got trained negotiators. You must try not to worry. These things almost always turn out all right.'

'But Jamie,' she cried. 'He'll be so frightened.'

Simon looked up. A man was standing by the glass doors, gesturing. 'The car's here,' he murmured.

He helped her up and held her firmly as she tottered towards the doors. It was the grey Cavalier. Simon helped her into the back seat and closed the door. Suddenly Briscoe was by the car, talking intensely to the young detective. After a moment Simon nodded and got into the front. Briscoe hurried around the car and climbed in the back.

'Why are you here?' Melissa's voice was a flat, toneless croak. She was huddled in a cataleptic state in the corner of the seat, her arms rigid and close in against her body.

'I may be able to help,' he said gently.

They didn't speak again until they were a long way down the motorway. A police escort had picked them up and they were in convoy with lights flashing and sirens wailing, moving at close to a hundred miles an hour.

Somewhere in Melissa's confused, horror-filled brain was a distant memory of travelling along the M3 at a similar speed in a dark green Daimler. She could also faintly recall, as if in a different life, a police convoy on a country road in New York State.

Slowly she became aware of Briscoe seated on the far side of the Cavalier's rear seat. 'You're not who you say you are, are you?' she murmured.

He turned from the window and gazed at her. 'No.' His voice was quiet.

'Who are you then? What are you?

He shrugged. 'I work for the United States Government.'

Her face hardened. 'Sent to spy on me.'

He made a face. 'And to look after you,' he said.

She contemplated him with big, tear-filled eyes. 'You haven't done a very good job.'

She turned away from him and looked to her front. She didn't speak again for the rest of the journey.

Dozens of police vehicles, their blue lights flashing, were parked on the green opposite the cottage. The Cavalier pulled up beside them. Scores of uniformed police officers were everywhere. Melissa allowed Briscoe to help her out of the car.

A big, middle-aged policeman with shiny buttons and silver braid on the peak of his cap, marched up to her. He told her his name and rank but she was too dazed to register details. Her eyes were fixed unwaveringly on the cottage, on the creaky, dark-oak front door behind which her son was suffering unimaginable horrors.

'Miss Semmington, Miss Semmington.' She dragged her eyes back to the policeman. 'I want you to know we have everything under control. We are doing all we can to ensure that your son and everyone else inside your home emerges safe and unharmed. We are trying to establish contact with the man inside. Once we've got that, we can start talking him out.'

He half-saluted and moved away as a uniformed policewoman put an arm around her shoulders and held on to her tightly. She watched Bob Briscoe follow the policeman and engage him in conversation.

The policewoman edged her back a few paces. 'I've got a flask of coffee,' she told her soothingly. 'Would you like a cup?' Melissa shook her head.

A dark green Daimler slewed to a stop outside the circle of police cars, kicking up little puffs of dust from the dry grass. A tall, familiar figure emerged instantly from the back of the car and marched across the green towards her.

'I came as soon as I heard,' Timmison said. 'Miss Semmington, I want you to know that we will do anything – anything – to make sure your son is safe.' His voice was stiff and brittle but she knew he meant it. 'You must understand that. Anything. Now, please excuse me.'

Without waiting for a response he strode away, moving towards where the senior policeman and Bob Briscoe were in deep discussion. Melissa's stupefied eyes followed him.

She saw him join the other two and frowned as she watched. It was clear Timmison knew the policeman, but his response when he was introduced to Briscoe was peculiar. The two men eyed each other guardedly. As if they knew of each other but had never met. Like rival suitors. She noticed they didn't shake hands. The three went into a huddle.

She turned to the policewoman. 'What are they doing?' she wailed. 'For God's sake, why are they holding meetings? Why is everyone standing around? Why aren't they doing something about getting Jamie out of there?'

'They are,' the woman placated her softly, tightening her grip around Melissa's shoulders. 'They're organising it. They have to do it right. Get him out without being hurt.'

'I want my son,' she howled. The tears coursed down her cheeks unheeded.

Another man joined the trio across the green. Melissa recognised him as one of the policemen who had daily sat in the blue Mondeo, guarding the cottage. *Supposedly* guarding the

390

cottage. They talked for a few seconds, then all four turned and advanced towards her. The policewoman let her go and moved a pace away. Melissa felt suddenly isolated.

'Miss Semmington,' the big policeman began, 'it's possible you may be able to help us identify the man inside the cottage.'

She shook her head violently. 'No I can't,' she cried. 'I don't know anything about him. All I want is my son. Get Jamie. Get him out of there.'

'Miss Semmington, we are doing what we can. But we must proceed with caution. The man inside your cottage is armed and very dangerous. It would help greatly if we knew something about him.'

'But that's why you must get Jamie. If he's dangerous he'll hurt him. If he's got a gun, he'll hurt Jamie.'

'We intend to prevent that happening. Whoever he is, he knows there's nothing to be gained by hurting your son. Or anyone else. He can't get away. The cottage is completely surrounded by armed-response officers.'

Melissa's tearfilled eyes slewed from the policeman's face to the scene in front of her. For the first time she noticed, beyond the groups of policemen standing out of pistol-range behind the cars, numerous blue-uniformed figures in armoured vests crouching by the hedge and the low garden fence. They had carbines levelled at the cottage windows.

'Oh no!' she cried loudly. 'Oh, no! You mustn't let them shoot. They'll shoot Jamie.' She surged forward, towards the cottage.

A pair of strong hands grabbed her and brought her up short. From somewhere far away she heard the policeman say: 'No one is going to shoot anyone, Miss Semmington. Least of all your son.'

'Melissa, Melissa.' The voice was low and intense. 'Look at me. Melissa.' The hands gripping her shoulders shook her softly. 'Look at me.'

The voice was almost hypnotic. She recognised it from somewhere in her past. The voice of a lover? Or of a traitor? Her befuddled brain couldn't tell.

She looked up. Bob Briscoe's face filled her vision. His eyes locked onto hers. Powerful, penetrating, dark brown eyes. 'Melissa, listen to me. You're losing it. You're letting go of reality.'

One of the others in the group made to interrupt. In her dazed state she saw Briscoe flash him a look. The man fell silent.

Briscoe's eyes bored into hers. 'You're on the edge of hysteria. No one blames you, but you're no use if you lose it, Melissa. Do you understand? You're no use to Jamie if you flip out. You cannot help him if you're out of it. To save Jamie you must get hold of yourself . . . get a grip. Now.' The hands shook her body gently.

She closed her eyes and swayed, confident in the strength of his grasp. The hysterical mist inside her head dissipated slightly. 'Yes, all right,' she whispered.

Briscoe retained his hold on her. 'The man in the cottage. The detective here says he's a big guy. Very big. Dressed in jeans and a blouson and check shirt. Does any of that mean anything to you? Do you know anyone like that? Anyone who would dress like that?'

She stared up at him. Did it mean anything? Curiously . . . it seemed to. She blinked.

'He has a gun,' Briscoe continued. 'He knows how to use it. We think he may have taken it off the policewoman in the cottage.'

Again, Melissa closed her eyes. Liz. Poor Liz. She had forgotten about her. It wasn't only Jamie trapped inside the cottage. There was Astrid and Liz. She was responsible for them as well. Oh God, it was all her fault.

She shook her head savagely, fighting to disperse the numbing fog of fear smothering her brain. 'Is it possible you might know who this guy is?' she heard Briscoe ask.

She kept her eyes shut, screwing them tighter, recalling another time and another place where she'd been surrounded by armed police. The man's description . . . there was an echo in her head . . . Chauncey Morton's voice.

'Is he American?' she whispered

'What?' Briscoe responded. 'Did you say American?' He glanced at the policeman. 'Is he American?'

'We don't know. He hasn't responded to the phone or the loudhailer.'

Briscoe squeezed her shoulders. 'Melissa, why do you think he's American?'

'We were attacked in a cabin in New York,' she mumbled. 'I think one of the people who attacked us was a big man in jeans and a check shirt. He was the one who got away. Sam Barber found out about him.'

'Sam Barber.' Briscoe's voice was suddenly animated. 'Who's Sam Barber?'

'FBI.'

'FBI?' he repeated urgently. 'Where, in Washington?'

She shook her head. 'San Francisco. The Economic Crime Unit.'

Retaining his grip on Melissa, Briscoe looked at the senior policeman. 'Do you have a command vehicle here? One that can get me a link with San Francisco?'

'Of course.'

Briscoe squeezed her shoulders. 'Well done,' he said warmly.

He relinquished his grip and nodded at the policewoman, who took her by the arm. Briscoe and the others hurried away.

The policewoman led her to a canvas chair in the lee of one of the cars where she sat her down and draped a blanket over her shoulders. It was then that she realised that, despite the warmth of the sun, she was shuddering. The policewoman gave her a cup of coffee in a plastic mug. She took it with a shaking hand and slopped half of it before she got it to her lips.

Briscoe and the others returned a few minutes later. 'We got Barber at home,' Briscoe told her. 'We're pretty sure the man in the cottage is a guy called Vinny Harold, one of the men who attacked you at the cabin. The FBI have him on their most wanted list. They haven't been able to trace him.'

'But why would he come here?' she cried

Briscoe gave her a dour look. 'He came here for you, Melissa. Maybe it was you he was after in New York.'

'Me? Why would he be after me?'

'It has to be something to do with your work. Right now, it doesn't matter. What matters is that this guy is one dangerous animal. He won't give up easily. It's obvious he came here for you, it went wrong, and now he's got Jamie.'

'Oh, dear God, what are we going to do?'

'We're going to do everything in our power to get your son out of there, Miss Semmington,' Timmison said gravely.

Her gaze switched between Timmison and Briscoe.

'The thing is,' Briscoe continued, 'we're pretty sure the guy is wounded. We think the policewoman put a bullet in him.'

'Wounded?' She stared up at Briscoe hopefully. 'Is that good?'

He grimaced. 'It's good and it's not good. It's good because he may be hurt bad. We know he's losing blood. That could be slowing him up. It's not good because . . . well, a wounded buffalo is even more dangerous. That's why I have to get inside the cottage.'

She puckered her face. 'You?'

He nodded. 'Yes.' He glanced at the senior policeman who was frowning unhappily and then at Timmison whose face was impassive. 'We've agreed. I've been trained for this kind of work. We figure it's the best way of handling the situation.'

'I thought you were supposed to be a venture capitalist . . . a financier?'

He smiled briefly. 'Sure, I know about that stuff too. But . . . well . . . this,' he gestured in the direction of the cottage, 'is my original line of work.'

She stared up at him dumbly, her face racked, her brain unable to come to terms with a world turned upside down.

'Listen Melissa,' Briscoe squatted by the side of her seat, 'we need a plan of the cottage. Both floors. Now.'

He reached up and the senior policeman handed him a pad and pencil. He plonked them in her lap. 'Can you draw us a plan?'

It took her some seconds to get her mind into focus and to recall the layout of her own home. She drew laboriously, watched in silence by Briscoe and the others.

Briscoe took the pad. 'This left-hand wall, there's no window on the ground floor except for the side window of your study, right? Upstairs, there's just the bathroom window on that side of the house. Is that right?'

'Yes.'

'Will it be locked?'

She thought of Astrid and her Teutonic obsession with hygiene. 'Maybe not. It could be open. Just slightly.'

Briscoe nodded. He stood up and turned to the others. 'That's the way to go,' he said decisively. 'He's blind on that side. He can't see what's happening there unless he leans out of the study window. In which case your guys can pop him.'

The uniformed policeman frowned. 'Or unless he's on the first floor and checks the bathroom.'

Briscoe shrugged. 'He may check upstairs from time to time but he won't stay up there. He has to stay here,' he jabbed at the pad, 'in this big room, the lounge. That's where he's got most control. Or in the kitchen. And if he thinks you're going to attack the house, that's where he'll expect it to come from.'

394

'That's ridiculous,' the policeman protested. 'He knows we would never attack the house whilst he has hostages in there.'

Briscoe shook his head. 'This guy is a wounded animal, cornered a long way from home. We don't know what he knows . . . what he's figuring. But if you're right, then he won't be expecting me, will he?' He began to move away. 'Now, I need a short ladder. And a handgun.'

'Bob.' Melissa let out a faint cry, like that of a small, wounded bird.

He stopped, half-turned and looked down at her. His dark, handsome features, which a moment before had been filled with concern, were suddenly set and menacing.

Already he was preoccupied with his mission.

She gazed up at him, the panic leaping in her face like flames. 'You will get Jamie out of there, won't you? Please? You will get him away from that man.'

He stared at her, iron-eyed. Slowly, he nodded. His voice was low . . . as dry and pitiless as the desert.

'I'll do everything I can.' He turned away.

Chapter Forty-Four

'He's asleep,' she wailed.

'What?' The blonde girl had a strange guttural accent. Maybe Kraut, he thought.

Big Vinny twisted his fingers deeper in her hair and yanked her head back. She whinnied with pain. 'What?' he snarled.

'He's asleep.' Her hands, tugging at his grip were as ineffective as butterflies.

'Where?'

'Upstairs.'

From where they were standing in the middle of the room, Vinny flashed a quick look out of the front window. The cop was still crouching by the car. From what he knew of cops the guy would stay put until back-up arrived.

'Show me.' He let go of her hair and grabbed her viciously by the arm.

He shoved her ahead of him up the narrow staircase. The puppy, now silent, followed them but found the stairs too steep. It stood at the foot of the staircase, whining pathetically.

Even moving slowly up the stairs was an agonising effort. The pain from his collarbone was intense, his left arm and most of his left side almost completely numb. They turned into a narrow landing with off-white plaster walls and dark irregular beams. The girl led him to a closed door at the end of the landing and stopped.

Bravely she tugged her arm out of his grip and turned to face him. 'He doesn't know you,' she said quietly. 'If you wake him he will get very frightened. He may have an attack. You must be quiet.'

She sounded like a goddam schoolmarm. Ordinarily he would have smacked the Kraut bitch upside the head but his shoulder was too painful. He wondered what the hell she was talking about? An attack? What kind of attack?

'Open the goddam door,' he told her, though he kept his voice low.

She eased open the door and they moved quietly into the room. There were toys everywhere and a kid's drawings on the walls. A small child was asleep in a bed.

'Shit,' Vinny whispered in surprise.

The kid was a moonface. Like his cousin Jethro. He frowned, remembering Jethro. The guy was fine most of the time and then for no reason at all would suddenly throw a fit. A hell of a fit . . . a knock down, drag out, slam bam fit. Now he knew what the bitch was talking about.

Vinny frowned, staring at the sleeping child.

If his original plan of getting into the cottage unseen had worked, he would have killed the kid straight away. Slit its throat as it lay sleeping. But now there was a good possibility he was going to need the boy to bargain with. The kid was a hostage. Vinny needed him alive.

What he didn't need was a kid going hysterical on him. It was better to leave him sleeping. He glanced around the room. It was secure enough. The kid, when it woke, would wander unsuspectingly downstairs. It wasn't going to go anywhere else.

He backed out of the room quietly, the blonde girl with him. She closed the bedroom door and he grabbed her. Shoving her ahead of him he quickly checked the other rooms on the first floor. The place was a nightmare. There was no way one man could defend it if the police mounted an assault.

But would they? he wondered. Would they try busting in while he had the girl and a moonfaced kid as hostages? No. The cops here would be like those at home. They'd try negotiation . . . talking him out before they thought of assaulting the cottage.

From the lead-mullioned windows of the big bedroom at the front he had a good view of the garden and the sunny green on the other side of the narrow lane leading past the house. Already there were police cars on the grass and uniformed cops running around and cordoning off the area. He glanced down at the armed cop crouching by the blue car.

With an assault rifle he could have taken the guy out easily. But with only a pistol . . .

The cop looked up and caught sight of him. Vinny shoved the blonde girl in front of the window, stepped to the side, pulled out the pistol and pressed it hard against the side of her head for the cop and all his buddies to see.

He saw the look of horror on the guy's face. Shit, he was half tempted to pull the trigger just to see how bad that look could get.

'Don't, please don't,' the girl pleaded. Her eyes were huge and fearful.

'Shaddup bitch.' After a moment he pushed the gun back into his belt and grabbed her. 'Downstairs.'

The puppy wagged its tail as it saw them coming. Vinny smiled and at the bottom of the stairs attempted to stroke the small ball of fur. The pain in his shoulder as he bent down was too much. He groaned and straightened up.

Seizing the girl once more, he checked out the room on the right of the hallway at the front. It was some kind of study. The door had a key in it. He locked it from the outside. At least, he thought, that was a little more secure.

He hustled the girl back into the big lounge. As soon as he released her she moved across to the fallen policewoman and knelt by her side. The woman groaned in pain.

'She is losing much blood,' the girl said.

'Yeah, so am I,' Vinny snarled.

He stared vengefully at the young woman lying on the carpet. The bitch had put a bullet in him. He ought to put one in her. Or finish the job with the knife blade in her heart.

But no, a wounded, half-alive cop was a lot more use to him right now than a dead one. She could be another bargaining chip. When the time came.

When the time came for what?

Big Vinny stared around the room. He needed a plan. He had to figure some way out of this goddam mess. It was important to think . . . and to think clearly. Only he couldn't. Not with the raging pain chewing inside his shoulder. It was almost impossible to take his mind off the agony. The first thing he needed was relief. So he could think straight.

He stumbled across the room and once more grabbed the girl by the hair. 'To hell with her,' he snarled, pulling her to her feet. 'You fix me first. Bandages, aspirin, where are they?'

She led him through into the kitchen. At the bottom of the garden half a dozen cops with carbines were running into position. Some, seeing him, pointed their weapons at the windows. Vinny scuttled out of the line of fire, aimed his pistol at the girl's head and ordered her to pull down the kitchen blinds.

Afterwards he made her help him off with his shirt. The collarbone was a bloody mess of torn flesh and slivers of white bone. As far as he could see there was no exit wound.

The girl bathed his shoulder in warm water and antiseptic before bandaging it as best she could and fashioning him a makeshift sling which held his left arm high up against his naked, hairy chest. Although blood was already oozing through the bandages, Vinny felt the pain ease a little. He emptied a bottle of aspirin onto the breakfast bar and threw half a dozen tablets into his mouth. He crunched them noisily.

In the lounge the phone started warbling.

He made to move out of the kitchen, but the girl insisted on filling a bowl with water and antiseptic and finding more bandages to treat the policewoman. Vinny let her. It would give the Kraut bitch something to do. He figured if she was looking after the cop she wouldn't be looking to escape.

He forced the girl to draw the lounge curtains before he lifted the phone. It was some limey cop. He killed the call instantly and left the receiver off the hook. A couple of minutes later a loudhailer started up from outside. It was the same guy, trying with soft, understanding words, to get him to talk.

Big Vinny forced himself to ignore the distracting noise. He would talk to the cops when he was ready. When he had a plan to break out. In the meantime he would let them sweat, not knowing who he was or what he wanted.

He lowered himself into an easy chair from which he could see the open doorway of the lounge and watched indifferently as the blonde girl attended to the policewoman's wound. From what he could see it looked like he had sliced her low down in her gut. It would be touch and go whether she made it.

He guessed the bitch was in a lot of pain. The notion gave him a sense of satisfaction. He could maybe use that, he thought. Maybe drag her to the phone and let the cops listen to her low, agonised moaning. That might be a useful distraction when he came to break out.

But how? How was he going to break out? That's what he had to figure. He would have to wait for night. That much was certain. The cops were bound to have spotlights on the house, but, maybe, if he could shoot a couple out and . . .

Stumped in his chair, Big Vinny began thinking of a plan.

The girl looked up from tending to the policewoman's wound. Her eyes remained large and fearful but her voice was steady. 'If she does not get help at a hospital I am afraid she may die,' she croaked.

Vinny shrugged indifferently. 'Tell me about it. She ain't going nowhere.'

The girl returned to her ministrations, gently pulling off the woman's skirt to get at the knife wound. The cop made no sound. Vinny guessed she had fallen unconscious. He stared at the woman's naked legs and at the blood seeping over her hip, unmoved by the sight of flesh. He had no yearnings in that direction. Sex was the last thing on his mind, even though he was sitting there half-naked without a shirt. The pain in his shoulder and the plight of his situation took precedence. His libido was turned off.

He noticed the puppy snuffling around the girl, jabbing its inquisitive nose at the policewoman's wound. The girl shoved it aside. It rolled across the floor and yelped. Vinny gave her a savage look. 'Leave the dog be,' he growled. 'Critter ain't done you no harm.'

He called it across to him. The puppy waddled over the carpet and Vinny reached down from his seat and stroked its ears. Fondling the dog helped him think.

His left arm lay heavy in its sling and his bandage was soaked, the blood dribbling down his chest and over his strong, heavy belly, matting the coarse hair of his body.

He wasn't sure how long he sat there, figuring out his escape. A couple of times he dragged the girl away from the policewoman to check the other rooms in the cottage, forcing himself upstairs despite the agony the motion of climbing stairs created in his shoulder.

Coming downstairs the second time he collected the aspirins from the kitchen and swallowed another half dozen to ease the throbbing pain.

He slumped into his seat and sat quietly, stroking the puppy's ears, watching but not seeing the blonde girl do what little she could for the fallen cop, hearing but not listening to the intermittent broadcasts of the police loudhailer.

After a while his mind began to formulate a plan of breaking out of the cottage. He had broken out of more than one VC ambush in his time: now he was beginning to see a way of breaking out of this. It would mean risks and maybe some shooting, but . . . yes . . . it could work.

After that he wasn't sure. The cops would have discovered the Mercedes by now so that was no longer an option. But there were plenty of other cars outside . . . cars in the darkness beyond the lights . . . cars belonging to the cops. And plenty of automatic weapons too.

He figured he would start talking to the cops in the early evening. That would make them think he was softening up. Then, come nightfall, he would kill the kid and the two women, break out and, in the confusion, whack a cop, steal his weapon and then . . .

He thought about the bitch he had come to kill. By nightfall she would be out there, going mad with worry about her kid. There was a possibility that in the confusion he might just get lucky and get to her. There was a chance of it. The last thing the cops would expect would be for him to stick around in the darkness. But his mission was still to kill the bitch. He hadn't forgotten that.

Big Vinny never forgot his mission.

Something intruded on his thoughts and he blinked. Something from outside. Something the goddam limey cop was announcing on the loudhailer. He listened.

'Vinny Harold,' the loudhailer boomed, 'pick up the phone. Come on, Vinny, talk to us. We can work this out.'

Shit. He stared in surprise at the curtains drawn over the front windows. The goddam cops knew who he was. How in hell had they . . . ?

A floorboard creaked upstairs.

He looked up and listened. Waiting.

Nothing.

He glanced over at the blonde girl. If she had heard it she gave no sign. Her attention was on the unconscious cop. He listened a while longer. No, it was probably nothing. This was an old house with real old-fashioned construction and . . .

Another floorboard creaked.

A different sound . . . a different floorboard.

Someone was moving about upstairs.

Big Vinny shot out of his seat, ignoring the sudden searing pain in his shoulder. The puppy, startled by his movement, barked and ran to shelter beside the girl. He pulled the SIG from the belt of his jeans.

'Come here,' he snarled at the girl.

She looked up. 'What?'

He pointed the pistol at her head. 'Come here, goddammit.'

She got up off her knees and moved towards him. He motioned her with the pistol to stand in front of him facing the open doorway of the lounge. She frowned at him quizzically.

From upstairs came the plaintive, muffled wail of a child.

The girl turned to Big Vinny. 'It's Jamie,' she said. 'He's woken up. I must go for him.'

For Christ's sake. Of course. The kid. The goddam kid had woken up.

Vinny grimaced. The child was bound to have woken up sooner or later, but what kind of reaction was it going to have when it saw him? With his arm in a sling . . . with blood soaking his bandages and drying in thin red rivers on his belly. Jesus, the last thing he wanted was the kid having some kind of fit. He should have killed it earlier.

Maybe he should kill it now. Have done with it. Damn.

The girl hurried out of the room, the yapping puppy scampering after her. Vinny followed. At the doorway he noticed something red splotching the white patches of the spaniel's fur. He frowned, staring down at the spaniel's back.

Blood.

Shit, the poor little critter was hurt. Goddammit, how had that happened?

Then he realised. Of course. The blood was probably from the cop.

He allowed himself a half-smile as he stepped into the hall.

The girl's body was flattened against the oak panelling of the staircase. Vinny's head came up in shock. His eyes flicked beyond the frightened, staring girl.

Crouching silently in the centre of the hallway was a man, his arms outstretched, his hands gripping a pistol aimed directly at Vinny's head.

The guy was inside the kill zone, less than a dozen feet away, and Vinny was exposed, his SIG down by his side.

He was dead already.

Big Vinny knew he was dead but he raised the SIG anyway, thinking in the instant before the man's gun roared and the first

9mm bullet exploded in his brain, that what had finally got him killed wasn't the cops or a bunch of dumb, drug-smuggling Mestizos, nor even Charlie Cong.

It was a moonfaced kid and a spaniel puppy.

Chapter Forty-Five

They heard three shots. Three sharp, flat, rapid reports from inside the cottage.

Then nothing.

Everything and everybody was instantly still, the groups of policemen and women suddenly silent, their eyes focused on the cottage, their breath indrawn.

Waiting.

There was the sound of a lock being turned and all eyes switched to the front door. Slowly, it creaked open.

Melissa watched two pistols, one after the other, fly out of the open doorway and land on the bright, sunlit lawn beside the garden path. From somewhere inside the hallway she heard a voice. It was Briscoe's. Loud and commanding. 'It's okay. We're coming out.'

Briscoe appeared first, his arms spread wide and half-raised. Immediately behind him was Astrid. She was carrying Jamie.

Melissa screamed and ran forwards. Steven Timmison caught her by the arm. 'Wait,' he ordered.

Briscoe saw them. 'Let her come,' he shouted. 'It's okay.'

Behind him, streams of armed police were storming through the open door.

Melissa raced across the green, over the lane and into the front garden. She grabbed Jamie out of Astrid's arms and clasped him tightly, tears streaming down her face. 'Jamie, my baby. Jamie,' she wailed.

She gazed at his face and was immediately surprised. He was rubbing sleep from his eyes and looking around him in amazement.

She shot an inquiring glance at Astrid who summoned a weak smile. 'He was asleep,' she explained croakily. 'He saw nothing. He is asking why are there fireworks.'

Melissa stared at her son for a moment then hugged him even tighter. She began laughing uncontrollably.

They were moved into a country hotel west of Winchester where they stayed for three weeks. On the second day Melissa gave Astrid some money and put her on a flight back to her family in Dresden. The girl was bearing up remarkably well but she had been through a lot: the terror of being threatened by Vinny Harold and the awful sight of seeing him gunned down had stretched her nerves to breaking point.

At the airport Melissa stroked the girl's hair and told her softly to spend as long as she wanted at home and if she didn't want to come back again to look after Jamie, she would certainly understand.

She phoned the hospital twice a day to find out how Liz was doing. On the third day a nurse told her the policewoman was out of intensive care and was expected to make a full recovery. Melissa felt an enormous weight lift off her. She didn't think she would have been able to bear it if a second policewoman had died on her behalf.

Someone, Timmison probably, had arranged for increased police protection and there were at least half a dozen plainclothes police resident at the hotel and watching over them. They were anonymous and unobtrusive and after a while Melissa hardly noticed their presence.

Timmison had told her to stay away from the cottage for as long as it took to have all the bloodstained carpets and furniture replaced. His department, he said, would pick up the bill. Someone phoned her at the hotel about her choice of replacements. She found it difficult to care and told them to find the closest match to the originals. Following what had happened, she wasn't sure she wanted to live in the place any more.

After a couple of days she called the office and spoke to Nigel Hawick. Timmison had briefed the senior partners on what had happened, he told her, and now as far as Rolay Richard was concerned she was on extended paid leave of absence.

His voice was filled with concern. How was she feeling? he asked.

She told him she didn't know. After all that had happened she felt numb, paralysed. She was still trying to get to grips with it . . . trying to get everything into some kind of perspective.

She needed time, she said, to work out her future. She told him where she was staying but insisted she didn't want anyone from the firm contacting her.

The weather was sunny and warm and she spent most of her days walking with Jamie in the pretty countryside around the hotel, their low-profile protection following at a discreet distance. She watched Jamie closely but it was obvious that what had gone on only feet from his bedroom door had escaped him completely.

He still asked, when he remembered, about the fireworks and why all the policemen had been there but it wasn't something that bothered him. He seemed delighted to be with her, walking the local footpaths and exploring the woods and fields with George following along on his stumpy legs. After the first week, though, she noticed he was getting bored.

Where was Astrid? he kept asking. And when were they going back home so he could sleep in his own room? And when was he going back to school to see his friends? He was keen to get back to his routine, and some of the pleasure Melissa felt at learning he had a life of his own was eclipsed by finding it wasn't entirely centred around her.

Towards the end of the week she felt strong enough to call Debbie and get her to cancel any outstanding meetings and reorganise her diary. She issued the secretary with a stream of instructions, finishing with the heap of documents from the Austerlitz Account she had piled on the table in the corner of her office.

'You'd better tidy them up and lock them away somewhere,' she said.

'But they're gone,' Debbie said.

'Gone. What do you mean, gone?'

'They're not there. They disappeared the day after . . . the day after the trouble at your cottage.'

'What, all of them? My notes included?'

'Yes. I thought you'd asked Boris Redbourn or Mr Hawick to move them for you.'

'No.'

'Well, maybe one of them did it anyway.'

'Boris wouldn't move things from my office. Nor would Nigel Hawick. At least I don't think he would. Not unless he thought they were . . .' She paused, then said: 'You'd better ask Nigel if he moved them.'

Debbie called back a few minutes later. 'I asked Mr Hawick. He said he moved the papers.'

'But why?'

'He didn't say.'

Melissa's face puckered in bewilderment. After a moment she said, 'Debbie, go and ask Nigel if he still has them.'

'What, now?'

'Yes.'

The secretary was back on the line in less than a minute. 'No. He says that man Mr Timmison asked for them. He has them.'

'Timmison?'

'Yes, Mr Timmison. Is that okay?' Debbie sounded worried. 'Is it all right if he has them?'

'Yes, that's okay. Don't worry about it, Debbie. Thanks.' Melissa replaced the receiver and stared unseeing out of her window at the cultivated parkland gently unfolding towards the smoky haze of the horizon.

One evening, towards the end of their second week in the hotel, she received a telephone call in her room. It was Bob Briscoe.

She was surprised.

He was downstairs in reception, he told her, and would like to buy her a drink.

She thought about it for a moment before catching sight of herself in a mirror. She had just put Jamie to bed and was dressed in a cream blouse and a crumpled navy skirt. She had no make-up on and was barelegged.

She stared at herself. 'All right,' she replied quietly. She brushed her hair and went down as she was.

He smiled at her but made no attempt to kiss her. They walked into the hotel bar where he ordered drinks before finding a quiet corner. They sat down by a set of French windows looking out over the hotel's formal gardens. A couple of unobtrusive policemen sat down on the opposite side of the big, oak-panelled room.

'I'm on my way to the airport,' he told her. 'I'm flying back to the States tomorrow. I wanted to say goodbye before I left.'

'You're a long way out of your way if you're going to Heathrow,' she murmured.

'I know, but I wanted to make the detour. It was important to see you.'

'Why?'

'To explain.'

The waiter brought their drinks. 'Actually,' she said when he had gone, 'I'm glad you came. I never thanked you properly for saving Jamie. It was all so confused afterwards, and . . .'

'Forget it,' he said.

'I'm hardly likely to do that. You saved my son's life. Whatever else, Bob,' she paused, 'is that your name by the way?'

'Yes.'

'Whatever else, I will always be grateful to you for that.'

He gazed at her and nodded. 'I'm glad it worked out the way it did. Is he okay, by the way?'

She smiled. 'He's fine. In fact we're both fine.'

They stared at each other. 'Good,' he said eventually.

She lifted her vodka and tonic and sipped it, watching him over the rim of her glass. 'You said you wanted to explain.'

'Yes. That time, at your offices, you said I'd used you. Said I had feigned affection.' He shrugged. 'Okay, well I understand you feeling that way but I wanted to tell you it wasn't true. At least not the affection part. I . . .' He paused. She could tell he was uncomfortable. ' . . . I liked you; I was fond of you. Genuinely.'

'But you did lie to me. You did tell me you were a venture capitalist when you weren't. You did tell me tales about financial deals you were working on, deals which were entirely make-believe. In fact, you told me a complete pack of lies. Didn't you?'

'Yes.'

'On behalf of the American Government.'

'Yes.'

'And did the American Government tell you to sleep with me?'

'No, that was my idea. I wanted to do that. I told you: I liked you. I was attracted to you.'

'But it didn't hurt all the same. Did it? I mean, screwing me meant we would be closer. Meant I would tell you a lot more about what I was working on.'

Her voice was acid. He grimaced but said nothing. 'That was the idea, wasn't it? To get close to me so I would tell you all about what I was doing.'

'Yes. Though I can't say it worked too well. You didn't give very much away.'

'Really? I thought I talked my head off.'

'No. Not really. You were very good about not talking. We had to try to piece together what you were working on from other sources.'

'But why?' she exclaimed. 'Why were you so interested in what I was doing?'

'You were working on a lot of critical stuff, Melissa. The people behind the Exchange Bank have compromised a big chunk of the American banking system. We needed to know what you knew . . . what you were finding out about these people.'

'Why? Didn't you think Rolay Richard would tell your government what I was finding out? You didn't think we would share that information with you?'

'Why should it? The American Government isn't a creditor of the Exchange Bank. Rolay Richard isn't working for the Americans. Your firm is working for the Bank of England.'

'So? The BoE or the Treasury or someone in the British Government would have told you what you needed to know.' He didn't reply. 'Well, wouldn't they?'

He shrugged. 'Who knows? Sometimes even friendly governments keep things from each other. Anyway, we needed to know what you knew . . . *when* you knew it. Not a helluva long time afterwards.'

She frowned and stared out of the French windows. The sun was sitting low over the topiary hedges, streaking the manicured lawns with a soft, golden light. 'Anyway,' she turned back to Briscoe, 'who is we?'

'I told you. The American Government.'

'Yes but what part? Surely the President didn't send you to over here to sleep with me.'

His chuckle was tinged with embarrassment. 'No.'

'So who?'

'I'm with a special department of the Federal Reserve. An investigations department.'

'What do you investigate?'

'Financial crime. I'm seconded to a committee called FATCAT. It's part of FINCEN.'

'Yes, I've heard of FATCAT.' A thought struck her. 'Oh God,' she exclaimed, 'you're with FATCAT. And you let me give you a lecture about money laundering. You must have been laughing your socks off. Me, telling you about hot money.'

He shook his head. 'It was about the best explanation I've ever heard.'

She appraised him through narrowed eyes. 'All the same, you're not a regular Fed man are you? Not really. I mean, the way you fought off those two men who attacked me. The way you got Jamie away from that man in the cottage. You said you were trained for that kind of thing. Not in the Fed you weren't. You didn't get that kind of training as a banker.'

'No.'

'So what are you? Some kind of agent?'

'That's right. Some kind of agent.'

'Well, what? What kind of agent?'

'It doesn't matter.' His voice was suddenly a stone wall. 'You don't need to know that.' He gave her a stiff look before swivelling in his seat and closing the subject. He signalled the waiter for another round of drinks then turned back to her.

'Who were those men, Bob? she asked quietly.

'The ones in the subway?'

'Yes.'

'What makes you think I know?'

She gazed at him 'I think you do.'

He stared back at her. 'Just a couple of lowlifes,' he growled. 'They weren't even anything to do with the mainstream of your work.'

'No? I thought they were supposed to be working for the Mafia. For the West Coast money launderers. Piagini . . . Pemblin . . . those people.'

He shook his head. 'The Mafia picks better people to handle a hit than those two bums. They were hired by a Turkish heroin pusher living in London. He had a lot of money go down with the Exchange Bank. The bastard thought he could stop you tracing it back to him by having those guys slice you into bits.'

She shivered slightly as she recalled her terror on the deserted platform. She saw the waiter approaching with their drinks and turned to stare out of the window at the idyllic, quintessentially English view. It was all over now, she told herself. All of it. Behind her. She paused for the waiter to leave before turning back to Briscoe. 'Did you kill them?'

'Me? No.'

'But you know who did.'

He was silent. 'How do you figure that?' he asked

'You didn't let me report the attack. Not straight after it happened. I suppose that should have made me suspicious. But I was too shocked. And too besotted. We'd made love the night before and then, like a shining knight in a fairy tale, you turned up in the nick of time to save me. It all worked out rather well for you, didn't it?'

An angry look passed over his face. 'I didn't set up that attack, if that's what you're trying to say. Part of my job was to look after you, prevent that kind of thing happening.'

'No, I don't think you arranged the attack. But you didn't want the police finding those men, all the same. Did you? You wanted to find them first.'

'I flew back to the States a few hours after it happened. Remember?'

'I've only got your word for that. And we both know how much you've lied to me.'

'Sure, you've only got my word. But I didn't kill those guys, Melissa.'

She considered him for a moment. 'But you know who did.' Her voice was low and intense. 'You arranged to have them killed. By some of your agent colleagues.'

He stared at her. Then he shrugged. 'They were a threat. We couldn't let you be threatened . . . allow your work to be jeopardised. So we fixed the problem.'

'Fixed the problem,' she repeated tonelessly. 'Two bullets in the back of the head fixes a problem?'

He nodded. 'Always.'

'And the heroin dealer?'

'Him too.'

'You know the police are looking for whoever killed those men?'

He shook his head. 'They'll have been told not to bust a gut looking.'

'I could tell them what you told me.'

He gave her a half-smile. 'They wouldn't thank you for it, Melissa. And anyway I really was in the States. So . . .' He shrugged.

'But why?' she wailed softly. 'Why kill them? God knows I hated those men, but I didn't want them dead.'

'Isn't it obvious? To warn off the others.'

'What others?'

'All the others who'd lost hot money when the Exchange Bank went into the tank. All those who figured on stopping you tracing it. Killing those guys was meant as a message – clear notice that anybody getting in the way of you doing your job . . . anybody taking a pop at you . . . was likely to wind up the same way.' He smiled icily. 'We probably saved you a lot of vicious attacks, Melissa.'

She grimaced. 'It didn't stop that man in the cottage. Or his friends in New York.'

Briscoe contemplated his whisky glass. 'Yeah. Those guys were different. I don't think anything was going to stop them.'

What about Akhtar Aziz?'

'Who?'

'The manager's assistant in the Exchange Bank.'

'The guy murdered with his family?'

'Yes. Was that anything to do with you?'

He appeared genuinely shocked. 'Shit, Melissa, what do you take me for?'

'I don't know. You've admitted you're a liar and an accessory in the murder of the men who attacked me.'

'Hey,' his voice was low but intense. 'Those two mothers were a couple of rats' assholes. So was their boss. Lowlife scumbags. They were always going to end up that way. If their professions hadn't got them killed, their personalities would have. But that guy Aziz and his family, they were civilians. We don't hit civilians.'

'So who murdered them?'

'It was an OC hit . . . a Mafia assassination. Word got out that he was talking to you, so the Mob had him and his family murdered.'

'For the same reason.'

'What?'

'*Pour encourager les autres*. It means . . .'

'I know what it means,' he replied sharply. 'Yes, it was meant to stop anyone else who was thinking of talking. The Exchange Bank did that if someone was suspected of disloyalty or had their mitts in the till. The guy you were after, Vito Kunzman, he was mostly the one who did the fingering. I guess you knew that. Maybe dead man don't tell tales, Melissa, but their deaths sure send messages.'

She stared at the table and shook her head. 'That poor little man. And his poor family.' She looked up. 'So much blood. And just for money.' She drained her vodka.

'It isn't always for money,' he murmured.

'No? Then what?'

'Sometimes, it's for what money represents.'

She gazed at him, trying to decipher what he meant. It was too enigmatic. Suddenly she felt tired . . . tired of talking about violence . . . tired of thinking about the Exchange Bank . . . tired of being with a man for whom she'd once had affection but who, she now knew, arranged assassinations.

She stood up. 'Thanks for the drink.' He rose to his feet. 'And thank you for saving Jamie. I really mean that.'

'I know.' He stared at her. 'I'm sorry . . . well . . . I'm sorry it went the way it did.'

She stared back at him and grunted. Slowly they walked through the bar.

'By the way,' he asked as they moved out into the broad, dark-panelled reception hall: 'as a matter of interest, how did you blow my cover?'

She stopped, staring at the large black and white tiles on the floor. 'In the end it was all too coincidental,' she said quietly. She looked up at him. 'I mean, a few coincidences I could live with, but wherever I was, you were. Wherever I was going, you were going.' They walked on.

'Sure, but that happens. Especially on the international finance circuit.'

'I know. That's why it didn't bother me. Not at first. But just when I was undecided whether to go to America, you phoned to say you couldn't come to London. Which, naturally, tipped my decision to go to America.'

She stopped and glared at him. 'God you must have thought I was as soft as blancmange. All you had to do was jerk my chain a little and I'd come running. It was easy, wasn't it?'

He looked pained but said nothing.

She took a few steps in silence before continuing in a low, venomous voice. 'Yet, as soon as I said I was leaving New York without seeing you . . . suddenly your plans had changed. Surprise, surprise, you had to come to England too.'

'And that made you suspicious.'

'I know it took a long time,' she said bitterly. 'I know I was too blind and besotted to see it initially, but, yes, in the end the excess of coincidences finally began to sink in.'

They walked out onto the broad gravel drive stretching away from the hotel's stone-arched entrance. Ahead of them the evening sky was streaked with layers of burgundy and violet. Wisps of high cirrus glowed salmon pink in an indigo sky.

'Okay, I understand that might have made you suspicious. But how did you compromise my cover? How did you know I wasn't who I said I was?'

'I called you from the Pierre and left you my number. Remember? Chauncey Morton,' she paused, 'the detective assigned to look after me, was worried about that. She said she would have to check you out.'

He nodded in understanding. 'Ah, okay, I see. So she told you.'

'No. She was shot dead before she had a chance. But before I left New York I asked Sam Barber to find out if Chauncey had got around to it. He called me in London and told me what she'd discovered.' She fixed him with a look. 'Which was that the Bob Briscoe I knew didn't exist.'

'I see.' They stopped beside his hire car, a navy Ford Scorpio. He turned to her. 'I'm sorry, Melissa,' he said quietly.

He saw the bitter look on her face. 'Well, what else can I say? Whatever, it would sound trite. Maybe it's best if I just say that I'm glad I knew you.' He held out his hand.

She frowned at it but made no move to shake it. After a moment he let it drop. 'Thank you for saving Jamie,' she told him. 'I'll always be grateful to you for that.'

He nodded. 'Yeah, well, that's okay. I hope he has a good life. And you too, Melissa. I don't suppose we'll meet again.' He turned to unlock the car door.

'No, I don't suppose so. I think maybe that's just as well. Yours is a very violent profession. If you don't mind me saying so.'

He shrugged, tinkering with the door. 'Yeah, well, we're both involved in pretty violent professions.'

She snorted softly. 'Hardly. You're some kind of agent and I'm a forensic accountant. There's no comparison.'

He stopped tinkering and looked sideways at her. He studied her face. 'You don't get it, do you?' He said it quietly, almost in wonder.

'Get what?'

'What's going on. After all this time, you still don't see it.'

'See what, for God's sake?'

'How much violence follows in your wake. So far, more than a dozen people have died in this Exchange Bank business. All of those deaths were connected with your work.'

'No they weren't. Not all of them.'

'Sure they were. Get real, Melissa. Think about it. Every death, from Aziz and his family right down to some redneck right-wing whacko, was linked to your job. Was connected with you chasing down a lot of hot money from the Exchange Bank.'

Something icy crawled up her neck and into her scalp. 'Are you trying to tell me I'm responsible for those deaths?' she blurted angrily.

'You? – No. What you do? – Yes.'

He turned to face her. 'Accept it, Melissa. Yours is a dangerous profession. All those billions . . . all those Exchange Bank accounts stuffed full of money . . . they're dangerous assets. People kill for them. Like you said . . . where there's money . . . there's blood. And you hunt the money.' He spread his hands. 'It stands to reason, sometimes you're gonna find yourself wading in blood.'

He saw the shocked look on her face. 'I'm sorry,' he said quietly. 'I thought you understood that.'

He stared at her for a few seconds longer, his gaze filled with affection . . . and something else. It took her a moment to work out what it was. Then she realised.

It was pity.

He shrugged, turned and opened the car door. 'Well, I gotta go.'

Melissa watched the car disappear into the dusk, following its lights until they faded into the dappling shadows of the huge lime trees lining the drive.

She turned back towards the hotel entrance.

The two big coachlamps on either side of the porch had been switched on, bathing the butter-coloured stone in a gentle light. Something caught her eye high in the darkening sky above the stark, dark silhouette of the building

It was a solitary star.

Chapter Forty-Six

Hunched in the back of the car, Barney Mullhane watched the big red bus in front edge slowly forward. It had been raining most of the morning and although it was only a light, summer drizzle, the London traffic was moving at the velocity of cold porridge.

It had taken the car five minutes to travel less than a quarter of a mile south along Regent Street.

'Jeesus,' Barney hissed: 'I could walk there quicker than this.'

Mullhane was scheduled for a midday meet with Steven Timmison and it looked like he was going to be late. He had flown to London the previous day, wondering on the long flight over what the hell was so important that the toffee-nosed Brit needed to see him personally.

There were several possibilities he could think of. Whichever it was, he knew he wasn't going to like it.

The car pulled into King Charles Street at twelve fifteen. After security had processed him he was accompanied by a gopher with a plummy accent around a large, magnificently decorated interior courtyard and up a wide marble staircase. Mullhane eyed the décor with a sardonic eye.

Halfway along a corridor the young man halted at a pair of polished double doors. He knocked, opened one and ushered Mullhane inside.

Steven Timmison was seated behind a desk the size of Texas. Mullhane noticed it had green leather inlay and, like the rest of the room, was about a century and a half old. Tall Georgian windows looked out onto a large square which looked to Mullhane like some kind of parade ground.

Timmison rose to shake his hand. 'Mr Mullhane, thank you for coming,' he said in his clipped, steely accent. 'Would you like some tea? Or perhaps you'd prefer coffee?'

Mullhane had tasted British Civil Service coffee before. 'Nothing, thanks.'

Timmison gestured to a seat in front of the desk. Mullhane eased himself into it cautiously. Timmison began: 'I take it by now you've had me checked out. You know who I am?'

Mullhane nodded. 'Sure. You're Chief of Staff of the Economic and Industrial Intelligence Unit attached to GCHQ. You report to the Joint Intelligence Committee of the British Cabinet.'

Timmison inclined his head. 'Absolutely right. Which means you and I, old boy, are in pretty much the same line of work. And at about the same level. So I think we should talk openly and off the record. Don't you?'

Mullhane shrugged. 'Okay, so you're a big shot in the business. But only at the bean-counting end.'

Timmison smiled his superior smile. 'Bean-counting is what matters, Barney. It's all about economics and industrial production these days. But of course you know that.'

Mullhane grunted. 'Yeah, I know it. I don't care for it too much but . . .'

'Which is why I've asked you specifically to come and see me.'

Mullhane frowned. 'What do you mean?'

'I want the CIA to dismantle its espionage apparatus in Britain.'

'What?'

'I want you to stop spying on us. We are supposed to be your friends. Remember? We are your allies.'

'Who the hell says we're spying on you?' Mullhane's voice was harsh and defensive.

'Come on, Barney, don't insult my intelligence. The CIA has been conducting a major campaign of industrial espionage in Western Europe and Japan since the end of the Cold War. Using the Exchange Bank as its primary source of funds. You were the one ordered to set it up, for God's sake. I know that; you know that. Now I have the proof. I'm telling you it has to stop.'

'Proof? What kinda half-assed proof would you have for a thing like that? What the hell makes you think the Agency has a network in Britain?'

Timmison snorted in irritation and laid a hand on a file sitting on his desk. 'I've got it all here. I know which front companies you're using and the names of the people you're employing here

417

and in Europe and in Japan. I've got chapter and verse.'

'Whatever you've got inside that,' Mullhane jerked his chin at the file, 'is just a crock of shit.'

Timmison leaned forward in his seat. 'Look, old boy, let's stop playing games. The American Government saves billions of dollars if it can tap into other people's R&D. Trade secrets are the name of the game now. Economic and commercial intelligence. We know your people have infiltrated both government and private research and development projects here. I'm telling you to pull them out. Disband your network in Great Britain. Now.'

Mullhane stared at the disdainful Englishman and decided there was little point in denying it. Nothing would be gained from stonewalling. Whatever else the arrogant bastard was, Timmison wasn't a fool. If Timmison said he had proof . . . he had proof.

'Yeah? So, how come you know all this?'

'The Exchange Bank of course. One of the liquidators uncovered funds being piggy-backed out of Nassau by a Mafia-connected company called Cyclix.' Timmison shook his head. 'I never know why the CIA uses people like the Mafia.'

Timmison's arrogance and holier-than-thou attitude was starting to rankle with Mullhane. 'Hell, you guys in British intelligence use some pretty unsavoury characters when it suits you,' he growled. 'The Mob are often the best people to use. They operate a lot of storefront corporations. Sure, they charge a fat fee for the job but they do it right and they don't ask questions. The big thing is . . . if they're caught they don't talk. Anyway, how come you knew we were piggy-backing the money through Cyclix? Who told you? That forensic accountant broad, Semmington?'

'Yes. You know about her?'

'Yeah, we were watching her for a while. We picked up on her when she was in Grand Cayman.'

'When she first latched on to Cyclix?'

Mullhane nodded. 'Yeah. But from what we know of her time in San Francisco, she was more focused on a West Coast launderer which had washed a few hundred million of hot Mob money.'

'She was. But something about the Cyclix funds intrigued her. So, she followed the money. You know how it is, Barney, if you follow the money . . . you find out the facts.'

Mullhane glowered at the man across the desk. The Englishman seemed to be enjoying himself.

'And we both know spying costs money. Especially industrial espionage. No one does that for love of country.' A faint smile touched Timmison's thin lips.

'Yeah, but how did she make the connection? Those funds were well hidden.'

'She traced a man called Kunzman. He was the Mafia's chief liaison with the Exchange Bank.' Timmison gave him a strange look. 'I hear you were looking for him too.'

'We were. We figure he was your deep throat.'

Timmison gave Mullhane another fleeting, noncommittal smile. 'Really?'

'Anyway,' he continued, 'Miss Semmington found Kunzman. At a cabin in New York State. Immediately she located him, she and her police guard were attacked by armed men, and Kunzman was mortally wounded. But before he died he gave Miss Semmington enough information to crack open a particular Exchange Bank account.' Timmison paused for effect. '. . . The Austerlitz.'

He watched Mullhane's face darken.

'Which, as you know, was a secure Exchange Bank account set up specifically by the CIA. For the purposes of funding industrial espionage.'

'This woman got inside Austerlitz?' Mullhane was anxious.

Timmison gave him a quizzical look. 'You mean you didn't know?'

'No I didn't know. Shit, if she got inside Austerlitz then she knows.'

'Knows?'

Mullhane frowned at Timmison, then made a gesture with his hands. 'She knows what you know.'

Timmison pounced. 'So you admit there is a CIA industrial espionage network operating in this country.'

For a few moments Mullhane continued to stare at the tall ascetic man across the desk. The guy's attitude was getting under his skin.

'Hey, what is all this *admit* shit?' he growled belligerently. 'Who the hell's playing games now? Yeah, so okay, we've got a network here. Don't tell me you're surprised. Don't tell me you haven't got people doing the same thing in America. So, okay,

419

now you know. Big deal. It's not you knowing that worries me. You're in the community. The problem is this goddam liquidator. She isn't. She's not one of us. She's a civilian. She's dangerous.'

Timmison shook his head. 'She knows nothing. Not for certain anyway. She's intelligent enough to be suspicious, of course. She can't understand why the Austerlitz Account was being run the way it was . . . so much security for so little money. But she doesn't know it was an Agency account. And she isn't likely to.'

Mullhane grunted. He wasn't convinced.

Timmison tapped the file on his desk. 'I've got her working papers. And she's no longer involved with the liquidation. Therefore, she isn't going to know. Only a few people here are aware of your set-up. So . . .' he leaned back in his seat, 'once you've dismantled it, no one will know anything.'

Mullhane leaned back in his seat. 'You're asking me to throw years of work down the toilet,' he growled.

Timmison frowned. 'I expect I am. But Her Majesty's Government doesn't care for its allies spying on us. We want that network taken apart.'

'Or what?'

Timmison looked surprised. 'Well, I know dog doesn't eat dog, old boy, but we couldn't possibly let you carry on as if nothing had happened. I expect we'd start leaking to the press that a number of the organisations listed in this file are CIA proprietary companies. We might even go so far as to declare certain American diplomats *persona non grata*. For industrial espionage. Very embarrassing for your State Department. And we could start prosecuting a number of American nationals resident over here. All very nasty and unnecessary.'

'Okay,' said Mullhane, 'I'll do a deal with you.'

'I don't think you're in any position to do deals,' Timmison responded coldly.

'I'll agree to close down the British network,' Mullhane continued. 'But the others: the French, the German, the Japanese . . . the others stay.'

'The French and Germans are our partners in Europe,' Timmison said. 'Are you suggesting we knowingly allow you to spy on them?'

'Sure. What the hell do you care?'

Timmison laughed sharply. 'But why should we agree to that?'

'Because you wouldn't want it known that you guys in British

420

Intelligence knew what was going on inside the Exchange Bank years before you closed it. You didn't *suspect* the bank was crooked, you *knew* it was. You knew it was laundering money, but you were using it yourselves. So you kept quiet. You allowed it to keep going. You were like the rest of us. You found it convenient to have a bent bank around.'

'You couldn't prove that.'

'No? I think I could. And anyway, who says I'd need to. You're not the only people who can leak a few items to the press.'

'Items? What kind of items?' There was a note of concern in Timmison's tone.

'Five years ago an Order In Council was made in your Department of Trade and Industry to allow your spy network at Cheltenham to monitor the bank. Which means all the Exchange Bank's communications were listened into by Cheltenham. Your DTI even obtained warrants to tap the bank's phones. For five years you've been monitoring their conversations . . . bugging their calls. You've been wise to what that bank was doing for all that time. You had enough to close it down years ago. GCHQ at Cheltenham would have given you all you needed.' Mullhane laughed sharply. 'That's one big advantage you Brits have over us Yanks. You're allowed to spy on your own citizens. Legally.'

'Even if we did monitor their traffic,' Timmison said dismissively, 'most of it was in code.'

Mullhane laughed sharply. 'Don't bullshit me. You got a Cray supercomputer at Cheltenham. That thing would cut through the bank's Data Encryption Standard or Rambutan like a chainsaw. A kid could break the codes the Exchange Bank used.'

'So, you want us to condone the CIA spying on our friends in Europe? Merely because you *think* we may have known something about the Exchange Bank?'

'Sure. It's a good deal. It's in your interests. If the media get to know the British Government had been listening in on the bank, you might have some tough questions to answer. Especially if the television and press boys believed you'd been using the Bank to fund illegal arms sales. Say to Iraq.'

Timmison blanched. 'You're fishing,' he said angrily. 'There's no way you could prove that.'

Mullhane gave him a scornful look. 'Hey, don't forget I've got a network operating in this country. I know you guys were helping businessmen manufacture and sell arms to the Middle

East. Those guys had to be paid somehow. So you fixed for them to be paid through the Exchange Bank. As soon as the Exchange Bank went into the tank, your intelligence people moved into the London headquarters, sealed a whole slew of documents and took them away. Nobody's seen them since. You and I both know those documents were about arms sales. I could release that information. The media would do the rest.'

Timmison was quiet as he considered the solid, grizzled man across the table. 'So what are you proposing?' he said finally.

'I guarantee to close down the Agency's British network. The rest of our activities – what we do in Europe and Japan – are nothing to do with you.'

The venerable room was silent as Timmison gave him a long, penetrating stare. 'No.' His voice was flat. 'I want more than that.'

Mullhane was surprised. 'More? Whaddaya mean more?'

'If you don't want us blowing the whistle on the fact that America has been spying on its allies, then I insist the CIA shares whatever industrial espionage it gets from its networks in Western Europe and Japan.'

'Shares?'

'With us. With my department.'

Mullhane gazed at the disdainful man opposite. After a moment he began to laugh, a deep booming laugh which rocked his solid gut. 'You want the Agency to stop spying on you. But you want us to go on spying on your partners in Europe. And to give you whatever skinny we dig up.'

'Yes.'

Mullhane's laughter subsided into low chuckles. 'Jeeesus, you really are something else,' he murmured. He continued to stare at Timmison. 'Okay,' he went on, 'like you say, dog don't eat dog. It sounds a good arrangement to me. Yeah, you got a deal.'

'Good.'

'Okay, that it?' Mullhane moved to stand up.

'There is one other thing,' Timmison said. He sounded like a schoolmaster.

Mullhane dropped back into his seat, waiting for whatever was coming next, his grey, stone-wall face masking his anxiety.

'During the course of her investigations, Miss Semmington was personally attacked three times. We know who sponsored

422

the assault in London, but the other two occasions – the attack by armed men in New York State and another assault at her cottage in Hampshire – we don't know who was behind them. Whoever it was, they were prepared to have their thugs use deadly force. Three police officers were killed at the cabin in New York.'

Mullhane frowned. 'So? Why are you telling me this?'

'I want to know if the CIA had anything to do with those assaults?' Timmison's voice was hard-edged. 'Was the Agency behind them? Did you sponsor them, Barney?'

'Me? What the hell makes you think I was behind them?'

'Because the CIA had most to gain from stopping Miss Semmington's work. Let's face it, the CIA lost millions of dollars in the shutdown. Even so, it's money you would rather lose than have her discover it was being used to fund industrial espionage on your allies. Therefore it would make sense for you to arrange to stop her. You've already said you were watching her. You knew she'd got onto Cyclix. Which meant she could have got on to Austerlitz.'

'And you figure we arranged to have her taken out?'

'The Agency is the obvious culprit. You didn't want her breaking into Austerlitz. So come on, Barney, did you sponsor those attacks?'

He stared hard at Timmison. 'Whatever happened to your Miss Semmington was nothing to do with the Agency,' he growled quietly.

'I don't believe you. Those attacks had to come from you.'

'The hell you say. Why me?'

'They were organised and sponsored in America. Using American nationals. That makes the CIA the obvious suspect. I think you were behind them.'

He shook his head. 'Well, you're wrong. I wasn't.'

He saw Timmison's look of disbelief and shrugged. 'Why the hell should I lie? We're both professionals. If the Agency had mounted a hit I'd admit it. But it didn't.'

'The CIA had the most to lose from her activities.'

'Yeah, who says so? Plenty other people had as much to lose. Outfits ranging from the Colombian Cocaine Cartels to the IRA wanted to stop her tracking their cash. Not to mention half the world's intelligence community. Any one of them could have been behind those hits.'

He paused, his face wreathed in thought. 'Hey, it could even be you! Maybe the British Intelligence Services wanted to stop her poking her nose in where it didn't belong. When it comes to the Exchange Bank, you've got as much to hide as the rest of us.'

'Are you telling me you didn't even consider putting a stop to her investigations? Having her attacked?'

'Sure we thought of it. We considered tipping off some of the bad guys using the bank and letting them drop her. But,' Mullhane shook his head, 'in the end we didn't do it.'

'You expect me to believe that?' Timmison pinioned him with a look.

'Sure I expect you to believe it.' He returned Timmison's gaze unflinchingly. 'What would be the point of whacking her? Sooner or later the liquidators would send someone else to do the job. And another one after that. And the Semmington broad is a civilian. Like I say, who whacks out civilians?'

Timmison's gaze remained riveted on his face. He frowned. 'So if it wasn't you,' he said softly, 'then who the hell was it? Who ordered those attacks on her?'

'Beats me. There are a helluva lot of contenders.' Mullhane saw an anguished look pass across Timmison's face. 'What's wrong?'

'Don't you see? If you're telling me the truth, then whoever sponsored the attacks is still out there. It's possible they'll attack her again.'

Mullhane frowned and rose to his feet. 'Yeah,' he growled, 'I guess they might.'

The worried look stayed on Timmison's face a moment longer before he stood up and marched around the enormous desk.

'Well,' he announced, 'we're agreed then. You'll close down the British end of your network immediately. But you'll keep us up to speed on whatever comes out of the rest of it.'

'Sure,' Mullhane grunted.

'Oh and one other thing, old boy. If, in the future, some part of the network is discovered . . . if what you're doing comes out . . . then, naturally, we didn't know about it. Her Majesty's Government had no idea what the CIA was up to.'

'Naturally,' Mullhane repeated acidly.

'Good. Well, all in all, old boy, not a bad day's work.'

Timmison opened one of the double doors and ushered Mullhane out ahead of him.

They walked together along the corridor and stopped at the head of the marble staircase where they shook hands.

'I think we should stay in touch,' Timmison said.

Mullhane grunted noncommittally and watched the tall, erect figure march away.

The guy moved like he had a billiard cue up his kazoo, he thought. All he needed was a bearskin hat and one of those quaint, old-fashioned uniforms and he could have been strutting his stuff on the parade ground outside.

The gopher with the cut-glass accent emerged from a side room and accompanied him out of the building.

The rookie leapt out of the car's passenger seat and ran around to open the rear door. 'Where to, sir?' he asked.

Mullhane didn't hear him. His face was contorted by a look of deep concern.

'Sir?'

Mullhane glowered at the young man.

'Drive around for a while,' he growled. 'I gotta think.'

Chapter Forty-Seven

The day Melissa moved back into the cottage Astrid phoned to say she was coming back. She missed Jamie too much to stay away, she said. Melissa met her at Heathrow where they fell into each other's arms and hugged long and fervently, crying tears of relief and joy as Jamie danced around them whooping with delight.

She spent a week at home before going back to the office, pottering in the garden, visiting Liz in the hospital and running Jamie to and from school.

With the return of Astrid, with Jamie settled back into routine and with George the puppy finally housetrained, life seemed almost to have returned to normal.

Timmison's people had done a good job in the cottage and the replacement furniture and carpets looked almost exactly the same as those ruined by the bloodstains. Any thoughts she'd had of moving were gone.

The only blot on her landscape was the police protection. It was inescapable. There were many more officers, and though she was grateful that at least now none were stationed inside, armed foot patrols were constantly to be seen at the front and the back of the cottage. Jamie kept asking why they were there and she was on the receiving end of some very dark looks from other residents in the village.

It was depressing.

Bleakly she wondered if a time would ever come when she could dispense with them. Or was she to be dogged by policemen carrying guns for the rest of her life?

The only obvious advantage to the protection was her first morning back at work when she was told that from now on a car would take her to the office and bring her back.

She had been away a month.

She walked through the enormous, open office of the fourteenth floor, marvelling at the curious familiarity of it all. It was like returning to the home of her childhood. The hiss of the air conditioning as she opened her door was a sound from another era.

Inside the fishtank she moved to the windows and for a while stared out over the river. There was a noise behind her. She turned. Debbie was standing in the doorway. 'Welcome back,' she said.

'Thanks.' Melissa took a deep breath and said: 'Okay, let's get to it.'

Everything relating to the Exchange Bank had been moved out of her office.

Debbie informed her that Nigel Hawick had divided the workload between Andrew Bailey and Frank Levinson. 'Any trouble?' Melissa inquired anxiously. 'I mean, any personal trouble?'

Debbie shook her head. 'None. They say it's all straightforward, routine work. The kind of thing FI does all the time.'

'Really.' She frowned.

She was finished with Debbie in less than ten minutes. For once in her life she had an empty schedule and a light workload.

Turning around in her seat she saw Nigel Hawick through the partition glass. He looked up and waved to her. She got up and wandered into his office.

'Welcome back!' he exclaimed. 'How are you feeling?'

'I'm fine, Nigel.'

He cocked his head to one side and considered her. She was looking particularly fine that morning in a beige Gucci suit with knee-length skirt and a pale cream silk blouse. The ensemble contrasted perfectly with the deep sheen of her hair and her grey-blue eyes. Her face was open and relaxed, the lines of tension and worry almost entirely gone. The only thing different was the needle-thin white scar on her cheekbone.

She closed his office door. 'This needs to be private,' she told him.

She seated herself in the chair opposite his desk and appraised her boss. 'Nigel, you were reporting to that man Timmison, weren't you?'

He nodded. 'Yes. Regularly. That was part of the arrangement with the BoE. I had to give him regular briefings on progress. Why?'

'Was it part of the arrangement with the Bank of England to report to the Americans too?'

'Pardon?' He looked shocked.

'You heard me, Nigel,' she said evenly. 'Was it part of the deal with the BoE and Timmison and whoever else was involved with the Exchange Bank liquidation that you tell the Americans everything that was going on?'

'Look, Melissa,' he protested, 'I don't know what you're talking about.'

'Yes you do, Nigel. I was picked up by a very good-looking American at Heathrow not long after I started on the Exchange Bank job.'

'So? I imagine that must happen a lot.'

She shook her head. 'I'd never let it before. But this one was different. He knew exactly the right things to say... the right buttons to press. It was as if he knew all about me. Which of course he did. You'd told him.'

'Melissa, what are you talking about?' Hawick's voice was strained.

She ignored his protest. 'After that, wherever I was, he was. Wherever I was going, he was going.' She paused, noticing a faint sheen of perspiration on Hawick's upper lip. 'He was even in Switzerland when I was there. Of course he wasn't in the same city as me.'

She stopped and frowned reflectively. 'At least he *said* he wasn't in the same city. But who knows? What I do know is that he was able to get into a hotel in Basel that I hadn't been able to book. Almost as if he knew where I was going. But, then again, he did. You were telling him my plans.'

'Melissa, if this man knew anything about your plans, then he must have got the information from Timmison. It was Timmison telling him. Maybe he wanted to give you extra protection.'

'Is that what they told you? The Americans? That's what this fellow told me too. He said he needed to be near me so he could look after me. Well, to be fair, he did that all right.' She raised her hand and lightly touched her left cheekbone. 'He saved me from those two thugs at Bank Station underpass. And he saved Jamie.'

Hawick nodded eagerly. 'Right. That's it. Don't you see, it must have been Timmison who set this man up with you.'

'No Nigel, it wasn't Timmison. I saw Timmison meet the American outside my cottage. They didn't know each other. What's more, it was obvious that, until that moment, Timmison didn't know *about* the American. No, it had to be you, Nigel. The guy told me as much.'

'What?'

'Yes. You see, the real point of him latching on to me was to keep tabs on what I was doing. Which meant getting me to talk. Only, apparently, I wasn't very forthcoming.' She paused again. 'At least, not in that department,' she added bitterly. 'So, he said they were forced to piece together what I was doing from other sources. There was only one other source, Nigel. You.'

'That's nonsense,' he blustered. 'There are plenty of other sources he could have used.'

She shook her head. 'No. There were no other sources. Nobody else knew everything about what I was doing . . . where I was going. Only you, Nigel. I know it was you.'

He stared at her. He looked like a small boy caught stealing.

'Look, I'm not going to do anything about this,' she went on. 'There isn't anything I could do, even if I wanted to. I couldn't prove anything. Besides. I don't want to. Believe me. I don't want to do anything about it. All I want is to know why. Why, Nigel? I mean you're supposed to be my boss. You're supposed to look after me. Why were you selling me out to the Americans?'

He gazed at her with a hangdog look.

From outside came the gentle buzz of the big office, from inside the quiet, sibilant whisper of the air conditioning. 'I wasn't selling you out, Melissa,' he finally murmured. 'You ought to know I wouldn't do that. They told me they needed to get someone close to you. To look after you.'

She had told herself she wouldn't get angry with him, but she couldn't help herself. She felt it billowing up and sweeping over her, straining her voice in resentment.

'For God's sake, Nigel. Didn't it occur to you that what they really wanted was to find out what I was doing? That they wanted me to talk? And that they'd use any method they could to soften me up?'

'Melissa, these people aren't the bad guys,' he whined. 'I wasn't talking to organised criminals about you. The people who contacted me were from a special department of the American Federal Reserve System.'

'I know that,' she snarled. 'I know where the fellow was from. He told me. But for Christ's sake, Nigel, what difference do you think that would have made? Do you think that would have stopped me going to jail if I'd talked and Timmison had found out? Bloody hell, Timmison was the one who insisted I sign the Official Secrets Act. I'm not supposed to talk to anyone about what I do. That includes the American Government.'

Her voice rose to a wail. 'Jesus, do you realise how much jeopardy you put me in? Supposing I'd been sent to prison. What would have happened to Jamie?'

'All right, Melissa, all right.' He held up his hands to placate her. 'I was only trying to protect you. They didn't say anything about getting you to talk. Honestly. Only about knowing where you were and what you were doing so they could keep an eye on you. Hell, Melissa, I was the one who wanted you to come off the Exchange Bank job. Remember? I wouldn't do anything to put you in danger. You should know that.'

She stared at him, struggling to bring her breath, and her anger, under control. 'Yes, all right, Nigel,' she said after a moment. 'I know. Maybe they used you like they used me. But why? Why the hell did you agree to it? Do these people have something over you?'

He looked down at the surface of his desk littered with papers. He was silent for a while. Then he looked up. 'It was when I was in the States,' he told her quietly. 'Setting up Rolay Richard over there. I was involved in an audit that looked very suspicious. But the owners of the company persuaded me that everything was all right.'

He shrugged. 'I was younger then. They had explanations for all the anomalies I was coming across. So, in the end, I produced an unqualified report. Not long afterwards it turned out the company was a front for the Mafia and the owners were completely bent.' He stopped, his face strained in anxiety.

'Go on,' she prompted softly.

'I was in a lot of trouble, Melissa. Believe me. It looked as if I had colluded in a false audit. I swear to you I hadn't but . . . it didn't look that way. Shit, I was frightened silly. Not only was my career with Rolay Richard about to go belly-up but I could have gone to prison. Then this fellow turned up. He said he was from the IRS and that if I agreed to help them in something they were doing, then I'd have no problems with the authorities over the audit.'

Hawick pulled a face and shrugged. 'What could I do?'

'What did you agree to do?'

'That was it. It was nothing. Or nothing very much. I kept them informed about another audit I was working on. Turned out to be a major case of tax evasion and capital flight. I gave them all the details and that was it. Never heard another thing. But once these people have got their hooks into you . . . once they've done you a favour . . . and got you to do them one in return . . . then there's always the chance they'll come back to you for more.'

'How many more favours have you done them?'

He shrugged. 'Two or three. All little things. Little bits of information. When I got the call about you and the Exchange Bank, it was the first time I'd heard from any of them in seven years. For God's sake, that business in the States was almost twenty years ago. I'd forgotten about it. But soon after we got the Exchange Bank job, the fellow from the IRS called and said he wanted me to help out some colleagues of his. Some people working for the Investigations Division of the Fed. I was to tell whoever called broadly what areas you were working on. Things like that.' He grimaced wryly.

'And you said yes?' There was a hint of incredulity in her tone.

'Come on, Melissa, he may have asked if I would help, but he certainly didn't make it sound like I'd got any choice in the matter. And anyway, it didn't seem very much. When this fellow from the Fed called, all he wanted was to know your travel itinerary and some detail of what you were working on. That's it. I swear. That's all he wanted.'

For a while she stared at him. Finally she shrugged. 'Okay, Nigel,' she intoned, 'it's all over now anyway. Only, it would have been nice if you had told me. It might have saved me a lot of heartache. I mean, if I'd known I could have told that bloody man to damn well sod off, couldn't I?'

'If you had, what would have happened in the underpass? And to Jamie?'

She made a face. 'Yes, that's the problem. I haven't got it straight yet . . . can't get my head around it. This man was using me and yet he saved me. And Jamie.' She grimaced in her effort to make sense of it.

Suddenly she wanted to get out of Nigel Hawick's office. To get away from him and everything else to do with the Exchange Bank. She stood up and moved to the door. 'Well thanks for telling me. Eventually,' she added acidly.

'Look, I really am sorry, Melissa.' His face was contrite as he gazed up at her from his desk. 'I didn't mean you any harm.'

She stared at him. 'No, I don't suppose you did,' she said softly, 'though I'm not sure what good you did me.' She half-opened the door before a thought occurred to her. 'Just as a matter of interest, when did the American first contact you. Was it as soon as the press announced we'd got the job?'

He thought about it. 'No. It was some time after.'

'When exactly?'

'I can't remember.'

'When your man called, did he ask you about what progress we'd made so far?'

Hawick looked sheepish. 'Yes.'

'And you told him.' He nodded. 'You didn't happen to tell him about Akhtar Aziz did you?' He nodded again. 'And the list he'd given me?'

'For God's sake, Melissa,' he moaned. 'It's bad enough having to admit all this as it is. What does it matter what I told him?'

'But did you? Tell him about the list? It could be important.'

He screwed up his face as if in pain. 'Yes,' he said after a moment. 'I did.'

'And did he seem interested in it?'

After a moment Hawick's eyes widened. 'Yes. Yes, as a matter of fact he did.'

'Any particular part of it?'

'What do you mean?'

'Any special part of the list. I mean, did he react specifically to any particular name? Say like Austerlitz?'

Hawick's face puckered. 'Yes,' he said slowly. 'It's funny you should mention that. Now I come to think of it, he asked me to spell it. And as soon as I mentioned that you'd got Kunzman's name he said it was important to get close to you.'

Hawick's frown deepened. 'In fact, that's when he said you would need protection.'

Chapter Forty-Eight

She couldn't leave it alone . . . couldn't stop thinking about it.

She was two days working on other things with most of her mind locked onto the mystery of the Austerlitz Account. It was a mystery she had been close to solving before the nightmare at the cottage and her month away from work.

Now, back behind her desk, there it still was. The puzzle stubbornly unresolved. It needled her, the enigma perversely embedded in her cerebral cortex like a piece of grit in her eye . . . like a sliver of meat in her teeth.

It was becoming an obsession. She could feel it happening; feel herself, like an addict, going down for the third time beneath the waves of her craving.

On the morning of her fourth day back at the office she gave in. Like an addict she abandoned herself to it.

Why not? she asked herself. She was an obsessive . . . she knew it. That was her character. That's what made her what she was . . . good at her job. She had to know; she had to get inside the Austerlitz Account and track the cash . . . hunt the money back to its lair. She had to understand the mystery.

She called Boris. 'Boris, did you keep copies of the searches you made on those companies in the Austerlitz Account?'

'Are you kidding?' he grumbled. 'This is Rolay Richard, Melissa. This is the great bureaucracy. Of course I kept copies. And you've got copies and probably Nigel Hawick has copies, and maybe by now a dozen other people have got copies.'

He sighed. 'Ninety-five per cent of the bloody documents in this building are copies of other bleeding documents in this building. Why the hell we have computers God alone knows. We should put all that stuff on . . .'

'For God's sake, Boris,' she snapped, 'spare me the sermon. If you feel so strongly, write a paper and copy in all the partners.'

He laughed loudly. 'In the meantime, I want copies of all those searches you conducted, plus the printout of the Austerlitz Account.'

'But I've already given you all that stuff once. Why do you want it again?'

'Boris,' she sighed, 'just do it. Okay?'

'It's a lot of work, Melissa.'

'No it's not. Just send me *your* copies. There's no need for fresh ones. You don't have to stand for hours over a red-hot photocopier.'

He grunted. 'Anyway, I thought they'd taken you off the Exchange Bank job. If you're not working on the bank any more, why do you need all this . . . ?'

'Boris . . .' she growled.

'All right, all right. No need to get your knickers in a twist.'

'That's sexist.'

'Bollocks.'

'So is that. Everything you've got Boris. In the next ten minutes.'

'Jesus, Melissa, you're worse than a . . .' She put the receiver down.

He arrived a few minutes later with a member of his staff. Both had their arms filled with a large pile of documents. She told Boris to put them on a corner of her desk. They exchanged banter for a few minutes before he made ready to return to his office.

'Are these your departmental copies?' Melissa asked indicating the pile.

'Yes.'

'Okay, I'll let you have them back when I've finished. Oh, and one other thing, Boris. I'd be grateful if you didn't tell anyone I've asked for them. Okay? I don't want anyone to know what I'm working on.'

He gave her a puzzled look. 'Fine by me. If that's what you want.'

'Yes, it is. No one is to know. Not Nigel, not anyone. If you're asked, you don't know what I'm doing. All right?'

He shrugged. 'Sure.'

She watched him amble across the open-plan office. He was wearing a pair of bright red cords.

She started work on the pile immediately, recalling as she

waded into it the gist of the notes and calculations she had made a month earlier. Within hours she was completely immersed, though she was disciplined enough to stop at five thirty and make her way down to the atrium and her official car.

After all that had happened, she was sticking with her resolution to be back with Jamie by seven every evening.

The research took her a working week . . . five solid days of tracking cash into and out of accounts, five days of innumerable calls and fax messages inquiring into the state and nature of scores of companies, organisations and individuals across the globe.

At the end of that week she had the answer. She knew.

Now she understood.

She stared at the explosive results of her work, a few pages of typed notes sitting within a plain, ordinary, manilla folder on her desk.

She had to tell someone. Straight away.

What she had uncovered was too important . . . too shocking . . . to be passed through channels in the normal manner. She must report it personally. But to whom?

Not to Nigel Hawick, she decided. Not after what he had told her. That was too risky. It would be better for him if he didn't know. But if not Nigel, who?

She lifted the phone. 'Debbie. Get me Steven Timmison.'

He agreed to see her immediately. She called security and by the time she arrived at the ground floor, her car with its two burly policemen was waiting at the kerb, glittering in the mid-morning sun. She hurried across the pavement clutching the slim manilla folder and slid into the back seat.

The young man with the Harrow tie preceded her swiftly around Durbar Court and up the marble staircase to Timmison's office. As soon as she was ushered in, Timmison rose to his feet.

'Miss Semmington, how nice to see you.' He paused long enough to give her a quick appraisal, taking in the manilla file. 'I must say you are looking remarkably well.'

His compliments were no less oleaginous than before.

'Please sit down. Tea?'

She nodded. 'Yes. Thank you. Mr Timmison,' she began, 'this is a report . . .'

Gravely he held up a hand as a middle-aged woman entered

through a side door. She was carrying the silver salver with the Spode tea set.

Melissa let out her breath and allowed herself to sink back into her chair as Timmison ceremoniously performed the ritual of pouring tea.

It occurred to her he was deliberately slowing the proceedings down, playing the game at his own pace, endeavouring to get her measure. As if he viewed her as opposition. He passed her a cup. 'Now, you were saying.'

She took her time sipping her tea. Two, she decided, could play at that game.

She put her cup on the desk and nodded at the manilla file. 'That's a confidential report,' she began, 'typed personally by me, about the Austerlitz, the locked-box account at the Exchange Bank.'

Timmison raised his eyebrows. 'But I thought your firm had reassigned you onto other things. I understood you were finished with the Exchange Bank.'

She smiled briefly. 'They have and I'm not. Not quite. I wanted to get to the bottom of what was happening inside Austerlitz.'

'Really? Why?'

'Because that bloody account almost got both me and my son murdered.'

'What makes you think that?'

'It was the only account in the bank *not* involved with organised crime. I'd always thought I was at risk from attack by the Mafia. That it was organised criminals who would use violence to stop me tracing their laundered funds. But the fact is, I was never in danger from them.'

'Come now, Miss Semmington, you're forgetting the men who attacked you here in London.'

'I'm hardly likely to forget them. Ever,' she intoned bleakly. Her fingers instinctively moved to the thin line on her cheekbone. 'But they weren't Mafia.'

Timmison's face was an impenetrable mask as his eyes searched her face. He was silent for a while.

'So, what's in this confidential report of yours?' he asked suddenly. His voice was low and controlled.

'I'm sure you know. After all, you had all my notes and files taken out of my office the day after the shooting at my cottage. When I came back I had to start the investigation all over again.'

436

Timmison stared at her. 'Yes,' he said slowly, 'I had not expected that.'

'It took me a week,' she went on, 'but I was determined to get to the bottom of it. I always knew there was something not right about that account. Which is why I went back to it.'

He smiled grimly. 'Given your famous instinct and determination, Miss Semmington, I suppose I *should* have expected that.'

'I checked out every company and organisation and trade association using the Austerlitz Account. All of them. Here and in Europe and in Japan. I even checked the individuals as far as I could.'

'And?'

'And they all have one thing in common. They're all working in economically strategic industries. Computer technology . . . defence . . . biotechnology . . . genetics . . . fibre-optics . . . All of them. And they were being paid money through the Exchange Bank from a source somewhere in America.'

'Do you know where?'

'Close enough. There are lots of sophisticated cutouts and false trails but those funds came out of Washington DC.'

'So what are you telling me, Miss Semmington?' The patronising tone made her frown in annoyance. He sounded like a schoolmaster.

'I'm telling you that the Austerlitz Account was the money conduit for a very large and organised spy ring.' She saw him affect a look of surprise.

'I don't mean your traditional kind of spy,' she went on, 'with fedoras and grubby raincoats. These people are far more sophisticated. They're state-of-the-art technology companies and highly qualified consultants, whizz-kid biotechnologists and computer engineers with PhDs. Austerlitz was funding economic espionage on a massive scale.'

'And you think the paymaster is American.'

Melissa snorted. 'You don't have to be very bright to work out who. Given sufficient time I could track those funds all the way back to CIA headquarters.'

'You think the CIA is funding espionage on its allies? That's rather far-fetched don't you think?'

'Of course not. In this day and age it makes perfect sense.'

'But all of this is surmise, isn't it? I doubt if your report

437

would constitute definite proof of your allegations.'

She stared at him icily. 'Mr Timmison, I am not stupid.'

'Of course not, dear lady. I wouldn't . . .'

'And please don't call me dear lady. I don't like being patronised.' Timmison's face stiffened. Two scarlet spots appeared high on his prominent cheekbones.

'Perhaps I should remind you that I'm a forensic accountant. My job is preparing financial statements and reports that will stand up in a court of law.' Melissa placed a hand firmly on the manilla file sitting on his desk. 'That is a report on my investigation into the Austerlitz Account. That investigation points to the existence of a major spy network. I know that and I'm absolutely sure you know it too.'

He was quiet for a while, staring hard at her. 'Have you reported this to Mr Hawick?'

She shook her head. 'No.'

He gave her a quizzical look. 'Really? Why not?'

It was her turn to feel her cheeks redden. She wasn't sure what to say. 'I don't know. I suppose because it's not mainstream money laundering. It seems more like a security issue to me. More your line of country.'

Timmison scrutinised her. 'Yes,' he drawled, 'I see.' She had the feeling he saw more than he was saying.

'Much of Rolay Richard's work is in America,' she hurried on, 'and as my report involves the American Government. I thought it simpler . . .'

'Ah yes,' he interrupted: 'divided loyalties. It's hard for people in the multinationals and the international accountancy firms to know where their loyalties lie, isn't it? Very difficult for someone like Mr Hawick.' There was something in his voice.

She eyed him levelly. 'I don't have divided loyalties,' she said quietly. 'I've discovered a big industrial espionage network operated by an intelligence agency belonging to a country that's supposed to be our friend. I've brought it to you.' She shrugged. 'That's it. I've done my job. Not that I need have bothered. The day after I told you I'd got inside the Austerlitz Account, you lifted my files and worked it out for yourself.'

He smiled icily. 'Like you, Miss Semmington, we are not stupid. But,' his smile softened a little and he relaxed into his seat, 'you did the right thing in bringing your report to me. Yes, we had worked out what the Americans were doing. I am currently talking to representatives of the American Government and insisting they dismantle their organisation. In the meantime, I must commend you on a really excellent piece of financial detection.'

She sipped her tea and allowed another of his compliments to slither past and die somewhere in a corner.

'There is something I should remind you of,' he went on.

Melissa put down her cup. 'The Official Secrets Act.'

'Quite. It would not be in anyone's interests if what you . . . we . . . have discovered came to light. You work in the real world, Miss Semmington. Public knowledge of this would not be in the national interest. I'm sure you understand that.'

She nodded. 'I understand. You want me to keep my mouth shut.'

She gazed at him wide-eyed and innocent. 'But does that also include the other matter? I mean that's not really anything to do with *our* national interest is it?'

His eyes darkened and he frowned. 'What other matter?'

'You mean you don't know?'

'Know? Know what?'

'You didn't check out all the companies using the Austerlitz Account?'

'Miss Semmington,' he barked, 'please come to the point.'

'One of the companies using Austerlitz was an American corporation. Based in Lexington. In fact it was the only American organisation in the whole account.'

'Yes, I know that.'

'But did you or your people investigate it? Check it out?'

'Yes, of course we did.'

'But not very deeply.'

He smiled his faintly superior smile. 'Well, we didn't think the Americans were spying on themselves, Miss Semmington. As far as we could see that company was just another channel for the money.'

'It was, but not for money to fund industrial espionage overseas. The CIA money going into the company was being tunnelled in another direction entirely. I know. I tracked the funds all the way home.'

His voice was cautious. 'Go on.'

'That corporation is owned by a research company which is linked to a trust. It's a complicated and tortuous route with a number of associated corporations and holding companies, but in the end I discovered that the beneficial owner of the ultimate holding company is a man called John Kilbride.'

'John Kilbride,' Timmison repeated.

'I expect it's a name you know,' Melissa continued. 'You may also know the name of his son, Philip. Phil Kilbride is a right-wing senator. He was in the press and on TV a lot when I was in America, pronouncing on the crisis in the American financial industry. The thing is, Phil Kilbride is strongly tipped to be the next American President.'

Timmison's frown returned. 'I know all that, Miss Semmington. What I don't know is why you are telling me it.'

Melissa tapped the manilla file on Timmison's desk. 'The explanation is in my report.'

Timmison's cool composure collapsed. 'Explanation,' he snapped. 'For God's sake, what explanation?'

'Simply that forty million dollars of CIA money has been passed to John Kilbride to help his son become the next President. The bottom line is that the CIA is funding a right-wing bid for the Presidency.'

Timmison's pale face hardened. It looked like a tombstone.

'What's more, I believe the people who have been trying to kill me and Jamie were sent by the CIA.'

Timmison stared at her with eyes as hard as bullets. 'That's nonsense,' he said abruptly.

'What is? That the CIA is funding Phil Kilbride for the Presidency? That's not nonsense. All the proof you need is there.' She tapped the file. 'That they were trying to kill me and my family? That's not nonsense either. But I don't have any proof, if that's what you're looking for. Except for the two attempts so far. And the fact that you are paying a great deal of money to protect Jamie and me from someone.'

'From organised criminals. Mafia money launderers.'

She shook her head. 'No, I told you, whoever is trying to kill me . . . it isn't the Mafia. Throughout this whole Exchange Bank investigation I have never been in danger from the Mafia.'

'How can you be so certain?'

'Because almost everything that happened to me was because of the Austerlitz Account. The further I got into it, the more dangerous life became.'

'You don't think it was because you were looking for Vito

Kunzman? After all, he worked for the Mafia. He stole their money.'

She shook her head. 'No. I'm not even sure it was Mafia money he stole. So many crooked people and organisations were using the Exchange Bank it could have been anybody's half billion. There's no evidence that the Mafia was ever looking for Vito Kunzman. But the CIA must have been?'

'Really? Why should they look for him?'

'Because he knew about the Austerlitz. He was the only person outside the CIA and perhaps John Kilbride who knew how to get inside it. Once the bank went down it would have been vital to get to Kunzman and eliminate him.'

'But this is all speculation, Miss Semmington. It's pure surmise.'

'The men trying to kill me in New York weren't speculation. Nor was the madman who got into my cottage. They were real. And so were the bullets that killed three police officers.'

Timmison leaned forward over his desk, his forearms resting on the green leather. 'Miss Semmington, I can assure you that whoever is trying to kill you, it isn't the CIA.' He did his best to make his voice reassuring but Melissa could detect the contrapuntal note of worry.

'I don't believe you.' She shook her head, her copper tresses sweeping across her shoulders.

'You must. I'm sure of it.'

'Well, if it isn't them . . . then who?'

'I don't know, but I am convinced it isn't the CIA.'

She gazed at him, her grey-blue eyes clouded by worry. She wanted to believe him but . . .

'I hope to God you're right,' she moaned. 'Because if it is the CIA, then sooner or later they're going to succeed.'

Chapter Forty-Nine

An hour later she was back in her office. It was almost lunchtime.

Before she left him, Timmison had once more laid heavy stress on the Official Secrets Act, emphasising the absolute confidentiality of her report about Kilbride and the CIA.

She had the feeling that what she'd said had alarmed him. His haughty demeanour had been badly dented.

Dropping into her seat, her eyes fell on the piles of files which Boris had brought up the week before. Now she had finished with the Austerlitz Account it would be prudent, she thought, to get rid of them.

She got Boris on the internal. He would send someone up for them sometime soon, he promised. Sometime soon with Boris meant sometime never. She called Debbie and nodded at the untidy stack of documents as her secretary walked through the door.

'Come on, I don't want all this stuff cluttering up the place. You and I can take them down to Computer Operations ourselves.'

Melissa was heartened to see Boris look suitably discomfited when they arrived laden with papers. He mumbled a few embarrassed words of thanks. She and Debbie piled the papers onto a desk in front of a monitor before Debbie went off to lunch.

'You want to see the model of the Austerlitz Account I constructed?' he asked by way of contrition.

She wasn't sure that she did. As far as she was concerned it was all over. Austerlitz was history. Still . . .

She shrugged. 'Okay, why not?' She hitched herself onto a corner of a desk.

He moved the mouse, pressed a few keys and the ubiquitous fat little arrows appeared, moving in colourful procession backwards and forwards across the screens. She watched the funds moving, courtesy of Cyclix, out of the Caribbean and into Central Europe before moving to America and finally disappearing back into the Caribbean and the account on Curaçao.

From there, thin, cursor-like icons shimmied across the screen to all the hi-tech companies, organisations and people in Europe and Japan she had spent the last week researching.

Boris shot her a look. 'What's it all mean? Do you know?'

'It was fraudulent conversion,' she lied glibly, her eyes still on the screens. 'A bunch of international businessmen siphoning off a lot of profits.'

'Oh.' He was satisfied.

'Boris?' She was still staring at the screen. 'What's that . . . there?' On the right-hand side of the computer map of America was a little orange icon with a question mark and a figure 190 next to it.

'That's the money going into the American company in Lexington.'

She frowned. 'What money?'

'I told you. Deposits were made directly into the Austerlitz Account on Curaçao that were nothing to do with the funds piggy-backed out of Basel. They were credited directly to the Lexington company.'

'I don't remember you telling me that.'

'Yes I did.'

'Did you?' Her forehead furrowed. 'But you haven't sent me details.'

'You didn't ask for them. You said you were tracking the money coming in from Basel. I didn't think you were interested in anything else.'

'So where did these funds come from?'

Redbourn shrugged. 'Don't know. It looks like they just turned up. There are no interbank transactions associated, no SWIFT records.'

'Boris, that's not possible. Money can't just turn up out of nowhere. Not unless . . .'

'Not unless what?'

'It arrived as cash.'

'What, a hundred and ninety million dollars in suitcases?'

Melissa smiled wryly. 'That was the usual method with the Exchange Bank. Especially in places like the Netherlands Antilles. How many deposits were there?'

'A couple of dozen or so. I can't remember. Anyway,' he frowned and looked up at her, 'didn't you pick them up when you were checking out the company in Lexington?'

She shook her head. 'I wasn't looking for them. I was focused on tracing the ownership of the company and backtracking the money piggy-backed by Cyclix. Not on bandit cash coming over the bank's counter.'

She turned from the screens and looked at Redbourn. 'Let me have what you've got relating to those deposits, Boris.'

'Come on, Melissa, I thought you'd stopped working on the Exchange Bank.'

'Not yet, Boris, not yet,' she told him softly. 'Not until I understand *everything* that was going on. So,' her tone hardened, 'I need whatever data you've got on those deposits.'

'Okay, I'll have someone bring it up to you.'

'No, I want it now, Boris.'

'Bloody hell, Melissa . . .'

'Now . . . Boris.' Her voice was steely.

The detail on the deposits amounted to one sheet of printout. Redbourn handed it to her. 'That's it?' she queried.

'That's it.'

'Right.' She pointed at the piles of files she and Debbie had dumped on the desk. 'I want that lot back in my office.'

'What?' he yelped. 'You've only just brought it down here.'

'And now I want it back. You can help me.' Swearing softly, he followed her with his arms full of files into the lift and back into her office.

As soon as he'd gone, Melissa extracted the thick file relating to the company in Lexington, went up a floor to the partners' photocopier, strangely quiet in the lunchbreak, and copied the file in its entirety.

Back in her office she sat at her desk with the copied file and started work.

Redbourn's call came soon after lunch.

His voice was verging on the hysterical. He sounded as though he was about to fall off a high cliff. 'Melissa. There's a man here.'

'A man?'

'From some department in Whitehall. He say's he's got a warrant. I've got to delete everything I've got on the computer about the Austerlitz Account.'

Melissa turned in her seat as Boris's voice wailed down the

phone. A middle-aged, bulky man was talking earnestly to Nigel Hawick in his office. Hawick caught her eye through the glass and waved her to come in.

'I mean, he can't just walk in here and demand I do that. Can he?'

'Yes, I'm afraid he can.'

'But who is he?'

'He works for our lords and masters. We've uncovered something they don't want us to know about. So they're making us eliminate all our records. To make it look like whatever we discovered never existed.'

'What did we discover?'

'Don't ask.'

'But he can't do that,' Redbourn echoed plangently. 'He can't make me destroy my records.'

She chuckled. 'Yes, he can, Boris. And he can make you keep quiet about it afterwards.'

'He's going to stand over me whilst I delete everything. Then afterwards I have to sign something. To say I've eradicated all the files.'

'It's an affidavit, Boris. You'll have to sign an affidavit.'

'To say there's nothing left.'

'Yes.'

Suddenly his voice was conspiratorial. 'I'm going to have to do it, Melissa. This guy is shit hot. He knows about computing. I don't think there's any way I can save stuff. I'm not going to be able to fool him.'

'Boris,' she said in concern, 'don't even think about it. Just do it. Do what he wants. Delete all the stuff relating to the Austerlitz, sign his bloody affidavit and forget everything you ever knew about it.'

'But what about all your work?'

She chuckled. 'Dear old Boris. Don't you worry. I've got what I want. You just do what the man wants. Okay? Now I have to go.'

She put the phone down, covered the papers on her desk with a few other files and strolled into Nigel Hawick's office. 'You've come about the Austerlitz files,' she said to the man in a pleasant voice.

He looked at her with small, suspicious eyes. 'You know about that?'

She shrugged. 'I had a meeting with your boss this morning. Since then I've been expecting you. As a matter of fact I imagine by now everyone in Rolay Richard knows why you're here.' She caught Hawick's questioning look. 'He has a colleague ruffling a lot of feathers in Computer Operations,' she explained.

'Do you have copies of files and papers relating to,' the man looked down at a notebook, 'the Austerlitz Account in your possession?' he asked.

'Yes. They are in my office.'

'And are those the only copies to your knowledge?'

'No. Your boss, Steven Timmison, has a set.'

The sharp, piggy eyes took on a duplicitous look. 'Who?'

She smiled. 'It doesn't matter.'

'Are you prepared to sign an affidavit that there are no other copies apart from the two you've mentioned?' the man demanded.

'In Rolay Richard? Certainly not,' she said haughtily. 'There could be a dozen copies of those papers by now.' She saw the man's jaw tighten in concern. 'Paper breeds in places like this. I am prepared to swear that those are the only copies in *my* possession. That's all.'

It took the man half the afternoon to catalogue the heap of files in her office. She watched him, wry amusement creasing into little lines at the corners of her mouth. At no time did he pay any attention to the innocent mass of papers littering her desk.

'Would you swear that I now have everything in your possession relating to this account?' he asked when he had finished.

She stared at him levelly. 'Yes.'

'Are there really more copies of those files in the building?' Nigel Hawick inquired nervously when the man had gone.

'I very much doubt it.'

He grimaced. 'Well, you might have told the fellow that. It wouldn't have hurt to be a bit more cooperative, Melissa. For the sake of the firm.'

'It's not part of my job specification to be nice to the likes of him, Nigel. Nor to Steven Timmison. People like Timmison want us to do their dirty work, but as soon as we dig up anything that might be embarrassing to the authorities, they rip it away and bury it. Then they have the gall to threaten us with affidavits and the Official Secrets Act.'

446

Hawick grunted. 'You may well be right but you do need Timmison at the moment. Don't forget he's the one providing you with protection.'

'Thanks very much for reminding me.'

'So what exactly is it that they're so worried about? What have you uncovered?'

She shook her head. 'It's better you don't know, Nigel,' she said, leaving his office.

From beneath the papers on her desk, she retrieved the file on the company in Lexington and carried on with her research.

It took her another twenty-four hours to finish. By late in the afternoon of the following day she had found the answer. Or what she thought was the answer. There was one piece of the jigsaw missing . . . a piece that could perhaps be supplied by someone she had thought she would never speak to again.

She grimaced as she picked up the phone and made the call.

'Hello,' she said when the call was answered. 'The Federal Reserve? I want your Investigations Division, please. I need to talk to someone calling himself Bob Briscoe.'

It took a while for her to convince the Fed she wasn't a crank. She knew it had an Investigations Division, she told the person at the other end and she wanted to talk to a man in it, or seconded to it, who called himself Bob Briscoe. She was told there was no such person working there. Melissa said she realised they had to say that but asked for her message to be passed on anyway. She left her name, spelling it slowly and distinctly.

Briscoe came on the line ten minutes later. She told him what she wanted.

He called her back the following day. They spoke for half an hour as Melissa made rapid notes, firing questions at him off the satellite and into the big square building on the corner of Constitution Avenue.

At the end she thanked him sincerely. He told her she was welcome and asked after Jamie.

After the call she stared at her notes Now she had the last piece of the jigsaw.

She broke her resolution to get back to Jamie by seven and stayed late in the office. Shortly after five thirty one of her policemen came up to the fourteenth floor and settled his reassuring bulk at Debbie's workstation. Melissa switched on her word processor and sat down in front of it.

It took her less time than she had expected to produce the couple of pages of typescript. She printed a single copy, and sealed it in a large, embossed Rolay Richard security envelope.

Her final act was to cross the floor of the huge, open-plan office to the shredder. She pressed the button and watched everything – her notes, and the photocopy of the file she had made a few days earlier – being sliced into thin ribbons.

She smiled at her policeman. 'Ready?'

She asked her driver to divert to King Charles Street, where she handed the envelope to a security man at the door of the office. 'This is an important report for Mr Timmison,' she told him. 'Please make sure he gets it at soon as possible.'

The security man gazed at her appreciatively. 'Don't worry, miss. I'll make sure he gets it.'

Chapter Fifty

Barney Mullhane's secretary called from the outer office. 'There's a Mr Timmison coming through on the safe line. You wanna take it?'

He'd have liked to say no.

He had only just arrived at the office, and the last thing he wanted to do was talk to Timmison. But he had the feeling he didn't have a lot of choice. Ever since leaving London and arriving back at Langley, Mullhane had been expecting another call from the tight-assed Brit.

'Yeah, okay,' he growled. He lifted the phone.

'I'm calling on a secure line,' Timmison's precise tones came through loud and clear. 'We need to meet.'

'What again?'

'Absolutely. Things have come to light. Believe me, it's in your best interests.' There was something in his tone. It sounded more like a threat than an inducement.

'Where?'

'Here.'

'Hell, I only just got back from London.'

'It's important. I recommend you come.'

Mullhane sighed. He was getting too old for all this shit. He was spending his declining years on aeroplanes, flying around the world at the behest of bean-counters.

He walked into the cafeteria close to 16th and N Street a little less than forty-eight hours later and made his way towards a booth close to the rear.

The place was undistinguished, filled with clerks and secretaries eating breakfast before starting yet another day of grunt work in one of Washington's innumerable government offices.

With his grey, spiky hair, lined face and crumpled suit,

Mullhane blended perfectly. He looked like one of them – with a lot more years on the clock . . . a middle-ranking accountant who had spent a lifetime of drudgery in the service of the Federal Government.

He found his booth and slipped into a seat. The man opposite didn't blend into the background at all. He was tall and distinguished, with a mane of silvery white hair. He looked out of place and uncomfortable.

'For God's sake, Barney,' John Kilbride whispered, 'why here?'

'Because here is safe. Take a look around, John. Nobody's got a wiretap into this place. You figure anything around here is bugged? This is one place in town we can talk.' A waitress approached the booth and Mullhane ordered coffee.

Kilbride, a half-full mug in front of him, shook his head. He gazed around the cafeteria, taking Mullhane's point. 'Okay, then what's so special that we have to meet in a place like this?'

Mullhane considered him for a few seconds. 'It's all up, John,' he said quietly. 'The roof has fallen in. What the Agency was doing was unconstitutional but you . . . Jesus Christ, you must have been fucking nuts. Anyway, we're pulling the plug.'

'What the hell are you talking about?' The waitress appeared with the coffee.

When she had gone Mullhane leaned across the table. 'John, don't shit me. You know what I'm talking about. It's all over. The question is, what are you going to do about it? I mean we got your boy Phil taken care of. But you . . . you're a problem, John.'

'What do you mean, you've got Philip taken care of?' Kilbride was suddenly anxious.

Mullhane shook his head. 'Phil's race for the White House just hit the skids. He's out of it, John.'

Mullhane pulled a plastic wallet from inside his jacket and dropped it onto the table. 'These were taken in Las Vegas about ten years ago. It's not just the Right who don't like that kinda stuff. It don't go down too well with a lot of voters. It don't look like your boy is supporting a lot of family values there, John.'

Kilbride stared at the pictures. 'Jesus, Barney, what are you giving me here? What is this? A shakedown? For Chrissakes, you wouldn't use these?'

'We have to. Hell, it's your own fault. You were working your own agenda while we were supporting Phil. You must have been crazy. Getting involved with some cockamamie private army that wants to stage a screwball revolution. Jeeesus, how dumb can you be?'

Kilbride stared at him. 'This country is going down the toilet, Barney,' he announced. His voice was quiet but vicious. 'Someone has to pull it out . . . put it back on its feet. By force if necessary. Hell, I thought you understood that. I thought that's why the Agency was helping Philip with his campaign.'

'Don't be a jerk. The Agency was prepared to help Phil because, once he was in the White House, he was prepared to help us. The Agency has taken a lot of knocks, John. It's having its balls sawn off. It's turning into a sewing circle for powder-puff public accountants. Phil supported the Agency: he figured our role should be sticking it to Castro and the Mad Mullahs and the Commies crawling out of the woodwork in Eastern Europe. That's what Phil wanted. Hell, that's what you said you wanted.'

Mullhane shook his head almost sadly. 'But you double-crossed us. You were cheating on the deal, John. You were using the set-up we'd established with the bank to fund this goddam army of yours.'

'Is that what this is about?' Kilbride spat. 'The account at the bank. Jesus, Barney, you allowed someone to get inside Austerlitz?'

Mullhane nodded. 'It's all out in the open. They know I was operating the account, that I was Mr Black. And they've found out about you. They found out you were working your own agenda inside Austerlitz, that you were Mr White. It's all out. Including the crazy scam you were working behind my back.'

'Then this is all your fault, Barney. You said nobody could get inside that account. You said nobody would know our business.'

Mullhane shrugged. 'Well, now they do. A snot-nosed Brit intelligence man knows for one thing. And he's putting the squeeze on. The Agency has got its dick in the wringer and this guy is turning the handle.'

'How? How does this man know?'

'The woman, Semmington, the forensic accountant with the bank's liquidators told him. She figured the whole enchilada.'

'And you couldn't stop her? What the hell, Barney with all the resources at the Agency's disposal you couldn't get rid of the bitch?'

Mullhane face was wreathed in anger. He glowered at Kilbride. 'Shit,' he sneered, 'in the end you're just another bean-counter aren't you, John? An amateur. Someone attempted a dumbass hit on this broad in upstate New York. We both know who. Only the goddam hit went wrong. Vito Kunzman was there and he got whacked but the Semmington broad didn't.'

Kilbride made to speak, but Mullhane's raised hand silenced him.

'The trouble was that, before he died, Kunzman told Semmington enough to get her into our account.'

'Jesus, I know all this,' Kilbride said hoarsely.

'Sure you know it. With your connections inside the community you knew everything that was going on. It was you who passed on all the dope about Semmington's movements. You thought you could control everything. But in the end, John, you're just another money man. A money man with a mission. They're the worst.'

Mullhane's eyes were like lowered howitzers as he glared at Kilbride. 'You were using us, John. Using the Agency and your connections in Justice . . . the DEA and the Bureau, to give you information to pass on to the toy soldiers. You gave them the where and when about Colombian drug runners so they could snatch the dope and sell it for guns. You told them about which banks they could hit, which diamond shipments to intercept, which Chilean warehouse was storing bullion.'

'All that was necessary. We had to have the funds.'

'And you hid them using the bank account we were using to help Phil.'

'An account you let some liquidator uncover,' Kilbride hissed. 'This is all your fault.'

Mullhane shook his head. 'Bean-counters,' he sneered. 'Always blaming someone else.' He leaned across the table belligerently. 'What do you figure would have happened if that dumbass hit on the cabin hadn't happened? Supposing Kunzman had merely been captured? You think he would have spilled his guts to some English pussy accountant about the Austerlitz Account? No way. He'd have been doing deals with whoever captured him about the half billion he'd stolen.'

He sat back in his seat. 'Anyway, there's no proof that Kunzman actually knew what we were doing inside that account. He may have guessed. But . . . did he know? But once he got shot and figured he was dying, he spilled his guts. To the woman. It was *she* who figured it all out She had the training to do it. You start shooting at people, John, and they figure you got something to hide. If you hadn't done that, we wouldn't have this God Almighty mess. Now, the Brits know our business and that limey bastard has got the Agency over a barrel. And it's all your fault. You and your toy fucking soldiers. That Brit is gonna be sticking it up us for years because of you.'

Kilbride's patrician features were strained. Suddenly he looked his age. 'So what are you going to do?' he croaked.

'Do? Me? I'm gonna retire, John. Real soon. Play golf at Burning Tree Country Club and forget all about you and the Agency and the rest of all this shit. Your boy Phil, well he's gonna be getting out of politics. He'll bow out gracefully and go back to his family. If they'll have him after those.' He nodded at the plastic wallet on the table.

'And what about me?'

Mullhane stared at him. 'Yeah,' he murmured. 'You're the problem, John. What do we do about you?'

For a week she heard nothing.

Andrew and Frank were said to be tracking down huge amounts of Exchange Bank money but they were reporting directly to Nigel Hawick and she wasn't involved. Which suited her perfectly.

Her workload was light and easy to handle and she was getting back to Jamie early. She was even planning a holiday. The only drawback in what, for once, seemed the idyllic life was the continuing presence of her police protection.

Debbie called as she was staring out of the window at the glittering river. It was a perfect summer's day and the view along the distant, snaking stretch of water to the Isle of Dogs was especially beguiling. 'It's that man Timmison,' she announced.

Melissa moaned. 'Couldn't you tell him I was out?'

'He wouldn't believe me if I did,' she retorted tartly and put the call through.

'Miss Semmington, I'm sorry I haven't been in touch following your report but I have some rather good news for you. I wondered if we might have lunch.'

'Lunch?' She was shocked.

'Yes. Anywhere you would like. I don't know where you City people like to eat but perhaps you might like to join me at the

Ritz. Or Le Gavroche. I feel my department owes you a decent lunch.'

Melissa stared at the phone uncertainly, trying to puzzle out what the hell Timmison could be wanting by offering her lunch.

The thought of being cooped up somewhere glitzy for a couple of hours with the cold, ascetic civil servant was even less appealing than sandwiches in her office.

And yet . . . She wondered what the good news could be.

'You want me to choose where?'

'Certainly.'

She glanced out of the window. 'All right,' she said slowly, 'why don't we have it in the Park.'

'Pardon?'

'Sandwiches in St James's. That would be rather nice, don't you think?'

She heard Timmison cough in surprise. She smiled. It was gratifying to be able to upset his precise, imperious world.

'Well,' he said slowly, 'I had in mind something a little more elegant, but if you're sure that's what you want . . . ?'

'Yes it is. I'd really like that.'

'Very well. Have your driver drop you at the Guards Memorial at twelve thirty.' He rang off.

Timmison was waiting, erect as any guardsman, when the car pulled up at the Memorial on Horse Guards Parade. Melissa got out, followed by one of her big policemen. Standing a little off to one side was the young man with the Harrow tie. Melissa noticed he was carrying a small rucksack. The policeman joined the young man as Timmison fell into step beside her.

He did his best to smile. 'It's not quite what I had in mind, but, as a matter of fact I think this is a rather good idea of yours. I haven't had lunch in the Park since I was a young man. I used to enjoy it.'

They found a vacant bench halfway between Duck Island and the footbridge. Melissa sat down as the young man placed the rucksack next to Timmison and moved away. The bench was warm from the sun. She noticed her policeman finding a seat on a bench close by.

Timmison took out a vacuum flask and handed Melissa a plastic beaker. He poured some liquid into the cup. She peered at it. 'What's this?'

A rather good Chardonnay actually.' He attempted a smile.

'It's against the law to imbibe alcohol in the Royal Parks so perhaps it's best to be a little discreet. The sandwiches are smoked salmon.'

The park was busy, the grass littered with sunbathers. Most of the benches were occupied by people like themselves, eating sandwiches in the sunshine.

Melissa gazed at the bright beds of Begonias and Marigolds before switching her gaze to the ducks: the Mallards, Pochards and Gadwalls paddling lazily in the water. A few Pelicans were sunning themselves in the water close to the island.

She turned to Timmison. 'You said you had good news for me.'

He nodded. 'Yes. I'm happy to tell you that you no longer need police protection. We will be withdrawing it.'

It was what she had been longing to hear. Yet, as soon as she heard the words she was afraid.

'Are you sure?' Her tone was doubtful. 'I mean, you've no idea how desperate I am to be see the back of armed policemen. But are you absolutely sure we're out of danger?'

'Yes. A man from the CIA called me yesterday to say that you and your son were safe.'

'So it *was* the CIA who attacked me.'

Timmison shook his head. 'No.' He dug inside the rucksack and retrieved a midday edition of the *Evening Standard*. He handed it to her.

Circled on an inside page was a piece about Philip Kilbride the presidential contender who had decided not to pursue his party's nomination after the publication of photographs depicting him in a *ménage à trois* with two prostitutes – one male – in a Las Vegas hotel room. Kilbride was expected to retire from politics.

In apparent reaction to the disgrace of his son, the article continued, John Kilbride – Washington insider, *eminence grise* and confidant of many postwar presidents – had been found dead at his home in Georgetown. The death appeared to be suicide.

Melissa looked up from the newspaper and frowned at Timmison. 'I don't understand.'

Kilbride smiled coldly. 'The man who was trying to kill you is dead.'

She was startled. 'What? You mean this man? John Kilbride?'

'Yes.'

'Are you saying it was Kilbride who tried to kill me? And Jamie?'

Timmison nodded. 'Yes. The CIA believe he personally briefed the man who got into your cottage.'

She stared at him in horror. 'You're sure it was him?'

'Absolutely. And now you are safe.'

Melissa dropped her eyes to the article and gazed at it for a few moments before handing the paper back to Timmison.

'With John Kilbride dead,' Timmison announced, 'the threat to you is over. You no longer require police protection.' He smiled again. 'It was your last report that did it. I showed it to a senior CIA man. No doubt the Agency arranged the rest.'

The shock returned to her face. 'You mean the CIA killed John Kilbride?'

Chapter Fifty-One

Timmison shook his head. 'I wouldn't go so far as to say that. I expect they encouraged him to fall on his sword.' He gave her a meaningful look. 'If you see what I mean.'

'But why?'

Timmison took a bite out of a sandwich. 'As your report implied,' he went on, 'Kilbride was betraying them. The CIA wasn't likely to forgive that. The Agency had set up the Austerlitz Account to fund industrial espionage, and then, later, Philip Kilbride's presidential campaign. John Kilbride was using it as a cover to purchase arms for an extreme right-wing movement called Manifest.'

'Manifest,' she repeated.

He nodded, his eyebrows raised and the superior look back on his face. 'No doubt taken from the silly notion the early Americans had that theirs was a manifest destiny.'

He finished his sandwich. 'These are very good,' he announced. He gave Melissa an appraising look. 'How did you get on to it . . . discover what Kilbride was doing?'

She was still staring at him, trying to come to terms with what he had said. It took a few moments for his question to sink in.

'We found a number of separate deposits amounting to a hundred and ninety million dollars in the Austerlitz Account. They were credited to the company in Lexington. But the money had come from nowhere. No paper trails, nothing. Which meant it had to be cash. I called a contact of mine in America and told him the exact amounts credited. A dozen or so corresponded with the proceeds of crimes in the United States. Bank robberies, bullion thefts, diamond robberies, that kind of thing.'

Timmison nodded. 'The money had come from crime.'

'Yes. Like a lot of the funds in the Exchange Bank. Anyway,

I followed the money. Kilbride's company was buying arms with it. There was a stream of funds to an account in Frankfurt controlled by a man I've come across before. He's an international arms dealer. I mean, I wasn't sure the guns were for some political movement. All I knew for certain was that the money was going for armaments. But, what with what's happening in America at the moment, and with Philip Kilbride being so right-wing, it seemed possible that that was what was going on.'

Timmison smiled grimly. 'It may have seemed possible to someone as clever as you, Miss Semmington. But I think it came as a shock to the CIA. Although they were betraying their charter to help Philip Kilbride, I don't think it even crossed their minds that John Kilbride was betraying them.'

She stared at him. 'Everybody betrays everybody else, don't they?' Her tone was flat and resigned. 'That seems to have been the theme of this entire Exchange Bank business.'

Timmison threw a piece of bread to a duck waddling across the grass. 'Really?'

He was scarcely listening. He looked mildly pleased with himself, with the hint of a smirk on his sharp, aquiline features.

'The American Government was betraying its friends and allies,' she went on in a monotone, 'whilst the CIA was betraying the American Government, and John Kilbride was betraying the CIA.' She shook her head. 'I've been wading chin-deep in treachery.'

She gazed at the bright summer scene – at the girls in their colourful skirts and blouses and the men in their shirtsleeves – and felt a faint, familiar stinging behind her eyes. 'And men who I thought were my friends were betraying me.'

'All the same, you have done an excellent job, Miss Semmington,' Timmison replied breezily. 'You've cracked the Exchange Bank wide open, traced a missing half billion dollars, got inside the Austerlitz Account . . .'

'So the only way to succeed is by betrayal,' she interrupted. 'Is that what you're saying?'

The smirk was replaced by a small frown. 'Well, I wouldn't go that far. After all, it's you who have been successful, Miss Semmington. And you haven't betrayed anyone.'

'Yes I have,' she murmured croakily. 'I betrayed a man called Akhtar Aziz. And his family. I told him I would protect him, that I would help him. But I didn't.'

'I think you are being extremely hard on yourself. All in all, this business has turned out extremely satisfactorily. You've traced a lot of money and resolved the matter of the Austerlitz Account with no fuss or publicity.'

'You mean I haven't talked.'

He smiled at her blandly.

'Nor am I going to. Am I? Not with your Official Secrets Act hanging over me.'

His cold blue eyes inspected her face. 'Quite.'

'Yet it appears that the only defence against treachery is to suspect everyone. Doubt everything you see, all you hear, everyone you meet.'

'Sadly, it would often seem so.'

She gazed at him. 'I'm learning that. Which is why I'm deeply suspicious of you.'

He chuckled and raised his eyebrows quizzically.

'In fact, the more I've thought about it, the more I've come to realise that you've been manipulating me. Right from the very beginning. Manoeuvring me into finding out what you wanted me to find out.'

The superior smile returned. 'Really? Why on earth should you think that?'

'You were never really concerned about me tracing the money laundered by criminals were you? Nor even in finding the half billion Vito Kunzman had stolen. You *wanted* me to concentrate on the Austerlitz Account. Which is why you said the men who attacked me were working for the West Coast money launderers. By taking me off pursuing Piagini, you forced me to focus on Austerlitz. But those men weren't hired by the Americans were they?'

'Come now, Miss Semmington, how could you possibly know who those men were working for?'

'Come to that, how could you? You said the attack was connected with my investigations into Piagini, but you never told me *how* you knew. In fact those two men were working for a local drug pusher.'

'Who told you that?'

'The man who arranged for them to be murdered. Bob Briscoe.' She checked herself. 'Or the man who calls himself Bob Briscoe. You remember him. The American who saved Jamie. He's in a similar line of work to yourself. But I'm sure you know that.'

Timmison's smile switched off.

'You weren't the only one interested in Austerlitz. Whichever department of the United States Government Briscoe works for, it also had a vested interest in me getting inside the account.'

'He had those men murdered?'

Melissa nodded. 'You probably know that too. Or you've guessed it. Not that you'd ever prove it. It was done to protect me. At least that's what he said. Though he was really protecting his investment. Just like you. When you offered me police protection.'

'I think that's a little unfair, Miss Semmington. I was concerned for your safety.'

'Maybe. But only enough to keep me on the job. You were far more concerned with me finding Vito Kunzman and opening up Austerlitz. Despite the danger you knew I might face, you kept manoeuvring me in that direction. And, of course, me being me, I fell for it. I was as interested in finding Vito Kunzman as you were.'

'Yes, that's right, you were.' He frowned at her. 'Why, exactly?'

She allowed herself a small smile. 'Because I thought he was your inside man.'

'Inside man?'

'Yes. Kenneth McKinnie at Berrenstein Lang first put us onto the idea. He thought the BoE had someone feeding them information . . . someone who had been on the inside of the Exchange Bank. After a while I came to the same conclusion. But like an idiot I thought that someone was Kunzman. I thought *he* was your inside man.'

She took a sip of wine from her beaker then threw back her head and allowed the sun to warm her face. She closed her eyes against the glare. Bright purple light swam lazily behind her eyelids.

'It was only much later I realized what a fool I was for thinking that,' she went on. 'How could Kunzman have been your mole? If Kunzman had been the one who'd spilled the beans about the bank, you wouldn't have wanted me to go looking for him. Would you? You wouldn't have wanted your snoop compromised.'

'What makes you think I knew anything about this man Kunzman?'

'Nigel Hawick was reporting to you as well as to the Bank of England. He told you and the BoE's supervisors about everything

I was working on. About Piagini and Pemblin . . . the funds Cyclix were piggy-backing . . . Kunzman . . . the Austerlitz Account. You were up to speed on everything I was doing.'

She opened her eyes and glanced at him. 'If Kunzman had been your snoop, you would have pulled me off that part of the investigation. Told me *not* to go after him . . . stopped me tracking him. Instead, you positively encouraged me to keep on searching for him with extravagant promises of protection in America.'

'Of course,' he pointed out stiffly, 'you have no proof that I or the Bank of England had *anyone* passing us information about the Exchange Bank.'

'Proof? Maybe not. But I know you had someone who had once been on the inside. Definitely. Only it wasn't Vito Kunzman. Was it?'

He didn't reply.

'If it had been, you'd have known a lot more about the Exchange Bank than you did. Especially about the Austerlitz Account. You'd have known pretty much everything you were wanting me to find out. Kunzman would have told you. It took me a while, but in the end I finally realised that.'

The superior smile returned. 'I must say your suppositions are very interesting, Miss Semmington. Your famous instinct again?'

'If you like.'

'So . . . what you're telling me is that you *believe* I had a source from inside the bank, but you don't know who it was. All you know is it wasn't Kunzman. It doesn't get us very far does it?'

'I didn't say that. I didn't say I didn't know who it was.'

'So would you care to speculate about who this mysterious inside man might be?'

'It isn't a man. It's a woman. Hidalgo Campeche's mistress . . . his personal assistant . . . she's the one who came to you.'

She saw the look on Timmison's face change.

'Sam Barber told me about the assassination in San Francisco. Campeche's mistress was known to have been in the tenement when he was shot. After that she disappeared. She came to you. And you've been protecting her since. It's obvious that's what happened. Only I was too stupid to see it.'

'Why should this woman come to me?' His voice had lost its jauntiness.

'I imagine she went to the Bank of England first. They put her onto you.'

'But why to us? The British? If this woman was going to reveal what she knew, why wouldn't she go to the American authorities?'

'Because she had an idea the CIA was using the Exchange Bank. She didn't know the details, but she probably knew some very powerful people in Washington had a vested interest in protecting the bank. She wouldn't have felt safe going to the Americans. She couldn't trust any of the American authorities. So she went to the British. After all, the BoE was the regulator for the Exchange Bank. It would make sense for her to come to Britain.'

Timmison was silent, his sharp eyes scanning her face.

'She gave you enough detail about the mainstream money laundering to allow you to close the bank down,' Melissa continued. 'I don't suppose she knew very much about Austerlitz. That was Vito Kunzman's baby. But she'd have heard whispers – enough to get you interested; make you think Austerlitz was worth investigating – that Kunzman was worth finding. So you used Rolay Richard, and specifically me, to do your digging for you.'

'Hardly surprising,' he said. 'You have the best reputation in London for tracking capital flight.'

'The best reputation in London for being a blind, trusting idiot,' she retorted acidly.

Timmison shook his head. 'I think you do yourself a disservice, Miss Semmington. Your work on the Exchange Bank has been extraordinarily competent. Of course I can't confirm any of what you say. Essentially you're guessing. But,' he inclined his head in a gesture of salute, 'I must say you are extremely perceptive.'

She laughed . . . a loud cynical laugh. A passing couple looked sharply at her. 'God, if only that were true. The fact is, I was completely blind. All along you played me for a fool.'

'Come now, I think that's a little unfair. It's true I was anxious to find out more about this Austerlitz Account. And I certainly thought that, if anybody could get inside it, you could. But playing you for a fool? Hardly. I don't consider you to be a fool, Miss Semmington.'

'Yes you do. You had me risking my life, and that of my son, finding out things you already knew.'

He laughed. 'Already knew?'

'Nothing of what I've discovered has come as a surprise to you, has it? I don't suppose it was much of a shock to find that the CIA had mounted a huge campaign of industrial espionage in Europe and Japan.'

'No, I can't say it was altogether a surprise. But your investigations provided us with details of their network . . . the names of their agents. It was an excellent piece of work.'

'And no doubt you'll put it to good use,' she said scornfully. 'You probably weren't too surprised to find that the CIA was helping a right-wing presidential candidate with funds for his election campaign. I don't suppose you were even surprised that John Kilbride was using the Exchange Bank to buy guns for a bunch of American fascists.'

He stared at her silently for a while. 'No,' he said quietly. 'None of it was a great surprise.'

'You knew,' she repeated.

'Knew? No. Guessed, perhaps. From what I knew of the Exchange Bank, as well as from what I learned from Campeche's mistress, I had an idea what might be going on.'

'You guessed Kilbride was buying guns to fund his right-wing militia?'

Timmison gave her a slight smile. 'You forget your Cicero, Miss Semmington. "Money is the sinews of war." Remember? You cannot have a revolution or a terrorist movement or anything remotely approaching it without money – a lot of money. And a bank – a compliant bank. A right-wing movement in America would need money for arms. Those funds would need a home and safe passage.' He spread his hands. 'The Exchange Bank was the perfect conduit.'

She nodded slowly. 'You've probably always had a notion of what the bank was up to. But now you have the facts. Chapter and verse. And the big plus is that you haven't had to reveal any of it yourself. It's all come out as a result of my work. If any of it comes to light you can say you never knew anything. The Exchange Bank liquidators found out everything. You and your department can stand back with clean hands and express shock at what's been going on.'

Timmison made a small, deprecating gesture. 'It's usually far better when a government department can do that. Keep out of the limelight. It's important that one's influence should be subtle. Don't you agree?'

'Which means, I suppose, that now you know the details you'll use them to apply a lot of subtle pressure on the Americans and the CIA and whoever else is involved.'

He took a sip out of his plastic cup. 'Something like that.'

'Perfidious Albion.'

Timmison laughed. 'I've always thought that expression rather a compliment. Especially from a Frenchman. But you must admit we've done quite a good job. We've been able to stop America moving to the right . . . getting itself some idiot, right-wing president. Getting itself involved in civil unrest and armed resistance. Yet,' he chuckled, 'it doesn't look like we've interfered in the process at all. The CIA got itself into the mess and now it's getting itself out.'

She frowned. 'You don't strike me as the type to oppose a right-wing government.'

He laughed. 'That's where you're wrong. Right-wing, left-wing, they're both irrelevant. I'm a realist. These days politics is beside the point. It is insignificant, Miss Semmington. The only thing that counts in today's world is economics. Economic power. Wealth. I would have thought you of all people would know that.'

She glowered at his patronising tone and stared at the ducks.

'Can you imagine what would happen to the world economy if America had a right-wing president? The American bond market is the central mechanism of world debt. What do you think it would do to world trade if America turned in on itself? Went isolationist? It was absolutely vital to stop that happening. Economically. Not politically. It's a small world and getting smaller. And we're all in it together. The only way we can keep the show going is if we all stay in step. A right-wing America wouldn't dance to the same tune as the rest of us. It wouldn't even know the music.'

She was silent for a while. 'You've got everything you wanted out of this, haven't you?' she murmured. 'I mean even the panic in America about the Mafia taking over the banks has boosted the British economy. All those funds . . . all that running money, flowing out of the States and into London. Very nice for us.'

He smiled. 'Yes, I must admit that's a useful short-term gain. Of course the money will soon move back. When the panic dies down. But, in the meantime, the London market is on an all-time high. All those dollars mean plenty of investment. We've been very fortunate.'

She shook her head and laughed cynically. 'I don't think you were fortunate. I don't think any of this was luck. I think everything has worked out pretty much as you meant it to work out when you sat down and devised this whole scheme. You *meant* all of this to happen.'

'Come now, Miss Semmington, you surely can't believe I'm as perfidious as that? Are you seriously suggesting I manipulated *all* these events?'

She nodded. 'Yes. Of course, I didn't see it at first.'

She was speaking almost to herself, staring at the pond and watching the light flittering over the ripples made by the ducks.

'At first I thought that, as the Exchange Bank had been set up by organised criminals for organised criminals, the Mafia was behind everything. Including Hidalgo Campeche's assassination. We knew many of the senior managers were robbing the gangsters behind the bank – moving assets around, falsifying accounts to hide losses, that kind of thing. So it was natural to think the Mafia had killed Dr Campeche. Perhaps they'd caught him out in some treachery. Yet the rumour was that Dr Campeche had been murdered by accident. He was the wrong victim. The word was it should have been Vito Kunzman.'

She shrugged. 'Okay, well maybe the Mafia had got it wrong. Maybe they had really wanted to kill Vito Kunzman and they'd made a mistake. But then I started asking myself, why should the criminals behind the bank want to kill either of them? They had an enormous money-laundering operation and everything was working smoothly. Why spoil it? Why would the Mafia want to kill either Campeche or Kunzman?'

She paused. 'So, I began to wonder. If it wasn't the Mafia, then who could it have been?'

Timmison looked expectant. 'Well, who?'

'As soon as I produced my report I decided it was John Kilbride. He was the one who had arranged to have Kunzman killed. After all, the people who had carried out the assassination were freelancers. It would be quite possible for them to get the wrong man.'

'Why would Kilbride have wanted to kill Kunzman?'

'It's obvious. Because he'd got wind that the Exchange Bank was about to be shut down. He wanted to prevent Kunzman revealing anything about Austerlitz if he was caught.'

She paused.

'Go on.'

But then I began to realise that scenario didn't fit either.'

'Why not?'

'Because if Kilbride had known in advance about the bank closing, he would have moved the funds out of Austerlitz. His first thought would have been to protect the assets. But he didn't move the funds. He couldn't. The bank's closure was a surprise. By the time he knew, it was too late for him to do anything. And at that stage there was no reason for him to make an attempt on Vito Kunzman's life. So, gradually, it became obvious to me that John Kilbride was not responsible for having Hidalgo Campeche killed. And if he wasn't . . . then who was? Who benefited from his death?'

Timmison smiled and shrugged. 'You tell me.'

'You did.'

'Me?'

'Yes. You.'

'Don't you think that's a bit far-fetched. Even for your famous instinct?'

She shook her head. 'You know, when I was with Vito Kunzman in the back of that police car, he said something about the assassination. He couldn't understand why anybody would want to kill him. And in a tenement in Caracas. He thought the attempt had been staged to put the frighteners on him. Someone wanted to make Campeche's assassination look like a mistake. To make it *look* as if the real victim was meant to be Kunzman. Well, I didn't think much about what he said at the time, but recently it all suddenly made sense.'

'Sense? What kind of sense would that make?'

'Because what would Kunzman do if he thought somebody out there was trying to kill him? He'd run. And to whom? Like Campeche's mistress, he couldn't trust the Americans. Which was what *you* were counting on.'

She stared at Timmison. His eyes were riveted to her face.

'You calculated he would run to you. To the British. You planned to have Campeche killed and thereby force Kunzman into your arms. Only he didn't do quite as you expected, did he? Instead of coming to you he stole half a billion dollars and went into hiding. But your luck held out because Campeche's mistress came to you instead. Even so, you still needed to find Kunzman and get inside that mysterious account he controlled.'

She shrugged. 'So . . . you employed me.'

Timmison put on a puzzled face. Melissa thought it looked contrived. 'But how would I have known to do all this? Why would I have bothered in the first place?'

'You've just told me that. You suspected America was developing a right-wing movement and that, if so, it would need funding. The Exchange Bank was the obvious source of money. The same would also be true if the CIA was undertaking industrial espionage. Money is also the sinews of spying, you know.' He smiled. 'You calculated that if you could get inside the Exchange Bank, you could find the answers.'

She let out a hollow laugh. 'Follow the money. It always works. I suppose you've been spying on the Exchange Bank for years. You would have known Vito Kunzman was important. Hence you devised your little scheme to make him run to you.'

He gazed at her. 'You really are most astute, Miss Semmington. But of course all this is highly improbable.'

'But when you have eliminated the impossible, whatever remains, however improbable, *must* be the truth.'

He laughed again. 'I suppose quoting Sherlock Holmes is appropriate under the circumstances. When it comes to financial detective work . . . tracking bad men and their money, Miss Semmington you are most certainly in a league of your own. Of course you cannot expect me to comment on any of this far-fetched scenario of yours.'

'No, I don't expect you to do that. But it *is* the only scenario that fits.'

Timmison finished his sandwich and brushed his long bony fingers together. 'Well, I've enjoyed our lunch,' he said. 'It's been most instructive. Not to say entertaining. I must say I am deeply impressed with you, Miss Semmington. Certainly, should the occasion arise I would be most happy to work with you in the future.'

'I don't think I'd ever want to work for you again.' She said it with feeling

'We shall see. However, there is one final thing . . .'

'If you're going to remind me about the Official Secrets Act, don't bother. I know I can't prove any of what I've said. I wouldn't

467

try. I won't talk, don't worry. I have too much to lose. We both know that.'

He nodded. 'Good.'

He appraised her for a moment, his eyes flicking over her face. 'By the way, I meant it when I said my department would pay for any remedial surgery you require.'

He nodded in the direction of her cheekbone. Melissa's fingers flew to the white line of her scar. 'I must say it doesn't look a lot to me, but I know you ladies are sensitive about your looks. So if you need surgery...'

Slowly she shook her head. 'No, I don't think so,' she said quietly. 'Someone I once knew told me it would give my face character. Perhaps it does. I don't know. But I think I may leave it for a while. Thanks all the same.'

His face showed a trace of surprise. 'As you wish.'

'Well,' he rose to his feet. 'Please don't get up.'

He extended a hand and despite herself Melissa shook it. 'It was a pleasure working with you, Miss Semmington. I hope we meet again.'

She watched him march away.

Her burly policeman got up from his seat and followed him. The young man with the Harrow tie appeared at the bench and packed the rucksack. Melissa handed him her plastic beaker. He took it without a word, then hurried after the rapidly receding figure of his boss.

For a while Melissa remained on the bench, watching the lunchtime crowds.

Curiously, with the disappearance of her policeman she felt exposed and vulnerable. She shook her head slightly to rid herself of the feeling. Her flowing hair glistened in the sunlight.

The job was done, she told herself. There was nothing more to fear.

It was over.

Slowly, she rose to her feet, conscious that things were returning to the way they always were. She was in the middle of a crowd and on her own.

She let out a small sigh and decided to take the rest of the day off. She would go home to Jamie.

She glanced up. High above, moving across the blue face of the sky, an aircraft was leaving a thin, white trail of vapour. She screwed up her eyes, trying to detect the glittering sliver of the plane. It was too high for her to see. Staring up, and vaguely aware of the quiet murmur of the people in the Park, she tried to determine in which direction, towards which point of the compass, it was travelling.

After a moment she gave it up.

It didn't matter.

More Crime Fiction from Headline Feature

Philip Friedman

REASONABLE DOUBT

'A quite splendid courtroom drama. Read it'
– THE SUNDAY TIMES

THE NEW YORK TIMES BESTSELLER

'Reads more like a true crime story than a made-up one' –
NEW YORK TIMES

It seems impossible, yet attorney Michael Ryan is asked to
defend his daughter-in-law in a murder trial. For Jennifer Ryan
is accused of beating a man's brains out in a Manhattan art
gallery and the victim is Michael's son, Ned.

There are powerful reasons, however, why Michael should lead
Jennifer's defence – not least his conviction that a defendant has a
moral right to the counsel of her choice. But if he takes the case
he will be forced to confront Ned's true nature – and expose the
worst secrets of his son's life in open court . . .

'Ingenious . . . you won't be able to guess the verdict' – NEWSWEEK

'A hard-to-put-down thriller . . . with menace lurking outside the
halls of justice and polished pyrotechnics within' – KIRKUS REVIEWS

'This is courtroom drama at its best' – ENTERTAINMENT WEEKLY

'Vivid and the action never lags . . . well done' – MYSTERY SCENE

'Undoubtedly the best courtroom novel I have ever read' –
LAWRENCE BLOCK

FICTION / CRIME 0 7472 3580 5

THE 13th JUROR

The compelling thriller from the author of
HARD EVIDENCE

JOHN T. LESCROART

'A heart-pounding page-turner . . . *The Thirteenth Juror*
is courtroom drama at its best' *Playboy*

Jennifer Witt is a woman who has suffered. Virtually
every man in her life has abused her, so who would
blame her if one day she struck back? Killed her doctor
husband Larry whose strictures and punishments have
made her life a living hell . . . But when Larry is shot
dead Jennifer, suspect number one, denies she was ever
beaten and consistently refuses to admit she killed him.
Dismas Hardy, agreeing to undertake her defence, tends
to believe her, especially since her seven-year-old son,
the apparent centre of her life, was also killed . . .

But as Jennifer's trial – a capital case – continues and
Dismas watches his own family life disintegrate under
the pressure of her defence, he begins to wonder if his
judgement has let him down. And if Jennifer Witt is a
cold-blooded childkiller . . .

'Unusual in his ability to combine courthouse scenes
with action sequences, judicial puzzles and dimensional
people, Mr Lescroart produces a full house of well-drawn
characters . . . A fast-paced text that sustains interest to
the very end' *Wall Street Journal*

'Engaging characters and a riveting plot that fans of
Scott Turow and John Grisham will love; recommended'
Library Journal

FICTION / THRILLER 0 7472 4760 9

DESPERATE MEASURES

David Morrell

Obituary writer Matt Pittman has reached the end of the line. Once a hot-shot investigative reporter with a loving wife and son, now he faces the future alone. Sitting in his bathtub with a pistol in his mouth, Matt prepares to end his life. But, as his finger tightens on the trigger, the phone rings.

On the line is a friend Matt can't refuse, his boss at the paper who needs one last task completed. So Matt postpones his death and finds himself on the wrong end of a man-hunt, wanted by the police and hounded by hitmen determined to silence him forever. As the killers close in, Matt is still determined to die but he's damned if someone else is going to pull the trigger . . .

FICTION / THRILLER 0 7472 4626 2

SILENT WITNESS

A FRIGHTENED CHILD HOLDS THE KEY TO A DOUBLE MURDER

GALLATIN WARFIELD

For State attorney Gardner Lawson, violent crime comes too close to home when his eight-year-old son Granville stumbles in on an armed robbery and double murder at a local grocery store. The boy is found unconscious, suffering from concussion and with the imprint of a gun barrel on his forehead. Though the only one who can identify the killer, he wakes up with no memory of the incident.

As the police search continues for a coldblooded murderer it is increasingly clear that Granville's memory must be restored – though that might expose him to mental trauma. Lawson is faced with a terrible dilemma.

Meanwhile two suspects have emerged: a rich student at a nearby boarding-school and a local thug with a police record. One of these is a dangerous psychopath who is almost certain to strike again.

Under gentle therapy, Granville is beginning to recall bits and pieces of the horrifying occurrence . . . But will he remember enough in time, and is his own life now in danger?

FICTION / THRILLER 0 7472 4065 5

A selection of bestsellers from Headline

BODY OF A CRIME	Michael C. Eberhardt	£5.99	☐
TESTIMONY	Craig A. Lewis	£5.99	☐
LIFE PENALTY	Joy Fielding	£5.99	☐
SLAYGROUND	Philip Caveney	£5.99	☐
BURN OUT	Alan Scholefield	£5.99	☐
SPECIAL VICTIMS	Nick Gaitano	£5.99	☐
DESPERATE MEASURES	David Morrell	£5.99	☐
A CERTAIN JUSTICE	John Lescroart	£5.99	☐
GRIEVOUS SIN	Faye Kellerman	£5.99	☐
THE CHIMNEY SWEEPER	John Peyton Cooke	£5.99	☐
TRAP DOOR	Deanie Francis Mills	£5.99	☐
VANISHING ACT	Thomas Perry	£5.99	☐

All Headline books are available at your local bookshop or newsagent, or can be ordered direct from the publisher. Just tick the titles you want and fill in the form below. Prices and availability subject to change without notice.

Headline Book Publishing, Cash Sales Department, Bookpoint, 39 Milton Park, Abingdon, OXON, OX14 4TD, UK. If you have a credit card you may order by telephone – 01235 400400.

Please enclose a cheque or postal order made payable to Bookpoint Ltd to the value of the cover price and allow the following for postage and packing:

UK & BFPO: £1.00 for the first book, 50p for the second book and 30p for each additional book ordered up to a maximum charge of £3.00.
OVERSEAS & EIRE: £2.00 for the first book, £1.00 for the second book and 50p for each additional book.

Name ....

Address ....

....

....

If you would prefer to pay by credit card, please complete:
Please debit my Visa/Access/Diner's Card/American Express (delete as applicable) card no:

Signature .... Expiry Date ....